Dover Public Library
Dover, Delaware 1990
302-736-7030

W9-DGB-163

Grace Livingston Hill

America's Best-Loved Storyteller

LOVE ENDURES

COLLECTION #1

BARBOUR
PUBLISHING

Dover Public Library
Dover, Delaware 19901
302-736-7030

The Beloved Stranger © 2012 by Grace Livingston Hill
The Prodigal Girl © 2012 by Grace Livingston Hill
A New Name © 2012 by Grace Livingston Hill

Print ISBN 978-1-62029-761-2

eBook Editions:
Adobe Digital Edition (.epub) 978-1-62029-995-1
Kindle and MobiPocket Edition (.prc) 978-1-62029-994-4

All rights reserved. No part of this publication may be reproduced or transmitted for commercial purposes, except for brief quotation in printed reviews, without written permission of the publisher.

All scripture quotations are taken from the King James Version of the Bible.

This book is a work of fiction. Names, characters, places, and incidents are either products of the author's imagination or used fictitiously. Any similarity to actual people, organizations, and/or events is purely coincidental.

Cover design: Faceout Studio, www.faceoutstudio.com

Published by Barbour Publishing, Inc., P.O. Box 719, Uhrichsville, Ohio 44683, www.barbourbooks.com

Our mission is to publish and distribute inspirational products offering exceptional value and biblical encouragement to the masses.

 Member of the
Evangelical Christian
Publishers Association

Printed in the United States of America.

THE BELOVED STRANGER

Chapter 1

1930s Eastern America

Sherrill stood before the long mirror and surveyed herself critically in her bridal array.

Rich creamy satin shimmering, sheathing her slender self, drifting down in luscious waves across the old Chinese blue of the priceless rug on which she stood! Misty white veil like a cloud about her shoulders, caught by the frosty cap of rare lace about her sweet forehead, clasped by the wreath of orange blossoms in their thick green and white perfection, flowers born to nestle in soft mists of tulle and deepen the whiteness, the only flower utterly at home with rich old lace.

Sherrill stooped to the marble shelf beneath the tall mirror and picked up a hand mirror, turning herself this way and that to get a glimpse of every side. There seemed to be no possible fault to be found anywhere. The whole outfit was a work of art.

"It's lovely, isn't it, Gemmie?" she said brightly to the elderly woman who had served her aunt for thirty years as maid. "Now, hand me the bouquet. I want to see how it all looks together. It isn't fair not to be able to get the effect of one's self after taking all this trouble to make it a pleasant sight for other people."

The old servant smiled.

"What quaint things you do say, Miss Sherry!" she said as she untied the box containing the bridal bouquet. "But don't you think maybe you should leave the flowers in the box till you get to the church? They might get a bit crushed."

"No, Gemmie, I'll be very careful. I want to see how pretty they look with the dress and everything. Aren't they lovely?"

She took the great sheaf of roses gracefully on one arm and posed, laughing brightly into the mirror, the tip of one silver shoe advancing beneath the ivory satin, her eyes like two stars, her lips in the curves of a lovely mischievous child; then, advancing the other silver-shod foot, she hummed a bar of the wedding march.

"Now, am I quite all right, Gemmie?" she asked again.

"You are the prettiest bride I ever set eyes on," said the woman, looking at the sweet, fair girl wistfully. "Ef I'd had a daughter, I could have asked no better for her than that she should look like you in her wedding dress," and Gemmie wiped a furtive tear from one corner of her eye over the thought of the daughter she never had had.

"There, there, Gemmie, don't go to getting sentimental!" cried Sherrill with a quick little catch in her own breath, and a sudden wistful longing in her breast for the mother she never had known. "Now, I'm quite all right, Gemmie, and you're to run right down and get Stanley to take you over to the church. I want you to be sure and get the seat I picked out for you, where you can see everything every minute. I'm depending on you, you know, to tell me every detail afterward—and Gemmie, don't forget the funny things, too. I wouldn't want to miss them, you know. Be sure to describe how Miss Hollister looks in her funny old bonnet with the ostrich plume."

"Oh now, Miss Sherrill, I couldn't be looking after things like that when you was getting married," rebuked the woman.

"Oh yes, you could, Gemmie, you've got the loveliest sense of humor! And I want to know *every*thing! Nobody else will understand, but you do, so now run away quick!"

"But I couldn't be leaving you alone," protested the woman with distress in her voice. "It'll be plenty of time for me to be going after you have left. Your aunt Pat said for me to stay by you."

"You have, Gemmie; you've stayed as long as I had need of you, and just everything is done. You couldn't put another touch to me anywhere, and I'd rather know you are on your way to that nice seat I asked the tall, dark usher to put you in. So please go, Gemmie, right away!

The fact is, Gemmie, I'd really like just a few minutes alone all by myself before I go. I've been so busy I couldn't get calm, and I need to look into my own eyes and say good-bye to myself before I stop being a girl and become a married woman. It really is a kind of scary thing, you know, Gemmie, now that I'm this close to it. I don't know how I ever had the courage to promise I'd do it!" and she laughed a bright little trill full of joyous anticipation.

"You poor lamb!" said the older woman with sudden yearning in her voice; the old, anticipating and pitying the trials of the young. "I do hope he'll be good to you."

"Be good to me!" exclaimed Sherrill happily. "Who? Carter? Why, of course, Gemmie. He's wonderful to me. He's almost ridiculous he's so careful of me. I'm just wondering how it's going to be to have someone always fussing over me when I've been on my own for so many years. Why, you know, Gemmie, these last six months I've been with Aunt Pat are the first time I've had anybody who really cared where I went or what I did since my mother died when I was ten years old. So you don't need to worry about me. There, now, you've spread that train out just as smooth as can be; please go at once. I'm getting very nervous about you, really, Gemmie!"

"But I'll be needed, Miss Sherry, to help you down to the car when it comes for you."

"No, you won't, Gemmie. Just send that little new maid up to the door to knock when the car is ready. I can catch up my own train and carry it perfectly well. I don't want to be preened and spread out like a peacock. It'll be bad enough when I get to the church and have to be in a parade. Truly, Gemmie, I want to be alone now."

The woman reluctantly went away at last, and Sherrill locked her door and went back to her mirror, watching herself as she advanced slowly, silver step after silver step, in time to the softly hummed wedding march. But when she was near to the glass, Sherrill's eyes looked straight into their own depths long and earnestly.

"Am I really glad," she thought to herself, "that I'm going out of myself into a grown-up married person? Am I perfectly sure that I'm not just a bit frightened at it all? Of course Carter McArthur is the handsomest man I ever met, the most brilliant talker, the most courteous gentleman, and I've been crazy about him ever since I first met him. Of course he treats me just like a queen, and I trust him absolutely. I know he'll always be just the same graceful lover all my life. And yet, somehow, I feel all of a sudden just the least bit scared. Does any girl *ever* know any man *perfectly*?"

She looked deep into her own eyes and wondered. If she only had a mother to talk to these last few minutes!

Of course there was Aunt Pat. But Aunt Pat had never been married. How could Aunt Pat know how a girl felt the last few minutes before the ceremony? And Aunt Pat was on her way to the church now. She was all crippled up with rheumatism and wanted to get there in a leisurely way and not have to get out of the car before a gaping crowd. She had planned to slip in the side door and wait in the vestry room till almost time for the ceremony and then have one of her numerous nephews, summoned to the old house for the occasion to be ushers, bring her in. Aunt Pat wouldn't have understood anyhow. She was a good sport with a great sense of humor, but she wouldn't have understood this queer feeling Sherrill was experiencing.

When one stopped to think of it, right on the brink of doing it, it was a rather awful thing to just give your life up to the keeping of another! She hadn't known Carter but six short months. Of course he was wonderful. Everybody said he was wonderful, and he had always been so to her. Her heart thrilled even now at the thought of him, the way he called her "Beautiful!" bending down and just touching her forehead with his lips, as though she were almost too sacred to touch lightly. The way his hair waved above his forehead. The slow way he smiled, and the light that came in his hazel eyes when he looked at her. They thrilled her tremendously. Oh, there wasn't any doubt in her mind whatsever that she was deeply in love with him. She didn't question that for an instant. It was just the thought of merging her life into his and always being a part of him. No, it wasn't that either, for that thrilled her, too, with an exquisite kind of joy, to think of never having to be separated from him anymore. What was it that sent a quiver of fear through her heart just at this last minute alone? She couldn't tell.

She had tried to talk to Gemmie about it once the day before, and Gemmie had said all girls felt "queer" at the thought of being married. All nice girls, that is. Sherrill couldn't see why that had anything to do with the matter. It wasn't a matter of nicety. Gemmie was talking about a shrinking shyness probably, and it wasn't that at all. It was a great awesomeness at the thought of the miracle of two lives wrought into one, two souls putting aside all others and becoming one perfect life.

It made Sherrill feel suddenly so unworthy to have been chosen, so childish and immature for such a wonder. One must be so perfect to have a right to be a part of such a great union. And Carter was so wonderful! Such a super-man!

Suddenly she dropped upon one silken knee and bowed her lovely mist-veiled head.

"Dear God," she prayed softly, long lashes lying on velvet cheeks, gold tendrils of hair glinting out from under lacy cap, "oh, dear God, make me good enough for him!" and then, hesitantly in a quick little frightened breath, "Keep me from making any awful mistakes!"

Then, having shriven her ignorant young soul, she buried her face softly, gently, in the baby roses of her bouquet and drew a long happy breath, feeling her fright and burden roll away, her happy heart spring up to meet the great new change that was about to come upon her life.

She came softly to her feet, the great bouquet still

11

in her clasp, and glanced hurriedly at the little turquoise enamel clock on her dressing table. There was plenty of time. She had promised to show herself to Mary, the cook, after she was dressed. Mary had broken her kneecap the week before and was confined to her bed. She had mourned distressedly that she could not see Miss Sherrill in her wedding dress. So Sherrill had promised her. It had been one of the reasons why she had gotten rid of Gemmie. She knew Gemmie would protest at her going about in her wedding veil for a mere servant!

But there was no reason in the world why she couldn't do it. Most of the people of the house were gone to the church. The bridesmaids left just before Gemmie, and Aunt Pat before them. Sherrill herself had watched the ushers leave while Gemmie was fixing her veil. Of course they had to be there ages before anyone else.

The bridesmaids and maid of honor had the two rooms next to her own, with only her deep closet between, and there were doors opening from room to room so that all the rooms were connected around the circle and back to Aunt Pat's room, which was across the hall from her own. It had been one of the idiosyncrasies of the old lady that in case of burglars it would be nice to be able to go from room to room without going into the hall.

So the rooms were arranged in a wide horseshoe with the back hall behind the top of the loop, the middle room being a sitting room or library, with three bedrooms on either side. Nothing would be easier than for her to go swiftly, lightly, through the two rooms beyond her own, and through the door at the farther end of the second room into the back hall that led to the servants' quarters. That would save her going through the front hall and being seen by any prying servants set to keep track of her till she reached the church. It was a beautiful idea to let old Mary see how she looked, and why shouldn't she do it?

Stepping quickly over to the door that separated her room from the next, she slid the bolt back and turned the knob cautiously, listening; then she swung the door noiselessly open.

Yes, it was as she supposed; the girls were gone. The room was dimly lit by the two wall sconces over the dressing table. She could see Linda's street shoes with the tan stockings stuffed into them standing across the room near the bureau. She knew them by the curious cross straps of the sandal-like fastening. Linda's hat was on the bed, with the jacket of her silk ensemble half covering it. Linda was always careless, and of course the maids were too busy to have been in here yet to clean up. The closet door was open, and she saw Cassie's suitcase yawning wide open on the floor where Cassie had left it in her haste. The white initials C.A.B. cried out a greeting as she crept stealthily by. Cassie had been late in arriving. She always was. And there was Carol's lovely imported fitted bag open on the dressing table, all speaking of the haste of their owners.

Betty and Doris and Jane had been put in the second

room, with Rena, the maid of honor whom Aunt Pat had wanted her to ask because she was the daughter of an old friend. It was rather funny having a maid of honor whom one hadn't met, for she hadn't arrived yet when Sherrill had gone to her room to dress, but assurance had come over the telephone that she was on her way in spite of a flat tire, so there had been nothing to worry about. Who or what Rena was like did not matter. She would be wholly engaged in eyeing her dear bridegroom's face. What did it matter who maid-of-honored her, so long as Aunt Pat was pleased?

Sherrill paused as she stepped into this second room. It was absolutely dark, but strangely enough the door to the left, opening into the middle room, had been left open. That was curious. Hadn't Carter been put in there to dress? Surely that was the arrangement, to save him coming garbed all the way from the city! But of course he was gone long ago! She had heard him arrange to be early at the church to meet the best man, who had been making some last arrangements about their stateroom on the ship. That was it! Carter had gone, and the girls, probably not even knowing that he occupied that room, had gone out that way through the other door into the hall.

So Sherrill, her soft train swung lightly over her arm, the mist of lace gathered into the billow that Gemmie had arranged for her convenience in going down stairs, and the great sheaf of roses and valley-lilies held gracefully over her other arm, stepped confidently into the room. She looked furtively toward the open door, where a brilliant overhead light was burning, sure that the room was empty, unless some servant was hovering about watching for her to appear.

She hesitated, stepping lightly, the soft satin making no sound of going more than if she had been a bit of thistle down. Then suddenly she stopped short and held her breath, for she had come in full sight of the great gilt-framed pier glass that was set between the two windows at the back of the room, and in it was mirrored the full-length figure of her bridegroom arranging his tie with impatient fingers and staring critically into the glass, just as she had been doing but a moment before.

A great wave of tenderness swept over her for him, a kind of guilty joy that she could have this last vision of him as himself before their lives merged, a picture that she felt would live with her throughout the long years of life.

How dear he looked! How shining his dark hair, the wave over his forehead! There wasn't any man, not *any* man, *any*where as handsome—and *good*, she breathed softly to herself—as Carter, *her man*!

She held herself back into the shadow, held her very breath lest he should turn and see her there, for—wasn't there a tradition that it was bad luck for the bride to show herself in her wedding garments to the groom before he saw her first in the church? Softly she withdrew one foot and swayed a little farther away from the patch of light in the doorway. He would be gone in just a minute, of course, and then she could go on and give Mary her glimpse and hurry back without being seen by anyone. She dared not retreat further lest he should hear her step and find out that she had been watching him. It was fun to be here and see him when he didn't know. But sometime, oh sometime in the dear future that was ahead of them, she would tell him how she had watched him, and loved him, and how all the little fright that had clutched her heart a few minutes before had been melted away by this dear glimpse of him.

Sometime, when he was in one of those gentle moods, and they were all alone—they had had so little time actually alone of late! There had always been so many other things to be done! But sometime, soon perhaps, when he was giving her soft kisses on her eyelids, and in the palm of her hand as he held her fingers back with his own strong ones, then she would draw him down with his face close to hers and tell him how she had watched him, and loved him—!

But—! What was happening? The door of the back hall, which was set next to the nearest window, was opening slowly, without sound, and a face was appearing in the opening! Could it be a servant, having mistaken her way? How blundering! How annoyed he would be to have his privacy broken in upon!

And then the face came into the light and she started.

It was a face she had seen before, a really pretty face, if the makeup on it had not been so startling. There was something almost haggard about it, too, and wistful, and the eyes were frightened, pleading eyes. They scanned the room hurriedly and rested upon the man, who still stood with his back to the room and his face to the mirror. Then the girl stepped stealthily within the room and closed the door as noiselessly as she had opened it.

Who was it? Sherrill held her breath and stared. Then swift memory brought the answer. Why, that was Miss Prentiss, Carter's secretary! But surely no one had invited her! Carter had said she was comparatively new in the office. He had not put her name on the list. How dared she follow him here? Had something come up at the last minute, some business matter that she felt he must know about before he left for his trip to Europe? But surely no one could have directed her to follow him to the room where he was dressing!

This all went swiftly through Sherrill's mind as she stood that instant and watched the expression on the girl's face, that hungry desperate look, and something warned her with uncanny prescience. So Sherrill stood holding that foolish bouquet of baby roses and swinging lily-bells during what seemed an eon of time, till suddenly Carter McArthur saw something in the mirror and swung around, a frozen look of horror and anger on his handsome face, and faced the other girl.

"What are you doing here, Arla?" he rumbled in an

angry whisper, and his bride, standing within the shadow, trembled so that all the little lily-bells swayed in the dark and trembled with her. She had never heard him speak in a voice like that. She shivered a little, and a sudden thought like a dart swept through her. Was it conceivable that he would ever speak so to her? But—of course this intruder ought to be rebuked!

"I have come because I cannot let this thing go on!" said the girl in a desperate voice. "I have tried to do as you told me. Oh, I have tried with all my might"—and her voice broke in a helpless little sob—"but I can't do it. It isn't *right!*"

"Be still, can't you? You will rouse the house. Do you want to bring disgrace upon us all?"

"If that is the only way," said the girl desperately, lifting lovely darkly circled eyes to his face, and suddenly putting her hands up with a caressing motion and stealing them around his neck—desperate clinging arms that held him fast.

"I can't give you up, Cart! I can't! I *can't!* You promised me so long ago you would marry me, and you've always been putting me off—and now—*this!* I *can't!*"

"Hush!" said the man sternly with a note of desperation in his voice. "You are making me hate you, don't you know that? Don't you know that no good whatever can come of this either for me or yourself? How did you get here anyway? Have you no shame? Who saw you? Tell me quick!"

"Nobody saw me," breathed the girl between sobs. "I came up the fire escape and along the back hall. This was the room I came to that day to take dictation for you when you had a sprained ankle and had to stay out here. Don't you remember? Oh, Cart! You told me then that someday you and I would have a house just like this. Have you forgotten how you kissed my fingers, and the palm of my hand, when they all had gone away and left us to work?"

"Hush!" said the man, his face stern with agony. "No, I haven't forgotten! You know I haven't forgotten! I've explained it all to you over and over again. I thought you were reasonable. I thought you understood that this was necessary in order to save all that I have worked so hard to gain."

"Oh, but Cart! I've tried to, but I can't! I cannot give you up!"

"You won't have to give me up," he soothed impatiently. "We'll see each other every day as soon as I get back from this trip. We'll really be closer together than if we were married, for there'll be nothing to hinder us from having good times whenever we like. No household cares or anything. And really, a man's secretary is nearer—"

There came a sharp imperative tap on the door of the sitting room. McArthur started and pushed the weeping girl from him into a corner.

"Yes?" he said harshly, going over to the door. "Has the car come for me? Well, say, I'll be there in just a minute. There is plenty of time by my watch. But I'll be right down."

There was a painful silence. Sherrill could see the other girl shrinking behind a curtain, could hear the painful breathing as she struggled to keep back the sobs, could see the strained attitude of Carter McArthur as he stood stiffly in the middle of the room glaring toward the frail girl.

"Arla, if you love me, you must go away at once," he said sternly, coming toward the girl again, and now he was within the range of the next room, and Sherrill had to shrink farther back into the shadow again lest he should see her.

Suddenly she saw him stoop, put both arms about the other girl, draw her close to him, and put his lips down on hers, hungrily, passionately, kissing her and devouring her with his eyes, just as he had sometimes on rare and precious occasions done to Sherrill! Sherrill clutched her bridal flowers and shivered as she shrank into the shadow and tried to shut the sight out by closing her eyes, yet could not.

A great awful cold had come down upon her heart, caught it with an icy hand, and was slowly squeezing it to death. She wanted to cry out, as in a nightmare, and waken herself—prove that this was only a hideous dream; yet something was stopping her voice and holding her quiet. It must not be that he should hear her, or see her! It must never happen that she should be drawn into this dreadful scene. She must keep very still, and it would pass. This awful delirium would pass, and her right mind would return! She was going pretty soon to the church to be married to this man, and all this would be forgotten, and she would be telling him sometime how she had watched him and loved him as he prepared to go forth and meet her, her dear bridegroom! He would be kissing *her* fingers and *her* eyelids this way. . . . But no! She was going crazy! That would never happen! A great wall had come down between them. She knew in her heart that now she would never, never tell him! He would never take her in his arms again, or kiss her lips or eyelids, or call her his! That was over forever. A dream that could not come true.

Then an impassioned voice broke the stillness and cut through to the depths of her being. It was his voice with that beloved quality she knew so well!

"Oh my darling, my darling! I can't stand to see you suffer so! There will never be any girl like you to me. Why can't you understand?"

"Then if that is so," broke out the weeping girl, lifting her head with sudden hope, "come with me now! We can get out the way I came and no one will see us. Let us go away! Leave her and leave the business, and everything. No one will see us! Come!"

The man groaned.

"You will not understand!" he murmured impatiently. "It is not possible! Do you want to see me ruined? This girl is rich! Her fortune and the connection with her family will save me. Sometime later there may come a time when I could go with you—not now!"

Then into the midst of the awfulness there swung a sweet-toned silver sound, a clock just outside the door striking the hour in unmistakable terms, and Carter McArthur started away from the girl, fairly flinging her in his haste, till she huddled down on her knees in the corner sobbing.

"Shut up, can't you!" said the man wildly as he rushed over to the mirror and began to brush the powder marks from his otherwise immaculate coat. "Can't you see you're goading me to desperation? I've *got* to go *instantly*! I'm going to be late!"

"And what about me?" wailed the girl. "Would you rather I took poison and lay down in this room to die? Wouldn't that be a nice thing to meet you when you came back from the church?"

But with a last desperate brush of his coat Carter snapped out the light and swung out into the upper hall, slamming the door significantly behind him and hurrying down the stairs with brisk steps that tried to sound merry for the benefit of the servants in the hall below.

The girl's voice died away into a helpless little frightened sob, and then all was still.

And Sherrill stood there in the utter darkness trying to think, trying to gather her scattered senses and realize what had happened, what might happen next. That something cataclysmic had just taken place that would change all her after life she knew; but just for that first instant or two after she heard her bridegroom's footsteps go down the stairs and out the front door, she had not gotten her bearings. It was all that she could do just then to stand still and clutch her great bouquet while the earth reeled under her trembling feet.

The next instant she heard a sound, soft, scarcely perceptible to any but preternaturally quickened senses, that brought her back to the present, the necessity of the moment and the shortness of time.

The sound was the tiniest possible hint of stirring garments and a stealthy step from the corner where the weeping girl had been flung when the angry, frightened bridegroom made his hasty exit.

Instantly Sherrill was in possession of herself and reaching forward accurately with accustomed fingers, touching the switch that sent a flood of light into the sitting room.

Then Sherrill in her white robes stepped to the doorway and confronted the frightened, cowering, blinking interloper, who fell back against the wall, her hands outspread and groping for the door, her eyes growing wide with horror as she caught the full version of her lover's bride.

Chapter 2

For just an instant they faced one another, the bride in her beauty, and her woebegone rival, and in spite of herself Sherrill could not help thinking how pretty this other girl was. Even though she had been crying and there were tears on her lashes. She was not a girl whom crying made hideous. It rather gave her the sweet dewy look of a child in trouble.

She stood wide-eyed, horror and fear on her face, the soft gold of her hair just showing beneath a chic little hat. She was dressed in a stylish street suit of dark blue with slim correct shoes and long-wristed wrinkled white doeskin gloves. Even as she stood, her arms outspread and groping for refuge against the unfriendly wall, she presented an interesting picture. Sherrill could not help feeling sorry for her. There was nothing arrogant about her now. Just the look of a frightened child at bay among enemies.

"How long have you known him?" asked Sherrill, trying to keep her voice from trembling.

The other girl burst forth in an anguished tone, her hands going quickly to her throat, which moved convulsively: "Ever since we were kids!" she said with a choking sob at the end of her words. "Always we've been crazy about each other, even in high school. Then after he got started up in the city, he sent for me to be his secretary so we could be nearer to each other till we could afford to get married. It has never been any different till you came. It was you—*you* who took him away from me—!" and the girl buried her hands in the soggy little handkerchief and gave a great sob that seemed to come from the depths of her being.

Sherrill felt a sudden impulse to put her face down in her lovely roses and sob, too. It somehow seemed to be herself and not this other girl who was sobbing over there against the wall. Oh, how could this great disaster have befallen them both? Carter! Her matchless lover! This girl's lover, too! How could this thing be?

"No," she said, very white and still, her voice almost toneless and unsteady. "I never took him away from you. I never knew there was such a person as you!"

"Well, you took him!" sobbed the other girl, "and there's nothing left for me but to kill myself!" and another great sob burst forth.

"Nonsense!" said Sherrill sharply. "Don't talk that way! That's terrible. You don't get anywhere talking like that! Hush! Somebody will hear you! We've got to be sensible and think what to do!"

"Do?" said Arla, dropping her hands from her face and flashing a look of scorn at the girl in bridal array. "What is there to do? Oh, perhaps you mean how you can get rid of me the easiest way? I don't see why I should make it easy for you I'm sure, but I suppose I will. I'll go away and not make any more trouble of course. I suppose I knew that when I came, but I *had* to come! Oh!"—and she gave another deep sob and turned her head away for an instant, then back to finish her sentence—"and you will go out to the church to marry him. It is easy enough for you to say 'hush' when you are going to marry him!"

"Marry him!" said Sherrill, sudden horror in her voice. "I could never marry him after *this*! Could *you*?"

"Oh yes," said the girl in a quivering, hopeless voice. "I'd marry him if I got the chance! You can't love him the way I do or you would, too. I'd marry him if I had to go through hell to do it!"

Sherrill quivered at the words. She was watching this other girl, thinking fast, and sudden determination came into her face.

"Then you shall!" she said in a low clear voice of determination. "You may get taken at your word. You may have to go through hell for it. But I won't be responsible for that. If you feel that way about it, you shall marry him!"

The other girl looked up with frightened eyes.

"What do you mean?"

"I mean you shall marry him! Now! Tonight!"

"But how could I?" she asked dully. "That would be impossible."

"No, it is not impossible. Come! Quick. We have got to work fast! Listen! There comes somebody to the door. Come with me! Don't make a sound!"

Sherrill snapped the light off and, grasping the gloved hand of the girl, she pulled her after her through the dimly lighted middle rooms and inside her own door, which she swiftly closed behind her, sliding the bolt.

"Now!" she said, drawing a breath of relief. "We've got to work like lightning! Take off your gloves and hat and dress just as fast as you can!"

Sherrill's hands were busy with the fastening of her veil. Carefully she searched out the hairpins that held it and lifted it off, laying it in a great billow upon the bed, her hands at once searching for the fastening of her own bridal gown.

"But what are you going to do?" asked the other girl staring at her wildly, though she began automatically to pull off her long gloves.

"I'm going to put these things on you," said Sherrill, pulling off her dress over her head frantically. "*Hurry*, won't you? The car is probably out there waiting now. They'll begin to get suspicious if we are a long time. Take off your hat quick! And your dress! Will it just pull over your head? Hurry, I tell you! What kind of stockings have you got on? Tan ones? That won't do. Here, I've got another pair of silver ones in the drawer. I always have two pairs in case of a run. Sit down there, and peel yours off quick! I wonder if my shoes will fit you. You'll have to try them anyway, for we couldn't get any others!"

Sherrill kicked her silver shoes off and groped in the closet, bringing out an old pair of black satin ones and stepping into them hurriedly. The jeweled buckles glinted wickedly.

Her mind was working rapidly now. She dashed to her suitcase and rooted out a certain green taffeta evening gown, a recent purchase, one that she had especially liked and had planned to take with her, in case anything should delay her trunk. She dropped it over her own head, pulling it down with hurried hands and a bitter thought of what pleasure she had taken in it when she bought it. If she had known—ah, *if she had known*! But there was no time for sentiment.

The other girl was fitting on the silver stockings and shoes, her hands moving slowly, uncertainly.

"Here, let me fasten those garters!" said Sherrill almost compassionately. "You really must work faster than this! Stand up. Can you manage to walk in those shoes? They're a bit long, aren't they? My foot is long and slim. Stand up quick and take off that dark slip. Here, here's the white slip," and she slid it over the golden head of the other girl. Queer, their hair was the same color!

Sherrill's mind was so keyed up that she thought of little painful things that at another time would not have attracted her attention.

"But I can't do this!" said Arla Prentiss, suddenly backing away from the lovely folds of ivory satin that Sherrill was holding for her to slip into. "I couldn't ever get away with it! Cart would kill me if I tried to do a thing like this!"

"Well, you were talking about killing yourself a few minutes ago," said Sherrill sharply, wondering at herself as she said it. "It would be only a choice of deaths in that case, wouldn't it? For mercy's sake, stand still so I won't muss your hair! This dress has *got* to go on you, and mighty quick, too!"

"But I couldn't get away with a thing like this!" babbled Arla as she emerged from the sweeping folds of satin and found herself clothed in a wedding garment, drifting away in an awesome train such as her wildest dreams had never pictured.

"Oh yes, you could," said Sherrill, snapping the fastenings firmly into place and smoothing down the skirt hurriedly. "All you've got to do is to walk up the aisle and say yes to things."

"Oh, I *couldn't!*" said Arla in sudden terror. "Why, they would know the minute I reached the church that it wasn't you! They would never let it get even as far as walking up the aisle. They would *mob* me! They would *drive me out*—!" She paused with a great sob and sank down to the chair again.

"*Get up!*" said Sherrill, standing over her fiercely. "You'll ruin that dress! Listen! There is someone coming to the door! Hush! Yes? Are you calling for me?" Sherrill spoke in a pleasant casual tone. "Is the car ready for me? You say it's been ready ten minutes? Oh, well"—she laughed a high little unnatural trill—"that's all right! They always expect a bride to be late. Well, tell the man I'll be down in a minute or two now!"

The maid retreated down the stairs, and Sherrill flew over to the bed and took up the wedding veil carefully.

"Now, stand there in front of the mirror and watch," she commanded as she held the lace cap high and brought it down accurately around the golden head. "Stand still, please. I've got to do this in just a second. And now listen to me."

"But I can't! I can't really!" protested the substitute bride wildly. "I couldn't let you do this for me!"

"You've *got to!*" said Sherrill commandingly. "I didn't get up any of this mess, and it's up to you to put this wedding through. Now listen! The man who is to take me—*you* in—is a stranger to me. His name is Nathan Vane. He's a second cousin of my mother's family and he's never seen me. He hadn't arrived yet when I came up to dress. Neither had the maid of honor, and she's a stranger to me, too. Her name is Rena Scott. They'll both be waiting at the door for you and will be the only ones who will have a chance to talk to you. All you'll have to do will be to smile and take his arm and go up the aisle. This is the step we're taking." Sherrill stood away and went slowly forward. "You'll see how the others do it. You're clever, I can see. And when you get up there, all you've got to do is answer the questions and say things over after the minister, only using your *own* name instead of mine. Ten to one nobody will notice. You can speak in a low voice. The maid of honor will take your bouquet, and you'll need to put out your left hand for the ring. Here! You must have the diamond, too!" and Sherrill slipped her beautiful diamond engagement ring off her finger and put it on Arla's.

"Oh," gasped Arla, "you're wonderful! I *can't* let you do all this!"

"Hold your head still!" commanded Sherrill. "This orange wreath droops a little too much over that ear. There! Isn't that right? Really, you look a lot like me! I doubt if even the bridegroom will know the difference at first—wedding veils make such a change in one!"

"Oh, but," gasped Arla, "Carter *will* know me; I'm *sure* he will! And suppose, suppose he should make a scene!"

"He won't!" said Sherrill sharply. "He hasn't the nerve!" she added cryptically, and suddenly knew that it was true and she had never known it before.

"But if he should!"

"He won't!" said Sherrill more surely. "And if he does we'll all be in it, so you won't be alone."

31

"Oh! Will you be there, too?" Arla said it in a tone of wonder and relief.

"Why, of course," said Sherrill in the tone of a mother reproving a child. "I'll be there, perhaps before you are."

"Oh, why don't you go *with* me?"

"That would be a situation, wouldn't it?" commented Sherrill sarcastically. "Former bride and substitute bride arrive together! For heaven's sake, don't weep on that satin—it's bad luck! And don't talk about it anymore, or you'll have me crying, too, and that would be just too bad! Here! Take your bouquet. No, hold it on this arm, and your veil and train over the other, now! All set? I'm turning off this light, and you must go out and walk right down the steps quickly. They are all the caterer's people out there; they won't know the difference. You really look a lot like me. For mercy's sake, don't look as if you were going to your own funeral. Put on a smile and *wear it all the evening*. And listen! You tell Mr. McArthur as soon as you get in the car on the way back with him, that if he plays any tricks or doesn't treat you right, or doesn't bring you back smiling to your reception, then I'll tell everybody here the whole truth! I'll tell it to everybody that knows him! And I mean what I say!"

"Oh!" gasped Arla, with a dubious lifting of the trouble in her eyes, and then, "*Oh!* Do we *have to come back* for the *reception*? Can't we just disappear?"

"If you disappear, the whole story will come out in the papers tomorrow morning! I'll see to that!" threatened

Sherrill ominously. "I'm not going to be made a fool of. But if you come back and act like sane people and go away in the usual manner, it will just be a good joke that we have put over for reasons of our own, see? Now go, quick! We mustn't get them all worked up because you are so late!"

Sherrill snapped out the light and threw open the door, stepping back into the shadow herself and watching breathlessly as Arla took the first few hesitating steps. Then as she grew more confident, stepping off down the hall, disappearing down the stairs, Sherrill closed the door and went over to the window that overlooked the front door.

The front steps were a blaze of light, and she could see quite plainly the caterer's man who was acting as footman, standing by and helping a vision in white into the car. The door slammed shut, and the car drove away with a flourish. Sherrill watched till it swept around the curve and went toward the gateway. Then she snapped on a tiny bed light and gathered in haste a few things, her black velvet evening wrap, her pearl evening bag, a small sheet of notepaper, and her gold pencil. She would have to write a note to Aunt Pat. Her mind was racing on ahead! The keys to her own little car! Where had she put them? Oh yes, in the drawer of her desk. Had she forgotten anything?

The bride's car had barely turned into the street before Sherrill went with swift quiet steps back through those two rooms again, into the back hall, cautiously out through the window that Arla had left open, onto the fire escape, and down into the side yard.

It was but the work of a moment to unlock her door of the garage. Fortunately the chauffeur was not there. He had taken Aunt Pat, of course, and everybody who would have known her was at the church. With trembling fingers she started her car, backed out the service drive, and whirled away to the church.

She threaded her way between the big cars parked as far as she could see either way from the church. Could she manage to get hidden somewhere before the service really began?

Breathlessly she drove her car into a tiny place on the side street, perilously near to a fire hydrant, and recklessly threw open her door. The police would be too busy out in the main avenue to notice perhaps, and anyway she could explain to them afterward. Even if she did have to pay a fine, she must get into that church.

A hatless young man in a trim blue serge suit was strolling by as she plunged forth from her car, and fortunately, for she caught the heel of her shoe in the billowy taffeta that was much too long for driving a car, and would have gone headlong if he had not caught her.

"I beg your pardon," he said pleasantly as he set her upon her feet again. "Are you hurt?"

"Oh no!" said Sherrill, smiling agitatedly. "Thank you so much. You saved me from a bad fall. I was just in a terrible hurry," and she turned frantic eyes toward the looming side of the church across the street. The young man continued to keep a protective arm about her and eye her anxiously.

"You're sure you're not hurt?" he asked again. "You didn't strike your head against the running board?"

"No!" she gasped breathlessly, trying to draw away. "I'm quite all right. But please, I must hurry. I am late now."

"Where do you want to go?" he asked, shifting his hand to her elbow and taking a forward step with her.

"Over there"—she motioned frantically—"to the church. I must get in before the ceremony begins."

"You ought to wait until you get your breath," he urged.

"I can't! I've *got* to get there!" and she tried to pull away from him and fly across the street. But he kept easy pace with her, helping her up to the curb.

"Don't you want to go around to the front door?" he said as she turned toward the side entrance.

"No!" she said, her heart beating so fast that it almost choked her. "This little side door. I want to get up to the choir loft."

"Well, I'm coming with you!" he announced, fairly lifting her up the steps. "You're all shaken up from that fall. You're trembling! Can I take you to your friends? You're not fit to be alone."

"I'm—all—right!" panted Sherrill, fetching a watery

smile and finding the tears right at hand.

"Don't hurry!" he commanded, circling her waist impersonally with a strong arm and fairly lifting her up the narrow winding stair that led to the choir loft. "You've plenty of time. Don't you hear? Those are the preliminary chords to the wedding march. The bride must be just at the door! Take it slow and easy!"

They arrived at the top of the stair in an empty choir loft. It was a church of formal arrangement, with the organ console down out of sight somewhere and the choir high above the congregation, visible only when standing to sing, and then only to one who dared to look aloft.

The whole quiet place was fully screened by plumy palms, and great feathery tropical ferns, and not even a stray from the street had discovered this vantage point from which to watch the ceremony. They had it all to themselves. No curious eyes could watch the face of the agonized bride-that-was-to-have-been.

Sherrill nestled in wearily against the wall behind the thickest palm, where yet she could peer through and see everything. She thanked her unknown friend pantingly with a hasty fervor, and then forgot he was still beside her.

Breathlessly she leaned forward, looking down, catching a glimpse of the bridegroom as he stood tall and handsome beside the best man, a smile of expectancy upon his face. Her bridegroom, watching for *her* to come! Her heart contracted and a spasm of pain passed over her face. She mustn't, oh, she mustn't cry! This wasn't *her wedding*! This was something she must nerve herself to go through. This was something tragic that must move aright or all the future would be chaos.

Then she remembered and her eyes turned tragically, alertly, down the aisle to the front door, her hand unconsciously pressed against her heart in a quick little frantic motion.

Yes, the bride had arrived! Of course she might have known that or the wedding march would not be ringing out its first stately measures! Yes, there was the huddle of rainbow-colored dresses that were the bridesmaids. How glad she was that none of them were really intimate friends. All of them new friends from Aunt Pat's circle of acquaintances. Her own girlhood friends were all too poor or too far away to be summoned. The first of them, the pink ones, were stepping forward now, slowly differentiating themselves from the mass of color, beginning the procession with measured, stilled tread; and back in the far dimness of the hall, silhouetted against the darkness of the out-of-doors, she could see the mist of whiteness that must be the bride, with the tall dark cousin beside her. Yes, the bride had come. Sherrill's secret fear that she might somehow lose her nerve and escape on the way to the church was unfounded. This girl really wanted Carter enough to go through this awful ordeal to get him! Besides, a girl couldn't very well run away and hope to escape detection in a bridal gown. Sherrill felt a hysterical laugh coming to her lips that changed into a quiver of tears, and a little shiver that ran down her back. And then suddenly she felt that strong arm again just under her elbow, supporting her, just as her knees began to manifest a tendency to crumple under her.

"Oh, thank you!" she breathed softly, letting her weight rest on his arm. "I'm—a little—nervous—I guess!"

"You aren't fit to stand!" he whispered. "I wonder if I couldn't find you a chair down there in the back room?"

She shook her head.

"It wouldn't be worthwhile," she answered, "the ceremony will soon be over. You are very kind, but I'll be all right."

He adjusted his arm so it would better support her, and somehow it helped and calmed her to feel him standing there. She had no idea how he looked or who he was. She hadn't really looked at him. She just knew he was kind, and that he was a stranger who didn't know a thing about her awful predicament. If he had been a friend who knew, she couldn't have stood with him there. But it was like being alone with herself to have him staying there so comfortingly. After it was over she would never likely see him again. She hoped he would never know who she was nor anything about it. She hadn't really thought anything about him as a personality. He was just something by the way to lean upon in her extremity.

The pink bridesmaids were halfway up the middle aisle now, the green at the formal distance behind, the violet just entering past the first rank of seats with the blue waiting behind. Their faces wore the set smile of robots endeavoring to do their best to keep the step. There was no evidence so far that either the wedding party or the audience had discovered anything unusual about this wedding or unexpected about the bride. She suddenly gasped at the thought of the gigantic fraud that she was about to perpetrate. Had she a right to do this? But it was too late to think about that now.

Sherrill's eyes went back to the bridegroom standing there waiting, his immaculate back as straight and conventional as if nothing out of the ordinary had occurred a half hour before. She remembered with a stab of pain the powder that he had brushed from his left lapel. Was there any trace of it left? She had a sudden sick faint feeling as if she would like to lay her head down and close her eyes. She reeled just a tiny bit, and the young man by her side shifted his arms, putting the right one unobtrusively about her so that he could better steady her, and putting his left hand across to support her elbow. She cast him a brief little flicker of a smile of gratitude, but her eyes went swiftly back to the slow procession that was advancing up the aisle, so slow it seemed to her like the march of the centuries.

The bride was standing in the doorway now, just behind the yellow-clad maid of honor, her hand lying on the arm of the distant cousin, her train adjusted perfectly; no sign on the face of the maid of honor that she had noticed it was the wrong bride whom she had just prepared for her appearance. They didn't know it yet! Nobody knew what was about to happen except herself! The thought was overwhelming!

Suddenly her eyes were caught by the little figure in gray down in the front seat. Aunt Pat! Poor Aunt Pat! What would she think? And after all her kindness, and the money she had spent to make this wedding a perfect one of its kind! She must do something about Aunt Pat at once!

Her trembling fingers sought the catch of her handbag and brought out pencil and paper. The young man by her side watched her curiously, sympathetically. Who was this lovely girl? What had stirred her so deeply? Had she perhaps cared for the bridegroom herself, and not felt able to face the audience during the ceremony? Or was the bride her sister, dearly beloved, whom she could not bear to part from? They truly resembled one another, gold hair, blue eyes; at least he was pretty sure this one's eyes were blue, as much as he could judge by the brief glimpse he had had of them here in the dimness of the gallery.

She was looking about for someplace to lay her paper, and there was none, because the gallery rail was completely smothered in palms.

"Here!" he said softly, sensing her need, and drew out a broad, smooth leather notebook from his pocket, holding it firmly before her, his other arm still about her.

So Sherrill wrote rapidly, with tense, trembling fingers:

Dear Aunt Pat:
I'm not getting married tonight. Please be a good
sport, and don't let them suspect you didn't know.
Please, dearest.

Sherrill

The young man beside her had to hold the notebook very firmly. He couldn't exactly help seeing the hastily scrawled words, though he tried not to—he really did. He was an honorable young man. But he was also by this time very much in sympathy with this unknown lovely girl. However, he treated the whole affair in the most matter-of-fact way.

"You want that delivered?" he whispered.

"Oh, would you be so good?"

"Which one? The little old lady in gray right down here?"

"Oh, how did you know?" Sherrill met his sympathetic gaze in passing wonder.

"I saw you looking down at her," he answered with a boyish grin. "You want her to read it before she leaves the church?"

"Oh yes, please! Could you do it, do you think?"

"Of course," he answered with confidence. "Do you happen to know if there is a door at the foot of these stairs opening into the church?"

"Yes, there is," said Sherrill.

"Well, there's no one else in the seat all across to the side aisle. I don't know why I couldn't slide in there without being noticed while the prayer is going on."

"Oh, could you do that?" said Sherrill with great relief in her eyes, and looking down quickly toward the front seat that stretched a vacant length across to the flower-garlanded aisle. "Would you mind? It would be wonderful! But there's a ribbon across the seat."

He grinned again socially.

"It would take more than a ribbon to keep me out of a seat I wanted to get into. Are you all right if I leave you for a minute?"

"Of course!" said Sherrill, drawing herself up and trying to look self-sufficient. "Oh, I can never thank you enough!"

"Forget it!" said the young man. "Well, I'd better hurry down and reconnoiter. *Sure* you're all right?"

"Sure." She smiled tremulously.

He was gone, and Sherrill realized that she felt utterly inadequate without him. But suddenly she knew that the procession had arrived at the altar and disposed itself in conventional array. Startled, she looked down upon them. Did nobody know yet? She should have been watching Carter's face. But of course he would have had his back to her. She could not have told what he was feeling from just his back, could she?

She moved a little farther and could see his face now

between the next two palms, and it was white as death, white and frightened! Did she imagine it? No, she felt sure. He had swung half reluctantly around into his place beside Arla, but he lifted his hand to his mouth as if to steady his lips, and she could see that his hand trembled. Didn't the audience see that? They would. They could not help it. But they would likely lay it to the traditional nervousness all bridegrooms were supposed to feel. Still, *Carter*! He was always so utterly confident, so at his ease anywhere. How could they credit him with ordinary nervousness?

But the ceremony was proceeding now, *her* bridegroom, Carter McArthur, getting married to *another* girl, and there she was above him, unseen, watching.

"Dearly beloved, we are gathered together in the sight of God and in the presence of this company to join together this man and this woman in the bonds of holy matrimony—"

Chapter 3

A great wrench came to Sherrill's heart as she looked down and realized that but for a trifling accident, she would even now be standing down there in that white dress and that veil getting married! If she had not tried to go through those two rooms without being seen, if she had not planned to go and show herself to Mary—poor Mary, who was lying on her bed even now thinking she was forgotten—if just such a little trifle as that had not been, she would be down there with Carter now, blissfully happy, being bound to him forever on this earth as long as they both should live. So irrevocable!

For an instant as she thought of it, her heart contracted. Why did she do this awful thing, this thing which would separate her forever from the man she loved so dearly? She could have slipped back into her room unseen; the other girl would have gone away, afraid to do anything else; and she could have gone to the church, and nobody would ever have been the wiser. She would have been Mrs. McArthur. Then what could Arla Prentiss do? Even if she had taken her life, few would have ever heard of it.

But she, Sherrill Cameron, even if she were Sherrill McArthur, would never have been happy. She knew that, even as she looked down into the white face of the staring, stony-eyed bridegroom. For between her and any possibility of joy there would always have come that look on his face when he had kissed the other girl and told her he would always love her best. She never could have laughed down nor forgotten that look. How many other girls had he said that to? she wondered. Was Arla, too, deceived about it? She evidently thought that she, Sherrill, was her only rival. But there might have been others, too. Oh, if one couldn't trust a man, what was the joy of marriage? If one were not the only one enthroned in a man's heart, why bind oneself to his footsteps for life? Sherrill had old-fashioned simple ideas and standards of love and marriage. But Sherrill was wondering if she would ever be able to trust *any* living man again, since Carter, who had always seemed such a paragon of perfection, had proved himself so false and weak! No, she could never have married him, not after seeing him with Arla. Oh, were all men like that?

And there he was getting married to the other girl, and not doing a thing about it! She was sure he knew now, and he was making no protest.

And then suddenly she saw her own heart and knew that somewhere back in her mind she had been harboring the hope that he would do something. That he would somehow—she didn't know how, for it wasn't reasonable—find a way to stop this marriage and explain all the wrong, and that joy would find its way through sorrow! But he wasn't doing a thing! He didn't dare do a thing! Fear, stark and ugly, was written upon his face. He *knew* himself to be guilty. He was standing there before the assembled multitude, the "dearly beloved" of the service, and not one of them knew a thing about what was happening but himself, and he knew, and he *wasn't doing a thing*! He *didn't dare*!

And then, just down below her in the front seat, a little motion attracted her eyes. A white ribbon lifted, and a figure slid beneath. A young man in a blue serge suit with a pleasant face had glided so quietly into the seat beside the little gray lady with the white laces that nobody around her seemed to have even noticed. He was handing her a folded paper and whispering unobtrusively a word in her ear. Aunt Pat had her note now, and in a moment she would know the truth! How would Aunt Pat take it? She was perfectly capable of rising in her delicate little might and putting a stop to the service. How awful it would be for everybody if she did that! Perhaps the note ought to have been held up until the service was over.

Then even with the thought came that frightful challenge. Was it only last night at the rehearsal that they had joked over it?

"Therefore if any man can show just cause why they may not lawfully be joined together, let him now declare it, or else hereafter forever hold his peace."

Her eyes were fastened on Aunt Pat in terror! What if Aunt Pat should arise and say she knew a just cause! Oh, why had she sent that note down so soon? If she could only recall it!

But Aunt Pat was sitting serenely with the note in her hand, reading it, and a look of satisfaction was on her lips, the kind a nice house cat might wear when she had just successfully evaded detection in licking the creamy frosting from a huge cake. Actually, Aunt Pat was looking up with a smile on her strong old face and a twinkle in her bright old eyes. It was almost as if she were *pleased*! The young man in the blue serge who had delivered the note was nowhere in sight, and yet she couldn't remember seeing him slip out again, though the white ribbon was swaying a little as if it had recently been stirred.

That deathly stillness settled down over the audience, an audible stillness, even above the voice of the organ undertone; and Sherrill, puzzling over Aunt Pat, turned fascinated eyes toward her former lover. How was he standing this challenge? Whichever girl he thought was standing beside him, surely he could not take this calmly. Oh, if she might only look in his face and see his innocence written there! Yet she knew that could never be!

But she was not prepared for the haggard look she saw on his face, a terror such as a criminal at bay might wear when about to face an angry mob who desired to hang him. The look in his eyes was awful! All their lively brilliancy gone! Only fear, uncertainty, a holding of the breath to listen! His hands were working nervously. She felt almost a contemptuous pity for him, and then a wrenching of the heart again. Her lover, to have come to such a place as that! Almost she groaned aloud, and looked toward the radiant bride, for radiant she really seemed to be, carrying out her part perfectly. Sherrill had felt she could do it. She was clever, and she had an overwhelming love!

And yet in spite of her horror over what was happening, somehow as she looked down there it seemed to be her own self that was standing there in that white satin gown and veil about to take sweet solemn vows upon her. What had she done to put her bright hopes out of her life forever! Oh, hadn't she been too hasty? Might there not have been some other explanation than the only obvious one? Ought she perhaps to have gone in and confronted those two in each other's arms?

Then suddenly the girl down there before the altar spoke, and her voice was clear and ringing. The great church full of people held their breath again to catch every syllable:

"I, Arla, take thee, Carter—"

Sherrill felt her breath coming in slow gasps, felt as if someone were stifling her. She strained her ears to hear, on through that long paragraph that she had learned so carefully by heart, her lips moving unconsciously to form the words before she heard them. And Arla was speaking them well, clearly, with a triumphant ring to them, like a call to the lover she had lost. Could he fail to understand and answer? Sherrill pressed her hands hard upon her aching heart and tried to take deep breaths to keep her senses from swimming off away from her.

Again she had a feeling as if that girl down there was herself; yet she was here looking on!

And now it was the bridegroom's turn!

Sherrill closed her eyes and focused every sense upon the words. Would he respond? Would he do something, or would he let it go on? For now he surely knew!

His voice was low, husky; she could scarcely hear the words above the tender music that she herself had planned to accompany the vow they were plighting. Afterward she fancied it must have been by some fine inner sense rather than the hearing of her ears that she knew what he was saying, for he spoke like one who was afraid!

"I, Carter, take thee, *Arla*—!"

Ahh! He had said it. He knew now and he had accepted it! He was taking the words deliberately upon his lips. Shamefully, perhaps, like one driven to it, but he had taken them. Her lover was marrying another girl!

He had not even tried to do anything about it!

With a little gasp like a deep-driven sob, she dropped upon her knees and hid her face in her hands, while the gallery in which she knelt reeled away into space, and she suddenly seemed to be hurled as from a parapet by the hands of her former bridegroom, down, down into infinite space with darkness growing all about her. Ah! She had been foolish! Why had she not known that this would happen to her? Love like hers could not be broken, torn from its roots ruthlessly, without awful consequences. How had she thought she could go through this and live through it? Was this the end? Was she about to die, shamelessly, and all the world know that she had a broken heart?

Ahh!

A breath of fresh air came sharply into her face from an opening door just as she was about to touch an awful depth, a strong arm lifted her upon her feet, and a glass of cool water was pressed to her lips.

"I thought this might be refreshing," a friendly casual voice said, not at all as if anything unusual were happening.

She drank the water gratefully, and afterward she wondered if it were only her imagination that she seemed to remember clinging to a hand. But of course that could not have been.

He looked down at her, smiling, as if he might have been a brother.

"Now, do you feel you have to stay up here till this

performance is ended and all the people escorted out below?" he asked pleasantly, "or would you like to slip down now and get your car out of traffic before things get thick? You look awfully tired to me, but if you feel you should stay, I'll bring up a chair."

"Oh," said Sherrill bewilderedly, "is it—are they almost—?"

She leaned forward to look.

"Just about over I fancy," said the man, who was steadying her so efficiently.

And as if to verify his words, the voice of the clergyman came clearly: "I pronounce you husband and wife. Whom therefore God hath joined together, let no man put asunder."

She shuddered and shrank back. The man could feel her tremble as he supported her.

"This would be a good time if you are going to slip away," he whispered. "There is just the brief prayer, and then the procession out is rather rapid. I fancy traffic will thicken up quickly after they are out. Or would you rather wait until they are all gone?"

"Oh no!" said Sherrill anxiously. "I must get back to the house if possible before they get there!"

"Then we should go at once!"

She cast one more glance down at the two who stood with clasped hands and bowed heads, and rapidly reviewed what was to come.

After this prayer there was the kiss!

She shivered! No, she did not want to see Arla lift her radiant head for that kiss. She had watched him kiss her once that night; she could not stand it again.

"Yes! Let us go quickly!" she whispered hurriedly with one last lingering glance, and then she stumbled toward the stairs.

Out in the cool darkness with a little breeze blowing in her face and the bright kind stars looking down, Sherrill came to herself fully again, her mind racing on to what was before her.

She was glad for the strong arm that still helped her across the street, but she felt the strength coming into her own feet again.

"I can't ever be grateful enough to you," she said as they reached the car, and she suddenly realized that she had treated him as if he were a mere letter carrier or a drink of water. "You have done a lot for me tonight. If I had more time, I would try to make you understand how grateful I am."

"You needn't do that," he said gently. "You just needed a friend for a few minutes, and I'm glad I happened by. I wonder if there isn't something more I could do? I'm going to drive you home, of course, if you'll let me, for you really shouldn't try yourself, believe me. Or is there some friend you would prefer whom I could summon?"

"Oh no," she said, looking frightened. "I don't want

anyone I know. I want to get back before they miss me—and really, I think I could drive. Still if you don't mind, it *would* be a great help. But I hate to take more of your time."

"I'd love to," he said heartily. "I haven't another thing to do this evening. In fact, I'm a stranger in town and was wondering what I could do to pass the time until I could reasonably retire for the night."

"You seem to have been just sent here to help in a time of need," she said simply as he put her into the car and then took the wheel himself.

"I certainly am glad," he said. "Now, which way? Couldn't we take a shortcut somewhere and keep away from this mob of cars?"

"Yes," said Sherrill, roused now fully to the moment. "Turn to the left here and go down the back street."

"I wonder," he said as they whirled away from the church with the triumphant notes of the wedding march breaking ruthlessly into their conversation, "if there wouldn't be some way I could serve you the rest of the evening? I'm wholeheartedly at your service if there is any way in which just a mere, may I say friend, can help out somewhere?"

"Oh," said Sherrill, giving him a startled look in the semidarkness, "you're really wonderfully kind. But—I hate to suggest any more, and—it's such a silly thing!—"

"Please," said the young man earnestly, "just consider me an old friend for the evening, won't you, and ask what you would ask if I were."

Sherrill was still a second, giving him a troubled look.

"Well, then—would you consider it a great bore to go back with me to that reception and sort of hang around with me awhile? Just as if you were an old friend who had been invited to the wedding? You see, I—well, I'm afraid I'll have to explain."

"You needn't if you don't want to," said the young man promptly. "I'll be delighted to go without explanations. Just give me my cue, and I'll take any part you assign me if I can help you in any way. Only, how the dickens am I going to a swell wedding reception in a blue serge suit?"

"Oh," said Sherrill blankly. "Of course, I hadn't thought of that. And I suppose there wouldn't be any place open near here where we could rent some evening things? Well, of course it was a foolish idea, and I oughtn't to have suggested it. I'll go through the thing all right alone, I'm sure. I'm feeling better every minute."

"No," said the young man, "it *wasn't* and *you're not*! I've got a perfectly good dress suit and everything else I'll need in a suitcase up in my room in the hotel, and it's just around that corner there. If you think it wouldn't make you too late, I could just park you outside a minute and run up and get the suitcase. Then I could put it on in the garage or somewhere, couldn't I? Or would it be better for me to get dressed in the conventional manner and take a taxi back?"

"Oh," laughed Sherrill nervously, "why, we'll stop at

the hotel, of course. It won't take you long, and they can't have started home yet, can they?"

"They haven't got the bride and groom into their car yet, if you ask me," said the young man blithely. "I doubt if they're out at the front door, to judge by that music. I've sort of been humming it inside since we started. You know, there's always a delay getting the cars started. Here's the hotel. Shall I really stop and get my things?"

While she waited before the hotel, she put back her head and closed her eyes, her mind racing ahead to the things she had to do. The worst nightmare of the evening was yet to come, and for an instant as she faced it she almost had a wild thought of leaving the whole thing, kind young man and all, and racing off into the world somewhere to hide. Only of course she knew she wouldn't do it. She couldn't leave Aunt Pat like that!

And then almost incredibly the young man was back with a suitcase in his hand.

"I had luck," he explained as he swung himself into the car. "I just caught the elevator going up with a man to the top floor. I had only to unlock my door, snatch up my suitcase, and lock the door again, so I caught the elevator coming back. I call that service. How about it?"

"You certainly made record time," said Sherrill. "Now turn right at the next corner, and go straight till I tell you to turn."

They were out in a quiet street and making good time when she spoke again.

"I've got to tell you the situation," she said gravely, "or you won't understand what it's all about and why I want you to help. You see, this was *my* wedding tonight."

"Your wedding?" He turned a startled face toward her.

"Yes, and I doubt whether very many have taken it in yet that I wasn't the bride."

"But—why—how—when—?"

"Yes, of course," explained Sherrill. "It all happened less than an hour ago. I was all dressed to go to the church, and I happened to find out about *her*. I—saw them together—saying good-bye—"

She caught her breath, trying to steady her voice and keep the tears back, and he said gently, "Don't tell me if that makes it harder. I'll get the idea all right. You want me to hang around and be an old friend, is that the idea?"

"That's it," said Sherrill. "I thought if I just had *somebody*—somebody they all *didn't know*—somebody they could think had been an old friend back in my home in the West before I came here, it wouldn't be so hard."

"I understand perfectly," he said. "I am your very special oldest friend, and I'll do my noblest to help you carry off the situation." His voice was gravely tender and respectful, and somehow it gave her great relief to know he would stand by her for the evening.

"You are wonderful," she said in a shaky little voice. "But, I never thought, is there—have you a wife or, or—somebody who would mind you doing that for a stranger?"

He laughed blithely, as if he were glad about it.

"No, I haven't a wife. I haven't even somebody. Nothing to worry about in that direction. Though I wouldn't think much of them even if I had if they would mind lending me for such an occasion."

"Well, I guess I'm not worth much that I'm letting you do it, but things are almost getting me. I was pretty tired and excited when it happened, and then, you know, it was less than an hour ago, and kind of sudden."

"Less than an hour ago!" said the young man, appalled. "Why, how did you work it to get the other girl there all dressed up?"

"I waited till he had started to the church. I guess I was dazed at first and didn't know what to do. I just dragged her into my room and made her put on the wedding things and sent her off in the car. You see, the man who was to give me away was a distant cousin who didn't know me, had been late in arriving, and the maid of honor was a friend of my aunt's who had never seen me either."

"But didn't the bridegroom know?"

"Not until he saw her coming up the aisle, or—I'm not sure *when* he knew, but—" There came that piteous catch in her voice again. "I don't know just *when* he knew, but he accepted it all right. He—used *her name* in the service, not mine. I haven't thought much yet about what I did. But I guess it was a rather dreadful thing to do. Still—I don't know what else I could have done. The wedding was all there, and *I* couldn't marry him, could I? Perhaps you think I am a very terrible girl. Perhaps you won't want to pose as my friend now you know."

He could hear that the tears were very near to the surface now, and he hastened to say earnestly, "I think you are a very brave and wonderful girl."

"Here's where we turn," she said breathlessly, "and I think that's their car down two blocks away. They have to go in the front drive, but we'll go on around here to the service entrance. Then we can get in before they see us."

"And by the way, oughtn't I know your name?" he said quietly. "Mine is Graham Copeland, and you can call me 'Gray' for short. It will sound more schoolmatish, won't it? All my friends call me Gray."

"Thank you," said Sherrill gravely. "And I'm Sherrill Cameron. That was my aunt Pat you took the note down to. She is Miss Catherwood. She didn't know either. I had to write and tell her."

"I couldn't help seeing some of the words," he admitted. "Will she stand by you?"

"I—don't know—!" Sherrill hesitated. "I thought I saw a twinkle in her eye, but it may have been indignation. She's rather severe in her judgments. She may turn me right out of the house after it's over. But if I can only get through the evening without shaming her, I won't care. She's been so very kind to me. I know this will be hard for her to bear. She stands very high in the community and is very proud. But she'll be nice to you. And then there'll be the bridesmaids and ushers. I'll introduce the rest of them. You won't be expected to know everybody. Here we are, and that's the first car just coming into the drive now! Oh, we're in plenty of time! Just leave the car right here. This is out of the way. Yes, lock it. Now, come; we'll go up the fire escape, if you don't mind, and then we won't have to explain ourselves."

Swiftly they stole up the iron stairs, Sherrill ahead, reaching down a guiding hand in the dark, giggling a little, nervously, as they stepped inside the window. Then she scuttled him down the back hall, opened a door to a small room that had been fixed up for the occasion as a dressing room, showed him how to find the front stairs, and directed him where to meet her as soon as he was ready.

Back through the two dim rooms where she had so recently come face-to-face with catastrophe, she hurried; only they were not in confusion now. The maids had been there straightening up. There were no traces of Cassie's suitcase nor Linda's street shoes. All was in immaculate order, the door thrown open to accommodate the expected crowds.

Sherrill slipped into her own room and fastened both doors.

Here, too, were signs of straightening. Her suitcase was closed, the closet doors and bureau drawers shut, everything put carefully away. But this room, of course, was not to be used for the guests. It was where the bride was expected to dress for going away.

Sherrill dashed to the dressing table and tried to obliterate as far as possible the traces of the past hour's experience from her face. She didn't care personally how she looked, but she did not want the assembled multitude to remark on her ghastly appearance. If she must go through this evening, she would do it gallantly.

She waited long enough to possess herself of a great ostrich feather fan that just matched the green of her frock. It would be wonderful to hide behind if need came, and give her a brave appearance. Then she put on the gorgeous necklace of emeralds, with three long pendants of emeralds and diamonds, a family heirloom that Aunt Pat had given her just that day. She must have something to replace the bridal pearls that were hers no longer. There were some rings and bracelets, too. She hadn't had much time to get acquainted with them. She fingered them over and chose one luscious square-cut emerald for her finger. Her hands also should go bravely, not missing the diamond which she had worn for the past four months.

She slipped the magnificent ring on her finger, closed her eyes for a second, taking a deep breath, then hurried downstairs.

There were sounds of approach at the front of the house, the lively chatter of bridesmaids disembarking from their respective cars. Aunt Pat was just entering the front door leaning on Gemmie's arm. Off in the far corner of the great reception room to the right, she could see Carter with his bride huddled under the bower of palms and flowers like a pair of frightened fowls between the clearing of two storms. The bride had her back toward the hall and was talking earnestly. Carter was half turned away, too, casting furtive frantic glances behind him, an ungroomly scowl upon his handsome brow. Poor Arla! Her hell had probably begun!

Sherrill unfurled her green fan and went bravely forward to meet Aunt Pat.

Chapter 4

Gemmie gave Sherrill a frightened scrutinizing glance, took the old lady's wrap and scarf, and fled, casting another worried, puzzled look behind her.

Sherrill took her aunt's arm. The old lady was smiling affably, but there was an inscrutable look about her. Sherrill couldn't tell whether it held disapproval or not. It was a mask—she could see that.

"What's her name? Who is she?" demanded the old lady out of the side of her mouth, without moving her lips or disturbing her smile. She was steering Sherrill straight toward the bridal bower. Sherrill had to speak quickly, keeping her own lips in a smile that she was far from feeling.

"She's his secretary, Arla Prentiss. He's known her for years."

"Hmm! The puppy!" grunted the old lady under her smile, and then raising her voice a little, "Come, let's get this line in order! Where's this bride and groom? Mrs. McArthur, Mr. McArthur—" Her voice was smooth, even, jovial and yet frigid, if such a combination can be imagined. Just as if she had not been calling the groom "Carter" for the past six weeks!

The bride and groom swung around to face her, the bride with a heightened color and a quick lifting of her chin as of one who expects a rebuff, the groom with every bit of color drained from his handsome face, and points of steel in his sulky eyes.

"I'm sure I hope you'll both be very happy," said Aunt Pat with a grimly humorous twist of her smile, implying perhaps that they didn't deserve to be, and then with just a tinge of the Catherwood haughtiness, she took her place in the line as had been arranged.

Now had come the most trying moment for Sherrill, the one spot in the program that she hadn't been able to think out ahead. It was as if she had blindly shut her eyes to the necessity of speaking to these two, unable to prepare the right words of formal greeting, unable to school her expression. And here she was facing them with that silly smile upon her lips and nothing in her heart to say but horror at the situation, which such a brief time ago had been so different!

And then, just as a strange constriction came into her throat to stop any words she might try to form with her cold dumb lips, and her smile seemed to her to be fading out across the room and getting hopelessly away from her forever, she felt a touch upon her arm, and there miraculously was Copeland, meticulously arrayed in evening garb, a cheery grin upon his face and merry words upon his lips: "Is this where you want me to be, Sherrill?"

The ice melted from Sherrill's heart, her frightened throat relaxed, fear fled away, and the smile danced back into her eyes. He had come in just the nick of time. A warm feeling of gratitude flowed around her heart, and her voice returned with a delightful little lilt.

"Oh, is that you, Gray? How did you manage to get back so soon? Yes, this is just where I want you. Let me introduce you to the bride. Mrs. McArthur, my friend Mr. Copeland of Chicago. Mr. McArthur, Graham."

Arla eyed the two keenly.

"Were you old schoolmates?" she asked the stranger brightly. "Carter and I went to school together from kindergarten up through senior high."

"Well, not exactly schoolmates," answered Copeland with an amused glance at Sherrill, "but we're pretty good friends, aren't we, Sherrill?" He cast a look of deep admiration and understanding toward the girl in green, and she answered with a glowing look.

"I should say!" She rippled a little laugh. "But come, Graham, they're all arriving in a bunch, and you've got to meet the bridesmaids and ushers. Here, come over to

Aunt Pat first!" and they swung away from the astounded bridal couple with formal smiles.

"Aunt Pat, I want you to know Mr. Graham Copeland of Chicago. He's been a really wonderful friend to me. She's Miss Catherwood, Gray. I've told you about her."

"And why haven't I been told about *him* before?" asked Aunt Pat as she took the young man's hand and gave him a keen, quick, friendly look. Then, as her old eyes twinkled, "Oh, I have met him before, haven't I? You had a blue coat on when I saw you last!" and her lips twisted into what would have been called a grin if she had been a few years younger.

"You're one of the conspirators in this practical joke we're playing, I suppose?" and her eyes searched his again.

"I trust I'm a harmless one, at least," he said gracefully.

And then there came a sudden influx of bridesmaids preening their feathers and chattering like a lot of magpies.

They gushed into the room and seemed to fill it with their light and color and jubilant noise.

"Sherrill Cameron! Whatever did you put over on us?"

"Oh, Sherrill, you fraud! All these weeks and we thinking *you* were the bride!"

"What was the idea, Sherrill? Did you expect us to fall over in a faint when we saw another bride?"

"But we all thought it was you for the longest time!"

"I didn't!" said Linda. "I knew when she got out of her car that there was something different about her!"

"Shh!"

Into the midst of the bevy of voices came Sherrill's clear, controlled one, sweet, almost merry, though Aunt Pat turned a keen ear and a keen eye on her and knew she was under great strain: "Girls! Girls! For pity's sake! Hush with your questions! Come and meet the bride, and then get into the receiving line quick! Don't you see the guests are beginning to arrive?"

The girls turned dizzily about as Sherrill, with a smile almost like her own natural one, approached the bride: "Arla—" The name slipped off her tongue glibly, for somehow with Aunt Pat and Graham Copeland in the background she felt more at her ease. "Arla—" The bride turned in quick astonishment to hear herself addressed so familiarly. "Let me introduce your bridesmaids. This is Linda Winters, and Doris Graeme—"

She went on down the row, speaking their names with more and more confidence, and suddenly the best man, who had been on some errand of his office, loomed frowning beside her.

"And oh, here's the best man! Carter, you'll have to make the rest of the introductions. I simply must get these girls into place! Here come all the ushers, too! I'll leave you to introduce them to your wife!" She said it crisply and moved away to make room for them, pushing the laughing bridesmaids before her and arranging them, with room for the ushers between, though everyone knew as well as she did where they ought to stand, having rehearsed it only the night before.

Then Sherrill slid behind them back to her place by Aunt Pat and the stranger, a place that had *not* been rehearsed the night before.

It was a hard place, a trying place, the worst place she could have been. She knew that when she chose it. But she had to face the music, and knew it was better to do it merrily at the head of the line than skulking at the foot where there would be plenty of time for explanation and questions.

So as the crowd of guests surged into the big lovely room, filled with curiosity and excitement, and ready to pull any secret one might have from the air and waft it to the world, it was Sherrill who stood at the head of the line in her lettuce-green taffeta, the little frock she had bought as a whimsy at the last minute, her second-best silver shoes, and the gorgeous Catherwood emeralds blazing on her neck and arms and finger. She was wafting her great feather fan graciously, and by her side was a handsome stranger! Would wonders never cease? The guests stepped in, gave one eager avid glance, and hastened to the fray.

Aunt Pat was next to the stranger, smiling her cat-in-the-cream smile, with twinkles in her eyes and a grim look of satisfaction.

"You ought to be at the head of the line, Aunt Pat," demurred Sherrill. "I really don't belong in this line at all."

"Stay where you are!" commanded the old lady. "This

is *your* wedding, not mine. Run it the way you please. I'm only here to lend atmosphere." She said it from one corner of her mouth, and she twinkled at the stranger. She was standing next to the bride and groom, but she hadn't addressed two words to them since her congratulations. However, they were getting on fairly well with the best man and maid of honor on the other side, and the stage was set for the great oncoming crowd.

Mrs. Battersea with her ultramodern daughter-in-law in the wake headed the procession, with the Reamers, the Hayworths, and the Buells just behind. They represented the least intimate of the guests, the ones who would really be hard to satisfy. Sherrill, with a furtive glance up at the tall stranger by her side, aware of his kindly, reassuring grin, felt a sudden influx of power in herself to go through this ordeal. It helped, too, to realize that several others were having an ordeal also. It probably wasn't just what this stranger would have chosen to do, to play his part in this strange pageant, and she was sure Aunt Pat hated it all, though she was entering into the scene with a zest as if she enjoyed it. Aunt Pat hated publicity like a serpent.

And there were the bride and groom. One could scarcely expect them to enjoy this performance. Sherrill cast them a furtive glance. The bride was a game little thing. She was holding her head high and conversing bravely with all those chattering bridesmaids, who kept surging out of line to get a word with her. And Carter, well, Carter had always been able to adjust himself to his surroundings pretty well, but there was a strained white look about him. Oh, whatever he might have felt for either of his prospective brides, it was scarcely likely that he was enjoying this reception. It was most probable that he would give all he possessed to have a nice hole open in the floor and let him and his Arla through out of sight.

So Sherrill drew a deep breath, summoned a smile, and greeted Mrs. Battersea, sweeping up in purple chiffon with orchids on her ample breast.

"Now, Sherrill, my dear," said the playful lady, "what does this all mean? You've got to give us a full explanation of everything."

"Why, it was just that we thought this would be a pleasant way to do things," smiled Sherrill. "Don't you think it was a real surprise? Mrs. Battersea, do let me introduce my friend Mr. Copeland of Chicago. Oh, Mrs. Reamer, I'm so glad you got well in time to come!"

Suddenly Sherrill felt a thrill of triumph. She was getting away with it! Actually she was! Mrs. Battersea had been not only held at bay but also entirely sidetracked by this new young man introduced into the picture. She closed her mouth on the question that had been just ready to pop out and fixed her eyes on Copeland, a new fatuous smile quickly adjusted, as she passed with avidity to the inquisition of this stranger. Here was she, the first in the line, and it was obviously up to her to get accurate information concerning him and convey it as rapidly as possible to the gathering assembly. Sherrill could see out of the corner of her eye this typical Battersea attitude, even as the guest put up her lorgnette to inspect the young man. She felt a pang of pity for her new friend. Did he realize what he was letting himself in for when he promised to stand by her through this? Oh, but what a help he was! How his very presence had changed the attitude that might have been, the attitude of pity for a cast-off bride! And, too, he had brought in an element of mystery, of speculation. She could see how avidly Mrs. Battersea was drinking in the possibilities as she approached.

But Sherrill drew another breath of relief. The young man by her side would be equal to it. She need not worry.

And there, too, was Aunt Pat! She would not let the first comer linger too long with the new lion of the occasion.

Even with the thought, she heard the woman's first question and saw Aunt Pat instantly, capably, if grimly, take over the Battersea woman. Whether Aunt Pat was going to forgive Sherrill afterward or not for making such a mess of the beautiful stately wedding which she had financed, she would be loyal now and defend her own whether right or wrong. That was Aunt Pat.

Yes, those two could be depended upon.

And then came Mrs. Reamer, fairly bursting with curiosity, and Sherrill was able to smile and greet her with a gracious merriment that surprised herself, and then interrupt the second question with, "Oh, but you haven't met my friend Mr. Copeland of Chicago yet. Graham, this is Mrs. Reamer, one of our nearest neighbors."

The Hayworths and Buells were mercifully pressing forward, eager to get in their questions, and Sherrill thankfully handed over Mrs. Reamer to Copeland, who dealt with her merrily. So with a lighter heart and well-turned phrases she met the next onslaught, marveling that this terrible ordeal was really going forward so happily, and presently she began to feel the thrill that always comes sooner or later to one who is accomplishing a difficult task successfully.

She was strained, of course, like one who pilots a blimp through the unchartered skies for the first time perhaps, yet she knew that when she got back to earth and her nerves were less taut, there was bound to be a reaction. Just now the main thing was to keep sailing and not let anyone suspect how frightened and sick at heart she really was, how utterly humiliated and cast out she felt, with another bride standing there beside the man who was to have been her husband. And he smiling and shaking hands, and overall conducting himself as if he were quite satisfied. She stole a glance at him now and again between handshakes and introductions, and perceived that he did not appear greatly distraught. His assurance seemed to have returned to him; the whiteness was leaving his lips, and his eyes were no longer deep, smoldering, angry fires. He really seemed to be having a good time. Of course he, too, was playing a part, and there was no telling what his real feelings were. Equally of course he was caught in the tide of the hour and had to carry out his part or bolt and bear the consequences of publicity of which she had warned him. She remembered that he had always been a good actor.

But there was another actor in the line who utterly amazed her. Arla, the bride, filled her part graciously, with a little tilt triumphant to her pretty chin, a glint of pride in her big blue eyes, an air of being to the manor born that was wholly surprising. There she stood in borrowed bridal attire, beside a reluctant bridegroom, wearing another girl's engagement ring, and a wedding ring that was not purchased for her, bearing another girl's roses and lilies, standing under a bower that did not belong to her; and yet she was carrying it all off in the most delightfully natural way. To look at her, one would never suspect that an hour ago she had been pleading with her lover to run away with her and leave another girl to wait in vain for him at the church. Well, perhaps she deserved to have her hour of triumph. She certainly was getting all she possibly could out of it. One would never suspect to look at her that she was a girl who had threatened just a little while before to kill herself. She looked the ideal radiant bride.

Sherrill's eyes went back to the face of her former lover for just an instant. It was lit with one of his most charming smiles as he greeted one of his old friends.

How she had loved that smile! How like a knife twisting in her heart was the sight of it now! Every line of his face, every motion of his slim white hand, the pose of his fine athletic body, so familiar and so beloved, how the sight of them suddenly hurt her! He was not hers anymore! He belonged to another girl! Her mind and soul writhed within her as the thought pierced home to her consciousness with more poignancy than it had yet done. He belonged to another!

But there was something worse than even that. It was that he never really had been what she thought him. There never had existed the Carter McArthur whom she had loved, or all this could not have happened.

For an instant it all swept over her how terrible it was going to be to face the devastation in her own life after this evening was over.

Then more people swarmed in, and she put aside her thoughts and faced them with a frozen smile upon her face, wondering why everybody did not see what agony she was suffering. She must not look at him again, not think about him, she told herself breathlessly as she faced her eager guests and tried to say more pleasant nothings.

At last there came a lull in the stream of guests, and Copeland turned to her confidentially, a cheerful smile upon his lips, but a graver tone to his voice: "I'm wondering what you've done about the license. Anything? It might make trouble for all concerned if that's not attended to tonight before they leave. I don't know what your law is in this state, but I'm sure it ought to be looked into right away. I'm a lawyer, you know, and I can't help thinking of those things."

Sherrill turned a startled face toward him.

"Mercy, no! I never thought of it. We had a license, of course. Wouldn't that do?"

He shook his head slightly.

"I'm afraid not. Do you know where the license was gotten? If we could get hold of the man—"

"Yes, I went along. But the office would be closed tonight, wouldn't it?"

"I suppose so. Still, if we knew the man's name, he might be willing, if there were sufficient inducement, to come over here at once and straighten things out for us."

"Oh, that would be wonderful! Perhaps he'd come for twenty-five dollars, or even fifty. I'd offer him fifty if necessary. It would be dreadful to have that kind of trouble."

Her eyes were full of distress.

"There, don't look so troubled," he said, putting on his grin again. "Remember you're a good little sport. This can all be straightened out, I'm sure. If you could just give me a clue to find that man. You don't know his name, I suppose?"

"Yes, I do," said Sherrill eagerly. "His mail was brought in while we were there, and I saw the name on the letters. Afterward, too, somebody called him by it, so I am sure it was he. The name was Asahel Becker. I remembered

it because it was so strange. Maybe we coul/
the telephone book. But would he have his stamp.
papers and seals and things? Could he get them, do you
think, if we offered him enough?"

"It's worth trying. If you will tell me where I can
telephone without being heard by this mob, I'll see what
I can do."

"There's a phone in the back of the hall under the
stairs, but I'll go with you, of course."

"No, please, if you are willing to trust me, I think I
can handle this without you. You have been taking an
awful beating, and this is just one thing you don't need
to do. Just give me the full names, all three. Here, write
them on the card so I won't make a mistake, and then you
stay right here and *don't worry!* If I need you, I'll come
for you."

He gave her a reassuring smile and was gone. Sherrill
found she was trembling from head to foot, her lips
trembling, too. She put up an unsteady hand to cover
them. Oh, she must not give way! She must snap out
of this. She must not remember yesterday when she
went joyously to get that license—and how her beautiful
romance was all turned to dust and ashes!

Just then the three elderly Markham sisters hovered
in sight, moving in a body, fairly bristling with question
marks and exclamation points, and she had plenty to do
again baffling them, with no Copeland there beside her
to help.

But blessed Aunt Pat turned in to help and soon had drawn the attention of all three.

"And this other bride," said the eldest sister, Matilda by name, leveling her gaze on Arla as if she were a museum piece and then bringing it back to Aunt Pat's face again. "Did you say she was a relative, too? A close relative?"

"Yes, in a way," said Aunt Pat grimly, "but not so close. Quite distant, in fact. It's on the Adams side of the family, you know."

Sherrill gasped softly and almost gave a hysterical giggle, just catching herself in time.

"Indeed!" said Miss Markham, giving the bride another glance. "I wasn't aware there were Adamses in your family. Then she's not a Catherwood?"

"Oh no!" said Aunt Pat with pursed lips. "In fact"—and her voice sounded almost like a chuckle—"the relationship was several generations back."

"Ohh!" sighed the inquisitor, lowering her lorgnette and losing interest. "Well, she seems to be quite attractive anyway."

"Yes, isn't she? Now let me introduce you—"

But suddenly Sherrill saw Copeland coming toward her, and her eyes sought his anxiously.

"You must be desperately tired," he said in a low tone as he stepped into the line beside her. "Couldn't we run away outside for just a minute and get you into the open air?"

"Oh yes!" said Sherrill gratefully. "Come through here."

She led him to the long french window just behind the line, open to the garden terrace, and they stepped out and went down the walk, where pale moonlight from a young moon was just beginning to make itself felt.

"It's all right," he assured her comfortingly, drawing her arm within his own. "He'll be here shortly with all his paper and things. He didn't want to do it at first, but finally snapped at the bait I offered him and promised to be here within the hour. Now, had you thought where we can take him?"

"Yes," said Sherrill, "up in that little room where you dressed. That is quite out of the way of all guests and"— she stopped short in the walk and looked up at her escort with troubled eyes—"we'll have to tell them—the bride and groom—won't we?" Her gaze turned back toward the house anxiously. He could see how she was dreading the ordeal.

"Not yet," he said quickly, "not till our man comes. Then I'll just give the tip to the best man to ask them to come upstairs. You leave that to me. I'll attend to it all. You've had enough worry."

"You are so kind!" she murmured, beginning to walk along by his side again.

He laid his hand gently over hers that rested on his arm.

"I'm glad if I can help. And by the way, I told this Mr.

Becker to come to the side entrance and ask for me, and I took the liberty of asking the butler to keep an eye out for him and let me know at once."

"Oh, thank you," she said. "I don't know what I should have done without you!"

"I am honored to be allowed to help," he said, glad that she had not taken away her hand from his touch, although he was not quite sure she was aware of it, she seemed so distraught. "As far as I am concerned," he went on brightly, "if it weren't that you are taking such a beating, I'd be having the time of my life!"

Sherrill gave him a quick convulsive laugh that seemed very near to tears.

"Oh, if it weren't all so very terrible," she responded wistfully, "I'd think it was almost fun, you're being so splendid!"

"You're a brave girl!" said Copeland almost reverently.

They had reached the end of the garden walk.

"I suppose we ought to go back in there," said Sherrill with a little shiver of dislike. "They'll be wondering where we are."

They turned and walked silently back a few steps, when suddenly a bevy of young people broke forth hilariously from the house, swinging around the corner from the front piazza and evidently bound for the garden.

"Oh!" said Sherrill, shrinking back. "We've got to meet them!"

"Isn't there someplace we can hide for a minute until

they have passed?" asked Copeland with a swift glance at their surroundings. "Here, how about this?" and he swung aside the tall branches of privet that bordered the path around the house and the hedge.

Sherrill stepped in and Copeland after her, and the branches swung together behind them, shutting them in together. There was not much space, for it happened that the opening in the hedge had been near the servants' entrance door, and the hedge curved about across the end, and at the other end it rose nearly twelve feet against the end of the side piazza where they had come out. It made a little room of fragrant green, scarcely large enough for them to stand together in, with the ivy-covered stone wall of the house behind them.

There in the sweet semidarkness of the spring night, where even frail new moonlight could not enter except by reflection, and with only a few stars above, they stood, face-to-face, quietly, while the noisy throng of guests trooped by and rollicked down to the garden.

Sherrill's face was lifted slightly and seemed a pale picture made of moonlight, so sweet and sad and tired and almost desperate there in the little green haven. Copeland, looking down suddenly, put out his arms and drew her close to him, just as a mother might have drawn a little troubled child, it seemed to her. Drew her close and held her so for an instant. She let her head lie still against his shoulder, startled at the sweetness that enwrapped her. Then softly she began to cry, her slim body shaking with the stifled sobs, the tears coming in a torrent. It was so sweet to find sympathy, even with a stranger.

Softly he stooped and kissed her drenched eyelids, kissing the tears away, then paused and looked down at her reverently.

"Forgive me!" he said tenderly in a low whisper. "I had no right to do that—now! I'm only a stranger to you! But—I wanted to comfort you!"

She was very still in his arms for a moment, and then she whispered so softly that he had to bend to hear her: "You *aren't* a stranger, and—you *do*—comfort me!"

Suddenly above their heads there arose a clatter inside the window of the butler's pantry.

"Quick, get those patty shells! The people are coming out to the dining room. We must begin to serve!"

Dishes began to rattle, trays to clatter; a fork fell with a silvery resonance. The swinging door fell back and let in another clatter from the kitchen. Hard cold facts of life began to fall upon the two who had been so set apart for the moment.

"We must go back at once!" said Sherrill, making hasty dabs at her eyes with her scrap of lace handkerchief.

"Of course," said Copeland, offering a large cool square of immaculate linen.

Then he took her hand and led her gravely out into the moonlight, pulled her arm possessively through his, and accommodated his step to hers.

When they came to the long window where they had escaped a few minutes before, he looked down at her.

"Are you all right?" he asked softly.

"All right!" she answered with a brave little catch in her breath, and smiled up at him.

He still held her hand, and he gave it a warm pressure before he let her go. Then they stepped inside the room and saw the end of the long line of guests progressing slowly down the hall and Aunt Pat hovering behind them, looking this way and that, out the front door, and into the vacated library. It was evident she was looking for Sherrill, for as they came forward her brow cleared, and she smiled a relieved smile and came to meet them.

Just an instant she lingered by Sherrill's side as Copeland stepped to the dining room door to look over the heads of the throng and reconnoiter for seats for them all.

"I don't know how you have planned," said the old lady in something that sounded like a low growl, "nor how long this ridiculous performance has been going on, but I thought I'd remind you that it will be necessary for that girl to have some baggage if you expect to carry this thing out. I don't want to interfere with your plans, but there's that second suitcase, the one that wasn't marked that we had sent up. It hasn't been returned yet, you know. I suppose you'll have to see that she has things enough to be decent on ship board, unless she has time enough to get some of her own. But if you let that lace

81

evening dress or that shell-pink chiffon go, I'll never forgive you. It's bad enough to lose the going-away outfit, but I suppose there isn't any way out of that. A couple of evening dresses and some casual things ought to see her through. Don't be a fool and give up everything!" And Miss Catherwood, with her head in the air and a set smile on her aristocratic face, swept on to the dining room.

Sherrill stood startled, looking after her doubtfully. Did that mean that Aunt Pat was angry? Angry yet going to stand by till it was all over to the last detail? Or did it mean that she understood the awful situation better than Sherrill knew? She was a canny old lady. How wonderfully she had stood and met that line of hungry gossip-mongers! But yet, she might still be angry. Very angry! To be the talk of the town when she had done so much to make this wedding perfect in every way. To have people wondering and gossiping about them! It would be dreadful for Aunt Pat!

Sherrill had a sudden vision of what it might be to face an infuriated Aunt Pat and explain everything after it was all over, and she had that panicky impulse once more to flee away into the world and shirk it—never come back anymore. But of course she knew she never would do that!

Then Copeland touched her on the arm.

"Please, do we follow the rest, or what?" and she perceived that they two were left alone in the room, with only the end of the procession surging away from them toward the dining room.

Sherrill giggled nervously.

"I haven't much head, have I?" she said. "I've got to go upstairs a minute or two and put some things in a suitcase. It won't take long. Perhaps I'd better go now."

"Yes," said Copeland thoughtfully. "Now would be a good time. I'll wait here at the foot of the stairs for you."

She flew up the stairs with a quick smile back at her helper. He was marvelous! It could not be that he was an absolute stranger! It seemed as if she had known him always. Here she had almost laid bare her heart to him, and he had taken it all so calmly and done everything needful, just as if he understood all the details. No brother could have been more tender, more careful of her. She remembered his lips on her eyelids, and her breath came quickly. How gentle he had been!

She hurried to her own room and miraculously found Gemmie there before her, the suitcase in her hand.

"Your aunt Pat thought you might be wanting this," said the woman respectfully, no hint of her former surprise in her eyes, no suggestion that anything was different from what it had been when the old servant left her there in her wedding dress ready to go to the church.

"Oh yes!" said Sherrill in relief. "You'll help me, won't you, Gemmie?"

With half-frenzied fingers Sherrill went to work, laying out things from her suitcase and bags, separating them into two piles upon the bed. The black satin evening dress, the orchid, and the yellow—those ought to be enough. Aunt Pat wasn't especially crazy about any of those. She put aside the things that were marked with her own initials; not one of those should go. She shut her lips tight and drew in a sharp little breath of pain.

Gemmie seemed to understand. She gathered those things up quickly and put them away in the bureau drawers. Gemmie's powers of selection were even keener than Sherrill's.

It did not take long, three or four minutes, and Gemmie's skillful fingers did the rest.

"There, now, Miss Sherrill, I can manage," she said. "You run back. They'll be missing you."

It was as if Gemmie was also a conspirator.

"Thank you, Gemmie dear!" said Sherrill with a catch in her voice like a sob, and closed the door quickly behind her.

Copeland was waiting at the foot of the stairs, and they found places saved for them close to the bride's table, a little table for two, and the eyes of all upon them as they sat down.

Sherrill saw the Markham sisters looking eagerly from Copeland to herself and back again, and nodding their heads violently to one another as they swept in large mouthfuls of creamed mushrooms and chicken salad. She had an impulse to put her head down on the table and laugh, or cry. She knew she was getting very near to the limit of her self-control.

But Copeland knew it also, and managed to keep her busy telling him who the different people were.

After all the ordeal was soon over, even to the cutting of the wedding cake by a bride very much at her ease and enjoying her privileges to the last degree. If Arla never was happy again, she was tonight.

And then after all the matter of the license, which loomed like a peril in Sherrill's thoughts, was arranged so easily. Just a quiet word from the butler to Copeland, a quiet sign from Copeland to the best man. Sherrill had put money in her little pearl evening bag, which she slipped to Copeland as they went upstairs together while the bride was throwing Sherrill's bouquet to the noisy clamoring bridesmaids down in the hall. Sherrill and Copeland were presumably escorting the bride and groom to their rooms to change into traveling garb, and no one noticed them enter the little room off the back hall where the representative of the law was waiting.

Just a few quiet questions from the grizzly old man who had come to make the legal part right, and who looked at them as only three more in the long procession that came to him day by day. They waited, those five, the best man doing his best not to seem too curious about it all, while those important seals were placed, and the proper signature affixed, and then Sherrill hurried the bride away to dress. A frightened, almost tearful bride now—afraid of her, Sherrill was sure.

Almost the last lap of this terrible race she was running! There would be one more. She would have to face Aunt Pat, but that she dared not think about yet. This present session with the bride who had taken her place was going to be perhaps the hardest of all.

Chapter 5

Sherrill led her white bride through the two middle rooms again, hurriedly, silently, remembering with sharp thrills of pain all that had happened earlier in the evening. She dreaded intensely the moment when they two would be shut in together again. One would have to say something. One could not be absolutely silent, and somehow her tongue felt heavy, and her brain refused to think.

But Gemmie was there! Dear Gemmie! Ah! She had forgotten Gemmie! What a relief! Gemmie with her most professional air of dignity.

The frightened little bride did not feel relief, however, at her presence. She faltered at the doorway and gave Sherrill a pitiful look of protest. Sherrill drew her inside and fastened the door, feeling suddenly an infinite pity for this girl among strangers in a role that belonged to another.

"Oh, here is Gemmie!" she said gently. "She will help you off with the veil and dress. Gemmie knows how to do it without mussing your hair."

Arla submitted herself to Gemmie's ministrations, and Sherrill hovered about, looking over the neatly packed suitcase and the great white box that Gemmie had set forth on the bed.

"Oh, you have the box ready for the wedding dress, haven't you, Gemmie?" said Sherrill, feeling she must break this awful silence that seemed to pervade the room. "That's all right. Gemmie will fold it for you and get it all ready to be sent to whatever address you say."

"Oh," began Arla, with a hesitant glance toward Gemmie and then looking Sherrill almost haughtily in the eye, "I couldn't think of keeping it. I really couldn't!"

"Certainly you will take it," said Sherrill sternly. "It is your wedding dress! *You* were married in it. *I* wouldn't want it, you know."

Arla answered with a quick-drawn, startled "Oh!" of comprehension. Then she added, "And I'm afraid I wouldn't either!"

Over Sherrill's face there passed a swift look of sympathy.

"I see," she said quietly. "You wouldn't want it, of course. I'm sorry. You are right. I'll keep it."

Arla was silent until she was freed from the white

veil and sheathing satin, but when Gemmie brought forth the dark slip and lovely tailored going-away outfit that Sherrill had prepared for herself, she suddenly spoke with determination:

"No," she said with a little haughty lifting of her pretty chin, "I will wear my own things away. Where are they? Did somebody take them away?"

"They are here," said Sherrill, a certain new respect in her voice that had not been there before. "But—you are perfectly welcome to the other dress. I think it would fit you. We are about the same size."

"No," said Arla determinedly, "I prefer to wear my own dress. It is new and quite all right. Wouldn't you prefer to wear your own things?" She asked the question almost fiercely.

"I suppose I would," said Sherrill meekly. "And I remember your dress. It was very pretty. But I just wanted you to feel you were perfectly welcome to wear the other."

"Thank you," said Arla in a choking voice, "but there is no need. You have done enough. You really have been rather wonderful, and I want you to know that I appreciate it all."

Gemmie, skillfully folding the rich satin, managed somehow to give the impression that she was not there, and presently took herself conveniently out of the room.

Sherrill looked up pleasantly.

"That's all right," she said with a wan smile, "and now listen! I've packed some things for you in this suitcase. I think there will be enough to carry you through the trip."

"That wouldn't be necessary either," said the other girl coldly. "I can get some things somewhere."

"I'm afraid not," said Sherrill. "You'll barely have time to make the train to the boat. The ship sails at midnight. You might be able to stop for a few personal things if you don't live too far out of the way, but you'd have to hurry awfully. You couldn't take more than five minutes to get them, and you couldn't possibly pack for a trip to Europe in that time."

"Then I can get along without things!" said the bride with a sob in her voice.

"Don't be silly!" said Sherrill in a friendly voice. "You can't make the trip into an endurance test. You've got to have the right things, of course. You're on your wedding trip, you know, and there may be people on board that Carter knows. You've got to look right."

She wondered at herself as she said all this coolly to this other girl who was taking the trip in her place. It was just like a terrible dream that she was going through. A wild thought that perhaps it was a dream passed through her weary mind. Perhaps she would presently wake up and find that none of all this nightmare was true. Perhaps there wasn't any Arla, and Carter had never been untrue!

Idle thoughts, of course! She pushed them frantically from her and tried to talk practically.

"I haven't put much in, just some casual things and three little evening dresses. Necessary underthings and accessories, of course. Some slippers, too, and there's a heavy coat for the deck. The bag is fitted with toilet articles. You won't need to stop for any of your own unless you feel you must."

"Oh, I feel like a criminal!" the bride said suddenly, and sank into a chair with her golden head bowed and her face in her hands, sobbing.

"Nonsense!" said Sherrill under the same impulse with which she might have dashed cold water in the girl's face if she had been fainting. "Brace up! You've gotten through the worst! For pity's sake don't get red eyes and spoil it all. Remember you've got to go downstairs and smile at everybody yet. Stop it! Quick!"

She offered a clean handkerchief.

"Now look here! Be sensible! Things aren't just as either you or I would have had them if we'd had our choice! But we've got this thing to go through with now, and we're not going to pass out just at the last minute. Be a good sport and finish your dressing. There isn't a whole lot of time, you know. Say, that is a pretty frock! I hadn't noticed it closely before. It certainly is attractive. Come, get it fastened and I'll find your shoes and stockings."

Arla accepted the handkerchief and essayed to repair the damages on her face, but her whole slender body was quivering.

"I've—taken your—hus–band—" she began with trembling lips.

"*You have not!*" said Sherrill with flashing eyes. "He's

not my husband, thank goodness!"

"You'd—have—been—happ–pp–ppy," sobbed Arla, "if—you—just—hadn't—found—out! It would have been much b–b–better if I had k–k–k–killed myself!"

"Don't you suppose I'd have found out eventually that he was that sort? And what good would your killing yourself have been? Haven't you any sense at all? For pity's sake stop crying! *You're* not to blame." Sherrill was frantic. The girl seemed to be going all to pieces.

"Yes, I am! I've taken your husband!" went on Arla, getting a fresh start on sobs, "and I've taken your wedding away from you, and now you want me to take your clothes—*and I can't do it!*"

"Fiddlesticks!" said Sherrill earnestly. "I tell you I don't *want* your husband, and if anybody wanted a frantic wedding such as this has been, they are welcome to it. As for the clothes, they're all new and have never become a part of me. I'm glad to have you have them, and anyway you've *got* to, to carry out this thing right! Now stop being a baby and get your shoes on. I tell you the time is going fast. Listen! I *want* you to have those things. I really do! And I *want* you to have just as good a time as you can. Don't you believe it?"

"Oh, you're wonderful!" said Arla, suddenly jumping up and flinging her slender young arms around Sherrill's neck. "I just love you! And to think I thought you were so different! Oh, if I'd known you were like this, I wouldn't have come here! I really wouldn't!"

"Well, I'm glad you came!" said Sherrill fiercely. "I didn't know it, but I guess I really am. Of course, I'm not having a particularly heavenly time out of it, but I'm sure in my heart that you've probably done me a great favor, and someday when I get over the shock, I'll thank you for it!"

"Oh, but I wouldn't have wanted to hurt you," sighed Arla, her red lips still quivering. "I really wouldn't. I've always been—well—decent!"

"That's all right!" said Sherrill, blinking her own tears back. "And I wouldn't have wanted to hurt you either. There! Let's let it go at that and be friendly. Now, please, powder your nose and hurry up. *Smile!* That's it!"

Just then Gemmie came back, a big warm coat over her arm, richly furred on collar and sleeves.

"It's getting late, Mrs. McArthur!" she suggested officially, and presented Arla's chic little hat and doeskin gloves with a look of approbation toward them. Gemmie had decided that the substitute bride must be a lady. At least she knew how to buy the right clothes.

Arla paused at the door as Gemmie stepped off down the hall to direct the man who had come to take the suitcase, and whispered to Sherrill: "I'll never forget what you've done for me! *Never!*" she said huskily.

"That's all right," said Sherrill almost tenderly as she looked at the pretty shrinking girl before her. "I'm just sorry you couldn't have had a regular wedding instead of one all messed up with other things like this."

"Oh, but I never could have afforded a wedding like this!" sighed Arla wistfully.

"Well, it might at least have been peaceful," said Sherrill with a tinge of bitterness in her voice. "But never mind. It's over now, and I hope a good happy life for you has begun. Try not to think much about the past. Try to make yours a happy marriage if it can be done."

They passed on together down the hall to the head of the stairs where Carter McArthur and his best man stood waiting, and as she saw her bridegroom standing there so handsome and smiling and altogether just what a happy bridegroom ought to look like, there came to Arla new strength. She lost her sorrowful humility and became the radiant bride again. That was her *husband* standing there waiting for her! *Her* husband, not another girl's! Only a short walk down the stairs now, a dash to the car, and she would be out and free from all this awfulness, and into a new life. She might be going into hell, but she was going with him, and it was what she had chosen.

Then suddenly, as Arla's hand was drawn within the arm of her bridegroom and they walked smilingly down the stairs with measured tread, Sherrill, falling in behind, felt greatly alone and lost. A sinking feeling came over her. Was she going to fall? That would be dreadful, now when it was almost over. Must she walk down those steps alone? Couldn't she just slip back to her room and stay there till they were all gone?

But just as she faltered at the top step, she felt a hand

under her arm, and a pleasant voice said in her ear: "Well, is it all over now but the shouting?" and she looked up to see the cheerful grin of Copeland.

She had forgotten his existence in the last few tense minutes, but he had been waiting, had seen her weakness, and was there just at the right moment.

"Did anybody ever before pick up a friend like you right out of the street in the dark night?" she asked suddenly, lifting grateful eyes to his face.

"Why, I thought it was *I* who picked *you* up!" he answered quickly with a warm smile.

"Well, anyway, you have been wonderful!"

"I'm only too glad if I have been able to live up to the specifications," he said earnestly and finished with his delightful grin again.

The people down in the hall looking up said to one another: "Look at those two! They look as if it were *their* wedding, don't they? Who is he, do you suppose, and where has he been all this time?"

Sherrill stood with the rest on the wide front veranda watching the bride and groom dash across to their beribboned car, which awaited them. She even threw a few of the pink rose petals with which the guests were hilariously pelting the bridal couple. Even now at this last moment, when she was watching another girl go away with her bridegroom, she must smile and keep up appearances, although her knees felt weak and the tears were dangerously near.

Mrs. Battersea had stationed herself and her lorgnette in the forefront, and she fixed her eagle eye especially on Sherrill. If there was still any more light on the peculiar happening of the evening to be gleaned from a view of the original bride off her guard, at this last minute, she meant to get it.

Sherrill suddenly saw her, and it had the effect of making her give a little hysterical giggle. Then Copeland's hand on her arm steadied her again, and she flashed a grateful smile up to meet his pleasant grin.

Mrs. Battersea dropped her lorgnette, deciding that of course this was the other lover appeared just at the last minute; only *how* did they get that other girl?

They were all gone at last. The last guest had joked to Aunt Pat about her wonderful surprise wedding; the last bridesmaid had taken her little box of wedding cake to sleep on and stolen noisily away. Just Aunt Pat and Sherrill and Copeland left standing alone in the wide front hall as the last car whirled away.

Copeland had stayed to the end, as if he were a part of the household, stayed close by Sherrill, taken the burden of the last conversations upon himself as if he had the right, made every second of those last trying minutes just as easy for her as possible, kept up a light patter of brilliant conversation, filling in all the spots that needed tiding over.

"And now," said he, turning to the hostess as the last car whirled down the lighted driveway, "I have to thank you, Miss Catherwood, for a most delightful evening. Sherrill, it's been wonderful to have had this time with you. I must be getting on my way. I think your butler is bringing my things."

Just then the butler came toward them bearing Graham Copeland's suitcase and high hat. Sherrill looked up in surprise. With what ease he had arranged everything so that there would be no unpleasant pauses for explanation.

But Aunt Pat swung around upon him with a quick searching look at Sherrill.

"Why, where are you staying?" she asked cordially.

"I'm at the Wiltshire," he answered quickly. "I hadn't time to get into proper garb before the ceremony, so I brought my things up here, and Sherrill very kindly gave me a place to dress."

"Well, then why don't you just stay here tonight? It's pretty late, I guess. We've plenty of rooms now, you know," and she gave him a little friendly smile that she gave only to an honored few whom she liked.

"Thank you," he said with an amused twinkle at Sherrill. "That would be delightful, but I've an appointment quite early in the morning, and my briefcase is at the hotel. I think I'd better go back to my room. But I certainly appreciate the invitation."

"Well, then, you'll be with us to dinner tomorrow

night surely. That is, unless you and Sherry have made other plans."

"I certainly wish I could," said the young man wistfully, "but unfortunately I am obliged to take the noon train to Washington to meet another appointment which is quite important."

Aunt Pat looked disappointed.

"I wonder," said the young man hesitantly, "I'm not sure how long I shall be obliged to stay in Washington—several days, likely, as I have some important records to look up at the Patent Office—but I shall be passing through the city on my way to New York sometime next week probably. Would I be presuming if I stopped off and called on you both?"

"Presuming?" said Aunt Pat with a keen look at Sherrill. "Well, not so far as I know," and she gave one of her quaint little chuckles.

"I do hope you can," said Sherrill earnestly with a look that left no doubt of her wish in the matter.

His eyes searched hers gravely for an instant, and then he said as though he had received a royal command: "Then I shall surely be here if it is at all possible. I'll call up and find out if it is convenient."

"Of course it'll be convenient!" said the old lady. "*I'm* always at home whether anybody else is or not, and I'll be glad to see you."

He bowed a gracious thanks, then turned to Sherrill as if reluctant to relinquish his office of assistant.

"I'll hope you'll be—" He hesitated, then finished earnestly, "All right."

There was something in his eyes that brought a warm little comforted feeling around her heart.

"Oh yes!" she answered fervently. "Thank you! You were— It was wonderful having you here!" she finished with heightened color.

"Oh, but you're not going that way!" said the old lady. "Gemmie, tell Stanley to bring the car around and take Mr. Copeland—"

A moment more and he was gone, and Sherrill had a sudden feeling of being left alone in a tumultuous world.

Now she must have it out with Aunt Pat!

Slowly she turned away from the door and faced the old lady, all her lovely buoyant spirits gone, just a weary, troubled little girl who looked as if she wanted to cry.

Chapter 6

"Well," said Aunt Pat with grim satisfaction in her voice, "you never did anything in your life that pleased me so much!"

"Oh, you darling Aunt Pat!" said Sherrill, her face glowing with sudden relief, and quick tears brimming unbidden into her eyes.

"Why, certainly!" said the old lady crisply. "You know I never did like that Carter McArthur. Now, come upstairs to my room and tell me all about it!"

"Oh, but aren't you too tired tonight, Aunt Pat?" asked Sherrill, struggling under the shock of relief.

"Bosh!" said Aunt Pat. "You know neither you nor I will sleep a wink till we've had it out. Run and get your robe on. I suppose you gave the grand new one to that little washed-out piece. Of course she had to have it. But put on your old one with the blue butterflies. I like that one best anyway. Gemmie"—raising her voice to the faithful maid who was never far away—"send up two plates of *every*thing to my room. *Every*thing, I said. We're hungry as bears. Neither of us ate as much as a bird while that mob was here. No, you needn't worry, Gemmie; it won't hurt me this time of night at all. I'm as chipper as a squirrel, and if I've stood this evening and all the weeks before it, I certainly can stand one good meal before I sleep. The fact is, Gemmie, things have come out my way tonight, and I don't think anything could very well hurt me just now."

"Yes, ma'am!" said Gemmie with a happy glance toward Sherrill.

A general air of good cheer pervaded Aunt Pat's room when Sherrill, in her old robe of shell pink satin with blue butterflies fluttering over it, and her comfortable old slippers with the lamb's wool lining and pink feather edges, arrived and was established in a big stuffed chair at one side of the open fire. Aunt Pat, with her silver hair in soft ringlets around her shoulders, sat on the other side of the fire robed in dove-gray quilted silk.

Gemmie brought two little tables and two heaping trays of food, and left them with the lights turned low. The firelight flickered over the two, the young face and the old one.

"Now," said Aunt Pat, "who *is* he?"

Sherrill looked up, puzzled.

"The other one, I mean. You certainly picked a winner this time if I may be permitted a little slang. He seems to be the key to the whole situation. Begin with him! Where have you been keeping him all this time? And why haven't I been told about him before? Is he an old schoolmate, to quote Mrs. Battersea, and how long have you known him?"

"I haven't!" said Sherrill with a sound of panic in her voice.

"You *haven't?*" asked her aunt with a forkful of chicken salad paused halfway to her mouth. "What do you mean, you haven't? You certainly seemed to know him pretty well, and he you."

"But I don't, Aunt Pat. I don't really know him at all."

"But—where did you meet him?"

"On the street."

"On the street! When?"

"Tonight."

"Mercy!" said Aunt Pat with a half grin. "Explain yourself. You're not the kind of girl that goes around picking up men on the street."

"No!" said Sherrill with a choke of tears in her voice. "But I did this time. I really did. At least—he says he picked me up. You see, I fell into his arms!"

"Mmmm!" said Aunt Pat, enjoying her supper and scenting romance. "Go on. That sounds interesting."

"Why, you see, it was this way. I parked my car in a hurry to get up into the gallery, and when I went to get out, I caught my toe in one of those long ruffles, or else I stepped on it; anyway, I fell headlong out on the pavement. Or at least I would have if this man hadn't been there and caught me. I guess I was so excited I didn't really realize that I was pretty well shaken up. Perhaps I struck my head; I'm not sure. It felt dizzy and strange afterward. But he stood me up and brushed me off and insisted on going across the road with me. I guess I must have been unsteady on my feet, for when he found I wanted to go upstairs to the gallery, he almost carried me up, and he was very nice and helpful. He took that note down to you and then got me a drink of water."

"Hmm!" said Aunt Pat with satisfaction. "He's what I call a real man. Nice face! Makes me think of your father when he was young. I couldn't make out how you'd take up with that little pretty-face McArthur nincompoop after seeing a man like this one."

"Why, Aunt Pat!" said Sherrill in astonishment. "I never knew you felt that way about Carter! You never said you did!"

"What was the use of saying? You were determined to have him. But go on. How did this Graham fellow get up here, and how did he get to calling you by your first name, and you him?"

"Well, you see, I slipped out just before the ceremony was over. He said I wasn't fit to drive; he'd either drive

103

himself or get some friend if I said so. But I was in a hurry so I let him drive. I wasn't thinking about formalities then. I knew I ought to get back home quickly. Anyhow, he was so respectful I knew he was all right."

"Hmm! There are respectful crooks sometimes! But never mind; go on."

"But really, Aunt Pat, I don't know what you'll think of me! I haven't had time before this to think what a dreadful thing it was I did, a total stranger, but it didn't seem so then. It seemed just a desperate spot in life. You'd let a stranger pull you out of the street when a mad dog was coming or something like that. I'm afraid you'll be horrified at me. But he was really very kind. He offered to do anything in the world, said he was a stranger in town with the evening to pass, before he met a business appointment in the morning, and if there was any way at all he could help—"

"For mercy's sake, child, stop apologizing and tell things as they happened. I'm not arraigning you."

"Well, I let him come home with me. I knew it would be easier if there was someone that everybody didn't know, and I let him come."

"Hmm!" said the old lady with a thoughtful smile that the firelight showed off to perfection. "Well, he certainly was clever enough. But how did he get a dress coat?"

"Oh, we stopped at the hotel and got his suitcase. He'd been to a dinner the night before in Cleveland. I let him dress in the little room at the end of the back hall.

We came in up the fire escape just before the first car arrived."

"Hmm! Clever pair!" commented the old lady as she took delicate bites of her creamed mushrooms. "Well, now, get back to your story. How long have you known about this other girl, Artie—was that her name?"

"Arla."

"Silly name! But go on. How long has this double business been going on?"

"I don't know," said Sherrill wearily. "Always, I guess."

"I mean, when did you find it out?"

"Just after you left the house for the church," answered the girl with downcast eyes. Now she was at the beginning of the real story, and it suddenly seemed to her as if she could not possibly tell that part.

The old lady gave her a startled look. She knew that they were now come to the crux of the matter. Sherrill had been so brave up to this point and had carried matters off with such a spirit that she had somehow hoped that Sherrill was not so hard hit. Hoped against hope, perhaps, that the final discovery was but the culmination of long suspicions.

"You don't say!" said the old lady, her usual serio-comic manner quite shaken. "But how? I don't see what— How—!"

Sherrill shut her eyes and drew a quick deep breath, then began.

"I was all ready. So I made Gemmie hurry on to the

church. I wanted her to be there to see it all, and I wanted to go and see Mary the cook. I'd promised her to come after I got dressed. I knew Gemmie would try to stop me, so I wouldn't let her wait as she wanted to. As soon as she was gone, I unlocked my door into the next room and went softly through toward the back hall." Sherrill had to stop for another deep breath. It seemed as though she was about to go through the whole terrible experience again.

"Well?" said the old lady sharply, laying down her fork with a click on the china plate.

"As I stepped into the end room, which was dark," she began again, trying to steady her voice, "I saw that the door into the middle room was open and the light streaming across the floor. I listened for an instant but heard nothing. I was afraid some of those strange servants would be snooping about. Then I stepped softly forward and saw Carter standing before the long mirror arranging his tie."

"Yes?" said the old lady breathlessly.

"I watched him just a second. I didn't want to stir lest he would hear me, and I wanted him to see me first as I came up the aisle—"

Sherrill's voice trailed away sorrowfully. Then she gathered strength again.

"But while I watched him, I saw the door beside the mirror open noiselessly, and that girl came in!"

"Hmm!" said Aunt Pat, allowing herself another bite of oyster patty but keeping her eyes speculatively on her niece. "She must have come up the fire escape or somebody would have seen her."

"She did," said Sherrill wearily, putting her head back and closing her eyes for an instant. Somehow the whole thing suddenly overwhelmed and sickened her again. It seemed she could not go on.

"Well?" said the old lady impatiently. "Did she see you?"

"No." Sherrill's voice was almost toneless. "No, but—"

"There, there, child! I know it's hard, but it's got to be told once, and then we'll close it over forever if you say so."

"Oh, I know," said Sherrill, sitting up and taking up her tale with a little shudder that seemed to shake her whole slender self.

"No, she didn't see me. She was looking at him. She went straight to him and began to talk, and I could see by his whole attitude that they were old friends. He was shocked when he saw her, and very angry. He ordered her out and scolded her, but she pled with him. It was really heartbreaking. Just as if he had been nothing to me. I couldn't help feeling sorry for her, though I thought her— Oh, at first I thought her the lowest of the low. Then I recognized her as his secretary, and of course I guess I thought still less of her, because she would have known that he was engaged."

"Yes, of course!" said Aunt Pat in a spritely tone. "Well, what else?"

"Well, she began pleading with him to go away with her. She reminded him that he had promised to marry her, and in his answer he acknowledged that he had, but oh, Aunt Pat! It is too dreadful to tell!"

"That's all right, Sherrill; get it out of your system. No way to do that like telling it all, making a clean sweep of it! Besides, sometime you'll want to look back on it and remember that you had the assent of someone else that you did the right thing. Even though you're sure you're right, there will come times when you will question yourself perhaps."

"I know!" said Sherrill quickly with that sharp intake of breath that shows some thought has hurt. "I have already!" Her aunt gave her a sharp keen look.

"Poor kiddie!" she said gently.

"Oh, I know I never could have married him," went on Sherrill heartbrokenly. "Only it is so dreadful to have my life all upset in one awful minute that way! To know in a flash that everything you've ever counted on and trusted in a person had no foundation whatever! That he simply wasn't in the least what I had thought him. Why, Aunt Pat, he had the nerve to tell her that it didn't matter if he was marrying someone else—that wouldn't hinder their relation. He reminded her that after he got home from the wedding trip, he would spend far more time with her than with me, and that whenever he wanted to get away for a few days, it would be entirely possible! Oh, Aunt Pat—it was too dreadful! And I standing there not daring to breathe! Oh!" Sherrill put her face down in her hands and shook with suppressed sobs.

"The dirty little puppy!" said Aunt Pat, setting down her plate with a ring on the table. Then she got up from her big chair and came across to Sherrill, laying a frail roseleaf hand on her bowed head.

"You poor dear little girl!" she said tenderly, more tenderly than Sherrill had ever heard her speak before.

For a moment then the tears had full sway, let loose by the unusual gentleness of the old lady's voice, till they threatened to engulf her. Then suddenly Sherrill lifted her face all wet with tears and drew Aunt Pat's hand to her lips, kissing it again and again.

"Oh, Aunt Pat! It's so wonderful of you to take it this way! You've done so much to make this a wonderful wedding, spent all this money, and then had it finish in a terrible scandal like this!"

"It's not a scandal!" protested the old lady. "You carried if off like a thoroughbred, and nobody will ever know what happened. You were the bravest girl I ever knew. You are like your father, Sherrill." Her tone was very gentle now, and soft. It hardly sounded like herself, and her sharp old eyes were misted with sweet tears. "And why wouldn't I take it this way, I should like to know, when I was pleased to pieces at what had happened?"

Then suddenly she straightened up, marched back to her seat, and took up her plate again. Her eyes were snapping now, and her tone was far from gentle as she said, "But it was far too good a thing to happen to Carter McArthur. He ought to have been tarred and feathered!

He deserves the scorn of the community! Go on. Tell me the rest! What excuse did he offer?"

"Oh, he said things about his business. He said he couldn't marry her; he had to marry influence and money! Aunt Pat, he seemed to think I had money, though I've told him I was poor and that you were giving me my wedding. Or else, maybe he was just lying to her; I don't know—"

"Well," said Aunt Pat, setting her lips wryly, "I suppose I'm to blame for that. I thought the thing was inevitable, and I told him myself that you would be pretty well fixed after I was gone. He likely was figuring to borrow money or something."

Sherrill's head dropped again, and she gave a sound like a groan.

"There, there! Stop that, child!" said the old lady briskly. "He isn't worth it."

"I know it," moaned Sherrill, "but I'm so ashamed that I loved a man like that!"

"You didn't!" said her aunt. "You loved a man you'd made up in your own imagination. Come, tell me the rest, and then eat your supper or you'll be sick, and then what'll Mrs. Battersea say?"

Sherrill gave a hysterical little giggle and, lifting her head, wiped away the tears.

"Well, then someone came to the door and told him the car was waiting and it was late, and he got frantic. He told her to go away, and then she threatened to kill herself, and suddenly he took her in his arms and kissed her—just the way he used to kiss me, Aunt Pat! Oh, it was awful. His arms went around her as if he was hungry for her! Oh, there was no doubt about how he felt toward her, not a bit! And then he kissed her again and suddenly threw her from him into the corner, turned out the light in the room, and went away slamming the door hard behind him."

"The poor fool!" commented Aunt Pat under her breath.

"I stood quite still holding my breath," went on Sherrill, "till suddenly I heard her move, and then I reached out and turned on both lights in both rooms and she saw me."

"What happened?" The old lady's eyes were large with interest.

"I believe I asked her how long she had known him," said Sherrill wearily, "and she said *always*, that they had grown up and gone to school together, and then he had sent for her to come here and be his secretary till he could afford to marry her—"

"A beast! That's what he is!" murmured Aunt Pat. "A sleek little beast!"

"She said it was not until I came that he turned away from her. She said awful things to me. She said it was all my fault, that I had everything and she had nothing but him, and I had ruined her life and there was nothing for her to do but kill herself! And when I told her to hush, that there wasn't much time and we had to do something, she thought I meant that she was to get away quietly so no one would know. She raved, Aunt Pat! She said it was all right for me, that I was going to marry him. And when I told her that of course I couldn't marry him now, and asked her if she would marry a man like that, she said she'd marry him if she had to go through hell with him!"

Aunt Pat's face hardened, though there was a mist across her eyes which she brushed impatiently away.

"Poor little fool!" she commented.

"So I dragged her into my room and made her put on my dress and veil. I guess that is all. She couldn't believe me at first. She said she couldn't do that, that he would kill her, but I told her to tell him that if he didn't treat her right, if he didn't go through the evening in the conventional way, or if he tried to throw it up to her afterward, then I would tell the whole world what he had done."

"Great work!" breathed Aunt Pat. "Sherry, you certainly had your head about you! And you certainly seemed to know your man better than I thought you did."

"Oh, Aunt Pat, it seems so awful for me to be sitting here talking about Carter when just a few hours before I thought he was so wonderful!"

"Yes, I know!" mused Aunt Pat with a faraway look. "I had that experience, too, once, ages ago before you were born."

"You did?" Sherrill looked up with wonder in her eyes.

"Yes," said Aunt Pat with a strangely tender look on her face, "I did. I was engaged to a young hypocrite once, and thought he was the angel Gabriel till I got my eyes open. Sometime I'll tell you about it. There isn't anybody living now who knows the story but myself. I thought I was heartbroken forever, and when my grandmother told me that he just wasn't the man God had meant for me, and that He probably had somebody a great deal better waiting somewhere, I got very angry at her. But that turned out to be true, too, and I did have another lover who was a real man later. It wasn't his fault that we never married. Nor mine either. He died saving a little child's life. But the memory of him has been better for me all my life than if I'd married that first little selfish whiffet. So don't let yourself think that the end of the world has come, Sherrill."

Sherrill sat looking at the old lady and trying to reconstruct her ideas of her, wondering at the mellowing and sharpness that were combined in her dear whimsical old face.

"There, now, child, you've told enough!" said the old lady briskly. "Eat your supper and go to bed. Tomorrow you may tell me about everything else. We've had enough for tonight. I'll talk while you eat now. What do you want to do next? Go to Europe?"

"Oh, not Europe!" Sherrill shrank visibly.

"Of course not!" snapped the old lady with triumph

in her eyes. "We'll go someplace a great deal more interesting."

"I don't think I want to go anywhere," said Sherrill sadly. "I guess I had better just stay here and let people see I'm not moping. That is, if I can get away with it."

"Of course you can!" lilted the old lady. "We'll have the time of our lives. They'll see!"

"The only place I'd want to go anyway would be out west by and by, back to my teaching. I'd like to earn money enough to pay you for this awful wedding, Aunt Pat!"

"Stuff and nonsense!" fumed the old lady. "If you mention that again, I'll disinherit you! You hurt me, Sherrill!"

"Oh, forgive me, Aunt Pat! But you've been so wonderful!"

"Well, that's no way to reward me. Go away when I'm just congratulating myself that I've got you all to myself for a while. Of course I don't fool myself into thinking I can keep you always. You're too good looking for that. And there are a few real men left in the world even in this age. They are not all Carter McArthurs. But at least let me have the comfort of your companionship until one comes along!"

"You dear Aunt Pat!"

"There's another thing we've got to consider tomorrow," said the old lady meditatively. "What are you going to do with those wedding presents?"

Sherrill lifted her face, aghast at the thought.

"Oh, mercy! I never thought about them. How terrible! What could one do?"

"Oh, send most of them back. Send Carter those *his* friends sent. Don't bother about it tonight. We'll work it out. You run along to bed now, and don't think another thing about it."

Ten minutes later Sherrill was back in her own room.

Gemmie had been there and removed every trace and suggestion of wedding from the place. Sherrill's best old dresses hung in the closet; Sherrill's old dependable brushes and things were on the bureau. It might have been the night before she ever met Carter McArthur as far as her surroundings suggested.

She cast a quick look of relief about her and went forward to the mirror and stood there, looking into her own eyes, just as she had done when she was ready for her marriage. Looked at her real self and tried to make it seem true that this awful thing had happened to her, Sherrill Cameron! And then suddenly her eyes wandered away from the deep sorrowful thoughts that she found in her mirrored eyes, with an unthinking glance at her slim white neck, and she started. Why! Where was her emerald necklace? She hadn't taken it off when she put on her robe. She was sure she had not. She would have remembered undoing the intricate old clasp!

Frantically she searched her bureau drawers. Had Gemmie taken it away? Surely not. She went to the little secret drawer where she usually kept her valuable trinkets. Ah! There was the box it had come in! And yes, the ring and bracelets were there! She remembered taking them off. But not the necklace! Where could the necklace be? Perhaps it had come unfastened and dropped in the big chair while she was eating her supper!

She stepped across the hall quickly and tapped at the door of her aunt's room.

"Aunt Pat, may I come in a minute?" she called, and upon receiving permission she burst into the room excitedly: "Aunt Pat! I've lost my emerald necklace! Could I have dropped it in your room?"

Chapter 7

For a moment Sherrill and Aunt Pat stood facing one another, taking in the full significance of the loss from every side. Sherrill knew just how much that necklace was prized in the family. Aunt Pat had told her the story of its purchase at a fabulous price by an ancestor who had bought it from royalty for his young bride. It had come down to Aunt Pat and been treasured by her and kept most preciously. Rare emeralds, of master workmanship in their cutting and exquisite setting! Sherrill stood appalled, aghast, facing the possibility that it was hopelessly gone.

"Oh, Aunt Pat!" she moaned. "You oughtn't to have given it to me! I—I'm—not fit—to have anything rare! Either man or treasure!" she added with a great sob, her lips trembling. "It—seems—I—can't—keep—*anything*!"

Aunt Pat broke into a roguish grin.

"I hope you didn't call that man rare, Sherrill Cameron!" she chuckled. "And for sweet pity's sake, if you ever do find a real man, don't put him on a level with mere jewels! Now, take that look off your face and use your head a little. Where did you have that necklace last? You wore it this evening, I know, for I noticed with great satisfaction that you were not wearing that ornate trinket your would-be bridegroom gave you."

"Oh, I thought I had it on when I came in here!" groaned Sherrill. "I just can't remember! I'm sure I didn't take it off anywhere! At least I can't remember doing it."

She rushed suddenly to the big chair where she had been sitting for the last hour and pulled out the cushions frantically, running her hands down in the folds of the upholstery, but discovering nothing but a lost pair of scissors.

She turned on the overhead lights and got down on her knees, searching earnestly, but there was no green translucent gleam of emeralds.

Meanwhile Aunt Pat stood thinking, a canny look in her old eyes.

"Now look here, Sherrill," she said suddenly, whirling round upon the frantic girl, "you haven't lost your soul, you know, and we are still alive and well. Emeralds are just emeralds after all. Get some poise! Get up off that floor and go quietly downstairs! Look just casually wherever you remember to have been. Just walk over the same places. Don't do any wild pawing around; just merely look in the obvious places. Don't make a noise, and don't say anything to the servants if any of them are up. I don't think they are. Gemmie thought they were gone to bed. I just sent Gemmie away. Then, if you don't find it, come up to me."

Sherrill made a little dismal moan.

"Oh, for mercy's sake!" said Aunt Pat impatiently. "It isn't as if you hadn't had a chance to wear them once anyway, and one doesn't wear emeralds, such emeralds, around every day. You won't miss them much in the long run even if you never find them. Now stop your hysterics and run downstairs, but don't make any noise!"

Sherrill cast a tearful look at her aunt and hurried away, stopping at her own room to get a little flashlight she kept in her desk.

Step by step she retraced the evening in an agony of memory. It wasn't just her losing the emeralds forever; it was Aunt Pat losing the pleasure of her having them. It was—well, something else, a horrible haunting fear that appeared and disappeared on the horizon of her mind and gripped her heart like a clutching hand.

When she came in her search to the long french window out which she and Copeland had passed to the garden such a little while before, she paused and hesitated, catching her breath at a new memory. If it came to that, *there* would be something she couldn't tell Aunt Pat! She couldn't hope to make her understand about that kiss!

Oh! A long shudder went through her weary body, and every taut nerve hurt like a toothache. How was she to explain it to herself? And yet—!

She unfastened the window with a shaking hand and, touching the switch of her flashlight, went carefully over the porch, and inch by inch down the walk where they had passed, not forgetting the grassy edges on either side. On her way back she stopped, and her cheeks grew hot in the dark as she held back the branches of privet and stepped within that cool green quiet hiding place. Oh, if she could but find it here! If only it had fallen under the shrubs. It would have been very easy for it to come unfastened while he held her in his arms. If only she might find it and be set free from that haunting fear. Just to know that he was all right. Just to be *sure*—! She felt again the pressure of his arms about her, so gentle, the touch of his lips upon her eyelids. It had rested and comforted her so. It hadn't seemed wrong. Yet of course he was an utter stranger!

But she searched the quiet hiding place in vain. There was no answering gleam to the little light that went searching so infallibly, and at last she had to come in and give it up. There was utter dejection in her attitude when she came back to Aunt Pat, her lip trembling, her eyes filled with large unshed tears, that haunting fear in their depths. For of course she could not help but realize that that moment when he held her in his arms would have been a most opportune time for a crook to get the emeralds.

"There isn't a sign of them anywhere!" she said.

"Well," said Aunt Pat, "you can't do anything more tonight. Get to bed. You look worn to a thread. I declare, for anybody who went through the evening like a soldier, you certainly have collapsed in a hurry. Lose a bridegroom, and take it calmly. Lose a bauble and go all to pieces! Well, go to bed and forget it, child! Perhaps we'll find it in the morning."

"But Aunt Pat!" said Sherrill, standing tragically with clasped hands under the soft light from the old alabaster chandelier, with her gold hair like a halo crowning her. "Oh, Aunt Pat! You *don't* suppose—*he*—took it, do you?"

"He?" said the old lady sharply, whirling on her niece. "Whom do you mean? Your precious renegade bridegroom? No, I hadn't thought of him. I doubt if he had the nerve to do it. Still, it's not out of the thinking."

"Oh, Aunt Pat! Not Carter! I didn't mean Carter." She said, astonished, "Of course he wouldn't do a thing like that!"

"Why 'of course'?" snapped Aunt Pat grimly. "He knew the value of those stones, didn't he? And according to his own confession, he needed money, didn't he? If he would steal a girl's love and fling it away, why not steal another girl's necklace? Deception is deception in whatever form you find it, little girl! However, I suppose Carter McArthur had enough on his hands this evening for one occasion, and he likely wouldn't have had the time to stage another trick. But I hope you are not trying

121

to suspect that poor innocent bystander that you dragged into your service this evening!"

"He was a *stranger*!" said Sherrill with white anxious lips and frightened eyes.

"Hmm! Did he act to you like a crook, Sherrill Cameron?"

"No, Aunt Pat! He was wonderful! But—"

"Well, no more buts about it. Of course he had nothing to do with it. I know a true man when I see him, even if I am an old maid, and I won't have a man like that suspected in my house! You don't really mean to say you haven't any more discernment than that, do you?"

"No," said Sherrill, managing a shaky smile. "I'm sure he is all right, but I was afraid *you* would think—"

"There! I thought as much! You thought *I* had no sense. Well, go to bed. We're both dead for sleep. And don't think another thing about this tonight! Mind me!"

"But—oughtn't I to call the police?"

"What for? And have them demand a list of our guests and insult every one of them? No emeralds are worth the losing of friends! Besides, nobody can do anything about it tonight anyway. Now get to bed. Scat!"

Sherrill broke into a little hysterical laugh and, rushing up to her aunt, threw her arms around her neck and gave her a tender kiss.

"You are just wonderful!" she whispered into her ear, and then hurried back to her room.

Before her mirror she stood again, looking sternly

into her own eyes. Such sorrowful tired eyes as looked back at her, such a chastened little face, utterly humble.

Somehow as she stood facing her present situation, it seemed weeks, almost years, since she had stood there in wedding satin facing married life like an unknown country through which she had to travel. If she had known when she stood there smiling with her wedding bouquet in her arms, and her wedding veil, blossom-wreathed, on her head, that all this was to be, how would the laughter have died on her lips! How trivial would have seemed her faint fears! Had those fears been a sort of premonition of what was to happen in a few minutes? she wondered. She had read of such things, and perhaps they were in the air like radio waves waiting to be picked up!

Oh, what a night! What an ending to all that lovely preparation! The tears welled suddenly into her eyes, and a great feeling of being overwhelmed came over her anew. Dust and ashes! How had all the beauty of her life faded in a few short minutes! And how was she to face the long desert of the future?

Ah! To have lifted the goblet of Life to her lips, and suddenly to have had it snatched from her without even a single sip! How was she going to bear it all?

It was like coming up to a great stone wall and not being able to scale it, a stone wall on every side, and not even a desire left to try to get over it. All that she really wanted just now was to drop down and sleep and forget.

Well, that was just what she had promised Aunt Pat

she would do, but even the effort seemed too much.

She turned from the mirror, too tired even to cry, and saw that Gemmie had laid out one of her plain simple nightgowns, nothing new and smart, just an old, soft, well-worn gown out of her pleasant thoughtless past. Gratefully she crept into it and got into her bed.

She was too tired to think, too burdened to toss and weep. All she wanted was to sink down into oblivion; and that was just what happened. Tired nature pulled a curtain about her, and she drifted away into deep sleep.

But it was not a peaceful sleep. There were troublesome times and buffetings. She was having to drive her car very fast over a rough wild road in a storm, and her wedding veil kept blowing over her eyes and getting tangled in her steering wheel. Carter seemed to be standing somewhere ahead in the darkness, waiting for her with a terrible frown on his handsome face, the frown he had worn when he first saw Arla enter that door. She was late for her wedding and out of breath. She seemed to be lost on a wild prairie, and was afraid, terribly afraid!

Over and over she dreamed this with variations. Sometimes it was snowing, and the sleet stung her cheeks and shriveled the lilies of the bouquet in her lap, but she had to go on until she finally arrived at a strange dark rendezvous in an unknown country, and plunged out of her car, letting it run away into the darkness without her. She groped about in the night to find her wedding, but there was only a closed and darkened church. She was filled with despair till a stranger, whom yet she seemed to have known all her life, came out of the shadows and helped her home. A stranger who kissed her gently when he left her at her door.

Chapter 8

A great gust of perfume from many flowers wafted out into the passageway as the steward threw open the door and ushered in Arla and Carter McArthur. Flowers everywhere! Sherrill's flowers!

Arla stepped back and closed her eyes quickly as if she had been struck in the face. Carter frowned angrily. He stepped inside and looked at the array. Flowers, fruit, candies. A haunted look passed over his face. This all represented what he had lost in the other bride. Popularity, wealth, influence! He began to examine the cards of the friends who had sent them. Sherrill's friends. All Sherrill's friends. None of his represented except the big basket of fruit from his underpaid office. He looked at it contemptuously. Smelton with his six children and sick wife, Johnny Farr the errand boy with a widowed mother,

Miss Gaye the assistant secretary who wore bargain-counter clothes and chewed incessant gum. Arla! Arla? Had Arla contributed to that basket of fruit, too? He cast a quick look at her, his wife, swaying there in the doorway looking white and miserable. Could it be possible that those poor wretches had asked Arla to contribute to a voyage gift for her rival? He had a passing sense of what it might have meant to her to be asked. The whiteness of her face showed she was not enjoying the festive array. Just for an instant he forgot his own annoyance and realized sharply what all this might have been to her. And yet how well she had gone through with it! So confidently, almost radiantly. It had been maddening to have her so confident, when she had dared to interfere, yet somehow it had also stirred his pride in her. After all, she was beautiful. No one could deny that! But she had gone beyond all limits in coming there to the house and precipitating this disaster. Yes, disaster! It meant destruction to his well-laid financial plans. And no matter how lovely this unsought bride might be, how well she might carry off her position as his wife, that could not offset the fact that he had in himself no position for her to carry off. It had all been a big bluff dependent on Miss Patricia Catherwood's fortune. And what he was to do now remained to be seen. However crazy he might always have been about Arla, that did not alter the fact that he cared for money and position more than he cared for any living woman. And he had in his mind the comfortable realization that he could always get the adoration of another girl if one failed him, or became for the time unwise.

Arla rallied her self-control and quietly entered in the wake of the bags, drifting unobserved into a corner until the steward had left and they were alone.

Carter readjusted the baggage, placing his own suitcase on top impatiently. He was one who always expected those serving to anticipate his slightest unexpressed wishes. He swung savagely around to Arla, stranded pitifully by the door, her arrogance and initiative all gone now, nothing but a frightened look in her eyes. She knew his moods. She understood that her time had come to pay for what she had done.

"Well, if that's what you wanted, there you have plenty of it!" he said, waving his hand toward the gifts. "Enjoy it while you can. It'll probably be the last you'll see of this sort of thing. If you could only have made up your mind to wait awhile, we might have had all this and more!"

The frightened look faded from Arla's eyes and lightning came instead. Her lips grew thin and hard. She turned away from him haughtily and busied herself removing her gloves. She looked very handsome and angry as she stood there not listening to him. He could not but see how smart she looked, how becoming her clothes. She knew how to dress. If only he could weather this crisis somehow, things might not be so bad after all. She really knew how to wear her clothes just as well as Sherrill, could perhaps make an appearance to suit his pride. And of course she was beautiful, of much the same type as Sherrill. That was what had attracted him to Sherrill in the first place—that she had reminded him of Arla. And perhaps Arla could learn. She could get rid of her provincialism. She had learned a lot already. But the money! If he only could be sure—!

He swung around and began to fumble with the baggage, stowing one big suitcase that contained his wedding garments back under the bed. Swinging another down and shoving it after. Of course the steward would attend to all that presently, but it suited him to be stirring, throwing things around. This was an awkward moment; various emotions were striving within him.

Arla stood where she had first entered, pulling off her long gloves deliberately, finger by finger, smoothing them carefully, thoughtfully. She was struggling to keep from bursting into tears.

The steward tapped at the door, and Arla made no move to answer it, but moved away and stood staring out of the porthole at the panorama of harbor lights. Already they were moving out into the stream, and she had a strange dreadful feeling that she was heading out into the midstream of life, leaving behind all that she knew, all that she had hoped, going into a wild lonely sea of problems and perplexities and going utterly unprepared and unloved.

Carter had gone to the door. She heard the conversation vaguely, as if it had nothing to do with her. It was something about a telegram. The operator wished to speak to Mr. McArthur. Carter went out and Arla wondered idly why he was sending a telegram now, on his wedding night, but she was filled with indifference concerning it.

Carter had left the door unlatched as he went out, and the draft from the open porthole cooled her hot cheeks. She turned to fasten the door, realizing that she was alone, a brief breathing space, and looked about her again.

Those flowers! How wonderful it would have been if they had been hers! If she had been a girl with friends who could send farewell greetings in such a costly style! Why, all these gifts, the wedding that had preceded them, had been but the fulfillment of her childish fairy dreamings—all the things she had most wished for in life—and now they had come, and how empty they were! How one's heart could starve in the midst of plenty!

She went about the room stealthily examining the cards, removing them with frightened hasty fingers. She would put them out of sight before Carter returned.

Some of the names she recognized as belonging to people who had been down the line and been introduced to her such a little time ago. They had gone through the motion of friendship with her, but that would be all. She would likely never see them again. For a brief moment she had walked with the elite and been recognized by them, but she was not a part of them, never would be. They were not of her world! Her highest dreams had been realized and yet had brought her no joy. Emptiness and sawdust! How she hated it all! How she wished for the old sweet simple days when she went to high school in pretty gingham dresses and Carter carried her books for her, looked down adoringly into her eyes, told her how lovely she was!

Oh, what had she done, how had things gone wrong, that they had come to this night? She remembered the look he had given her as he waved his hand toward the flowers and told her to enjoy them while she could, that it was probably the last of that sort of thing she would see. She shivered with anguish as she felt his contempt all over again, and realized that he was not the Carter of her happy school days, not even the whimsical lover who had sent for her to be his secretary. She must face that fact and not give way to sorrow. Then her lips became set with determination, and she stepped calmly to the bell and rang for the stewardess.

When the woman presented herself, Arla waved toward the flowers.

"I would like you to take all those away," she said coldly. "They sicken me. Take them down to the steerage, please, and give them to the old women and the little children."

When Carter came back, the flowers were all gone. The boxes of expensive candies were gone. There was left only the basket of fruit from the office standing alone on the dresser.

"Why—where—what—?" asked Carter, looking about and sensing the emptiness.

"I told the stewardess to take them down to the steerage and give them to people who could enjoy them," she said in a cold steady voice.

Carter looked at her half startled. He had had so many startling things flung at him already this long terrible evening that one more or less made little impression. Then his eyes swept about the room again and he noticed the fruit.

"Why not that one, too?" he asked, his lips settling into their habitual sneering curve.

"Because that one is yours!" she answered steadily. "Because *I* paid for that myself!"

"You paid for it yourself?" he exclaimed, looking at her in astonishment.

"Yes, I paid for it myself!" she answered, folding her gloves smoothly together again and laying them out on the table.

"But—*why*? Why should you pay for them? Why not the others? Who got up the idea?"

"It wasn't gotten up. I did it all. They don't even know about it. They hadn't any money to put into gifts. They have all they can do to keep from starving. Johnny's mother is likely dying tonight. He won't be able to get any flowers for her funeral! Smelton's wife has had a relapse, and one of his children has a broken leg; the only child who had any job at all. Miss Gaye needs all her salary for gum. Who would you think would send you fruit from the office if I didn't?"

"But why *you*?" he asked again, a strange incredulous look in his eyes.

"Why I?" answered the girl with a flash of her tear-drowned eyes and a sudden quiver of her lovely lip. "Why I? Because I was a *fool*! Because I'll always be a fool, I suppose, where you are concerned! Because I *thought* I loved you, and wanted you to have all the honor there was, even from an office like ours! It was just after you told me that I had always been— Oh, what's the use! I won't say those empty words over. I had a spirit of self-sacrifice. I thought I loved you enough to sacrifice myself! That was before I found out I couldn't stand it! It was before I told your other bride that I'd go through hell to marry you. It was even before I understood what hell was like!"

"Did you tell her that?" His face was white with anger and a strange wild remorse.

"Yes, I told her that when she said she wouldn't marry you after what she'd seen, and asked me if I would, and I said I'd go through hell to marry you! But I didn't know what hell could be like then, even at the beginning. I thought I was in it then, but I *wasn't*."

A wave of shamed color swept over his face, leaving it white as death. He almost staggered and put out his hand to steady himself against the wall.

"You don't care that you're putting me through hell, do you?" he whined impressively.

She gave him a withering glance.

"You deserve it," she said fiercely. "I don't! I've always tried to be as decent as you would let me. I never played fast and loose with you. I've loved you always—and—I love you—now! God help me! Why do I love you? Oh, why? You are despicable! You know you are! How could anybody love a little handsome selfish beast like you? And yet I do! Oh, what a wedding night!"

She threw herself suddenly down upon the bed and wept bitterly. And he, trembling, almost ashamed, filled with passionate remorse and angry retaliation, turned the light off and crept humbly to her side, kneeling, groping for her hand. Her words had lashed him through fury into a sudden brief fleeting vision of himself.

"Arla!" he said, reaching after her in the dark. "Arla! Don't cry that way! I do love you!"

Chapter 9

Sherrill awoke in the morning with a gorgeous sunlight streaming across the lovely old blue rug, lighting her familiar room cheerfully.

Then instantly, as if someone had struck her across the heart with a club, there came to her a remembrance of all that had happened since she awoke in that room so joyously yesterday morning. The future, drab and desolate, stretched itself away before her, a dreary prospect.

Sherrill's soul turned sick at her own desolation, and all the horror of her situation rushed over her with a realization of details which she had not had time for last night in the sudden stress and need for immediate action.

And now of course the first thought that occurred was, had she done right? Was her action too hasty? Had there been any other way? What would other girls have done? *Could* she have married him knowing the truth about him?

Of course, if there had been the least doubt about it, if there had been any chance at all that she was misjudging him, she would have been wrong not to have given him an opportunity to explain, to clear himself if he could.

But she had heard his own words. She had seen him clasp that other girl and kiss her with the same passionate fervency with which he had kissed her. She had seen his face as he took her in his arms. She could never forget it. Yes, she had heard his own confession that he still loved the other girl, and that after his marriage and wedding trip they would be freer than ever—! *Ah!* She caught her lips between her teeth with a trembling breath. How that sight, those words had stabbed her! Oh no, there was no possibility of doubt. He was false-hearted. He had *meant* to be false!

If he had just been weak and fallen into this situation, one could forgive. Forgive, but not marry. She could never marry a man whom she could not trust.

But he had been deliberately false, and she could scarcely be sorry for him. No, she could only be sorry for that poor desperate girl who had been willing to go through hell to have him.

Well, there was such a thing as hell on earth, of course. Her own present outlook seemed not far situated from such a location, and yet she knew if she had to go through even a mild kind of hell for the rest of her life, she would rather take it alone than tied up to the man whom just a few short hours before she had been joyously preparing to marry. No, she must be thankful that a kind Providence had even in such a tragic moment prevented her from marrying Carter McArthur.

And yet though all that was true, Sherrill Cameron lay with wide desperate eyes staring out at a sunlit desolation.

She closed her eyes again and tried to wish herself back to sleep, but the eyes flew open like a doll's that had lost their weights. She knew that she was definitely awake for the day and could not drop back into merciful oblivion again even for a brief space. She must face what was before her.

So she lay staring about the room that had sheltered so much of her joy and happy anticipation, and suddenly from every wall and corner things jumped out at her that had been connected with her courtship. A great bunch of dried grasses that she and Carter had gathered the day they took their first walk together. It filled a thin crystal vase on the mantel and made a thing ethereally lovely. Gemmie never would have known that it was a reminder of dear dead days.

High over her white marble mantel was fastened a pennant. It spoke of the first football game she had attended with Carter, less than a year ago! Gemmie wouldn't have realized that the pennant spoke eloquently of a lost past.

Knotted carelessly on the corner of a signed etching on the opposite wall, for no apparent reason at all, was a bow of scarlet ribbon, a memento of last Christmas, kept because Carter had tied it about her hair the morning they were skating together, and then had drawn her face back and kissed her behind a sheltering hemlock tree that hid them from the view of the other skaters on the creek. And that was another memory that she must cut out and throw away. It did not belong to her and never had belonged, it seemed! Gemmie had no idea what that red ribbon meant.

Over on her desk that bronze paperweight! Gemmie never had known that it had been on his desk the day she first went with Carter to his office. She had admired it and he had given it to her. That was before Arla came to be his secretary! Ah, but he had known and loved Arla first! He loved her enough *afterward* to have sent for Arla. And yet he had gone right on with his intimacy with Sherrill! The bronze, too, must go into the trash!

And over on the bureau, that little ivory figurine! Gemmie had always admired that. But she did not know that Carter had bought it for her in a curio shop the day they went together to New York.

Oh! She could not bear these memories! She must not! She would give way and weep. And weeping was not for her today! She must keep a mask of happiness on her face. She must not let anyone suspect that her life was shattered by that wedding as it had come out last night. They must think it was all planned or at least that a definite and friendly change was made before the ceremony. She could not go around and explain the whole thing as it had happened. Even if she were willing on her own part, she could not explain what involved others' secrets. No, she must play her part through to the end and keep a brave, cheerful, even merry face. How was she to do it?

Then suddenly she could not bear the sight of those things on her wall, and she sprang up and dashed the bunch of grasses down, sweeping them into the fireplace where Gemmie had carefully laid a fire.

The vase was only a plain little thing from the five-and-ten-cent store, but it seemed to understand what was expected of it, and as Sherrill lifted the grasses swiftly from it, it toppled and rolled slowly, deliberately down upon the hearth and smashed into a thousand pieces.

Sherrill stood for an instant looking at it regretfully, almost as if it had a personality. Poor fragile thing! Too bad for it to lose its existence through no fault of its own. It had been part of a lovely bit of beauty, but at least now she would not have it around to remind her of the grasses and the day that they were picked!

She stooped and swept the pieces quickly with her little hearth broom into a newspaper, and wrapped them carefully, putting them into the wastebasket. Now they were gone. Even Gemmie wouldn't be reminded to ask where the grasses were.

Then she touched a match to the fire, and it swept up and licked the grasses out of existence in one flash.

Sherrill turned to the room again. She mounted a chair and pulled down the pennant, stuffing it fiercely into the wastebasket. She snatched the bow of ribbon from the picture frame and dropped it into the fire. She caught up the bronze paperweight. That wouldn't burn! Nor the ivory figurine! What could she do with them? Give them away? They might somehow come back to face her someday, and she wanted to be utterly rid of them. Ah! There was one place where she would never be likely to see them again. She might send them to Carter's office. But no, that would be only to bring back to his mind the days they had had together, and that she did not want. She wanted only to sever all connection with him, to wipe out from both his memory and hers, insofar as was possible, all thought of one another. Then only would she be able to lift up her head and breathe freely again.

She unlocked a little secret drawer in her desk to put the bronze and ivory out of sight, and came on a packet of notes and brief letters from Carter. There hadn't been many because he had been right there to see her every day. She had almost forgotten these letters and some programs and clippings. She seized them now and flung them into the middle of the fire, closing her eyes quickly that she might not see the flames licking around her name in that handwriting that had been so beloved, turning her back lest she should repent and snatch them out to read them over again. She must not! No, it would unnerve her! It would make her heart turn back and lash her for what she had done in giving her bridegroom over to another girl. She must not because he never had been hers! He was not worth the great love she had given him.

And now she remembered how unworthy she herself had felt to marry him, and how she had prayed and wondered. Was this awful thing that had happened in some mysterious way an answer to her prayer? Oh, it was all a mystery! Life itself was a mystery. Joy one minute and awful sorrow and desolation the next! Sorrow! Sorrow! Sorrow!

Suddenly from the next room through the closed door there came a burst of wild sweet song:

"When I have sorrow in my heart,
What can take it away?
Only Jesus in-ah my heart
Can take that sorrow away."

It was Lutie, the fresh-cheeked young girl who came in certain days in the week to help with the cleaning. Lutie had the windows of the guest room open and was beginning her weekly cleaning. Sherrill's windows were open, too, and that was why the words came so distinctly. But how strange that such words should come to her just now when she was so filled with sorrow!

Lutie was banging things around, drawing the bed out, and the bureau, setting chairs out of the way and running the vacuum cleaner over the floor. Sherrill could hear the thump as the cleaner hit the baseboards now and then. And Lutie's voice rang out clear again in the next verse:

> *"When I have fear in-ah my heart,*
> *What can take it away?*
> *Only Jesus in-ah my heart*
> *Can take that fear away."*

Sherrill began slowly, languidly to dress, listening to the song. Fear in the heart. She considered herself. Did she have fear in her heart? Yes, she recognized a kind of dread of the days that were before her. Not fear of anything tangible, perhaps, but fear of gossip, criticism, prying eyes. Fear of having to face all that would come in the wake of that wedding that was hers and yet was not. Fear of a drab future, a long lonely way ahead, no home of her own. She could never have a home of her own now, nor anyone to care for her and enjoy life with her. For she would never dare trust a man again, even if she ever found one whom she could love.

> *"When I have sin in-ah my heart—"*

piped up Lutie joyously,

"What can take it away?
Only Jesus in-ah my heart
Can take that sin away."

Sherrill was not especially interested in sin. She had never considered herself to be much of a sinner, and her thoughts wandered idly, considering her own case more than the song as she listened to the lilt of Lutie's voice in the closing verse:

"When I have Jesus in-ah my heart,
What can take Him away?
Once take Jesus into my heart
And He has come to stay!"

There was a pause in the singing and the sound of voices in the hall. Thomas, the house servant, had come up to get the rugs to give them a good cleaning in the backyard. Lutie was demurring, but finally tapped hesitantly at Sherrill's door.

Sherrill in her negligee opened the door.

"Miss Sherrill, Thomas was wanting to get your rug for cleaning, but I guess you aren't ready yet, are you? I wasn't sure whether you were in your room or not."

"That's all right, Lutie," said Sherrill, stepping through into the next room where the girl was at work. "Tell him to go in and take it. I can finish without a rug."

Sherrill went to the guest room bureau and began to

arrange her hair, and Lutie came back after helping the man roll up the rug.

"That's a curious song you were singing, Lutie," said Sherrill pleasantly. "Where in the world did you get it? It sounds like a spiritual."

"I don't guess it is, Miss Sherrill," said the girl, pausing in her dusting. "I got it down to our Bible class. It is pretty words, isn't it? I like that part about Jesus taking your sorrow away. I sing it a lot."

"But you've never had any sorrow, Lutie," said Sherrill wistfully, eyeing the girl's round rosy cheeks and happy eyes.

"Oh, Miss Sherrill, you don't know," said Lutie, sobering suddenly. "I've had just a lot! First my mother got awful sick for two whole years, and then when she got better my sister just older'n I died. And my little brother has hurt his hip, and they don't think he'll ever walk again."

"Oh, Lutie," cried Sherrill in dismay, "that is a lot of trouble!"

"Oh, but that's not all," said the girl, drawing a deep sigh. "My dad got some steel filings in his eye about nine months ago, and they think he's going blind, and now they've laid him off the job, so my brother Sam and I are the only ones working, except Mother now and then when she can get a washing to do. And our house is all mortgaged up, and the bank closed last week where we had our money saved to pay the interest, and now we'll maybe lose the house; and Mother needs an operation, only she can't stop working to go to the hospital. And"— the girl caught her lip between her little white teeth to hold it from trembling, and Sherrill could see that there were tears in her eyes—"and—then—my boyfriend got mad and started going with another girl because I wouldn't run off and get married and leave the family in all that mess!"

The big tears rolled out now, and down her round cheek, and Lutie caught a corner of her apron and brushed them hastily away.

"Excuse me, Miss Sherrill," she said huskily. "It just sometimes gets me—"

"You poor dear child!" said Sherrill, putting down her hairbrush and coming over toward her. "Why, you poor kid, you! I never dreamed you could have all that to bear! And *yet* you could sing a song like that!" She regarded the girl earnestly. "You certainly are brave! But Lutie, you know a boyfriend that would do a thing like that isn't worth crying after." Sherrill said it and suddenly knew she was speaking out of her own experience.

"I know it!" gulped Lutie. "I know he ain't, but sometimes it all just comes over me. You see, I was right fond of him."

Then she flashed a smile like a rainbow through her tears and brightened.

"But I don't feel like that much now since I got Jesus in my heart like the song says. He really drives the sorrow away, and I'm mostly glad just to let Him have His way with me. If it wasn't fer Him, I couldn't stand it. He really does take the sorrow away, you know. I guess you likely know that yourself, Miss Sherrill, don't you? But you see, I haven't known Jesus so long, so I just have to talk about Him and sing about Him most all the time to keep myself reminded what a wonderful Savior I've got."

Sherrill turned a searching, hungry look upon the little serving maid.

"Where did you get all that, Lutie?"

"Down at our Bible class, Miss Sherrill. I been going there about a year now. We got a wonderful teacher down there. We study the Bible, and it's just wonderful what he makes us see in it. I just wish you'd come down sometime and visit, Miss Sherrill, and see what it's like."

"Maybe I will—sometime," said Sherrill slowly, still studying the girl as if there were some strange mystery about her.

"It ain't a very grand place," said Lutie apologetically. "Maybe you might not like it. It's just a plain board floor, and the walls are cracked and the seats are hard. It ain't like your church. The windows are painted white because they look into an alley. Maybe you wouldn't think it was good enough for you. But I'd like you to come once and see. The singing's just heavenly, and the teacher's grand! Everybody loves it so, they just can't bear to go home."

"Why, I wouldn't mind things like that!" said Sherrill earnestly. "Indeed I wouldn't. I'll come sometime; I really will. I'd like to see what it's like. When do you meet?"

"Monday evenings!" said Lutie with dancing eyes. "Oh, Miss Sherrill, if you'd come I'd be that proud!"

"Why, of course I'll come!" said Sherrill heartily, relieved that she could do anything to make Lutie's eyes shine like that, half curious, too, to see what it was that had made this simple girl happy in the face of such terrible troubles.

Sherrill carried the memory of the girl's face with her as she went back to her room to finish her dressing. What a light had come into her eyes when she said what a wonderful Savior she had! Savior! Savior from what? Her sorrow? Her fear? Her sin? Lutie couldn't be such a great sinner. It was probably just a lot of phrases she had picked up in some evangelistic meeting, poor thing, but if she thought she was comforted by it, there must be some good in it. Anyway, Sherrill decided she would go and find out. If there was any cure for sorrow, surely she herself needed it. And she drew a heavy sigh and went downstairs to face the morning after her own wedding day without a bridegroom.

She tried as she walked down the broad front stairs to forget how that other bride had looked, smiling and proud, holding her head high. And how Carter had looked, haughty, handsome, carrying it all off just as if it had been planned that way.

Carter! What had he thought? How had he taken it? Strange that he had not shown a sign, nor spoken a word to her. Did she fancy it, or had there been a furtive look of fear in his eyes? Anyhow, it was plain enough that he had avoided looking straight at her. Not once had he looked her in the eyes. Not once attempted to draw her aside and speak to her. She did not know from his looks whether he was very angry or only relieved to have had things work out this way.

Her heart was very heavy as she thought of this. It seemed to blot out the happy days of the past, to make Carter into an utter stranger. Yet of course it was better so. That was what she wanted; only somehow the awfulness of his attitude overcame her anew as she came down to the setting of the last act of that tragedy that had ended her high hopes. How was she going to bear the future?

And then, suddenly, just at the foot of the stairs she remembered the emeralds! The emeralds and the stranger! And down upon her like some gigantic bird of prey swept her fear of the night before!

Chapter 10

Miss Catherwood was already at the breakfast table looking as fresh and chipper as if she had gone to bed at nine o'clock the night before. She was opening her mail, and there was a smile of satisfaction on her face. She gave Sherrill a keen look as she came into the room.

"Well, I'm glad to see you're still a good sport!" she said with her funny twisted grin. "But you didn't sleep very well, did you? There are dark circles under your eyes. Sit down and eat a good breakfast. Oh, I know you think you don't want a thing but a cup of coffee, but that's not the way to act. You've got a few hard days before you, and you've got to keep your looks through them or people will say you are mourning after that sap-head, and you don't want that. Come, set to work. We've got to get at sending back those presents. You'll feel better when they

149

are out of the house."

Sherrill gave a little moan and dropped her face into her hands.

"Oh!" she groaned. "How impossible it all seems! But if I could only find the necklace, I wouldn't mind any of the rest!"

Aunt Pat flung a wise glance at Sherrill's bowed head.

"That'll turn up all right," she said. "Come, child, perk up. I've been wondering. Can you think back and be sure when you last had it?"

Sherrill shook her head.

"No. I've been trying, but I can't be sure. If I only could, it would take a big load from my mind."

"Well, *I* can!" said Aunt Pat. "You had the necklace on when you sat in the dining room eating your supper after you came in from outside. I know, for I sat and watched the lights in those stones, and I remember thinking how well they became you, and how they brought out the color in your cheeks and the gold in your hair."

Sherrill's head came up suddenly with a light of hope in her eyes and a soft flush on her cheeks.

"Are you *sure* you saw them on me at the table, Aunt Pat? Perfectly sure?"

"Perfectly sure," said Aunt Pat steadily, studying the girl quietly.

"Well, that's something!" said Sherrill with a sigh of relief. "At least I didn't lose it—in the garden!"

"No, you didn't lose it in the garden," said Aunt Pat

with a wicked little grin. "Now don't think anything more about it. Let's get at those presents. First you sit down and work out a little model note sweet and gracious that will fit all the presents and not tell a thing you don't want known."

Sherrill presently brought it to her aunt for her approval.

My dear—

The sudden change in our plans for the wedding has left me in an embarrassing situation, having in my possession a lot of lovely gifts that do not by right belong either to me or to Mrs. McArthur. I am therefore of course returning all the gifts and apologizing for having been the unintentional cause of so much trouble to the donors.

But I do want to add just a little word of my appreciation for your beautiful gift, and to thank you for your delightful intention for my pleasure. It is so wonderful to see such gracious evidence of friendship.

Very sincerely,
Sherrill Cameron

"I think that is quite a nice bit of English!" said Aunt Pat with satisfaction when she had read it. "It says all that needs to be said and tells nothing. It ought to be published. It would be so helpful to other girls caught in like predicaments."

Sherrill broke into hysterical laughter.

"Oh, Aunt Pat! You're a scream! As if there were ever another girl caught in such a predicament!" she said.

"I don't know," said the old lady dryly. "You can't tell how many girls have had a situation like yours; only most of them likely didn't have the nerve to handle it the way you did yours. There must have been some girls who were too great cowards to back down from a church full of wedding guests, and the wedding march just on the tiptoe to begin. They probably paid afterward, and paid double, too. Surely, Sherrill, you aren't the only one who ever found at the last minute that her lover was made of coarse clay. Don't ever fancy, no matter how hard a thing you have to go through, that your experience is unique. This old world has been going on a good many hundred years, and there are precious few situations that haven't happened over and over again. Cheer up, child; that's a model letter, and you're a good little sport!"

Miss Catherwood handled the return of the presents in a masterly manner. Her secretary and Sherrill wrote the notes while Gemmie and the butler under her supervision repacked the gifts. It was amazing how quickly the things were marshaled from the tables into their neat original packages, each with its dainty note attached. Sherrill grew so interested in seeing how much she could accomplish that she almost forgot her anxiety about the emeralds.

It comforted her greatly that the necklace had not been lost while she was out with Copeland. But later in the day something occurred which brought back her uneasiness and that nameless fear again. Oh, to know certainly, who if anyone was connected with the disappearance of the jewels!

It was late in the afternoon and Miss Catherwood had just said they had done enough for today and must stop and rest. Just then the hall door opened timidly and Lutie showed a deprecating face.

"Please, Miss Catherwood, might I come in and speak to you a moment?" she asked shyly.

"Why, of course, Lutie. Come right in," said the old maid cheerily. "What is it?"

"Why, Miss Catherwood, I found something," she said earnestly, holding her two hands cupped, the one in the other. "Maybe it isn't much account, but it looked to me as if it might be something real. It's only a little thing, and I thought if I gave it to any of the other servants they might laugh, but I knew you would know whether it was valuable or not."

Lutie dropped a delicate bit of brightness into the old lady's hand and stood back waiting shyly.

Aunt Pat held the bit of jewelry in her delicate old hand for an instant and examined it carefully. Then she looked up at the girl.

"Where did you find this, Lutie, and when?"

"Just now, ma'am, in the little back room off the

servants' hall. It was on the floor just under the edge of the little writing table, and I almost swept it up, but then I saw it glittering, and it first looked like a bit of Christmas-tree tinsel, but when I looked closer it seemed like something real."

"Hmm!" said Aunt Pat significantly and, looking up at Sherrill, added: "It's from the emerald necklace, Sherry, a whole inch of chain and part of the clasp!"

Sherrill gave a startled exclamation, and the old lady turned to Lutie again.

"Thank you, Lutie, for bringing it straight to me. Did you speak to any of the other servants about it?"

"No," said Lutie. "I was afraid they'd laugh at me. They tell me I'm fussy about little things."

"Well, that's a good trait sometimes," said the old lady. "I'm glad you brought it straight to me. Yes, it's valuable. It's part of something we had lost. You might keep your eye out while you're cleaning to see if you find any more of it. Now, suppose you come and show us just where you found this." They followed Lutie to the little room in the servants' hall.

"Thank you, Lutie," said Miss Catherwood when she had showed them the exact spot. "I shan't forget this!"

"Oh, that's all right, ma'am. I'm glad you weren't angry at my bothering you."

Lutie withdrew with a shy flame blazing in her cheeks.

Aunt Pat turned to Sherrill, who was searching the

room over, vainly hoping to find more of the necklace.

"Now, Sherrill," said Aunt Pat, "tell me just who was in this room and where each one stood. What were they here for, anyway, in this back room?"

"They came to get the license fixed up with the right names," said Sherrill, half shivering at the memory. "We sent for the clerk and he sat right there in that chair all the time he was here."

"And where did you stand?"

"Most of the time over there by the door. Once I stepped over to the table while I was explaining to him that I had changed my mind about marrying Carter."

The old lady gave her a swift look.

"Where was Carter at the time?"

"He stood just back of me."

"Hmm! How did he look when you explained that you had changed your mind about marrying him?"

"I didn't look at him. I was trying to keep my voice from trembling."

"Did he say anything or make any motion that seemed like a protest?"

"He cleared his throat in a nervous kind of way. I had a fancy that he was afraid I was going to tell more than I did. He stirred uneasily."

"And didn't he speak at all?"

"Only to answer the questions that were put to him by the clerk. Of course Mr. Copeland had explained the situation to the clerk in a general way, and the questions that were put were mere form. He just assented to everything. Mr. Copeland had really made it very easy for us all."

"Hmm!" said Aunt Pat thoughtfully and then reverted to the bridegroom.

"And Carter assented to all the questions, did he? He made it very plain that he was marrying that other girl by intention? He didn't make any protests nor attempt any explanations?"

"Not a word." Sherrill's voice told how deeply that fact weighed upon her.

"Little whippersnapper!" ejaculated the old lady indignantly. "Well, it's just what I would have expected of him! He hasn't the backbone of a jellyfish. He was born a coward! Perhaps you can't blame him so much. He probably had ancestors like that. Well, now, tell me, how long did you stand there?"

"I stepped away immediately after he had answered his questions and made a place for her—for the bride—to stand."

"And did you watch Carter's face while she was being questioned?"

"I wanted to, but just then he dropped his handkerchief. He acted very nervous, and he stooped over to pick it up. It seemed to take him a long time. He didn't seem to want to look at me. I tried to make him. It seemed as if I must make him look at me just once so that we could get adjusted to things. Just a look from him that he was ashamed, or that he felt I had done the right thing, would have made it so much easier. I felt so unhappy and frightened!"

"I know you did, dear child. Of course! But don't have any question but that you did the right thing. Well, who else was there? Carter and that girl and the clerk and you? Was Mr. Copeland in the room?"

"Not at all," said Sherrill quickly. "He stood outside in the hall every minute. I'm sure of that."

"He didn't even step back into the room when you all came away?"

"No," said Sherrill with assurance. "I'm positive of that, for he waited for me at the door and walked across to the middle room with me, and Carter and Arla were behind us. The clerk went ahead, down the back hall and the back stairs the way he had come. He went out of the room before any of us left it."

"Who was in the room last?"

"Why, Carter—and his—that is—the—bride!" she finished with a quick sharp breath.

"You're sure?"

"Yes, I looked back and called to her to follow me and that I would help her get ready. Carter was just behind her. He had apparently dropped his handkerchief again and was stooping to pick it up."

"Hmm! What did he do with it?"

"Why, I think he put it in his pocket."

"And he didn't look up even then?"

"No." Her voice was grave and very sad. "He seemed as if he was ashamed. He almost looked—well—frightened!"

"Probably was," said Aunt Pat dryly, "ashamed and baffled. He had been hoping to get a lot besides a bride in marrying you. I didn't tell you, but I came on him looking at the emeralds the morning I gave them to you. He seemed tremendously impressed with them. In fact, he looked as if he were just gloating over them. He didn't know I saw him. He thought he was alone. But I can't help thinking if he'd gotten them he'd have pawned them before the night was over."

"Oh, Aunt Pat!" exclaimed Sherrill in dismay. "Why—he—really spoke very beautifully about them. He said he was so proud that I should have regal jewels. He said he only wished that he were able to give me such things but he hoped someday he could."

"Oh yes, he could talk!" sniffed Aunt Pat. "He was mealy-mouthed. But don't try to defend him, Sherrill. I know it hurts to have him turn out that way, but you might as well understand the truth at once and not go to getting him up on a pedestal again. Now, I've got to think what to do for Lutie. I like to encourage the sort of thing she did, bringing that bit of chain straight to me. She's a good girl, and probably needs help. I wonder if I should give her money."

"Did you know that she has a little lame brother, Aunt Pat?" asked Sherrill. "And her father is going blind and her mother needs an operation?"

"Mercy, no!" said Aunt Pat, looking up from the bit of chain she was examining. "Why, how did you find that out? We must do something for them right away."

"Yes, they are afraid they are going to lose their house, too. They can't pay the interest on their mortgage. The bank closed where they kept their savings, and she and her brother are the only ones working."

"Well, for mercy's sake!" said Aunt Pat, greatly disturbed. "And to think they never said a word! Why wasn't I told of this sooner? When did you find it out, Sherrill?"

"Just this morning," said the girl, thinking back through the day. "I heard Lutie singing in the next room to mine where she was cleaning. She was singing about what to do when you had sorrow in your heart, or something like that. I asked her where she got the song and said I guessed she never had a sorrow, and then she told me all about it."

"Hmm!" said Aunt Pat thoughtfully.

Then she opened the door and called to Gemmie, who was never very far away from her mistress's call.

"Gemmie, go see if Lutie has gone home yet. If she hasn't, tell her I want her a minute."

Then she turned back to her niece.

"Sherrill, this is the setting of one of the tiny emeralds from that chain, see, one of the wee ones up near the clasp. Now, where do you suppose the rest of it is? You know, the clasp used to be weak, but I had it fixed; at least I supposed I had. I sent it to the jeweler's before I gave it to you. See! This evidently has been stepped on, or else yanked from the chain! How the links are crushed! Now, the question is, where did the necklace drop, and who was there when it happened?"

Sherrill looked up with troubled eyes, the haunting fear coming back to her soul, but Lutie came in just then, and she had no opportunity to answer her aunt.

"I sent for you, Lutie," said Miss Catherwood pleasantly, "because I want to tell you that there is a reward for finding this chain and for bringing it straight to me."

Lutie had been a bit troubled at being sent for, but now her face showed great relief and swift protest.

"Oh no, ma'am," she said breathlessly, "I couldn't think of taking anything for just doing my duty."

"Well, you're not; I'm giving it! That's different! I'm giving it because I'm grateful, and you've done me a big favor, one that no money can pay for. You've given me one little clue to something valuable and cherished that I've lost. And now, listen. I've just found out that you've got a lame brother, and your father has trouble with his eyes, and your mother needs an operation. In that case I want to help. Yes, it's my right! You don't suppose we were put into this world to be pigs with what God gave us, do you? I want to see your mother on her feet again, and if there's anything that can be done for your father and brother, I want to help do it. Sometimes operations will do wonders with eyes, you know. Another doctor might put your father where he could go to work again."

"Oh, Miss Catherwood! You're too good!" began Lutie, tears of gratitude rolling down her cheeks and her lip trembling into a big smile like a rainbow upside down. "I don't know as my mother would think it was right to take help from anyone, but it's wonderful of you to suggest it."

"She'd think it right to take it from God, wouldn't she?" snapped the old lady crisply. "Well, this is just God's money, and He told me to give you what you needed. There's no further use in discussing it. I'm coming to see your mother in a very few days."

"Well, maybe"—Lutie hesitated, her eyes shining with the great possibility—"if you'd let us work afterward and pay it off when we can."

"Pay it back to somebody else, then, not me," chuckled Aunt Pat in full form now. "I don't want you to have that on your mind. If you ever get able, just help somebody else out of trouble. I tell you God told me to give you what you need, without any strings to it! And, oh yes, Lutie, if you should find any more of this, just bring it to me at once no matter how busy I may be. It was a necklace, and it had green stones in it. Big ones and little ones."

Lutie's eyes grew wide.

"I wonder if that green bead I picked up was one!" she exclaimed. "It was just a tiny little bit, looked like glass.

161

At first I thought it was a bead, but then I thought it was glass, and I swept it up with the dust. It hadn't any hole like a bead in it."

"Where did you find it, Lutie? What did you do with it?"

"Why, I found it in the big crack between the floorboards over under the bureau. I had to pry it out with a hairpin. I gathered it up with the dust when I thought it wasn't anything but glass and put it in the waste for Thomas to burn. Wait, I'll run down and see if I can find it. Thomas went down to the grocery for Cook. I don't think he's burned the trash yet!"

Chapter 11

Lutie sped on swift feet and was presently back again, her eyes shining, a tiny green particle held in the palm of her hand.

Miss Catherwood examined it carefully and Sherrill drew close.

"It is, *it is!*" cried Sherrill. "It's one of the wee little stones by the clasp, Aunt Pat!"

"Yes," said Aunt Pat grimly. "Whoever got away with the rest of the stones missed this one anyway."

Then the old lady turned to Lutie.

"Well, you've done me another favor, Lutie. Here's a bit of money I happen to have in hand. Take it and run home now and get something extra nice for supper just for my thanks offering. Tell your mother I'll be over soon."

When Lutie had finished her happy and incoherent thanks and gone, Sherrill came and put her arms around the old lady's neck.

"You are wonderful, Aunt Pat!" she said and kissed her tenderly.

"Nonsense!" said the old lady with an embarrassed grin. "Nothing wonderful about it! What's money for if it isn't to help along your fellow men and women? And besides, you don't know but I may have my own selfish reasons for doing it."

"A lot of people don't feel that way about it, Aunt Pat!"

"Well, that's their opinion!" she answered. "All I've got to say is they miss a lot, then."

"But Aunt Pat, aren't you going to do anything more about this now? Aren't you going to call the police and report the loss, or—ask anybody, or anything? Aren't you even going to tell the servants?"

"I've already told the servants that someone who was here last night lost a valuable necklace, and offered a good-sized reward for finding it, but only Gemmie knows it was your necklace. Gemmie would miss it, of course, when she came to put your things away. She was always very fond of those jewels and was pleased that I was giving them to you. She would have to know. But Gemmie won't say anything."

"But dear Aunt Pat! I do want everything possible done to find it even if it makes a lot of unpleasantness for me. I'd rather have it found. To think that you kept it all these years and then I should lose it the very first time I wore it! Oh, Aunt Pat, I must get it back to you!"

"Back to *me*!" snorted the old lady, quite incensed. "It's not mine anymore. It's yours, child, and I mean to have it back to you, if possible of course, but if not there's nothing to break your heart about. Stop those hysterics and smile. You are just as well off as you were last week. Better, I think, for you are rid of that selfish pig of a lover of yours!"

Sherrill suddenly giggled and then buried her face on her aunt's shoulder.

"Aunt Pat," she said mournfully, "why do you suppose this had to happen to me? Why did I have to be punished like this?"

"I wouldn't call it punishment, child," said the old lady, patting Sherrill's shoulder. "I'd say it was a blessing the Lord sent to save you from a miserable life with a man who would have broken your heart."

"But if that is so," wailed Sherrill, "why didn't He stop me before it went so far? Before it would hurt so much?"

The old lady was still a minute and then said, "Perhaps He did, and you wouldn't listen. Perhaps you had some warnings that you wouldn't heed. I don't know. You'll have to look into your own life for that."

Sherrill looked at her aunt thoughtfully, remembering little happenings that had made her uneasy. The time Carter had gone away so hurriedly back to his former home without explanation. The letter addressed to him in a girl's handwriting that had fallen from his pocket one day, which seemed to embarrass him but which he put back without a word. The telegram he sent her to say he was called to New York when afterward she discovered he had been west again, and when she innocently asked about it he gave but a lame excuse. The conversation she had overheard about him on the trolley calling in question his business principles. The strange way he had acted about not wanting to purchase her necklace at a certain store where she had admired a string of pearls, but had insisted on choosing one from another place. Oh, little things in themselves, but they had made her vaguely uneasy when they happened. Had they been warnings? Perhaps she should have paid more attention to them. But she had been so reluctant to believe anything against him, so determined to shut her eyes to any fault of his!

There was that day, too, when she had come to the office unannounced and found Arla sitting very close to Carter, her hand in his, her head on the desk, crying. They had jumped apart, and Arla had gone quickly out of the room with her handkerchief to her eyes. Carter had been angry at her for coming in without knocking, and had explained that Arla's mother had just died and he had been comforting her; there was nothing else to it. That incident had troubled her greatly, and they had had more than one discussion about it, until her own love and trust had conquered and she had put it away from her mind. What a fool she had been!

She had argued afterward that of course he was not perfect and that when they were married she would help him to overcome his faults. He seemed so devoted! Then there would surge over her that feeling of his greatness, his ability and good looks, his many attractions, and she would fall once more under the spell of wonder that one so talented as he should love her.

Sharply, too, there came to memory the night before when she had stood looking into her own mirrored eyes, wondering and shrinking back. Was that shrinking the result of those other fears and warnings? Oh, what a fool she had been! Yes, there had been plenty of warning. She was glad of course that she was mercifully delivered from being married to him, but oh, the desolate dreariness of her present situation! A drab life of loneliness to be looking forward to. To have thought herself beloved, and then to find her belief was built on a rotten foundation!

They had come out now, crossed the servants' hall and the back sitting room where Carter had dressed for his wedding, and paused at the head of the stairs for a moment. Sherrill slipped her arm lovingly about the old lady's shoulders, and Aunt Pat patted her hand cheerfully. Then as they stood there they heard the doorbell ring, and some packages were handed in, two great boxes.

"More presents!" gasped Sherrill, aghast. "Oh, if there was only something we could do to stop them!"

"Well," said the old lady with a grin, "we might send

out announcements that you were not married and 'Please omit presents' at the bottom of the card."

Once again Sherrill's tragedy was turned into ridicule, and she gathered up her courage and laughed.

"You're simply wonderful, Aunt Patricia! You brace me up every time I go to pieces. That's just what—!" Sherrill stopped suddenly, and her cheeks got red.

"That's just what what?" asked the old lady, eyeing her interestedly.

"Oh, nothing! You'll laugh at me, of course. But I was only going to say that's just what that stranger did last night. He seemed to know exactly how I was feeling and met me at every point with a pleasant saneness that kept me going. I shall always be grateful to him."

"Hmm!" said Aunt Patricia approvingly. "Well, I thought he had a lot of sense myself."

Then Gemmie came forward with more boxes.

"We're not going to open them tonight, Gemmie, no matter what it is," said Miss Catherwood decidedly. "We're just too tired to stand the sight of another lamp or pitcher or trumpet, whichever it is. We'll let it go till morning."

"But it's flowers, ma'am," protested Gemmie. "It says 'Perishable' on them, Miss Catherwood!"

"Flowers?" said the old lady sharply, giving a quick glance at Sherrill as if she would like to protect her. "Who would be sending flowers now? It must be a mistake!"

"It's no mistake, ma'am; there's one for each of you.

This small one is yours, and the big one is Miss Sherrill's."

She held the two boxes up to view.

Sherrill took her box wonderingly. It seemed as if this must be a ghost out of her dead happy past. For who would be sending her flowers today?

She untied the cord with trembling fingers, threw back the satiny folds of paper, and disclosed a great mass of the most gorgeous pansies she had ever seen. Pansies of every hue and mixture that a pansy could take on, from velvety black with a yellow eye down through the blues and yellows and purples and browns to clear unsullied white. There were masses of white ones arranged in rows down at the foot of the box, with a few sprays of exquisite blue forget-me-nots here and there, and the whole resting on a bed of delicate maiden hair fern.

The fragrance that came up from the flowers was like the woods in spring, a warm, fresh, mossy smell. Had pansies an odor like that? She had always thought of them as sturdy things, merry and cheery, that came up under the snow and popped out brightly all summer. But these great creatures in their velvet robes belonged to pansy royalty surely, and brought a breath of wildness and sweetness that rested her tired eyes and heart. She bent her face to touch their loveliness and drew a deep breath of their perfume.

The card was half hidden under a great brilliant yellow fellow touched with orange with a white plush eye. She pulled it out and read the writing with a catch in her breath and a sudden quick throb of joy in her heart. Why should she care so much? But it was so good to have flowers and a friend when she had thought all such things were over for her.

"I hope you are getting rested," was written on the card just above his engraved name, Graham Copeland.

A sudden chuckle brought Sherrill back to the world again, the warm glow from her heart still showing in her cheeks, and a light of pleasure in her weary eyes.

"The old fox!" chuckled Aunt Pat.

"What is the matter?" asked Sherrill in quick alarm.

"Why, he's sent me sweetheart roses! What do you know about that? Sweetheart roses for an old woman like me!" and she chuckled again.

"Oh, Aunt Pat! How lovely!" said Sherrill, coming near and sniffing the bouquet. "And there are forget-me-nots in yours, too! Isn't it a darling bouquet?"

"Yes, and the fun of it is," said Aunt Pat with a twinkle of sweet reminiscence in her eyes, "that I had a bouquet almost exactly like this when I went to my first party years ago with my best young man. Yes, identical, even to the lace paper frill around it, and the silver ribbon streamers!"

Aunt Pat held it close and took deep breaths with half-closed eyes and a sweet faraway look on her face.

In due time Patricia Catherwood came out of her brief trance and admired the box of pansies.

"Aunt Pat," said Sherrill suddenly, her great box of

sweetness still in her arms as she looked down at them a little fearfully, very wistfully, "he wouldn't have sent these if he had—"

"No, of course not!" snapped the old lady. "I declare I'm ashamed of you, Sherrill Cameron. Can't you ever trust anybody anymore just because one slim pretty man disappointed you? Just get on the job and learn how to judge real men, and you won't have any more of that nonsense. Take those flowers to your room and study them, and see what you think about the man that sent them."

"Oh, I trust him perfectly, Aunt Pat. I'm quite sure he is all right. I *know* he is! But I was afraid you would think—!"

"Now, look here, if you are going to keep charging me with all the vagaries that come into your head, 'you and I will be two people!' as an old nurse of my mother's used to say. For pity's sake, forget those emeralds and go and put your flowers in water. Unless, perhaps, you'd rather Gemmie did it for you!" she added with an acrid chuckle.

"Oh no!" said Sherrill, quickly hugging her box in her arms, her cheeks flaming crimson. "Look, Auntie Pat. Aren't they dear? And yours are dear, too. Almost as dear as yourself."

There was a tremble in her voice as she stooped and kissed the old lady on the sweet silver waves of hair just above her brow, and then she hurried away laughing, a dewy look about her eyes.

It was so nice not to feel utterly forgotten and out of things, she told herself as she went to her room with her flowers. It was just like him and his thoughtfulness to do this tonight! This first night after that awful wedding that was not hers! Somehow as she took the pansies out one by one and breathed their sweetness, laid them against her cheek with their cool velvety touch, the weariness went out of her. It seemed to her as if by sending these blossoms he had made her understand that he knew this was a hard night and he was still standing by, although he could not be here, helping her through. She thought the joy that bubbled up in her heart was wholly gratitude.

"Pansies for thoughts!" she said to herself and smiled with heightened color. "Is that why he sent them? Forget-me-nots! Oh—!"

She rang for a great crystal bowl and arranged the flowers one at a time, resting on their bed of ferns, and she was not tired any longer. She had lost that sense of being something that was flung aside, unwanted.

She got herself quickly into a little blue frilly frock for dinner and fastened a few pansies at her breast, pale blue and white and black among the fluffy frills. She came down to find the old lady in gray chiffon with a sweetheart rose at her throat, and the bouquet otherwise intact in a crystal vase before her.

It was after all a happy little meal. The two had lost their sense of burden. They were just having a happy time together, getting nearer to each other than they ever had been before, and the hazy forms of a youth of the past dressed in the fashion of another day, and a youth of the present very much up to date standing in the shadows behind their chairs.

"I've been thinking of that question you asked me, why all this had to come to you," said the old lady. "I wonder—! You know, it might have been that God has something very much better He was saving for you, and this was the only way He could make you wait for it!"

"I shall never marry anybody now, Aunt Pat, if that's what you mean!" said Sherrill primly, though there was a smile on her lips.

"Hmm!" said Aunt Pat, smiling also.

"I could really never again trust a man enough to marry him!" reiterated Sherrill firmly, nestling her chin against the blue velvet cheek of the top pansy.

Aunt Pat replied in much the same tone that modern youth impudently use for saying "Oh yeah?"—still with a smile and a rising inflection—"Ye–es?"

"This man is just a friend. A stranger sent to help in time of need," explained Sherrill to the tone in Aunt Pat's voice.

"Hmmm!" said Aunt Pat. "It may be so!"

Chapter 12

Arla's triumph was brief. She found Carter anything but a lover the next morning. He was surly and crabbed to her at breakfast, found fault with her attire and her makeup, told her her lips were too red for good taste, even went so far as to say that Miss Cameron never stained her fingernails. Arla felt as if she had been stabbed. She could scarcely finish her breakfast.

But because she had determined to make this marriage a success, she bore his criticism, even ignoring his reference to his other bride though the tears were not far away, and a smoldering fire burned in her eyes. Was this other girl to be held up to her as a paragon the rest of her days? Oh, he was cruel!

She studied his sullen face, his selfish lips, and saw these traits in him for the first time!

And she, by marrying him in that underhanded way, had forfeited a right to protest against such words. She could not flare out at him and tell him he had loved her enough to marry her and therefore he need not compare her with another. He had not married her by his own initiative; she had married him, and taken him as it were unaware, where he could not help himself.

The cold flamed into her face and then receded, leaving it deathly white and making the redness of her lips but the more startling!

Then when they went on deck, almost the first person he sighted was a man from whom he had borrowed largely but a few days before on the strength of his marriage into the Catherwood fortune.

Without explanation he dashed around a group of deck chairs, upsetting one in his haste, colliding with a man, and swinging around to the other side of the ship without any seeming reason at all.

Arla followed him breathlessly, trying not to appear to be running a race. She was nonplussed. What was the matter with Carter? She had never seen him act in such a crazy way.

When she at last came to a stop, panting at the secluded hiding place that he had selected, she watched him in dismay. His face was actually lowering.

"What in the world is the matter with you, Carter?" she asked, almost tenderly. She began to think perhaps all that had happened yesterday had unsettled his mind.

"Everything in the world is the matter with me!" he said in a harsh tone. "Everything terrible that could happen to a man in any position!"

Arla studied him, still with that troubled look in her eyes, knowing that he would presently explain himself. She had not been his secretary for some months without knowing his habits.

"That was Mr. Sheldon that we passed as we came up the companionway. Didn't you recognize him?" He turned and glared at her as if she were responsible for Mr. Sheldon being on board.

"Sheldon? What Sheldon?" asked Arla in a pleasant tone. "I don't know any Mr. Sheldon, do I?"

"No!" said Carter. "You don't *know* him, socially of course, but it's not many hours since you witnessed his signature on some papers in the office!"

He paused impressively.

Arla looked puzzled and waited again, but Carter was still trying to impress her. At such time he could take on a fairly ponderous look, though he was not a large man, by merely swelling up proudly and looking down at her.

"Well, what of it?" asked Arla half impatiently after she had waited a reasonable time for explanation.

"What of it? And *you* can say what of it! You who wrote out those papers for him to sign, you who heard the whole conversation and know that it was on the strength of my expectation of being able to raise a large sum in the near future that he loaned me the money I needed to finance—" He stopped abruptly, conscious that this very wedding trip was a part of the business he had to finance, the ring that sparkled on her finger, the pearls she had worn to the altar. He couldn't quite tell her that! Even in his present state of mind, he couldn't be as raw as that.

"Well—?" she said again almost haughtily, watching him narrowly. His whole attitude toward her, his very tone had become offensive.

"*Well?* No, there is nothing well about it!" he snapped. "That man is a friend of the Catherwoods. He knows the Catherwood lawyer intimately. And he knows Sher— he knows Miss Cameron by sight. I have been with her when we met him. Don't you realize—? You can't be so blind as not to know that it would be nothing short of disastrous for him to know what has happened! Why, it's even conceivable that he might stop payment on that check now. He could radio a message to his bank, you know. And then I'd be in a worse hole than I'm in already. You know as well as I do."

"Well, but he couldn't possibly know what had happened from merely meeting us together on deck!" said Arla haughtily.

"Couldn't he? You don't think he's sharp enough? Well, let me tell you he's keen. How long do you think it would take him to cancel his agreement if he discovers that instead of marrying an heiress I am tied to a penniless secretary?"

The words cut to the quick! Arla caught her breath

and set her lovely teeth sharply in her red underlip, trembling with humiliation and anger.

He cast a furtive glance at her and grew only the more hateful, realizing perhaps to what depths he had descended.

"Well, you needn't cry-baby about that!" he said sharply. "You might as well understand what kind of a hole you've put me in!"

"*I've* put you in—!" said Arla fiercely. "*I!*"

"Yes, you!" said the man, now beyond all bounds of self-control. "I didn't do it, did I? It was *you* who came to the Catherwood house fifteen minutes before the hour set for the wedding and got hysterics all over the place and drove me crazy so that I didn't know what I was doing! It was *you* that staged a scene with Sherrill and got yourself married to me, wasn't it? I didn't know anything about it, did I? What could *I* do?"

There was an ominous silence while Arla struggled to control her voice. Presently she spoke in a tone of utter sadness as if she were removed from him by eons of time.

"Then all you told me last night was untrue!" she said. "Then you lied to me about your great love that you said you had for me!"

Suddenly the man grew red and shamed looking.

"I didn't say it was a lie!" he said. "This has nothing to do with that!"

"No, but I did!" said Arla. "And it has everything to do with that! I went through agony and humiliation to save you from marrying a girl you did not love because I believed you still loved me, and had only fallen for her because you needed her money. I was trying to save you from yourself, to save our love that in the past has been so sweet and true. And this is what I get! You tell me I have put you in a hole! Well, I'm in the same hole! What do you think it is for me to be married to a man that talks that way? Do you think I'm enjoying a wedding trip like this?"

"Well, it was none of my doings!" said the man, shrugging his shoulders angrily. "I told you what kind of a fix I was in. I explained the whole matter to you, didn't I?"

"Not until you had failed to get me to go out west on a vacation where I couldn't find out about it until afterward! Not until your wedding invitations were about to come out," said Arla steadily.

"Well, I *tried* to tell you before. I tried to let you know by my actions—!"

"Yes, you tried to be disagreeable to me!" said Arla. "I suppose I ought to have understood you were trying to cast me off like a worn-out garment. But I didn't! I thought you were worried about your business. I forgave everything because—I—loved you!"

The man gave an angry exclamation.

"There you are bawling again! Oh, women! They do nothing but make trouble, and then they weep about it. A man is a fool to have anything to do with women!"

Arla lifted angry eyes.

"You would have talked that way to your paragon of a Sherrill Cameron, I suppose?" she said, dashing away her tears.

He gave her a furious look.

"Can anything be more tantalizing than a jealous woman?" he sneered. "Well, I think we've gone far enough. I didn't come up here to listen to the kind of talk you've been giving me. I wanted to make you understand that we're in a very critical situation and we've got to do something about it! We've simply got to avoid meeting people, at least together."

"Just what do you mean by that?"

"Just what I said! We can't afford to have Sheldon get onto this. And he isn't the only one on board that knows us. I met Bixby this morning in the smoking room. He asked after Sh—he asked after the bride, of course, and made some silly joke about having admired her first, and I had to tell him you were seasick, that you were a bad sailor and might not be able to appear at meals during the voyage. He knows Sheldon, you know, is a sort of a henchman of his, and it won't do to have him talking. I think that's our best bet anyhow to save complications; just you stay close in your cabin, except late at night we can slip out and take a walk on deck where the rest don't usually come."

A wave of indignation passed over Arla's beautiful face.

"So that is the way you intend to treat me on my wedding trip!" she said bitterly. "Keep me shut up in my room! Your bride! Well, I'll know how much to believe the next time you tell me you love me! How about you staying in and letting me do the talking?"

"But don't you see that wouldn't do? They all know Sh—that is, they all knew Miss Cameron."

"I see that you are perfectly crazy about money. You love money better than honor or decency or me."

"Now you're being unreasonable!" said the man irritably. "I've told you our fortune hangs upon what happens in the next few days. I can't help it, can I, that my investments failed? Everybody else is having the same trouble. If the wedding had gone through as planned, there wouldn't have been any trouble about money. I could have gotten around the old lady and gotten a loan of a hundred thousand or two to tide me over. But now—"

"But now, since she found you out and the fortune isn't available, you mean to take it out on me—who really is the wronged one from the beginning. Well, I won't stand for it, that's all! I'm not going to stay shut in and have you roaming around perhaps with some handsome brunette who has another fortune lying around!"

Her eyes were blazing wrathfully. Her tone was low but very angry. He watched her furtively. It wouldn't do to let her get started on that line. She could mess things up a lot more if she chose to.

"Look here, Arla!" He swung around upon her. "Be sensible! Haven't I told you that my business will go under completely and leave me utterly bankrupt if I can't tide over the next six months and pay my indebtedness? And now, just when I think I'm going to be able to swing it, you get childish and balk at helping me."

"I'm not childish, and I don't balk at helping you when it's right and reasonable. But I won't be lied about, and I don't intend to allow anybody to mix me up with the girl you didn't marry, not to save twenty businesses. Besides, I don't see what a mere fifty thousand matters. Even if Mr. Sheldon does refuse to pay the twenty-five thousand now, and the other twenty-five thousand in two or three months, you still have a lot more thousands that you can't do anything about. You can't save your business any way you try, and it's better to realize that and give it up. Just let them take over what you have, and don't try to launch out. Begin again in a small way and I'll help you!"

"Ah, but there's where you are mistaken, Arla! I've found a way. I'm sure I've found a way to swing the rest of that. Just last night a way came. I can't tell you about it yet, but it's sure! And we shall be on easy street yet, my girl! Just have a little patience. A day or two after we've landed on the other side, I shall have everything all fixed up."

His eyes narrowed and he looked at her cunningly.

She gave him a quick furtive glance.

"And suppose you didn't? Suppose you are mistaken?" Her breath came sharply. "Don't you know you are throwing away something sweeter and finer than any money or any business that you could ever have?"

Perhaps because her words went deeper than she understood, they angered him the more.

"Get out of my way!" he roared, forgetting he was on an ocean liner. "If you're my wife, take my orders, then! Don't you dare to stir out of the cabin again in daylight unless I say you may. Go! I don't want to see you anymore; you make me tired! Talk about wedding trips? *I'm* having a glorious one!"

"Hush!" said Arla imperatively in a low controlled voice. "There's your Mr. Sheldon just below you coming up the stairs!"

Carter turned and saw the puffy red face of the financier advancing pompously up to where he stood, but when he turned back to give Arla a warning scowl, she was not there. There seemed no way that she could have gone, but she was gone. Carter was left embarrassed and awkward to meet the dignified scrutiny of the man he wished to placate. He wished frantically that he knew how much of his conversation had been overheard.

Chapter 13

By a way that her need had come to her in the sudden crisis, Arla had fled to her stateroom. Having locked her door, she stood for an instant with clenched fists down at her sides, her teeth set in her trembling underlip, fighting back the tears that filled her eyes, fighting down the anger, the remorse, the dismay that threatened to overwhelm her. Then she began to walk up and down the small room like a young lion in a cage.

Suddenly her mood changed. She grew calmer. She took a book and a warm coat, went out on the deck, found an out-of-the-way nook where Carter would have to hunt to find her, and sat down, pretending to read, but really thinking out the way before her step by step. If she had to go back twenty-four hours, would she have been willing to marry Carter? She refused to answer that question. It was too late. She must go forward!

She stayed in her hiding place until long past the lunch hour, subsisting on the cup of broth that was brought around on deck in the midmorning. Still Carter had not found her, or perhaps had not chosen to seek her. Then soon after lunchtime a young man came breezily by her chair, paused, hesitated, and then cried out, "Great Caesar's ghost! If this isn't Arla Prentiss! Say now, what do you know about that? I'm in luck, aren't I?"

Arla looked up, dismay in her soul, for there before her stood the soda clerk from her hometown drugstore, crude and breezy and familiar as ever. He had known her all her life, had bestowed various boxes of candy upon her, had attempted to pay her attention sometimes, though she had always been able to laugh him off. Still, he was genuine, and somehow the real hearty admiration in his eyes now warmed her heart, even while she was wondering what Cater would say when he found that Hurley Kirkwood was on board.

But there was no dismay in Hurley Kirkwood's heart. He was joyously glad to see her. He had been somewhat like a stray cat till he sighted her, having no acquaintances on board, and being adrift in the world for the first time in his life.

"Say now, this is great!" said Hurley, quickly drawing up a camp stool and settling down to enjoy himself. "Say now, Arla, are you alone? Taking a trip to Europe alone? Say now, if I can be of any service!"

Arla gave a little shiver.

"No, I'm not alone," she smiled. "My husband is around here somewhere! I'm on my wedding trip, Hurley!"

"Boom! Just like that!" said Hurley, slapping his hands together noisily. "Hopes busted at the first word! Well, I congratulate you, Arla. But say now, when did it happen? You kept it mighty still, didn't you? Didn't any of the home folks come to the wedding? Your aunt Tilly wouldn't have missed it, I'm sure, if she'd known."

Arla suddenly realized that there was another part of her world yet to be dealt with.

"Yes, it was rather sudden," said Arla. "You see, Carter found he had to go abroad, and of course it made a splendid wedding trip. I had practically no warning whatever. We just got married and rushed off to catch the boat."

"Well, you certainly put one over on the hometown," said Hurley. "Sorry I didn't know about it. You might have called. There's about a dozen I know would have come on to see you off. And me, why, I could have made it easy. I been in New York three days just bumming!"

Arla tried not to shudder again at the thought. It seemed to her that nothing could have been more perfectly the last straw at that terrible wedding of hers than to have had Hurley Kirkwood appear on the scene. She registered a distinct thanksgiving that she had been saved so much at least.

And yet, as he talked on, giving her homely items

of domestic interest about her aunt Tilly's rheumatism, old Mrs. Pike's having lost all her money when the bank closed and going to the poorhouse, Lila Ginn's latest escapade of running away with a drummer, and the party the high school kids had at a roadhouse that made all the school board sit up and take notice, somehow Arla felt the tension in her taut nerves relax. After all, it was comforting just to hear of home folks and hometown and things that happened in the years before Carter had loved and tried to marry another woman. It was good to forget if only for a few minutes the problems and perplexities of her own present situation.

Hurley Kirkwood made a good soda clerk. He knew how to kid everybody in town with a special brand of kidding for each individual. There was something vivid and interesting about Hurley in spite of his crudeness, and presently Arla forgot herself so far as to be laughing heartily at some of the stories Hurley told.

Hurley had saved up his money, and he was just explaining to Arla how he had always wanted this trip to Europe and mapping out the course of travel he had planned for himself, when suddenly a stern and forbidding Carter arrived on the scene. He fairly glared at the poor soda clerk, whom he had never liked, mainly because he presumed to be friendly with Arla. Carter had never approved of Arla's being friendly with Hurley. Just because she had gone to school with him did not give a mere soda clerk the right to take the girl of a man like himself to *anything*! Not even a ball game in the early evening played in his own neighborhood! Not even if he started out alone and just *met* Arla and sauntered with her to the grandstand and bought her peanuts, which is what had happened one summer evening when Carter's interest in Arla was in its initial stages.

Therefore Carter glared at Hurley and gave him a passing: "Oh, Hurl, you here! Not serving in your official capacity as drink slinger on board, are you?"

There was utter contempt in Carter's tone. All the venom and fury that he had been holding in his heart for Arla during the morning because she had not obeyed him, and had been evading him, he vented in that one contemptuous sentence.

And Hurley, happy, crude, a bit obtuse, not easily hurt, could not but recognize the unfriendliness and grew red and embarrassed. He attempted to rise to the occasion by slapping the dignified Carter on the shoulder and offering congratulations in his native style.

"My sympathy, Cart!" he said with a guffaw. "I hear you been getting tied! Only wish I'd been there to be best man. I'd have given you a great send-off! But say now, isn't it great we both got on the same little old boat together! My word! I got something to write home to the little old hometown now! Mebbe that won't make 'em all sit up and take notice! Cart and Arla got tied at last! We been looking for news and an invite this long while, and then you went and done it on the sly! But say now, I certainly do wish you a lotta happiness!"

Carter's face had grown more and more stern during this tirade, and now his tone was like a slap in the face as he made another attempt to put this fool from home in his place.

"I am sure Mrs. McArthur and I are greatly obliged to you for your interest," he said disagreeably, and then turned to Arla sternly.

"My dear, I shall have to ask you to come down to the stateroom at once. There is a matter I must discuss with you."

But Arla was resenting her husband's attitude. A sudden loyalty for the hometown and the people and things that used to be dear to her surged over her. Carter had no call to insult this well-meaning but ignorant youth who stood there red and hurt and wondering over the unnecessary coolness in Carter's tone. She knew that Carter was venting upon him all the injury and indignation he felt for her, and she turned lightly away from the command and answered, "All right, Carter, I'll be down presently. I want to finish my talk with Hurley first. He's been telling me all about the people at home."

Carter could scarcely believe his senses. Arla was standing out against him. He stared at her in consternation a moment with an icy look, then turned on his heel and marched away.

She did not look after him as he went. She did not dare to think what effect her attitude would have upon him. It was the first time in her acquaintance with him—which had dated from her very young childhood—that she had ever defied him. She had pled with him, she had wept, she had been sweet and submissive, but she had never openly defied him before, and she was trembling over it. She found herself almost panic stricken. Perhaps he would never speak to her again. Perhaps he would divorce her. Yet it was what she had resolved in those morning hours of meditation that she would do, defy him, show him that he could not order her about. Would she be able to carry it out?

For another half hour she asked questions about the people at home, questions in which she had not the slightest interest, but which she knew would bring forth voluble answers, long enough to protect her from having to say much back. Hurley was delighted. In all his acquaintance with her taken altogether, he had never had this much speech of her. He admired her greatly and was tremendously flattered that she had stayed to talk with him. He was so flattered that he forgot Carter's insulting tone.

When Arla had finally ceased to tremble and felt that she had sufficient control of herself to carry out the program she had planned for herself, she arose sweetly.

"Well, now, I really must go to that longsuffering husband of mine," she said, smiling. "It's been so nice to meet you again, to hear all the news from home, and to know you're going to have such a lovely trip." And then she was gone, and Hurley knew that he was dropped as definitely as she had always dropped him in the old days when he brought her candy and she accepted it graciously, but always had a reason why she couldn't go to the movies with him.

Hurley went and stood by himself, staring off at the sea and wondering why it was. Here he had been having as nice a time with her as anyone would need to ask to have, and all of a sudden he was out of it, just out! That was all! He knew as well as if she had told him that he wouldn't likely come in contact with either of them the rest of the voyage. Oh, maybe meet and bow or something like that, but nothing more. And here he had been fool enough to fancy that now that he had money enough to take a trip abroad, they would be friendly and he would have somebody to talk to now and then, just be friendly with anytime he liked! Well, maybe it was just his imagination. He decided he'd forget it. Probably they'd be all right the next time he met them. Maybe he'd try to get at their table, and then they'd have to be friendly.

When Arla reached the stateroom, Carter was not there. She was likely being punished. So she put on one of Sherrill's prettiest negligees and lay down to rest. That is, her body was resting, but her mind was madly working. She was looking life in the face, realizing all sorts of possibilities. Well, that other girl had been right. It was no enviable path she had chosen for herself, but having chosen it, being married, the thing she had so much desired, she must make it a success if that were a possible thing to do. She had not attained her wish unless she was able to hold him. And she saw keenly enough that this was the crucial time. What she did now would count through the years. Oh, for wisdom to know what was the best thing to do!

Carter did not return to the stateroom until it was nearly time for dinner. He found Arla attired in black satin and looking fairly regal, putting the last touches to her facial expression. She turned an indifferent glance at him, and in spite of his smoldering anger, he was startled at her beauty. Sherrill had never been more beautiful! Arla certainly was a stunning-looking woman. There was some satisfaction in that for the future. If he ever pulled through this hard time, he could be proud of her. There was an air about her that he had never seen before, a certain smartness that he had always admired in Sherrill. He did not realize that Arla was wearing one of Sherrill's outfits which was the work of an artist and had cost a fabulous sum. He simply saw that Arla was looking more wonderful than he had ever seen her look before. For a moment he was almost ready to forgive her and take her into his arms. Then she turned and gave him a haughty indifferent glance and his anger boiled again.

"What are you all rigged up like that for?" he snarled,

even while his eyes gloated over the lovely curves of her throat and white shoulders. "You're not planning to do what I forbade you to do—?"

"Forbade?" said Arla with slightly uplifted eyebrows. "Really! I shouldn't recognize any such word as that between us! That isn't what marriage means. Not in this age and generation! If you mean am I going down to dinner, I certainly am. If you don't want to go with me, that's entirely up to you. I am sure Hurley Kirkwood will be delighted to take me in to dinner. I can tell people you are seasick, you know. But as this is the first ocean voyage I've ever had, and maybe the last one I'll ever get, I intend to enjoy every minute of it in spite of your disagreeableness."

"You don't care what happens to me and my business, then? I thought you professed to love me!" he said after a long silence during which he went and stared out the porthole.

"Why, I supposed I did, too," said Arla lightly, "but as for caring what happens to you and your business at such a price as you demand, I'm not so sure that I do."

He was still a much longer time now, staring out at the endless waves of the ocean.

"Then do I understand that you refuse to comply with my request and stay out of sight during the voyage?"

"Yes, I do!" said Arla coolly, taking up her hand and mirror and examining her profile carefully and the wave of her lovely gold hair.

"But why, Arla? You have always wanted me to get on. You know I want it for you as much as for myself—!"

"Oh!" interrupted Arla in a surprised voice. "No, I didn't know that!" Her tone was sweet and innocent. "Did you want it for me as much as for yourself when you were going to marry Sherrill Cameron?"

He gave a quick angry exclamation.

"Can't you leave her out of the question now we're definitely done with her?" he asked desperately.

"I'm sorry," said Arla. "I'd like to, but the trouble is she somehow won't be left out. You see, she was there, and I'm not so sure she's definitely out of it either."

"Well, then, if you must bring her in, yes, I did do it for your sake as much as my own. I thought an alliance with her would bring the needed funds and position, and later, well—there are such things as divorces, you know!"

She turned a steely eye to him.

"Carter, if you had been brought up in the social world of today, there might be some excuse for your daring to say a thing like that to me, but both you and I had decent mothers who didn't believe in such things, and when you say that, you are insulting both Miss Cameron and myself. You said something of that sort last night, I remember, just before you flung me off in the corner and went out to marry your other bride. I don't know how I ever forgave it in you enough to be willing to marry you except that I thought you were beside yourself and didn't realize what you were saying. It was preposterous, you know! And if I didn't think you were still rather beside yourself, I certainly wouldn't stay here with you now and listen to such talk."

"Very well, now, if you are so interested in me and my business," he said at last, "what would you suggest that we do? You know the facts, that I need a large sum of money to tide me over, and if I can get it I can keep my business floating till this depression is past. If I don't, I either have to give up and lose everything or else probably go to jail!"

"I would *not* go to jail!" said Arla. He gave her a sudden quick startled look. But Arla went steadily on talking, not looking at him. "I would take the next boat back as soon as I landed and arrange to give over my business interests in such a way that while it might be a total loss of all that has been gained through the last three years, your name would be cleared, and you could go honorably into some more modest business and have a chance of making good. You will remember I happen to have been present in the office when an offer was made to you which would have made that possible!"

"Oh!" exclaimed the man angrily. "I'm not an utter fool!"

"Are you sure?" asked the woman. "Sometimes I wonder!"

After a long silence the man spoke again in a voice of smoldering wrath: "Well, come on. I suppose you've got to have it your way and go down to dinner even if it wrecks everything! It was bad enough before, but now that the situation is further complicated by the appearance of that country bumpkin from home, I don't see how we can possibly get by without trouble. How in the world are you going to explain him to people if he chooses to barge in on us?"

"I don't expect to explain him or anybody else we may happen to meet. This is not a private boat, and anybody has a right on board who pays his fare. Please remember that I had nothing whatever to do with his being here. As far as I am concerned, I see no reason why we shouldn't go about our business as anybody else does. If your business were on an honest basis, we could go about freely and enjoy ourselves without watching out for what people think."

"Women know nothing about business!" glowered Carter. "Well, come on, let's get this over."

So Arla in Sherrill's costly lace gown from an exclusive Paris house walked regally beside her husband and never showed by the flicker of an eyelash that she had recognized across the saloon another two people from home, a young man and his wife who had been in the same class in high school with Carter and Arla. It would be time enough for Carter to know they were on board when he had to meet them. They would be another element in this problem she was trying to solve.

Chapter 14

There was a sense of peace in Sherrill's room the next morning. The fragrance of the pansies pervaded the place. The delicate perfume spoke to her at once even before she opened her eyes. It brought the memory of the pleasant stranger, as if his presence were still lingering not far away to help.

Then she opened her eyes to see the pansies on the low bedside table where she had placed them. She reveled in their soft brightness and was glad they were just pansies, not any of the more conventional flowers. They seemed to emphasize the simple frank friendship that had begun on the street, just plain honest friends helping one another. Pansies might grow in anybody's garden, only these of course were sort of glorified pansies. But it was a comfort that they did not recall the bridal bouquet nor any of the flowers in the church. Just simple pansies that she might love and lay her face against.

She reached out for the card that lay beside them

on the table. Somehow that hastily penned line seemed to have a deeper meaning than just a wish that she was rested physically. It seemed to carry a desire that she might be healed in spirit from the deep hurt to her life that he could not help knowing that wedding must have been to her.

Little memories of the kindness in his eyes, merry eyes that yet held tenderness, came back to her; the turn of a sentence that made her laugh when he must have seen the tears were very near to coming; his pleasant grin. They all filled her with a warmth and comfort that were restful and almost happy.

She lay there thinking about him. How kind he had been! She was rejoicing in the presence of the pansies in their lovely fern setting when Gemmie tapped at the door and entered with a breakfast tray.

"Miss Patricia said you better eat before you get up," she announced, setting her tray down on a low table and drawing back the silk curtains.

Gemmie brought her negligee and put it about her, adjusting her pillows. Then she bustled over to the hearth and lighted a fire that was ready, though it was scarcely needed that bright spring morning. Sherrill began to perceive that Gemmie had something on her mind. She never bustled unless she was ill at ease. But Sherrill was too comfortable just at that moment to try to find out what it was, so she let Gemmie go on setting things straight on the dressing table and then setting them crooked again. At last she spoke.

"It's right awful about that necklace being gone, Miss Sherrill!"

Boom! A great burden of stone seemed suddenly to land back again in Sherrill's heart, just where it had been the day before, only a trifle heavier if possible.

"Yes," quavered Sherrill, pausing in her first comforting swallow of coffee.

"Seems like we ought to do something about it right away," went on Gemmie. "Seems like we oughtn't to let the time get away with us."

"Yes, Gemmie," said Sherrill distressedly, "but Aunt Pat wants to work it out in her own way. I think she had some idea about it, though she doesn't want to tell it yet. We are not to tell anybody about it, you know."

"Yes, I know," said Gemmie severely as if she disapproved greatly. "But Miss Sherrill, it doesn't seem reasonable, does it? That necklace didn't have legs. It couldn't run away of itself, could it?"

"Not very well, Gemmie." Sherrill lay back against her pillows with distress in her eyes.

"There was only one stranger there, wasn't there, Miss Sherrill? I was wondering if you knew him real well. Was you right sure about him?"

"Stranger?" said Sherrill coldly. "Did you mean the clerk who came in to witness the license papers signed?"

"Oh, laws! No! Not him. I've known him for years. He used to live next door to my best friend, and he wouldn't steal a pin. He's too honest, if you know what I mean. But wasn't there a stranger there, Miss Sherrill? I came across him in the back hall just after I got back from the church. I went up to leave my hat and coat, and I found him wandering around trying doors all along the hall."

"Oh, you mean my friend Mr. Copeland," said Sherrill with elaborate coolness. "No, I brought him there, Gemmie. He'd just come from the train and brought his suitcase to change here. I met him at the church. He's from out near my old home in the West, you know, Gemmie. I put him in that little end room where we afterward signed the papers. He's quite all right!"

Sherrill explained it all out slowly, her voice growing more assured as she went on, and ending with a ripple of laughter, though she felt that awful haunting doubt creeping into her mind again with the accompanying heaviness of heart.

"You know him right well, do you? You're sure he wouldn't yield to temptation, are you? You know those stones are wonderful costly, Miss Sherrill!"

"Oh, for pity's sake, Gemmie! What an awful suggestion to make about a friend and guest of ours! You'd better not say that to Aunt Pat. She certainly would not be pleased. Of course he is entirely above suspicion. Why, he is a friend, Gemmie!"

"Well! I didn't know how well you knew him," said Gemmie offendedly. "I never heard you speak of him before, and I didn't know but what he might be somebody you hadn't seen in a long time, and didn't know how he'd turned out now he's growed up."

Sherrill managed a real laugh now and answered, "No, Gemmie, nothing like that! Now, if you'll take this tray, I'll get up. I want to get at those presents again. We got a lot done yesterday, didn't we?"

"Yes, Miss Sherrill, but you've not eaten your breakfast, and Miss Patricia will be all upset."

"All right, Gemmie, I'll eat a little more if you'll run and see if the morning mail has come yet. I'm expecting a letter. Aren't my flowers lovely, Gemmie? Mr. Copeland's the one that sent them to me."

Gemmie eyed the flowers half suspiciously.

"Yes," admitted Gemmie reluctantly, "for flowers that aren't roses, they're above most."

Then Gemmie, leaving a mist of insidious doubt in her wake, swept firmly out of the room, and Sherrill had a silly feeling that she wanted to throw the whole breakfast after her and burst into tears. How outrageous of the stupid old thing to get such a notion and try to rub it in! Of course her kind stranger friend was all right! She would not let such sickening doubts creep into her mind. Aunt Pat didn't think any such thing. She didn't herself. As she remembered the fine merry countenance and wide frank eyes, she felt that it was utterly ridiculous to suspect such a man even though he was a stranger. Yet there was that heaviness planted for the day again, planted in the very pit of her stomach just like yesterday.

Then she suddenly put her face down into her pillows and cried a few hot, tempestuous, worried tears till she remembered Gemmie would soon return with the mail and she mustn't have red eyes. So she stopped the tears, and before Gemmie could come into the room again, she sprang up and buried her face in the dewy sweetness of the pansies, touching her lips to their coolness hungrily. Oh, why did evil and suspicion and sin have to come in and spoil a world that would otherwise be bright? She would not, *would not* believe or entertain the slightest suspicion against Graham Copeland. They had made a compact of trust and friendship, and she would abide by her own intuition. Yes, and by Aunt Pat's judgment also.

And so when Gemmie entered, Sherrill was bending over her flowers, touching them delicately with her fingertips, lifting a pansy's chin lightly to look better into its face, and smiling into their cheerful little faces with a whimsical fancy that some were grinning just as their donor had done.

But Gemmie wore an offended air all that day, and went about poking into corners everywhere trying to find that necklace.

"I don't see why Miss Patricia won't have the police up here!" she declared. "I shan't be happy till that necklace is found! Who was that girl anyway, that bride? Did you ever see her before? Seems to me this is the strangest doings that ever was had about this house. I don't understand it myself. We never had doings around here that was out of the ordinary before. I mus' say I don't like it myself. Did you know that girl, Miss Sherrill?"

"Oh yes, Gemmie," said Sherrill, summoning a brave tone. "She was an old friend of Mr. McArthur's. In fact, they had been sort of engaged for several years, and—then—well, they got separated. . . ."

Sherrill's voice trailed off vaguely. She knew she was treading on very thin ice. How was she to make this all quite plausible to this sharp-eyed, jealous servant who loved her because she belonged to her beloved Miss Patricia, and yet not tell all the startling facts?

"You see, Gemmie," she went on bravely, taking up the tale and thinking fast, "she came just after you left with a message for Mr. McArthur, and I happened to find out about it, so we had a little talk and fixed it up this way. It was rather quick work getting us dressed all over again, but I think we got by pretty well, don't you?" Sherrill finished with a little light laugh that sounded very natural, and Gemmie eyed her suspiciously.

"I ought to have stayed here!" she declared firmly. "I knew I oughtn't to've gone when I went. That was *your* wedding dress, not hers, and she had no business with it!"

"Oh, that!" laughed Sherrill cheerfully. "What did that matter? You see, she didn't happen to have her own things with her, so we fixed it up that way, and I thought everything came off very well. She looked sweet, didn't she?"

"I didn't take notice to her," said Gemmie sourly. "When I saw it wasn't you, I was that put out I could hardly keep my seat. I didn't think you'd be up to any tricks like that, Miss Sherrill, or I wouldn't have left you. If I'd have been here, I'd not have let her by having your wedding dress, not if she never got married. And your wedding, too. It was a shame!"

"Oh no, Gemmie, it was lovely! Because you see, when I found out a few things, I didn't want to get married myself just then, so it turned out quite all right. I wouldn't want to marry a man who loved another woman, would you, Gemmie?"

"I wouldn't want to marry any man that lives!" sniffed Gemmie. "They're all a selfish, deceiving lot. Not one good enough for a good girl like you."

"There you are, Gemmie! You think that and yet you are angry that I let another girl marry him!"

"Well, he was yours by rights after he'd went that far!" sniffed Gemmie, getting out her primly folded handkerchief and dabbing at her eyes.

"Well, I didn't happen to want him when I found he really belonged to another girl," said Sherrill soberly, and she wished that her heart didn't give such a sick plunge when she said the words. They were true, of course, and yet her soul was crying out for the lover she had thought she had, though she didn't intend that this sharp-eyed woman should find it out. "And now, Gemmie, keep it all to yourself and let's forget about it. I'm back here to stay awhile, and I'm going to have the best time a girl can have. Do you happen to know where that little pale green knit dress of mine is, with the white blouse? I think I'd feel at home in that. Hasn't it got back from the cleaner's yet?"

"Yes, it came back three days ago, but I put it away in the third-floor closet. I didn't think you'd be needing it yet awhile."

"Oh, get it for me, Gemmie, will you? That's a dear! It's just the thing for this morning."

Sherrill hurried with her dressing, and when Gemmie came back with the dress, she slipped into it and with a happy little wave of her hand hurried downstairs, looking much brighter than she felt.

The next two days were full of hard work. It seemed that Miss Catherwood was in a great rush to get those presents out of the way.

But there does come an end to all things, even unpleasant ones, and Sherrill finally came to her aunt and laid a neatly written envelope in her lap.

"There, Aunt Pat, that's the last one of those awful notes I have to write. The very last one! And I'm glad! glad! glad! Now, what next?" and she looked drearily out of the window across the wide sweep of lawn and garden.

"Next we're going to rest," said the old lady, leaning back in her chair with a gray look about her lips. "I believe I'm tired, and I know you are. I've watched you getting thinner and thinner hour by hour. You've been a good sport, but now we've got to rest a little."

Sherrill sprang into alarm at once.

"You dear precious Aunt Pattie!" she cried, and was down on her knees beside her aunt's chair with her arm about her, looking earnestly into the tired old face.

"Oh, it's nothing," said Aunt Pat crisply, trying to rouse herself. "I just want a nap. I guess I've caught a bit of a cold perhaps. You need a nap, too, and then afterward we'll plan what we'll do next. How would you like to take a trip somewhere? You can be thinking about it while you're going to sleep."

Chapter 15

The next day was Sunday. Sherrill had been dreading it. Aunt Pat always went to church. Sherrill would be expected to go also, and she shrank inexpressibly from entering that church again, the church that had been decorated for her wedding, the church in which she had gone through that horrible experience, watching her bridegroom given to another woman. She almost decided to beg off, say she had a headache or something, only she knew a headache would bring alarm to the dear old lady and perhaps bring on a lot more complications that might be even worse than going to church. But oh, how she dreaded the soft lights from the stained glass, the exquisite music that would stir her soul to the depths and make her remember all the lovely things she had dreamed of and lost.

A dozen times during the early morning she thought of new excuses to stay at home, and even after she had her hat and gloves on and was on her way downstairs, she had half an idea of telling Aunt Pat plainly how she longed to escape this experience, just this one Sunday anyway.

But when she got downstairs, she found that the old lady was already in the car waiting for her, and there was such a pleasant light of expectancy in her eyes that Sherrill had not the heart to suggest that she would not go.

"I got to thinking," said the old lady almost shyly, "I'd like to go to an old church where I went once with my best young man. Would you mind, Sherry?"

"Oh, I'd love it of course," said Sherrill, deep relief in her voice. It would be so good to go to a new place where she would not have to go through that awful wedding again all during service. So good not to have to face the battery of eyes that would be watching to see just how she was taking life without her bridegroom. It would be such a relief not to have to sit and feel them wondering about her, thinking up things to say about her when they got home to their various dinner tables. Oh, many of the people in the home church were friends, nice pleasant people whom she liked, but it was good not to have to be watched this first Sunday after her world had been turned upside down.

Dear Aunt Pat! She had known, of course, that

she would feel like that, and had planned this to have something different.

"You see," said Aunt Pat suddenly, right into the midst of her thoughts, "James and I went out to this church a great many years ago. We started quite early Sunday morning for a walk to get away from everybody else for a while. We didn't plan where we were going—or at least, maybe James did—he was like that; he thought of nice things and planned them out ahead—but we just started along the road."

Sherrill turned bright, interested eyes on her sweet old aunt.

"We held hands," confessed Miss Patricia with a little pink tinge stealing into her soft roseleaf cheek. "It was very early when we started, and there were no people about, not even a carriage on the road. We had a wonderful time. I had some caraway cookies in my silk bag that hung from my arm by little velvet ribbons. Soon there was dust on my best shoes, but I didn't care. We stopped before we went into church, and James dusted them off. There were narrow velvet ribbon laces to my shoes, crossed at the ankle and tied in a little tassel bow."

Aunt Pat's eyes were sweet and dreamy.

"We talked about what we would do when we were married," went on the sweet old voice. "We planned a house with pillars and a great window on the stairs. I was going to do my own work. I had written down a list of things James liked to eat, and I was learning to cook them."

"Oh," said Sherrill, bright-eyed, "it's just like a storybook."

"Yes, it was," said Aunt Pat. "I was very happy. We walked a good many miles, but I wasn't tired. I didn't get tired in those days, of course, but James slipped my hand through his arm, and that made it like walking on clouds!"

"Dear Aunt Pat!" breathed Sherrill.

"When we came to that little white church, we knew we had come to the place we had been looking for, though we hadn't known what it was or where it was. But it was our church. We both exclaimed over it at once."

Sherrill nestled her hand in her aunt's hand.

"It was still early when we got there. The old sexton was just ringing the first bell, and it sounded out over the hills like music. The bell may have been out of tune, but it sounded sweeter than any orchestra has ever seemed to me. We went and sat on a flat gravestone in the little cemetery under a tall elm tree and ate our seed cakes, and James put his arm around me and kissed me right there in the graveyard. It made me glad with a deep sweet gladness I had never felt before. It seemed just like heaven. And a bird high up sang a wonderful song that went through my heart with a sweet pain."

The little old lady had forgotten for the moment that Sherrill was there. Her eyes were dreamy and faraway.

"People ought never to get married unless they feel like that about each other, Sherry."

"No," said Sherrill, still gravely, "I don't think I did. I was just happy. Having a good time!"

There was a long minute of stillness; then Sherrill said shyly, "Tell the rest, please, Aunt Patricia."

"Well," said the old lady, her eyes still on the faraway, "after a while the people began to come. They drove up in buggies and carriages, and a few in old farm wagons with boards across the sides, for seats, and carpet on the boards. Then we got up and walked around among the white stones and read the names and dates until the sexton rang the second bell, and then we went in. A young girl with a pink ribbon and daisies on her hat played an old cabinet organ, and I remember they sang 'Nearer, My God, to Thee,' and God seemed very near to us and we to Him."

"Yes?" said Sherrill, nestling closer in a pause.

"We sat in the very last seat back by the door," went on the sweet old voice, "and James held my hand under the folds of my ruffles. I had on a very wide bayadere striped silk skirt with three deep flounces, and they flowed over the seat beautifully. I can remember the strong warm feel of his hand now."

The tears began suddenly to come into Sherrill's eyes.

"We sat all through that service hand in hand and nobody the wiser," said Aunt Pat with a bit of her old chuckle, and then a softened light came into her eyes.

"We planned to go back there someday and be married in that church when James had gotten a good job. We loved that church! But Sherry, we never went back there again! The next day they brought my James home with the mark of a horse's hoof on his temple."

She paused an instant, looking far away, and added, "Lutie's mother was the little child whose life he saved!"

"Oh, Aunt Patricia!" said Sherrill in a low, awed voice. She understood now why helping Lutie's family was so important to Aunt Pat.

"I've never been back till today."

"My dear!" said Sherrill softly.

They were at the church now, a little white building set among the trees, with a quaint old graveyard surrounding it. A young sexton was tolling the bell. He would be perhaps the grandson of the old sexton who was there when the young Patricia walked up those steps with her James.

There were smart cars parked in the old sheds where farm wagons drawn by plow horses, and buggies and carriages drawn by the family horses, used to be hitched so long ago. People were coming along the road dressed in stylish modern clothes. But as Sherrill looked at the pleasant white church, she seemed to see the young Patricia in her wide hooped skirts with silken flounces and a broad flat hat with streamers, walking with her James up the steps of the house of God, and she made much fuss of brushing the tears away before she got out of the car, for people were hurrying by them in happy groups, eyeing them curiously as the shining limousine drew up before the flagstone path.

Sherrill watched her aunt furtively as they walked together up that path to the church. Her bright eyes had suddenly grown old and tired looking, and the soft cheeks and lips seemed to sag a little wearily. She walked without her usual spring, and when Sherrill drew her hand within her arm, she leaned down heavily upon her as if she were grateful for the support. Her eyes were searching over to the right among the old mossy headstones. Sherrill felt she was looking for the place where she and her young lover had sat so long ago.

They went into the church and found a seat halfway up. People stared in a kindly way and whispered about them, pondering who they were. There were quaint windows about the walls made of long panes of clear colored glass put together in geometrical forms like a kaleidoscope. The sun was casting long bright rays through them, making quaint color effects of green and blue and yellow on people's chins and noses, and stabbing the old red ingrain carpet in the aisles with a sickly purple and red that did not match. But there was one window, at the back of the pulpit, high above the head of the minister, a gorgeous window, that was the work of a real master. It pictured an open tomb and an angel in a garden of lilies, with a wondrous blue light in a leaden sky where morning broke the gloom and shed a veil of loveliness over the lilies. Underneath in small clear letters were the words SACRED TO THE MEMORY OF JAMES AND PATRICIA and, JOY COMETH IN THE MORNING. Then a long-ago date in characters so small they were hardly discernible.

Sherrill stared at it, startled. So that was what Aunt Patricia had done! Given this little stranger church a window! A window with a story that nobody understood! Aunt Pat had likely done it through her lawyer, or someone who did not even know her except as a client.

Sitting there in the weird light of stark mingled colors, studying that one lovely window, Sherrill worked it all out: the tragedy and the sweetness of Aunt Patricia's long lonely life, the patience and utter cheerfulness that characterized her. What a lesson to a whining world! She wondered if Aunt Pat had anything besides her own strong self to rely upon. Did she know Lutie's secret? She was never one to talk religion or to preach. She went regularly to church at least once a Sunday, and there was a little worn old-fashioned Bible on her bedside stand, but Sherrill had never seen her reading it, had never thought of her as being a strong religionist. Could it be that in her quiet way she, too, like Lutie, had something in her heart, some great mysterious power beyond the earthly, that sustained her?

There was a little old wheezy cabinet organ played by a young girl with jingling silver bangles on her arms. The choir sat on a raised platform behind the organ and whispered a good deal among themselves. When they sang it was rousing. Not all the voices were cultured. When they sat down the green and purple from one of the windows played across their features grotesquely. An old man in the pulpit with the young minister prayed plaintively, yet there was something exceedingly sweet and uplifting in it, and Sherrill stole a look at the old lady by her side. There was a look of utter peace upon her face, as if a prayer of her own were winging upward to heaven beside the old man's petition.

The minister was a young seminary student, a bit crude, a bit conceited, and greatly self-conscious. His words did not seem to mean much in relation to life. Sherrill was thinking of her aunt, and strangely, too, of Lutie's mother, the girl who had been rescued from death at such a cost. Now why was that? In all human reason it would seem that the young James with such a bright prospect of life, with such a partner as his Patricia, would have been worth infinitely more to the world than just Lutie's mother, a quiet humble mother of a servant girl. If there was a God supreme above all, surely He would manage His universe wisely, economically. And it seemed such an economic waste to kill a man with great possibilities that humble serving people might live. It did not seem reasonable.

And yet, in the great economy of life, was it possible that the servant had some duty to perform, some place in the plan of things, that was important?

It was a baffling question to think upon, and Sherrill had not solved it when she rose to sing the last hymn. She only knew that her soul had been stirred to the depths, but more by Aunt Pat's story than the sermon, more by the great window with its resurrection story than by the service.

Kindly hands were put out shyly in welcome when the service was over as they passed down the aisle and out the door. The stately old lady walked sweetly among them, nodding here and there, smiling with that faraway look in her eyes, loving the gracious country folk collectively, because of one Sunday morning long years ago, and a lad who was long gone Home. You could see that they regarded her almost as if it had been an angel visiting their ancient place of worship. And Sherrill walked humbly in the shadow of that sweet soul's humble greatness.

The people stood back and hushed their chatter to watch the old lady away, but when she was out on the flagged path again, she did not go down the walk but turned aside to the graveyard.

"This way," she breathed softly, and stepped on the young spring grass.

She led the way around to the side of the church, far back from the road, under a great elm tree.

"It was there we sat." She said it more as if talking to herself, and indicated with a little wave of her hand a great flat stone with an ancient date almost obliterated by lichens.

Then she turned about but a yard or two to the right and stood looking down at a small white stone with a single name, JAMES, cut deep in its side, and a date of a generation ago.

Sherrill stood still, startled, looking down at that name, realizing all it meant to her aunt to be standing there this morning, the first time she had come there since that beloved lost lover was laid there.

Just a moment they stood silently, Sherrill feeling the awe of the presence of a funeral pall. Yet there was nothing gloomy about the place. Clear spring sunshine flooding the spot, flicked with shadows of elm branches tossing in the light spring breeze. Birds caroling joyously overhead. The sound of friendly voices of the worshippers was just a few paces away, young laughter, the whirr of a motor starting from the church.

Unquestionably the young lover had not lain there all these years, his body crumbling to dust. He must be somewhere, doing something. Love and bravery and courage did not just blink out. That conviction came to Sherrill as a fixed fact, though she had never thought of such things before. Where was he, this James, and what faith had Aunt Pat that one day joy would come in the morning?

She thought of her own life, blighted right at the start. Would there be joy, too, in some morning for a life like hers that had found a lover false-hearted?

The old lady spoke.

"I'd like to have what's left of me put here when I am gone!" she said, laying a hand on Sherrill's arm. "There's plenty of room. It doesn't matter, of course; only it is pleasanter to think of being here than up under that great Catherwood monument at Laurel Hill. They can put my name there if they like, but I'll lie here. It'll be nice to think of getting up together in the morning."

"Dear Aunt Patty!" said Sherrill, struggling with a constriction in her throat.

"I've put it all in my will, of course, and the stone's been made ready, just 'Patricia' and the date. But I thought I'd like somebody that belonged to me to understand."

"Of course!" said Sherrill tenderly, catching her breath and trying to steady her voice. "But—you're not going yet, dear—not for a long time. You wouldn't leave me—alone!"

"Why, certainly not!" snapped the old lady with one of her quiet grins. "I've got to look after you for a spell yet. Come on, let's walk around. We don't want a lot of people staring at us. There's no need for them to know we're interested in just one grave. Let's walk around the church. There are some curious stones there, very old. James and I found them that day and talked about them. And there's a view—look! Away off to the hills! I think it's a lovely spot!"

"It is indeed," answered Sherrill, and almost envied her aunt for the joyous look on her face. How she had taken her sorrow and glorified it! Sherrill wondered if she, in like situation, could have risen to such heights, and felt how impossible it would have been for her. Felt how crushed she was by this her own sorrow, which she recognized at once was so much less than what the old lady had borne for years unmurmuring, and said again to herself that there must have been some sustaining Power greater than herself, or human weakness—even human strength—never could have borne it.

There was something glorified in the rest of that day. Sherrill felt that she had been allowed a glimpse into an inner sanctuary of a soul, and life could never again be the trivial, superficial thing that it had seemed to her before.

Aunt Pat was very tired and slept a great part of the afternoon, but in the evening she came down to the living room and sat before a lovely fire that Gemmie had kindled for them. She made Sherrill play all the old hymns she used to love. It brought tears to hear the quavering voice that still had a note of sweetness in it, wavering through a verse here and there, and Sherrill, trying to sing with her felt her own voice breaking.

Yet there was nothing gloomy about the old lady that night, and presently she was joking again in her snappy bright way, for all the world like a young thing, and Sherrill's heart was less heavy. Aunt Pat wasn't going away to leave her. Not now anyway.

Chapter 16

Sherrill needn't have worried about her aunt, for the old lady was up the next morning chipper as a bird, eating her breakfast with a relish.

"We're going to see Lutie's mother right away," she said. "We've got to get that family straightened out before we plan to do anything for ourselves."

"Oh, that will be wonderful!" said Sherrill, who had arisen this morning with a great pall over life. Since there was no immediate action necessary, she could not get hold of anything in which she was interested. But to help another household who were all in trouble intrigued her. It didn't occur to her either to realize that the canny old lady was wisely arranging to fill her days too full for her to brood over the past.

So they went to the neat little house where Lutie

lived. Sherrill was amazed to see how attractive the little weather-beaten house had been made. There was lack of paint on its ugly clapboards, lack of grace in all its lines, lack of beauty in its surroundings, for there were slovenly neighbors all about and a great hideous dump not far away to mar what otherwise might have been a bit of landscape.

But the ugly house had been smothered in quick-growing vines. The ugly picket fence that also needed painting had been covered with rambler roses now beginning to bud; the yard had a neat patch of well-cut lawn, with trim borders where young plants were beginning to give a good showing; and a row of pansy plants showed bright faces along the neat brick walk. The pansies winked brightly up at her like old acquaintances.

An ugly narrow court between houses had been concealed by tall privet hedge trained into an arched gateway, and there were nice white starched curtains at the windows upstairs and down. They might be only cheesecloth, but they made the house stand out like a thing of beauty in the midst of squalor.

"Hmm!" said Aunt Pat appreciatively. "Pretty, isn't it? I don't know why I never thought to come here before."

The mother opened the door, wiping her hands on her apron, which was an old towel girded about her waist. There was a fleck of soapsuds on her arm, and her face, though the morning was only half gone, looked weary and worn.

"Oh, Miss Catherwood!" she said to Aunt Pat, her tone a bit awed.

She opened the door wide and welcomed them in, casting a troubled eye over the room behind her to see if it was surely all in order.

"But you oughtn't to be washing!" objected Aunt Pat as she reached the top step and looked into the neat front room. "I thought you were sick. I heard you ought to go to the hospital."

The woman gave a helpless amused little laugh, not discourteous.

"No, I'm not sick," she said rather hopelessly. "I'm not near as bad off as some. I'll be all right when Father gets well. Come in, won't you?"

Aunt Pat marched in cheerfully.

"Now, I'm not going to take up any more of your time than is necessary," she said as she sat down in the big old stuffed chair. "You go and shut off your dampers or gas or whatever it is that's worrying you, and I'll talk to you just five minutes, and then you can get back and finish up what you've started. I suppose that's got to be done in spite of everything, but I've got something to say that's even more important."

The woman cast a sort of despairing look at her caller and with a half-deprecatory glance toward Sherrill, who had settled down on the old haircloth sofa, she vanished into the back room where they could hear her turning on water, lifting dripping clothes from one tub to another, pulling a tin boiler across the top of an old-fashioned iron range, and slamming the dampers back and forth.

She returned, pulling down her neat print sleeves and fastening a clean apron over her wet dress.

Sherrill meanwhile had been looking around the little room, noting carefully the pretty trifles that Lutie had used to make the place homelike. There was even a little snapshot of herself that Sherrill recognized as one she had thrown in the wastebasket. It was framed in glass with a black paper binding and stood under the lamp on the small center table. Poor Lutie! Sherrill was deeply touched.

"Well," said Aunt Pat, "I'll get right to the point. My niece found out from Lutie that your husband is sick. How is he? Getting well fast?"

"No," said the woman sadly, "he doesn't improve at all now. He's pretty well discouraged. He said last night he guessed he had got to the end, and the sooner it came the better off we'll all be."

The woman was blinking the tears back and swallowing hard. Her lips quivered as she spoke.

"Fiddlesticks!" said Aunt Pat briskly. "We'll see if something can't be done about that. Have you got a good doctor? Who is your doctor?"

"We haven't any doctor now," said the woman with a hopeless note in her voice. "We've tried three, and he only got worse. He would not hear to having any more bills run up that we never can pay."

"Hmm!" said Aunt Pat. "What doctors did you have?"

"Oh, we had the company doctor where he worked first, and he went on for two months and didn't make a mite of difference. And then we got Dr. Green. He was the doctor that examined him for his insurance several years ago, but he said just out plain he couldn't do him any good. And then we tried a specialist somebody recommended at the office where my son works, but he charged ten dollars every time he saw him, and ordered things that cost so much we couldn't get them, and said he ought to go to a private hospital for observation where they charge fifty dollars a week, and we had to give that up. Now we owe them all, and Lutie is paying them fifty cents a week, and Sam pays sometimes a dollar when he can spare it; dear knows when we'll get them all paid off."

"Well," said Aunt Pat with satisfaction, "then the coast is clear. That's good. Now, I'm going to send my doctor up to see him. How soon would it be convenient for him to come?"

The woman flushed.

"Oh, we couldn't really afford another doctor," she said in a worried tone. "It's very kind for you to take an interest in us, but you see, we just couldn't pay him now, and it only worries Father and makes him so he can't sleep."

"Yes, but you see, my doctor won't cost you anything," said Aunt Pat. "He does these things as a favor for me.

He's an old friend of mine, and he's been our family physician for years. He's very skillful, too, and he'll tell me the truth. If anything can be done for your husband, we'll find out what it is. And as for money, dear woman, aren't you and I both God's children? I've got some money that is just crying out to be spent somehow. They're after me to build an art school with it, but if it could make your husband better, I'd a lot rather have it used that way. And I take it God would be a great deal better pleased."

"Oh, but Miss Catherwood, I couldn't! You're awfully good and I'll never forget it—but we couldn't! Oh, we never could!" The woman was crying openly now, into her nice clean blue-and-white checked apron. Sherrill had a sudden feeling that she would like to go over and put her arms around Lutie's mother and kiss her on her tired, seamed forehead. Suppose it had been her mother? Sherrill's mother seemed so very many years away!

But Miss Catherwood was sitting up very straight now. "Fiddlesticks end!" she said crisply. "As if you'd put pride between when it comes to getting your husband well! Listen! The Lord told me to come over here this morning and see what needed doing and do it. See? And you're not going to block the way. You're just going to be a dear sweet woman and do what you're told. How soon can you be ready for the doctor?"

"Oh!" sobbed the woman. "You're too good to us! Lutie said you were the salt of the earth—"

"Now, look here," fumed Aunt Pat, "stop that kind of

225

talk. We don't need any salt around here just now. Wipe your eyes and tell me how soon I can have the doctor stop. Can you be ready for him by two o'clock? I think it likely he could be here about then. And while he's here I'm going to tell him to take a look at the little boy. Lutie said he had trouble with his hip."

"Oh yes," wailed the mother as if the admission stabbed her to the heart. "They tell me he'll never walk again. He doesn't know it yet, poor kid. He keeps talking about when he's going to get well enough to play baseball with the other boys."

"Well, we'll see what can be done," said Aunt Pat with satisfaction. "And now, is there any way we can help you with this washing? Because, you see, we want you to be ready to have the doctor give you an examination, too, and then we'll know where we stand."

"Oh, but I'm all right!" beamed the mother eagerly. "I don't need the doctor now. If my husband and boy could just get cured I'd be all right. It's just been the worry—"

"Well, that's all right, too, but you're going to have the examination, and then we'll find out what the doctor says about it. If he says you're all right, why, then no harm is done, but if he says you need an operation, you're going to have it right away."

"Oh, but I couldn't be spared while my two men are sick," said the woman in alarm.

"Oh yes, you could, my dear!" said the old lady

determinedly, "and it's a great deal better for you to be spared now than to wait until it's too late to help you. Don't be silly! Here comes Lutie. She'll look after the house and her brother while the three of you are in the hospital."

"Hospital?" said the woman frantically. "But we couldn't afford—!"

"Oh yes, you could. It's all fixed, I tell you. Here comes Lutie. How about that wash out there, Lutie? Can't you finish that up while your mother gets your father and brother ready to go to the hospital?"

"Oh, Miss Catherwood! Wouldn't that be too wonderful!" cried Lutie, her cheeks growing red as a winter apple and her eyes starry. "Of course I can finish up the wash. Only"—and she paused in consternation— "I'm supposed to go up to your house to help with the ironing at eleven o'clock."

"Well, that's off for today. I'll explain to the housekeeper. We've plenty of people there to finish the ironing for this once, and if we haven't, it can go unironed. Now go to work quickly, and don't let your mother get all fussed up about things."

When they got up to go, Lutie looked at Sherrill wistfully.

"I been wondering if you really was going with me to the Bible class tonight," she said in a low tone. "I've been telling the other girls about you, and they're so anxious for you to come. But now I don't know as I can go this week. Maybe I'll be too busy here."

"Bible class?" said Aunt Pat, scenting something interesting. "What's that? Where were you going with her, Sherrill?"

"She's been telling me about a class she attends," explained Sherrill. "Why, yes, I guess I can go tonight if you can find you can. I'd be interested to see what it's like."

"Of course you mustn't miss you Bible class, Lutie," said her mother with a wan smile. Then, turning to Miss Catherwood, she explained, "Lutie's been that taken up with her Bible study, and I'm glad she's got something since things have been so awful bad. But perhaps, Lutie, you'll be too tired."

"Oh, I'm never tired," said Lutie eagerly. "I'll go. Shall I come round to the house for you, Miss Sherrill?"

"No, I'll call for you with the little car," said Sherrill with sudden inspiration. "Then you won't have to walk when you are tired."

"Oh, that would be wonderful!" said Lutie as if Sherrill were offering her a ride in a chariot of state.

"Here, Lutie, help me down these steps. I want to ask you some questions," said Aunt Pat imperatively.

Lutie helped the old lady carefully down the steps, and as they walked out to the car, Miss Patricia snapped out the questions.

"My niece said you lost some money. What bank?"

Lutie told her.

"Hmm!" commented Miss Patricia. "Who owns your mortgage?"

Lutie gave the necessary information.

"Hmm!" said the old lady. "I know them. I'll see what can be done. Don't you worry about losing your house. Just get your mother comfortable. And by the way, if your folks all have to go to the hospital, you won't have time to work at the house till they get on their feet again, will you? It'll take about all your time to keep house here, won't it?"

"Oh no, Miss Catherwood!" said Lutie in consternation. "I just couldn't afford not to work. There won't be anything for me to do but get Sam's breakfast and dinner and put up his lunch. I can give you just as much time as you want."

"That's all right, then, Lutie. Don't you worry. But if you need to take a vacation for a few weeks, why, you just come to me, and we'll fix it up so you won't lose anything by it. Now, Sherrill, are we all ready to go?"

They drove away amid exclamations of blessing from Lutie and her mother, and Sherrill felt a big lump rise in her throat as she looked back and saw them standing in the doorway, the mother waving her apron.

"That was wonderful of you, Aunt Pat!" said Sherrill eagerly. "That was dear of you! But it's going to cost you a lot of money."

"Well, you see, child, I figured if James gave his life to save Lutie's mother, it was maybe my job to look after the rest of the family. And what's money in a case like that?

If God thought saving her life was worth a man's life, then surely the least that I can do is to look after her, or somebody else's family if there hadn't been this one. I've you to thank for finding this out for me. I never thought to ask anything about them before, and Lutie never opened her lips. If I thought anything about them at all, I supposed they were all well and hearty and everyone with a good job and thrifty. Lutie looks that way. What's this thing you're going to tonight?"

"Why, when she was singing that happy little song the other day, I asked her where she got it. She told me about a class where they study the Bible and learn to be glad even when there's trouble. I said I would go with her sometime."

"So she's that kind, is she? Well, I'm glad. Now, here's the doctor's, and I'll just run in and give him his orders. I'm hoping he isn't full up every hour today with operations or something. I'd hate to go back on my word."

A few minutes later she was back.

"He's going to see them at three o'clock. It's the best he can do. He's very busy. But I told him all about them, and he promised me he'd do his best to put them all back in normal health again. Now, Sherrill, what did I do with the card Lutie wrote that mortgage company's address on? I want to stop and see my lawyer a minute and get him to fix that up, and then we can go home and rest awhile. We've done a big piece of work."

"A wonderful piece of work," mused Sherrill. "Oh,

Aunt Pat! You've done more with your life than any woman I know!"

"Fiddlesticks end!" said Aunt Pat scornfully. "I've not done the half that I should. Now, Sherrill, while I'm seeing my lawyer I'd like you to do a little shopping for those people if you will. They'll need things to go to the hospital with, dressing gowns and robes and things, and decent suitcases to carry them in. I want them to be comfortable while they are there. That poor woman doesn't look as if she's had a day's rest since she was born, and I mean she shall have. Get her a real pretty robe, and brushes and things. Nice pretty ones. She likes pretty things, I'm sure. Look at the way they've fixed up that old ramshackle house with just plants and vines. Not even paint! I'll give you the money, and you get the necessary things. And I'm glad you're going to that Bible class. There are a lot of things in the Bible I don't understand, but I believe it from cover to cover, and I'd like to know more about it. I'm too old to study now, but you're not, and you can tell me all about it."

When they got home they found a stack of mail awaiting them. Notes of commiseration and protest from the people who had received their wedding gifts back again. Some letters, intended to cheer up Sherrill in her lonely estate of maidenhood, which made her very angry. A few giving her loving wishes from far-off friends who hadn't yet heard of the change in the wedding arrangements.

She looked up listlessly from her lap full of letters and gave a deep sigh. How much more worthwhile was the world of helpfulness to which she had just been with her aunt, than this social world built around such an unstable foundation. She could sense through all these elaborate phrases that some of her old friends and playmates actually thought less of her because she had allowed herself to be washed up on the shore of maidenhood again, after she had once landed a man and gotten so far as wedding invitations.

Aunt Pat looked up sharply at the second sigh and handed over a letter.

"Well," she said triumphantly, "they haven't put your emeralds on the market yet, whoever it was that took them. Of course there has hardly been time for anybody to get them to Europe. But if they attempt it, it won't be long before we know who did it."

"Aunt Pat!" said Sherrill in astonishment. "Then you have done something about it after all!"

"Why, of course, child! You didn't think I was a fool, did you? I called up the private detective who was here at the wedding and had a talk with him. He's been quietly watching all the places where they would be likely to be put on the market. They're all registered stones, you know. Any jewel dealer of repute will be on the watch for them. Sooner or later they would have to turn up at the right place to get a reasonable price for them. I talked to my lawyer about them, too, told him I didn't want publicity, and he's working quietly. So that's that and don't worry! They'll turn up if you were meant to get them back, and if you weren't, all the worry in the world won't help you."

After lunch Sherrill went to lie down and had a long restful sleep. She had a sort of feeling when she woke up of being stranded on a desert island, and now that she was coming near to that Bible class that she had promised to attend, she found a keen aversion to going. Why had she promised Lutie? Lutie was well enough herself, but Lutie had spoken of other girls who wanted to see her. They would be common girls without education, of course. They would have heard a lot of gossip about her wedding and how she didn't get married after all, and would be watching every move she made.

She half started to the telephone to tell Lutie that she was tired and would go another time, and then the eager look in Lutie's eyes came back to mind, and she couldn't quite get the courage to call off the engagement. So she dressed herself in a plain quiet little knit dress of blue wool, and a small felt hat to match. It was one of her oldest sport dresses, and quite shabby now she thought. But she did not want to make Lutie feel that there was too much difference between them.

Miss Catherwood looked at her approvingly as she came into the room at dinnertime.

"Some people wouldn't have known any better than

to put on an evening dress," she remarked irrelevantly and smiled her peculiar twisted grin. "Well, I hope you have a good time, and be sure to listen for me."

Chapter 17

Dubiously Sherrill parked her car and followed Lutie into the plain wooden building. If she hadn't promised Lutie, she never would have gone tonight. She had lost her first curiosity about Lutie's source of peace, and if she had not seen how eager and pleased Lutie was about taking her, she would have invented some excuse.

The building was not inviting. It was old and grimy. There had not been much money for fresh paint, and the floor was bare boards. A large blackboard and a battered old piano were the only attempts at furnishings besides the hard wooden benches, and the only decorations were startling Bible verses in plain print on white cards here and there about the walls.

"All have sinned and come short of the glory of God" was announced on the right; and Sherrill, entering, felt a shade of resentment at being classed with sinners. She had a feeling that her family had never been in that class.

There were other verses, but she had no time to read them, for several young girls came up and Lutie introduced them.

One put a hand on Sherrill's arm intimately and with a sweet little smile said, "We're so glad you have come. Lutie has been telling us about you, and we hope you will like it here. We just love it."

Again there was just the least bit of resentment in Sherrill's aristocratic soul that these girls should think her of their class, and expect her to be coming more than once. Yet there was something so winning about her smile, and so gentle in her manner, that Sherrill began to wonder if perhaps she had been wrong. Perhaps these girls were not all in Lutie's class. It was difficult to tell. They wore nice clothes; one had a pretty little pink crepe dress and a white beret, like any girl who had been out to play golf or tennis. There was an earnest air about them that made Sherrill like them in spite of herself. Could it be possible that she, Sherrill Cameron, was a snob? She must get out of this state of mind. She would not come here again likely, but while she was here she would be one of them, and do her best to enter into the things. She would be a good sport. She would be in their class, even if they were not in hers. After all, what was her class anyway? She was just a girl by herself who would have had to earn her own living somehow if Aunt Pat had not invited her to live with her. The fact that she had earned it until then teaching school instead of cleaning rooms and ironing as Lutie did, really made no difference, of course. It was all silly anyway.

So Sherrill put out a friendly hand and greeted all the girls with her own warm smile, and they loved her at once. The strangest part about it was that somehow she couldn't help liking them. They were all so friendly and eager, what was the use of trying to act exclusive?

There was one thing she couldn't understand. She heard one of those girls just behind her speaking to Lutie. The words came out between the clamor of the people who were gathering. "She's lovely, isn't she? Is she *saved*, Lutie?" And Lutie murmured something very low that Sherrill couldn't catch. Somehow she knew they were talking about her. And then the other girl said, "Well, we'll be praying for her tonight," and slipped away up front with a group of others, and whispered to them. They nodded, gave quick glances back, and a moment later Sherrill could see them off at one side bunched together with their heads bowed. A quick intuition told her they were praying for *her*, and the color mounted into her cheeks. Her chin went up a trifle haughtily. Why should she, Sherrill Cameron, need to be prayed for? And why should they *presume* to do it unasked?

But the room was filling up rapidly now. Lutie led her to a seat halfway up and gave her a hymn book. The little group of praying ones had scattered, one to play the old piano, two others to distribute hymn books and Bibles, and suddenly the room burst into song, but she noticed that two or three of them still kept their heads bent, their eyes closed as if they were yet praying.

Sherrill looked around her in amazement. Here was a crowd of people, almost all young people, and they were singing joyously as if it made them glad to do so. They were singing with that same lilt that Lutie had had while she was working, and their faces all looked glad, although some of them obviously must be very poor, if one might judge from their garments and the weary look on their young faces, while others again were well dressed and prosperous looking.

Presently they began to sing Lutie's song:

"If I have sorrow in my heart,
What can take it away?"

And Sherrill, without realizing she was doing so, began to sing it herself, and felt a little of the thrill that seemed to be in the air.

She fell to thinking of her own interrupted life and wondering why it all had to be. Why couldn't Carter have been all right, the perfect man she had thought him? Why did it all have to turn out that way, in that sudden mortifying manner? If it only could have happened quietly! Not in the face of her whole invited world as it were.

But suddenly she felt the audience bowing in

prayer, and was amazed to hear different voices taking up petitions, so many young people willing to pray in public! And so simply, so free from all self-consciousness apparently. It was extraordinary. Even little Lutie beside her prayed a simple sentence.

"Please, dear Father, don't let anything in us hinder Thy light from shining through us, so that others may see and find Thee."

Dear little soul! How had Lutie learned all this sweet simplicity? Just a little serving maid, yet she seemed to have something really worthwhile. What was this mysterious power? Just an idea? A conviction?

One of the prayers impressed her deeply. It came from a girl's voice up toward the front, perhaps one of those who had been introduced to her. It was "Dear Father, if any have come in here tonight not knowing Thee as Savior, may they find Thee and not go out unsaved." Sherrill had a strange feeling that the prayer was for her, although she couldn't exactly understand why she needed saving.

Then the prayers changed into song again, a rousing one:

"I've found a friend who is all to me,
His love is ever true;"

Ah! That was what she wanted, Sherrill thought, a friend whose love was ever true. It was almost uncanny, as if someone here knew just what she needed.

> *"I love to tell how He lifted me,*
> *And what His grace can do for you,"*

sang the audience, and then burst into that tremendous chorus that thrilled her, though she only half understood its meaning:

> *"Saved by His power divine,*
> *Saved to new life sublime!*
> *Life now is sweet and my joy is complete*
> *For I'm saved, saved, saved."*

Sherrill ran her eye through the rest of the verses and lingered on those lines—

> *"I'm leaning strong on His mighty arm;*
> *I know He'll guide me all the way"*—

and experienced a sudden longing. If there were only someone who could guide her! Someone who could take away this utterly humiliated, lost feeling, and make her sure and strong and happy again; the way she used to be before all this happened to her!

Then another hymn was called for, and the eager young voices took on a more tender note as they sang just as earnestly, only with deeper meaning to the words than any of the other songs had carried. Sherrill followed the words, and to her amazement found a great longing in her soul that she might be able to sing these words and mean them, every one.

"Fade, fade, each earthly joy."

That was what had been happening to her. The life that she had planned and that seemed all rosy before her had suddenly in a moment faded out.

"Jesus is mine!"

How she wished she might truly say that!

"Break every tender tie,"—

Ah! Her case exactly.

"Jesus is mine!"

rang the triumphant words. She glanced about at the eager young faces, so grave and certain. How could they be certain that Jesus was theirs? What did it mean anyway to have Jesus? Was it just a phrase? A state of mind? She studied several of them intently.

"Dark is the wilderness,
Earth has no resting-place,
Jesus alone can bless,

241

Jesus is mine!"

The tears suddenly welled into her eyes, and she blinked them back angrily. She certainly did not want these stranger girls to think she was soft and sentimental.

The leader arose after the hymn was ended and prayed, just a few words, but it seemed to bring them all to the threshold of another world, an open heaven. Sherrill had never had such a feeling in a meeting before, not even in the solemn beautiful church where Aunt Patricia worshipped. And this was all so simple, and without any emotion except gladness!

There was a little stir all over the room. Everybody was opening Bibles. Lutie found the place and gave Sherrill one, and they all began to read together.

At first Sherrill did not pay much attention to what she was reading because she was so busy watching the others and feeling astonished. But gradually the words began to make themselves felt in her mind. She looked up at the speaker, startled, to see if he were looking at her. She almost thought he must have known of her trouble and selected the passage because he knew she was to be here.

"Beloved, think it not strange concerning the fiery trial which is to try you, as though some strange thing happened unto you—"

It was strange, though, thought Sherrill; how could she pretend it wasn't?

"But rejoice," the voices went on in unison, "inasmuch as ye are partakers of Christ's sufferings; that, when his glory shall be revealed, ye may be glad also with exceeding joy."

Christ's sufferings! How could her trouble have anything to do with what Christ had suffered on earth? He had never had anyone go back on Him as she had; He had never been made a public laughingstock by anyone who was supposed to be His special friend—or wait, perhaps she was wrong! Had not His own disciple been the one who turned against Him, betrayed Him, laid the plot that led to His being nailed to the cross before the mocking multitudes?

These thoughts flashed through Sherrill's mind as she looked up from her Bible to give a grudging attention to the speaker.

"Let us see," he was saying, "to whom these words are addressed. Peter was writing a letter to Christians who had fled from their homes because of persecution. At the beginning of the letter he says that they, and himself with them, are 'begotten again' unto a living hope—" Sherrill winced; her hopes were all dead.

"These words describe those to whom the letter is written. No one else has a right to the promises in the letter except those who are 'begotten again'—born again. We must understand that clearly before we go on with the letter. If you want the joy that Christ can give even in the midst of suffering, remember that it is for you only if you are a child of God, born into His family by believing that Jesus Christ the Son of God was nailed to the cross because of your sins. He rose from the dead, and He can give you life, but your new birth comes from more than just believing this *about* Him! Believing about Christ never saved anyone. It must be believing *in* Him. Believe that He took your condemnation upon Himself, and accept Him as your own personal Savior."

Sherrill's eyes were fixed on the teacher's face now, utterly absorbed. She had never heard anyone talk like this before. It was quite possible she had sat in church often under sermons that included such doctrines, but they had never been able to reach her heart before, perhaps because her mind was too full of her own plans and thoughts. In fact, it was probably the first time in her life that she had even read a portion of scripture with her mind on it. Her mind had always been politely aloof when she entered God's house, or found it necessary to take up a Bible.

A living hope. How she wished she might get one. This teacher was talking just as Lutie had talked, only more convincingly. And these people in the room looked at their teacher eagerly, earnestly, as if they understood from experience what he meant. She looked about on them wistfully. Could she get what they had? The teacher had said it came by believing in Christ, but how could one believe in someone who died so many years ago? How could one believe unless one knew and was convinced?

As if the man had read her thoughts and were answering them, he went on.

"Belief is not an intellectual conviction. Belief is an act of the will, whereby you throw yourself on the promise of God and let Him prove Himself true. If someone asked you to take a ride in a new kind of airplane, you might not be able to go over every bit of its machinery and be sure that it was in perfect order; you might not understand the principle by which it worked, nor be sure it could carry you safely; you might not even know the man who made it, nor have the wisdom to judge the principle under which it operated, but you could get into the plane and take a ride and let it prove to you what it claimed to be able to do. If you were in need of getting somewhere in a desperate hurry, you might not even stop to think very carefully about it. You would say: 'This plane has taken others. I believe it will take me. At least I am going to trust myself to it.' And so you would get into the plane and fly away. Afterward when you have safely reached your destination, then you are convinced that the plane can fly, for it has safely carried you. You have experience, but faith comes first. Now turn to Hebrews the twelfth chapter."

The room was filled with the rustling of Bible leaves as heads were bent and the place was found. Sherrill blundered around among the books of the Bible like a person in a strange city trying to find a street. She was beginning back somewhere near Genesis, and her cheeks were a bit red with confusion. All these young people were turning straight to the right page with confidence. She tried to see over Lutie's shoulder without seeming to do so, to get the number of the page. Surely Bibles had pages, didn't they? Why didn't he tell the page? Again that feeling of resentment at being caught in a humiliating position welled up in her. Why did she let herself come here to be made a fool of? All she could remember was Matthew, Mark, Luke, and John, and that in connection with some old nursery rhyme.

But Lutie came to her rescue now and made short work of finding the place—Lutie the little maid who did the cleaning and ironing! Wise in the scriptures!

Then every voice in the room began to read, and Sherrill read, too, startled at how the words seemed meant just for her.

"My son, despise not thou the chastening of the Lord, nor faint when thou art rebuked of him: for whom the Lord loveth he chasteneth, and scourgeth every son whom he receiveth. If ye endure chastening, God dealeth with you as with sons; for what son is he whom the father chasteneth not?"

The teacher stopped them for a moment.

"The literal meaning of the word 'to chasten' here is 'to train a child.' Although you may be born again, a son of God, you are not to forget your subjection to the will of the Father. I wonder how many of you have been wondering why you have had to pass through some peculiar trial or testing? Have you found out yet that God was giving you that hard thing just to teach you to know Him better? Sometimes we are so taken up with the world, or with our own plans and selves, that we haven't given a thought to God, and He just had to take away the thing in which we were interested to make us give our attention to Him, that we might know His will and get the full blessing He has prepared for us.

"I have sometimes seen a mother take away a toy from a little child in order to make him listen to her teaching, and God often has to do that for His dearest sons. Go back to First Corinthians 11:31: "'If we would judge ourselves, we should not be judged. But when we are judged, we are chastened of the Lord, that we should not be condemned with the world.' The sons of God— that is, believers—cannot be condemned with the world, and if they do not judge their careless and unworthy ways, then the Lord must deal with them and make them experience His chastening."

Sherrill wondered in passing if Aunt Pat had ever studied the Bible in this way. Did she know how the Bible fit people's daily lives, and that a verse in one book explained a verse in another book?

And then the teacher whirled them back to the Old Testament for an illustration, and Sherrill had to have Lutie's help once more in finding the place. By this time she had determined that before another week—if she decided to come to that class again—she would learn the books of the Bible.

The teacher was making plain now how God yearned for the love and fellowship of His children. He showed how disappointed God must be in them because they are so filled with themselves, so forgetful of the fact that they are on this earth only temporarily, getting ready for an eternal life.

It was a new view of God. Sherrill had never thought of herself as having any relationship to God at all, and now it seemed one had to be either a son or a deliberate rejector of the wonderful love and grace of God toward sinners. Sinners! As the teacher went on, bringing more and more verses to their attention, Sherrill had a view of the Lord Jesus and began to get the realization that everybody was a sinner. She was appalled to think of herself under such a classification.

When the meeting finally closed with another wonderful prayer, Sherrill was in a maze of bewilderment. She wanted to get away alone and think. There were so many questions that had come to her mind that, as she watched the young people gather around the teacher, eagerly asking questions, she wished she had the courage to join them.

Lutie had excused herself to take a message to a girl across the room, and Sherrill, left alone for the moment, turned to the book table at the back of the room. What an array of little paper-covered books with startling titles! They were all on topics she was in the dark about.

A sign above them said they were only fifteen cents apiece. Sherrill picked out half a dozen and got out her purse, paying the pleasant-faced boy who had charge of the table.

"Got a Scofield study Bible?" asked the youth, waving his hand toward a collection of Bibles in various bindings.

"Why, no, what is a Scofield Bible?" asked Sherrill shyly, and realized at once as the youth stared at her that she had shown great ignorance.

"Oh, it's the regular text, of course," he explained politely, "only it has a lot of helpful notes that make it pretty plain about the dispensations and symbolism and covenants and things. It helps a lot to have them right there on the page with the text, that's all."

"How much are they?" asked Sherrill, reaching for a small limp-covered one in real leather.

"Well, that's about the most expensive one we have," said the boy, looking at her with a new respect. "We have cheaper ones."

"But I like this one," said Sherrill and paid for it feeling as if she had bought a gold mine. Now perhaps she had something that would answer some of her questions!

When Lutie came back, apologetic for being so long, Sherrill had a package all done up ready to take home.

"They are wonderful books!" said Lutie, casting wistful eyes at the book table. "I've got two or three for my own. We girls get different ones and lend them around among ourselves."

When Sherrill got home, she went straight to her aunt's room.

Aunt Pat had gone to bed but was lying bolstered up with pillows reading, and Sherrill noticed that her little Bible lay on the bed beside her.

"I've been buying some books," said Sherrill, half shamefaced. "See what you think of them."

She undid her package and displayed them.

Miss Catherwood took up the Scofield Bible first and examined it curiously.

"I've heard about this," she said thoughtfully. "I'd like to look it over sometime. Maybe I'll get one, too. They say it's very enlightening."

Then she went over the other books one by one.

"Yes, I know this one. It's by a president of a theological college, a wonderful man, they say. I came across a notice of this book in a magazine. And this I know and love. I used to have a copy, but someone borrowed it and never brought it back. But these others I never heard of. You'll have to read some of them aloud to me. I'd like to know what they are. The titles look wonderfully interesting. Well, how did you like the meeting? Was it a meeting?"

"Why, no," said Sherrill thoughtfully. "It wasn't exactly a meeting, nor exactly like a school. I don't just know what to call it, but it was wonderfully interesting."

"Begin at the beginning and tell me all about it," said the old lady, studying the vivid face before her.

Sherrill hadn't worn that look of interest since the wedding night. The desolate haunted expression was almost gone.

After that first night Sherrill began to be fascinated with the study of the Bible. She realized, of course, that she had only as yet touched the outer fringes of the great truths it contained, but she really longed to know more, and she found that this, more than anything else, was able to help her forget her changed estate.

It was the second Monday night that she lingered till most of the others were gone and asked a few questions that perplexed her about salvation. For she had come already to see her own need, and she finally in great simplicity said she would accept the Savior.

When at last the teacher was free and turned to her, she shyly asked, "Mr. Mackenzie, how can one tell—does anybody really know—that is"—she hesitated—"how would *I* know whether I am all right with God or not?"

She finished in a blaze of embarrassment. She had never spoken to anyone before about the thoughts of her own heart concerning God. She had a feeling it was almost immodest, for the people she knew never did it.

But with Spirit-taught gentleness and understanding, the man of God answered her, putting her instantly at her ease, and treating the question as most natural and supremely important.

"Indeed you can know, most positively, Miss Cameron. Let me ask you first, have you ever realized that you—that we all of us—are sinners in God's sight, utterly unfit for His presence?"

"Yes, I have," said Sherrill earnestly. "I never did before, but last week I saw that."

"Then do you realize that you need to have the sin taken away that separates you from God?"

"Yes, oh yes!" The tears sprang to her eyes.

"Then 'behold the Lamb of God, who taketh away the sin of the world!' Just look to the Lord Jesus Christ as the One who bore on the cross all the guilt penalty for your sins. God poured out on His own Son all His righteous wrath against us. 'For all have sinned, and come short of the glory of God; being justified freely by His grace through the redemption that is in Christ Jesus.' Do you believe that?"

"I do," said Sherrill solemnly.

"Then read this aloud."

Mr. Mackenzie opened his Bible and pointed to a verse. Sherrill read, "'Therefore being justified by faith, we have peace with God through our Lord Jesus Christ.'"

"Read it again, very slowly, please."

Sherrill read it again, very slowly, letting the truth sink deep. Suddenly a radiance broke through the puzzled earnestness of her face.

"I see it now," she said. "It's all right!"

"Then let's thank Him for so great a salvation," said Mr. Mackenzie.

The rest had all gone but Lutie, and the three knelt together as Mr. Mackenzie poured out a thanksgiving for the newborn child of God.

So Sherrill went home that night with real news for Aunt Pat that kept that old saint awake half the night praising her heavenly Father.

Chapter 18

Presently the days settled down into regular normal living again, the lovely pansies had faded, and nothing more had been heard from the stranger.

Sherrill tried to put him out of her mind, tried not to start and look interested whenever the doorbell rang or a package arrived. She tried to curb the feeling of disappointment each night when she went up to her room, that he had not come that day.

"He has forgotten us long ago," she told herself. "It was a mere incident in his life. He was just a passing stranger. He probably felt that he had done his entire duty toward us by sending those flowers. They were only sort of a bread-and-butter letter, and saved him the trouble of writing one. He has likely gone back to Chicago by this time and gotten immersed in business again. If he ever thinks of us again, it will be to laugh sometime with his friends and tell about the unusual wedding he once attended. Why should I be so silly as to keep on watching for him?"

But still she could not forget the stranger. And still there came no word of the lost jewels.

Aunt Pat kept a watchful eye upon Sherrill. She sent for maps and guide books. They studied routes of travel, considered various cruises, planned motor trips, and all the while watched over Lutie's family, agreeing that they must not go away anywhere till the operations were all over and the invalids back at home doing well.

When the third Monday night came, Lutie was up at the hospital waiting to hear the result of her mother's operation. Lutie's mother was in a very serious condition. Sherrill was restless and finally decided to go to the Bible class alone.

To her surprise the whole loving group of people at the mission knew about Lutie's anxiety and spoke tenderly of her. When the time of prayer came, Sherrill listened in wonder to the prayers of faith that went up from many hearts for the life of Lutie's mother. Sherrill was amazed that they dared pray so confidently, and yet always with that submissive "Nevertheless, Thy will, not ours, be done."

She had a feeling as she listened that she had been sitting in a dark place all her life, and that during the last three weeks light had slowly begun to break. It seemed that tonight the light was like glory all around her.

These people actually lived with God, referred everything to Him, wanted nothing that He did not send. They were in a distinct and startling sense a separated people, and she was beginning to long with all her heart that she might truly be one with them.

The meeting was more than half over, and the lesson for the evening was well under way when the woman who sat next to Sherrill on the end seat next to the aisle, with a whispered word about catching her train, got up silently and slipped out. A moment later Sherrill became aware that someone else had taken her place, someone who had possibly been standing back by the door.

He came so silently, so unobtrusively, that Sherrill did not look up or notice him till he sat down, and then suddenly she seemed to feel rather than see that he was looking earnestly at her.

Startled, she glanced up to find herself looking straight into Graham Copeland's smiling eyes!

Then Sherrill's face lighted with a great gladness, and something flashed from eye to eye. He reached quietly over and clasped her hand, just a quick clinging pressure that no one would have noticed, and her fingers returned it. Then something flashed again from hand to hand, some understanding and knowledge of mutual joy.

It was like finding a dear old friend after having lost him. It was the knowledge that everything precious in the world had not been lost after all.

She lifted another shy glance and caught that look in his eyes again, and was thrilled to think he was here. What a wonderful thing this was! Never in all her acquaintance with Carter McArthur had there been anything like this, but she did not think of that now. She was just glad, glad, glad!

He took hold of one side of her Bible when another reference was announced, their hands touched again, and joy ran trembling in the touch. Shoulder to shoulder, their heads bowed over the sacred Book, they read the holy words together, and new strength and hope and sunshine seemed suddenly to come to Sherrill. Her friend had come back. He was all right. Her strange unwelcomed fears had been unfounded. Now she knew it. She had looked into his eyes and all was right. She was even gladder for that than that he was here.

This meeting with him might last only a few minutes more—it might never come again; but she was glad that he was this kind of man.

The class was crowded that night, and the chairs were very close together. The aisles were narrow. Yet the nearness was pleasant, and the fellowship with God's people. She stole a glance at her new friend's face and saw that he was watching the speaker, listening interestedly. He was not bored. He had not come here just to take her away home and make a fashionable call upon her. He seemed to be as glad to be here as she was to have him, and to have entered into the spirit of the hour like any of them. Was that just an outstanding characteristic of his that he could adjust himself to any surroundings and seem to be at home?

But no, she felt he was truly in sympathy here, more even than he had been at the wedding reception. To a certain extent he had been an outsider there, entering in only so far as would help her, but it really seemed as if he belonged here. Or was that just her imagination?

She wondered if she ought to suggest going home. Perhaps he had only a short time. But he settled that by suddenly turning and smiling into her eyes and whispering, "He's very fine, isn't he?" and suddenly her joy seemed running over so that she could hardly keep glad tears from her eyes. To have a friend like this, and to have him feel as she did about this sacred hour. Why, that was greatest of all!

Then it came to her that just the other day she had felt that all the troubles in the world were crowded into her small life, and now all at once they had lifted. What did it mean? Was God showing her that He had infinitely greater joys in store for her somewhere than any she had lost?

These thoughts raced swiftly through her mind while her companion fluttered the leaves of the Bible, finding the next reference as if his fingers knew their way well about the greatest book in the world, and then their hands settled together holding it again.

Well, thought Sherrill, *I seem to be losing my head a*

little, but I'm just going to be glad while gladness is here.
And then somehow their spirits seemed to go along
together during the rest of the meeting, flashing a look
of appreciation when something unusual was said.

The rest of the hour seemed all too short. It was like
a bit of heaven to Sherrill. When it was over Copeland
spoke graciously to the friends about her and greeted the
teacher when he came down to speak to them.

"You know, we have a great Bible school out in my
city, too," he said with a smile as he shook hands with the
teacher. "I don't get as much of it as I would like. I'm pretty
busy. But sometimes I run in there for a bit of refreshment."

Out into the sweet darkness of the summer evening he
guided her, his hand slipped within her arm in a pleasant
possessive way. He seemed to have already located her
car, and as they went toward it he said in vibrant tones,
"I didn't know you were interested in this sort of thing.
I'm so glad. It gives us one more tie for our—friendship.
I'm sure now that you must know the Lord Jesus."

"And oh, *do you?*" Sherrill's voice was vibrant, too.
"I've only known Him a very short time, and I'm very
ignorant, but—I want to learn."

Sherrill's hand was clasped in his now, but she did
not realize it till he put her in the car.

"Shall I drive?" he asked, as if he had been taking care
of her all his life.

"Yes, please," she said eagerly, "and tell me, how did
you happen to be there? How did you know I—?"

"Your aunt told me the way," he said, anticipating her question. "I got to the house just after you had left. She told me how to find you and I came at once."

"Then—you had been there some time?"

"Yes. I came in during the singing just before the lesson. They certainly can sing there, can't they?"

"Oh yes. But I'm sorry I didn't see you. I could have come out—" She hesitated.

"Wasn't it better to stay?" he asked, smiling, looking down into her face. "It was a sweet and blessed fellowship, and I needed something like that. I've been in a feverish sordid atmosphere ever since I left here, and I was glad to get the world out of my lungs for a little while. Besides, I enjoyed watching your face. I got a double blessing out of the meeting from enjoying your interest."

"My face?" said Sherrill in sudden confusion. "Oh!" and she put up a hand to her flushed cheek. "Were you where you could see me? I didn't know there was anything in my face but ignorance and amazement. I can't get used to the wonders of the Bible."

"It was very—" He hesitated, then added, "Very precious to watch," and his voice was almost reverent as he spoke.

"Oh!" said Sherrill, at a loss for a reply. But he helped her by going on to speak in a matter-of-fact voice.

"I'm glad to get here at last," he said. "I've been going through a strenuous siege of work, in Washington and New York, back and forth, sometimes in such haste that

I had to fly. No time to call my soul my own, and then an unexpected business trip to the south which kept me working night and day. I thought I would be able to stop off for a few hours before this, but I couldn't make it. I was afraid you would have forgotten me by this time."

"No," said Sherrill quickly. "I could not forget you. You came to me in a time of great trouble, and I shall never forget how you helped me. I'm so glad to have another opportunity to really thank you. I didn't half know what I was doing that night."

"Well, I'm glad to be back at last," he said. "I didn't want to lose this friendship. It seemed to be something very rare sent to me right out of the blue, you know."

He gave her a wonderful smile that set her heart thrilling.

I'm surely losing my head, she told herself. *I mustn't be a fool. But I can't help being glad he is like this even if I never see him again.*

Sherrill was sorry when the short ride was over and they had to go into the house and be conventional. She treasured the little quiet talk in the darkness. It was easier somehow in the dark to get acquainted and not be embarrassed at all they had been through together.

Aunt Pat was waiting for them eagerly, and Sherrill felt her kind keen glance searching her face as she sat down.

"Now," said Aunt Pat, "before we begin to talk, how much time have we got to get acquainted? What time did you say you had to leave?"

"I think your local train leaves about ten after eleven," answered Copeland. "I have a taxi coming for me in plenty of time, so I do not have to keep thinking about that. But perhaps I shall be keeping you up too late?"

He looked eagerly at the old lady.

"Late?" said the old lady, laughing. "We're regular night hawks, Sherry and I. We often sit up till after midnight reading. I'm only sorry you have to go so soon."

All too rapidly the brief time fled. He seemed so like an old acquaintance that he fit right into their pleasant cozy evening. Aunt Pat discovered that they had mutual acquaintances in Chicago, and Sherrill sat listening to their talk and wondering how she could ever have entertained that haunting fear about this wonderful stranger. It was such a relief to have the fear gone forever. Not that she ever really suspected him herself—she still loyally maintained to her own heart—but she had been so afraid that others would if it ever came to an investigation.

Then he would turn and look at her suddenly and smile, and something would happen to her heart, something wild and sweet that never had happened before. She did not understand it. Never in all her acquaintance with Carter McArthur had there been anything like this. It was like finding an old friend after having lost him. It was knowing that she had not lost every precious thing in the world after all. It was rest and peace and joy just to know she had a friend like that.

The lovely color flooded into her face, and joy was in her starry eyes. That pinched look of suffering that Copeland had seen in her face the first night was gone. He looked again and again to make sure. It was not there anymore. The glance in his eyes when he turned toward her always with that wonderful smile thrilled her as nothing had ever done before.

In vain she chided herself for feeling so utterly glad just because of his presence. He was only making a call, she told herself. But that gladness would keep surging over her like a healing tide that was washing away the pain and anguish she had received the night she found out that Carter was false to her. He might go away in a few minutes and she never see him again perhaps, but still she would be glad, glad that he had come tonight and reassured her that he was just what she had thought him at first. New strength and life and hope seemed to come to her as the moments flew by.

Aunt Pat took herself off upstairs for a few minutes to hunt for a book they had been talking about, and Sherrill had a little time alone with him.

"You are feeling better?" he said in a low tone, coming over to sit beside her on the couch, scanning her face searchingly.

"Oh yes," she said, deeply touched at the tenderness of his tone. "I'm beginning to see some reasons why it all had to be. I'm beginning to understand what I was saved from!"

He reached out and laid his hand quietly over hers for an instant with a soft pressure.

"That is good to know!" he said gently. "You were very brave!"

"Oh no!" she said, her eyelids drooping. "As I look back, I'm so ashamed at the way I played out. It was dreadful the way I let you stand by and go through all that awful reception! But I'm so glad to have this opportunity to really thank you for what you did for me that night. As long as I live I will always feel that that was the greatest thing any man ever did for any woman in trouble. An utter stranger! You were wonderful! If you had been preparing all your life for that one evening, you could not have done everything more perfectly."

"Perhaps I had!" he said very softly, his fingers closing about hers warmly again, his eyes catching hers as they lifted to look wonderingly at him, and holding her gaze with a deep sweet look.

Then suddenly Gemmie appeared at the door with her rubber-silent tread bearing a small table and placed it, covering it with a festive cloth. Gemmie, seeming to see nothing, but knowing perfectly, Sherrill understood, about those two clasped hands between them there on the sofa.

Gemmie brought coffee in a silver pot with delicate cups and saucers, tiny sandwiches, cinnamon toast, little frosted cakes, and then an ice. Gemmie managed to remain nearby until Aunt Pat returned with her book.

Gemmie watching like a cat!

And the two talked, pleasant nothings, conscious of that touch that had been between them, conscious of the light in each other's eyes, glad in each other's presence, getting past the years of their early youth into a time and place where there was only their two selves in the universe. Wondering that anything had been worthwhile before, thinking, each, perhaps, that the other did not understand.

Aunt Pat came back with her book and ate with them, a happy little meal. She watched her girl contentedly, watched the young man approvingly, and remembered days of long ago and the light in a boy-lover's eyes. That was the same light, or else she was mightily mistaken.

Then all at once Copeland looked at his watch with an exclamation of dismay and sprang to his feet.

"It is almost time for my train!" he said. "I wonder what has become of my taxi! The man promised to be here in plenty of time."

"Gemmie! Look out and see if the taxi is there!" called Aunt Pat.

"No, ma'am, there's no taxi come. I been watching out the window!" said the woman primly with a baleful look at Copeland as if his word was to be doubted. Gemmie thought he likely hadn't told the taxi man to come at all. She thought he likely wanted to stay all night.

"It isn't far; I'll try to make it!" said Copeland. "I'm sorry to leave in such a rush. You'll forgive me, won't you?

I've had such a wonderful time!"

"Why, I'll take you, of course," said Sherrill, suddenly rousing to her privilege. "My car is right outside. Come, out this side door. We've time enough."

"But you'll have to come back alone!" he protested.

"I often do!" she laughed. "Come, we can make it if we go at once—although I wish you could stay."

"But I mustn't!" said Copeland. "I must get back at once. It's important!"

He took Aunt Pat's hand in a quick grasp.

"You have been good to let me come!" he said fervently. "May I come soon again?"

"You certainly may!" said Aunt Pat. "I like you, young man! There! Go! Sherrill's blowing her horn. You haven't any time to waste!"

With an appreciative smile he sprang to the door and was gone. Aunt Pat watched them drive away and then turned back with a smile of satisfaction to see Gemmie standing at the back of the hall like Nemesis, looking very severe.

"That's what I call a real man, Gemmie!" said Aunt Pat with a note of emphasis in her tone.

"Well, you can't most always sometimes tell, Miss Patricia," said Gemmie primly with an offended uplift of her chin.

"And then again you *can!*" said Aunt Pat happily. "Now, Gemmie, you can wait till Miss Sherry comes back, and then lock up. I'm going to bed."

Out in the night together Sherrill kept the wheel.

"I'd better drive this time," she explained as she put her foot on the starter. "It will save time because you don't know the way. You be ready to spring out as soon as I stop, if the train is coming."

Sherrill flashed around corners in the dark and pulled up at the station a full two minutes before the train was due.

"I have my ticket, and my baggage is checked in the city," said Copeland, smiling, "so this two minutes is all to the good."

He drew her hand within his arm, and they walked slowly up the platform, both conscious of the sweetness of companionship.

"I'm coming back soon," said Copeland, laying his free hand softly over hers again. "Your aunt said I might."

"That will be wonderful!" said Sherrill, feeling that it was hard to find words to express her delight. "How soon?"

"Just as soon as I can get a chance!" he said, holding her hand a little closer in his own.

Then they heard the distant sound of the train approaching and had to turn and retrace their steps down the platform.

"I'll let you know!" he said.

Somehow it took very few words to complete the

sweetness of the moment. The train thundered up and they stood there waiting, her arm within his.

"I wish you were going along," he said suddenly, looking down at her with a smile. "It's going to be a long lonely journey, and there is a great deal I would like to talk to you about, but we'll save it for next time."

The train slowed down to a stop, and the few passengers from up the road came straggling out.

Copeland and Sherrill stood back just a little out of the way till the steps should be passable, and as they looked up, Mrs. Battersea hovered in sight through the car door, coming back from an evening of bridge with some friends in the next suburb.

"Isn't that your Battledore-and-shuttlecock lady of the reception?" murmured Copeland with a grin.

Sherrill giggled.

"Mrs. Battersea," she prompted.

"Yes, I thought it was something like that."

The lady brought her heavy body down the car steps and arrived on the platform a few feet from them.

Copeland stooped a little closer and spoke softly: "What do you say if we give her something to talk about? Do you mind if I kiss you good-bye?"

For answer Sherrill gave him a lovely mischievous smile and lifted her lips to meet his.

Then Mrs. Battersea, the conductor just swinging to the step of the car and waving his signal to the engineer, the platform and all the surroundings, melted away, and heaven and earth touched. The preciousness of that moment Sherrill never would forget. Afterward she remembered that kiss in comparison with some of the passionate half-fierce caresses that Carter used to give, kisses that almost frightened her sometimes with their intensity, and made her unsure of herself, and she knew this reverent kiss was not in the same world with those others.

With that sweet tender kiss, and a pressure of the hand he still held, he left her and swung to the lower step which the conductor had vacated for a higher one as the train rolled out of the station.

He stood there as long as he could see her, and she watched him, drank in the look in his eyes, and suddenly said to her frightened happy heart, "He is dear! *Dear!* Oh, I love him! I *love* him! He is no longer a stranger! He is beloved! The Beloved Stranger!"

Then as the train swept past the platform lights into the darkness beyond, with her heart in her happy eyes, she turned, and there stood Mrs. Battersea, her lorgnette up, drinking it all in! Even that last wave of the hand that wafted another caress toward her before he vanished into the darkness!

Sherrill faced her in dismay, coming down to earth again with a thump. Then with a smile she said in a cool little tone, "Oh, Mrs. Battersea! You haven't your car here. May I take you home?"

And Mrs. Battersea, bursting with curiosity, gushed

eagerly, "Oh, Sherrill Cameron, is that really you? Why, how fortunate I am to have met you. I've just twisted my ankle badly, and my chauffeur is sick tonight. I expected to take a taxi, but there doesn't seem to be any."

Then as she stuffed herself into Sherrill's little roadster, she asked eagerly, "And who was that attractive man you were seeing off on the train? That couldn't have been the charming stranger who was at the wedding, could it? Oh—Sherrill! Naughty, naughty! I thought there was a reason for the changes in the wedding plans!"

Sherrill was glad when at last she reached her own room and could shut the door on the world and shut herself in with her own thoughts and memories. But a moment later Gemmie knocked at the door and brought a message from her aunt that she would like to see her for a minute.

Gemmie looked at Sherrill's lovely red cheeks and smiling lips coldly, distantly. Sherrill felt as if she would like to shake her. But she gave her a brilliant smile and went swiftly to her aunt's room.

"Well," said the old lady from among the pillows of her old-fashioned four-poster bed, "I hope you see now that he never stole that necklace!"

"Aunt Pat!" said Sherrill in an indignant, horrified tone. "I never thought he did! I *knew* he didn't! But I wanted him to come back to prove to *you* that he hadn't! He was *my* stranger. I knew he wasn't that kind, but I couldn't expect other people to realize what he was. I was afraid you would always suspect him if he didn't come back."

"Hmm!" said the old lady contemptuously. "I know. You didn't give me much credit for discernment. Thought you had it all. Now, run along to your bed, child. You've had enough for one evening. I just wanted you to know I think he's all right. Good night!"

Chapter 19

Sherrill awoke the next morning with a song in her heart, but while she was dressing she talked seriously with herself. It was utterly impossible, she told herself, that a splendid man like Graham Copeland could care about a girl he had seen only a few hours, and especially under such circumstances. There was that precious kiss, but it had been given half in fun, to carry out the joke on Mrs. Battersea. Men didn't think much of just a good-bye kiss—most men, that is. But her heart told her that this man was different. She knew that it had meant much to him.

Then she told herself to be sensible, that it was wonderful enough just to have a real friend when she was feeling so lonely and left out of everything.

Of course he was very far away. He might even forget

her soon, but at least he was a friend, a young friend, to tide her over this lost, humiliating spot in her life.

And he had said he would come soon again! Well, she mustn't count too much on that, but her heart leaped at the thought, and she went about her room singing softly:

"When I have Jesus in my heart,
What can take Him away?
Once take Jesus into my heart,
And He has come to stay."

The trill of her voice reached across the hall to Aunt Pat's room, and the old lady smiled to herself and murmured, "The dear child!" and then gave a little wistful sigh.

It was raining hard all day that day, but Sherrill was like a bright ray of sunshine. It was not raining rain to her; it was raining pansies and forget-me-nots in her heart, and she did not at all understand what meant this great lightheartedness that had come to her. She had never felt toward anyone before as she felt toward this stranger. She had utterly forgotten her lost bridegroom. She chided herself again and again and tried to be sober and staid, but still there was that happy little thrill in her heart, and her lips bubbled over into song now and then when she hardly knew it.

Aunt Pat sat with a dreamy smile on her lips and watched her, going back over the years to an old country graveyard and a boy with grave, sweet eyes.

Three days this went on, three happy days for both Sherrill and Aunt Pat, and on the morning of the fourth day there came a great box of golden-hearted roses for Sherrill, and no card whatever in them. An hour later the telephone rang. A long-distance call for Sherrill.

With cheeks aflame and heart beating like a trip-hammer, she hurried to the telephone, not even noticing the cold disapproval of Gemmie, who had brought the message.

"Is that you, Sherrill?" came leaping over the wire in a voice that had suddenly grown precious.

"Oh yes, Graham!" answered Sherrill in a voice that sounded like a caress. "Where are you?"

"I'm in Chicago," said a strong glad voice. "I want to come and see you this afternoon about something very important. Are you going to be at home?"

"Oh, surely, yes, all day," lilted Sherrill, "but how could you possibly come and see me today if you are in Chicago?"

"I'm flying! I'll be there just as soon as I can. I'm starting right away!"

"Oh, how wonderful!" breathed Sherrill, starry eyes looking into the darkness around the telephone, almost lighting up the place, smiling lips beaming into the reciever. "I—I'm—*glad*!"

"That's *grand*!" said the deep big voice at the other end of the line. "I'm gladder than ever that you are glad! Are you all right?"

"Oh, quite all right!" chirruped Sherrill. "I'm righter than all right—*now!*"

"Well, then, I'll be seeing you—shortly. I'm at the airport now, and I'm starting *immediately!* Good-bye—*darling!*"

The last word was so soft, so indefinite that it gave the impression of having been whispered after the lips had been turned away from the phone, and Sherrill was left in doubt whether she had not just imagined it after all.

She came away from the telephone with her eyes still starrier and her cheeks rosier than they had been when she went to it. She brushed by the still-disapproving Gemmie, who was doing some very unnecessary dusting in the hall, and rushed up to her aunt's room.

"Oh, Aunt Pat!" she said breathlessly. "He's coming! He's flying! He's coming this afternoon. Do you mind if we don't go for a ride as we'd planned?"

"Who's coming, child?" snapped Aunt Pat with her wry grin and a wicked little twinkle in her eye. "Be more explicit."

"Why, Graham is coming," said Sherrill eagerly, her face wreathed in smiles.

"Graham indeed! And who might Graham be? Graham Smith or Graham Jones? And when did we get so intimate as to be calling each other by our first names?"

For answer Sherrill went laughing and hid her hot cheeks in the roseleaf coolness of the old lady's neck. The old lady patted her shoulder and smoothed her soft hair as if she had been a baby.

"Well," said Aunt Pat with her twisted smile, "it begins to look as if that young man had a great deal of business in the east, doesn't it? It must be expensive to travel around in airplanes the way he does, but it's certainly interesting to have a man drop right down out of the skies that way. Now, let me see, what are you going to wear, child? How about that little blue organdy? You look like a sweet child in that. I like it. Wear that. Those cute little white scallops around the neck and sleeves remind me of a dress I had when I was sixteen. My mother knew how to make scallops like that."

"I'll wear it, of course," said Sherrill eagerly. "How lovely it must have been to have a mother to make scallops for you. But I don't know as that is any better than having a dear precious aunt to buy them for you. You just spoil me, Auntie Pat! Aren't you afraid I'll 'spoil on you' as Lutie's mother says?"

"Well, I've tried hard enough," said the old lady, smiling, "but I can't seem to accomplish anything in that line. I guess you are the kind that doesn't spoil."

All the morning Gemmie came and went with grim set lips and disapproving air, going about her duties scrupulously, doing all that was required of her, yet saying as plainly as words could have said that they were all under a blind delusion and she was the only one who saw through things and knew how they were being deceived by this flying youth who was about to appear on the scene again. She sniffed at the gorgeous yellow roses when she passed by them and wiped her eyes surreptitiously. She didn't like to see her beloved family deceived.

But time got away at last, and Sherrill went to dress for the guest, for they had been consulting airports and had found out the probable hour of his arrival.

Sherrill was just putting the last touches to her hair when Aunt Pat tapped at the door and walked in with a tiny string of pearls in her hand, real pearls they were, and very small and lovely.

"I want you to wear these, dearie," she said in a sweet old voice that seemed made of tears and smiles and reminded one of lavender and rose leaves.

Sherrill whirled about quickly, but when she saw the little string of pearls, her face went white, and her eyes took on a frightened look. She drew back and caught hold of the dressing table.

"Oh, not another necklace!" she said in distress. "Dear Aunt Patricia. I really couldn't wear it! I'd lose it! I'm afraid of necklaces!"

"Nonsense, child!" said the old lady, smiling. "That other necklace is going to turn up sometime, I'm sure. Remember I told you those stones were registered, and eventually if someone stole them, they will be sold, will ultimately arrive at some of the large dealers and be traced. You're not to fret about them, even if it is some time before we hear of them. And as for this necklace, it's one I had when I was a little girl, and it is charmed. I always had a happy time when I wore it, and I want you to wear this for me this afternoon. I like to see you in it, and I like to think of you with it on. You'll do it for me, little girl. I never had a little girl of my own, and so you'll have to have them. I'm quite too old now to wear such a childish trinket."

So Sherrill half fearfully let her clasp the quaint chain about her neck, and stooped and kissed the dear old lady on the parting of her silvery curls.

Sooner than Sherrill had dared to hope, he came. She watched him from behind her window curtain while he paid the taxi driver and then gave a quick upward look at the windows of the house. No, she had not been mistaken in her memory of him. That firm, clean, lean look about the chin, that merry twinkle in his eyes. The late-afternoon sun lit up his well-knit form. There was a covert strength behind him that filled her with satisfaction and comfort. He was a man one could trust utterly. She couldn't be deceived in him!

Then Gemmie's cold voice broke stiffly on her absorption: "The young man is here, Miss Sherrill!"

"Oh, Gemmie," caroled Sherrill as she hurried laughing from her window. "Do take that solemn look off your face. You look like the old meetinghouse down at the corner of Graff Street. Do look happy, Gemmie!"

"I always look as happy as I feel, Miss Sherrill," said Gemmie frigidly.

But Sherrill suddenly whirled on her, gave her a

resounding kiss on her thin astonished lips, and went cheerfully past her down the stairs, looking like a sweet child in her little blue organdy with the white scallops and pearls, and her gold hair like a halo around her eager face. The small blue shoes laced with black velvet ribbons about her ankles fairly twinkled as she ran down the steps, and the young man who stood at the foot of the stairs, his eyes alight with an old, old story, thought her the loveliest thing he had ever seen.

Aunt Pat had managed to absorb every single servant about the place, suddenly and intensively, and there wasn't a soul around to witness their meeting, though perhaps it would not have made the least difference to them, for they were aware of nobody but their own two selves.

She went to his arms as to a haven she had always known she possessed, and his arms went around her and drew her close, with her gold head right over his heart, her cheek rubbing deliciously against the fine serge of his dark blue coat. Dark blue serge, how she loved it! He had worn a coat like that when she first found him!

He laid his lips against her forehead, her soft hair brushing his face, and held her close for a moment, breathing, "Oh, my darling!"

Then suddenly they drew apart, almost embarrassed, each afraid of having been too eager, and then drew together again, his arm about her waist, drawing her into the small reception room and down to the small sofa just inside the portiere.

The man laughed softly, triumphantly.

"I was afraid to come," he said. "I was afraid it would be too soon, after—after—that other man!"

"You mean Carter?" said Sherrill, and then with a sudden inner enlightenment, "Why, there never was any other man but you." She said it with a burst of joy. "I thought there was, but now I know there *never* was! At least I thought he was what you are! There has *always* been you—in my thoughts, I guess!" and she dropped her eyes shyly, afraid to have too quickly revealed her heart.

"How could I have been so mistaken!" she added with quick anger at herself. "Oh, I should have had to suffer longer for being so stupid!"

But he drew her within his arms again and laid his lips on hers, then on her sweet eyelids, and then, his cheek against hers, he whispered, "Oh, my precious little love!"

Suddenly he brought something from his pocket, something bright and flashing, and slipped it on her finger. Startled, she looked down and saw a great blue diamond, the loveliest she had ever seen, set in delicate platinum handiwork.

"That marks you as mine," he said with a wonderful look into her eyes. "And now, darling, we've got to work fast, for I haven't much time."

"Oh!" said Sherrill in instant alarm. "Have you got to go back again right away?"

"Not back again," he laughed, "but off somewhere else. And I don't know what you'll think of what I've come to propose. Maybe you'll think it is all wrong, rushing things this way when we've scarcely known each other yet, and you don't really know a thing about me or my family."

"That wouldn't matter," said Sherrill emphatically, without even a thought of the emerald necklace, though Gemmie at that moment was stalking noisily through the hall beyond the curtain.

"You precious one!" said Copeland, drawing her close again and lifting one of her hands, the one with the ring on the third finger, to his lips.

"Well, now, you see, it's this way. I'm being sent quite unexpectedly to South America on a matter of very special business. It's a great opportunity for me, and if I succeed in my mission it means that I'll be on Easy Street, of course. But I may have to stay down there anywhere from six weeks to six months to accomplish my purpose—"

"Ohhh!" breathed Sherrill with a sound like pain.

He smiled, pressed her fingers close, and went on speaking.

"I feel that way, too, dearest. I can't bear to be away from you so long when I've only just found you. And I've been audacious enough to want to take you with me! Do you suppose you could ever bring yourself to see it that way, too? Or have I asked too much? I've brought all sorts of credentials and things with me."

"I don't need credentials," said Sherrill, nestling close

to him. "I love you." And suddenly she felt she understood that other poor girl who had said she would marry Carter McArthur if she knew she had to go through hell with him. That was what love was, utter self-abnegation, utter devotion. That was why love was so dangerous perhaps to some. But this love was different. This man knew her Christ, belonged to Him. Oh, what had God done for her! Taken away a man who was not worthy, and given her one of His own children!

His arms were about her again, drawing her close, his words of endearment murmured in her ear.

"You will go?" he asked gently. "You mean *you will go*?" There was an awed delight in his voice.

"Of course!" said Sherrill softly. "When would we have to go?"

"That's it," he said with a bit of trouble in his eyes as he looked down on her anxiously. "I have to go *tonight*! Would that be rushing you too much? I'd make it longer if I could, but there is need for great haste in my business. In fact, if it could have waited until the next boat, I wouldn't have been sent at all; a senior member of the firm would have gone in my place. But just now neither of them could get away, so it fell to my lot, and I had no chance to protest."

Sherrill sat up and looked startled.

"Tonight!" she echoed. "Why, I could go, of course—but—I'm not sure how Aunt Patricia would take it. She's been wonderful to me, and I wouldn't like to hurt her. I ought to ask her—!"

"Of course!" said Copeland. "Where is she? Let's go to her at once! I'll try to make her see it. And—well—if this thing succeeds, I'll be able perhaps to make it up to her about losing you so suddenly. It might just happen that I would be put in the east to look after a new branch of the business. We could live around here if that would make it pleasanter for her."

"How wonderful!" said Sherrill. "Let's go up to her room! I know she'll be kind of expecting us."

So they went up the stairs with arms about one another, utterly unaware of Gemmie, peering out stolidly from behind the living room portieres.

They appeared that way in Aunt Pat's doorway when she had bidden them enter, for all the world like two children come to confess some prank.

"I see how it is with you," said Aunt Pat with a pleased grin as they stood a second, at a loss how to begin. "I expected it, of course."

"I know you don't know a thing about me," began the lover, searching around in his legal mind for the things he had prepared to say, "but I've brought some credentials."

"Don't bother!" said Aunt Pat indifferently. "I wasn't quite a fool! You didn't suppose I was going to put my child in danger of a second heartbreak, did you? I looked you up the day the first flowers came."

"Why, Aunt Pat!" said Sherrill, aghast. "You said you trusted him utterly! You said you knew a man when you saw one!"

"Of course I did!" said Aunt Pat, not in the least disturbed. "I knew he was all right. But when it was a matter of you, Sherrill, I knew I had to have something more than my own intuition to go on. I wasn't going to go and give you away to every stranger that came along with a nice face and a pleasant manner. Someday I expect to go to heaven and meet your father and mother again, and I don't want them to blame me, so I called up my old friend Judge Porter in Chicago and asked him to tell me all he knew about this young man. Don't worry, young man, I made him think it was some business I wanted to place in your hands. But I found out a lot more than your business standing, and I knew I would, thanks to my old friend George Porter. I went to school with him, and he always was very thorough in all he did. So it's all right, young man. You have my blessing!"

Copeland's face fairly blazed with joy, but before he had time to thank the old lady, Sherrill spoke.

"But there's more, Aunt Pat! He wants us to be married right away!"

"That's natural," said Aunt Pat dryly, with her wry smile.

"Yes, but Aunt Pat, he's being sent to South America, and he has to go tonight!"

"Tonight!" said the old lady alertly. "Hmm! Well, it's fortunate you have a wedding dress all ready, Sherrill."

"Oh," said Sherrill with a quick look of astonishment. "I hadn't thought about it. Could I wear that? I could just

284

wear my going-away dress, of course."

"No," said Aunt Pat. "Wear your own wedding dress! Don't let yourself be cheated out of that just because you had to lend it to another poor girl for a few minutes. Get your mind rid of that poor fool who would have married you and then made you suffer the rest of your life. Don't be foolish. It was *your* wedding dress and not hers. And she couldn't have hurt it much in that short time. Don't you think she ought to wear a real wedding dress, Graham?" asked the old lady briskly, turning to the young man as if she had known him since his first long trousers.

Copeland's eyes lighted.

"I'd love to see you in it!" he said, looking at Sherrill with adoring eyes.

"Oh, then I'll wear it, of course," said Sherrill with starry eyes. "It was really awfully hard to give up wearing it—it was so pretty."

"Of course!" said Aunt Pat brusquely. "And why should you? Forget that other girl, and the whole silly muddle. Now, young man, what is there to do besides getting her suitcase packed? Have you got the license yet?"

"No, but I know where to get it, and I'm going for it right away."

"Very well," said Aunt Pat. "I'll have the chauffeur take you. Sherrill, what about bridesmaids? Yours are all scattered."

"Do I have to have them?" asked Sherrill, aghast.

"I don't see why," said her aunt. "I suppose we'll have to ask in a few friends, a dozen perhaps, just Cousin Phyllis and her family and maybe the Grants, they're such old friends. I'll think it over."

"And I wouldn't have to be given away or any of that fuss either, would I? It all seems so silly," pleaded Sherrill. "I thought before that if I had to do it over again, I'd never want all that. Couldn't Graham and I just walk downstairs together and be married without any elaborate extras?"

"You certainly could," said Aunt Pat. "If your Graham doesn't feel that he is being cheated out of his rights to a formal wedding."

"Not on your life!" grinned Graham Copeland. "I'd hate it all! But of course I'd go through a good many times that and worse to get her if it was necessary. All I want is a simple ceremony and your blessing."

"Blest be!" said Aunt Pat. "Now, get you gone and come back as soon as possible. Sherrill, send Gemmie to me, and tell her to send up the cook. We'll scratch together a few green peas and a piece of bread and butter for a simple little wedding supper. No, don't worry. I won't do anything elaborate. What time do you have to leave, Graham? All right. She'll be ready!"

Sherrill stayed behind after her lover had gone, to throw her arms around her aunt's neck and kiss her many times.

"Oh, Aunt Pat! You are the greatest woman in the

world!" she said excitedly.

"Well, you're getting a real man this time, and no mistake!" said the old lady with satisfaction. "When you have time, I'll show you the letter my friend Judge Porter wrote about him, but that'll keep. You had better go and get your things together. I'll send Gemmie to help you as soon as I'm done with her."

So Sherrill hurried to her room on glad feet and began to get her things together. She went to the trunk room and found her own new suitcase with its handsome fittings, still partly packed as it had been on that fateful wedding night. She went to the drawers and closets and got out the piles of pretty lingerie, the lovely negligees, dumped them on the bed, and looked at them with a dreamy smile, as if they were long-lost friends come back to their own, but when Gemmie arrived, stern and disapproving still, she had not gotten far in her packing.

"Miss Patricia says you're to lie down for half an hour right away!" she announced grimly. "And I'm to do your packing. She says you're tired to death and won't be fit to travel if you don't."

"All right!" said Sherrill with a lilt in her voice, kicking her little blue shoes off and submitting to be tucked into her bed, blue organdy and all.

Gemmie, with a baleful glance at her, shut her lips tight and went silently about her packing, laying in things with skillful hand, folding them precisely, thinking of things that Sherrill in her excited state never would have remembered. And Sherrill with a happy sigh closed her eyes and tried to realize that it was really herself and not some other girl who was lying here, going to be married within the next few hours.

But there are limits to the length of time even an excited girl like Sherrill can lie still, and before the half hour was over she was up, her voice fresh and rested, chattering away to the silent woman who only sniffed and wiped a furtive eye with a careful handkerchief. It was all too evident that Gemmie did not approve of the marriage. But what could one do with such a woman who had been perfectly satisfied with a man like Carter? She was beyond all reason.

Sherrill went over to see her aunt for a few minutes and have a last little talk.

Aunt Pat invited just a very few of their most intimate friends, and some of those couldn't come on such short notice. "Just to make it plain that we're not trying to hide something," she said to Sherrill with her twinkly grin. "People are so apt to rake up some reason to gossip. But anyway what do we care? The Grants are coming and they are the pick of the lot, and Cousin Phyllis. She would never have forgiven us if she hadn't been asked. She did complain about the shortness of the time and want it put off till tomorrow, but I told her that was impossible."

Then Sherrill told her what Copeland had said about

the possibility of his being located in the east when he returned, and Aunt Pat gave her first little mite of a sigh and said with a wistful look like a child, "Well, if he could see his way clear to coming here to this house and living, it would be the best I'd ask of earth any longer. It'll be your house anyway when I'm gone, and I'd like you to just take it over now and run it anytime you will. I could sort of board or visit with you. I'm getting old, you know. You speak of it sometime to him when it seems wise, but don't be hampered by it, of course." Aunt Pat sighed again.

"You dear!" said Sherrill, bending over her and kissing her tenderly. "I'd love it, and I'm sure he would, too. Now don't you worry, and don't you feel lonesome, or we'll just tuck you in the suitcase and take you along with us to South America."

Aunt Pat grinned and patted Sherrill's cheek smartly. "You silly little girl! Now run along and get your wedding frills on. It's almost time for the guests to be here, and you are not ready."

So Sherrill ran away laughing and had to tell Gemmie to please bring the big box containing the wedding dress.

"You're not going to wear *that*!" said Gemmie, aghast.

"Certainly I am, Gemmie," said Sherrill firmly. "It's my dress, isn't it? Hurry, please. It's getting late!"

Gemmie gave her a wild look.

"I should have been told," she said coldly. "The dress should have been pressed."

289

"Nonsense, Gemmie; it doesn't matter whether there is a wrinkle or two, but there won't be. You put tissue in every fold. Anyway, you can't press it. It's too late!"

Gemmie brought the great pasteboard box, thumped it down on the bed unopened, and stalked into the bathroom, pretending to have urgent work there picking up damp towels for the laundry.

Sherrill, feeling annoyed at the stubborn faithful old woman, went over to the bed and lifted the cover of the big box.

There lay the soft white folds of the veil like a lovely mist, and above them like blooms among the snow the beautiful wreath of orange blossoms, not a petal out of place. Gemmie had done her work perfectly when she put them away. And beneath the veil Sherrill could see the gleam of the satin wedding gown. Oh, it was lovely, and Sherrill's heart leaped with pleasure to think she might wear it again, wear it this time without a doubt or pang or shrinking!

She turned away humming a soft little tune and went about her dressing.

Gemmie had laid out all the lovely silken garments, and it was like playing a game to put them on, leisurely, happily.

When she was ready for the dress, she called Gemmie, and then Aunt Pat came in, already attired in her soft gray robes, looking herself as lovely as any wedding could desire.

"I'm glad I can have a little leisure this time," she said, settling into a big chair and smoothing her silks about her. "Last time I had to be hustled off to the church when there were a hundred and one things I wanted to attend to at home. I don't know that I care much for church weddings anyway unless you *have* to have a mob."

Gemmie's eyes were red as if she had been weeping, and she came forward to officiate at the donning of the dress with a long sorrowful look on her face.

It was just at that moment that there came a tap at the door, and the maid handed in a package.

"It was special delivery," she explained. "I thought maybe you'd want it right away."

"You might've known she'd have no time to bother with the like of that now," said Gemmie ungraciously, taking the package from the girl.

"Oh, but I want to see it, Gemmie," cried Sherrill. "Thank you, Emily, for bringing it up. I want to see everything. You don't suppose anybody is sending a wedding present, do you, Aunt Pat? Don't tell me I've got to go through all that again!"

"Open it up, Gemmie!" ordered Aunt Pat. "It might be something Graham has had sent to you, you know, Sherrill."

With something like a sniff, Gemmie reached for the scissors and snipped the cords.

"It'll not be from him!" she said tartly. "It's from across the water!"

"Across the water? Europe?" said Sherrill and reached for the package.

"Hmm! Across the water!" said Aunt Pat, sitting up eagerly. "Open it quick, Sherry. It might be interesting!"

Chapter 20

If Carter McArthur had been told on the first day out from New York that before the end of the voyage he would be almost reconciled to his fate as husband of a penniless bride, he would have been astonished. But it was nevertheless true.

Arla Prentiss had always been a clever girl, and Arla McArthur driven by necessity became almost brilliant in managing her difficult affairs. She had taken the material at hand and used it. Even Hurley Kirkwood and the two old high school classmates became assets in the affair. Before the voyage was over, she had even won out with the man Sheldon and used him to her own ends.

How they came to be seated at a table in a pleasant but obscure corner of the dining room with Hurley Kirkwood, Helen and Bob Shannon, and a very deaf old man who paid no attention to any of them, was never known to Carter McArthur. He was very angry when he discovered it, and put Arla through the third degree, but in the end he saw it was a good thing. There was nobody at the table they needed to be nervous about. The three old acquaintances had never heard of Sherrill Cameron and her gorgeous wedding at which she was not the bride, and would be very unlikely to hear now, at least before the voyage was over. Moreover, they were good company, and there was a certain pleasant intimacy that it could not be denied relieved the strain under which both Arla and Carter had been. There was no danger of some embarrassing question coming up.

Carter grew quite genial and like his old youthful self in their company, accepted the stale jokes about his fondness for Arla with the same complacency that he used to do in the old days when they first began to go together, and actually treated Arla with a degree of his former devotion. If he realized that Hurley Kirkwood was sending home daily bulletins of the honeymoon to a devoted group of fellow citizens, it only filled him with a vague satisfaction. It comforted his self-esteem to feel that his hometown still honored him even though Sherrill Cameron had found out that he was a scoundrel.

Besides all this there was a certain amount of protection in having one's own private little clique. It was almost as good as if Arla had been willing to stay in her stateroom and pretend to be seasick.

Then one evening, near the end of the voyage, Carter, coming out on deck to seek Arla where she usually sat, found her walking the deck arm in arm with the great financier, conversing with him vivaciously and seeming to be entirely at her ease.

She was wearing the loveliest of Sherrill Cameron's evening dresses, the orchid chiffon, and with the moonlight gleaming on her gold hair, she looked like a dream. Evidently the financier thought she did also, for he was bending graciously to her and smiling.

Carter withdrew to a distance and watched them from afar, his eyes narrowing, his admiration growing for his lovely wife. Either she was going to be his utter undoing, or else somehow she had managed to wrap Sheldon around her little finger.

They had it out that night in the stateroom, very late, in a brief session. Carter poured abuses upon her, to which she listened absently, and then laughed.

"Oh, Carter, excuse me," she said condescendingly. "All that excitement is so unnecessary. You see, Mr. Sheldon thinks I am Sherrill Cameron. He told me how much he had always admired my lovely hair and eyes, and said my aunt Miss Catherwood was a marvelous old lady!"

It was some minutes before Carter recovered from the shock of that and asked for details, but before they were finished he actually came to telling Arla that she was a wonderful woman, and that he loved her beyond anything on earth.

"If I had only realized how really clever you are, Arla, I would never have looked at Sherrill Cameron!" he said, and Arla drew a sharp breath and wished he had not said that. Wished that somehow she might get back her illusions about him. Sherrill Cameron had been right, of course. One could not be happy with a man who had been torn from his pedestal. And yet, wasn't there some way to put him back there? To keep him from doing the things that made her despise him?

Several times after that Arla walked and talked with the great man, and Carter's temper was improving daily.

It was about three hours before they were expecting to land.

Arla had scribbled a letter to her aunt Tilly in her hometown telling briefly of her hasty marriage, because she knew that Hurley would spread the news widely, and her aunt would be hurt if she did not receive some personal word. She had just returned from posting it and found Carter pulling out the suitcases from under the bed. He stacked them up in two piles, the ones that were to be left with the shipping company for the return voyage, and the ones they were to take to the hotel with them. His own suitcase was on the top of one of the piles.

Suddenly he remembered some letters he had written which he wished to post on shipboard. He rushed out, slamming the stateroom door behind him, and an avalanche of suitcases careened over to the floor. The top one burst open—perhaps it had not been securely latched—and some of the contents flowed out upon the floor.

Arla sprang forward to pick up the things before Carter's return. She had begun to realize that that was to be her perpetual attitude, always being ready to smooth the way before her husband if she wished to live peaceably with him. That was his wedding suit lying sprawled upon the floor. It would not be a wise note to introduce just at this stage, a reminder of that awful wedding.

Arla stooped and picked it up, and as she lifted it, she felt something slip out from between the loosened folds—or was it out of a pocket, the trouser pocket perhaps?—and slither along the floor.

She looked down quickly. Was it money? No, something bright and sparkling with green lights in it! Something gorgeous and beautiful lying there on the floor before her startled eyes!

She stopped and stared. What was it? Where had she seen that rarely wrought chain before and those wonderful green stones? Emeralds! They were Sherrill Cameron's emeralds. The necklace she had worn the night of the wedding! The necklace that everybody in the room had been talking about and admiring!

For an instant Arla stood there almost paralyzed, facing the possibilities of how that necklace got into her husband's pocket. Over her face the whole gamut of emotions played in quick succession. Astonishment, horror, disgust, scorn, fear, and then a great determination.

Frantically she dropped the garments she held and grasped the glittering necklace, cradled it in her hand for an instant, caught the gorgeous lights in the beautiful gems. Was Carter planning to sell these rare jewels to get the fortune that was to have come from the alliance that her coming to the Catherwood house that night had foiled? Was that what he had meant, that he had found a way to get the rest of the money he needed to save his business schemes?

And was he excusing himself by saying that the jewels were a part of the wedding presents and therefore he had a right to take them? She knew that Carter was capable of such quibbling. Her heart sank. Was she also to have a thief as well as a trifler for a husband?

Outside the door she could hear footsteps coming along the passageway. He might return at any moment! A great panic came upon her. He *should not* be a thief! She would foil that as well as his attempt to marry the other girl!

Her first impulse was to hurl those stones from the porthole and destroy the evidence against him, but as she swayed to take a step in that direction, she realized what she was doing. Those were Sherrill Cameron's jewels. Hurling them into the sea would not make Carter any less a thief, even if no one ever found it out. And Sherrill Cameron had been wonderful to her, generous in the extreme. She could not do that to her, throw her costly jewels in the sea! That other girl had already suffered greatly through herself; she should not also lose her property. No, the only possible way to undo the wrong that Carter had done was to return them to their owner. Somehow she *must* return them and yet shield Carter! Shield him from going to the penitentiary!

Hastily she wrapped the jewels in a clean handkerchief, tied the corners securely, and hid it in her own suitcase beneath the lingerie. Then she hurried back to pick up Carter's things. If she could only restore them to their place before he returned!

She schooled herself to go carefully, folding each garment without a wrinkle, laying everything smoothly back in its place. It seemed to her that it was hours before that suitcase was fastened and back on the top of the pile where he had left it.

Then she went to her own suitcase and began frantically hunting through it among the various contents for a suitable container for the jewels. If she could only get them in the mail before it closed! She glanced at her wristwatch. There was a little over half an hour. She must not fail to get them in. She *must* get them wrapped in time! He should not be *allowed* to be a thief! He might have done many crooked things in business, doubtless had; she could not help the past, but insofar as she was able, he should not be allowed to steal a lady's jewels! She never could endure life with that over her, that she had helped him to take the necklace of the girl who had given him up to her. It was too low and contemptible! He wouldn't be thinking himself of doing it if he weren't so utterly frantic about money! He had been decently brought up, just as decently as she was. He wasn't naturally a crook. She must protect him against his worst self.

And she must protect the necklace from her own weakness, too, she realized. If he should discover she had it, should look at her with his beautiful eyes, kiss her the way he did last night, ask her to surrender it, could she resist? She doubted her own strength. She must put that necklace where neither he nor she could ever get it again.

She found in the suitcase a little leather case containing lovely crystal bottles of perfume and lotions. She took out the bottles and packed the jewels carefully, swiftly, among soft folds of Sherrill's own fine handkerchiefs. Then she scribbled a hasty note.

> *You must have dropped this when you were packing. I found it in the suitcase. I hope it has not caused you any anxiety.*
>
> *Arla McArthur*

With the leather case wrapped in a bit of silk lingerie and then in paper, she went hurriedly out and procured a mailing carton from the stewardess, addressed her package at a desk, and was not satisfied until it was safe in the keeping of the ship's mail service.

When she went back, Carter was directing the steward about the baggage. She was silent and abstracted, putting a few last things in her suitcase. The baggage was all going up on deck at once. The whole ship was in a state of getting ready to land.

Carter, too, seemed absorbed in his own thoughts. Just before they left their stateroom, he remarked briskly that they would go directly to the hotel and he would leave her there for the morning. He had some business to be transacted that must be attended to the first thing. Then he would be free to go about with her if all went well.

All during the slow process of arrival and landing and on the way to the hotel, Arla was thinking what to do when her husband should discover his loss. Now that she was safe on land and the package in the return mail was presumably safe on its way to America, she felt more sure of herself.

Nevertheless, when they arrived and were at last left alone in their room, even before Carter began fumbling with the latch of his suitcase, she found she was trembling. She could hardly take off her hat; she was afraid Carter would see that she was shaking.

She busied herself hanging up their garments, putting away her hat, washing her hands. Anything not to seem to be noticing Carter, who was frantically flinging his things about on chairs, on the bed, the floor, anywhere, and finally turning his suitcase upside down and shaking out its corners.

"I've lost something!" he said when she came out from the closet, where she had been arranging her dresses on hangers, and found him standing amid confusion.

"It's something very important," he said, beginning again to pick up things and fling them about, to feel in pockets, poke into the fittings of his bag.

"Can I help you?" asked Arla, trying to steady her voice.

"No! No one can help me!" he said, flinging a house-coat across to the bed. "I can't find— Oh, it's here somewhere, of course! It couldn't have gotten away!" He seemed to be talking more to himself than to her. He seemed almost to have forgotten her existence.

"Oh, to think I had to be forced into such a situation!" he groaned at last, flinging himself down in a chair and covering his face with his hands. "Was ever any man tormented as I have been?"

Arla came over and stood beside his chair, laying an icy hand on his bowed head. She was shaking from head to foot, but she tried to make her voice calm.

"I'd like to help you, Carter!"

"Well, you can't help me!" he said flinging rudely away from her. "It's all your fault anyway that I'm in such a situation. You put me here—how could you help me? It's too late! If you had wanted to help me, you'd have done what I told you sooner, and then everything would have come right. No, you can't help me. You don't even know what it is I'm hunting for, and if you did you wouldn't understand!"

Arla stood still for a minute, and then she went and sat down across from him.

"Listen, Carter!" she said in a cold, clear voice. "I understand perfectly what you are looking for and what you meant to do. You are looking for Sherrill Cameron's emeralds, and you won't find them because they are on their way back to her!"

He sat like one stunned for an instant, and she thought he had not understood her. Then suddenly he sprang to his feet and glared at her. His hair was awry, his face was distraught, and his eyes glittered like a madman's. For an instant she thought he was going to strike her. He looked as if he might even have killed her for that minute, if he had had the means at hand. He was beside himself.

"You—! You—! You *dared*!" he screamed and poured out upon her a stream of curses that made her shudder with their cruelty.

But she must not cry. She must not show that she was afraid of him. This was the time she had to be strong. She had saved him from the penitentiary, and now she must make him understand what danger he was in. Her courage rose to the necessity.

"Yes," she said steadily, "I dared! For *your* sake I dared!"

"For my sake!" he sneered. "You say you did it for *my* sake?"

"Yes, I did it for your sake. Remember you tried to

marry another woman once for my sake. Well, I didn't do a thing like that, but I took away the knife that would have cut your throat. You didn't know what you were doing, perhaps; you had been through so much. But afterward you would have realized and been ashamed. And I didn't intend to have a common thief for a husband!"

"Thief?" he cried furiously. "I had a perfect right after all that had been done to me. An underhanded—!"

"Stop!" said Arla coldly. "You are not the one to talk about anything underhanded. And you would not have found your argument would have stood before a court of law."

"It would never have come to a court of law. They wouldn't dream who had them. Besides, I had arranged to sell them at once!"

"You poor fool," said Arla. "Didn't you know that that necklace was registered? Those stones were well-known stones. I heard them talking about it at the reception. You couldn't have got away with it even if I hadn't interfered. You would have been in the penitentiary before three months were passed."

The man was white to the lips now and sank back in his chair groaning. It was a piteous sight! Tears filled Arla's eyes in spite of her resolution.

Then he suddenly raised his head and glared at her again with his bloodshot eyes.

"And I suppose you don't think they'll trace your package and come after me to every country in Europe?"

he snarled, terror in his face.

"No," said Arla coolly, "I wrote a note inside the box and told her she must have dropped the necklace into the suitcase when she was packing."

He was still, staring at her, the strained muscles of his face gradually relaxing. Then he dropped his head into his hands again and groaned aloud, groan after groan until Arla felt she could not stand another one.

At last he spoke again.

"Everything is lost!" he moaned. "I might as well be in the penitentiary. I can't meet my obligations! I can't ever get on my feet again! I am disgraced before the world!"

"Listen, Carter!" said Arla in a tone that demanded attention. "You are only disgraced if you have done something wrong. I saved you from doing one wrong thing. I'm glad I could. I never could respect you again if you had done that! But it's undone now. The necklace is on its way back, and no harm will come to you but losing your business. I'm glad you're losing that. I hate it! It is what made you forget your love for me and go after another woman. Oh, she may be a great deal more attractive than I am, and all that, but you belonged *to me*. By all that had gone before, you were mine and I was yours. You knew that! By your own confession these past few days, you know it now. Now stop acting like a baby and be a man! How do you think I feel having a husband like you?"

"What can I do?" he groaned.

"Sit up and stop acting like a madman," said his wife, turning away to hide the sorrow and contempt in her eyes. "If you'll get calm and listen, I'll tell you what you can do, and I'll stand by and help you! What you should do is take the next boat back and hand over your business to your creditors. Then let's go home and start anew. You can do it, and I can help you. Won't you listen to reason, Carter, and let us be honest, respectable people as our parents were?"

Carter, slumped in his chair, made no reply for a long, long time. Arla sat tense, every nerve strained, waiting. She knew that her words had been like blows to him. She felt weak and helpless now that she had spoken. It was like waiting to see whether someone beloved was going to die or live.

But at last he lifted his head and looked at her. She was shocked at his face. It had grown old and haggard in that short time. He had the terrible baffled look of one who had walked the heights and been flung to the depths. She had never seen him before with his self-confidence stripped from him utterly.

"I could never get back to that!" he said, and his voice was hoarse and hopeless.

"Yes, you could!" said Arla eagerly. "If you'd just be willing to give it all up and start over again!"

"Oh, you don't know!" he said, still with that hopeless look in his eyes. "You don't know it all!"

"You'd be surprised!" said Arla, springing up and

going over to kneel beside him with her arm about him. "I know a lot more than you think I know. You left your books out one day, and I thought they were the books you told me to look up that old metropolitan account in. I hadn't an idea what I was coming on until it was too late."

He looked at her, startled, blanching.

"And you knew all that, and yet you married me?"

"Yes," said Arla, her voice trembling.

He suddenly dropped his head upon her shoulder.

"I'm not worthy of you," he groaned. "I guess I never was!"

"That has nothing to do with it, Carter!" she said almost fiercely. "I love you, and *you shall* be worthy! Say you will, Carter, oh, say you will!"

Her tone fairly wrung the promise from him.

"I'm a rotten low-down beast!" he said between his clenched teeth. "I can say I will, Arla, but I don't even know if I can do what I say I will."

"Yes, you can!" said Arla in the tone of a mother determined to save her young. "You *shall*! I'll help you! I'll make you. When you're weak, then I'll be strong for you! I've got to! I'll die if you can't be brought back to be a decent man again!"

For a long time his face was hidden on her shoulder, and his whole frame shook with emotion, but her arms were about him, and she held him close, her tears raining down unheeded upon his bowed head.

At last he said in a low tone husky with emotion, "If you can love me like that after all I've done to you, then perhaps I can! I'll try!"

Then eagerly she lifted his face to hers and their lips met, their tears mingling.

It was sometime after that that Arla spoke, gently, quietly.

"Now, oughtn't we to be doing something about a boat to go back on?"

Carter looked up and his capable business expression came upon him.

"I think first, perhaps, I'd better cable to that man that made the offer about the business. He'll maybe go back on it, or have done something else already, you know."

"You're right!" said Arla. "Let's go together. I can't be separated from you now till it's all fixed."

"Yes, come!" he said, catching her fingers. "Oh, Arla, there's maybe something for us somewhere, when you can love me like this!"

Thus Arla entered on her life undertaking of making a man.

"This diamond," she said thoughtfully, looking at the gorgeous ring on her finger, "and those pearls. Are they paid for, Carter?"

She watched him keenly as the slow color mounted to his forehead again, and his eyes took on a shamed look.

"Because if they're not," she hastened to say, "let's send them back, I mean take them back or something.

They're not really mine, you know. They never were. You got them for her, and I think of it every time I look at them. Someday when we can afford it, you can get me some of my own, and I'd like that much better."

Carter went and stood by the window, looking out with unseeing eyes. His perceptions were turned inside to himself. He was seeing just what kind of a contemptible failure he had been. Seeing it as nothing else but utter failure could have made him see.

"There's no end to it!" he moaned hoarsely.

"Yes, we'll get to the end of it, only let's make a clean sweep now once and forever. Suppose we sit down while we're waiting for the answer to that cable and write down a list of things that have to go back or be sold or something, and debts that have to be paid. Don't forget anything. Let's just look it all in the face and know where we stand."

"We don't *have* a place to stand!" said the disheartened man. "Every foot of ground under us is mortgaged. That's what you've—what we've—what *I've* brought you to, Arla!"

Arla's eyes had a strange light of hope in them as she looked at him. He hadn't said she had brought him to that. He had started to, but he hadn't said it. He had acknowledged that he had done it himself! There was some hope.

They had about a week to wait for the boat they had decided to take, and they went to cheap lodgings and made little excursions here and there on foot, seeing what they could of the old world in a humble way. Perhaps nothing could have better prepared Carter to go from a life of extravagance into plain homely economy like taking their pleasure without cost. For Arla wouldn't let them spend an unnecessary cent. She had everything down to the last penny now, and was determined that they should get free from debt.

"Someday," said Carter, watching a young couple, obviously on their wedding trip as they entered a handsome automobile and drove happily away, "someday I'll bring you over here, and we'll see Europe in the right way."

"Perhaps not," said Arla, her lips set with determination. "We've got to get over expecting things like that. If we ever get rich, it might happen, and then of course it would be great, but it isn't likely, not for a long time anyway, and we're not going to expect it nor fret that we haven't got it. It's wanting things we haven't got that has nearly wrecked our lives, and we're going to stop it! We're going to have a good time on nothing if we have to, and just be glad."

There was disillusionment in her voice and eyes, but there was cheer and good comradeship. Carter looked at her in wonder and was strangely comforted.

But Arla turned away her disillusioned eyes and struggled to keep back sudden tears. She was getting on very well, it was true. Carter had been far more tractable than she had hoped, and that gleam of self-abasement had been hopeful, yet she knew it was but transient. He was weak. He was full of faults. He would fall again and again. He would lapse back into his old self. The world was too full of temptations and ambitions for her to hope for a utopian life with him. Hell was there with its wide-open doors, and her strength was so small! She suddenly felt like sinking under it all. Just courage, her own courage, just determination, couldn't pull him out of this and make him into a decent man again, a man in whom she could trust, upon whom she could lean. Oh, for some strength greater than her own! Oh, for some power to right their lives! Happiness in such circumstances? She knew it was impossible. A good time on nothing? Yes, if they loved and trusted each other perfectly perhaps, but not when one had constantly to bear the other up.

Oh, she would go on as she had promised, stand by him through everything. She loved him. Yes, she loved him. But there was a desolate desperateness about it all. She knew it. She knew it even while she set her beautiful strong red lips in determination to go on and succeed. She knew intuitively that there was something lacking! Some great need that would come, some need for help outside of themselves. Just human effort couldn't accomplish it.

Would Carter ever come to see that he was radically wrong, not just unfortunate? Would his remorse over his failure ever turn to actual repentance?

Oh, for something strong and true to rest down upon!

And vaguely even while she tried to set her courage once more for higher attainment, she knew that what she was trying to do was just another of the world's delusions. She never by her own mere efforts could save Carter from himself. She might help perhaps, better things in great degree, make life more bearable, more livable, but still in the end there would be failure! What was it they needed? Oh, there must be something, some way!

So with desperation in her eyes, a vision of a future full of useless efforts, she turned back to her heavy task.

Chapter 21

Sherrill, filled with a startled premonition that clouded her eagerness over the package, tore off the wrappings and pulled out the little bundle in its cover of silk, shook out the bit of lingerie, a sort of consternation beginning to dawn in her face. This was her own, one of the things that had been in Arla's suitcase!

Then she recognized the little leather case and snapped open the catch, dropping out the note that Arla had written. It fell unheeded to the floor.

But there were no lovely little bottles in the case! What was this, just handkerchiefs? She pulled them out, just catching the heavy little lump knotted in the handkerchief, before it fell.

With hands that trembled now with excitement, she unknotted the corners of linen that Arla had tied so hastily, and stood staring as the gleam of the great green stones flashed out to her astonished gaze.

"Oh, Aunt Pat! It's *come*! My emerald necklace has *come back*! Look! The stones are all here! Gemmie! Oh, Gemmie! Where are you? The emerald necklace has come back! It's *found*! It's found! Oh, isn't it wonderful that I should find it just now?"

Gemmie hurried in from the bathroom where she had been pretending to pick up the towels and place clean ones. Her eyes were still suspiciously red, and she came and stood there looking at the jewels, the most amazed, embarrassed, mortified woman whom one could find, heartily ashamed at all she had been thinking and doing, almost half suspicious yet.

"Where did they come from?" she asked sharply. "Who took them?"

"What does it matter now?" sang Sherrill. "They're here and I don't have to worry anymore! Oh, I'm so glad, so glad!"

"What's this on the floor?" said Aunt Pat, whose sharp eyes had sighted the twisted note.

Gemmie stooped down and handed the note to Sherrill, and Sherrill read it aloud. Read the name, too, Arla McArthur, and never thought how that last part was once to have been her own.

"Oh, Miss Sherrill!" Her voice was shaking with emotion. "It certainly is wonderful. And I'm that ashamed! And me thinking all this time—!"

But nobody was listening to Gemmie. Aunt Pat asked to see the note, and Sherrill handed it happily over to her. She read it carefully, and then with her little wry smile and a twinkle in her eye, she remarked, "So you dropped it in the suitcase when you were packing! Well, it may be so, Sherrill! Of course it may be so!"

Then when Gemmie had gone out of the room on some errand, she said, "Well, Sherrill, I'm glad you learned to trust him before it turned up!" and met with a wicked little grin and another twinkle of her bright eyes her niece's indignant denial that she had ever done anything but trust him.

An hour later, dressed once more in her wedding satin, with the long silvery folds flowing out behind her, and the soft veil blossom-wreathed upon her head, Sherrill stood before her mirror. The faithful Gemmie knelt beside her, arranging the folds of her train.

Someone tapped at the door and handed in a big box.

"It'll be your flowers," said Gemmie in an awestruck voice. She brought in the box and opened it, carefully taking out the lovely bridal bouquet of wedding roses and lilies.

"It's much, much nicer than the other one, Miss Sherrill," she said in deep satisfaction as her eyes gloated over the flowers. "They're a better quality of flower; they are indeed! And I like the white ribbons much better than the silver. It comes from the most expensive place in the city, too; it really does. They have all the quality orders—they! They really do!"

"Oh, you dear old silly," said Sherrill affectionately. "But it is lovely, isn't it? I like it better, too!"

"Well, I like yer man, Miss Sherrill, I'll say that!" added Gemmie shamefacedly. "And now I'll just be running over to see if Miss Pat wants anything. And mind you don't go to playing any more pranks on us, slipping in another woman on me for a bride," she added anxiously.

"No, Gemmie, I'll stay right here this time," laughed Sherrill. "I won't give this man up to any other girl!"

So Sherrill stood before her mirror in her bridal array once more and looked into her own mirrored eyes. Happy eyes this time, without a shade of fear or hesitation in them. Eyes full of trust and hope. And suddenly as she faced herself, she closed her eyes and lifted her head and spoke into the silent room: "Dear God, I thank You that You took away what I thought I wanted, even though it hurt, and gave me what You had kept for me. Oh, make me worthy of such joy, and make me always ready to yield to Your will."

Silently she stood with bowed head for a moment more, and then with a lovely light in her face, she lifted her head and went to meet her bridegroom at the head of the stairs.

The little assembly of congenial guests were waiting

for them as the two walked down the stairs. An old musician friend of Aunt Pat's was playing the wedding march on the piano, and the minister stood waiting before a hastily assembled background of palms and ferns. Sherrill walked into the room on the arm of her bridegroom and took her place to be married, her heart swelling with joy and peace.

It was a simple ceremony, few words, solemn pledges, another ring to go with her diamond, and dear people coming up to congratulate her. There was one fine old gentleman among them, a friend of Graham's father, who told her what a wonderful man she was getting, and wished her the simple earnest wishes of a bygone day.

And there were amazing presents. Some of them had been sent here before and returned, and returned again now, laughingly, because their donors had had no time to get something new. And there was a happy little time with a few tears at the end. Then Sherrill kissed Aunt Pat and Gemmie, too, and in her pretty dark-blue going-away dress that she had never worn until now, was whisked off in Aunt Pat's car to the airport, and taken in an airplane to New York. An hour later the ship weighed anchor and set sail for South America. It didn't seem possible that all this had happened since the golden-hearted roses arrived that morning.

Sherrill and her beloved stranger husband stood at last on deck in a quiet place alone. They watched the lights of their native land disappear into the distance, looked at the great moonlit ocean all about them, and clung closer together.

"To think that God saw all this ahead for me, and saved me from making such a terrible mistake!" said Sherrill softly.

"He knoweth the end from the beginning," quoted Graham, holding her hand close in his own and looking down into her sweet eyes.

"Yes, but the best of all is," said Sherrill after a little pause, "that He brought me to know Himself. Graham, if I hadn't been stopped in what I thought I wanted most of all in the world, I would never likely have known the Lord Jesus, nor have found out what a wonderful book the Bible is."

"And I perhaps would never have found a girl who knew my heavenly Father!" said Graham. "His will is always best."

Then softly he began to sing, and her voice blended with his tenderly:

"Have Thine own way, Lord! Have Thine own way!
Hold o'er my being absolute sway!
Fill with Thy Spirit till all shall see
Christ only, always, living in me!"

THE PRODIGAL GIRL

Chapter 1

As soon as the letter came that practically promised the contract for which he had been bending all his energies for the past six months, Chester Thornton sat back in his chair and let his mind relax.

For the first time in a year he took a deep breath without a tremble of anxiety at its finish. Now he could look things in the face and know that instead of a gradually increasing deficit there would be a good profit. This new connection would mean the backing of half a dozen of the best firms in the country; it would mean prestige and widening interests, unlimited credit and respect. It spelled success in large letters and filled him with an ecstasy such as he had not known since he was a carefree boy and went fishing.

He stared across at the file cabinets unseeingly and tried to think what it would mean to his home and family! Why, they could even buy a new house, a palatial place up on the Heights, and choose their own place in the world. In three or four years the firm would be one of the wealthiest in its line in the country; they might even open up a foreign office!

He drew himself sharply back from daydreams into the present. It would mean right now that he could do a lot of things that had needed to be done for a long time, little repairs to the house, not extensive of course, if they would be moving in a year or so, but enough to put things shipshape and livable again until they could look about them and choose just the home that they wanted. They might have to build. Why, of course they would build, that was the idea—*build*, and have just what they wanted! And in the meantime, whatever he had to do to their present home would only enhance its value for sale.

Then, too, Christmas was coming in a few weeks!

For the first time in his life he would be able to purchase real Christmas presents, gifts that were worth something and not just scrimped necessities. He really had never enjoyed giving Betty that wristwatch, platinum though it was, and set with some good little diamonds, because he had to lie awake so many nights planning just how he could make up for having spent that money on it. But Betty was the dearest daughter in the world; she deserved all that he could give her. Then his thoughts turned to Eleanor, and his soul swelled with joy; now he could buy that string of pearls he had wanted for so many years to give her and never dared. It wasn't expensive as those things went, not the one he wanted, very simple and lovely, not a long string, for Eleanor liked quiet things.

A lover-like smile hovered over his lips for an instant at the thought of the gentle-faced woman who was his wife. Then his released ambitions leaped forward.

Well, Betty could have the car now that she had been coaxing for for over a year. Of course she was a little young for a car, only a trifle over seventeen, but all her friends had them, and it would relieve the situation for Eleanor wonderfully if she could have the family car free for herself and not have it continually off with Betty and her friends.

Of course Chris would be upset over Betty having a car, but Chris could wait another year or two. A boy wasn't really fit to own a car till college age, though of course some of them did. But there were other things for Chris, and his time would come later. And there was Jane and the twins! Oh, it would be rare to buy Christmas gifts this year with no grim ghost of want hovering behind to restrain his every impulse!

Thornton left the office at three o'clock that afternoon for the day. Things were in good shape, and he really could not hold himself down to work; he felt so happy. It seemed as if he must do something about it.

Acting on this desire, he went at once to the showrooms of the new Mermaid Eight. If he was going to get that car for Betty by Christmas it was high time he was looking into the matter. It ought to be ordered at once.

The Mermaid Eight proved to be far more fascinating than he had been told, and it was almost time for the five-thirty train to leave the station when he came puffing into the last car and dropped into a seat by the door.

He sank with a sense of satisfaction into a comfortable position, cast a quick, furtive glance around hoping there were none of his close acquaintances near to whom he must talk, and unfurled the newspaper, which he had bought from habit as he dashed past the newsstand. He did not want to talk to anyone just now. He wanted to enjoy this new sense of freedom from care and think over his afternoon's experience.

Which one of those three Mermaid Eights would Betty rather have? The yellow one was out of the question of course, entirely too loud for a young girl. Perhaps it would be better to let her choose but no, that would spoil the joy of the surprise. This first real gift that was really worth anything he would choose just as he wanted it to be.

And he knew in his heart that the deep rich green like the heart of the woods would be his choice. Of course the blue was good, too, but blue was so common now. No, that green one with the sporty little gray top and the nickel trimmings was distinguished enough for any girl. Yes, he would get the green one. Perhaps he would not even tell Eleanor about it. He would just surprise them all.

His gaze wandered from the newspaper, which he was not reading, to the window with its lights flashing past. How beautiful it was out there with the river far below surrounded by lights clustering along its banks, little red lights like red berries on the barges tied up at the empty wharfs. Smoke billowing softly, cloud-like from the tall stacks of factories, more lights in clusters, stars above, stars below. Why, how beautiful it was! What a world to live in anyway, when even the riverbank down by a factory could appear beautiful at night. Someone ought to write a poem about it. The beauty of a city at night. Perhaps someone had. Perhaps others had noticed this beauty; he never had. It took an easy mind to just sit down and see beauty. He must remember this and get more time to look around him, see the beauty in the world before he got old!

It certainly was good to feel that great load of anxiety gone that he had carried now for ten years. Success in sight and writ large! His heart swelled gratefully.

It was then that the words struck him. They hurled around his protective newspaper and got him by the throat like so many demons taking him unawares to destroy him.

He had heard those two young voices; boyish, silly, vacuous, he had unconsciously labeled them when their conversation reached his averted consciousness. He had heard without knowing what they were saying, until suddenly his daughter's name was mentioned followed by a loud, nasty laugh, the kind of a laugh a demon from the pit might give after a dastardly deed of depredation.

Instantly the father's senses were alert, stung into horror, unable to believe his ears. If the two youths who were so frankly talking over their conquests could have seen his face, could have known who was sitting behind them listening to their depraved confidences, they would have slung themselves with little delay from his earshot. But in cheerful ignorance of his proximity, and with confident casualness, they proceeded, in no hushed voices, boastfully comparing experiences and girls!

"Little rats! Little dirty rats! Vile dirty devils!" A voice from Thornton's soul away off in the distance seemed to be crying, "Throttle them! Choke them! Rub their faces in the dust of the earth! Strangle them! Pull out their tongues by the roots! *Exterminate* them!" The words seemed to be tumbling over and over in his brain, while his heart turned cold with horror and anger, and his brain seethed with helpless phrases. For a moment he knew how a murderer felt. He must kill them. Of course he must kill those vile creatures who had presumed to speak of his upright, precious daughter in such vilely intimate terms.

And yet when he tried to throw down the paper and rise, his hands trembled and had no power to release the sheet from his hold! And the power was gone from his feet! He could not move his eyes to see those two who were blaspheming his child in his hearing. An icy hand had his throat by a terrible grip, and something was binding his heart with fearful pressure so that it seemed as if the very veins in his temples would burst. Was he having a stroke? Was this paralysis that held him hand and foot from dragging those low-lived youths the length of the car and flinging them from the platform into a passing field?

Gradually his heart beat more steadily, and he could think a little. His eyes, which had been staring so blindly, began to see the larger letters on the sheet before him, although he did not comprehend their meaning. He was groping, reaching out, trying to steady himself. Perhaps he had been overdoing lately. Those blinding headaches to which he had been subject the last few months were a result of overwork and worry, and now that the pressure was relieved somewhat he was feeling a reaction. Surely he *must* have only fancied that he heard those awful words, the loathsome laughs that were like crawling serpents coming toward him, menacing the one he held so dear. What had they said anyway? He recalled the words, forced himself to bear again the shock of their meaning. Surely, surely they were lying! Boasting to one another! Trying to outdo one another, the dirty little vermin! Surely, they only chose his daughter's name to accompany such boasts because she was so high, so pure, so far above any possibility of a breath touching her reputation that the boast was all the greater! Of course it could not be true—his *daughter*! Betty! Why, *little Betty! They must be made to suffer for this!* It was not true! He must do something about it, though! He must take them out when the train stopped, take them somewhere perhaps to the garage and put them through a grilling and then wallop them till they were sick. Would that be sufficient for such a hellish offense? He must control himself. He must remember his daughter's fair name. He must not bring her into the public eye by attacking the criminals here in public. He must put a hold upon himself.

He was startled at the strength of the fury that had been unleashed within him—righteous fury!

Yet there he sat frozen in his seat, and those boastful voices were speaking further of his Betty, setting forth her personal charms with a frankness that was more than revolting, comparing her exquisite intimate loveliness to that of some other girl whom they called Judy! Why did he not reach forward now and grip that boy by the throat? Call the conductor and have him arrested! What was it that held him this way from making a single move?

Was it? Could it be that he was afraid lest Betty? No! But *had* Betty been *indiscreet*? Could she have allowed intimacies without realizing, meaning to? Innocently of course. Oh, no—impossible!

His Betty! But yes, that must be what held him back!

He thought of her exquisite rose-leaf body as a baby lying softly in the white blanket when he and Eleanor had looked at her alone together for the first time, almost to worship her, so fresh and sweet she was from God, like a bud dropped down to earth from heaven. It had seemed a sanctuary just to stand and look at her. Her father's heart had turned to God more closely at that moment than ever before, when he realized that God had trusted him with such a flower of perfect life to love and guide. It had made him feel that he must somehow purify his own life to be worthy of so great a trust. And through the years when she had been growing up he had always felt this more or less whenever he looked at her glowing beauty. He felt almost like worshipping her, giving her reverence for her exquisite purity and beauty.

And now, these swine dared to joke about her charms as if—

He paused and stared about him as the train came to an abrupt halt at his home station, and passengers arose all about him swarming out.

He let his paper fall from his numb fingers and tried to stand upon his feet. The two youths in front of him were noisily dragging one another up, laughing irresponsibly. The one who had spoken those first terrible words caught the falling newspaper and returned it to Thornton's nerveless hand. The father lifted his stricken eyes and recognized the youth as the son of a neighbor, a classmate of Betty's in high school. Thornton's face was ashen, but the boy was not looking at him. He was still employed in a whispered line of jokes with his companion, his eyes following a girl who had just come down the aisle. The little swine! He had not even known that the father of Betty had heard what he had said! Would he have cared if he had noticed?

The stricken father stood there dazed, filled with loathing of life, trying to think what he should do. He seemed to lack the power to move out of the car. Yet he knew that when all the others were out he must get out quickly and go after those boys and— What should he do? What could he do that he would not have to explain and thus bring his Betty into disgrace! Oh, he understood now why men sometimes became murderers!

But when he had gone out to the platform and the train had passed on its way, he seemed dazed by the dark. He tried to look around for those boys, but they were gone. Before long everyone else was gone, too, and he was left standing alone on that platform with the rows of lights and the sound of the station agent slamming the late baggage into the baggage room, getting ready for the next train down to the city.

He dragged his heavy feet across the track. He had the feeling his heart was a great burden that he had to carry home and that his feet were too frail for the task. His head, too, bothered him. He could not think. He could only hear those awful words about his Betty beat over and over in his brain, and he could not decide what to do. Should he go to Dudley Weston's house, ask for Mr. Weston senior, and demand— What should he demand? What was adequate for a young girl's name and intimate sweetness defamed even in thought?

He knew of course that there were stories being told about the frankness of youth, the lengths to which they would go, the orgies, the debaucheries— But these were not young people like his own. Such a thing could never touch his family, reared in refinement, guarded and taught the right from babyhood with such a home and such a mother! No, of course not! Betty would never allow intimacies! And yet these boys had dared— Had said that she—

He would get to that point and every time would halt and recall the boy's words, phrases what Betty had said, what Betty had— Oh, God! Could there be any punishment for desecration like that?

Oh, yes, the boys and girls had stolen kisses when he was young, and thought it smart, had held hands on a sleigh ride or a hayride, or coming home in the moonlight. But nothing like *this*!

Petting parties! Was that what they meant when they mentioned in the papers and magazines the doings of young people? And referred to them lightly! The writers could not have understood! Oh, it could not be that a thing like this, a loathsome cancer, could steal into the heart and life of a rose of a girl like his Betty and defame it!

Yet all the while in the back of his mind was that fear growing as he dragged his heavy feet along the path, the fear that Betty had inadvertently been a party to the whole thing. Giddy and pretty, fun loving, daring, she might have led her companions on unwittingly He got no further than that. Yet it was something that might bring shame on her sweet self if brought to the light of inquiry, and what was he to do?

He groaned aloud so that a passerby hurrying down to the next train turned and looked after him and wondered if he ought to offer help.

And now the necessity for getting home and seeing Betty rose within him like a frenzy. One look at her sweet flower face would of course dispel these groundless fears and give him strength to go out and bring vengeance on her maligners. He felt sure that all he needed to set his spirit right and give it the accustomed strength to act was to look in his Betty's eyes and see her sweet, pure smile. His little daughter Betty!

And then he came within sight of his home, a comely stone dwelling with welcoming windows set with shaded lamps and a glow of firelight in the cheerless night.

He paused a moment to look at it all once more and think how dear it was before he stepped within and learned the truth. Before its charm could be shadowed by anything that could sadden the beautiful life they had lived within. Why had he thought they needed another home? This one had been so gracious, so wonderful, so satisfying. Even if he came to have millions, why should he change such a home as this for the fairest mansion earth could offer?

There was Eleanor standing by the fire, one foot resting on the fender, and Doris hanging on her mother's arm. Jane was playing something on the piano, a dashing little jazzy melody that rang out cheerily through the closed window. Chris was seated in the window reading the sports page of the evening paper, and John was working away in the corner with his radio. Thornton saw all this as he stepped up on the porch and hungrily looked in the window. His home! Why hadn't he been more mindful, more grateful for having such a home?

And they were all waiting for him. He must be very late! It seemed ages since he had got off the train and started to walk home. He could see through the open door beyond that the table was ready. The pantry swing door opened a crack, and the maid looked in crossly and out again.

But where was Betty?

His heart contracted sharply, and he hastened to open the door and step within to dispel that ghost of fear again.

Betty was just coming down the stairs as he closed the door and looked around. She was dressed in a little rosy taffeta, slim and straight to her narrow waist and then hooped on the hips and flaring out like the petals of a lovely flower. Her exquisite head with its sleek gold cap of close-cut shining curls was tilted delicately as if she knew her power, and her slim, white lovely arms and neck gleamed against the darkness of the staircase as if they were also of the texture of the rose. She poised on her little high-heeled silver shoes, fussing with a spray of silk roses on her shoulder and called crossly to her father where he stood staring by the door.

"Well, is that you, Chester, come at last? You better cut this out! *I've* got to go out this evening, and I can't be kept waiting all hours! We were just going to eat without you! I didn't see any sense myself waiting all this time. Come on, Eleanor, he's here at last, and you better give him a dose of medicine. He looks like a stewed prune. Do get a hustle on, I can't wait all night!"

Chapter 2

The lovely little daughter pirouetted lightly on the lower step of the stair till the light over her head showed full upon her loveliness, accentuated here and there—a touch of carmine on the pouting imperious little mouth; a soft blush on the cheek that he had always called her lovely complexion; a darkening of lash and brow; a shadow under the great blue eyes that somehow wore a dashing look of boldness and impertinence tonight that he had never seen before. It seemed that the hall light was cruel. Those overhead lights were always severe. When she got out to the table he would see her as she really was, and then this horrible fear that was gripping his heart now so that he could scarcely breathe would leave him forever. Just let him get a good look into her dear eyes and see her smile. He wished she wouldn't call him Chester in that pert tone. It didn't sound respectful. When she had first taken it up playfully it had been a joke, but tonight—well—tonight it hurt!

The ghost stepped nearer and gripped him by the throat. He must drive this awful thing away. He must get to the dining room quickly! Perhaps he was going to be sick! He must swallow a cup of coffee. That would make it all right, of course. There was nothing in all this. Of course there was nothing at all—nothing at all!

Seated at the table, he passed his hand over his eyes and looked about on them all, trying to focus his eyes on Betty's petulant face. It was plain that Betty was displeased with him. Yet somehow her face did not look quite so disturbing here as it had under the weird light of the hall chandelier. It was better blended, less suggestive of paint and powder. Of course he was quite accustomed to the ever-present powder puff that all girls nowadays played with in public, but it had never entered his head that his daughter wore anything like what people called "makeup." That was low and common to his thinking, and quite unflattering for a girl of respectable family.

Chris broke in upon his thoughts with a sudden request for money.

The father tried to summon a natural voice:

"Why, Chris, you had your usual allowance, and it is only ten days into the month. What do you want of more money?" he asked, feeling that his voice sounded very far away and not at all decided. His mind really was on Betty.

But Chris seemed almost to resent his query:

"Well, I *want* it!" he said crisply, as if his father had no right to ask the question.

"What's the matter with your allowance? You'll have to give an explanation. What have you done with it?"

"He–he–he's lost it playin' pool!" chimed in Johnny joyously with a grin of triumph toward his older brother.

"Shut up! You infant! You don't know what you're talking about!" said Chris angrily.

"I do so! I was lookin' in Shark's window with Bill Lafferty when you lost. I heard Skinny Rector tell you he's goin' ta tell our dad if you didn't pay up tonight!"

Chris shoved his chair back noisily.

"Aw, baloney! Dad if you're gonta listen to an infant, I'm done! *Keep* yer money. There's plenty of places I can get money if you won't give me what I want! Other boys don't get this kinda treatment in their homes—want ta know every nosey little thing, and listen to an infant!"

He complained all the way through the hall in a loud voice, and the front door slammed on his final word.

The family sat in a perturbed silence for an instant till the mother broke it in a worried voice that had a hidden sob in its texture.

"He hasn't eaten a mouthful, Chester."

"Well, what can you expect?" reproached Betty. "You can't treat a young man as if he were a three-year-old. If Chester wants Chrissie to stay at home, he'll have to shell out a little more liberally from now on. Chrissie's almost grown up and isn't allowed anything compared to other boys. Why, we're the only two in our set that haven't got cars to come to school with, and I think it's scabby! I'm getting ashamed to go out of the house."

"That'll be about all from you, Betty!" said her father in a cold voice that was so new to him that he felt frightened at it. Was he actually talking to his little Betty this way?

"On second thought, you needn't go out anymore until we've had a thorough understanding on this subject and a few others," he added.

Betty stared at him in astonishment for an instant and then burst into a mocking laugh:

"Try and do it!" she sneered. "How do you get that way, Chet? It isn't in the least agreeable."

"Now Betty," began her mother anxiously, "don't hurt your father. You know he didn't mean—"

"He better not!" said Betty imperiously.

"We gotta boy in our school ut says ya don't havta obey parunts," broke forth ten-year-old John. "He says, 'What they gotta do about it?' He says they ain't got any more right ta say what ya shall do an' what ya shan't 'n we have. He says we all got the same rights—"

"John, leave the room this minute!" said his father sternly.

Johnny looked up aghast, his well-loaded fork halfway to his lips. He was not used to hearing his father speak like that.

"Go!" said Thornton.

Johnny hastily enveloped the forkful.

"But I was just gonta tell you about the club we got. It's called 'Junior Radicals.' We—"

"Johnny, your mouth is too full to talk," pleaded the distressed mother.

"Go!" There was something in his father's voice that Johnny Thornton had never heard before. He made sure of another forkful of chicken stuffing and reached for a second hot biscuit as he rose reluctantly from his chair, but his father's hand came out in a grip like a vise and rendered his small sinewy wrist utterly useless. The biscuit dropped from his nerveless fingers dully on the tablecloth, and Johnny Thornton walked hastily toward the door, a little faster than his feet could quite keep up, propelled by a power outside his own volition. He had never known his father could be so tall and strong.

"Great cats!" remarked Betty contemptuously as the dining room door closed sharply. "Chester must be crazy! I never knew him to be so off his feed before! I'm going to get out of the picture before anything more happens. Tra-la-Eleanor. I wish you joy! You better beat it yourself till the weather clears."

"But Betty! Your father said—" began Mrs. Thornton.

But Betty was gone out through the kitchen and up the back stairs to her room. Her closing remark as she sped through the swing door into the pantry was:

"Bilge!"

The door upstairs into Johnny's room was heard to close firmly and a key to turn in the lock. Then Thornton's steps came slowly, unsteadily down, almost haltingly, his wife thought. Could Chester have been drinking? But no, of course not. He hated the stuff. He never touched it. It must be business. She ought to have told Betty to be more considerate.

When he opened the dining room door again his face was white as a sheet and his eyes were staring ahead as if he saw a ghost. He marched sternly to his seat and sat down, but he made no attempt whatever to eat. Instead he looked around his depleted dinner table.

"Where is Betty?" he asked in a voice that was husky with feeling.

"Why, I think she's gone up to her room, dear," said his wife placatingly.

Thornton's face did not relax, and Jane who had been biding her time silently, mindful of the fig pudding, which was her favorite dessert, decided to leave while the going was good. But when she slid stealthily from her seat to go out, her father's voice recalled her.

"Sit down!" he said severely. "And don't leave the table until dinner is finished."

Jane stuck up her chin indignantly:

"I was just going up to my room," she said defiantly. "I've got some 'mportant studying to do."

"Sit down!" thundered her father uncompromisingly.

Jane slid into her seat sullenly.

Mrs. Thornton looked at her husband almost tearfully and explained in a low voice to the sulky girl:

"Daddy comes home tired out and doesn't want to be worried. He isn't feeling well, I'm sure. He wants it to be quiet and orderly and not everybody jumping up and running out—"

"He went out himself," said Jane impertinently.

"Hush!" said the mother with a fearful glance at her husband. But little Doris diverted the attention suddenly, contributing her bit to the conversation, having been turning over her mind for a suitable topic ever since her brother's summary exit. It seemed the dramatic moment for her to enter the limelight also.

"We got a new book in school today. Our teacher read it to us. It's a story about a lady that lived in a tree and could do things with her toes just as well as with her hands. And by 'im by she got to be a real lady and came down outta the tree and lived in a house. She was one of our aunt's sisters, the teacher said."

"You mean *an*cestors," corrected Jane, coming out of her sulks with a giggle to correct the baby of the family.

"No, aunt's sisters!" insisted Doris. "She 'estinctly said aunt's sisters."

"What does all this mean, Eleanor?" said Thornton, looking at his wife. "Do you mean they are stuffing that kind of bosh down babies? In *school?*"

"It's her science class," asserted Jane importantly. "They're just starting to learn about how the earth began, all gases and things you know, and how everything developed of itself, and then animals came, and some of 'em turned into men. We had it all two years ago, but now they're beginning it in the first grade."

"What utter nonsense!" said Thornton angrily. "It's all well enough for some highbrows to think they believe in evolution if they want to, but they have no right to stuff it down children's throats, not *my* children, anyway. And in the *public* school. Eleanor, haven't you taught these children *any* of the Bible?"

"Why, of course, Chester," quavered his wife soothingly. "They had all the Bible stories read to them. You know about Adam and Eve, darling. Why, Jane you got a prize once in Sunday school for telling the story of creation. How can you let Daddy think that you don't know—"

"Oh, of course I remember all that, Mud," said the thirteen-year-old, "but that's all out of date. Didn't you know, simply *nobody* believes the Bible anymore? My teacher said the other day, simply *nobody* that really knows *anything* believes it anymore. She said there were some places in the New Testament that were true to history, but the rest was all fanciful, kind of like legends and things, especially all that about Adam and Eve. It was just like mythology, you know. Didn't you and Daddy *know* that? I suppose you haven't been paying attention to what went on since you stopped school, you know, but my teacher says almost *nothing* in the Bible is true anymore. It isn't *scientific*! Why, even the children in the elementary school know that!"

"That will do!" thundered Thornton furiously. "Eleanor, this is unspeakable! Why haven't you known what kind of bosh our children were being taught? Where are the rest of them? I want to sift this matter out and know just where we stand! This is *awful*! Send for them all to come back! I want to see them right away."

Mrs. Thornton looked distressed. She had been listening to Betty's tiptoeing feet overhead, and now she knew they had ceased. She was even sure she had heard the creak of the back stairs and the opening of the kitchen door. Therefore she stalled:

"Suppose we go away from the table, anyway, Chester," she suggested, "so that the maid can clear away. You've scarcely eaten a thing. Jane, you and Doris take your pudding up to the sitting room while your father finishes. He is all tired out and ought not to be disturbed while he eats. Take another cup of coffee, Chester, dear. Your nerves are all worn out. You must have had a hard day today. I'm afraid things haven't gone as well as you hoped at the office. But never mind, dear! Don't let it worry you. Whatever comes, we've got each other. Remember that and be thankful."

"Got each other!" exclaimed Chester strickenly. "But *have* we?"

"Of course we have," cheered his wife. "Now dear, drink that hot coffee and you'll feel better. Come, and then we'll go into the library and you'll lie on the couch and tell me all about it. Then by and by when you are rested I'll call the children and you can talk to them, or perhaps tomorrow morning. You know you are in no frame of mind to talk calmly to them, and in the classes I've been attending about child rearing they say it is simply fatal to talk excitedly to a child, that it arouses antagonism, and that really is the worst thing we can do. You know really they are human beings like ourselves and have to be given a chance to express themselves. They won't stand for radical discipline such as you and I passed through. Really Chester, the children of today are quite, *quite* different from a few years ago. You know things have changed, and young people have *developed*. There is a more independent attitude—"

"Stop!" cried Thornton. "Stop right there! Eleanor, if you have swallowed that rot whole and are going to take that attitude I shall go mad. *Express* themselves! I feel as if the whole universe has gone crazy."

"But Chester, dear, you are overwrought—!"

"I should say I am overwrought. Eleanor, you don't know what you are talking about. Listen!"

"Well, drink your coffee," she said soothingly. "At least drink your coffee before I ring for Hetty, and then we'll go into the other room and you shall tell me everything. You poor dear, I'm afraid you are going to be sick!"

"I don't want any coffee! I can't eat! I tell you, Eleanor, I must see the children! I must see *Betty* first! No, I can't tell you anything till I have a talk with Betty. It is too dreadful! I want to understand the whole thing better before I tell you. Come, quick! Get Betty. I must see her at once."

She tried to persuade him to lie on the couch and let her cover him up before she called her daughter. She poked the fire into a blaze and stalled for time by turning the hall light out so it would not shine in his eyes, but he pranced back and forth and refused to even sit down.

So at length she went upstairs to call Betty.

But Betty's room was a whirlpool of garments: little silk doodads, trailing negligees, powder puffs, with an eddy of diminutive high-heeled shoes in one corner and a strapped pile of schoolbooks submerged in a chair under a torn evening frock. But no Betty!

It was as her mother had expected. Betty had made good her escape.

Mrs. Thornton passed through the confusion with deft hands, picking up and straightening as she went, hanging the flimsy little inadequate rags her daughter called clothing on the hooks in her closet, sweeping the clutter of ridiculous shoes into a quiet bag on the door, smoothing the bed, tidying the bureau. She stalled again for time. If only Chester would fall asleep he would be more reasonable. He would not blame the children. Something terrible must have happened in the business world that he should come home like this. He was usually so fond of the children, so interested in all that they had to tell about school life, so proud of Betty's looks, and Jane's music.

Probably the deal that he had hoped for so long had fallen through, and she knew that that meant a great loss of money. But he would pull out of it. He always did. And he was yet a vigorous man, young for his years, and keen in business ability, beloved and respected. All would be right. All she had to do was to soothe him now for a little while. If he would only fall asleep—

She heard his voice calling her impatiently:

"Where is Betty? Why doesn't she come down at once?"

The mother hastened down with a placating air:

"Chester, I'm afraid she's gone, but she ought to be back before very late. Suppose you just lie down here and tell me all about it. You know that always makes things better—"

But he interrupted her:

"Gone? Where has she gone!" There was alarm in his voice and in the startled eyes he turned on her.

339

"Why, you see, Chester, she had plans this evening—"

"Yes, I believe she told me so," he shouted, "but I told her at the table that she was to stay at home!"

"Hush, Chester, the maids will hear you! Let me explain. You see, Chester, she really *couldn't* stay at home. It was an engagement of two weeks standing. She had promised!"

"*Couldn't!*" he said, his voice still loud with alarm and excitement. "Couldn't obey her father? Well, I'd like to know why not?"

"Why, because there were other people involved. Chester, you really didn't give her any chance to explain, you know, and it was getting late. You remember you kept us waiting for dinner—"

"Involved? Who else was involved? Where has my daughter gone? I want to understand this thing perfectly. Where *is* Betty?"

"Why, Chester!" said his wife, aghast. She had not seen her husband so roused in years. He must be losing his mind.

"Listen, dear, she has only gone to a little high school dance. She'll probably be home before long now. They don't usually stay very late."

"But why should that be more important than obeying her father?"

"Because she had promised to go with one of the boys, one of her classmates, and she couldn't leave him without a partner."

He wheeled on her.

"*Who* has she gone with?"

"Why, Chester, how strangely you act! Just one of the boys she has known all her life."

"*WHO?*"

"Only Dudley Weston, our neighbor," said the mother complacently, sure that the name would cool her husband's heated temper. But his eyes fairly blazed.

"Dudley Weston!" he cried, and his voice was like a moan. "That little *viper!*"

"Why, Chester! Now I'm sure you must have a fever or something. It is only yesterday you told me he was growing into a fine manly fellow, and said how handsome he was as he went down the street."

The man groaned.

"Well, I don't think so anymore. Betty might as well have gone with the devil from hell."

"Now, Chester, you are swearing! I never heard you swear before. Oh, what shall I do?"

But he paid no heed to her words. He was searching behind the hall table for his hat that had fallen on the floor.

"Where *is* that dance?" asked Betty's father.

"It is at the high school hall," said Mrs. Thornton. "Oh, Chester! What are you going to do? You are not going *after* her? You are not going in public to mortify our daughter! Our little Betty! Oh, Chester! She will never forgive you! She won't come! I'm sure she won't come. She is very angry at you already. If you do a thing like that you will alienate her forever. Chester, you *mustn't!*"

She was crying now, great tears rolling down her cheeks, though she seemed unaware of them. She caught hold of his coat and held him with all her slender strength.

Something in her frail sweetness and agony touched him even in his wrought-up state. He looked down at her, and for a moment his eyes softened with deep pity and tenderness.

"Listen, Eleanor, you don't understand. You must trust me in this. I know what I'm about. And our Betty is in terrible danger. That boy is rotten! I heard him talking tonight in the train! About our Betty! Saying unspeakable, loathsome things about her! Oh, I would have saved you this if possible. He was boasting—I can't tell you all, not now anyway, there isn't time. I must get Betty before it is too late. Where is Jane? Call Jane. I want her to stay with you. *Jane!*"

He sprang up the stairs and flung her door wide, but there was no Jane there. He turned to his wife who had come stumbling up the stairs after him, the tears still flooding her face.

"Where is Jane?" he asked now with that strained white look about his eyes returning.

"She has just gone over to Emily Carter's to study her lessons. She asked me if she might go. They often study together. She'll be home by nine o'clock."

He glanced at his watch.

"Nine o'clock! Why, it's past nine now! I'll just step around and bring her back. I don't like her running around the streets at this hour of the night even a block. She's too young, and there are too many devils around. Besides, I want her to stay with you."

Then with sudden tenderness he stooped and kissed her.

"Don't cry, Eleanor. I didn't mean to be harsh. But you didn't understand. It was pretty bad and shook me a good deal, but we'll pull out of this somehow."

Then he was gone out into the night, leaving his wife with the worst alarm in her heart she had had in all the years of her married life. What would Betty do now? And what might not Chester do, when he found that Betty would not obey him in public? She recalled all the recent lectures on child rearing and sat weakly down on the lower step of the stairs and wept again.

Then out from the little front room near the linen closet at the end of the hall where Johnny had his haunts there arose a raucous voice singing from Johnny's radio:

> *"I'm a little boy,*
> *And I love a little girl!"*

And the mother on the stairs wept and wondered what the lecturer would tell her to do under the circumstances.

Chapter 3

The Carters lived halfway down the next block.

Thornton reflected that he had better take the car to save time. He could explain to Jane on the way home that her mother was feeling worried about something, and he wanted her to stay up with her till he returned. Then he could drop her at the door and drive right on to the high school.

But when he stopped at the Carters' door he was surprised to find the house all dark, both upstairs and down. Probably the children were up in some back sitting room studying, or in Emily's bedroom. He frowned anxiously as he rang the bell and waited impatiently. It seemed terrible to think that Betty had gone off with that unspeakable boy! And how was he to go about it to explain it to her? He would probably have to let her mother do it. It would be such a humiliation for his delicate-minded Betty to hear the foul words that had been used about her. Perhaps a hint from her mother would be sufficient without having to humble her by having her father tell his awful experience. That would have to be her mother's part. His was to deal with the lad.

He brought his mind back from his unhappy reflections to ring the doorbell again. Surely these people had not retired at half past nine! And if so, what had become of Jane?

He rang a third time, this time prolonging the pressure until he could hear the distant whir of the bell from the front steps.

A window was pushed up slowly above his head, and a voice called casually.

"Who down dar? What you-all want? Ain't nobuddy hum 'cept jes me an the baby."

"I'm Mr. Thornton," explained Chester. "I've come for my daughter, Jane. Won't you tell her to come right down? I'm in a hurry."

"Her ain't hyear no moh! Her 'n' Em'ly went out som'ers. Said they wuz goin' down t' the drugsto' at the cohneh fer a soda. Reckum they'll return d'reckly. But you cawn't nevvah tell. Mistah Cahteh an' his wife don' gon' ta town ta the *thee*-a-tre, an' Em'ly she gene'lly does as she please when dey out. I can't be bothahd! You jes' try the drugsto' ef yoh wants yoh gal in a hurry. Mebbe yoh find her! I gotta go back. The baby's cryin'!"

The window went down with a slam.

A sudden sense of fury descended upon Chester Thornton. Why did all these things have to happen to him at once! Just when things were looking up and everything was hopeful! Here was life in a terrible mess! Little Jane, too! Just a baby! Wandering around the streets at night with another child. He never did like those Carters. They were common! *Common!* That's what they were! Or the girl would know better than to take another child out alone at night.

He climbed wrathfully into the car and stepped furiously on the gas, startling a furtive cat into a streak of shadow.

Now, where should he look for Jane in case she was not at the drugstore? But perhaps Jane had already gone home. Yes, of course, that was it. Jane wouldn't go to corner drugstores alone at night. Jane knew she was to go home. That was the explanation. She had been told to return at nine o'clock. She was not common herself, even if she did like to go sometimes with a common child. Probably it was not in the least necessary for him to hunt further; of course she had gone home, and he had missed her in the dark. Nevertheless, now that he was here he would make sure.

He parked his car hastily in front of the brightly lighted store, and leaving the engine going he sprang out to look in the window.

There was a crowd in the drugstore. The soda fountain was always popular of course at this hour of the evening, even in winter. The nearby college and prep school supplied a continuous flow of patrons.

Thornton stopped at the window, lowered his head to look under a poster of a bold miss advertising a new brand of cigarettes, but the crowd inside the window was too close for him to get a good survey of the entire store. He went up the steps and flung open the door, and just as he did so the crowd parted to let out an elderly woman with a large bottle and an anxious air of haste. For an instant Thornton got a glimpse of an open space beyond the crowd, and a young delicate little face strangely familiar, whirling giddily before a circle of admiring spectators.

Almost instantly the crowd closed up again, and a noisy cheer followed. Several rough young voices called out familiarly:

"Go to it, kid!"

"Give us another one of those high kicks, Jane!"

With strange premonition Thornton pushed aside the crowd of college fellows that stood in his way and brought himself inside the circle of onlookers, unmindful of the resistance of the youths who blocked his way.

"Say, what's your haste, old gent?" one flung up at him as he elbowed his way to the front.

And there was *Jane*, his little child Jane, with her short kilted skirt tucked up like a ballet girl, her delicate features aflame with excitement, a bold, abandoned challenge in her big blue eyes, her close-cropped dark curls quivering, her bare childish knees above their rolled down stockings flashing white against the dark background of the mahogany showcase. Jane, dancing in solo, to the clamor of a jazzy radio in some unseen depth of the store's recesses. Jane, dancing for the amusement of a score of lustful-eyed youths who watched her all agog and cheered her on with none-too-delicate phraseology. Seemingly regardless, she danced on light as thistledown yet vulgarly suggestive in a dance that might have had its origin in the slums.

As her father entered upon the scene Jane was in the midst of an intricate whirl of arms and legs, white knees all mixed up with rippling skirts and flying arms, white hands fluttering, one dark lock of hair longer than the rest, waving like a crest over the pretty forehead. Her vivid little face with its forward impudent smile flashed back and forth so rapidly that for an instant Thornton did not know his own child. Then, as the shaft of bitter assurance entered his soul, she finished with several high kicks and a lazily graceful handspring, coming upright with shining eyes and glowing cheeks and a little saucy tilt of triumph, openly aware of the admiration of her audience.

The irreverent onlookers broke forth into coarse jests and cheers once more, raised neglected cigarettes, and quickly wove a blue haze of smoke about their favorite; they gathered closer about her, reaching for her with bold, intimate hands.

Suddenly they fell back and a hush came over them all. Jane had seen her father!

Jane's delicate little features grew suddenly drawn and mature. Jane's big dark eyes stood out in her little white face, the color ebbed away, and a kind of panic of fright spread over her face. Even the shell-pink ears, so carefully uncovered by the barber's shears, so boyish in their bareness, were white as if they were dead. Jane stood and stared at her father, for she had never seen such a look on his face as she saw now. Not at least since the day in her babyhood when she had put her mother's diamond ring down the sewer pipe in the street, and her father had taken her to his study and given her the soundest spanking she ever remembered to have had. Jane stood still in her tracks and watched him come, felt a sudden leadenness in her knees and hands, and wished for a nice convenient hole to open through that tessellated marble floor and let her down anywhere; she did not in the least care where.

Emily Carter, standing at the soda fountain counter with a young man almost twice her age, sucking soda through a double straw, watched him come and giggled excitedly. The crowd of college boys with a sprinkling of prep boys, away without leave to purchase cigarettes, saw the fright in their favorite's eyes, and a long low murmur like a young menace swept among them; but Chester Thornton came on with two long strides and gripped his daughter by the arm.

Without a word he led her out, her boyish head held high, a side sweep of frightened grimace on her face turned toward her former audience.

One or two of the bolder boys tried to step in his way and protest against the removal of their entertainer, but Chester Thornton swept them aside as if they had been made of cardboard, and took Jane out to the car.

"Get in!" he said sternly. His voice sounded like a knell.

Jane tried to summon a natural voice:

"I've left my coat and hat behind," she said, as if it were quite a natural thing to have done in a corner drugstore at ten o'clock at night. "I'll have to go back and get them, Daddy." Her voice had reached almost a cheerful tone now.

"Get in!" commanded her father.

"But Daddy! It's my best hat and coat!"

Thornton shoved his daughter forcefully into the seat and

slammed the car door shut.

Jane began to cry. She was angry at herself for crying, but she could not keep the tears back. She had never seen her indulgent father act like this. It must be true, as Betty had said, that Daddy had gone crazy.

"I'm cold!" she chattered.

He paid no heed to her.

As the car turned around she saw Emily Carter come to the door to watch her with an awed, sober look; then she heard a jeering laugh ring out from one of the boys, and her face grew crimson with mortification. He had no right! Her daddy had no right!

"I've got to stop at Emily's and get my books," she said as they whirled down the block. "I've got very important lessons to study for tomorrow."

"You should have thought of that before you went down to display yourself before the loafers of the town," he said curtly.

"Why, Daddy, I only went down for a minute. Emily had to get some toothpaste her mother had sent her for this afternoon and she had forgotten, and then the boys asked me to give the dance we are going to have in our school play!"

Thornton was silent and grim, driving hard. They flashed past the dark Carter house, and Jane put a detaining hand on his arm.

"This is the house, Daddy! I really must get those books. I'm going to have to sit up late now to get done. There's a test tomorrow—"

"You're mistaken!" said her father crisply. "The test was tonight! And you *have* failed! You needn't worry about your books. You'll not need them anymore. You're done with that school forever!"

"Daddy!"

Jane sat frozen in silence, trying to fathom the horror of what had just been said to her. Did it mean that Daddy was so angry he was going to send her away to boarding school? She would like that! It would be a regular lark. But what if he were to have her taught at home! That would be unbearable!

They stopped abruptly at home, and Thornton took his daughter by the arm firmly, almost painfully, and escorted her to the house.

Eleanor was still sitting on the lower step of the stair, weeping. She looked up anxiously as the door opened, hoping, half expecting Betty, almost afraid to look at her face. But instead there stood Jane, with a sullen, defiant, frightened look and tears on her face, rolling slowly, heavily down from wide eyes.

"Why, Janie, dear, you didn't go out on a night like this without a coat, did you?" her mother asked, springing to her feet anxiously.

"No," said Jane fiercely. "Daddy wouldn't wait till I got them on, and I'm all in a shiver."

"Why, Chester, that was dangerous!" said his wife, turning worried eyes on him.

"So was the place I found her in," said Thornton grimly. "Eleanor, put her to bed, and *watch* her till I get home. It isn't safe to let her out of your sight."

"Why, Chester! You frighten me!" said his wife, her hand fluttering to her breast. "Where did you find her?"

"I'm sorry," said Thornton gravely, "but it was necessary to frighten you. I found her in the corner drugstore 'expressing' herself for the benefit of a lot of lewd fellows who were cheering her on and calling out dirty remarks."

Mrs. Thornton's eyes sought Jane's sullen ones in horror:

"Janie!"

Jane's eyes went down to the toes of her small shoes, and she shrugged her shoulders indifferently.

Thornton looked at Jane in a kind of helpless despair.

"Now, I'm going out to hunt our other daughter," he said in a choking voice. "Goodness knows what I'll unearth this time. We seem to have run amok."

He paused and looked at his wife compassionately, as if he

would like to say something comforting, when there wasn't anything comforting to say. Then he turned toward the door.

"Well,"—with a tone that had a choking sound—"I must go—"

"Don't you think, Chester, don't you think maybe you'd better wait?" began his wife anxiously. "Betty will be sure to be home soon now—"

A look of finality came quickly into his face.

"No!" he said and was gone, then opened the door again to say:

"If Chris comes in, tell him to wait up till I get back. I've *got* to see him!"

Five minutes later Thornton parked his car in a long line that stood around the athletic field of the high school and took his way up the broad steps to the assembly hall where the dance was being held.

"Strange!" he said to himself. "*Dancing* in a school! When I was young they used to say such things detracted from the studies and made the student unfit for work the next day."

The stairs were bordered with couples seated close together holding hands, giggling, eating candy, smoking a furtive cigarette. He thought he saw a girl's delicate fingers toying with one, but of course he was mistaken. Not a high school girl, openly like this. Not in Briardale, anyway. They might do it out in the world but not in Briardale!

He scrutinized the faces as he came slowly up the stairs, which somehow seemed to be a mile long and very steep.

Of course Betty would not be sitting out on the stairs. Her mother would have brought her up better than that. And yet, young people were thoughtless. He might find her there. He remembered when he and her mother used to slip out and sit on stairs, and talk. There was nothing terrible in that—unless—unless she was talking to that young hound of a Weston! He couldn't bear it if he found her with that boy! She must be made to understand that she must never speak to him again. He was like pitch. It was a desecration to even think of him.

The sound of jazz from the high school orchestra led him on. He reached the door of the assembly hall, with difficulty, through the giggling, roughhousing crowd of boys and girls, and looked about anxiously for Betty. Several couples were dancing in the center of the great floor, dancing in a way that brought disgust to the father's heart. Was that the kind of thing his Betty had been going out for! Did Eleanor know how they danced today? He drew a deep breath and took a resolve. If he ever got Betty out of this—

But he got no further, for he heard a furtive whisper just behind him:

"Oh, there's Betty Thornton's old man! Won't she be furious! I'll bet he's come spying on her! Great cats! If my dad would try to put anything like that over on me, wouldn't I kick!"

He turned and looked in the speaker's face, a pretty, painted, bold face, coarse in its bravery of cheap taffeta, flimsy tulle, and lengthy earrings, a girl who lived two doors from his home and whom he had known by sight for several years.

She met his gaze defiantly, coldly.

"Can you tell me where to find Betty, Clara?" he asked, hating himself for having to ask her, yet not knowing where else to turn.

"Betts? Oh, why, she must be round here somewhere," answered the girl carelessly. "Did you see Thorny anywhere, Jim?" she called to a young man who was ambling past with a tray of ice-cream dishes.

"I sure did," grinned the boy. "She and Dud just passed by. Dud said it was too slow here, and they were going up to Todd's Tavern where they could get something real."

Something familiar in the set of shoulders held Thornton's stern glance as the youth passed, with a leer, nimbly on among the dancers. It was the other boy from the seat in front on the evening train!

He watched him for an instant, as some strong lion in a temporary cage might have watched his prey, and then turned to go down the stairs. It became apparent to him that a group of young people were watching him and snickering openly. He held his head haughtily and compelled himself to walk steadily down the stairs, although they seemed to have become insecure and to rise and fall with each step. He was conscious of holding the words of the lad suspended in air, as if they were something like a missile flung to hurt him, which he had caught just in time, but which had come close to wounding him fatally. It was as if he had yet to sense the import of their meaning, though the words had been going over and over like a chime of horrid bells in his brain, keeping time with his every move.

When he reached the outside steps he stood still, looking up to the quiet stars overhead, trying to steady his mind and understand. Repeating the lad's answer over now, alone with the stars, he took home the terrible truth. Betty was out alone with that filthy youth, Dudley Weston! Todd's Tavern! They could go to no worse place in the whole region round about. It bore a reputation that stood for all the modern sins!

He had just sense enough left to hope that Jim Harkness might have been trying to pull over some kind of a sickly joke. From the tone of his conversation earlier in the evening, and from the leer on his face when he was asked where Betty was, he could easily judge that a joke of just that kind would appeal to Jim Harkness. In fact, wasn't Jim the kid that used to carry Betty's books to school a couple of years ago? Perhaps there was a tinge of jealousy in the affair.

With momentary relief from his fears he drew a deep breath and pressed his white lips firmly.

Nevertheless, there was no time to be lost. If Betty had gone to a place like that she must be rescued before she could step a foot inside it. Fortunately he had a car that bore the reputation of being able to outdistance anything on the road, though he seldom had occasion to put it to the test. But now as he climbed into it, he threw in his clutch with a determination that made the engine jump.

Out at the school gate he came to a sudden halt and accosted a row of elementary school boys sitting on the curb smoking in the dark.

"Did you see a car drive out here a few minutes ago?"

"Yep! A Knowland Six! One eye on the blink. Taillight no good either!" they responded definitely.

"Which way did it go?" Thornton asked as if life and death hung on the answer.

"Out de pike!" was the prompt answer.

Grimly Thornton gave rein to his steed.

Chapter 4

The car shot forward like a racehorse suddenly put to track. It curveted around the next corner and dashed into the pike at fifty-five, barely escaping a darkened bus on the express lane from Washington, threaded a precarious way between two Fords dizzily driven, and an old-fashioned coupe piloted and passengered by elderly frightened women. He careened down the long hill by the Plush Mill, across the trolley tracks as if they were hurdles, and rocked up the hill beyond the bridge crazily. If he had seen another man drive as he was driving he would have said he was out of his mind. And perhaps he was, he thought, and strained his eyes to see ahead, watching for the fluctuating wink of a red taillight.

Occasionally as he fled along through the darkness, leaving the town behind and penetrating farther and farther into the country district, he wondered vaguely what had happened to the satisfaction he had felt as he entered the evening train on his homeward way that night. Surely, all of this was a bad dream! Surely he would wake up soon and discover he was still on his train, dozing, and hear Briardale called out and hurry home to tell Eleanor about the car

354

he was going to buy for Betty.

But no. The memory of the scene at the dinner table spoiled that. It passed before his mind like a panorama. A series of catastrophes, each one in itself enough to lay a burden on a father's heart. Even the twins seemed to have suddenly sprung into activity with their rationalistic talk. He must look into that school at once. Some fool teacher was likely amusing herself teaching such rubbish to the children. Some half-baked little country girl who had gathered a few wild ideas in college, which she thought were higher education. He would find out who it was and have her fired at once. What was the school board thinking about? But of course they did not know. He would see that they were informed before another day dawned. He probably ought to have accepted that nomination as a member of the board last spring instead of pleading that he had not time. Well, this was his punishment. But if he *had* accepted the position he would have done his work better than the others seemed to have done. Nobody who taught things like that would have got by him.

These ideas served to take his thoughts for a few minutes from the awful fear that was growing in his mind about Betty as he plunged on in the darkness, yet each time he sighted a blinking red light ahead his heart would fail him again, and a smothering sensation between horror and fierce anger would rise and almost choke him. The blood seemed to be all in his head and beating through his eyes, as if he were on his own feet running a race. His heart could not keep up and felt as if it would burst. He wondered if perhaps he might be having a stroke. But he must not, he must not, not till Betty was safe.

He overtook three different cars ahead, only to find them filled with staid elderly couples or family parties sleepily jogging home.

He had almost persuaded himself that Betty was safely at home by this time instead of driving off across the country with a wild youth. That was it, of course. Dudley Weston had been taking Betty home. Betty would never consent to go to a place like Todd's Tavern.

355

Betty was too well bred for a thing like that. Of course she would not know what kind of a place she was being taken to, but she would understand that it was too late at night to go off on a drive anywhere with a young man. It wasn't respectable. Betty would have made him take her home, of course. Eleanor had said she would be there pretty soon. Eleanor had seemed very sure. He was a fool of course to have taken this long jaunt on a chance word of a jealous boy who wished to put something over on him.

He had reached this point when he came in sight of Todd's, set far back from the road in the midst of a lonely grove on the top of a little hill, in a wild and lonely countryside. There were no lights anywhere in sight in any direction on hill or valley, save the fringe of red and yellow glare that edged Todd's Tavern. They blared through the night with a garish lure that sent the shudders down Thornton's back. That *his* child should be taken to a place like that even against her will was unthinkable! He would *somehow* have that Weston fellow arrested!

His car plunged on through the night, over ruts and humps without regard to its going, till he came at last to the high-arched gate with its single bright globe streaking across the dark of the road in a great gash of light above the dark winding drive that led by devious ways up to the inn.

Then caution suddenly seized him. He backed down into the shadow, parked his car as silently as possible, and proceeded on foot. As he trod the dry grass at the edge of the gravel making his footsteps as inaudible as possible, he began to think that it was going to be awkward to appear in that tavern and search for his daughter, *HIS DAUGHTER*! Supposing she was not there? He must let no one suspect that he even thought she was. He would have to be searching for someone else if he had to account at all for his appearance. He shrank inexpressibly from the ordeal. And yet it must be gone through with. If only he were sure whether she was really there; he could enter with more dignity. Perhaps there was a window unshuttered where he might look in and make sure, and possibly save being seen at all. It might be those high school children were entirely mistaken. Dudley Weston had perhaps taken some other girl to this abominable place, and his Betty might be even now at home asleep in her own bed. He must proceed slowly. It would not do to let even people who came to a place like this know that he feared Betty was here.

He dragged his heavy feet up the winding way till he came out on the level and was suddenly aware of a long line of cars parked in the dark edges of the drive. Somehow the sight of them brought a premonition. Was that— Could it be the Weston car? The last one in the line, parked boldly quite near the driveway?

Carefully, silently, he stole nearer, peering through the darkness. Yes, that was a Knowland, the same lines at least, and the taillight was out. So were the headlights. But he was sure about the car. He was used to seeing it go by his house every day. Perhaps he had better step up close to be positive. That would give him something to go on. Perhaps it would be well just to boldly go up to the door of the tavern and ask for Dudley Weston.

Thornton had taken the precaution to bring his flashlight from the car before he left it, and now as he stole toward this dark car his hand gripped it, ready for use when he should get close enough to see. One flash would make it plain. Besides, if he remembered rightly the Weston initials were on the door.

With the flashlight drawn and his finger on the switch, he crept close and raised the little lamp, but even as he did so he became aware of strong cigarette smoke and two red sparks glowing at him like two eyes from the backseat of the car.

It was too late to retreat, for the fingers had obeyed the order his brain had given, and his big searchlight blared out full in the faces of the two occupants, discovering to Thornton's horrified gaze his daughter Betty lolling in the embrace of Dudley Weston and puffing away at a cigarette.

The flashlight went dark, and there was an angry stir in the backseat of the car. Two glowing sparks of lights sped through the darkness like fireflies and were extinguished in the grass on the far side of the car. Then two angry young people issued forth and confronted him: Dudley Weston and his daughter Betty!

There was nothing about his daughter to show either that she had been lured into the present situation against her will or that she was a penitent sinner brought to overwhelming judgment. Wrapped in a fur-trimmed velvet evening cloak, which Thornton recognized as his wife's, she stood out against the blaring background of Todd's illumination almost regally, her slim body drawn to its tallest, her little sleek head held haughtily, like an angry princess. She surveyed him, and her voice was cold like showers of icicles as her words buried their sharp points in her father's heart:

"Well, Chester, what do you seem to think you're up to now? It strikes me somebody had better keep an eye on you. I'm about convinced that you've taken leave of your senses! What's the little old idea anyway?"

Then, suddenly confronted by her unbroken morale, Chester Thornton could think of nothing to say in reply. He even flashed the light upon her again, with an aimless idea that he had made a mistake somehow and this was not his Betty, his little girl, talking that way to him, not ashamed at all of what she had been doing! She bore the scrutiny of the light and his searching, pitiful, gaze without flinching. Her eyes were cold and hard, and her lips were scornful.

He tried to speak, and no sounds came from his parched throat.

Betty stepped coolly out of the spotlight and laid her hand on her companion's arm:

"Come on, Dud, let's go back and have another dance," she said nonchalantly. "If Dad thinks he can pull anything like this he's got another think coming. Let's go!"

A laugh of triumphant defiance broke hoarsely from the young man as he turned to obey. But suddenly Chester Thornton's senses were set free, and fury arose within him. Was this young reptile to defy him and lead his daughter away while he stood by? He had not forgotten the tricks he learned in college, and a quick well-directed blow under the chin sent young Weston sprawling on the hard bare ground to the utter astonishment of Betty, who whirled furiously on her father, a look in her eyes that was not good to see. It was a look that he was to remember long years after, a look like a blow that left a scar.

But Thornton was alert now and keyed up to the fighting point. He picked young Betty up in his arms as if she had been a feather and strode off down the hill.

Betty struggled furiously at first and then was still for an instant in sheer astonishment. When she began to struggle again, silently he held her like a vise.

"Look here, Chester, you needn't think you can treat me like this. I won't stand for it!" she defied him when she saw she could not get away.

But he strode on through the night without a word. "I'll scream!" she said threateningly. "And then what will they think of *you*? There are plenty of people in that tavern, and they will come out and laugh at you. A silly old parent that thinks he has just come out of the ark!"

Still Thornton strode on down the hill. It was taking all his breath, between his anger and helplessness and the weight of his daughter, which he had by no means been training for during the years.

They were almost to the car, and Chester Thornton was wondering whether he could hold out, when Betty dealt her final blow.

In a cold, hard, matter-of-fact tone she said:

"Well, I *hate* you, and I'm *off* you for *life*!"

The impact quivered through his trembling flesh like an actual blow. He realized that here was another thing with which he would have to live out the years, and never forget!

Betty! His little Betty! His first baby girl!

There was an instant's struggle again as they reached the car. Betty was determined not to be carried home ignominiously. But he held her fast.

"Will you get in quietly, or shall I have to tie you?" he asked in a strange panting voice that somehow startled her in spite of her hardness.

"Oh, have it your own way," she said, relaxing suddenly into indifference. "I'm getting terribly sleepy anyway and might as well go home." She summoned a casual yawn.

How had the universe got turned around? *This* was his Betty! The child for whom he had but a few short hours before been planning an expensive Christmas surprise and exulting in her probable delight in it. How had all this awful change come about?

He tried as he drove along through the night to think of a wise mode of approach, for he must have it out with her before he reached home. He would have to tell her all those awful words that that foulmouthed boy had said. There was no way to spare her from it. She ought to know the truth. Her humiliation would have to be complete before she could be brought to her senses.

Betty was leaning back, feigning sleep.

Very gently, very tenderly, with the deep, hurt love in his voice and words chosen from the depths of his suffering heart he began:

"Betty, it is because I love you—" he started in a voice she used to love.

"Rot!" said Betty sleepily. "Save your breath, Chester. That kind of mush is out of date."

Appalled, he summoned new words, sharp with truth, and began to tell her what he had heard in the train.

She listened through to the finish, and then her scornful laugh rang out like a flashing knife:

"Oh, is that all you've got on your chest?" she scorned. "I thought you were off your nut. But you've only got a Victorian complex after all. Poor Dad, you'll recover, but you've lost out as far as I'm concerned. I thought you had an open mind!"

"Betty! What do you mean? Don't you— Aren't you—?"

"No, I don't think Dud is a beast! No, I'm not shocked or humiliated or any of the other things you want me to be. This is an enlightened age, and things have changed since you were young. I have my doubts whether they were so very sanctimonious as you try to make out even then, but of course you want me to think they were. But as for Dud, he's all right. He's no worse than all of the rest of us. We're just frank and honest. All the boys talk like that. That's nothing. We're just living our lives in the new free way, that's all. You lived your life, and it's our turn now to live ours as we please, and there's no use in thinking we're going to be tied now by any antiquated whims that people tried to kid themselves into a century ago, for we won't do it."

"My child!" he said sadly. "Right and wrong do not change. God is always the same. There are certain laws—"

"Oh, bilge!" broke in Betty. "You don't really believe that. That's all baloney!"

Appalled, at last he gave it up and silently drove her to her home. There was nothing left to tell her, nothing to say, because she did not care for any of the standards he set up. She had torn them down with a laugh and flung them to the breeze. She had declared her inalienable right to do as she pleased and flouted the idea that there *was* such a thing as right and wrong.

He groped for the right word and wondered what it had been in his youth that had held him back from many things. Sin—that was it, a sense of sin. Why, *she seemed to have no sense of sin at all!*

He spoke the word as if it were a talisman, a sword that he had mislaid and was glad to find again.

"Betty, it is *sin*—" he said.

361

She laughed.

"What is *sin*?" she said pertly, imitating his voice as he pronounced the word.

An old answer came from out of his past, learned back in the years of long, dear, drowsy Sabbaths, with a smell of spiced cookies and gingerbread in the air, and his mother's sweet face as she sat in the rocking chair by her window on the old farm and read her Bible while he learned his catechism:

"Sin is any want of conformity unto or transgression of the law of God," he said.

Betty stared and laughed again.

"Where did you get that, Chet? Sounds like some highbrow lawyer. Whatever it is, it's moth eaten. What right would God have to make laws for us? If He put us here on the earth and made us live whether we wanted to or not, it's up to us to have as good a time as we can, isn't it? If there *is* a God," she added mockingly.

He was silent with the shock of it, the humiliation.

He had never taken time to live by them himself, but he had all the doctrines thoroughly defined, laid carefully away in a neat napkin in his mind ready for any time of need. He was an elder in the church! A warm advocate of all things orthodox and biblical! And his child was talking like this! This was rank atheism!

He was silent as he drove up to the door, on his face such a look of haggard despair that Betty turned, in a kind of hard pity, as she got out of the car:

"Listen, Chester," she said with a bit of fine condescension in her voice. "You needn't worry about me, really! Dud isn't as bad as he seems to you, and anyway, *I* know how to take care of myself. *All* girls do nowadays!"

With that she was off into the house, and the door closed lightly behind her.

He sat in the car for a minute more staring at the house, staring through the dark at the door where she had passed, hearing over again the awful things she had said to him—actually *said* to her father!

He moaned and leaned his weary head down against the wheel for a moment. Then laboriously he started his car again and drove slowly into the garage.

His wife was waiting for him when he came in. She had hot coffee and a nice little tray with delicate chicken sandwiches and a cup of custard in a china cup. She had stirred the fire when she heard him come, and his chair was waiting, drawn up before it with the tray on a little table at the side and only a dim shaded light at the far end of the room. She knew how to do all those exquisite little comforting things so perfectly. Just her presence was a rest.

But tonight, he waved her aside. How could he tell her? Betty's mother, pure as the snow! How could he tell her that Betty's lovely lips had uttered words of perdition, and that the very breath on which they were brought to his ear was rank with stale tobacco smoke, and a tang of something stronger! Betty's little rosebud lips! Betty's baby lips that had been so pure and sweet and wonderful!

He sank into the chair by the fire with a groan and covered his face with his hands. He shook his head when she tried to press the coffee upon him, and groaned again. How could he tell Eleanor? And yet he must. This was something they must bear together, work out together. Could he make Eleanor understand the horror of it all? And if she did understand, would it perhaps *kill* her?

Into the midst of the turmoil of his mind and the distress of his wife, there came the sound of a key turning cautiously in the lock, a key that was unsteadily fitted into place and turned reluctantly. At last the door opened, and Chris lurched into the hall. In his clumsy attempt to be quiet about it he knocked over a vase of flowers that stood on the hall console and then tried to mop it up with his hat, muttering that it was all right. No place for weeds anyway!

Something thick and unnatural in his voice caused both father and mother to look at him with startled eyes, and his father drew himself sharply out of the comfortable chair and went toward him:

"Chris!" he said, and his voice was like an electric current. "What is the matter with you? Where have you been?"

"Tha's none o' your business!" replied the boy, trying to straighten up and look steadily at his father, his dripping hat back again on his head. "You refused to gimme the dough I needed, an' I went where I knew I could get it! Tha's all! Wha's that t'you? Got m'debts all paid an' three dollars lef' over. Pretty good, what? You ain't got a single kick comin'—"

Chris's voice trailed off suddenly in a kind of choking sound as a strong hand seized his collar.

"That's enough!" said Chester Thornton authoritatively. "Don't say another word in your mother's hearing!"

He threw the boy's hat off, pulled off his overcoat, and taking him firmly by the arm propelled him up the stairs to the bathroom, his face sternly white, the boy dragging back and protesting.

"Wha's yer hurry, old soak?" Chris asked his father blearily. "Got all night, ain't we? I know I'm half-stewed, but wha's that? It's happened once or twice before—"

The bathroom door slammed over the last words, and Eleanor Thornton, listening in horror at the foot of the stairs, heard the water turned on furiously in the bathtub.

As if he were assisting at some horrid rite, Chester Thornton helped his son to remove his clothing, and then against his most earnest protests plunged him into a tub of cold water.

Minutes later, sobered, ashamed, well rubbed down and arrayed in dry, warm pajamas, Chris crept to his bed, and Chester Thornton came slowly, heavily down the stairs like an old, old man.

"Eleanor!" he said gropingly, as she came toward him from the darkened parlor and stood beneath the hall light, "Eleanor, I—"

It was then that everything went black before his eyes, and clutching for the stair railing and missing it, he fell and struck his head against the newel post. Then all the world fled away from his consciousness.

Chapter 5

Her mother's scream brought Betty to the head of the stairs calm, superior, in a hastily assumed robe. But when she saw her father lying at the foot of the stairs with blood on his forehead and her mother kneeling beside him wiping his face with her handkerchief and endeavoring ineffectually to lift him to a sitting posture, her assurance fled, and a white, scared look took its place. For angry as she was with him, she adored her father.

She flew down the stairs taking command as she came.

"Now Mums, you keep cool," she said. "I'll call the doctor. How did it happen?"

"He fell," said her mother reproachfully. "I think he was dizzy— He— Your brother—*You*— He's been—"

But Betty was already giving the doctor's number at the telephone and waiting, for no orders proceeded efficiently to the kitchen for water and ice and pieces of old linen.

The doctor arrived almost at once. Betty had caught him just as he came in from a late call before he had retired.

They laid Thornton on the couch in the living room, and Betty stirred the fire and put on fresh wood. She brought glasses and spoons and blankets and hovered silently in the shadows of the room until the quivering eyelids opened at last, and she saw her father's searching glance go hurriedly around the room, heard his deep, profound sigh as returning consciousness brought back his problems. Then she stole silently up to her room and lay down in the dark with her door open, listening. She was frightened at the white look of her father's face, but angry, too. It didn't seem quite decent of Chester to collapse this way just because he had discovered a few trifles about his children that he hadn't known before. He had no right to be so far behind the times that he would expect them always to be infants! When he got better she would have to take him in hand, bring him up to date and open his eyes to a few facts. Times were changed of course, and Chester hadn't realized it, but she had never expected him to show weakness, physical weakness, just because his whims were crossed. Whims! They were worse than that. They were antiques, wished on him by a former generation. How could he have been so blind as not to have seen before this that the world had outgrown them?

Yet she lay and quivered at the thought of her father ill. Her dad had always been so strong, so ready to give her anything she wanted.

She stole out to the hall and listened when the doctor talked in a low tone to her mother, straining her ears and trying to hear what they were saying. She could not sleep until she knew he was out of danger.

Then she heard her father call to the doctor. His voice sounded weak, strained, yet insistent.

The doctor went into the living room again, and Mrs. Thornton came slowly upstairs. Betty could see that she was weeping even before she lifted her tear-stained face.

"He's all right now, I hope, dear!" said the mother. "The doctor wants him to get to sleep. I'm going to put a hot water bag in the bed and get his things out. The doctor doesn't think the bruise was serious."

There was a quiver in the end of her voice that gave Betty a strange uneasiness.

"It's not like Chester to pass out!" said Betty with a half return of her habitual flippancy.

The mother shrank visibly from the words.

"I wouldn't, Betty dear," she said in a half-apologetic tone. "Your father doesn't like you to call him that. It doesn't sound respectful—"

"Rats!" said Betty inelegantly. "Are *you* trying to be an old stiff, too?"

"Betty! Really! Your father is very sensitive just now, and the doctor says we must be very careful. He says he is in a very dangerous state. He says this has been coming on for a long time—"

Betty gave her a startled look.

"For what reason?" she said and pinioned her mother with her glance.

"I'm afraid it's business," she said with a catch in her breath. "He's been lying awake at nights, oh, for weeks and perhaps longer. I don't know. He didn't tell me till recently. And then this tonight—"

"Business? What's the matter with business?" asked Betty sharply.

"I'm afraid things are in a very bad way."

"Whaddaya mean, bad way?"

"Well, I'm not sure, but I'm afraid your father has failed. I'm afraid it's just as bad as it can be. I know he was expecting something to happen yesterday that would turn the tide either way. And just now when the doctor asked him if he couldn't get away from business and take a real rest he said, 'Oh, the business doesn't matter anymore!' just like that, as if everything was all over. And I think that he is kind of desperate about it. I feel that we shall have to do everything we can to make him happy and make him understand that it doesn't matter whether we have any money or not if he only gets well. The doctor said that this was a warning. He didn't say just what, but from the questions he asked I'm sure he was afraid of stroke, or paralysis, or some of those terrible diseases. Betty, we must be *awfully* careful not to worry your father. But there! I believe the doctor is persuading him to come up. Get that other pair of pink striped blankets and lay them on the radiator. We might need them. He said he was so cold—"

Betty eyed her mother keenly. Evidently Dad had not told her yet. That was decent of him. No need in stirring Mother up.

Betty flew around efficiently, helping her mother, thinking her keen, stubborn young thoughts, trying to look a new situation in the face, and rebelling furiously at having her young life disrupted by any financial catastrophe. It wasn't like her dad to go flooey and leave them all in the mud. He must have done something awfully foolish to get things all in a muddle. She couldn't keep a kind of resentment out of her thoughts as she worked.

Yet when she caught sight of her father's white face again as the doctor helped him up the stairs, while she stood in the darkened back hall and watched, her heart failed her. Poor Dad! Poor Chester! He had always been such a good sport! Perhaps he would pull out of it! He had to. He would have to *borrow* money or something till times got all right again. Of course, that was it. He would borrow money. Everybody did nowadays anyway. It was old-fashioned to worry because you couldn't pay your bills right on the dot. Oh, Chester would pull out, of course. She couldn't think of them as settling down to be *poor*. Of course not. It wasn't to be tolerated!

And so, comforting herself, she crept back to her bed, and having heard the doctor go down stairs and out the front door, she composed herself to sleep.

~⁓

Mrs. Thornton tiptoed around her room putting things in order for rest, laying her slippers and warm robe on a chair by the bed for possible sudden need in the night, switching on a night-light in the hall just outside her bedroom door, switching off the brighter light. She slipped softly into bed, making the least movement possible that she might not disturb her husband.

She curled down gratefully under the blankets, let her tired head sink into the pillow and closed her eyes, for the evening had been a long, hard one and the culmination had been appalling. She had done a good deal of weeping, which was always exhausting, and her senses were almost benumbed with the various shocks they had received. But the things that had happened during the last hour had left the earlier events somewhat in the background. The unpleasant scene at the dinner table, and the incidents of Jane and Betty seemed comparatively unimportant in the light of later developments.

What, for example, had been the meaning of Chris's strange actions and his father's unprecedented treatment? Could it be possible that Chris was growing wild? She could not get away from the memory of the smell of liquor about him when he came into the house. She shuddered involuntarily as she thought of his unsteady step and incoherent speech! Chris! Her first little son, Chris, scarcely grown out of childhood, just coming into strength and beauty. Chris of whom she had always been so proud! Her first son! Chris gone wrong so early! And gambling! Could it be true? Surely it was someone else's fault, not Chris's. Why, Chris had been brought up to respect himself and his family! And that family had always stood for temperance and right living! His father an elder in the Presbyterian church, too! Surely Chris would not have knowingly disgraced his family!

She tried to think who Chris could have been going with that she might have someone else beside her son to shoulder the blame. That Harold Griswold, very likely. He had an expensive sports car and all the pocket money he wanted, and Chris had been determined to be in that car every waking minute out of school. They tore by the house forty times a day like a mad torpedo bound for destruction, and Eleanor had formed the habit of catching her breath and closing her eyes in a quick prayer whenever she heard the screech of the junior Griswold's car, for she was always certain that her own son was clinging somewhere about its rigging, if he was not actually driving it. She fully expected to see him flung white and lifeless across the pavement sometime, from mere momentum, as the reckless bunch of wild youths hurled by. Several times she had been on the point of appealing to Chris's father about it, only she knew that her husband was already overburdened with anxiety, and she kept hoping that Chris would find some new attraction, and it would not be necessary to worry his father with it. She did so hate to have Chester blame Chris for anything. He seemed at times so hard on the boy. As if he did not remember being a boy himself.

But now, surely, this Griswold boy was the one who had led Chris astray.

Having settled this matter and made up her mind to suggest this to Chester the first thing in the morning so that he would not blame Chris so severely, she turned to other troubles.

Chester. The doctor had said he was nervously run down and needed a change. The nerves around her heart gave sick, sore thrills of anxiety as she recalled the doctor's warning. Assuredly it must be managed and at once. If only Chester would be reasonable and see the thing as it was.

It would be fine if he could take an ocean voyage. The Batemans were going on the Mediterranean trip. It would be great if Chester could go with them! Of course he would object to going without her, yet he would not want to leave the children alone, especially after what had happened tonight. And of course it would be cheaper for Chester to go alone. He might even balk at any expense on his own account, but expense was not to be considered where his health was at stake.

Poor Chester, he must have had an awful day at the office, worn to a thread! And he had been so hopeful in the morning! Probably that was the explanation of his being so excited over Betty and her affairs, and even the children at the table, and poor little Jane. Jane was only a child. She had sobbed herself to sleep. She hadn't an idea she was doing anything wrong to show the boys her little school dance when they asked her, just a few of the college boys who had been friendly. But of course she must be made to understand that it wasn't nice to have done what she did. She must give Jane more attention, let her invite her little friends home, and have parties, so that she wouldn't be continually asking to go with the Carter child. Probably it was all the fault of the Carter girl. She was ill bred. She ought not to have allowed Jane to become so close till she had had time to get to know her mother. But she had been so busy! Those club meetings, and the child rearing class had been one straw too much. Yet it had seemed important to know the latest discoveries in child psychology.

Suddenly from out of the still darkness came her husband's voice: "Eleanor, are you awake?"

How did he know? She had not stirred. She was alert at once, a pang of fear at her heart.

"Yes, what is it? Do you feel worse?"

His voice sounded as if it came from far away, years ago; as if a great many things had happened since they last talked. He ignored her question as if it had not been.

"Eleanor, would it crush you entirely to give up our life here, in this house, in this town?"

He asked it anxiously, apprehensively, as if he knew he was asking a great thing and was sad for her to have to answer such a question.

Fear gripped her heart, and for an instant all speech left her. It had come, then! Chester had failed. In spite of his bright hopes, all was lost. They were going to be *poor*! Somehow she had never considered

371

that possible. Poor Chester! How terribly he must feel!

Then her brave heart rose to the occasion, and she summoned a cheer that she was far from feeling.

"Why, of course not, Chester. I wouldn't think of letting a thing like that crush me. If you are only well we can make a lark out of anything else. If that's what you are worrying about, forget it and go to sleep. It's really most important that you get your sleep. The doctor told me so. Now just put everything aside and try to relax. We'll talk everything over tomorrow and fix up some nice plan."

"You don't understand, Eleanor," he said, almost sternly. "This isn't something that can be put off. We've got to act, at once. It is imperative! Eleanor, we've got to begin our life all over again! I haven't told you everything—"

"Don't try to, dear," she said eagerly. "Just let it wait. I'm ready to do whatever you think best, of course, but you really must get some rest."

"I can't rest until this is settled," he said decidedly. "I've got to act immediately, the first thing in the morning. There isn't an hour to lose. I've been thinking it over in every detail, and there's only one thing to do. But I've got to have your hearty cooperation or it will be a failure."

"Haven't I always cooperated, Chester?" she asked half tearfully, feeling a premonition of even more than she had feared.

She leaned toward him, and her hand stole within his. He gripped it feverishly, eagerly, as if it was something strong and comforting to hold to.

"You certainly have, dear, always. You're a wonderful woman. That is why I shrink from putting this all upon you, especially just now when I had so hoped that I was going to be able to make life beautiful and easy for you from now on. But I see no other solution for our problems."

Bravely she rose to the occasion as she always had for lesser troubles:

"Then, Chester, let's accept it and get a good time out of it somehow, as we always have."

"Bless you, my dear!" said Chester, folding her hand closer and giving it a firmer clasp. "Well, then, wonderful little woman, how soon can you be ready to start?"

She caught her breath with the thought of all she was going to give up. Their lovely home into which they had put so many comforts and sweet memories. Their host of friends! The good schools—all the things that were so superior and had brought them to Briardale in preference to any other suburb. It came over her like a great shock. She had never thought it could come to this. She had expected possible economies but not to have to go away. Then she rallied her strength and forced her voice to be steady:

"Why, let me see, the dressmaker is coming next week—"

"You'll have to cut that out. It won't be necessary anyway, now."

"Oh," said Eleanor, with another shock, "perhaps not." Poor Chester! "Why, I can't tell without thinking. There'll be a lot of packing and sorting to do, you know."

"Not much!" said Chester crisply. "We'll only need to take the barest necessities, of course good warm things, and bedding."

A new fear gripped her. Then the failure must have been complete.

She was still for a minute trying to take it all in, and then her voice trembled back to steadiness as she asked:

"But what will we do with the house—and—and the things we are leaving behind? Won't we have to sort—and—and—pack—"

"No," said Chester quickly. "I'd thought of that. Hannah will be here, and she knows where everything is, and we can send for anything we may have forgotten. There are professional movers, you know, if there is anything Hannah and John can't manage. There won't be anything like that to hinder."

Appalled, she considered again. At last she asked falteringly:

"Why, how soon did you think we could get off, Chester?"

"About noon tomorrow," he answered crisply, as if it were the greatest relief in the world to have the announcement made.

Chapter 6

"Tomorrow!" she gasped. "Why, Chester, it is tomorrow already, and you haven't been to sleep yet! You know the doctor wouldn't possibly give his consent to your traveling tomorrow!"

She said the last in a soothing tone as one would speak to a sick child who demanded cake and ice cream.

"The doctor has nothing whatever to do with this," he said impatiently. "It is something you and I have to settle. As a matter of fact, if it comforts you any, I mentioned it to the doctor that I might be going away on a long trip tomorrow, and he seemed to think it would be the best thing I could do."

She lay still, growing cold at the thought of the inevitable, unable for the moment to take in all that had befallen her in one short night.

She was still so long that he thought she had gone to sleep.

"Eleanor," he asked cautiously, "you're not asleep? Why, Eleanor, you're not crying, are you?"

"N–no, Chester," she managed with a little catch of her breath. "I'm just—just—thinking! It's been rather sudden, you know."

"You poor darling! Yes, I know. How I wish I might have saved you all this. It seems as if I couldn't stand it for you—I—"

But Eleanor roused to protest once more:

"Don't think of it, Chester. It's not a bit harder for me than for you. And so long as we bear things together they won't get the better of us."

"You were always brave, Eleanor. But I'm afraid this is going to be particularly hard for you. Going away from comfort and convenience into comparative primitive living. I'm not sure you will be able physically to stand it. And yet I can think of no other way at present."

Primitive! She turned a startled look at him in the dark.

"Where—had you thought of—going, Chester? Had you any plan?"

"There is only one place. The old farm in Vermont. It's ours, you know, and I've always meant to remodel it someday, make it livable for a summer home. There are associations of my boyhood that I've always clung to. But now it seems like a haven, and I guess we'll have to put up with it as it is for a while, till we can get on our feet again and know what to do."

Eleanor's heart sank. Vermont! And he talked as if it was to be permanent! It must be that he was already out of the firm, or he would not think he could run away at a moment's notice this way. He must be really down and out. She had never seen him give up like this. How terrible!

She roused to her maternal tone.

"Nonsense!" she said briskly. "It will be a lark! I've always wanted to go there, and we never seemed to get around to it. Don't worry another second. Go right to sleep, now. If it isn't comfortable we'll make it so, somehow. And it will be good for us to have to go without some of the luxuries we've been surrounded with so long that we don't really have sense enough to be grateful for. What do you think I am? A butterfly? A peacock?"

"But there's no running water, Eleanor—" he explained anxiously.

"Well, there's likely some kind of water, isn't there? And we can do the running ourselves." She actually summoned a bright little laugh. "The twins will just enjoy carrying water."

"And no electric lights or gas—" went on the sad, honest voice.

Eleanor was appalled, but she only hesitated a minute.

"We'll make a bonfire then," she flashed at him. "Now, will you go to sleep?"

"And you are willing to start tomorrow?" he asked anxiously.

"If you feel well enough in the morning," she promised. "Come, go to sleep quick, or I can't get up in time to get ready!" and she deliberately turned over on her pillow and pretended to settle down for sleep.

"It will be very cold up there, Eleanor. You'll need all the warm clothes you can get, and blankets."

"All right!" said Eleanor briskly to hide the plunk of a great tear that was rolling down her cheek.

"You'll have to wear flannel, *real* flannel, you know. You can't get along with flimsy silk stuff such as you wear down here."

Eleanor was still a minute over a new thought:

"Hasn't that house been shut up for several years? Won't it be very damp? Do you think it will be safe to go in? We might all get sick!"

"There's been a caretaker living in the back part until a month ago. His son-in-law got hurt, and they went down to Albany to live with the daughter and help her out. It can't be so very damp. And there are stoves. It won't take long to rustle a fire."

There was almost eagerness in his voice, a yearning toward the scenes of his boyhood.

Eleanor's heart sank again. Rustle a fire! What mysterious thing was that! She had never made a fire in her life, nor come any nearer to it than to set a match to the fire in the fireplace, or stir it up and put on a stick. What was the new life going to mean? Surely, surely, it couldn't last. But she must be brave. Something would turn up to lighten the burden! When Chester got better he would be back in business again and would soon right their fortunes. At least the change would not be bad for him now. She could see he was almost attracted by it! But the children! How would they take it? Such a shame to take them from their schools where they were doing so well and were so attached. Suddenly she voiced her trouble:

"You don't think, Chester, that maybe there would be some way to—well, to hold it off a little till the school year was up? Or maybe leave the children here with friends to finish? It's going to be so embarrassing for them not to get their credits for the year's work when they have been doing so well. Helen Winslow would take Betty, I'm sure, and maybe Jane. Of course it wouldn't matter so much about the kiddies. They are young yet. But Chris and Betty ought to finish the grade and not miss a whole year or even six months."

"Eleanor!"

Chester Thornton sat up abruptly, regardless of the bandage on his head.

"Eleanor! You don't understand! I wish you didn't have to either, but you must. No, don't try to stop me. I'll have to explain now. Do you know where I found Betty tonight? Up at Todd's Tavern at the side of the road, in a dark car, lying in the arms of the foulest-mouthed boy it has ever been my fate to hear speak, and she was smoking a cigarette!"

"Oh, Chester!" cried Eleanor as if he had stabbed her, the tears flowing unguarded down her cheeks now. "Oh, Chester! Surely, surely you must be mistaken. Isn't that *awful*! Oh, but at least—I cannot think it was Betty's fault! Someone else has—"

"I'm not so sure!" said Betty's father grimly. "Do you know what she said when I spoke with her? She called me an antique and said I had a Victorian complex! And when I tried to tell her what that little viper had said about her in the train she only laughed and said he was no worse than any other boy of their set, that *every*body talked 'frankly' nowadays. People didn't have foolish reserves the way they used to, and it was a great deal better. She even hinted that she thought that you and I had probably indulged in the same indecencies when we were young. And she added quite significantly, that I needn't worry, that she *knew how to take care of herself*."

Eleanor gasped and sobbed brokenheartedly for a minute then pleaded sadly:

"But Chester, really, Betty wouldn't have *meant* all those things. She really *wouldn't*. You know that kind of talk is a kind of fad nowadays. The girls put on that sort of thing, but they don't *really mean* it all."

"Eleanor!" said Chester Thornton, and his voice was sternness itself. "Is it possible that *you* can excuse a thing like that?"

"Oh, no, no, of course not," said Eleanor quickly, stifling the great sob that seemed to engulf her. "No, I wouldn't *uphold* it, of course not! Only really, I don't think *Betty* had an idea of meaning all that. She must just have been copying some of the other girls—"

"Well, we'll put her where she won't have any of that kind to copy, then," said her father firmly. "Eleanor, where have we been? What have we been doing? Sleeping? That this thing could have burst upon us full fledged? Do you know our eldest son came in drunk tonight? Positively drunk? Do you know he had been in one of the lowest places in this city all the evening gambling? He told me so. He was drunk enough not to realize what he was revealing!"

"Oh, Chester! Chester!" said Eleanor. "*Surely* someone else was to blame for that. Someone gave it to him without his realizing what he was drinking. I'm sure he wouldn't drink—not *really drink—our Chris*! Or if he did I'm sure he never did it before—"

"I'm afraid not," said the father sadly, "I found a flask in his pocket with his initials on it from some fool of a girl, and it was not a new flask, either. Chris knew well enough what he was doing, Eleanor!"

Eleanor crumpled down into her pillow and felt as if the world had come to an end. How could all these awful things have come to her in one brief evening!

"And little Jane," went on the father, as if he were but thinking aloud. "Little Jane. If you could have seen her, leering, making eyes at those fellows, flinging her legs around in the most indecent way for those great loafers to watch her. I won't repeat the words that passed between them. It was too disgusting. Where have we been, Eleanor, that our children could have got away from us this way? Oh, we have been asleep!" He groaned aloud.

"Oh, don't, Chester!" begged Eleanor. "I can't bear you to take it like that! I *have* been worried," she confessed. "They've told such terrible things at the child rearing class. Really, you'd hardly believe—"

"After tonight I can believe *anything*!" said the father grimly.

"But they warned us not to oppose the children," Eleanor hastened to explain. "They said this was a new generation, and we must deal with them carefully and not antagonize them. They said it was a phase that would pass, a phase of adolescence!"

"Rubbish!" Chester snorted. "Rubbish! And you swallowed that? Eleanor, I'm surprised!"

"Well, no, I didn't exactly swallow it," said Eleanor, mopping her hot, weary face with a soppy handkerchief. "I thought about it, and I've been very careful. Of course I've always tried to put *positive* thoughts, good suggestions forward, and not negative ones. They say you must not say 'don't' anymore, that it merely rouses antagonism."

"Bosh!" said Chester angrily. "They all need a good, sound spanking! A lot of them! We've been all wrong, Eleanor! We've been too easy! I see it now. And those women in that club, Eleanor, they need to be spanked, too! They weren't spanked enough when they were young. They are fools, Eleanor! What in thunder did you ever see in a bunch like that? I declare, I shall go crazy, *insane*, if I don't get out of this town before tomorrow night!"

"Of course," said Eleanor, suddenly rousing to remember that her husband was sick, and the doctor had warned her that he must be kept very quiet and not get excited. "Chester, if you will just lie down and go to sleep now, I understand it all, and I'll get ready to go. I'll be ready whenever you say! There, dear! Do lie down! It's all right now, I understand. It'll be *all right*!"

Chester Thornton lay down, suddenly feeling very weak and tired, and murmured:

"Eleanor, you're the best little woman a man ever had for a partner!" And in spite of all her troubles, Eleanor Thornton somehow felt her heart warm and knew that *every*thing was not quite lost.

She laid a soft hand on the hot forehead of her husband and was rewarded in a few minutes by hearing his low, steady breathing and knew he had fallen asleep.

But she herself lay down in a daze and could not even close her eyes.

Over and over again she heard the awful words of arraignment of her children. Over and over she rehearsed certain sentences of Chester's, which she took to relate to his business affairs, and her heart sank lower and lower till there seemed no glimmer of light at all.

But so curious a hold has money and the things of this world on a human heart, that strangely enough the loss of the money loomed almost as large in Eleanor Thornton's scheme of things as did the misdemeanors of her children. Not that she did not hate sin as much as her husband, and shrink from having it come near her own, but that she simply could not believe that things were as bad as Chester had said. Chester was excited and weary and had seen things writ large. Chester would learn later that the children were not quite gone to perdition yet. They had only been experimenting a little and would soon come to their senses. In a healthy atmosphere these things would pass off. And of course, in a way, there was some advantage even in hiding themselves in a desolate Vermont farmhouse for a time.

But the morals of her children did not deeply trouble her as much as the immediate problem of how they would take their father's failure and what she was going to do herself about many little embarrassing details that were going to arise in the morning if Chester carried out his program of leaving the city at once.

There, for instance, was her civic committee. It was supposed to meet with her tomorrow, and the psychology class immediately following. The little cakes that she would serve with tea and bonbons were even now reposing in the tin cake cupboard, each one perfect in its snowy icing.

There was her bridge club the next day, and her old friend Genevieve Whitely just back from Japan and coming! And there was the committee for decorating the church at Christmas. It was to meet that Sunday night, and the plans were all made. She was chairman! She would have to write out the directions fully. No one else would understand, and the greens were all ordered. They would wonder why she had bought so many yards of laurel unless she drew a plan for the festoons. And there was the dressmaker! She would be annoyed, because she had changed three customers to give her these special days next week. There was Chalkley's bill she had promised to pay at once. She must not forget to make out the check the first thing when she got up.

So heavily did all these things weigh upon her that she almost contemplated getting up at once and beginning, only that she knew it would be sure to arouse Chester, and he really must get his sleep. Before long when he was surely sound asleep, she would just slip out and make out some lists, so that she wouldn't forget anything.

There would be all the children's clothes to pack, for they wouldn't have sense enough to select the right things. Betty would want to take all her party dresses, of course, and right then there would be a conflict if she tried to explain what kind of a place they were going to. They would all rebel at flannel underwear and woolen stockings. Thank goodness there was a whole trunk full of things like that stored away in the attic, packed safely in camphor, and all clean and mended. She had intended to get them out and send them in some missionary box pretty soon. They were put away one spring before it was certain that flannel was taboo for the rest of the time. She foresaw that she must pack such things without the knowledge of the children or they would manage some way to throw them out. Then there were the galoshes. They all had new ones, but she must not forget them.

She began to enumerate the list on her fingers: "Notes, telephone, checks, flannels, galoshes—" trying to relate one to the other in such fashion that she could remember them. If she only had a pencil and paper.

She reached stealthily out in the dark to see if she had left her little notebook on the bedside table and rejoiced to find it under a magazine. Carefully she drew it toward her. Yes, the pencil was inside.

She turned to a back page of the book where she knew nothing was written and began to set down the items, writing as well as she could by sense of feeling, hoping it would be readable in the morning. At last when she had written all she could think of, she put the book back on the table with a sense of relief and closed her eyes. It was a mountain of work to be accomplished in one short morning, but she thought she could do it if it was thoroughly organized.

She decided to get up as soon as daylight came and go up to the attic while the household still slept, filling the old suitcases with flannel underwear, old sweaters, and woolen stockings, and thus escape any chance of argument on that score. Then after breakfast she would make the children— No, that would entail constant argument if they did it. Better get them out of the way. That was it. She would arise *before* daylight and write her notes: write the ladies of the committees, and the bridge club, and a substitute for her Sunday school class, that she had been suddenly called away. Write her checks, and write as many notes instead of telephone calls as she could possibly get done before the children awoke. Then she would send the children with the notes and get them out of the way, leaving free time for her to select the things that were to go along. She could rush through it by going through every closet and bureau drawer systematically.

She meant to keep Chester in bed till the last minute possible.

She was just trying to decide how to tell the children of the sudden cataclysm that had befallen them, or whether to let Chester do it, when most unexpectedly she fell asleep. And when she summoned her thoughts and opened her eyes the sun was streaming broad across her bed, and Chester was not in the room!

Chapter 7

She sat up in a panic and called him, but there was no answer. The whole house seemed to be most silent. Oh, she had overslept! And Chester had escaped!

She looked at the little clock on the bureau, and it was quarter past eight! With sudden premonition she sprang up, threw her robe about her shoulders, slipped her feet into slippers, and went down the hall to find the escaped invalid. But there was no one in the hall or bathroom. The children's doors were all open, and no one answered her call.

She hurried downstairs to the dining room, but there was no one there. The table showed signs of a few hurried breakfasts, but no one answered when she called again.

She went out to the kitchen, and Hannah was just emerging from the back kitchen, her arms full of milk bottles and fresh loaves of bread from the baker's cart that usually passed about this hour.

"Oh, are you ready for your breakfast, Mis' Thornton?" asked Hannah, quite in her every morning usual tone.

"Why, Hannah, where is Mr. Thornton? Did he come downstairs?

I must have overslept!"

It began to seem to her that she must have dreamed all those awful things that had happened last night. Probably none of them were true. Probably they were not going away to Vermont this morning, and all was as usual.

But Hannah broke that illusion.

"Yes, ma'am, Mr. Thornton was down at half past five. I was up because I'd forgot to put the note in the milk bottle to leave that cream for whipping. I give him a cup of coffee right at once, and he went down to the office. He said he couldn't wait, but I made him eat some bread and butter and scrambled eggs, and while he was eating he told me I was to put up a lunch, a good big one, so I got the sandridges all made, ham, an' chicken, an' jelly ones. I used that half a roast chicken was left from last night. You all didn't half eat yer dinners an' there was plenty. I got some little blackberry tarts in the oven now, and I've made a sponge and a nut cake. I guess you'll do. And there's some o' that spice cake left, too. Mister Chris he likes that. An' I'm boilin' the eggs now fer hard boils—"

"Oh, Hannah!" cried the frantic mistress. "You're an angel! And to think I overslept when I was so very anxious to get down before anyone else."

"'S awright!" said Hannah indulgently. "The mister said I wasn't to disturb you till half past nine. He said you was all tuckered out an' needed the sleep."

Eleanor gasped.

"Oh, he ought to have woken me up! I don't see how I'm ever to accomplish everything. Hannah, do you know where the children are?"

"Why I rackum they've went to school," said Hannah placidly. "I didn't say nothin' to 'em. Miss Betty she come down late as us'l an' drunk two cups of coffee an' beat it. Jane she was down furst off, soon's her pa got outta sight, said she had some lessums to study an' she'd lef' her books over ta Nemly's."

"But didn't they see their father, didn't he tell them—"

"I guess not, Mis' Thornton. They didn't come down till he was gone. The twins come down just after Jane, and I scrambled 'em some eggs, and they went. Come to think I don't know if Mr. Chris come at all. I ain't heard him—"

Eleanor caught her breath and did some swift thinking.

"Oh, all right, thank you, Hannah," she said and turned back upstairs.

Perhaps it was just as well that the children were out of the way for the time being. She would get a lot done toward the packing before they knew, and forestall *all* contention. Of course she would have to do the work single handed, but perhaps that was easier. And if worst came to worst she could cut out the telephone calls and send telegrams on the way saying she had been suddenly called away.

She dressed hastily and fairly flew up to the attic.

It took but a few minutes to sort out the woolen things and dump them into the suitcases that stood close at hand, to pile a few extra blankets and coverlets at the head of the stairs ready to be taken down. She added a roll of old linen and sheets. If they had to return to the primitive life, they would need old rags.

She resurrected several old traveling rugs and sweaters and a thick coat or two and began to wonder how all these things were to be carried in one seven-passenger car that would have seven full-sized passengers in it when they were all in. The trunk would have to be reserved for their wearing apparel and would scarcely be adequate even then. But perhaps Chester meant to pack a box and send it express. At any rate, the things were there, ready to put right in somewhere.

She went downstairs with a feeling of relief that the worst item of her list was finished.

Betty's room was the first to attack. Betty would be the worst to deal with in case she came back soon. Perhaps Chester had sent her to school to get her books and say good-bye.

She went through Betty's things hurriedly, worriedly. It would seem that there was not much of Betty's apparel that was suitable for an occasion like this. A few rather expensive casual dresses, one a silk and wool jersey; one silk pleated skirt with an exquisite angora sweater, whose only claim to going along was that the sweater was warm; and a little knitted dress for which she had just been wheedled into paying an exorbitant price. Betty was wearing her most sensible dress today, a rich soft brown. That was well, for she needed something warm and dark for the drive, and it would have been a struggle to make her put it on perhaps if she hadn't chosen it herself.

As she reasoned, she began to be aware that she was almost afraid of Betty, of what she might say and do. That was not right, of course. Perhaps she ought to have been more firm with Betty. In spite of the child rearing class, she might have made a mistake. Betty used to be a tractable little girl.

There was scarcely any underwear among Betty's garments that was suitable for a winter life on a northern farm, but mindful of the plentiful stock in the attic she packed a few of Betty's most sensible underthings, added a couple of pairs of silk stockings for dress up— although what dress up could there possibly be for poor Betty out on that dreary farm? Was Chester doing just the wisest thing? Would not Betty and all of them in fact rebel at such summary tactics? However, it might not last. Chester might find some other way out. Perhaps it would prove to be merely a nice Christmas vacation for them all, and there would be a way out of their catastrophe in a little while.

She folded Betty's things neatly and laid them in piles on her bed, trying to put everything into as small a compass as possible. Shoes, warm gloves, hairbrush, comb. . . None of those ridiculous bottles and jars of cold cream would be needed. She need not bother about jewelry, either. A little dose of simple life would do Betty good.

She discovered as she went toward Jane's room that the three big suitcases that fitted into the automobile trunk were standing ready in the hall. Poor Chester, himself ill, yet thinking of all these things, even telling Hannah about a lunch! Oh, would he get through the day without breaking? She sent up a swift prayer for him and hurried on with her work.

It did not take so long to lay the neat piles into a suitcase. There was going to be more room than she feared. She even in pity stuck in a string or two of Betty's beads. The child would feel utterly lost without something of the sort.

Jane's garments were less of a problem. Jane still wore gaudy woolen stockings with fancy tops on occasion. Jane wore pleated skirts and sweaters. Jane had several warm, pretty dresses. She made short work in there. Also the twins were no problem at all. They had their good sensible clothes. Betty would have her new fur coat, of course, and her old one, which she was supposed to wear to school—and seldom did now because she liked the new one better. The old one would do for Jane.

She worked swiftly. By half past nine she arrived at Chris's door, suddenly remembering that Hannah had said she had not seen him that morning.

There he lay deep in sleep, and the hard lines of his young face, the weak sag of his handsome mouth, startled her. Chester had been right. They needed to get away at once. Eleanor went swiftly from drawer to closet, working with frenzied fingers, the tears running down her face, but Chris lay sound asleep and did not stir.

After she had packed the things she thought he needed, leaving out those he would have to wear, she turned toward him and laid her hand on his forehead.

He stirred uneasily and drew away from her touch.

But this was no time for sentiment. The minutes were flying, and she needed Chris's help.

"Chris!" she called clearly, close beside him, but Chris slept on.

At last she brought a cold, wet cloth and washed his face. It would not do for his father to come back and find him sleeping while his mother was doing all the work alone.

He started awake angrily, furious at the cold water, not sparing his mother any rudeness that came into his cloudy mind.

"Chris," she said firmly, "you'll have to get up at once! I need your help. Your father has been very sick, and we have to go away. The doctor thinks it's imperative!"

"What the deuce!" said Chris, flinging himself back on his pillow and blinking at her. "Dad was all right last night. I'll say he was. What's he trying to put over on us?"

"Chris, that's not the way to speak of your father. And you must get up at once and get to work. There is a great deal to be done, and your father is a sick man. He's gone down to the office for a few minutes, but he may be back any minute, and it would be dreadful if he were to find you still in bed. It's half past eleven. Chris, your father has been going through a terrible time. I'm afraid he has lost all his money—everything! You'll have to be very gentle and helpful! Hurry! I've several important errands I must send you on. Don't waste time, get up at once."

She left him, closing the door and going at once to her own packing of which she made short work, folding into the remaining suitcase her own and her husband's plainest garments.

Hannah came up while she was doing it.

"Now, Mis' Thornton, wha' kin I do? I got the supper packed in the hamper, an' I got a pot of soup on fer you all ta eat. What you want I should do after you all leave?"

She began as she spoke to smooth up the bed and tidy the room with a deft touch here and there that made it much easier to sort out things and pack.

Mrs. Thornton could hear Chris splashing about in the bathroom and knew that in course of time he would appear, so she gave Hannah a few directions and sat down to write some of the notes that she felt were imperative to send before she left. If Chris got ready in time he could take them, if not she would leave them for Hannah to deliver.

But Chris when he appeared was not inclined to deliver notes.

"What's all this about going away?" he asked his mother, frowning as he stood imperiously in the door of her room and stared around at the suitcases and the general air of devastation the packing had wrought in his mother's usually neat room.

His mother was finishing an important note and did not answer at once, and Chris further addressed her:

"I want you to jolly well know that *I'm* not going along! I've got important things to do here at home. If Dad's broke I've got to get some money somehow, even if I have to accept a job somewhere! And you can just take my things outta that suitcase! I'm staying at home!"

His mother looked up sorrowfully, and it seemed to her that she had not really noticed before how her boy had changed. He seemed to have been suddenly transformed in a night, or was it that her eyes had suddenly been opened and she was awake now?

"Chris, there probably won't be any home here to stay in," she said sadly, the enormity of the situation sweeping over her anew, and the tears coming unbidden into her eyes and rolling down her cheeks.

"Whaddaya mean?" demanded Chris furiously. "No home. Whaddaya mean?"

"I mean just that. We're going to have to leave here. I have not had time to talk with your father beyond a few minutes of planning for the immediate future, but I feel positive that the business has been swept away, at least so far as your father's part in it is concerned. Your father has been going through a terrible ordeal, and the doctor told me last night that unless he gets immediate relief from the strain he will have a stroke of paralysis or something terrible like that. So, you see that if you make it any harder for him you may be responsible for his life!"

"Great cats!" said Chris irreverently. "Has Dad been speculating? I thought he had some sense! He had no business to let things get into a mess when he had us to take care of! A man has no right——"

"Christopher!" said his mother. "A mere boy has no right to criticize his father! Don't let me ever hear you speak of your father like that again! You ought to be ashamed!"

"Aw well," said Chris, walking into the room with an air of a young prince. "Looka hear, Muth. This leaves me in an awful fix. I'm broke. D'ya understand? And I've practically promised to buy Hal's automobile day after tamorra. I swore I'd have the first payment for him, an' a fella can't let a thing like that go flooey. I ask you, cannee?"

"Chris, you don't mean that you have bought an automobile without telling your father? You know what he said about not allowing you to drive yet!"

"Oh now, come off, Muth, don't begin that! This is an offul good bargain. I could fix it up and sell it fer fifty or a hundred bucks more'n I paid, see? It would give me something steady to do outsida school, see? Dad's always harpin' on my being employed. As if a fella oughtn'tta have a little fun now an' then."

"Chris, for pity's sake, don't let's talk about such things now. I want you to go up in the attic and bring down the large trunk over in the corner, the one with Grandfather's initials on it. Bring it right away, quick! I'm in a great hurry. And then go back and bring down that pile of blankets at the head of the stairs."

"Awwright, Muth, only waitaminute! I wanta ast you something. Say, Muth, this is very important to me. How much money have you got, Muth?" He lowered his voice anxiously, "B'cause, if you lend me some—about two hundred say, I'll pay it up soon's my allowance comes in, I mean over time, of course. I'll pay half of my allowance every month till it's all paid. Honest I will, Muth——"

"Chris!" said his mother, looking at him with a blanched face. "What are you talking about? What in the world could you possibly want with two hundred dollars? And you know what your father said about borrowing from me or anyone else. I couldn't lend you any money if I had it, and I haven't got it. I've just made out checks for bills we owe, which takes all but a dollar or two of what I had in the bank, and I don't know when your father will be able to give me any more. You don't seem to understand that your father is financially ruined. Now, will you get that trunk?"

"But Muth, I *gotta* have it! Right now, I gotta have it."

He looked at her pleadingly, his miserable eyes piercing her very soul. She felt as if the earth beneath her was reeling. What had Chris got into now? At another time, even the day before, if Chris had come to her with eyes of anguish and pleaded like this she would have turned heaven and earth to get the money for him. She would have covered it up and thrown some kind of a sop to her conscience for helping him evade his father's law about borrowing. But her eyes had been opened, at least halfway. She began to suspect that there was something wrong, something more than just what Chris put on the surface.

Downstairs the twins had come bursting into the house, home from school for lunch, and Jane's voice could be heard outside calling merrily to her companions.

"Oh bother!" said Chris. "Oh *heck*! Muth, I simply *gotta* have that money 'fore night! I'm up ta my eyes. My *honor's* at stake!"

"*Your honor?*" said his father's voice in the doorway behind him. "Your *honor*! Just what is it you call your honor, Chris?"

Chris turned as red as a beet. His eyes drooped, and he wheeled and faced his parent like a thing at bay. When he lifted his glance to see how angry his father was, his eyes fell again as if they had been struck.

Eleanor came forward anxiously, her eyes on her husband's white face:

"It's nothing you need bother about, Chester," she said. "It's just a little matter between me and Chris. You needn't worry. I'm just as firm as you are when it comes to things like this. You go and lie down and let me deal with this."

Chester's eyes looked at her sadly, and then he turned back to the boy again, who had already brightened under his mother's tone.

"Just a little matter of two hundred dollars," he said, as if it were a sword that he had held back from doing damage.

"Chris, step into your room for a few minutes. I have something to say to you."

"Why, I can't just now, Dad. I promised to get a trunk down for Muth," said Chris with a show of haste. "She's waiting for it."

"Very well," said Chester. "I'll wait."

Chris tugged the empty trunk down the attic stairs, with many a thump and a snort as if it were very heavy indeed, and then went back for the blankets while his father waited at the foot of the stairs courteously, until the task was completed.

"Now, if you're quite ready, Chris, we'll step into your room," said Chester.

When the door closed behind the two, Eleanor Thornton sank back into her chair again and buried her face in her hands. She was so tired and frightened and worn out with various emotions that it seemed to her she must just sink down on the bed and cry.

The clamor downstairs roused her. Jane was teasing the twins, or they were teasing Jane. It didn't matter which. There was sound of breaking crockery and Hannah's sharp voice remonstrating. This was no time for weeping. She had promised to be ready.

She hurried downstairs and started the children to eating. Jane was clamoring that she must hurry back. They had a rehearsal of the play fifteen minutes before the afternoon session. She begged that she might have bread and butter and plum preserves and go right back, eating it on her way.

"Sit down, Jane. You're not to go back to school today. We're going away!"

"Going away?" screamed the twins in chorus. "Gee! Where? Can we go, too?"

"Yes, we're all going. Now eat your lunch. There isn't time to talk. There's a great deal to be done. Jane, sit down! Didn't you hear me?"

"Mamma, I can't go anywhere today," said Jane, assuming Betty's best manner for the occasion. "I think it's the limit for you to go away somewhere when you know I can't go. You know the rehearsal lasts all this afternoon—"

"Jane, sit down, and I'll explain. You are not going back to school. We are going away. They will have to get along without you at the rehearsal."

"But they can't, Mamma," said Jane with her mouth full. "I'm in every scene. I'm really the *star*! It wouldn't be *honorable* of me to go away and leave them in a hole!"

Honorable! There was that word again. What a strange sense of honor her children seemed to be suddenly developing.

Eleanor tried to explain.

"Circumstances have taken a most unexpected turn, Jane. I haven't time to explain to you now. But your father or I will see that your teacher is notified. It isn't as if there isn't plenty of time before the play to supply your place, and you told me yourself that at least two of your classmates were both eager and able to take your place, so we shall not be seriously inconveniencing anybody."

"Do you mean that you're not going to let me be in the play at all?" asked Jane, aghast.

"We will not be in town, Jane. We are going away this afternoon."

"I won't *stand* it!" Jane shouted with a quick burst of angry tears. "I won't, I *won't*! You *shan't* do a thing like that to me! I'll run away! I'll—I'll—I'll stay at Emily Carter's." She paused in her outburst and brought out a tempestuous little smile with a tilt of her small chin and a toss of her curly head. "*That's* what I'll do, Mamma. I'll stay at the Carters' till you come back, or—or—till after the play's over."

"Under no circumstances will you stay at the Carters', Jane. And your father is quite unwilling that you shall either act or rehearse in that play even once more. He saw quite enough of your part last night. If I had known what it was that you were doing, if I had understood—"

"Why, Mamma, it wasn't like what I did last night. I changed it just for fun. There's nothing you couldn't like about the play, really. If you'll just come over and watch me rehearse, Mamma. Please—"

"Jane, sit down!" said her mother severely. "Sit down and eat your lunch. We have no time for further discussion. I'll explain everything later. As soon as you are through, go up and change to the dress that is lying on your bed, and be quick about it!"

But Jane in a storm of tears dashed into the living room and flung herself upon the couch to howl.

"Jane, you must stop this noise at once," said Eleanor, following her. "Your father has been very ill, and you will make him worse."

Jane wept on, growing louder.

John appeared on the scene, his face smeared with plum jam and a blackberry tart in either hand:

"Aw, cut it out, Jay," he called. "We're goin' ta have a corkin' time. Hannah says we haven't any money anymore an' we're goin' away off to live on a farm where they have pigs and cows and a haystack to slide down and ponies and a wheelbarrow."

Jane sat up and looked at him. She made a face at him, and then she went on crying.

"I—shan't—g–g–g–go!" she sobbed out tempestuously.

About that time the door of Chris's room opened upstairs, and Jane heard her father's footsteps, heard his voice in grave tones. She remembered his grip of her arm last night and got up from the couch. She came slowly back into the dining room, mopping her red nose and eyes and catching her breath in broken sobs as she slid into her seat at the table.

The dining room became very quiet. Even the twins were still, eating tarts and drinking more milk.

Chris was walking downstairs behind his father.

"Yes, sir!" they could hear him say in a subdued tone. "Yes, sir. I will."

They came into the dining room silently and took their seats. Chris did not look at his mother. He sat down and began to eat from the plate Hannah gave him. He asked for coffee, but he did not look at anybody. His eyes were down upon his plate as if he was ashamed, or afraid, his mother could not tell which. Her heart began to quake with new fears.

Chapter 8

"Where is Betty?" asked Chester Thornton, looking with troubled gaze around the table.

"She got off to school before I woke up," said Eleanor apologetically, "and I haven't had time to send word for her to come home."

"But she ought to be here by this time," said her father, looking at his watch.

"She ain't comin' home," volunteered John. "I saw her go into the cafeteria with some kids fer lunch. She told me to tell Mamma she wouldn't be here."

"I had better telephone for her," said Eleanor, rising anxiously.

"No!" said Chester sharply. "Just get her things ready, and we'll stop for her on the way. We haven't time to wait for her to come home."

Eleanor sank back into her chair once more, finished the coffee, and took one more bite of her bread and butter, but she felt as if she could hardly swallow anything.

"The truck will be here soon," said Chester. "There'll be room for a trunk or two and all the blankets and pillows you need to take. How soon will you be ready?"

"Oh!" said Eleanor feebly. "Why, yes. Very soon."

"Chris and I have an errand to do," announced Chester. "It may take us fifteen or twenty minutes, and when we get back I'll be ready to start whenever you are. I noticed you had my things pretty well packed."

Eleanor marveled at the restrained voice of her husband. He seemed deathly white, and she feared for him. She wondered what the errand was that was important enough to take him away even for fifteen minutes. She looked keenly at Chris, but he went on eating with his eyes downcast. Her heart seemed heavy like lead. She swallowed the scalding coffee and rose without attempting to eat anything more.

"I'll go up and put the last things in," she said. "Jane, you had better come with me."

Jane looked at her father.

"Daddy?" she said with a quiver in her voice. "Daddy, do I have to go?" Her question ended in a wail.

"Yes!" said Chester, looking at the little girl with a reminder of last evening in his eyes, until she quailed.

"But—Daddy"—her lips were quivering with the pretty, pitiful plea that had always won her what she wanted—"Daddy, I can't leave my teacher in a h–o–o–ole!"

"I will explain to your teacher," said Chester Thornton. "Jane, your mother needs you upstairs."

Jane arose slowly, reluctantly, sobbing into her handkerchief despairingly, but her father and Chris went out without noticing her. Chris walked as though he was about to face an ordeal.

When they had gone out the front door Jane returned to the dining room to retrieve the last tart from the twins and went slowly upstairs, emitting crumbly sobs occasionally.

"Jane, sit on this suitcase while I fasten it," called Eleanor, and Jane, discovering her old last year's sweater and cap, grew suddenly interested. She looked around and discovered the other suitcases and the big trunk. Somehow the affair took on new meaning. There might be something interesting in it all, even if one didn't get to act in the play. There would be other plays, and they would likely be coming back someday. It was rather fun after all to be taken out of school and go off on a mysterious trip.

Chester and Chris did not come back in fifteen minutes. Eleanor watched the clock anxiously, not because she cared how late they started but for fear of what might be unearthed of Chris's misdoings.

Then Michael, the driver, arrived with the truck, and she had her hands full getting the right things loaded in. Of course having the truck come made things a thousand times easier. She could just wrap a lot of things in an old quilt and have it piled into the back, without bothering to pack.

During this episode Jane disappeared and was discovered just turning the corner of the street. It was Michael who ran after her and brought her back.

"I was only going to get some things I left at Emily's and then run around and say good-bye to the school," she explained sulkily.

Eleanor set her to work scrubbing the tart off the twins, and searching in the hall closet for all the galoshes.

"I don't see what we need these for," said Jane. "We're going in a car, aren't we? Where are we going, anyway?"

"To a nice place where Daddy used to live when he was a boy," explained Eleanor. "We're all going off to have a good time, because Daddy is all tired out and needs a rest."

Jane eyed her keenly. She had a lurking suspicion that the migration had something to do with her performance at the drugstore, but she said nothing.

Then Chester arrived with a subdued-looking Chris. Eleanor

tried in vain to read from their faces what had happened but could not in the bustle of leaving.

Hannah came down to the car to take last directions, and there was no more time. She had to count up the suitcases, run back to look through all the rooms, and make sure that nothing important had been left behind.

Then they all piled in, Eleanor in the backseat with Doris in the middle leaving a place for Betty; Jane, still sulky, and John, too excited to sit down, in the middle seats. Chris was in the front, with Chester driving.

Chester slammed the door shut and put his foot on the clutch. Hannah came running with the other thermos bottle of hot chocolate for the twins and an extra milk bottle, and Eleanor looked back at the home she so loved and wondered if she would ever see it again.

The twins were excited now and were talking.

"Daddy, will there be plenty of pigs?" asked John.

"Cut it!" growled Chris importantly and then subsided again as if he suddenly remembered.

The car started and went down the street. Jane looked hungrily toward the Carter house and twisted her neck to get a last glimpse of the drugstore on whose steps lounged two prep boys, smoking illegal cigarettes. She gave them a grimace with her tongue in her cheek, which was not unnoticed by her mother, and then settled down to the excitement of going on a journey. Jane was not at the stage of life where an impression had very deep hold. A new one could easily erase it.

They turned down the street on which the high school was located, and suddenly Eleanor's heart gave a thud of fear. There had been so many that day. Now what would Betty do? Make a scene, probably. What would that lecturer have suggested in a case like this? But then of course that lecturer would never have allowed things to go as far as this. She would likely have said that the children had a right to express themselves. They had their own lives to live, and if they did not want to live them as their father and mother wanted them to do, they should not be forced into it. Bah, what foolishness it all was. Something was wrong. Why had she not seen it all before? It was a wrong basis to start out on. Expressing themselves! What were "themselves" anyway when they didn't know what it was all about yet?

Chester stopped the car and got out. He walked briskly up the steps of the high school and disappeared within the great doors. Jane had a satisfying reflection that Daddy would meet his match in the superintendent. Perhaps there was still hope that they might not have to go anywhere until school was over. What a lark it would be *then* to go off on a mysterious journey to a new place!

Betty was applying lipstick to her pretty mouth, carefully, thoroughly, vividly, behind her largest study book propped up on her desk.

Her seat happened to be at the back of the room, and as the teacher was busy with a class in the front of the room she was not likely to be discovered. It was counted a misdemeanor to apply makeup in school, especially so in that teacher's precincts, but Betty felt a little pale, and the class meeting to be held immediately after school was one of the places she liked to be particular about her appearance.

Betty never attempted anything but the faintest makeup around home. She knew her mother did not consider it good taste, and her father could not endure it, so she always went early to school and paid a good deal of attention to patting her face into order behind the door in the cloakroom before she went into her classroom. It was annoying to have to plan, and be stealthy, just to be decent. A pity one's parents were so behind the times!

She was thinking about it as she put the finishing touch to

the gory little cupid's bow she was making of her mouth, her lips pursed up like a cherry, when she heard her name called and felt the searching eyes of Miss House come down and pierce behind her Latin textbook.

Lipstick and mirror went down like a flash. Out came a small white handkerchief and gave a quick polish to her chin while she assumed an interested manner and lifted innocent eyes to her teacher's call.

"Miss Elizabeth Thornton, you are wanted in the office at once!"

Betty arose, annoyed. Surely Miss House wouldn't send her down to the office just for brushing up her lips a little, all so quietly in the back seat with no one sitting near to watch her. She had waited till the psychology class came in to recite before she even started, and it hadn't taken her but a minute.

Betty went down to the desk haughtily to protest, but Miss House waved her toward the door.

"Someone in the office waiting to see you. Professor Morley said you were to come at once!"

Wondering, yet somewhat relieved, she made her way down the hall.

Someone to see her! Who could it be? Surely Dud hadn't taken this way of communicating with her. He wouldn't dare openly. He would likely call up and make an appointment in code sometime late in the afternoon. But who on earth could it be?

As she turned the knob of the door there came a sudden thought of her father like a sharp little pain going through her heart. Perhaps something had happened to her father! Perhaps he was worse, and her mother had sent for her! How terrible if one's father should die, as Hattie Blaine's father had done last week!

Then girding herself up and lifting her chin a little haughtily she entered the door and stood face-to-face with her father.

She stared at him, half-relieved, half-frightened. Had Chester gone crazy, tracking her around this way? What could have happened? She forgot entirely the vivid color that she had just applied to her lips and could not understand the startled stare her father gave her for an instant before he spoke. Then his voice sounded harsh and stern as he said:

"Get your hat and coat, Betty, and come with me! Professor Morley understands you're going, so you need wait for nothing but to get your things. Hurry! I will explain it all to you on the way. We are late already!"

Betty's face darkened ominously, and her little red lips went thin and hard with determination.

"I couldn't possibly think of it," she said. "Wherever you're going, Chester, you'll have to go without me. I've got commitments all the afternoon, and I haven't a minute to spare. I've one more recitation before three o'clock, and I'm not quite ready for it."

"You are excused from recitations, Betty. I have arranged all that."

"But I have a class meeting and an important report to give. I couldn't possibly go if it were a trip to Europe. And we have basketball practice this afternoon."

"That has nothing to do with it, daughter. Something far more important has come up, and you will have to come with me at once! If you have any message to send to anyone I am sure Professor Morley's secretary will take it for you."

He turned to the girl at the desk who was discreetly making out index cards.

"Will you kindly let my daughter's friends know that she was suddenly called away by her father and will not be able to be at her class meeting this afternoon, or her basketball practice?"

Betty bit her red lips hard; she was so angry with her father for mortifying her this way. She tried to think of some way out, but he stood waiting for her and she turned, slowly, reluctantly, and went across the hall to the cloakroom, looking eagerly either way in hopes of seeing some of her special friends that she might send a hasty word of explanation to one of the boys who had asked her to take a ride in his new car that afternoon. She had really been planning to slip away from basketball. But no one whom she dared trust came by, and she had lingered as long as she dared in the cloakroom with her father standing just outside the door. She finally had to come out and follow him down the steps.

Once outside the school she made another stand.

"See here, Chester, what's all this about? I simply *can't* go away anywhere today. I really have things that I must do. You don't understand what a responsibility a girl in my position has. I'm class president, and we've just found out some of the class are trying to put something over on us. Trying to influence the faculty to say we can't wear anything but plain white muslin dresses at commencement, and a lot of folly like that, and I've simply *got* to go back and put a stop to it. If the vote goes their way it will make us no end of trouble. We'll have to get up a school strike to undo the mischief."

Chester Thornton took his daughter's arm, firmly, but with a friendly touch:

"You'll find it won't affect your future in the least, Betty," he said in a kindly voice. "There are several things you do not yet understand, and I will have to explain, but the main one just now is that you are to come with us *at once!*"

"Us?" said Betty with a sudden quick glance down the walk at the car that she had merely taken for granted before. "Us?" incredulously. "Really, is this a family picnic? It is a poor time to choose," she remarked coldly. "Thanks, I don't care to attend."

And she stopped short in the walk and looked defiantly up at her father.

He looked down into her face with eyes that were sharp with the pain of disappointment. There was even a look of disgust about the glance he gave her, and his voice sounded entirely unlike the indulgent father she had always known.

"Betty," he said, "I am quite capable of taking you up and carrying you to the car as I did last night. But, there are several young people up at the window over the front door. They have evidently recognized you. Do you wish to leave the schoolhouse in that manner, or will you walk down and get into the car in the usual way?"

Betty looked up startled, recognized the boy of whom she had been in search talking to a girl she disliked, gave a quick nod and a cheerful wave of the hand to them, and tripped down the walk to the car, vanishing into the place left for her in the backseat with much the same manner that an arrested man dives from the patrol car into the door of the courthouse when a crowd is standing around watching.

Chester was in his seat almost as soon, and the doors slammed shut. John pulled down his little middle seat, and off they went.

As soon as they had turned the corner Betty sat up, her cheeks flaming brilliantly under the generous coat of white she had applied to them a few minutes before and her eyes flashing like two naughty stars.

"Well!" said Betty with the air of a royal princess kidnapped. "I should like to know what possible explanation there can be to this extraordinary performance."

She fixed her mother with her eyes, but her tone was loud enough to reach easily to the front seat.

Eleanor busied herself with folding back the sleeve of Doris's sweater that had come down below her coat sleeve and did not pretend to try to answer. Chester was threading his way carefully through traffic, going in the opposite direction from home. Betty grew angrier with every second.

"Is somebody dead? And are we all going to the funeral?" she asked contemptuously. "I'm sure I don't know who it could possibly be that would demand our instant presence before the afternoon session of school closed. Now, I shall lose my marks on my report, and every mark counts from now on whether I win the college scholarship or not."

But no one answered. Chester was too much preoccupied in getting through a snarl of vehicles at the railroad crossing to be expected to reply, and Eleanor had stooped to recover her handbag, which had slipped to the floor of the car.

"I'm perfectly furious!" said Betty, sitting up the straighter and looking angrily at first one parent and then the other and then around the ring of brothers and sisters.

"So we all observe!" said Jane quaintly, settling back sanctimoniously. Having suffered herself, it was good to be able to watch someone else take a grilling. Besides, the affair had begun to take on the proportions of an adventure in Jane's eyes. She was already forgetting what she had left behind in the joys of what might possibly be ahead. Jane was still half a little girl.

But the road wound on out of Briardale, down toward the city, and finally turned into the state highway. Still nobody had answered.

When the car dashed out of Briardale and toward the city line, Betty turned to her mother.

"I insist on knowing where we are going," she said in a tone that made Chester feel like slapping her. When did Betty develop into such a little minx? He hadn't noticed it coming on.

"Your father will explain presently," said Eleanor in a gentle tone. She was still engaged in settling some of the little bags and boxes that had been tossed into the car just as they started. She had avoided her daughter's eyes, because she could not bear to see the fury in them and so had not noticed her makeup.

"Gee!" said John, turning around and suddenly getting a good look at his oldest sister. "Gee! You look like Lily Whiffletree!"

Now Lily Whiffletree was a maiden of uncertain age and an unsavory character who lived with her blind and deaf old father on

406

the outskirts of Briardale, and her daring outfits and notorious deeds were the talk of the town.

Chester and Eleanor both turned suddenly and looked at Betty, Chester with open annoyance, and Eleanor with horror. Betty became suddenly aware of herself and sought her scrap of a handkerchief in her coat pocket. Her mother's reproachful "Oh, Betty! How could you be so common?" only served to anger her the more.

"I'm going to get out!" she said and burst into passionate tears.

"Yes," said Chester, "you're going to get out, right down there by that brook on the edge of the Willowvale Golf Course, and wash your face!"

Chapter 9

He drew up at the side of the road and opened the door of the car.

"Get out, Jane," he ordered.

Jane got out with a leer on her elfin face.

"Get out, Betty!"

Betty resisted, but her father reached in and drew her out.

"Now, go down there and wash your face! You can get some of the flour off at least, and if the red doesn't come off with water we'll stop at the drugstore and get some acid or something to take it off. I'm not going through the world with my daughter looking like a bad woman."

"Doesn't she look funny, Mamma?" laughed Doris. "Doesn't Betty look funny, all red and white like a circus clown! Why, Mamma! You're crying. What'r ya crying for, Mamma? Are you crying 'cause Betty looks like Lily Whiffletree? Mamma, *say*!"

"Aw shut up, can't ya!" growled Chris, suddenly entering into the conversation. "Such a *life*!"

Betty returned with her father from her trip to the creek, looking several shades more lifelike, and climbed into the car indignantly.

"I never heard of a girl of my age being treated this way in my life!" she remarked as she settled back and turned her face toward the window of the car with an air of withdrawal from the world.

Chester Thornton climbed back into the car and slammed the door shut. He waited an instant with his hand on the wheel, and then he turned around and faced his little family, a yearning look on his tired, drawn face that went to his wife's heart.

"Now," said he, "we have quite a journey to take before night, and we haven't any time to waste in talking. There are things that I intend to explain to you when we get to a place where we have leisure. At present, it is enough to say that it is your own doings that have brought this journey about, and that your mother and I feel that it is for the best in every way. Now you know, however much you may pretend that you are your own masters and mistresses, that that isn't the case at all. You are all *our children*, and in the eyes of the law—you are still underage and therefore under our control. Also, you have a moral obligation, whether you own it or not, to obey me as long as I am supporting you, whether you like it or not.

"I am taking you on this journey because I feel that it is for your own good, and I shall go into no more detail at present. There will probably be some unpleasant things, and hard things in what is before us, and I expect you to be good sports and take them as all in the day's work. If you do this you may find that the journey will be a pleasant one. It will be, of course, just what you make it. We shall also incidentally discover who of you are loyal to the family. That's all. Now, shall we go?"

"All set!" rollicked out John joyously. It was plain that John had no objection to the family flight.

Chester stepped on the gas, and the car shot forward into the clear, cold winter afternoon.

For an hour or more no one spoke save John and Doris who

eagerly watched every car they met, counting how many of the different makes they passed and discussing their various qualities. Their chatter reminded Chester of his happy errand about this time yesterday hunting a Mermaid Eight for Betty and planning his Christmas presents. Now, what would Christmas be? Had he done right to bring them all off into a desolate place just as the holiday season was arriving?

But a glance in the mirror showed him Betty's hard, angry face, fierce in its concentrated fury. Betty was by no means subdued.

He recalled her struggles the night before and her resistance at the schoolhouse. Betty was a problem indeed.

Chester was very tired. He had had scarcely any sleep for twenty-four hours, had eaten almost nothing since noon of the day before, and suddenly he felt the strain. His weary eyes longed to close and his body to relax. His heart seemed to go slower and slower and the tenseness of the atmosphere among his family was almost more than he could bear. Yet he knew he had been right to come. It seemed as if there had been someone leading, choosing this way for him, almost as if he had no choice in the matter.

Eleanor was terribly weary. She longed to put her head back on the cushion and cry, yet she knew she must keep a steady front. It would not do to break down. She felt Betty's presence like a stranger, as if she had suddenly become an enemy. Her own little girl! It wrung her heart.

And Chris sat slumped beside his father, his eyes down, or out of the window, with a strange embarrassment upon him. What could have happened to subdue him so? He did not even make any display of more than a passing interest when they came upon the wreck of two cars at the turn of a hill. There was a little group of people standing about it, and a state policeman taking names and asking questions. There was no need to stop, and Chester drove straight ahead. Betty seemed frozen to ice. She never moved a muscle and kept her unseeing eyes fixed out the window, as if she had withdrawn to another universe and had nothing in common with any of them. Jane too was sullen and unhappy as if she would like to cry but wasn't sure it would do any good. She had a kind of frightened look about her self-willed little mouth that reminded her mother of the time five years before when she had run away from her call straight into a mortar bed in front of a new house and got into liquid lime to her waist. It was a frightened, defiant look.

To judge by their looks there did not seem to be an over amount of loyalty in any member of the party.

It was Doris who finally voiced the question that was trembling on all their lips and brought their thoughts to a climax:

"Well, anyway," she said after a long silence in which not even John had spoken. "Anyway, I gotta go back by next Friday. We have our party then, and Miss White wants me to give a speech. I know it all now, and I've got to have a new dress to wear. They are all gonta have new dresses. Mine has gotta be red. I'm a holly berry! Say, Daddy, when are we goin' back? I gotta get ready for the party."

"I can't answer that now, Doris. I'm not sure that we shall ever go back," he said gravely, sadly.

A new consternation settled down upon the group. Betty's face grew even harder to read, as her mother glanced furtively toward her. Chris seemed to slump farther down in the seat. After that not even Doris spoke anymore, and before long Eleanor found that the tears were rolling down her cheeks silently. She drew the little girl into her arms and patted her.

"Don't cry, darling," she whispered. "I think we'll have a nice time where we're going."

"But—I—wanta—be—a—holly berry," sobbed the little girl.

"Well, perhaps we'll find some real holly berries where we're going," whispered her mother, summoning a smile and wiping Doris's tears away.

Jane still sat sullen and thoughtful, as the car rushed on through little towns and big ones, out on the great highway, detouring into byways now and then to avoid traffic near a town, and back again to the highway.

Suddenly Chester broke the tension by turning to Chris:

"Want to drive awhile now, Son?" he asked in a kindly tone as if nothing had happened to precipitate a cataclysm in the family.

Chris accepted with alacrity, almost embarrassed, eager to be of service. Chris liked to drive beyond everything, but his father seldom allowed him to do so. They stopped and made the change, and something tense in the atmosphere seemed to break away. Chester gave a few suggestions about keeping to a certain spot in the road and avoiding the rough edge. The boy warmed under the kindly tone and seemed to feel his self-respect returning. It relieved Eleanor to see them more like companions again. Chris was only a boy yet!

But Betty, who still wore her air of offended princess, resolved to have nothing further to do with the family. Jane was wriggling restlessly and at last she announced:

"I'm hungry! When do we eat? Aren't you going to stop somewhere pretty soon?"

"We can't waste daylight stopping," said her father, with more of the old fatherly tone than he had used since the evening before. "I guess your mother has a snack along somewhere if you are hungry."

That was the signal for a general sigh of relief.

"Right there in the hamper at your feet, John. Hand it up here. There are special packages for tonight. Hannah has it all organized."

She opened the hamper with John's eager assistance and began to hand out sandwiches all neatly wrapped in waxed paper, delicate chicken and ham between waferlike slices of bread and butter, a tang of mayonnaise, or was that a spiced pickle? Appetizing egg sandwiches and cookies that would melt in your mouth. Jane bloomed into good nature at once and filled both hands and her mouth eagerly. Doris and John accepted the little tin cracker containers that held their portions, and promised to be very careful not to drop any crumbs. Chris folded his lips about a whole small sandwich and went on driving with a look of feeling great responsibility for the car. Even Chester swallowed gratefully the cup of steaming coffee his wife poured from the thermos bottle. Only Betty refused to take part in the general good cheer. She would eat nothing. She would not drink any coffee, and she scorned the cup of milk from the other thermos bottle that Doris offered her. She sat with haughty demeanor, staring out at the gathering dusk, a princess in exile, chafing at her bonds.

When the hamper was all packed away again everybody seemed to feel better, everybody but Betty. One would almost have thought Betty was not there, so still she sat, so cold, so angry and immovable.

As it grew dark the twins got sleepy. Jane began to laugh and call attention to houses they passed and then to tell something funny she had heard that day, and the atmosphere cleared visibly.

Chester offered to take the wheel again, but Chris said in a grown-up tone, quite as if he were used to saying what should be done:

"No, Dad, you're all in! I'll drive carefully. You rest!" and Chester relaxed into the seat and watched his boy, watched also, furtively in the mirror, the dark, hard little face of his Betty and sighed, wondering if it was too late for little Betty. His Betty!

It was about this time that Chris discovered that a Ford truck was following them, had been for a number of miles, had turned whenever they turned, stopped a good distance behind them whenever they paused at traffic lights, and when they bore out on the lonely highways, came steadily on with them, as if it belonged.

"If I didn't know we were miles away, I'd say that was Mike sitting on the front seat," said Chris importantly, eyeing the dark car that came on like a distant shadow.

"It is," said Chester. "Michael and his brother."

"No kiddin'?" asked Chris in amazement. "Are they going with us?"

"They are bringing up some supplies," said Chester, and opened his lips as if he would have said more, but closed them again.

The children grew silent again thinking what this might mean. It would look as if this were even a more serious business than it had at first appeared, this being kidnapped by one's father. There seemed to be no nonsense about it. They were really going into exile. It occupied them fully for a little while, this thought of what it might mean for them if it was really true as their father had said, that they might never be returning.

Doris crept into her mother's lap, before long, and went to sleep, and John stuffed a blanket between his seat and Jane's and camped down with his head in Jane's lap. Jane herself rested her head against the upholstery of the door and drowsed off, and then it all grew silent again save for a word now and then between Chris and his father.

Eleanor's arms ached and her head swam, but she made herself fairly comfortable in her corner with Doris in her arms, and she too fell asleep. But Betty maintained her stiff, hard gaze out of the window, hungry and weary, but refusing to rest or to eat.

About midnight they came to a halt beside a long low, old-fashioned building that looked as if it might have been a country tavern sometime back in the 1870s. It was neatly painted and its wide, low-browed verandas, the lower one level with the sidewalk, gave it an appearance of being centuries old. Betty frowned at it in dismay. What could her father be thinking of to stop at a place like this? They had just passed a quite modern-looking brick hotel a couple of miles back, and here Dad had chosen this out-of-the-world, impossible-looking place! It was disgusting! It was all consistent with the rest of the crazy expedition. Dad must have gone out of his mind. But what could Mother be thinking of to allow this farce to proceed?

Chester got out and went into what seemed to be the office,

though it was little less than a wide hallway with a big desk. He had a few words with the proprietor and then came out accompanied by a boy who began to take out suitcases.

Chester opened the car door and said, "Come!"

Jane shook John awake, and he stumbled out, more asleep than awake. Chris got out at his mother's direction and helped Doris out, making her stand on her feet and helping her into the great wide parlor where she collapsed into sleep again on a convenient couch.

Eleanor gathered up some of the little things that had been stowed about her and followed. Betty was last. Her father waited patiently and then turned the car over to Michael who by this time had driven the Ford truck up behind them.

The parlor into which they had been shown while Chester went through the formalities of registering was a strange, quaint place, very long and spacious, but low of ceiling. The floor was covered with beautiful old oriental rugs, and the room was furnished completely and luxuriously with some of the finest old pieces of mahogany that Eleanor had ever seen. She could not help stopping to exclaim over their beauty, tired as she was. Three great sofas of priceless pattern, gateleg tables, leaved tables with lyre pedestals, rare old chairs covered with real needlepoint and carved by an expert's hand, a whole dozen mahogany straight chairs all perfect, and all matched! How had they been preserved through the years! Some fine old engravings were on the wall, and a few oil portraits that bore the unmistakable hallmarks of a master's brush.

"Chester! Where did you find such a place? How did you hear of it?" exclaimed Eleanor with the true connoisseur's delight in the antique and the precious.

"Gartley told me about it this morning. Said it was worth a trip just to stop here overnight," said Chester, looking around with eyes that seemed rested already. "I wasn't sure just what it would turn out to be."

He cast an anxious eye toward Betty who was standing in the doorway with curling lip. Nothing could be more out of harmony with Betty Thornton's present mood than this quaint bit of yesterday in the guise of a hotel. She swept the long, lovely room with a scornful glance and turned on her little high heel with a shrug of her trim shoulders.

Chris was standing in the front door looking out disconsolately on a deserted square in the midnight, its bare, cobbled surface as empty as if it had been swept. On the opposite side were nothing but warehouses, softened by tall willows standing at intervals along the curb.

Betty took a quick step and was at her brother's side, speaking low.

"For heaven's sake, Chris, give me some cigarettes! I'm just ready to pass out!"

"Same here!" said Chris gloomily.

"Do you mean you haven't got any?"

"Not a one," said Chris, "and not a red cent to get any if this dumb dump had any place to buy 'em. I tried to get Mike to give me some, but he said he had only a pipe and he wanted that himself, and his brother don't smoke. Whaddaya know about that? A full-sized man and don't smoke. But say, Betts, what's the matter with you lending me some money? I'll go fifty-fifty."

"I left my purse in my desk," said Betty sadly. "I hadn't an idea there was anything like this being put over. Dad wouldn't wait a minute for me to go back."

"Tough luck!" said Chris. "Guess I'll have to part with my class ring. I don't see going without."

"I've nothing but a vanity case," said Betty, frowning. "I can't spare that. I'd stand a fat chance of getting another, and I'd be a fright to go anywhere if I ever get out of this."

"Come, Betty," said her father just behind her, so close his voice made her start. How much had he heard of their conversation?

Chapter 10

Come, Son! The rooms are ready, and I guess we're all ready for bed," urged Chester.

"Think I'll take a little walk around and see the town," ventured Chris suddenly, with a swagger that was a trifle overdone.

"Not tonight, Son," said Chester, laying a firm hand on the shrinking shoulder of the boy. "We've a hard day's ride before us tomorrow, and it's high time to turn in. We've quite a mileage to our credit so far already. Come!"

There was no alternative but to turn their reluctant feet and walk upstairs. Well, perhaps there would be a chance to get out a window or something after the family had retired. Betty tried to convey the idea to Chris with her eyebrows as they straggled behind the others, but when they reached the second floor, they saw there had been unexpected arrangements made. Only two rooms were available, the larger one with two double beds, the other containing a double bed and a cot. Each had its private bath and both were clean and quaint and altogether attractive.

"Eleanor, you and the girls had better take this room," said

Chester, looking around appraisingly at the larger room. "The boys and I will get along famously in the smaller one. Turn in now, quickly, and don't waste time. I want to get started at least by eight o'clock, if you feel that will not be too early."

"Are you sure it will not be too much for you, Chester, to start again so early? Remember, you had hardly any sleep last night, and you've been on the run all day. You are a sick man, you know."

"Don't you believe it!" said Chester, giving Eleanor a wan smile. "We're off for a lark, and every hour that passes rests me. I feel that we've left all care behind."

It was maddening! Betty turned away with a sick, empty feeling at the pit of her stomach and every nerve in her crying out for the stimulant to which she had been for months accustoming herself.

But in turning she caught sight of the little tin box of sandwiches, which Eleanor had taken the precaution to bring in, and swiftly, while her mother was still talking with her father, she reached for it and sneaked out several, hiding them in the folds of her coat and slipping into the bathroom to eat them behind a locked door.

When she came back into the bedroom again her temper was by no means improved, though her stomach was not quite so empty.

"I'm sure I don't see why Dad picked out such a perfectly poisonous place to stay all night," she growled bitterly. "What was the idea of herding us all into one room as if we were so many sheep? Why couldn't I have a room to myself? I'm not a baby."

Eleanor refrained from telling her that she was acting like one.

"Why, we thought this arrangement would be better, dear. You see, we don't like to put the twins in separate rooms. They are so young to be in a hotel alone, I asked Daddy to fix it this way on their account. And then, too, you know it's much cheaper to have only two rooms."

"Oh, hen!" said Betty inelegantly. "Is it as bad as that? Are we really poor?"

"I'm afraid we are, dear!" said Eleanor, a pathetic note stealing into her voice. "Do, dear, try to be pleasant. Your father has a great deal to bear already—"

"Well, what did he let himself get into such a heck of a mess for, then?" said Betty. "I'm sure I think he was to blame!"

"Betty!" said her mother. "Hush! Don't speak again tonight! You are unbearable!"

Betty slid out of her dress and, declining the sensible night array that Eleanor had selected for the journey, flung herself into one of the beds in the brief, flimsy silk affair that she was pleased to call underwear. She turned her back on a dreary world, resolved that she would find a way back into her own life again, somehow, even if the rest of the family had to go on and be poor. She felt that life owed her a good time, and she meant to have it, and no stuffy old father and mother were going to keep her from it.

As she closed her eyes she resolved not to sleep a wink and to be the first one out of the room in the morning. She simply had to manage a smoke somehow or she would go to pieces.

But in spite of her resolves, sleep took her unawares, and she was the last one to wake up in the morning.

Jane was poking her when she finally struggled up to face a bitter world once more.

"Wake up, Betts! Dad says we must be down to breakfast in five minutes."

Eleanor felt refreshed. In spite of the rebellion of her children, and the approach of poverty, her heart somehow was lighter. They were all together. They were on their way—somewhere—and Chester seemed almost happy as he knocked at their door and asked how near ready they were. There was the old glad lure in his voice that there always had been when they all went off anywhere for a frolic. The journey that had begun in gloom and sadness might yet end in victory and a reasonable amount of comfort. She resolved to enjoy it while she could. If Chester had sad news to tell her tomorrow when he had settled down to face the future, she would try to bear it sweetly and help him in every way she could. It would be good to have this one more day together to look back upon just as if nothing had happened to interrupt their glad life.

And, too, there was a sense of security about having the children all there together where she could be sure what they were doing and what they were not doing. All the fears of the day before, all the awful happenings that had made her afraid to think about her children, seemed to have vanished with this morning's sun, and not even Betty's gloom as she arose and donned her brief apparel at her mother's command could quite put her back in her wretchedness.

Breakfast was a dream.

A wide, low-browed room with a great open fireplace stood at one end, high enough and wide enough for one to stand within its enclosure, the fire leaping over great back logs as if it loved them, as if it were a part of a happy, pleasant place. The walls were painted white, with sheer white ruffled curtains tied back from the small-paned, old-fashioned windows. The floor was wide old boards scrubbed to glistening white and sanded. The tables and chairs were painted apple green, and the linen that dressed them was glistening white and immaculate. It was as if they were guests in a comfortable old farmhouse where everything was ordered for beauty and peace. The neat maids in simple print dresses and white aprons brought oatmeal that would put to shame its sister cereals in other stopping places; brought rich yellow cream in fat little apple-green pitchers; brought sausage and fried potatoes so crisp and well seasoned that they seemed some lordly dish; brought golden-brown wheat cakes, light as a feather, and coffee fit for a prince to drink. There were plates of golden honey in the comb, and willow baskets filled with deep-purple grapes. The children ate and ate and could not bear to leave a crumb.

Betty drank two cups of that strong delectable coffee and felt better. So did Chris. They had eaten of everything, even the despised oatmeal, until they were ready to burst, and when they finally gathered their effects and packed themselves once more into their car in the wide cobbled square, they were reluctant to leave the odd old-fashioned inn. There was in their general attitude more of the spirit of holiday than any of them had felt the day before, and they rode away into the morning with a certain feeling of adventure that was almost enjoyable. They had almost forgotten that they were being kidnapped.

The sun was shining when they drove away. The bare brown branches stood out against the sky like brown lace. The little streams they passed glistened in the sunlight. The brightness flooded everything and made the meanest home they passed seem cheerful. There was a briskness in the air that brought a smile to the faces of people on the street.

The sun was still shining fitfully as they skirted New York to avoid the heaviest of the traffic, though deep-blue clouds the color of ink stains were looming on the horizon.

Chester eyed them anxiously as he speeded on every clear stretch of road and pressed on long after the others had confessed they were hungry.

"We're going to have some bad weather, I'm afraid," he said once when they came to a long detour that was bound to delay them.

They had a late afternoon luncheon at a small, smug town hotel, not half so well cooked as their breakfast had been, nor nearly so intriguing in its menu. Underdone chicken and heavy biscuits, elaborate salad on wilted lettuce, elaborate desserts, ice cream and pie and pastry, but it did not satisfy as the morning meal had done.

Chester hurried them out to the car again, paused to give a few careful directions and point out something on the map to Michael, then, with another anxious look at the sky, he put Chris at the wheel and they started on again.

The sun was making no pretense of shining now. It seemed to have erased itself from the heavens. The sky was overcast with thousands of clustery blue-black fragments of cloud, hurrying busily here and there at cross purposes, some lazing and blocking the way for others. It gave the sky an uneasy, restless appearance. The whole family felt it. Doris and John fidgeted, and wanted to get out and walk, wanted to stretch out full length and rest, wanted to ask innumerable questions. The whole little company began to have a breathless feeling as if they were running a race, and even Eleanor began to look out at the clouds anxiously and finally suggested timidly that perhaps they ought to find a place to stop for the night if there was going to be a storm.

Then suddenly they came upon a forest, standing up before them in serried ranks, like beautiful soldiers in battle array, lifting dark, lovely arms of fir and balsam and pine. Spires of white birch were etched delicately against the plumy branches of the evergreens. The road was covered with pine needles, hushing their going till the way seemed almost enchanted.

Down into a narrow dirt road they dashed, amid the winter grandeur, a moss-banked brook at the side, with a sudden bridge across it made of great logs put corduroy fashion, rumbling like thunder as they flew over; a road so narrow that two cars could not pass. They wondered what would happen if another car came in sight. But none came.

A chance railroad leaped across in front of them in an occasional break in the woods, no sign of its being, no voice of engine or warning word, no hint of station or possible train to travel it, just a shining track left there alone in a great crack in the vast forest. It seemed like some forgotten toy of a forgotten generation.

Now and then they came out of the forest for a mile or two to skirt some gleaming lake, its waters like the polished sheen of gunmetal in the gloom of the cloudy winter afternoon; then into the forest again, and on, through the narrow, quiet road that seemed to wear an eerie light of mystery. The tinkling brook was much farther below them now, and at the next turn, close below them, they saw a great stone covered with vivid moss and lichens in the midst of a tiny torrent.

"Oh," the children exclaimed. "Oh, Daddy! Let us get out and climb over on that stone!"

"Yes, Daddy! Stop! I never saw a stone like that!" cried Jane.

"There will be other stones," said Chester. He was looking up at the clouds.

They began to climb upward, and still the serried ranks of trees seemed to be climbing with them. But when they came out into the open again, across another chance railroad that ambled through the wilderness, there were slow, lazy flakes drifting down through the leaden air, and the sky overhead seemed menacing.

It was not half an hour before the few lazy flakes had become millions, great fat, wide flakes, like small blankets, hastening, blurring and blotting the landscape from sight. They clung to the windshield, and when the windshield wiper slushed them off they froze again in a fine blur over the glass and made it almost impossible to see the way ahead.

Eleanor was almost glad when the road wound into the woods again because here the snow was not so thick, being held off by the branches overhead; and yet, there was a kind of feeling of insecurity about it all that made her apprehensive. She began to wonder if it had been wise to come away like this in the dead of winter into a strange, wild place where they knew nothing about anything, or anybody. She eyed her husband anxiously, but though his face was grave, he did not look worried, more as if he were eager.

They were passing few villages now, although there were lakes with summer cottages circling about them. But in the gathering dusk they were hardly cheerful with their boarded-up windows. There were no stars, and the moon seemed to have been blotted off the heavens.

Chester had taken the wheel again himself during the last hour and was driving ahead as if he saw a definite goal not far away. He seemed to be well satisfied at each small landmark, never hesitating which way to turn at a crossing.

"Are you sure you know the way, Chester?" Eleanor ventured at last. "It looks so all alike," she added fearfully.

"Positive!" said Chester cheerfully. "I knew every twig and stone for miles around this region when I was a boy."

"It would be some stunt for you to get lost in a dump like this!" sneered Betty.

The children looked at their father wonderingly and stared out into the dark night again. Somehow he seemed unfamiliar. It had never been a reality before to them that he had been a boy. Chris stared out at the murky shadows and grew thoughtful. He wondered what it would have been like to have been a boy with Dad. He was a pretty good sport sometimes. He would have been a peach of a kid.

"Didya go a fishing?" suddenly called out John, who was supposed to be asleep.

"I sure did," said Chester. "Remember that great boulder we saw down in the creek below the log bridge this afternoon? I used to sit on a boulder like that hour after hour and fish for trout. I'm not sure, but that boulder may be there yet. We'll take a look someday."

"Gee!" said John sleepily and dozed off again.

It began to seem as if the last forest they had entered was interminable, but suddenly they came out upon a fairy scene—the dull sheen of dark water, set in white velvet, and lit by the clustering constellations of a little town on its farther bank.

"There she is!" exclaimed Chester excitedly, almost as John might have said it. "Right across there. That's the town where I used to go Saturdays to buy things for my mother: shoes, and sugar, and corn to feed the chickens!"

Betty sat up and stared coldly at the few bright lights.

"Is that all there is of it?" she asked contemptuously and relapsed into her corner again as if she had no further interest.

They drove through the little country town that lay snugly under its new white blanket of snow. The roofs were blanketed and hung with festoons already, and the streets looked deserted. Only a few houses showed lights in the lower floors, for the hour was growing late for country folks. The stores were closed and shuttered. To all intents and purposes it was midnight in the main street of Wentworth.

Chester slowed down the car and looked eagerly about him, driving as if he loved it all. Even under the snow it looked clean and good and homely to his weary eyes. If only he could find his mother waiting at the journey's end as he used to in the boyhood days! If only he might take Eleanor to her, and his children. She would have known what was the matter with his children. She would have told him what to do with them! Had he drifted away from her teaching that he did not know himself what to do for them?

At the end of the short street Chester made a sharp turn to the right, up a hill, and was plunged once more into midnight darkness, with the tall forest on either side.

Eleanor's heart sank.

"Don't you think, dear," she said leaning forward and speaking hesitantly, "wouldn't it be a good idea to just go back to that little town and stay at the hotel all night? You are so tired—we all are tired."

"Hotel's closed this time of year."

"Well, then, somebody must take strangers. Couldn't we inquire?"

"No, Eleanor, it wouldn't do. You know I telegraphed to Jim Hawley to expect us. He has the key, and I told him to have the fires lighted and the lights going. He might wait up all night for us. It's only a couple of miles farther now."

The children began to stir restlessly, breathing on the windows and trying to peer into the impenetrable darkness. Eleanor's heart grew strangely heavy. What was coming next? She was so weary it seemed as if she could bear no more strain.

A few minutes later they stopped at a little shanty of logs, where a lantern was slung out over a crude porch.

Chapter 11

A woman opened the door as the car stopped and came out shading her eyes with a worn hand.

"Is this Mrs. Hawley?" asked Chester, lowering the window and speaking into the snowy atmosphere. His voice sounded strange and shut in as voices sound when children play under a tent of quilts.

"Yes. I'm Jim's mother. And this'll be Mr. Thornton. I remember you when you was a little kid."

"Jim got my telegram, then?" asked Chester, impatient to be gone. "Is he over at the farm?"

"Yes, he got the telegram, leastways I did. Murdock brought it over this morning on his way back from his milk route. But Jim, he's broke his leg, Mr. Thornton. A tree fell on him and busted him all up. He's flat on his back fer a spell, I guess. Don't 'spose he'll be much use till spring now. Yes, he's awful sorry he couldn't do nothin' fer ya, Mr. Thornton. Yer Ma was allus so awful good to him when he was a little kid and sickly like. But you'll find plenty o' wood. Jimmy, he stowed it up in the woodshed thinkin' it might be needed. An' I managed to git up there myself today an' dust around and lay a few fires. You ain't got nothin' to do but touch a match to 'em. Sorry I can't take you all in, but we ain't got a fire only in one room, and the rest o' the house is cold as charity. You'll be more comfortable in yer own place. But I kin make ya a pot of hot coffee ef you'll wait—"

"No, Mrs. Hawley," protested Chester. "We won't wait for that. We've plenty of coffee in our thermos bottle, and we'd better be getting on. Thank you just the same. Have the key?"

"Yes, I'll get it—"

She hobbled back into the house, and they noticed that she was lame.

"To think she should have taken all that trouble," said Eleanor with compassion. "Chester, that was dreadful!"

"Yes, she is a good woman," said Chester and then reached out for the key that the old woman had brought.

"Mrs. Hawley," he said, "we feel it keenly that you should have felt it necessary to leave your own work and go to the farm. I wish I had known. I'm very sorry to have put this on you when you had enough trouble of your own."

"Oh, that's all right. It was good for a change to run over, and Jim, he was that fidgety; till I did I couldn't get nothin' else done."

"Well, we're deeply grateful, and we'll come over to see Jim and shall hope to be able to return your kindness, as soon as we get ourselves settled."

They started on again, leaving the old woman holding the lantern high over her head, peering after them through the snow.

"Oh, Chester! What are we going to do? Won't the house be fearfully cold?"

"We'll soon have it warm if the fires are laid. She's a faithful soul. Fancy her toiling around laying fires for us! I'm sorry it turned out this way, Eleanor, for your sake. I wanted you to see the house first under pleasant circumstances. But it can't be helped now, and we are lucky to get here before the snow gets any deeper, I guess. I've been rather worried the last hour or so."

With that he turned the car with a lurch suddenly straight to the right and plunged into the deepest, darkest road that Eleanor had ever experienced. There seemed no opening in the thick growth of trees. She wondered how her husband knew where the trail was.

The headlights of the car picked out the white pathway foot by foot and lit up a little brown rabbit standing startled right in the way. The children came to life at this, and even Betty, thrilled with the thought of being out there in that dense woods in the snow, stretched her neck to see the little creature of the wild. It was like being in the scene of an educational movie.

"For Pete's sake, where are we going?" asked Betty at last, roused to a shivering idea of discomfort. "What's the little old idea, anyway, Chester? Do you want us to freeze to death? It looks to me as if you were trying to see how far you could go before you finished us all. And you call this a lark!"

Chester's lips shut in a thin, firm line, but he did not reply. He was driving carefully over ruts a foot deep, and the car lurched from side to side and wavered on like a foundering ship at sea.

It seemed hours that they were plowing along in that narrow, dark trail, though in reality it could not have been more than five minutes, before they suddenly emerged to a wide, clear space, deep with snow, the air thick with great flying flakes. It was like coming to the top of the world and looking out on winter. Gradually as they hitched along more slowly yet, there emerged from out of the thick whiteness an outline of a low, rambling building, dark and snow crowned, like an old woman hunched into a shawl with a heavy wool hood over her eyebrows.

Chester drew up at the side of this building and shouted to Michael to pull in also. They all looked out in dismay. It seemed terrible to think of getting out into that whirl of driving, blinding snow.

Chester, with his flashlight in his hand, got out and unlocked the door. He went inside, and they could see the bobbing of the flashlight through the doorway and the windows as he went into another room. Then there flickered up another light, yellower, steadier.

They sat and waited, and in a moment more another flare lighted up the room, wide and yellow and cheering, and the long, low, old farmhouse came alive. Chester had lit a fire in the great old fireplace, and welcome leaped out to meet them.

Chester appeared at the doorway again, an eager smile on his tired, dirty face.

"Come!" he shouted through the blizzard. "It will soon be warm in here! Chris, help your mother and the girls out while I light the other fires. We'll have a warm house in no time!"

Chris clambered out stiffly and helped out his mother and Betty. Then he went back and carried Doris in, dumping her on a couch, and going back for wraps and bags.

Michael and his brother had already backed up the truck and were unloading boxes and bags, great packing cases of canned goods, and the trunks and bales of blankets.

"They all came through in great shape," smiled Michael to Eleanor, as he threw down the last bale of blankets.

Betty was walking about disdainfully studying the rooms. She felt that prison walls were about to close in upon her.

Eleanor was busying herself pouring out hot coffee from the thermos bottle for the two men, Michael and his brother.

"It seems dreadful, Chester," Eleanor was saying, "to let them go out in this storm again tonight after driving all day."

"I'm bound to get down that mountain, ma'am," said Michael, smiling, "afore this snow gets any deeper. There's goin' to be drifting before morning, an' I'll feel easier if I get beyond the pass before I sleep. Jim an' I'll be all right, ma'am, don't you worry, an' I wantta get back where I can telegraph my wife, fer she'll be that worried if she don't hear."

"Of course," said Eleanor sympathetically. "But are you sure it's safe to go back now in the dark?"

"Perfectly safe, ma'am, while the snow lies still, but if a wind should come up, an' she might any minute now, it wouldn't take long to put that pass twelve or fifteen feet deep. O' course there's other roads, but not so quick, and Jim and I figure we'll get down the mountain and beyond the pass now while the goin' is passable, and then we'll take our rest. Good-bye, ma'am, an' I hope you find everything all right, and get along fine—"

Betty and Chris listened as though they heard the keys to their cell turning in the lock. So, Michael and Jim were going back! Then who was going to do things for them? Were there servants in this strange, desolate place to which they had been brought?

Chester stayed out in the snow with Michael and Jim for a few last words, but Eleanor shut the door and came over near the fire.

"Isn't this wonderful!" she said cheerily, though they could see she was terribly worn and tired. "I've dreamed of a fireplace like that! I was beginning to be chilled clear through."

"I'd much rather have a hot water radiator!" said Betty contemptuously.

"We'd better undo these blankets at once and spread them out to take the chill off them before we start to make up the beds. Come Betty, get to work."

Betty reluctantly drew off her gloves, and Chris without being asked untied the big ropes that bound them together.

"I can't see what was the idea of prancing off here to do all this hard labor," said Betty. "Why not stay at home and work if it had to be? Is it just a gesture, or what?"

But nobody answered her. Eleanor was spreading out the blankets in front of the fire.

"Isn't it funny having no electric lights!" giggled Doris, waking up to look around.

"Look out, Doris, don't go near the table. A candle is a dangerous thing. We'll have to get the lamps in shape as soon as possible." Eleanor lifted the candle and set it on the high mantel.

"Lamps!" said Betty, aghast. "For cat's sake! You don't mean kerosene lamps? I draw the line at that. You can count me out if that's what you have in mind. I never saw such folly! It's perfectly *poisonous*! Chester must have gone crazy!"

"And now," said Chester, coming back, stamping the snow from his feet, "isn't this cozy?" He beamed about on them with almost a happy look on his tired, lined face.

"I'll say it is," said Betty contemptuously. "Cozy as the tomb! I should have thought you could have found a cemetery nearer home, but perhaps this one is cheaper!"

Chester looked at her as if she had struck him, an ashen shadow stealing over his face, but Eleanor, deliberately cheery, called forth:

"Yes, dear, it is wonderful! I'm going to love it, I'm sure. Now Chester, we need some more light, and let's see how many beds we can get ready in a jiffy. These children need to be put to bed; they are too cross to live with."

"Yes," said Chester. "I have five pounds of candles here." He picked up a box by the door. "If I remember rightly there are candlesticks in every room. We'll light the fires in the airtight stoves, and you don't know how quickly you will have nice comfortable rooms, everywhere. Old-fashioned stoves beat the furnaces for quick heat every time."

He led the way up a quaint staircase leading from a large hall covered with old oilcloth in tessellated gray and black blocks. The stair rail was mahogany, and the risers were painted white.

Eleanor followed Chester, urging sleepy little Doris. The other children remained huddled in the big living room where they had arrived, looking about with alien eyes.

"Some dump!" commented Chris, slumping into a grandfather

431

chair that would have been almost worth its weight in gold in a New York antiques shop.

"Isn't it perfectly poisonous!" responded Betty, turning from a survey of a snow-plastered windowpane. "I've a notion to go out and sit in the car."

"You can't," said Chris shortly. "It's gone!"

"Gone? What do you mean? I mean our car."

"Well, I say it's gone."

"But how could it go?"

"Jim drove it. Whaddaya 'spose he came along for?"

"You don't mean we're stranded in this desert without a car?"

"I said it."

"Chris Thornton! I shall go raving insane!"

"Good stunt!" responded Chris. "Might enliven the desert."

"Chris, did you manage to get anything?"

"Not a red."

"I'm just ready to pass out."

"Same here."

Jane eyed them knowingly.

"You needn't be so terribly mysterious. I know what it is you're talking about. Cigarettes. I'm not dumb! I guess I've smoked cigarettes, too!"

"Shut up, you baby! We were speaking of chocolates. If you go babbling what we say you'll get what's comin' to you, that's all," threatened Chris.

"So will you if you call me baby anymore," said Jane impishly. "I'm going upstairs and choose the best bed!" And she vanished into the hall.

The big old farmhouse had a hall running through the center upstairs with rooms on each side, and then down three steps from the top of the stairs, rooms rambled off again over the back wings of kitchen and sheds. They seemed vast chambers with their great, old four-poster beds and their fine, old mahogany chests of drawers. Eleanor, tired as she was, could not refrain from laying an admiring hand on the rare old wood and exclaiming over some particularly fine old specimen of a chair or little bedside table.

She chose the right-hand front room for Chester and herself, with the room connecting just in back of it for Jane and Doris. Betty was assigned to the room across the hall from her mother's, and Chris and John in the room in back of that. There would be plenty of room for each of the children to have separate quarters later if it seemed feasible, but tonight the main thing was to get everybody to bed as comfortably and quickly as possible. There were airtight stoves downstairs with drums in the two back upper rooms, and a gradual warmth was beginning to penetrate the whole house, though it still felt damp and chilly.

"Chris," called Chester, "you and John come with me and bring up several armfuls of wood. We've got to keep fires going all night."

"We can't go out in all this snow and get wood," growled Chris.

"You don't have to," laughed his father. "Come this way. If I'm not much mistaken you'll find the kitchen shed full. Come on, you wouldn't make much of a pioneer."

"I should say not!" responded Chris disgustedly. "I think the world has got beyond that stage. There's no sense in living the primitive life in these days!"

He flung a meaningful glance at Betty with whom he had just been discussing their father's failure in merciless terms. They both felt that he had no right to fail when he was responsible for them. They felt that he was taking their discomforts in altogether too blithe a manner and needed reproving.

Chester carried a candle and set it on a high shelf in the kitchen and put another in the kitchen shed. Chris came slowly after him. He stared about at the great rambling shed with its rough floor and high rafters, unlike any room he had ever looked upon before, reaching out into weird shadows of seemingly illimitable proportions. It might have been a barn or storehouse, a warehouse perhaps, but what a peach of a gym it would make! His mind wandered to basketball vaguely. Perhaps if one worked things rightly there might be some fun left in the desert after all, that is provided there were any natives near enough in the wilderness to make up two teams.

Along the entire length of one wall was a huge pile of wood, neatly cut in stove lengths and fireplace lengths, and over it the one candle shed the weirdest play of light and shadow. Chris reluctantly consented to carrying an armful of wood into the living room, and slowly returned for another, while John, fully awake now and delighted with the kitchen shed, carried three.

Betty and Jane meantime had been requisitioned for bed making, and the house took on an atmosphere of liveliness, with cheerful voices calling back and forth and candles flickering in every room. The old house had not seen the like for almost twenty years. Chester came up the stairs with an armful of wood humming an old tune: "We'll stand the storm, it won't be long. We'll anchor by and by—"

Unconsciously he had chosen an old favorite of his father's. It seemed somehow to have been a part of his childhood waiting for him in the old house, come to his heart to welcome him. As he went down the stairs for another load he began to hum and the old words came back to him unconsciously:

"Should earth against my soul engage, soul engage,
Should earth against my soul engage, soul engage,
Should earth against my soul engage, and fiery darts be hurled,
Then I can smile at Satan's rage,
And face a frowning world. We'll stand—"

"Listen to Dad!" said Betty with a wondering look on her face as she paused in the flinging of a warm, sweet-smelling sheet across her great-grandmother's bed to Jane, who was supposed to be helping make the beds. "I never heard him sing like that! Never!"

"*I* think it's going to be *fun!*" declared Jane, catching the sheet and vigorously tucking it in on her side.

Betty suddenly froze into a frown.

"Help yourself!" she said bitterly. "Not me! I'm not accepting things like this when they're wished on me."

"What'r ya going to do about it?" mocked Jane.

"I'll find something to do, mighty quick, and don't you forget it, Jane!" affirmed Betty mysteriously.

"Well, if you want my opinion, Betts, you're a fool not to take the fun while it's going. All us here together like this, and Dad and Mother playing along with us, I think it's going to be great."

"It's poisonous, Jinny, just perfectly poisonous! And you'll find out quick enough. Just wait till you have to fill a lamp, precious! I've heard about lamps. They smell to heaven, and you never can get your hands clean afterward. Sort of a Lady Macbeth act, darling. Not all the rain in the sweet heavens and all that sort of thing. You know you've had that in school. Only in this case it would be snow, of course. Did you ever see snow like that? I ask you. Look at the windowpanes, perfectly obliterated, and there's a pile of snow, on every windowsill! Will you look? Isn't this the grandest dump for the Thornton family to arrive in, caught like rats in a trap."

"I think it's fun!" said Jane stoutly.

"Help yourself!" yawned Betty. "I pass."

"Betty, dear," called Eleanor, "come down and get something to eat."

"Thanks! But no way!" shouted Betty rudely. "I'm going to bed."

So Eleanor climbed the stairs once more and brought Betty a long, thick nightgown with long sleeves that she had just unearthed from the old attic trunk.

"What! Wear that thing?" refused Betty. "Not while there's life left in me to protest! I'd never expect to emerge if I once put on that antique. That's one that Noah wore in the ark, Mums."

"You'll be glad of it when you find out how cold it is here," urged Eleanor earnestly.

"Then I'll wait till I'm glad, but I think you've guessed wrong. I'll never be glad, and I think I prefer to die to the cause of suitable garments for sleeping. So if you find your little Elizabeth frozen stark in the morning you can lay it to bringing her up to the North Pole against her will, and not to the lack of Grandmama Noah's best nightgown."

"Never mind, Eleanor," said Chester, coming by the door just then. "She'll come to it. Let her find out for herself. That's the best way."

Betty cast him a gleam of hate and resolved that she would freeze solid before she ever put on a thick nightgown.

At last they were all stowed away in their beds, most of them glad to get the thick garments from other days and the hot water bottles that Eleanor had tucked in beside them. There were heaps of blankets and down quilts over all, and piles of wood by every stove. The house had lost its freezing atmosphere and was filling with a healing warmth, and only Eleanor's teeth were chattering as she crept in at last to a well-earned rest and put her tired head on the pillow. Too weary she was to realize that it was less than forty-eight hours since she had lain and worried about this trip, and now here she was! Just glad to lie down and be warm, and know that her brood were safe for the night at least. There were thousands of things that might happen tomorrow, of course, but for the night they were safe.

The candles left in the hall burned down to the sockets and blinked out. The house lay dark and still. The fires banked down, stopped crackling, and all the family slept. While outside in the wide, wild night the soft flakes continued to come down, wilder and faster as the night wore on.

And the next day was the Sabbath.

Chapter 12

When the morning dawned it was scarcely perceptible, the air was so altogether filled with the beating, flying, drifting snow. Snow from above, snow from below, snow from all sides, out and over and under, a new white world, such as the children had never seen before. The old rambling farmhouse seemed almost snowed under, and only the smoke from the big-mouthed chimneys gave any signs of life.

They slept till nearly noon, and when they awoke, the whiteness prevailed over all the earth, and the air. It was as if they had been let down, house and all, to the bottom of the ocean, and were there amid the drifting, hurling, eddying deep, only that the water was white, white snow in tempestuous motion. They were as isolated as if they had been wrecked at the bottom of the ocean. They stood at their various windows and looked out with varied feelings.

Chester's face was almost exultant. They were here! They were *all* here! And none of the terrible things that had attacked his children could get to them! Not for a while at least. So far they were safe.

If they had waited a day later they could not have made it up the mountains. The drifted snows would have shut them out, and perhaps he would never have been able to manage it again, never have been able to save them from the world, the flesh, and the devil. But now they were here, and God had shut them in with His snow and His terrible cold.

It was curious how old phrases from the Bible kept continually coming to him and fitting in with things. Was it just because he was here where these walls had so often echoed to the reading of the scripture, and where his father's and mother's voices in prayer had so often been heard? Had these things perhaps lingered in the atmosphere, and some undiscovered arrangement of his soul had become a human radio to set them vibrating once more? He had read that someone was trying to perfect an instrument so delicate and so far reaching that we might sometime be able to hear the voices of Moses and the prophets, of Jonah and Paul, and Washington and Lincoln again. Well, perhaps some such thing had happened here. He turned from the window with a reverent look in his eyes and called:

"Eleanor, come and see the world! We must have slept till Christmas!"

Eleanor's first word was an exclamation of anxiety:

"Chester, what can have happened to Michael and Jim?"

Chester's face sobered.

"I think they are all safe," he said. "An hour would have got them down through the village and over the pass. After that it was all clear sailing, just a big snowstorm. They reached a good hotel and were fast asleep probably before we got to bed last night. Michael said there was no risk whatever. Besides, remember it is high noon, twelve full hours since they left us. There weren't three inches of snow in the pass when we crossed it, and it did not start to blow till after daylight. I was up putting more wood on the sitting room stoves, and I heard it commence."

Eleanor looked up at him and found to her surprise that he did not look as worn as she had expected.

"I believe you are enjoying it, Chester," she said wistfully. "I believe it was the very thing you needed."

"Is it going to be so very hard for you, dear?" he asked with sudden anxiety.

"Oh, no!" she said, veiling her apprehension. "I believe it is almost interesting. This is such a fine old house, and there is so much to see. And we haven't been all alone together like this without anything coming between or anything we had to do since the babies were little."

"Do you feel that too, dearest?" he said and stooped to kiss her.

Across the hall Jane was wriggling into her clothes underneath the sheets to keep from having to stand on the cold floor, and Betty was protesting at being woken up.

"For Pete's sake, get out of this bed!" said Betty crossly.

"Mamma says to get up. It's time to get dinner. Did you know we had slept all the morning, Betts?"

"I don't care if I sleep all the afternoon, too," snapped Betty. "Go away and let me alone. There's nothing to do in this dumb dump but sleep. I don't care if I never wake up."

"Oh, but Betts! You wanta wake up and look out! It's grand. The sky and the earth are all mixed up, and you can't see anything. Not anything but just snow!"

"Well, I'm sure I don't see what there is nice about that. I think it is poisonous! Just perfectly poisonous!"

"Oh, but it's going to be fun! It's going to be wonderful!"

"It isn't my idea of fun," growled Betty and turned over to sleep more.

The twins, however, were overjoyed at the snow. Later when Jane had succeeded in rousing Betty, they all sat down to a belated meal, which was neither breakfast nor lunch. Chris began to ask questions about sledding and skating.

"Oh, for the matter of that," said Chester, "there is a place only a few miles from here where they ski. It's one of the famous hills where they have the big contests. Some record jumps have been made by the great ski champions there, both Canadian and American."

"Really?" said Betty, surprised out of her gloom.

"Absolutely!" said Chester with something of his old twinkle in his eyes.

Betty remembered her role and relapsed into silence, but Chris began to ask questions again.

"Have you ever been to one of those contests, Dad?"

"I sure have," said Chester, his eyes taking on a pleasant look of reminiscing. "It was the last time I was up here in winter. I went over with your uncle Clint. Let me see, that was, I'm not just sure what year. Surely I've told you about it before."

"Oh, gee! Why weren't we along?" breathed Chris.

"It must have been the winter your mother had you all down in Florida, the time Betty was so sick. I thought surely I would have told you about it, though. It was wonderful.

"You know the whole course up there is outlined with evergreens, and strung with a perfect blaze of pennants of all colors. It looks like a vast border of flowers against the whiteness of the snow. People come from all around to see one of those meets. Perhaps we'll find a way to get there sometime ourselves. They come in sleighs and automobiles from miles away. It is a great affair. Bing Anderson made his big record leap that day of one hundred and ninety feet."

"Gee, I've seen 'em in the movies," said Chris, greatly excited, "but I never realized they leaped that far."

"Oh, yes. I've read that Nels Nelsen several years later leaped over two hundred and forty feet!"

Chris edged his chair nearer.

"I certainly would like to see that!" he exclaimed excitedly. "I don't see how it's done!"

"We'll go over someday and look at the track. There's always somebody over there practicing. You know how the course is built, don't you? It's like this—here's the takeoff, here's where they gain their first momentum—"

Chester took knives and salt shakers and laid it all out, with Great-Grandmother's Wedgwood sugar bowl for the starting hill and crumpled napkins for other points.

"This is an iced groove—" Chester tilted a silver knife against the crumpled linen hill. "Here is a tower for the judges"—he drew toward him a bottle of olives that Betty had set on the table—"and the bystanders are all along here. Why, at the carnivals I'm told even amateurs do some pretty high jumping."

"Oh, boy! I'd like to get in on something like that!" remarked Chris wistfully. "Any chance for a fella that isn't in their clubs?"

"Why, I don't know," said Chester thoughtfully, looking interestedly at his son.

"I've seen *girls* in pictures doing that," said Jane pointedly.

"It might be that there'd be a chance for you all to try skiing somewhere around here. We'll inquire when we get settled," said her father. "That depends. . . ." But he did not say what that depended upon.

There was a distinct silence while the children thought it over, got a thrill from just the idea of going out and skimming through space.

"It's like what I dream sometimes," said Jane thoughtfully. "I think I'm walking along on the street, and suddenly my feet somehow rise up a little off the ground and I go along just the same sort of walking on the air, getting faster and faster, only when I go real fast I have to be awfully careful not to lose my balance or I go up higher than I meant, and it kind of scares me, and sometimes I'm afraid my feet will get up over my head, they go so fast, like when you're in the water, you know—"

"Why, I've dreamed that!" said Betty, forgetting herself once more and then went hurriedly on with her eating.

They finished the last of the sandwiches—only stopping to make coffee.

"We must clean out the lunch box first and not waste anything at all," said Eleanor, "for there's no telling how long this storm will shut us in from getting fresh supplies."

"Don't worry about that," said Chester. "I called up the grocer and told him to pack canned goods and groceries to last for some time. I think also there are a lot more things that Hannah put in the truck. You better investigate; some of them might not keep."

"I have," said Eleanor. "There is a pair of roasted chickens and a great, beautiful baked ham. I'm sure I don't see how she managed to get it all done in so short a time without my knowing a thing about it. There's a great big tin box full of doughnuts, too."

"M–m–m–m–m–m–mmm!" said the children in chorus.

"Well, Hannah went out before seven o'clock and got the things as soon as the stores were open," said Chester. "I just gave her a little hint that we might be needing them."

"It is really wonderful what you accomplished," said Eleanor. "We shan't have to cook for several days, and that will be nice. We shall have a chance to get acquainted with our house and put things away."

Betty cast a frowning look at the imprisoning snow.

"How long do they keep up, storms like this?" she asked at last. "I think it is perfectly poisonous to have it snow this way. I don't see how on earth we're ever to get away from here. How deep does the snow get?"

"Sometimes six or eight feet when it drifts. In fact, there have been times when we have had to tunnel through worse drifts than that. When I was a boy I remember a storm that began just like this and lasted for three days and nights!"

"Oh, murder!" said Betty under her breath, casting a frightened look toward the window.

"We don't often have such blizzards. That was the worst I ever remember. When it finally stopped snowing we could hardly get the door open. There was a drift all across the front of the house, away up to the top of the first-story windows. You had to go upstairs to see out! My, but it was a beauteous sight! I remember we all went up to the attic to look out and see whether our neighbors were snowed in. It looked like velvet, spread everywhere, and all the valleys and ugly rocky places covered. It was like fairy land. The trees— But there! You'll see for yourself when the sun comes out."

"I don't think it's ever coming," said Betty disagreeably, but Chester went on with his story.

"We cleared the way from the back door to the well and out to the cow yard and barn. That was comparatively sheltered, and it didn't take long with all us boys working. There was John and Sam and Clint and our father; and I was almost eleven years old and did a good share myself."

The children sat back from the table and looked at their father, trying to think of him as only eleven years old.

"Gee!" said John and grinned toward his mother.

"Then we started to clear away the drift in front of the house, and it was some drift! In places you could reach the top of it from the second-story windows."

"Ohhhh!"

"It was Clint that suggested we had better find out if anybody else needed help before we began to fancy digging around the place, and he was the one that first thought of going up to the attic to look."

"How could you tell up in the attic?" asked Chris.

"Why, you could see most of the houses in the valley from there, and you could easily tell if anybody was snowed under."

"Why didn't you telephone?" asked Jane.

"They didn't have telephones then, silly!" said Chris.

"Yes, the telephone had been invented, but it hadn't penetrated these parts then," said Chester, "and if it had we couldn't have afforded to have one. People were poor in those days. We got our living from the soil. But when we looked we could see smoke coming cheerfully up from most of the houses, showing that they had fires, and in some places we could see that the men were out digging paths around the houses. But there was one house, just below the brow of a windswept hill, that seemed to have been utterly obliterated. There wasn't even a dark streak where the chimney ought to have been, and not a wisp of smoke in the air above it."

"How did you know there was any house there at all?" asked Doris eagerly. She was sitting on a little old-fashioned stool by the fireplace now, her cheeks red as roses, and listening with all her might. Doris loved a story.

"Oh, we knew every house in the neighborhood of course, just as you know everyone who lives on your own street. And besides, that special house was where Letty Cameron and her mother lived alone, and they were very poor. Mr. Cameron had died the year before after a long illness, and Letty and her mother had had a hard time getting on. They took in sewing, and Letty taught in the district school over on the other side of the hill. Letty was a pretty girl, and Clint had been going with her more or less, taking her to singing school and going over there to cut wood for them sometimes. And when there wasn't any sign of smoke coming from the chimney, I could see Clint was very much disturbed, and so was Father.

"He asked Clint how much wood he had cut the last time he was there, and Clint said, 'Plenty.' They talked about it a minute or two, and then Father said we must go and see. They got out the old bobsled and hitched up the horses, but the drifts were so deep they had to keep stopping to shovel themselves out. I remember Mother didn't want me to go along, but Father said, 'Oh, let him go! He's got to learn to be helpful, and he's getting a big boy now.' I was so proud to be allowed to go along. But it was a long time before we got down to the road. By that time they had got out the old snowplow down in the village, and part of the way the road was broken. We stopped and got some other men and boys to go along and then struck into the back road that led to the Cameron cottage. It was an exposed road and terribly drifted. I remember wishing several times that I had stayed at home; my hands got so cold, and my feet felt as if they didn't belong to me. But there were eight or ten men with us by that time, and at last we reached the Cameron house. But it was all snowed under except one or two windows on the second floor.

"When we shouted, nobody answered, and when at last we tunneled through to the side door and knocked, nobody answered. The men talked about it a minute or two and decided the Camerons had gone to somebody's house to stay till the storm was over, but Clint insisted that we ought to go in and see, and so at last Father put his shoulder to the door and wrenched it open.

"I remember how solemn we all felt, just as if we were house-breakers as we went marching solemnly in. Father told Clint to go ahead as he was kind of a friend and was often there, and when they got into the kitchen where they lived mostly, they saw why there hadn't been any smoke from the chimney. There was plenty of wood piled around the hearth, as if they had brought it in from the shed to be ready for cold and storm, but the fireplace was completely smothered in snow, and snow lay away out over the floor for a couple of feet. You see, the stone that is put across the top of the chimney to keep things from falling down had blown off in the storm, and the snow had come down and put out the fire, probably fallen down in great quantities. The Camerons were unconscious, almost frozen to death. They were huddled in each other's arms in the bed, with all the blankets they had piled over them, but it was bitter cold, and the wind and storm had been rushing down the chimney for hours.

"I don't think either of them ever quite recovered from the shock. Mrs. Cameron had pneumonia the next winter, and Letty was never strong after that. My brother Clint married her a few weeks later and went to live down at their house. He seemed to have aged during that day. I never saw anyone work so hard in my life as Clint did, digging that tunnel to the house. He was all bound up in Letty."

"Was that my aunt Letty that died?" Jane asked with awe in her voice.

"Yes, she only lived about five years after their marriage, and Clint has never got over it. He can't seem to settle down, just travels from one place to another, doesn't care to have a home anymore."

Betty got up suddenly and walked to the window, blinking out at the deep white lace of the snow on the pane.

"I think this is a *terrible* place!" she said in a choking voice. "I don't know why anybody would stay in it, *ever*! It's perfectly *poisonous*!"

"Aw, cut out that poison business, Betts. You've overworked that word for two days now!" declared Chris gruffly.

"Well, now," said Chester with compunction in his voice. "I'm sorry I've given you that feeling, little girl. I was just reminiscing. It didn't occur to me that it would be depressing. This really is a lovely place, and I want you to grow to like it as much as I did."

"I never shall!" said Betty violently. "I hate it! It's just like a prison. It's perfectly poi—"

"There you go again, Betts, with your poison!" interrupted Chris. "You're a pain in the neck, you are! If we can't have a little holiday, sort of a vacation—"

"Holiday!" uttered Betty witheringly. "Do you call this a holiday? A vacation? Come out here to smother under a blanket of snow! The worst of it is there won't be anybody to dig us out when the storm is over, if it ever is!"

Chester cast a look of despair on Eleanor and sighed heavily.

Eleanor laughed, although she was far from cheerful herself.

"Well, you know, Chester, that wasn't exactly a cheerful story you told about people freezing to death. Come, let's do something pleasant. Betty, why don't you look over those books? Perhaps you'll find something really interesting to read. There ought to be some rare old books in a collection like that. I confess I'm curious to see them."

"There wouldn't be anything among those fusty, old-fashioned things to interest me," said Betty with her nose in the air and a fine contempt sitting on her shrugged shoulders.

"Yes, there would, Betts, here's the very thing. Suits you just to a T. *Foxe's Book of Martyrs.* Come and try it!" said Chris, holding out a faded old volume with tattered edges to its yellowed pages.

"I think you're all perfectly horrid!" said Betty, bursting into tears and rushing up the stairs to her bed where she was heard to fling herself down and weep.

Chester started to follow her, his face full of distress.

"Let her alone, Chester," said Eleanor. "Let her cry it out. She's all strung up. You must remember you never crossed her in anything before in her life. It is hard for the child."

Betty cried herself to sleep and did not come down again until night had settled over the world, and a pleasant smell of something cooking came luringly up the stairs.

Chapter 13

There were lamps burning brightly in all the rooms and a great fire of logs in the fireplace in the living room. Now and then a spit of snow came down the chimney to sizzle in the fire as a reminder that the blizzard was still in full force outside, but the house had a cheerful look.

They had all been at work getting things into order. The suitcases were gone from the living room, the packing boxes had vanished from the dining room, the canned things were standing in neat rows on the big old pantry shelves on clean newspaper shelf covers, and the two roasted chickens were in the oven sending out a delicious smell every time the oven door was open. There was really something like a regular dinner set out on the table. Bread freshly cut from the loaves that Hannah had providently wrapped in double waxed paper, a plate of butter, a dish of preserves, another of olives, potatoes roasted in their skins, a corn pudding just out of the oven. Really, they had done wonders for their first real meal in the house. Betty slid into her vacant chair and when she had eaten looked less forlorn.

"Now," said Eleanor when they had finished, "we'll all work

together putting things away. Jane, you and Daddy may put the food away in the closet we cleaned. You know where everything belongs now. I will wash the dishes, and Chris and Betty may wipe. Thank fortune we have plenty of dish towels. Hannah remembered to put them in. I never would have thought of them. Here, Betty, put this apron on. You mustn't get that dress dirty. There's no cleaner here to call every Tuesday and bring things back Friday. We'll have to look out for our cleaning ourselves. John, you and Doris wash your hands and be ready to carry the dishes to Jane to put in the cupboard."

It didn't take long when they all worked, and though Betty did not enter into the affair with any degree of heartiness, she yet managed to do her part, and in a very short time the kitchen was cleared up and the table set for breakfast the next morning.

"Now," said Betty dismally, consulting her little wristwatch. "For Pete's sake, what shall we do? It's only seven o'clock and a long evening ahead!"

"Not so long, Bettykins," said her father gently. "People go to bed at nine o'clock in the country, you know."

"For cat's sake, what for?" said Betty.

"Well, because they have to get up in the morning, I guess."

"I don't see how they exist!" moaned Betty.

"Come on," said Eleanor, coming in from the kitchen rolling her sleeves down. "We're going to sing now. Jane and I found the old melodeon this afternoon, and Chris mended one of the reeds so it goes pretty well. Where are those old singing books you said you found, Chester?"

"Right here on the shelf," said Chester eagerly. He was pleased as a boy at the prospect.

"Oh, heck!" groaned Betty but accepted the book and slunk down on the corner of the old sofa that Chris had drawn up to one side of the fireplace.

"Try number ten," said Chester eagerly, sitting down near a lamp.

"We always used to begin with that every Sunday night. Father liked it. He had a good deep bass voice, and Clint always sang tenor."

Jane went to the melodeon and pumped away vigorously at the pedals.

"On Jordan's stormy banks I stand,
And cast a wishful eye
Toward Canaan's fair and happy land,
Where my possessions lie."

they sang, only Chris gave Betty's foot a brotherly kick and loudly substituted Briardale for Canaan with a meaningful look at his sister.

"How perfectly tortuous that instrument is!" said Betty as they finished the seven verses and began to turn pages over in search of another.

"Torturous is good," said Chris, "only don't overwork it like you did the poison."

"Shut up!" said Betty and curled up disconsolately in one corner of the sofa again.

They sang "The Lord's My Shepherd," "Rock of Ages," "Just as I Am," and then they sang "Happy Day" and "Happy Land" for the children, and Chester's face looked so rested and happy as he sang the old tunes to the cracked accompaniment of the old melodeon that even Betty refrained from further contemptuous remarks.

"We always sang in the evening," said Chester when they were quite hoarse with singing. "It's a pleasant custom. I wonder why we never kept it up!"

"I don't see how you had time," said Betty sarcastically.

"What did they have to do?" said Jane. "They couldn't farm in the nighttime."

"Oh, we had plenty to do," said Chester. "There was wood to cut and pile in the woodshed, and if we stayed out skating after school, we had it to do after supper. There were lessons to learn, and we all sat around the table with the big student lamp in the center and studied till nine o'clock. Then my father always got the big Bible and drew up to the table, and we children scattered around the room, Emily by our mother's side, and the boys around the room, and we sang first, two or three hymns."

"Who played?" asked Jane quickly.

"Nobody," said Chester. "We just sang. The melodeon was an importation of later years, bought for Emily to take lessons on. She got so she could play for worship about the time I went away to college, and I only remember that when I came home at vacations."

"Aunt Emily was the one that married a missionary and went to Africa, wasn't she?"

"Yes," said Chester with a sad note in his voice. "We never saw her again. She died of jungle fever after she'd been there about five years, but she was a dear little sister. Pretty, too. She looked a good deal like Betty. I remember the last worship we had before her wedding. Father read the ninety-first psalm, and I shall never forget his prayer that night."

He was silent for a moment, and Eleanor spoke, as if for the moment she and her husband were alone together.

"Yes," she said thoughtfully. "I've often missed it. We always had family worship in my home, too, you know. I never cared so much about it when I was a girl, but after I went away I really missed it sometimes. It is strange how sweet home grows when we once get away from it forever."

"I don't know why we never had it," said Chester. "I've often thought I'd start it someday. It seemed the right thing to do, especially since they made me an elder in the church, but somehow the time never seemed to come."

"Yes, I know," said Eleanor. "I don't see how we could, with school so early and you having to rush off to business meetings at night so much. But it would be nice. The children don't realize what they've missed."

Betty looked bored, and Chris began to whistle a tune from the hymnbook, although it sounded much more like the jazzy thing they sang in the poolroom the night he played his last game than it did like any conceivable hymn.

"Of course we could have it here," said Eleanor hesitantly.

There was a long pause. Chester looked a little startled. At last he said:

"I suppose we could."

He rose and went over to the old bookcase that ran from floor to ceiling on both sides of a corner of the room and selected a large, old, worn book. He came slowly back, turning the pages.

"Here's the old family record," he said. " 'Emily, born April 7th, 1880; Clinton, born November 10th, 1885; Esther'—that's the little sister that died when she was only a month old. My! How this carries me back! There, Eleanor, you read something to us!"

He laid the old Bible down in Eleanor's lap and retreated to his chair, sitting down with his hand shading his eyes. The children watched him curiously, embarrassedly. This was not the father they knew, who joked and kidded them, and bought them grand presents, and humored them, and went off to business most of the time. This was somebody they would have to get acquainted with all over again.

Eleanor opened the book hesitantly, studied the record for a moment, then turned the pages aimlessly.

"Where was it you said your father read the night before Emily went away?" she asked fumbling among the pages.

"The ninety-first psalm."

Eleanor found the place and read:

"He that dwelleth in the secret place of the most High shall abide under the shadow of the Almighty. I will say of the Lord, He is my refuge and my fortress: my God; in him will I trust. Surely he shall deliver thee—"

The words sounded strangely to the children as they sat wondering, shy, wishing it was time to go to bed. Yet the words fitted the strange setting of the quaint old room, lovely with furnishings of the past, flicker of firelight, candle glow, and the wild, dark storm clashing at the windowpanes.

A sudden gust shook the kitchen door and set it banging, and John tiptoed to shut it, glad of the relief from sitting still so long, wishing he might find a mouse in the pantry, or a strange dog in the kitchen to break the monotony.

When he came back his mother's voice was still reading:

"There shall no evil befall thee, neither shall any plague come nigh thy dwelling. For he shall give his angels charge over thee, to keep thee in all thy ways."

It seemed comforting to the twins. They stopped wriggling and began to listen. Somehow the storm did not seem so powerful after those words. Only Betty was not listening. Betty was pulling a hair out of the old horsehair sofa. She felt out of place.

When Eleanor's voice ceased and she closed the book, Chester sat for a moment and then took his hand down from his face.

"Well," he said, looking about on them with a look that was almost shy. "Well, I suppose we should pray next."

He waited a moment and no one spoke. Then he rose and knelt beside his chair, and Eleanor, too, knelt, swiftly, as if she was accustomed. The children looked around startled, hardly knowing what to do. Jane followed her mother's example first, then Doris, half giggling, got down upon her knees and covering her face with her hands peeped through her fat fingers. John slid off his chair tentatively, to one knee. Finally Chris, his eyes suddenly raised to a swift survey as if he had but just realized what was going on, got himself casually to his knees.

And now only Betty was left, curled up on her sofa staring at them all with hostile eyes. What did they all want to do that for? Were they all gone nutty together? It was the storm that had got them. Well, no wonder, but she would not go crazy, too!

She sat bolt upright while her father seemed to wait for her, or was he hesitating for words? It was a strange, unpleasant experience. It was almost as if she were alone facing God who stood out there in the middle of the room somewhere and looked at her. Not harshly, only gently, as if she was doing something impolite to Him.

Then suddenly Betty, too, seemed to melt down into her sofa, head on the arm, body reclined, one knee half on the floor, a sort of a compromise between kneeling and sitting, her eyes shut to keep out the feeling of God out there in the room watching her sitting up and declining to yield to family worship.

It was a new thing for Chester Thornton to have to search for words. He was the one of all others who was always being called upon for an impromptu speech, in his business club, at banquets, or on social occasions in the church. Yes, and he was a standby to be called upon to pray at meetings of presbytery, or session, or on the few occasions of late when he had found it convenient to present himself at the midweek prayer service. As the church janitor aptly put it: "Mr. Thornton certainly can compose a handsome prayer!" And it was the general opinion of the whole church.

Yet, there was Chester Thornton upon his knees in the old home of his childhood, surrounded by sacred and precious memories and only his wife and children present. Every word that he had ever known seemed stricken from his vocabulary.

But at last the habit of later years came upon him as he struggled and sought for words, and he opened his mouth and let habit guide it:

"Oh, Lord, we thank Thee that we are permitted to meet here tonight—"

What was he saying? That was the way he usually prayed at prayer meeting after a longer absence than usual! He paused and hesitated—tried to get back to the beginning again—"Oh Lord"—and he an elder in the church! What would his children think of him? How was he to get out of this? What was it he was struggling after, that he had come up here to find? Why had he actually walked into this worship? Why, because he was longing to get for his children what his father and mother had given to him in his childhood, something clean and fine and strong that would anchor them—

"Oh—Lord—*Father*!" with a desperate ring to his voice. "Show us all what to do! Amen!"

There was a moment's tense silence, and then they all rose, awkwardly, in the garish candlelight, blinking because their eyes had been closed, and there had been near tears behind their lashes.

Only Eleanor had an exalted look upon her face.

Betty had stolen away silently, while a log in the fireplace fell down in a shower of sparks and made a soft, lush sound of parting ashes. Stolen up the stairs so quietly and swiftly that no one noticed her going. She might not have been there at all that evening for all they were aware of her.

Upstairs she was undressing, swiftly, silently, in the dark; creeping into bed, that she might not seem to have been present at that strange solemn ceremony downstairs, so disturbing, so somehow humiliating. She could not bear to think of her father kneeling there silent, ill at ease, in that ridiculous posture, humbling himself before an unseen Being that was not there! Of course it was all tradition, this God business. Nobody believed in it anymore. Why did her father want to make himself ridiculous with such performances! Just because it was the fashion to have what they were pleased to call family prayers when he was a kid!

Betty crept under the blankets shivering and pulled them up over her head with a dry sob, swallowed instantly. She pressed her fingers

THE PRODIGAL GIRL

hard upon her eyeballs, trying to shut out the memory of her father kneeling there in the firelight with the flicker of a candle wavering back and forth in weird shadows across his head and face. But the more she tried to hide from the memory the clearer it became, until the thought of that One, whom she thought of as God, standing across the room and looking at her, became intolerable. Then she flung back the sheets and said aloud to herself:

"I *won't* let this get me! I'll go nuts, too, if I do!"

When they all came up to bed Betty was apparently fast asleep. Sometime in the night the wind ceased, and the snow stopped sifting down. The stars came out, cold and white and still.

When morning dawned there was dazzling brightness over the earth, a new created world, white as the first soul God made.

When Betty awoke she heard Jane singing like a blackbird down in the kitchen. The glare of the sun through the snow-clogged glass blinded her so that at first she could not open her eyes. There seemed to be something electric in the air, something joyous and different. In spite of her firm resolve not to yield to it, not to let anything make her enjoy what this terrible exile had to present in place of the joys she had lost, she found herself hurrying eagerly to get dressed, rushing down the stairs to see what it was all about, healthily hungry and ready for bacon and eggs and toast. Yes, even ready for despised oatmeal or anything that was to be had.

The boys went out with their father immediately after the meal was finished, and Jane was not far behind, in one of the old despised sweaters and some strange woolen leggings, her feet in galoshes and her hands in an old pair of socks she had found in a knitting bag in the living room. Betty took a broom and followed.

It was very exciting.

Father and the boys had only cleared about a foot from the door yet, and she had to wait until there was room for her to work also. It was most amazing, this great white wall that shut out all sight of the outer world, high as the door, even higher in places, hardly room to get the handle of the shovel out.

Father seemed to know just how to slide the great snow shovel in to take out a mountain of the white feathers and fling it far out of the way, over where the wind had blown a place almost down to the ground. Chris was smaller, not so tall nor stout as Father, yet he was managing pretty well, too. And soon Chester got Jane and John to work going toward the back while he and Chris worked toward the front. At last there was a path out into an open place where there were no drifts and where the snow was only about a foot deep, blown hard and dry and crusty, and they could all come out and stand.

Eleanor put on her fur coat and came, too. And there they got their first view of the new white world. They stood in awe and silence and looked, their eyes almost blinded by the glare of the snow. Out across the wide sweep of snow-clad meadow, sloping gently away and down, where gaunt birches waded knee deep, and sometimes almost neck deep, in plumy whiteness, and where heavy laden evergreens dipped lacey dark fingers into the foam. They looked to endless other hills of whiteness just like theirs, hill beyond hill, rising to shadowy mountains, snowcapped and furred with heavy hanging hemlocks.

It is safe to say that none of them save Chester had ever looked on such an awe-inspiring, breathtaking scene before, and they stood and gazed, without even the wish to speak, so beauty startled were they with the sight. They looked till eyes went blind with the glory of it and bodies shivered with the clear cold. Yet when they went in they had to come straight out again, as if it would be gone before they could get back. Such wonder! Such daunting beauty! Such spotlessness! So much of it in such vast reaches! Even Chris could hardly keep on working.

"Good night! If some people could see that! If they just could! Why, good night! We might advertise and charge admittance! Oh, boy! Wouldn't we get rich quick! Nothing poisonous about that, is there, Betty?"

But Betty had gone inside. It was too great! She could not bear it. She felt as if she had been snatched away from the regular commonplace world of reality to which she belonged and set down in a spirit world where she was all out of harmony, and it was choking her. She went in and went upstairs and made all the beds! She actually did, virtuously, without being told, absenting herself from the great world show downstairs. Not even trying to look through the impenetrable tracing on the windowpanes.

Till suddenly, reaching her mother's room in her round, she came full upon the display of lacey frostwork lit up by the full blaze of the winter's sun. She had to stop and exclaim in ecstasy.

Such elfin blades, with fairy towers, and fern work, such carvings and fretwork, and little flower faces peering at her here and there from unexpected dells of asphodels—what was that phrase—yes, "celestial asphodels." All the poetry she had ever read came rushing round her asking to be expressed in words for this lovely sight.

One window was thrown up to air the room, and she seemed to be atop of the world as she advanced to close it and saw the vast whiteness from a new angle. She caught her breath with the beauty, the almost fearsome beauty of it all, caught hold of the window frame to steady herself from the feeling that she was going to fall down the world.

And as she looked, there below her lay a little house half-hidden beneath the slope of the hill, a little house with a low-hanging roof, a tall chimney wide and generous, and soft, lazy smoke like a plume penciling itself against the sky in a little curly smudge.

That must be the house where Aunt Letty lived so long ago and almost froze to death in a snowstorm like this! And here was she, a young girl, too, alive and warm and vivid, and not hurt at all by the storm. What would it have been to have lived so long ago and be old-fashioned? Wear strange clothes and long hair, teach a country school, build fires, be Victorian, and have a family worship every night. Oh heck! Just think of it!

Betty put the window down with a slam and switched the bed into shape, tucking the old patchwork quilt in viciously, not stopping to regard the delicate stitches of Great-Grandmother Thornton's sampler, exquisite and microscopically small.

Head up and chest out she stalked into Chris's room at the back of the house, feeling very virtuous that she was making beds without request. Here, too, she found the window wide and the sun streaming in. The view was entrancing, for there below her, down a sharp incline of whiteness, lay a great smooth table of white, almost round in circumference and fringed by close, crowded trees. Across it, windblown and smooth as metal, flashed a broad space of silver like a great mirror giving back the sunlight in a flood of blinding light.

Chapter 14

It was some minutes before Betty's eyes could stand the brightness enough to figure out what it could be, so startling it was, there amid the quiet white hills. A white valley like all the rest, fringed by snow-decked trees, except for that flash of silver! It seemed mysterious, uncanny, as if the earth had somehow manifested a new phenomenon.

But of course! It was a lake, round and beautiful, hidden there among the pines and frozen over likely before the snow began, for where the wind had swept it it was perfectly glassy and smooth. How wonderful! A lake all their own, and frozen like that, so perfectly! At home they had skating for only a week or ten days, or sometimes only a day or two at Christmas, and for the rest of the year they had to go to the rink, and Daddy didn't like that very much. There had always been a fuss if she let it be known she was going. He said it was too public. But skating! There might be compensations after all. Life wasn't quite so poisonous as it had looked before.

She closed the window and made the bed thoughtfully, taking care with the smoothness of each sheet and blanket. Skates! How could they get their skates? It would take ages to send home for them, and maybe the skating would be all gone by the time they got here. In fact, would they ever be able to communicate with the outside world until spring? She doubted it, all that wilderness of snow, oceans deep and impenetrable. Well, there must be some skates to be found somehow. Perhaps the attic might yield a store of strange old things that could be made to do.

She went downstairs with her face almost bright.

"Come on out, Betts, it's wonderful!" said Chris, coming in for something to wear on his hands, having hopelessly split the fur-lined gloves he had started out with.

Eleanor opened up the trunk of old flannel underwear that had been deposited in the woodshed the night they came and found mittens galore, old and darned and ugly, leftovers from the years, but good and warm and welcome now. Betty, peering out at the tunnel they had already completed to the pump, scurried back and donned anything in the way of warm garments she could lay her hands on, everything except those despised galoshes. She came out in a red sweater, gray cap and scarf, and woolen stockings drawn over her shoes.

As she stepped back to the kitchen she stopped and called joyously, with a ring to her voice that sounded almost like the old-time Betty of two years before:

"Oh, Mums! You brought our skates! You old darling! Did you know there is a perfectly precious lake down in the backyard?"

That was a morning of utter joy and excitement. Even Betty forgot that she was an exile and worked away with a broom and a shovel till her back ached and her cheeks needed no rouge to make her utterly beautiful.

Eleanor in the kitchen, looking out occasionally from a windowpane that Chris had cleared for her, forgot her weariness and anxiety, her tormenting doubt whether they had done right to bring the children away from school just at the critical time of the year, with examinations coming on and Christmas so near. She forgot everything but the joy of seeing them all together working away, father and children like so many comrades shoulder to shoulder intent on getting paths everywhere and making a way of communication with the outside world.

Their voices rang out happily, calling how many feet they had done and how deep the drift was in his or her particular space. Happy tears welled into Eleanor's eyes as she turned away and went back to the kitchen, resolved to have a wonderful dinner ready for them when they came in hungry and tired after their task was finished.

She stood amazed for a minute and read the names on the cans and packages and bags. Flour and sugar and cornmeal, hominy, rice, oatmeal, and a sack of buckwheat. Tins of crackers and biscuits and cakes, glass jars and tin cans of fruits and jellies and vegetables. Baking powder, cocoa, chocolate, even some boxes of shredded coconut. Bars of chocolate, cans of coffee, boxes of tea, salt and codfish and kippered herring. She could hardly think of anything that she could possibly make that did not have its ingredients all there before her. How had Chester managed it? But of course he had put it into the hands of some clerk to select the things. Poor Chester. He didn't realize how expensive that would be. She ought to have given the order and asked prices carefully, now that they were going to be poor. Well, she would hoard the delicacies and deal them out little by little, making them last a long time so that more would not have to be purchased again soon.

It was almost pleasant to get back to the kitchen lore of her early married days. She was hampered a little by not understanding the wood range and constantly forgetting to poke wood down its voluminous throat, which it seemed to devour in a second and die down in another if she did not poke it in again. It was also bewildering to have to use iron pots and pans instead of her nice smooth aluminum, which she doted on at home. But a further search revealed the fact that Hannah had even managed to put in a few of those—saucepans of different sizes and some of the cake and pie pans. That would make things easier.

Just as she had selected the materials for the meal she was planning and turned to leave the pantry, she heard Chester's voice outside the window as he slid the big shovel into the top wall of the drift that covered the pantry window and came into contact with Chris's shovel on the other side of the drift.

"Hello, kid!" called Chester. "That you already? Good work! Having a good time?"

"I'll tell the world!" shouted back Chris happily.

She paused and watched through the window. She could just see both their faces through the top pane where the light stole down inside the big drift in a jagged line. They were working away on either side of the drift a foot apart, and the snow was giving way before them. It was hard work, too. She knew they had to carry some of it back ten or twelve feet through the narrow passage they had made to get to an open space where they might deposit it.

When she turned back to the kitchen again there came the girls' ringing laughter, Betty the loudest of them all. She and Jane had formed a partnership, pelting John and Doris with snowballs in return for those they had thrown while the girls were shoveling.

Who would have believed that the Betty of yesterday could be this cheerful creature, playing like a child in the snow!

John had started a snowman out in an open space where the wind had blown the ground almost bare. He was rolling a great ball almost as tall as himself, and now the girls stopped snowballing and helped. When they got it as large as they could roll, they made another smaller one and put it on the top of the first for a head. Jane tore some blue woolen balls from the knit cap she was wearing and stuck them in for eyes. Betty fashioned a nose from snow and found a bit of red ribbon in her pocket that she applied like lipstick. They made arms and put mittens on for hands, and Jane took off her cap and scarf and put them on him, and then they all stood back and shouted for Dad and Mother and Chris to come and see. Altogether it was a wonderful morning, and a great deal of work got itself done.

Hungry as wolves they came in when Eleanor rang the big farm dinner bell, all talking at once, all eager to tell Mother how much each had shoveled.

It appeared they were nearly down to the road that led to the little log house at the turn. When they got there, they would be in touch with the world again and could arrange for milk to be left at the gate each morning and the mail and the daily paper to be brought up. But why care, after all? The load of fretfulness and anxiety to get back to the world seemed to have dropped from every shoulder.

"And Daddy," said Betty, forgetting her recent affectation of calling him by his first name. "Is that really a lake down behind the house, and is it truly frozen over, or is it only a mirage? It looks like a sheet of silver in the sun."

"Why, yes, certainly, haven't I mentioned the lake?" asked Chester composedly, helping himself to baked beans—real bean-hole beans from a can that Eleanor had doctored with molasses and seasoning and butter and browned again in the oven. "Yes, that lake is always great. We boys used to spend every afternoon there until dark when we didn't have chores to do. And sometimes when it was moonlight—"

"Oh–h–h–h–h–hhh!" chorused the excited young people. "*Could we?*"

"We could!" said Chester happily, watching the play of pleasure on Betty's beautiful little face.

Oh, Chester was glad now he had come. He knew he was glad. He felt his prayer was being answered.

"Did you know that Mums brought our skates?" announced Betty with the air of conferring a great secret. "Yes, sir, all of them," she said as Chris turned an eager questioning face. "I wonder how long it will be before we can get down there?" continued Betty. "It looks miles deep in snow."

"Ah, but there's a path if you only know the way. We'll have to do a pretty bit of shoveling, and it may be a day or two before we get around to the lake, but we'll get there," promised Chester.

They all slept like logs that night, going to bed at half past eight. Not even Betty made a protest. But she went to the window of Chris's room before she went to her own, and looked out on the luminous valley with its one clear little streak of moonlight from a tiny thread of a new moon, and caught her breath again at the loveliness. Strange, unreal world of beauty. It seemed as if it was all a dream. What a splendid place for a house party. If it wasn't for that old business going bad she would ask Chester to let her invite the whole class up for Christmas week, and they could give a dance, and maybe invite some of the people around the neighborhood if there were any people worthwhile. What a mess that Chester should have failed! She never thought a thing like that could happen to her, to be the daughter of a poor man and have to live on a farm!

And so in spite of the silver sheen in the valley and the heap of skates in the woodshed and the little thread of a new moon hanging over the frozen lake, Betty went to bed with an evil spirit attending and a grudge against her father growing again in her heart. Also she longed for a cigarette, feverishly, wildly as she lay down on the old cord bed that creaked and groaned even with her light weight. A cigarette! If she could have just one. Here it was two whole days since she had had a smoke, and she hadn't been that long without one for over two years! It was fierce! Perfectly poi— But at that stage Betty fell asleep, for shoveling snow does not tend to make one wakeful.

It took two days to get shoveled down to the lake, because there was so much else to do that they couldn't work at it constantly. It was maddening to have to come in and wash dishes and carry wood. But finally the last step in the steep hill was cut and a path shoveled out on the ice to meet the windswept silver, and they all raced up to the house to get their skates.

Mother was making doughnuts, and there was a great platter full of the hot delicious circles, freshly powdered with sugar, standing on the table. Good cheer fairly exuded from every face as they stood around eating as many as they pleased with not a word of objection from Eleanor. She would have to mix up more dough, but after all, why not let them enjoy them while they were hot? The cold air and exercise would help to digest them, and they would likely stay out till all hours now that the ice was ready.

So they ate till they could eat no more then shouldered their skates and flew down to the ice.

The sun was just sinking behind the farthest mountain as they came out of the house. It looked like a ball of fire opal against the golden glitter of the departing day. Long ruby rays slithered over the crusty snow. Fine brown pencilings of birch trees made pictures against the distance.

"It looks just like a Christmas card!" said Jane. "Look, Betty!" And Betty, pausing on the top of the hill to finish her last bite of doughnut, felt something like a faint thrill of appreciation for the grandeur spread out before her. Then she whirled down to the ice and, putting on her skates, glided away into the sunset filled with the joy of living, a child on wings flitting over the fairy dazzle of glass as lightly as a bird. Just a happy child, all her tantrums and half-developed passions held at bay by the pure animal joy of flying along on the ice.

The next day a letter came from Dudley Weston and two other letters from Betty's best girlfriends. Betty was a woman again, with all her pride of self-will, all her arrogance and fury at being kept in prison when the world she had left behind her, her world, was swinging on with dizzying whirl without her.

Betty locked herself in her bedroom to read her letters, though everybody but her father and mother were down on the ice, and even they were in conference behind closed doors over some letters they had received.

Thorny, old girl, it began,

I call it pretty lousy of your old man to step in and disconnect you the way he did up at the Tav. I must say I think he owes me several apologies, knocking me stiff right out of the blue that way. If he hadn't been your dad I'd have knocked him cold for that, and next time I'll do more than that if you know what I mean. Better warn him!

But anyway, what's the little old idea doing the vanishing act? I called up your house twice yesterday and got nowhere. Gyp Magilkey says she thinks it's some parent stuff, that your dad was mad as a hatter up at the high dance, but I told her you wouldn't stand for anybody monkeying with your rights.

Still, if the old man has got you pinned and you can't help yourself, me for the rescue! How'd you like to get married? We might try the companionate way, it seems to be the latest now—or just go off, that's really less trouble and lots are doing it, though it isn't quite so new. Probably companionate would make less kick; it's more formal, you know.

But say, we could get away with it in vacation and nobody the wiser, and then sometime if anybody makes a kick about anything, or we want to pull something, we could spring it on 'em. Whaddaya say? Mebbe I could get Gyp and Sam to come along. They'd do for witnesses. But you must let me know. Make it snappy. I'll have to make arrangements. We could make a getaway after school the Friday before Christmas. Gwen has a house party and all of us are going, of course, and nobody would miss us till we were off for good.

I can't seem to find out where you've gone. Everybody is vague. You send directions, and I'll meet you where you say, and when; only don't keep me waiting and spoil the game. Better wire if you accept.

Yours to get drunk,
Dud

P.S. *The play went rotten. They put Sue Rounds in your place, but I kicked and now Gwen's going to get it, but no worries if you wire O.K. I shan't be there to see. Here's hoping, and MAKE IT SNAPPY!*

Chapter 15

$\mathcal{M}$ary Magilkey, otherwise Gipsy, had given more gossip:

Betts, you little beast! You're the limit!

Here I give up a perfectly good date to spend the night with you and help you fix up that faun costume so your mother wouldn't find out, and when I get to your house there's nobody but that ugly old woman, and she says she doesn't know when you'll return. She won't even say where you've gone, but I'm sending this through the post office. Of course they'll forward it to you if you're really away for long.

But say, you certainly did one dirty trick leaving before rehearsal. It certainly was a scream. I thought I'd pass out. Sue Rounds volunteered to take your part, said she knew it all. You know she's a wow for learning everybody's part. She's dying to get into a play sometime, and she's just hanging around ready for any little old chance like you handed out to her. But oh, boy! If you could have seen her flirt with Dud! He glared at her like a jazz pirate and she rolled her eyes and got in that line,

470

you know—"Oh, my dearest love! You have come back to me at last!" I nearly died! And Lois snickered right out and Miss House shut her lips hard and shook her head severely at her. But Sue went right on with her mushy speech. I thought Dud was going to knock her down, but he caught sight of Housey's face and grabbed her round the waist like a bag of beans and said, "Come, let's get out of here where we can talk!" and he sounded just like the chief of police come to arrest her. Honest, we all simply screamed and went into spasms, and Dud put out his foot and tripped Sue, and she fell flat! It was great! Housey finally dismissed the rehearsal and said there "wouldn't be any play at all if this happened again," etc., you know, like she always does when she's mad. But afterward I heard Dud asking Gwen Phillips to take the part if you didn't come back. He said he'd make it right with Housey. He'd threaten not to act himself. So you'd better get a move on you, Betts. You don't want Gwen to nail him, and she will! I could see she was flattered when he asked her to take the star part with him. You can't trust any man, Betts. Out of sight is out of mind. But perhaps you don't care. Of course, Gwen is giving a house party in vacation and all that, but perhaps you know. She is going to have a big dance at Shillingsworth's, too, and Dud'll probably drive her to that if you don't get back. But perhaps you've already had your invitation.

And oh, yes, Fran's uncle has let her ask the class to a trip on his yacht during Christmas week. You'd better get back. I'm having a couple of new casual things made just for the occasion. And Estelle has a new dress her aunt brought her from Paris. She calls it a "frock" but it looks like a patchwork quilt and hangs something fearful on her!

Now, darling, write me at once and tell me what you want me to say when Gertie Gates gets to prying about where you've

gone and why; and whether it is true that your dad thrashed
Dud Weston and told him never to come near you again; and
whether you and Dud have really had a fuss; and all that. You
know Gertie. Besides I'm dying of anxiety about you. I shall
pass out absolutely if I don't hear by Wednesday. And precious,
one word of advice, don't let your parents put anything over on
you! You're almost of age and have a right to do as you please!
They *did*, of course!

Passionately,
Gyp

Frances Allison's letter was brief and to the point:

Betts, old thing:
    This is just to let you know that there's a new man in our
class. He came the day after you left, and he's simply stunning!
But he belongs to me, so hands off. He's taken me out twice in
his car, and it's a humdinger. He lives in the old Foster place
and his uncle is T.Y. Pettingill, the real estate man. They have
simply scads of money, and he's awfully generous. I think he
would make a wonderful class president, in case Willie Boyer
doesn't get well enough to come back this year. We really ought
to have somebody who looks the part, don't you think?
    And Betts! He has a cousin coming at Christmas, a college
man. I've seen his picture, and he's almost as good looking. If it's
really true as Gertie Gates is telling round that you and Dud
are angry with each other I'll introduce you to him first and
give him the high sign. So you better hurry home.

Your adoring Fran

Betty read these effusions through and then turned back to Dudley Weston's, reading it again with thoughtful brows. Gone was the childlike look and the glow of the morning, gone the far view of distant mountains and sunsets and the vivid joy of skimming over perfect ice. Betty was back in her high school days, as if there had been no interval. Her heart burned hot with pride of possession, possession of her man—or what she was pleased to call a man. A flame of jealousy shot through her heart at the thought of Gwen Phillips and her house party. Dud used to go with Gwen down in the eighth grade. She *should not* get him back again!

Nor was Betty averse to attracting the new man from college, especially if he was good looking. It was just as well for Dudley Weston to see that he wasn't the only one that admired her.

All the same Dudley had been fairly upright. Hadn't he asked her to marry him? And that really was as much as he could be expected to do after her father had knocked him down. Yes, quite decent, suggesting a companionate marriage or any old thing she chose!

Betty narrowed her eyes and stared unseeing off at the mountains out of her window, trying to decide which she would prefer of the three.

It would be thrilling just to go off. She had always dreamed of that, albeit fearsomely. Some fragment of antiquity, perhaps, still lingered in her blood. One couldn't quite get away from one's stuffy ancestors, and even the psychologists admitted that a certain percentage of your character was inheritance, though not nearly as much as they used to think. The rest was environment, and of course if one had the courage to make one's environment what one wished, why one could be *anything*—almost anything in the universe!

Betty's heart swelled within her, and she rose, her head uplifted and her soul full of aspiring thoughts. What if she should go off with Dud? Just go off! Still, that was old stuff of course as Dud had said. People had been doing it for centuries. Of course companionate marriage was newer, and nobody in Briardale had tried it yet. It really sounded a lot better than just going off and made it easier to change around providing things didn't go so smoothly. As for getting married, real downright, respectable getting married, of course every girl had that in the back of her mind as she grew up, veil stuff and white satin and orange blossoms. But one couldn't have that and a thrill, too, and really nowadays most people would choose the thrill. There really wasn't much you could get a kick out of in a wedding after all. There simply *weren't* any new combinations of colors for bridesmaids unless one dared have them garbed in black velvet with big white horsehair hats trimmed in something severe, perhaps a tail of monkey fur—just one, like a tassel hanging down over one shoulder and drawn through the hat in a pinched fold!

Betty narrowed her eyes again and studied the mountain intensely. Of course a bride would have to wear white, and it wouldn't look exactly right to trim it in black, even though black and white were awfully smart just now. But wait! Why *did* a bride always have to wear white? Why couldn't the bride wear black? Black velvet, that was it, with a dash of ermine, and the bridesmaids in white organdy. They could still wear the monkey fur tassel on their hats. That certainly would be different from anyone else, and the headlines in the newspapers could read THE BRIDE IN BLACK! Black had always been attractive on her, and Mums would never let her wear it; she said it was too old for a young girl. Mums was extremely old-fashioned. But of course she couldn't pull off any outfits like that if she *were* married at home or in the church. Well, one ought to consider all those things, but everything taken into consideration it would really be easier, and she'd get far more of a kick out of accepting Dud's suggestion.

And wouldn't it make a sensation at school? She could fairly see Miss House's irate complexion turn brick color when the news came out. And wouldn't the girls envy her? Of course she would drive Dudley's car whenever she liked after that, even before she told that she was married. But perhaps, after all, she and Dudley wouldn't bother to go back to high school. Why should they? Married people didn't need a diploma. It was only a gesture.

Into the midst of her reflections came a clear call for supper, and Betty was hungry. She had been skating all the afternoon and she was ravenous. She went down to the dining room and mingled with the family, taking part in the conversation and seeming to be just as she had been two hours before, but her mind was running on other things. She was thinking all the time, *What would they say if they knew I was going to be married in a couple of weeks? Am I?*

So she toyed with the idea, laughing a good deal with Jane and Chris to cover her self-consciousness, playing paper dolls with Doris most obligingly and a game of checkers with John on an old checkerboard he had found in the desk drawer.

"What if I should?" she kept saying over and over to herself. "What if I should? But of course—how could I?"

By the time she went up to bed she had reached the stage of wondering how she could get a telegram off to Dudley Weston. *If* she should decide to do it, how could she send him word without the family becoming aware of it? Of course she might send a letter, but she doubted if it would get by the family censorship. Chester Thornton had told his daughter she was to have no communication whatever, *ever*, with Dudley Weston; that he was not fit for a decent girl to speak to. If her father should see a letter addressed to Dudley lying with the letters to be carried down to the mail when he drove down to the village as he did almost every morning with the milkman, he would be sure to destroy it and forbid her to write again. Well, she might enclose it to Gyp, or Fran, and ask them to mail it or give it to Dud, but could she really trust them with an errand so momentous? If anything happened that they left it around or told anybody else—Fran might tell that new man, for instance, or

Gyp might think she would steam the letter open and read it or hold it up to the light and get a few words. Gyp was very curious and she might think as she was her best friend that she had a right to find out how matters stood between her and Dud. No, a letter sent that way was not really quite safe, and besides, there was Gwen Phillips, and no telling how much influence she might have over Dudley in the meantime. Even a day was precious. She really ought to send a telegram. Dud would be upset if she didn't do as he suggested, even though it was unreasonable of him. She must somehow manage. Couldn't she steal out of the house early in the morning and catch the milkman down at the foot of the lane? Dad didn't go in town every day. She could send it tomorrow perhaps.

She lay awake a long time after the family were all asleep thinking about it, making plans. By this time she had fully made up her mind that she was going. How could any girl give up a chance like that?

Having decided to go, Betty now turned her thoughts to the wording of a telegram.

It must be brief. It must be businesslike. It must be misleading to all but the one concerned. Phrase after phrase formulated itself only to be rejected, but at last she settled on the following words as covering the case satisfactorily:

"Will arrive railroad station Springfield, Massachusetts, noon Saturday. Companion preferred."

She solaced her conscience by saying that it would be easy enough to call it off later if she changed her mind, and so thinking went to sleep.

But she missed her calculation and overslept, and the morning was far on its way before she awoke. There was no alternative but to get her father to take her with him when he went down to the village next time, trusting to luck to get away and send her telegram.

As she went about her dressing, thinking this all out, she remembered with sudden dismay that she had no money to send that telegram, and how was she to get any? Of course she could send it collect, but that didn't seem just right. Betty was a proud little thing. But at last that problem, too, was solved.

At the supper table the night before, the conversation had run on Christmas and the prospect of no gifts, each one of the children bewailing the fact that they had not bought nor brought anything that would do for that purpose. Their mother had looked up with a quick smile that nevertheless contained a swift warning look toward their father and said, quite as if it were a usual thing to do:

"We'll have to *make* our Christmas presents this year. I was thinking about that last night. I believe it will be interesting. Just make some little thing, each of you for each of the rest, and we'll give a prize for the most original gift."

"But there's nothing to make them out of," mourned Jane.

"Oh, plenty!" said Eleanor, still smiling. "There is a wonderful attic full of beautiful things, and there's all the outdoors also. When I was a girl I made a braided rug for my mother for Christmas once, out of old rags that were to be thrown away. She loved it, and I enjoyed the making, too."

"What's out of doors, I'd like to know?" asked Chris.

"Well, pinecones and acorns and acorn cups. We used to make picture frames out of those. And you have your camera. There are plenty of beautiful pictures that someday you can have enlarged. Once my father made me a dollhouse out of a packing box—"

"Oh–hh," said Doris, looking from one to another of the family hopefully.

Betty remembered this now and turned it over in her mind. It gave her an idea, and one idea brought another. Later when they were washing dishes together she said:

"Mother, could you give me about a dollar or two? I want to get a new thimble. And my toothbrush keeps shedding bristles. I broke my comb, too, and I'd like some decent letter paper. I thought I'd ask

Dad to let me go along down to the village tomorrow if he goes. I hate to ask him for money, since you say he hasn't any."

"Why, I think I can manage that much," said Eleanor, smiling. It seemed a reasonable request. But Betty went up to her room feeling like a liar and a thief. She had done far worse things than that at home sometimes, without being troubled, but somehow this seemed a more flagrant offense, because she was deliberately planning to bring trouble and sorrow to her mother and father. Yet she went straight on with her planning.

The next morning Betty went down to the village on a farmer's sleigh, an old farm wagon with runners beneath and straw for upholstery. Chester went to the hotel to do some telephoning. He told Betty to float around and do her shopping. He pointed out the shopping district: a general merchandise store, dry goods and groceries combined; a drugstore combined with the post office; and the railroad station a little farther down the street.

Betty went to the last one first and got a timetable to make sure she could reach Springfield at the hour named. She also sent her telegram and discovered the price of a ticket to Springfield. How was she ever to get enough together even for so short a journey? She must hoard her money. Her mother had given her two dollars, and there was not much over a dollar left after sending the telegram. She must have some cigarettes, too!

The man in the drugstore gave her a sharp look when she asked for cigarettes, and she thought for a moment that he was going to refuse her. But she told him she was buying them for her brother, and he finally went and got them. She bought Chris some, too. It seemed only fair, since Chris would have done as much for her if he had the chance. Then she went back to the hotel and wrote a letter to Dudley Weston. It had necessarily to be brief lest her father appear before she finished, and she wanted to mail it if possible today. She wrote:

Old thing,

*You've said it! Parent stuff. Pinned all right. Broke, too.
All kinds of a time getting wire off. Meet you in Springfield
railroad station at noon, Saturday the 22nd. If school closes
early Friday afternoon you ought to make it by then. If you
write don't put your name on outside of envelope. Forbidden
stuff! Hard going! If you want to send anything, make it
chocolates with a layer of smokes inside. This is a perfectly
poisonous place. Empty as a flask! Be sure to bring Gyp
and Sam, or else get Fran and somebody. And let's make it
companionate. That sounds newer. Don't be late.*

Thorny

Chapter 16

Betty slipped out and mailed her letter and then came back and sat down in the funny old stuffy parlor and waited. She stared out of the window at the little empty street with its mountains of snow on either side and its far vista of frozen lake at the end. The lake was surrounded by a huddle of closed summer cottages and boathouses shivering on the bank like worn old ladies in white fur capes and hoods. She was thinking that she had done it now. The word had gone out of her hand that she would marry Dudley Weston. She could not call it back! It was under the United States stamp and seal! It had to go with its message. If she wanted to retract she would have to go back on her word, and there was an unwritten law that one who did that had a streak of "yellow." Betty had never showed a streak of yellow. She was known all over school as a "game kid." She would have to carry it through now, no matter what.

Her cheeks glowed and her eyes shone. It was going to be a lot of fun, anyway, something to break the horrible monotony of this snowbound dump to which they had brought her.

When her father came back to her she was looking almost happy, and her cheeks glowed so brightly that he gave a relieved sigh. Betty was standing the exile better than he had dared to hope. Perhaps if they stayed long enough she would forget all about the dreadful things she had left behind her and become again the pure, sweet child she had been. If only it might prove that he had not discovered things too late! He had just arranged to have a telephone put into the old house, which would make it possible for him to stay all winter, with only a trip to the office now and then.

"Well, Betty, did you get everything that you wanted?" he asked pleasantly.

Betty looked up then answered evasively:

"Well, no, not everything. Some things cost more than I thought. I didn't have enough money."

"Not enough money?" he said, smiling, and dropped a five-dollar bill in her lap. "Run along and get what you want. I want to write a letter, and then we'll be ready to go when Mr. Brown comes back."

Betty took the money, her cheeks growing very red, and went slowly over to the store. She would have to get something or her mother would ask about it. She felt as if she were taking her father's lifeblood in that five-dollar bill. She almost ran back to give it to him and tell him she didn't need the things, that he had better keep it for necessities, that she knew he couldn't afford it. Then she reflected that it would go far toward making her journey to Springfield possible; and after all, when she was gone, there would be one less in the family to support.

She bought a twenty-five-cent toothbrush, a ten-cent thimble, a thirty-cent box of letter paper, and came slowly, almost shamefully, back to her father, feeling that she ought to give the change back, yet knowing she did not mean to do so unless he asked her.

Chester did not ask for the money. Betty got into the old sleigh and settled down in the straw, telling her conscience that she wasn't doing anything criminal. The money would be there in her pocket if

481

either her father or mother asked for it back again. She wasn't stealing it. They had given it to her. She reflected, as she drove back to the merry jingle of the sleigh bells, that she had done very well to get things so far under way for her going, and she could afford to be nice and pleasant the rest of the time she had to stay. Of course they were going to be terribly upset with her for a while, and perhaps it was a rather rotten thing for her to do. Yet after all, it was rotten of them to bring her away from her friends and park her up in a mountain to die! They had no right! It was her own life, and she had to live it. She was preparing to live it to the limit, and the thought made her fairly sparkle with goodwill toward her family.

As a sort of atonement she entered at once into plans for Christmas as soon as she got back to the farm. She instituted an expedition to the attic immediately after lunch in search of materials and professed to have great ideas for what she was going to do. But she said nothing at all about the other ideas she had developed while hunting through the old trunks and bandboxes and chests. She came down with her arms full of old velvets and satins and silks, but she did not tell about the rose-colored taffeta she had found in the depths of the biggest trunk. It had been a part of Great-Aunt Elizabeth Thornton's ancient trousseau. She brought it down wrapped in an old hand-embroidered nightgown of firm, fine linen embroidered in delicate vines and flowers. The taffeta was made with a silk fitted waist and a long, full skirt, very much like the present-day fashion of evening dresses. It had a low, round neck and a bertha collar of priceless old lace. Why, wouldn't it do to take along for a dance frock? She had nothing whatever fit to appear in before her own world except the little jersey dress she had worn away from school that day. She scorned all the sensible garments her mother had brought along. Of course when she got home, after the marriage and a suitable interval for some kind of a honeymoon, depending on how much money Dud could rake up, she would be able to get into the house and perhaps find some of her own clothes. Surely everything must be there just as when they left it. The house couldn't have been sold with all their clothes in it, not so soon anyway. Of course Mother and Dad had had a lot of conferences behind closed doors and hadn't breathed a word. There was no telling what had been done. Mother looked awfully sad sometimes when she came out, and once Betty had caught her crying. It was hard on Mums, of course. After she was married and living in luxury she would invite Mums a great deal to visit her. Of course she would be living in luxury, for Dud's father was said to be fabulously rich, and he had been awfully generous with Dud. When he found he was really married and settled down he would of course likely build him a house and furnish it. Too bad Dad couldn't get her a decent trousseau, but going off this way would really let him off. Nobody could expect him to do anything when he hadn't been told, and of course he would be angry for a while. That would be natural, and people wouldn't expect anything of him till he got over it. Then by that time he would likely have pulled up in his business, and of course Dad would come across handsomely with chests of silver and things as fast as he got into shape. He had always been generous.

So reasoned Betty as she locked her door against intrusion, turned her back on Great-Aunt Elizabeth's limp china doll that she had brought down to dress for Doris for Christmas, and arrayed herself in the rose-colored taffeta. It certainly was attractive, with its fall of rich old lace about the shoulders, almost down to the slim little waist. The skirt was put onto the waist with a cord and hung about her deliciously. If she could only manage to curve up the hemline in front a little, it would make it more chic, but on second thought that might be dangerous, with no long mirror by which to get the effect and no one to help her pin it up. Besides, there were many dresses made nowadays with straight hems, and it would be charming to say it was being worn just as her great-aunt had worn it on her wedding trip! All it really needed was ironing, and she could easily manage to bring up an iron and an ironing board or something and smooth out the wrinkles. This business of making Christmas gifts for each other was going to make it quite possible for her to do a lot of things in privacy without exciting suspicion, because they were all working behind closed doors.

She whirled about to let the rich, rosy waves of silk swish around her and the lace collar foam around her shoulders. She spread out her young white arms before the old mirror where perhaps her aunt had once stood in that same dress. She put her head to one side and sighed happily. It looked as if a real thrill was on the way.

Then she suddenly shivered. It wasn't as warm up in that old Vermont farmhouse bedroom, heated only by a drum from the sitting room below, as it was in her steam-heated bedroom at home in Briardale. Primping and admiring herself might be at the expense of a cold, and she mustn't run that risk now or she might not be able to get away with her plan.

So she slipped out of the rosy silk and folded it safely away in its shrouding of embroidered linen in her bottom drawer, locked the drawer, and put the key in her sweater pocket. Then she put on her warm farm garments again and stole downstairs to read by the fire. She had found an old book that was thrilling and wanted to finish it. It told of lords and ladies and quaint old times of persecution when knights fought for ladies fair, and love was supreme. The essence of the story somehow mimicked what Betty was planning to do. She began to idealize the noble Dudley as her rescuer.

Yet she had a very tender feeling toward her mother and the rest of the family. She even laid down her book and went to the kitchen door to ask if she could help her mother when she heard her sigh as she shut the oven door on a couple of big apple pies she had just made.

"No, dear, it's all done now," said Eleanor gently, "but you may set the table if you will. Then everything will be ready for supper, and we won't be in such a rush when they all come in."

So Betty set the table, listlessly, bored, leaving off half the things that make a smooth and quiet meal, and went back to her book with a conscience at ease. After all, was she not a dutiful daughter, even though she was planning to run away with a man of whom her parents disapproved! But then one must live one's own life!

Betty came reluctantly at the third call, in the midst of the most exciting chapter of all, to eat the delicious meal that her mother had prepared. She ate rapidly with enjoyment and was about to excuse herself and go back to her book when her father halted her.

"Sit down, Betty!" he said. His tone was kind but firm. There was a new note in it, which Betty in her preoccupation failed to notice.

"No way, Chester," she said with an impudent laugh. "I'm right in the thrill of my book, and I can't wait another minute."

She had not called him Chester since they came to the farm, and somehow with the use of the disrespectful term her old bravado returned. It would not be long now before she was free from this kind of submission. She tilted her chin impertinently and turned away from the table.

"I said, '*Sit down*,' Betty!" And now there was something unmistakable in his voice, though it was quiet and self-controlled.

Betty flashed at him a defiant look as she took another step toward her book, and then suddenly, she did not quite know why, she came back and sat down, her face overclouded by a sudden sullen anger.

But Chester paid no attention to her attitude. He continued to look at her steadily, with that quality of searching justice in his eyes that made her uncomfortable in spite of her anger. It seemed an age that he looked at her so, until she wished to drop her eyes from that steady glance, but could not do so.

"Betty, while you are in my house—"

Betty gave him a sudden, quick startled look. Why did he say, "While you are in my house," as if he knew? Could he possibly have found out? Had he followed her down in the village without her knowledge?

"While you are in my house," went on the steady voice, "you will not call me by that name anymore. What began in jest has ceased to be amusing and has become disrespect. It is part of the disrespect of the age. It is what we came here to get away from. It was perhaps partly our fault that you were allowed to fall into such habits. But it will not be our fault if you continue in them. Your mother and I are determined to undo as far as possible what has been done while we had our eyes shut. Now, I hope that is thoroughly understood—"

His eyes went around the table and searched each young face with a meaningful glance. There was something about his expression that showed he was not to be trifled with.

"This is something that applies to you all," he added, "a principle that must be observed. We want no more flippant remarks and no more refusals to do what you are told to do."

Chris turned red and began to put more butter on a piece of bread, though he had seemed to have quite finished his supper. Jane folded her napkin in tiny plaits and pretended not to have heard him, but it was plain that each recalled some recent offense and understood what he meant.

"Excuse me, Mums," said Chris, hurriedly stuffing the last bit of bread and butter into his mouth. "I wantta get in that wood. It might snow again tonight, and we'd need it."

"There is apple pie," said Eleanor, looking troubled and rising quickly. "And cottage cheese the milkman brought. You like that!"

She started toward the kitchen.

"Wait!" said Chester in that arresting tone. "Sit down, Eleanor, please. There is something else I want to say first. It is time you children began to help your mother and to keep her from waiting on you all the time. It is time the work of the house was divided among you and not all left for your mother to do. I came in here a few minutes ago and found your mother sitting down with a dizzy head, as white as could be, and all in a tremble from cooking all the afternoon. She is scarcely able to sit up at the table now, and yet you have all let her wait on you hand and foot, and you were going to let her continue to do so. Eleanor, can't someone else get that pie? You sit still. Betty, get the pie!"

"For Pete's sake, aren't we ever going to have a maid again?" said Betty impudently.

"Perhaps not," said Chester coolly. "Betty, get the pie!"

"Well, if we weren't in such a poisonous dump you might get some kind of a job somewhere and *get* a maid!" said Betty furiously and flounced out to the kitchen.

Eleanor cast a reproachful look at her as she went. Betty felt fiercely glad as she picked up the pie and came back, glad that they had given her reason to rebel. Life seemed once more all wrong, and the only way to right it was to accept Dudley Weston's rescue. She gave her conscience a slap and told it to be quiet, and she carried the pie in and put it down in front of her mother with a thump.

"You may bring the pie to me," said Chester, noticing how tired Eleanor was looking.

Betty slammed the pie in front of her father.

"I thought children of respectable families were supposed to be sent to school," she said as she slumped into her chair again.

"Perhaps we are not a respectable family," said Chester, eyeing the pie. "I have had strong suspicions during the last week that we were not. Jane, will you get me a knife and some plates?"

"Well, aren't we going to school anymore?" asked John eagerly as if he personally would be quite willing to dispense with that conventionality.

"Certainly," said Chester evenly. "There are several different kinds of schools. I felt that a change would be most beneficial at this time. You are about to engage in a course in domestic science and agriculture."

"Agriculture?" asked Chris contemptuously. "At this time of year?"

"At this time of year," said Chester. "Woodcutting and carrying has a large part in the winter work of the farmer. In the interim it will not hurt you boys to get a little touch of domestic science along with your sisters. To that end, we are all going to wash the dishes tonight and put them away. Tomorrow I am expecting a man to put in our telephone, and after that I shall be busy most of the mornings and afternoons, but after five o'clock I shall expect to do my part toward the running of this house with the rest of you, and I shall expect each one of you to do your share without complaint. I believe your mother has some plan for division of labor, and she will tell you about it tomorrow. But I want you to understand there is to be no shirking. I brought you up here partly to give you an understanding of some of the hardships of the world of which you have so far seen very little, and they can only be understood by experience. Therefore we are going to have experience."

"Great cats!" said Chris.

"I abhor housework!" said Betty wrathfully. "I don't see any sense in people with brains having to do it, either."

"Were you under the impression that you had brains?" asked her father half amusedly.

Betty flushed angrily and swallowed her last bite of pie before answering. Then she arose haughtily, gathering up her dishes with the air of a degraded princess:

"Well, if this sort of thing is going on," she said as she opened the kitchen door with her piles of dishes, "I for one shall leave!"

"Indeed!" said her father calmly. "Just where would you go?"

"There are plenty of places I can go!" she tossed her head mysteriously. "Lots of girls are leaving home today, getting jobs and things like that. I don't blame them either if this is the sort of parents they have to endure!"

With that Betty went out and shut the door behind her. A moment later they heard her stamping noisily up the narrow back stairway.

Chester opened the door into the hall, and his voice met her as she reached the door of her own room:

"Betty, you may come down at once. Your part of the evening's work is not done."

Betty came down, her eyes stormy. Silently she went about doing what she was told to do, and doing no more. Silently until she was dismissed she remained, and when the lamp in the kitchen was put out she rushed up to her room and had it out with herself, telling herself that she was glad she had sent word to Dudley. Such antique oppression was not to be tolerated. Then she cried a little, angry tears of self-pity, to think that her proud family had come to such straits as this. But it was not for the sake of the family she cried, but for her own. She was full of self-pity. And she began to think harsh thoughts against her previously indulgent father. What could have come over him to act this way, after all his years of kindness? He surely must be losing his mind!

But Chester Thornton was not losing his mind, heavy though his heart might be. As he worked away at the great banks of snow that hindered their moving about and down to the road as they would, his thoughts were busy trying to discover where the fault lay that his children who had apparently started out so well in life had run amok of all the modern trash and eagerly embraced it. Perhaps he was trying to blame someone else, for what he was slowly coming to see had been at least partly his own fault.

His full enlightenment came the evening he found his mother's old Bible, with a few faded words from her own trembling hand written on the flyleaf.

> *To my children,*
>
> *I leave this old Book as the best heritage I can give. Study it carefully, and you will find the way to peace and righteousness and happiness as I have done. If there is ever anything wrong with your lives, come back to this book as if it were a mirror, and it will clearly show you what is the matter. And when you are lost in the world, it will guide you home.*
>
> Mother

The tears rolled unexpectedly down Chester's cheeks when he read that. His mother's message across the years, like a voice from the grave showing him what to do! As if he had put to her the very questions that had been troubling him and she had handed him this book as an answer!

He read until far into the night. Read until Eleanor came down in robe and slippers with a worried look upon her face and asked what was the matter.

The strange part of it was that the first page he had opened to had been the story of Eli's two sons who were misbehaving and the curse that God told Samuel to bring upon Eli.

He had begun to read the story because it had been one that his mother often read to him and his brothers when they were little children, sitting on their low stools about their mother's knee on Sunday afternoon. The child Samuel! How well he remembered what charm it had for him at five years old! But the story itself had grown vague and its meaning utterly obscured. The part that Eli and his two profligate sons played in it began to appear like writing that has been done in invisible ink and brought near the fire. Eli stood out as a picture of himself: Eli, who meant to be a good man, but who had been too indulgent with his children! His heart burned within him as he read, and ever he could hear the sweet voice of his mother through the words. No, it was not as it had seemed at first, a miracle, that the worn old book should have fallen open at the third chapter of first Samuel. Often and often had it lain open there upon her knee while they listened entranced to the story.

And now as he read the once familiar sentence against the old easygoing father-priest the words stabbed themselves into his heart, and it was as if his own name were substituted for Eli's, and his own neglect became a sin, heinous as Eli's.

In that day I will perform against Eli all things which I have spoken concerning his house: when I begin, I will also make an end. For I have told him that I will judge his house for ever for the iniquity which he knoweth; because his sons made themselves vile, and he restrained them not. And therefore I have sworn unto the house of Eli, that the iniquity of Eli's house shall not be purged with sacrifice nor offering for ever.

Over and over he read the awful words of the Lord God, and as they forced their way into his soul he seemed to be being judged of the Lord Himself, for the iniquity in his own household.

Back to the years of the babyhood of his little children he was carried, when he stood beside the pink and blue laced and beribboned cribs and watched the tiny buds of life unfold in beauty with such high hopes of what their lovely lives would be. All his own faults and follies were to be carefully erased from them, all guards and helps put about them to direct them into perfection. Perfect they had come from God, and perfect they should grow up to show what perfection in men and women could be. No children had ever been so fair and sweet and promising as his.

How hard he had worked during the years to make the home a

fitting background for their youth, to pile up money with which to lavish upon them all the best that the world could give. Early had he sought out the best institutions of learning and carefully arranged that their initial education should be such as to prepare them for the requirements of the great universities that he had chosen. Never had they asked for anything that other children had, but he had given it if he could, and if he could not he generally managed soon to make it possible. He had ever been their comrade, playing with them when he could, taking time as often as possible for extended holidays, or at least sending them and their mother on holidays. He had chosen the best church in town, that is, the church where the best people, the really cultured, educated, refined people went. He had insisted that they be identified with its activities, although now he recalled that Betty's sole effort in that line had been the playing of the star part in a great religious pageant where she had posed as some indefinite, angelic, personified principle looking more than angelic, and receiving enough praise to turn any girl's head. Jane, too, had done a little childish act, a feather dance, between parts. After all, had that sort of thing helped them heavenward? Yet, too, he remembered now a carnival held in the public hall of Briardale, for the benefit of the new church community hall that they were trying to build. Betty had entered into the drive for raising funds enthusiastically. She had presided over a fountain of lemonade dressed in some outlandish garb of a heathen goddess. He remembered she had been barefoot, and that he had protested, but the committee had carried the day, saying she wouldn't look the part if she wore shoes. Oh, his children had always looked the part in whatever they had done, even church work. But what had been the matter?

They were all members of the church, the whole family, himself an elder. They entertained the other elders once a year, royally; he always contributed generously, loaned their car, and sent flowers and cake to whatever was going on. They even sang in special choirs on occasion and helped decorate the church for holidays and holy days. And yet, they had made themselves *vile*! That phrase kept repeating itself over and over in his weary brain. "Thy sons have made themselves vile! Thy house shall not be purged by sacrifice nor offering for ever!" He had forgotten Eli. He seemed to hear the words spoken to himself. *Thy sons! Thy children!* At times it came over him with overwhelming shame.

So, tonight, when Betty had gone upstairs and all was still, a kind of gray, ashen look came over the father's face. He was hearing those words again: "Thy children have made themselves vile! Thy house shall not be purged with sacrifice nor offering for ever!"

Chapter 17

Eleanor had gone up early to bed with the younger children. She looked utterly worn out. Chester knew that the scene at the supper table had not rested her. These things pierced her like a sword. Eleanor loved peace and loved to see the children happy. It distressed her beyond measure to have dissension. He could see that every word that Betty spoke had hurt her.

Chris was in the woodshed, with a lamp on the high shelf by the door, pounding and sawing away at a dollhouse he was trying to make for Doris for Christmas. He seemed to be fairly interested, and that was something to be thankful for. Jane had locked herself in her room professing to be working at Christmas presents also, and there was no longer need to keep up an appearance of cheerfulness. Chester slumped in an old rocking chair by the stove, the gray look overspreading his face like a fast-traveling cloud that was blotting out the light.

He sat for a long time with his elbows on his knees and his face buried in his hands, seeing things he had never seen before, feeling his need of something that he had never missed before, feeling his utter helplessness, unable to bear the weight of his little girl Betty's defection.

The chair in which he sat had been the one in which his mother had rocked her babies long ago. She had put those gentle, loving arms around them; he could feel the frailty of them now, so slender and so warm and so tender, and yet so strong, holding his little hot body when he had a fever, her fingers touching the burning forehead, so cool, so dear! He had felt so safe in her arms, his little gentle frail mother! If he only could go to her now, kneel before this same chair, put his aching head in her lap and pour out his troubles!

And she had sent him word down through the years to go to the Book she had left, for guidance! Well, he had gone, and it had only brought him condemnation. Utter, hopeless condemnation! He groaned aloud, and Betty, lying wide eyed above the big old base burner with its upstairs drum to warm her room, heard the groan through the echoing stovepipe and stared and shrank. Was that her dad, groaning like a woman? Heard and despised him for it. Heard and hardened her fierce, rebellious young heart. He had no right to act like that! He had no right to be so old fogeyish and care that way about things nobody else believed in anymore!

Half an hour later as she lay in her bed, still staring at the dark ceiling, still thinking bitter thoughts about him, she heard his footsteps coming slowly up the stairs. He stopped at her door and opened it gently, listened a moment, and spoke:

"Betty, are you asleep?"

Betty stirred and coughed. She could not think how to reply. Something in her soul refused to let her answer directly.

He came over beside the bed and touched her gently on the forehead.

"Betty, little girl," he said, and his voice was very tender, the way she remembered it when she was a tiny child. "Your father loves you!" His voice was wistful. "I've been thinking about it, child, and I'm

495

afraid I haven't been the right kind of a father to you!"

Of all things! What a horrible thing to say! That was sob stuff! That was against the code. Her father talking *mush* like that!

"Shall we begin again, little girl, and try to straighten things out, try to understand and help each other?"

"Don't!" said Betty, jerking away from his touch. "Don't!" in a sob that was almost a scream and burst into angry hysterical tears, flinging herself as far away from him as she could get and letting the great sobs rack her slim young body.

Her father stood there in the dark room, with the light from the hall casting a long, bright finger sharply on the floor through the crack under the door. He waited, hoping she would turn back, perhaps answer him, when the storm of tears should have passed. But the shaking sobs went on, and before long he went round to the other side of the bed and, stooping, kissed the bit of hot, wet forehead between the guarding fingers, and so passed out of the room.

And Betty lay and sobbed and hated her father for bringing back that awful feeling of the presence of God in the room, God standing out there in the middle of the dark room, condemning her! God!—and there *wasn't* any God! Everybody said so nowadays. Just everybody!

She cried harder. She felt that she would like to take poison or something just to show them how she hated it all. There was a fierce resentment in her wild, uncontrolled nature. She had her own life to live, and they should not hinder her. She felt if this kind of thing went on that she would not be able to go away with Dudley Weston. And yet she *would*! Nothing should hinder her now! This was a perfectly awful place, all shut in by fierce cold and snow, and God out there in the middle of the room looking at her in the dark. God! When there really *wasn't* any God at all!

The next day the morning mail brought trouble. A telegram that had been put in the mail and brought up by a neighbor passing that way. There was word from the bank. Chris had forged a check for two hundred dollars! Chris was closeted with Chester for two hours in the little room off the sitting room. He came out at last with red rims around his eyes and a more shamed look than ever on his hard, young face; came out hastily and hurried into the woodshed where he was heard for a long time chopping kindling.

Eleanor had been openly weeping, and nothing was said about the new regime of work. Indeed Eleanor made no move toward getting the midday meal. She went to her room and lay down with the door shut. Jane, loitering to ask a question about something she was trying to sew for one of the boys for Christmas, thought she heard a sob, and came away.

"Oh, heck!" she said, doing a handspring on the kitchen floor for Doris's benefit. "I wish we could go home. This place is rotten!"

Chester went down to the village, walking because there was no other transportation at this hour. The gray look on his face had deepened perceptibly. He seemed twenty years older. It was nearly four o'clock when he came back; everybody was hungry, and nobody knew what it was all about. Chris had gone out to the barn after he finished chopping the wood and remained there. He did not come back to the house till his father came home. He slipped in then and up to his room like a rabbit trying to get by without notice.

Betty came down about noon and began a few works of virtue. Everybody had gone crazy. They should see that she was sane.

She washed the dishes and straightened the dining room. Then she made some toast and scrambled some eggs for the children. That was about the extent of her culinary knowledge. She had never had time to learn anything more. There had been too many dances and high school plays and basketball games.

She felt most virtuous when she had finished. She reflected that it would be good to leave a sweet savor of good works behind her when she went. She had a generous, forgiving spirit toward her parents this morning. They never had been young—at least it was so long ago. And anyway, life had scarcely been worth living in their day. Such prudish, impossible notions! She wondered what could be the matter with Chris. But even Jane's most accomplished snooping failed to make plain the cause of Chris's depression, and when she finally dared to waylay him on the stairs during one of his restless excursions out to the barn and ask him what was "eating" him, he pushed her roughly aside and said:

"Aw, nothing! Shut up, won't ya? Yer a pain in the neck! A fella can't take a step without finding you underfoot!"

The telephone had been installed, and Chester Thornton retired into the library and carried on long conversations with "long distance." But the room was not under any of the bedrooms nor near any of the stovepipes, which carried sound so beautifully, and not one word of the low-voiced communications leaked out to the curious children. Nor did the heavy oak doors that shut their father and their brother in give away any secrets.

Chris slid in furtively and stayed hours with his father. An occasional tinkle of the telephone bell gave sign that something important must be going on. When the two came out for meals Chester was grave and preoccupied, and Chris wore a white, frightened look.

Nor was Eleanor any more communicative. When Jane, who was the boldest of the group, attempted to question her, she answered, "Oh, just business. You wouldn't understand."

Three days like this went by, depression in the very atmosphere, Eleanor giving a low-voiced question when Chester came to meals, or maybe a mere lifting of the eyebrows that seemed to mean "Have you heard yet?" and Chester answering by a mere negative movement of his eyes, scarcely perceptible.

It was terrible! Betty wished she had said she would come at once to Briardale. She could have sold something—her watch, perhaps—

her precious platinum watch! Anything to get away from this terrible place! It seemed as if the judgment day was about to dawn upon them all.

To add to the general gloom there was a thaw, and mist and steam began to ascend to a gloomy threatening sky with intermittent sunshine. Nobody went down to skate, nobody went down to the village. The sled that Chris and his father had found and had been repairing for family sledding stood dismantled in the woodshed with one runner off. There was nothing left for Betty to do but dress Doris's doll and throw together an outfit for herself from the old chests in the attic. Betty did a great deal of ransacking in those days, unearthing some most interesting garments. Her mother was entirely too preoccupied to notice when she asked if she might have them, so Betty had a free hand with several rare old dresses and primped and pinned and cut and slashed to her heart's delight. Jane, meanwhile, was also conjuring Christmas presents out of old things from the attic. And occasionally Betty, between outfits, worked awhile at Doris's doll, making many lace ruffles on green silk for its party dress.

Doris and John were the only really happy members of the family. They made endless snowmen and snow houses and snow forts, and reveled in the great out-of-doors, coming in with rosy cheeks and shining eyes to get a handful of unguarded cookies or doughnuts when driven by hunger, and back again to the fray.

But at last there came a day a little after noon when the door of the closed room suddenly opened and Chris came out with his old brisk manner. Not closing the door carefully with that funeral-in-the-house air that he had been doing.

Betty was in the dining room setting the table for lunch because she was hungry and hoped it would bring her mother downstairs to suggest something about lunch if she jingled the dishes loud enough.

Betty had a strong conviction that her mother was up in her bedroom most of the time praying. Not that Eleanor had up to this point been inclined to much obvious prayer, but Jane had burst into the room one morning and found her kneeling by her bed and reported that her face was all red and tear stained. Eleanor always came downstairs with that wistful, unhappy look in her eyes that Betty naturally connected with prayer. Why should one pray unless one was in a terrible strait? What could be the matter? Business couldn't be so awful that they would feel it like that! Why, one could always get a new business if the old one failed. And besides, what could Chris have to do with that? He was too young to help in business.

Betty heard Chris come out of the old library and go upstairs with a spring, two steps at a time. He sounded almost as if he was whistling. Yes, that was a whistle. He was stamping around his room and opening and shutting closet doors and bureau drawers, and *whistling*! Betty drew a sigh of relief.

Then Eleanor came swiftly down the stairs and went into the library, just as Chester was coming out. His face looked as if a great burden had rolled off from his shoulders, and Betty heard her mother exclaim, "Oh, thank the Lord!" and then she saw her put her face down on her husband's shoulder and cry. Betty hurried into the kitchen and stood looking out of the window at the distant mountains overhung with clouds, and just as she was watching, the sun burst through and sent golden bars down through the purply gray and blue of the sky.

Then Chris came clattering down the back stairs and greeted his sister for the first time in four days.

"Hello, Betts!"

Betty turned a disturbed face on him:

"What's the matter, Chris? For Pete's sake, tell me!" she pleaded.

"Absolutely nothing!" declared Chris joyously. "Everything's okay. *Absotively*! Say, Betts! Aren't there any doughnuts left or something? I'm holla as a log, an' I gotta beat it down ta the village with a business letter fer Dad. It's gotta go on the next train. Get me something, can't ya? Something I can take in my hand. Where's the rest of that apple pie, that'll do. And gimme a hunk of cheese! Thanks awfully. Dance at yer wedding and all that sorta thing!" He was gone into the front part of the house. She could hear him breezing into the library and calling out excitedly to his father in his old confident tone.

But Betty stood still in the pantry; the dishcloth she had been holding in her hand dropped to the floor. Now why did Chris say that about dancing at her wedding? She felt weak and upset. Of course Chris hadn't an idea about her plans. He just said it. It didn't mean a thing. But it certainly did make her head reel.

Well, it was a relief to have the atmosphere cleared again, of whatever it was. She almost felt like singing herself, or whistling or something. Perhaps she didn't want to go away. But of course that was nonsense. She must. She had promised. But now she could show Mums the doll's dress. It certainly was pretty. Mums would like it. And she had made it all herself.

It was like having life freed from some great obstruction. Now things could go sparkling on like a stream in the summer sunshine.

Jane appeared at the door, her face full of satisfied curiosity.

"Oh, Betts! You've dropped the dishcloth! That means company, and we're going to have it. The minister from that funny little white church down in the village, with the sharp steeple and the big bell in a square box under it, is coming to call. He just telephoned, and Daddy said it was all right to come. He's coming *this afternoon!*"

"Oh, heck!" said Betty ungraciously. "Let's go down and skate!"

"We can't!" said Jane. "Daddy said the ice is all slushy on top. He says we'll get our feet awful wet. And he says if it'll only be a nice still night and turn cold without any wind that the ice'll be good again."

"Jane, have you heard what's been the matter? What's Chris been up to?"

"Oh, that!" said Jane nonchalantly. "Didn't you find that out yet? You aren't very keen, Betts. It's something about Jim Disston's

Packard that Chrissie has been buying with some money that wasn't his, or a check or something."

"For cat's sake! I thought Chris had more sense!" said Betty, looking off at the hills with her cheeks growing red. What would they all say when it was discovered that she had run away and got married?

"Well," she went on after a minute, "we can go somewhere when that minister comes. I've had all the glooms I can stand for one week. When we see him coming we'll beat it out the back door and run down the hill out of sight. Get your coat and galoshes and leave them down in the kitchen so you won't have to go back after them."

There was no opportunity however to disappear when the minister arrived, for he came walking up the snowy lane with no sleigh bells to announce his coming.

Betty and Jane had been kept busy all the afternoon in the kitchen. Eleanor had come out with her face wreathed in thankful smiles and put the finishing touches to the lunch that Betty had prepared, and immediately after lunch she challenged them to help her do some baking.

It really was almost interesting, with their mother in such a mood, to put on big aprons and roll up their sleeves and learn how to make real pies and cookies and biscuits. Betty made a cake, too: chocolate layer with the black butter frosting, and it turned out wonderfully. She was so proud of it that her eyes took on their old childish shine, and her cheeks were glowing, and when Chris came in from his long walk of six miles, hungry as a bear, he stood in the door and admired it.

"Oh, boy!" he said, licking his lips eagerly. "Oh, boy! Some cake! When ya going to give us a sample, Betts? You don't mean you made it all by yourself? Sure 'nough? No kiddin'?"

Suddenly the home seemed dear. Just because she had contributed to its comfort. She had forgotten that she was leaving it so soon. She had a choking feeling in her throat as if she was going to cry.

"Well," she said to herself, "at least we won't starve. Mums always said people had to learn cooking before they got married. I guess I'll try pie. Though I don't really suppose I'll ever have to cook. The Westons have plenty of servants, more than we ever had. But it's likely I might have to tell a servant how to make a chocolate cake someday. Anyway, it's fun!"

And right at that point the minister walked into the kitchen!

"Excuse me!" he said. "I knocked several times but nobody seemed to hear, so I just followed your voices. I'm Dr. Dunham. Is this Mrs. Thornton?"

Eleanor dried her hands and greeted the minister, introducing the children.

"Shall we go into the sitting room?" she said, preparing to lead the way.

"Well, it smells mighty good out here," said the minister, looking around with a twinkle in his eyes. "I'd be entirely satisfied to sit right down here and let you go on with your work."

Jane slid up to him in her elfish way and presented a plate of hot cookies just out of the oven that she had been helping to make, and they each took a cookie and went munching into the sitting room.

The minister won Betty's heart by pausing at the table where she had just finished icing her wonderful chocolate cake.

"Well, that certainly is a cake to be proud of!" he said. "Are you the cook that made that work of art?"

Betty swelled proudly and forgot that she had meant to be haughty and superior if any minister tried to make up to her.

Chester appeared on the scene with a hearty welcome, and Chris entered a moment later with an armful of wood. He had just finished building up the fire on the hearth, and the flames snapped and roared up the great old chimney with old-time good cheer. Betty slid into a chair, pleased, interested, just tired enough with her cake making to be glad to sit down and listen.

She saw Chester turn to Chris with a quick flash of anxiety: "Did you make the train, my boy?" he asked in a low tone. "I didn't know you had got back."

"I sure did!" said Chris with a proud ring to his voice. Betty looked up at him wonderingly. It seemed almost as if Chris had added a year or two to his voice, it sounded so manly. She caught a quick glance of relief from her father before he turned back to talk with the minister. How glad Chester had looked! Did he care so much about what Chris did as all that? He would care a lot about her, too. It was a rotten deal she was going to hand him! But why did she have to keep thinking of those things all the time? There was a whole week before she had to go, and she wanted to enjoy it as much as she could. She must keep such thoughts out of her mind or she would be turning "yellow," and that would never do. She would lose all her reputation at school for being "hard boiled," and she was very proud indeed of that, though it must be admitted that she had a very vague idea of what it really was intended to mean.

The minister had beautiful silver hair, and keen blue eyes that could either twinkle or look straight through one. His cheeks were rosy like two winter apples, and his shoulders were sturdy as if he knew how to carry burdens as well as stand in the pulpit.

He showed at once that he had a sense of humor by telling two or three stories that fascinated the children and sent them off into peals of laughter. Betty found herself wondering why a perfectly good, fine gentleman like that wasted himself in being a minister; it seemed such a dull profession.

He spoke of his son as being away studying for the Christian ministry, and Betty thought:

Oh, how poky! How perfectly poisonous for any man to wish that on a young man. Just burying him alive! What a rattling shame!

"David is coming up at Christmas to see us," said David's father, beaming with pleasure at the idea. "His mother and I can hardly wait for the time to come! He can't get here till Christmas Day, probably, and he may be delayed a day or so later on account of having to take some services for a fellow student who is ill, but you understand, Christmas doesn't occur for his mother and me till he gets here! I'd like him to meet you. There aren't so many young people around in the winter months, all off to college or a job in the city somewhere, you know. David is a great man for sports. He just revels in them while he's home, and the snow is fine this winter."

"Our young people have been trying to fix up an old sled for sledding," said Chester heartily. "Perhaps your son will come up and join them. The old hill out behind the house used to be something worthwhile."

"I'm sure he will if you'll let him," beamed the father. "He has a sled that he thinks is rather fine, a 'humdinger' I think he calls it. Perhaps you'll let him bring it up."

What a bore! thought Betty. *Of course he's just a country clod. But then, I'll be gone, and it won't matter!*

Chester was quite eager about it. He was saying that his children had been somewhat lonely since they came. Now how did Chester know that? They certainly didn't want any native talent around. Still, the old man was kind of a good sport. The son might not be so bad. Only any young man in this age that would submit to having himself made into a minister was simply off the map so far as she was concerned. She let the conversation drift past her while she began to think about Dudley Weston and wonder why she hadn't heard from him again. Surely Dud couldn't back out now, after having asked her to marry him! No, Dud was game! H wouldn't stand her up.

When her thoughts came back to the room again the minister was talking about skiing, describing a great meet over at Brattleboro.

"David has always been interested in it," said David's father. "When he was quite a little lad he got hold of a pair of skis, and he used to drive his mother almost insane jumping off mountains and disappearing and turning up on the top of another somewhere."

"Oh, can he do that?" said Betty suddenly, before she realized she was saying it. "I should think that would be a real thrill! I'd do anything in the world if I could learn."

"Well, it's a thrill to watch it," said the father, "and David is rather a wonder at it. I have no doubt he'll teach you if you ask him," smiled the minister. "He's taught a great many."

"I shall certainly ask him," said Betty eagerly and then remembered she wouldn't be there when David came! What a shame. Perhaps she could get Dud to come back after a few days and visit, and they would try it together. That would be a great stunt! Dudley was always ready for anything new. That was one reason why she liked Dudley better than most of the other boys, because he never stopped at anything she proposed and then always went her one better in proposing something still more daring.

When Betty came back to the conversation again from her thoughts, her father was proposing a most astounding thing. He had actually asked this apple-cheeked minister, this native of the backwoods, to open a school there at their house for them! Of course the man talked very well, and probably knew something about stuffy old theological books, but not anything modern. Ministers had to be pretty well educated or people wouldn't call them to churches, but imagine an old fossil like that who didn't know any of the up-to-date ideas, of course, trying to teach them anything! Why, even Doris would know more of what was going on in the world today than he would be likely to know.

But Chester seemed to be in earnest. He was even getting it down to the number of hours a week. They were talking about how in Scotland the minister always used to be the teacher of any higher education. Chester was saying that he wanted his children to get back to the good old ways. He was actually talking about Latin and Greek! Greek! Imagine it! That would be a scream! What would Dud and the girls think if they heard of it, Betty Thornton studying Greek!

Chester and the minister talked on, speaking of literature, how rotten the books of today were. What did an old fossil like that know about the books of today? He couldn't possibly have heard of some of the Russian novels they had to read in lit class. He would probably be horribly shocked even to know what they were! Imagine!

"I think perhaps I could spare the time," the minister was saying. Great cats! Was Dad actually going to try to pull off a thing like that? Well, she was thankful she was out of it.

"There is no book like the old Book," the minister was saying. There was almost what one might describe as a glow of tenderness in his voice.

"If people would really study the Bible more they would find in it a liberal education. They would find wonders in it that have never yet been revealed. But they are being discovered now. It is marvelous how the scriptures have been opened up in even the last ten years. Discoveries, history, the shaping of nations, archaeology, are all giving keys to that which has long been locked away from the knowledge of man, and it will not be long before the world is startled into knowing that the old despised Book has all the time contained the germs of all knowledge."

What a scream he was. The idea of talking about archaeology! When everyone knew that they were digging up bones of extinct animals that were living millions of years ago, just perfectly proving that the Bible was all off, and evolution was the only thing. But of course, a minister had to pretend to believe all those things or he wouldn't be paid his salary.

Thus irreverent youth kept up a running comment.

But what was this that her father was saying?

"I would like my children to study the Bible, too. Yes, that is the very thing! I would like them to know all there is to know about the Bible!"

For Pete's sake! Was Chester really going to try to put a thing like that over on the kids? Study the Bible! And with that old fossil! Wasn't this the limit? Well, she would be off in a few days and give them something else to think about!

But the minister was speaking to Betty, and Betty could not help liking his pleasant pink smile.

"I shall have to tell David what wonderful chocolate cakes you make up here. I am sure he will be knocking at your door the very first day he gets home! He's great for chocolate. His mother can hardly keep up with the demand while he's home."

But Betty hardened her heart against the thought of a David who would let himself be wished into a minister, and she secretly hugged the thought that she would be gone when David arrived.

Chapter 18

The house took on a very different atmosphere now. Chris went around whistling everywhere and keeping up at least a show of work. The wood boxes overflowed with wood, and the fires were always replenished when he was about. Also he wore a more manly, respectful air toward his father and mother, as if somehow they had plucked him from some danger and he was grateful. If Betty had not been so occupied with her own affairs she would have wondered about it. As it was, he was a very pleasant brother to have around, developing a gallantry altogether new and an anxiety to please everyone that was most delightful. He had taken Betty into his confidence, and she spent one whole afternoon making lace curtains for the dollhouse out of a piece of old net she found in the attic, papering the different rooms, and gluing together the minute stairs that Chris had sawed out. It really was becoming tremendously interesting, this getting ready for a homemade Christmas.

The still, clear cold came down as Chester had predicted it would, and the lake became a glassy sea, spreading like silver in the sun. Then the days were all too short for the wonderful skating, and they went down after supper once or twice, father and mother and all, and it was fun to watch the parents glide away together like two young people, Eleanor, after the first wild clutch and flounder getting her girlish poise and sailing off with fair rhythm.

It was great fun, the whole family skating together! It seemed as if time had given them a reprieve and they were all children together. There were times, hours together, when Betty forgot her contempt of the country, and her plans to get out of it, and enjoyed everything wholeheartedly.

Christmas would fall on Tuesday this year.

It was the Thursday before Christmas that they went out to get the tree, Betty with the rest, and Eleanor along on the bobsled to help pick it out.

The air was clear and keenly cold, but the dryness made it most exhilarating. The white-clad mountains with their fringe of evergreens looked like vast Christmas cards in the distance, and even Betty felt a new kind of Christmas excitement in the air. There had been days when she wept and mourned for her class plays and her dances and her giddy little friends, but she was fast becoming interested in the new vast world to which she had been transplanted. If it had not been for Dudley and what he would think of her, and the howl that would arise from those of her friends to whom he had undoubtedly by this time confided their plans, she would have been glad to forget him and enter heartily into the holiday.

But a troubled mind is not a mind at rest, and Betty was ready at the slightest inconvenience to burst into contempt or fury and pour her scorn on her family.

It was an afternoon to remember. The tramping over the crisp crust of the snow to find the particular tree that would just fit into the place in the big sitting room where Father remembered the tree always used to stand; the glitter on the snow as they stood around while Father and Chris took turns cutting down the tree; the resinous smell of the chips as they flew from the axe; the plumy sweep of the spruce boughs as the tree finally toppled and bowed its lovely tip slowly, almost with a sweep of pride to the ground. All those things were imprinted on Betty's mind, and something like a plaintive song in her heart kept going over and over, *You're going away! You're not going to be here to see this tree all decked out with paper ornaments and popcorn and cheap homemade stuff!* and something hurt at the thought.

"Sob stuff!" said Betty to herself, turning sharply on her heel and walking away from the rest, determined not to think about it. She had her life to live! They had no right to hold her here in this poisonous dump!

Mother opened a basket of lunch she had brought along, and they all ate raisin gingerbread as they rigged the tree on the sled. Then all hands took hold to pull it home, everybody but Eleanor who walked smiling beside the tree and looked as young as any of them. Once Betty turned around and caught a glimpse of her mother's face looking so pleased and full of delight, and it came to her suddenly as a new thought that Mums must have been a very pretty girl indeed! Would she look mature and serious all the time after she had been married for a while? Well, perhaps, but she doubted it. She didn't intend to work as hard as Mums had done. She would lie in the lap of luxury.

They carried the tree home with much shouting and laughter and made a ceremony of getting it set up. There was a great bundle of hemlock branches Chris had cut and lashed to the tree with a piece of rope, and Betty took pleasure in decorating the room with these, putting them over pictures and windows and on the mantel.

Dan Woolley from the next farm brought in the mail just as they were sitting down to a belated supper. There was a letter for Betty.

She hid it in her pocket and did not open it until she had a chance to run upstairs while the others were lingering at the table, excusing herself to go after her apron.

It was from Dudley. She had recognized it, though he had evidently tried to disguise his handwriting. It was brief and to the point:

Old girl,

> *O. K. You've said it! Suits me! We'll paint the town red! Sam and Gyp have renigged. Too much pull for Gwen's shindig! But I know another kid in New York and he can get a girl easy enough. Don't you be late. We might want to take in Gwen's ourselves later. We better get tied in New York if you think that's necessary. If you keep me waiting I'm off you for life.*
>
> *Dud*

It wasn't exactly the kind of letter a bride would expect to receive from her lover two nights before she expected to be married, but it stirred Betty with a strange excitement. Perhaps there was beneath it all in her heart a trace of unrest and disappointment at the lack of something, call it romance if you like—Betty termed it "thrill"— something that the world for generations has taught its children to expect of love and courtship. But Betty reflected as she stuffed the precious letter into her pocket that this was a frank and progressive age, and she was a modern girl. There was no mushy stuff nowadays, everything was matter of fact. She had prided herself on attaining that attitude for the past two years, and this was no time to retract. She was going out into the world on her own, and she must be firm and carry the thing through gallantly.

She came flying downstairs, with her eyes feverishly bright and her cheeks aglow, and offered to do the dishes all by herself. Chester looked up with a pleased smile.

"It agrees with our Betty up here," he said happily. "Look at her cheeks, Eleanor. She doesn't need any rouge or lipstick now. That was the way nature meant to have the cheeks painted."

Betty caught her breath and hurried into the kitchen with a pile of plates. Something in her father's tender glance made her suddenly vaguely afraid, a wild homesick throb of fear, or was it only that she was so excited? But she mustn't let things get her this way. She had to carry this thing out right, and she mustn't let Dud see she had wavered.

They all insisted on helping with the dishes, however. They would not leave her alone a minute. And afterward they went into the sitting room and sat around the fire, with the lamp in the hall so that they sat only in the firelight with the soft glow over the crisp, resinous spines of the great, beautiful tree, the sweet piney smell mingling with the fragrance of wood smoke. Betty was stabbed with a sudden throb of the dearness of her family that she never had suspected before. She realized that she would never forget that moment.

They sang Christmas carols for half an hour, and then suddenly Chester stood up and said:

"I think we'll have to thank our heavenly Father tonight!" His voice was almost wistful as he looked around in the firelight and smiled, and before Betty realized they were all kneeling again with the shadows playing over them while Chester brought them each to the Father's notice in words that were matchless for tenderness and pleading. It seemed to Betty that she could not stand it. For there was God standing out there in the room again, looking at her, and there was her father telling God all about her in such tones as if he could see Him. See a God who was not! Poor old-fashioned Chester! And she was planning to steal out of the house tomorrow toward morning when they were all asleep and run away to be married! It was awful! If she had only known her father would do that strange, absurd thing again, she would have slipped off before they sang, said she was sleepy or something.

She stole a quick glance around to see if there was a way open to the stairs, that even now she might disappear. She saw her father, with the glow of flickering light on his graying hair and over his tired face, her father in that humble attitude, and she shrank from it. If only she had not looked! For she knew again that this was something she would never forget, and she did not wish to remember it. It was something that paralyzed the spirit that was driving her on into life, something that disarmed her and made her weak and humble, something that would reach out clinging hands and try to keep her from going.

The day had been full of eager plans and mysterious secrets. Mrs. Woolley had sent down a can of mincemeat. She said it was made after Mr. Thornton's mother's own recipe, and no mince pies could beat old Mrs. Thornton's.

Betty and Jane had made molasses taffy and had great fun pulling it and cutting it into neat shapes and arranging it on waxed paper. Mrs. Woolley sent down some cranberry jelly; and the turkey, a great twenty pounder, was from a nearby farm, also sent as a love gift in memory of the departed grandmother who had been a blessing to the whole neighborhood. The house had been full of good spicy smells, and laughter from morning to night, and Betty had worked harder than any of them, her conscience driving her most mercilessly.

"For I won't be here long to help," she said to herself a hundred times.

Why, Betty is waking up, the dear child! thought Eleanor, and Chester's pleased smile was constantly upon her, making Betty almost writhe as she met it, for she kept hearing in contrast her father's stern voice as it had sounded that night he took her away from Dudley Weston. And now another day would bring that hard look back to his face.

But he will forgive me all right when it's all over, promised her heart cheerfully whenever she faltered; and she had filled the hours so full that there was no more time to think.

All this went over in Betty's mind while her father prayed, and when she rose from her knees she hurried up to her room, not daring to stay around the fire and talk any longer. She had yet her little gifts to tie up. The quaint old china doll in its modern, up-to-date green silk was already reposing in a box for Doris. She was leaving her string of coral beads, which she had had on the day she left Briardale, for Jane. Jane loved them, and she could think of nothing else. She had bungled a necktie out of an old piece of silk for Johnny, hemstitched a handkerchief each for Eleanor, Chester, and Chris out of a piece of fine linen from the attic, and embroidered initials on them. It was all she knew to make.

After they were all tied and labeled she looked at them unhappily and reflected that if Dud brought money enough along she would buy some really nice things for them in New York and send them up after she was gone.

There remained yet a note to write. Young girl elopers always wrote notes to their angry parents. The only trouble was hers were not angry just now, and she had been having a really wonderful time for the last two or three days. Still, she had a duty to herself. She had her life to live.

So she bolstered up her failing courage.

There was a pleasant bustle in the air next morning when she awoke, and it seemed unreal that she was planning to go away. The very smells in the house made her tingle with excitement. Wood smoke stealing deliciously up through the cracks around the old stovepipe. Scent of pine tree, fragrant from its recent living in the great out-of-doors; odor of hemlock mingled with other faint suggestions of sage, onion, thyme, and sweet marjoram; pickles and cloves and spice. It wasn't at all the time to leave home: Christmas! Christmas belonged to home and Mother and Father and the children. But of course, she was going out into the world now to make her own Christmas, and it was too late to draw back.

Betty sprang up and dressed quickly. So much conscience as she still retained told her that at least she must do all she could for the common good this last day.

She came down with a docile conscious air, but everybody was too busy and too eager to notice her much.

Someone brought the morning mail—it might have been the milkman on his way home from his route. The neighbors did such kindly things. Betty was wiping the dishes at the time. She looked fearfully toward the pile of letters, half hoping there would be one from Dudley calling off the wedding. If Dudley should want to put it off till after Christmas she wouldn't feel half-bad, she told herself.

But there was no letter for Betty. There was one for Chester, however, something about Chris, it seemed, for Chris and his father retired to the library and read it. Chris came out smiling and went whistling back to his work. Whenever he spoke his voice was so glad it sounded almost like singing. Betty looked at him curiously once or twice and thought how dear he suddenly seemed. Betty could hardly understand herself all that day. Sometimes she wanted to cry. Even when they all went down that afternoon to skate for a couple of hours, her heart seemed in her throat.

Night came and sitting round the fire. Betty couldn't stand that. Chester was telling a long story about his boyhood, the night of a blizzard when there was a sick lamb, and he and his brother Clint had to dig a tunnel to the barn and bring it in the house and feed it with warm milk in a bottle. Next there would come some singing and then perhaps another prayer. If she had to kneel through another prayer she would scream! She simply could not carry that picture of her father on his knees away with her into the world. It would spoil everything.

So she slipped to her mother's side and whispered that she was very sleepy and must be excused to go to bed.

Everything was all ready for her flight. Her own little suitcase that she always carried when she went to visit some girl for the weekend was all packed in the closet, hidden under an old sweater beside her little overnight bag, also fully packed. A coil of clothesline was tied through their handles. She meant to let them down through the window after the family came upstairs and have them already there for morning.

Quickly she undressed and put on the frail undergarments she meant to wear on her trip, scorning the heavy flannel underwear her mother had brought along, which she had gladly been wearing to keep out the unusual cold.

Then she put on the heavy flannel nightgown over her underwear and crept into bed shivering. Coming as she had from the warm, cheery room downstairs, the room seemed colder than usual, even with the stovepipe hot enough to burn to the touch. A rim of light around the stovepipe seemed to bring her in close touch with the room below.

Yes, she was right, she had come away just in time. They were singing that strange old song that Chester loved, just because his mother used to sing it, likely:

> *"Rock of ages, cleft for me,*
> *Let me hide myself in Thee,*
> *Let the water and the blood*
> *From Thy riven side which flowed,*
> *Be of sin the double cure,*
> *Save me from its guilt and power."*

Rocks and blood! An odd old song. How could Chester bear to sing it? Sin! As if anybody believed in it anymore. There wasn't any such thing. Sin was supposed to be something that God had said you mustn't do, and if there wasn't any God, if there was only a force of nature or whatever you called it, what bunk it all was, and why did anybody want to put anything like that over on the world anyway in the first place?

Betty covered up her ears and shut her eyes, trying to draw her spirit away from the consciousness of it all, but the words sang clearly up the old stovepipe and seemed not to mind the bed quilts at all.

"Nothing in my hand I bring,
Simply to Thy cross I cling."

As if a cross could do anything for anybody! Such superstition!

"Naked come to Thee for dress,
Helpless look to Thee for grace;
Foul I to the fountain fly;
Wash me Saviour or I die."

There! There was that horrid word, *foul*. Chester had used that when he spoke of Dudley. He said he was a foulmouthed rascal! Betty shivered again and drew her head farther under the sheets. Foul! That meant unclean. Dirty! That was ridiculous! Just because people were frank and spoke of things that everybody knew. Just because they happened to be younger than a few other people, they were called dirty! Well, that wasn't fair! That was injustice, and the young people of today were not taking anything like that handed out to them. *Not on your life,* thought Betty!

There, there was that other horrid verse, the worst of them all:

"While I draw this fleeting breath,
When my eyelids close in death!"

518

A shudder passed over her, and she put her fingers in her ears. But still there came faintly, because she had to listen in spite of herself, the words,

"When I soar to worlds unknown,
See Thee on thy—"

She stuffed the blanket into her ears, but she knew the rest was "judgment throne," and she hated it! Why did she have to be judged? Just because she was following out her nature! She didn't! She wouldn't! And she didn't want to hide in any rock no matter how many ages it had lived and fooled people.

The singing died away, and now she had to listen again, and she heard them kneeling down. She might as well have stayed, for she could hear every word that Chester said. And, great cats! He was praying for *her*. By *name*! "Our little Betty!" He had no right! He had no *right*! "Give her a meek and quiet spirit. Help her to learn to do right!"

This was the limit!

And there were tears on her face, very wet tears, that made the sheet and pillow damp and would not stop. Oh, she was frantic! This was poisonous! Perfectly poisonous! Would Chester never stop? It would have been almost better if she had stayed down. He would not have made it so personal then. But if he had she would have cried right there before them all, and that would have been awful! Nobody cried anymore. It wasn't the thing to do at all. Everybody would howl if they knew she cried at old sob stuff like that! And the strange part about it was that she hadn't gained a thing by coming upstairs, for there was God, out here in her bedroom looking at her, just the same as He had done downstairs when she knelt with the rest. God! Just an idea! But there He stood looking at her with such strange, wistful, almost loving eyes, the way Chester looked at her

519

sometimes, only more so. And she couldn't get away from Him even with her eyes shut. She couldn't get away from Him even with all the sheets over her head. Well, she would get away from Him when she went with Dudley, that was certain. Dudley hadn't much in common with God!

Now they were rising from their knees, and the vision of God was gone. She felt great relief and turned over her pillow, arranging the spot where her tears had wet the sheet so Eleanor would not feel it if she came in to say good night. She lay down and tried to breathe very regularly, her face turned away from the door. They were coming up now. Chester was banking down the fire on the hearth and locking the door. The key turned with a grating sound. She had meant to put a drop of oil in that lock and had forgotten it.

She could hear Jane tiptoeing by the door, and now Eleanor opened it softly and looked in. Her father was coming up the stairs with the lamp in his hand. She could see the flare of the light on her opposite wall through the fringes of her lashes.

"She seems to be sound asleep," she heard Eleanor say in a whisper. "Poor child, she was tired! I guess I won't go in, it might wake her!"

She closed the door softly, and Betty missed her mother's kiss.

Cautiously she stole out of bed and lifted her window. The night air bit at her thin garments like ice. The old-fashioned catch slipped from her excited fingers once and the window slid down with a thump. She held her breath, but no one seemed to notice. She could hear her mother talking in low tones in the room across the hall. She tried the catch once more and this time it held, and the cold air poured in about her again, bitterly, romping with the flannel nightdress and chilling her bare feet.

She went softly to the closet, brought out the suitcase and bag, let them down till they touched on the crisp snow below and slid a little way before catching in the stalks of a tall old lilac bush. She looked at them for an instant, half-frightened. There they were! They had started! And soon she, too, would be on her way, very, very early in the morning.

She cast a fearful eye at the sky. It was clear as a bell. The stars seemed larger than she had ever seen them before, and a new moon hung like a silver boat in a sapphire sea. Across the distance the mountains were dimly shadowed against the night. It was a wonderful scene, almost formidable in its cold, sparkling beauty. There was one star that was larger than the rest, looking down straight at her. It seemed to pierce her like an eye. She remembered that idea of God coming into her room and watching her, and she turned quickly away from the window and crept into bed, pulling the blankets over her head again. She must get some sleep. This was no way to pull off a stunt. What would Dud think of her if he knew? It was weird. It was perfectly fusty.

She deliberately set herself to go to sleep, but sleep seemed far from her. She seemed to be holding her body up from the bed, holding her breath, somehow imagining that her secret would make itself known if she breathed aloud.

Chester and Eleanor were still talking. She could hear their pleasant tones. It was good to go away when they were happy. Perhaps Chester had had some good word about business.

Then she remembered that she had meant to put the rest of her clothes by the bed so that she would make less noise leaving when the time came, and she slid out in the cold air again and brought her dress, the pretty jersey dress she had worn to school the last day, and her shoes and placed them on a chair by the bed. She went back to the closet and got her fur coat and hat, and on second thought her galoshes, and put them where she could reach them without moving about on the floor, for she did not trust the old flooring. Some boards creaked horribly under the least step.

All these excursions with the window open chilled her to the bone, and she crept back to bed with her teeth chattering and finally fell asleep.

Chapter 19

It was still dark with the stars shining when she awoke, but she could see a streak of dawn over against the horizon, and she knew it must be getting toward day. She listened and soon the old clock in the hall that Chester had put in running order the first day they arrived chimed out four.

Betty had heard that four o'clock was the time that sleep was the deepest, so she had chosen that hour for her going.

It took all the courage she had to even reach out into the cold and pull in her dress under the covers. She had not realized it would be so cold. She ought to have closed her window.

Neither was it an easy thing to put on her dress under the sheets without making the bed creak wildly in the still, old house. The clock had struck the half hour before she was really ready, hat on, fur coat buttoned. She stuffed her shoes inside her galoshes and stole out upon the floor in her stocking feet. Slowly she reached the door, step by step, with intervals between, lifted the latch with infinite pains, released it as carefully, and moved with almost fairy tread into the hall, down the stairs, half leaning on the railing and sliding down. It seemed an age till she reached the door, and another till she had slid back the rusty old bolt, turned the key, and was out at last with the door shut behind her.

She stopped an instant and listened. The house was as still as if it were empty. The branches of the maple tree stirred with the wind and hit against the upper hall window, clashing like sabers. They startled her. Surely, someone would wake at that sound! But all was silent.

The stars were still out, though the sky was paling, and off to the east a rosy light was appearing now. She must get on her way at once.

She had put on her shoes and galoshes before she opened the door. She stepped out upon the snowy path, and her footsteps crunched like the little lumps of confectioner's sugar under the rolling pin when she was making that butter icing for the cake yesterday. She only dared take one step at a time, and wait between lest someone would wake and hear her.

Slowly she made her way to the side of the house where the bags waited under her window, reached out on the smooth crust for the end of the rope, which she had purposely flung as far toward the path as she could from her window, and drew it toward her. The bags were caught in the lilac, but she finally managed to free them and draw them slowly toward her. At last she was out on the open path that led to the lane.

She drew a long breath when she finally turned into the lane and the shelter of the thickly grouped birch trees. She was hidden now by the shadows at least, and no one could see her here from the house. She would have to make a detour around the log house by the highway, but she had planned that all out. Besides, no one there would be up yet, and she felt reasonably sure that she would beat the milkman down by a full hour at least. No one else would know her, and anyway, by the time they could get word to her family she would be safely hidden in the station, or in the train if it was on time.

But it was hard walking on the rough snow, with baggage to

carry, and the three miles to the village loomed ahead like a trip around the world. Her back soon ached, her arms grew heavy, her feet were very cold, and her hands in their thin kid gloves were frozen numb. She had to stop several times and take off her gloves and put her hands inside her fur coat to get any feeling into them at all. She wished she had brought her mittens along, but it was too late to go back now. So she wound a couple of handkerchiefs around her hands over her gloves and took up her heavy suitcase again. If she had only brought that rope along she might have dragged it on the snow, but that was now too far away.

She tried walking on the crust of the snow, but in places it was soft, and once she went through and floundered around, getting snow inside her clothing until she was most uncomfortable. She wished she had worn her thick underwear until she got to the station at least. She might have thrown it away afterward. She had no idea it would be so mortally cold at this hour in the morning.

She was on the verge of tears when at last she staggered into the highway and began the long hard walk down the hill. If it had been up the hill she could not have managed it, for the suitcase and even the little overnight bag were growing heavier every minute.

The thread of a moon like a silver boat hung low in the sky now, almost over the brink of the horizon, just tilted a little lazily, as if its work for the night was done, and it was about to drop over into another world to rest.

The woods on either side of the road seemed dense and full of awful shadows. One could almost expect bears or bandits to walk out of them at any minute, and behind her she kept imagining a continual procession of people coming on to catch up with her, but she made her painful way mile by mile and saw not a soul. Once off in the distance she heard sleigh bells, but they stopped soon, and the next time she heard them they were farther away.

Unharmed, she came at last through the woods and down into

the still sleeping village. She drew a deep breath and put down her burdens on the outskirts of town to rest and warm her hands inside her coat. Her feet were numb, and when she tapped them on the snow to try to get the blood moving they stung painfully. She wished she had worn her heavier shoes or brought the warm woolen stockings her mother insisted upon her wearing for skating.

As she walked down the village street, the frozen lake with its huddle of cottages and boathouses had turned to pink and gold, and a new world burst upon her jaded sight. She had never seen such early morning before. It was lovely. But she was by this time too frightened and too tired to appreciate it.

She was petrified with anxiety when she found the station was not open. Off in the distance about two blocks she saw a light in the kitchen of a house. She might go there and get warm, but they would ask questions, and besides, she might miss the train. So she settled down on her suitcase on the sheltered side of the station, covered her feet as much as possible with her coat, and waited for the day to break and the train to come.

It came at last, and she had to get on without buying a ticket, for the station agent was just taking down his shutters as the train crawled round the curve, and there was no time for tickets.

It rather frightened her to see how little money she had left after paying her fare to Springfield. For the first time it occurred to her to wonder what she would do if Dudley did not keep his word.

But she was too weary and too sleepy to think long about anything just now. It was warm in the car, too warm, and she soon curled up in the corner of her ill-smelling seat and went sound asleep.

Back at the farm things had been happening also.

Eleanor was putting a pan of muffins in the oven when the telephone rang. Jane was setting the table.

"I don't see why Betty can't come down and do this," Jane complained. "It's her turn to set the table."

"Never mind this time," said Eleanor. "She can take two turns the next two days. I wouldn't wake her this morning; she seemed so very tired last night. Go tell Daddy his phone is ringing."

Jane called up the stairs to her father, and Eleanor came to the kitchen door with a troubled look.

"Don't make a noise, Janie, dear. Really, it isn't kind. Betty was not feeling well last night."

"Oh, rats!" said Jane crossly. "Perhaps I wasn't either. Betts just lies down on her job every time and you let her! I'm sick of it. When are we going back home? I want Hannah! This is a heck of a life!"

"Janie!" said Eleanor in dismay, tears sounding in her voice. "Why, Jane dear, I thought you liked it here! You've seemed so happy and have been working so well."

"Oh, it's all right!" shrugged Jane. "When everybody works together I don't mind, but when Betts gets this princess complex, it makes me tired! Who crowned her, I'd like to know?"

But Eleanor had no chance to answer that. Chester came out of the library excitedly:

"It's too bad, Nell, but I've got to go back home to sign some papers. There isn't time to get them here and back again, and it involves a great deal of money. But it can't be helped. Can you get along without me for a couple of days?"

"Oh, Chester!" gasped Eleanor in dismay, feeling as if the earth were reeling under her. "And Christmas— The children!"

"I know! It's too bad! But I hadn't any choice. I'll make it back before Christmas Day is over if it's a possible thing. We'll make it up to them somehow!"

"Now Daddy, I think that's *rotten!*" burst out Jane. "No Christmas! And you gone! I wish I was de–e–e–ead! Well, I *do!*" And Jane broke into a torrent of angry tears and flung herself down on the couch, shaking with sobs.

Chester turned impatiently toward Eleanor, looking suddenly gray with anguish.

"It can't be helped!" he said almost hoarsely in his excitement. "I've got to go, Eleanor. Can you come upstairs and help me a minute? John Dowley is going to stop for me and run me down to the train. I just telephoned him. There's barely time for me to catch it. Could you put some buttons in a clean shirt for me, Eleanor?"

"But you must sit down and eat something first," began Eleanor.

"I haven't time, I tell you!" said Chester excitedly and tore up the stairs. "I can get something on the train."

"Get up, Janie, and make some coffee quick for Daddy!" called Eleanor as she vanished up the stairs.

"Good night!" said Chris, appearing at that moment from the woodshed where he had been getting an armful of wood. "What's eating you, Jay? This certainly is some house!"

Jane sat suddenly up and glared at her brother, eyes blotched with tears, lips puckered with disappointment, shoulders shaking with more sobs:

"Daddy's got to go back home! He won't be here for Chris–s–s–muss!"

"Dad going home!" exclaimed Chris, turning suddenly white and frightened. "W–w–w–what for?"

"Oh, I du-no!" bawled Jane. "Some old papers he's gotta sign. I think this earth is a horrid old place. This Christmas'll just be *l–l–l–l–ost*! That's what it'll be! I w–w–w–ish we could *all* go home and get back to real life again!"

But Chris was up the stairs three steps at a bound and made no reply. He appeared at his father's door white and anxious.

"What's the matter, Dad?" he asked, a note of almost fright in his tone. "Anything more about that check?"

Chester paused one instant to take in the look on his son's face and flashed him a smile.

"No, Son, that's all right. This is the office. A contract that I have to sign and something about a loan that has to be put through early Monday morning. There isn't time to get the papers here for signature and back again for Monday. You look after Mother and the kids, won't you, Son? Sorry about Christmas, but I may get back before the day is over. You do what you can to make up. You're the man of the house."

"Yes sir!" said Chris, looking pleased and relieved. "Yes *sir!*"

The next ten minutes were strenuous. Chris went to the attic for his father's suitcase and manifested a man's intelligence in getting the right things together to put into it. Eleanor sewed on a missing button and hunted clean collars and cuff links. Even Jane roused herself, sobbing, with the tears still blurring her eyes, and poured a cup of coffee for her father, creaming and sugaring it just as he liked it and making two dainty sandwiches for him to eat on the way.

It seemed no time at all till Chester was striding from the door, too hurried even to kiss them, calling back directions, and waving good-bye in the early morning sunshine, as the old farm sleigh bumped its way over the ruts and out down the lane.

The family turned back to the house that seemed suddenly deserted and empty.

"Aw, gee!" began Chris, and then caught a glimpse of Eleanor wiping a furtive tear from her eye, and changed his tone. "Say, Mums, you go sit down and eat a good breakfast. You've been on the double jump ever since you got up. Here, Janie, you put back those muffins in the oven and get 'em hot. Let's all sit down and eat. That'll make the time go. And while we eat let's plan some surprise for Dad when he gets back. Say, Mums, can't we put off Christmas till Dad gets here? Make it daylight saving or something, just set back the clock a coupla days or something? What say? Nobody round here'll know what we're doing, so we can't be interrupted by any nosey people that wantta know why we're doing it. Just pretend it isn't time yet. How'll that do?"

His voice was cheerful and even enthusiastic, and Eleanor stifled the sigh that was in her heart and smiled.

"Surely!" she said. "Why not? This interruption was something we couldn't help so we might as well make the best of it."

Jane looked up hopefully.

"Do you think Daddy will bring some candy or something back with him?" she asked.

"Well, I'm not sure," said Eleanor, hating to spoil the child's ray of hope. "You know Daddy will be very busy every minute he is there; no time to go out and buy anything, even if he could afford it—"

"Oh, I forgot the old money!" said Jane disconsolately. "Won't he ever have any money again?"

"Why, I hope so," said Eleanor, trying to banish the fear that clutched at her own heart. "I haven't talked about money to your father since we have been here. The doctor told me he ought to get away from everything for a little while and have a real rest. I thought the main thing was to be cheerful. But I imagine there must be some hope somewhere for the business or he would not be going down to sign a new contract, although it may be just something about settling up with their creditors. I didn't have time to ask him. But such things don't really matter, Jane dear, if we are all together and all well. We'll pull out of the troubles. Let's just get ready for Daddy's homecoming and make him have a good time so he will forget if he has had any business troubles while he was gone."

"But what shall we do?" asked Jane mournfully. "We're all ready for Christmas now."

"How about popcorn balls?" said Eleanor brightly. "Would you like to make some of those? And we must string a lot of popcorn for the tree and cut out things to put on it. Oh, there's a lot to do. There'll hardly be time to get it all done. Here, John, you and Doris eat your breakfast and begin to shell the popcorn. The milkman brought a lot of it over yesterday. And Chris, there's an old popper hanging in the woodshed. You might try scouring it a little. I think it would be all right if some of the rust was rubbed off."

"Oh, how darling!" said Jane, sunshine coming back into her face as suddenly as it had gone. "Shall I go wake up Betts? She'll like making popcorn balls, I'm sure."

"No, don't wake up Betty yet," said Eleanor. "Let her sleep till she feels like herself again. She'll feel more like working if she's had her sleep out. Let's get everything ready first, the table all cleared off and the dishes washed. I thought about making some cookies in the shape of stars, too."

"Fine!" said Chris. "And Mums, how about me cutting out some tin stars from the tomato can tops for the tree."

"Why, that's a wonderful idea. I was wondering how we were going to get something silver on it."

"And say, Mother," put in Doris, "couldn't you make some gingerbread men with currants for eyes, like the story in my book at school?"

"I think I could," laughed Eleanor, her heart growing lighter as she saw each one of the children beginning to take hold of the idea of a delayed Christmas. Now if only Betty would be as cheerful, everything would be all right. She dreaded Betty's coming down, lest she would cast discouragement and blight upon all the others. She decided to let Betty sleep as long as possible.

Meantime the horse that John Dowley had hastily harnessed to take Chester to the early morning train was racing down the road with a wicked stride as if he rather enjoyed the errand, and his sleigh bells jingled a merry tune in the frosty air.

"Stand a pretty good chance of makin' her," said John Dowley as he wrapped the reins around his big sheepskin mitten and gave the secret cluck to his horse that let him know he might go his best pace.

"I'm afraid not, if my watch is correct," said Chester, taking it out again and looking at it anxiously as if it might have something encouraging to say about it. "Is this train ever late?"

" 'Times it is," said John Dowley, "when there's a blizzard upstate. But we'll make her."

The horse skimmed over the rough road, and the sleigh bumped along, almost upsetting at times, and then righting itself amazingly. Chester sat grimly in his seat holding on to the sleigh and trying to plan what he should do if he missed the train and stopped at every crossroad and watering trough as it were.

They had climbed the hill now and were coming down the other side. The little village lay spread out before them, the station a mere red dot at one side. The sun on the lake flashed back at them, dazzling their eyes. The black gash in the whiteness of the landscape that was the railroad track wound away in the distance, and at the extreme end there was a plume of smoke.

"She's on her way!" said John Dowley with set lips. "But we'll make her."

"Is that the train off there?" asked Chester with anxious eyes watching the little plume of smoke pause, spume up again, and begin to move.

"That's her!" said John Dowley. "She's stoppin' at the crossin'! Up, Blackie, we gotta make her!"

The horse seemed to understand and plunged on, and Chester went through the mental process several times of gripping his suitcase and sprinting for the train at the last minute.

The train came on and was lost to view as the sleigh dashed into a little wood, but they could hear the whistle, shrill and defiant, echoing among the hills. Chester's heart beat fast, and he felt as if he were running with the horse.

The train was just screaming into town as they rounded the corner by the little white church and took the shortcut behind the stores to the station. But someone had left a truck across the road, and Blackie had to turn out for it and wallow a wild minute or two to get around it. Chester's heart sank once more. It seemed hopeless now and no use to get out and sprint, for the drift was too deep to run in. Then Blackie righted himself, pulled free of the snow, and was off again. John Dowley stood up in the sleigh and gave the horse the reins, and truly the horse seemed to understand.

The train was just pulling out of the station as they drew up at the far side, out of sight of the engineer who might have waited if he had known. Chester sprang from the sleigh, suitcase in hand, just as he had planned, and sprinted for the slowly receding end of that train. He almost lost his footing on a spot of ice but caught himself and whirled on, catching the last car and reeling to the step with something of his boyhood's agility.

It took him several seconds on that bottom step before he could gather breath to pull himself up and into the car. He dropped into the last seat and sat back relieved. It was not so much that last few feet of sprinting that seemed to have taken the strength from him. It was the whole tempestuous episode, the having to leave Eleanor and the children just before Christmas, the terrible need of getting that train because of the crisis that had arisen at home, the agony of watching that little plume of smoke coming nearer and nearer, and only one brave horse to bridge the distance. It seemed to him he would never forget the sound of that fiendish whistle as the train began to gain on them, as if it knew it was racing with humans.

In due time Chester's mind calmed, and he got out his papers and began to do some important figuring, while station after station slipped by without his notice.

And all the time, in the second car ahead, curled up fast asleep in her seat, his daughter Betty rode.

Chapter 20

At Springfield he looked up, got out his watch and the timetable to see if they were on time. Well pleased that they were, he glanced out again and watched the crowds idly. As the train started on, he noticed a pretty girl who looked extremely like his Betty, standing on the platform. If he hadn't just left Betty at home in her bed asleep, he would have been almost startled, this girl looked so much like her. Dressed as Betty did at home, too. A fur coat just like hers and a little black hat. He turned his head to watch her, keeping up the illusion pleasantly. She walked like Betty, too, carrying a little suitcase, with her small head tilted proudly and her back straight as a pipe stem.

The girl disappeared into the station and Chester went on with his figuring and thought no more about it. In due time he arrived in New York, making perfect connection with his home train. He was filled with satisfaction at the way things were coming out.

Meantime, back at home the family were making popcorn balls and gingerbread men and tin stars and cookies. They were busy and happy and did not even notice when a few lazy flakes began to come down.

It was not till they had cleared off the things and began to get lunch that Chris looked up.

"Aw! Gee! Look, it's snowing again! Now we'll havta sweep off that lake; it'll spoil the skating! Gee, I hope it don't snow all night. I don't know how we'll manage to get the lake clear without Dad!"

"Never mind," said Eleanor soothingly, casting an anxious glance at the sky. "It doesn't look so very dark. Perhaps it won't snow long. Doris, you may go and wake up Betty now. Lunch is all ready to put on the table."

But Doris came back with word that Betty wasn't there.

"Oh, you're a baby!" said Jane, speeding past her. "She's in some other room. She's probably gone in my room to borrow something."

"No, she isn't, Janie," cried Doris, aggrieved. "She isn't anywhere. I looked in all the rooms!"

"She's probably up in the attic getting some more stuff for Christmas presents," said Eleanor, setting a steaming dish of potatoes down beside another of creamed codfish. "Come, get up in your chair, Doris. We want to eat while the things are hot."

But Jane came flying back wide eyed.

"She isn't anywhere, Mums. I don't think it's fair. We thought she was asleep and here we did all the work, and she's probably off hiding, reading an old book or something."

"Aw, she's in the attic," said Chris. "Call her, can't you? I'm holla as a log. Let's get ta eating."

"I went up in the attic," affirmed Jane. "I looked behind all the trunks and everything. I bet she's gone skating all alone. I say that's not fair. Let's eat all the lunch up!"

"Mercy!" said Eleanor. "I hope she hasn't gone skating alone. Your father said yesterday there was a hole in the ice. It might not be safe!"

"Aw, her skates are here, Mums! She couldn't have gone skating. Run back, Jane, and look again. You'll find her. Call. Tell her about the popcorn balls. That'll bring her. Hurry!"

"I tell you, I looked everywhere, and I'm not going to look again!" said Jane sulkily. "Betty won't come for me anyway, ever. She thinks she's too big to mind me!"

Then suddenly Eleanor dropped the dishcloth she was holding and sped up the stairs. A strange premonition had come to her. Something had happened to Betty!

Chris found his mother, five minutes later, sitting by the bureau in Betty's room crying, a letter lying on the floor by the chair. Eleanor's face was covered by her apron, and she seemed to be stifling great sobs, which shook her whole body. Chris had never had anything hurt him so as it did to see his mother cry like that, as if everything was lost. He went over and put his arms around her, gathered her up like a little child, and sat down on Betty's bed with her still in his arms, his little mother!

And suddenly all the bad, wild, careless things he had ever done rose up and stood around him to shame him, and his face grew red and shy. He patted his mother awkwardly and tried to think what Dad would have done if he had found her instead. He was the man of the house now. He shook off the condemning past and rose to meet his manhood.

"Wha's z' matter, Mums?" he crooned shyly. "Don' cry, Muth! I say, Muth, wha's z' matter? Tell a fella, can't ya? Aw, c'mon!"

For answer, Eleanor suddenly buried her face in her boy's neck and cried harder, and Chris's eyes went wildly round the room wondering what he should do next? What did men do when women cried? He had always been the one to be comforted before. How did they do it? He had done his awkward best, and it did no good.

"Muth!" he said helplessly, almost reverting to the uncomforted one himself, feeling baby enough at this minute to cry himself and seek comfort from her.

Then suddenly his anguished, wandering gaze touched the letter lying on the floor. Betty's handwriting!

Why had Betty written a letter?

Some vague fear menaced his continued peace. He strained his eyes and tried to read the words, but only one here and there was readable from the crumpled paper lying so far away. "Christmas," he saw and "poisonous." "Perfectly poisonous" that must be. It would be if Betty wrote it. And, was that "Dudley"? Yes, that was a *W* after the Dudley. What had Dud Weston been doing? That *mutt*! Thought he was king! What did Betts see in him? Was that last word "Good" or "Good-bye"?

"Muth!" he cried in alarm. "Muth, where's Betts?"

"She's gone!" said Eleanor with a quick little sob that sounded like a knife.

Chris's arms went round his mother tighter, protectingly, and his mouth shut in a thin, firm line that made him look like his father.

"Now, look here, Muth, be sensible! Betts can't have gone far. We'll get her. Where's she gone?"

"She says she's gone to get married," said Eleanor, in smothered sobs, as if the son who were comforting her were older than herself. She seemed to be utterly dazed at the thought. "There's her letter; read it," and she motioned toward Betty's note lying on the floor.

"Good night!" said Chris in horror. "Here, I'll put you on the bed, Muth! You lie still and let me han'l this! Good night! Why, Muth! Betts is only a child! A mere child!"

He laid his mother gently on the rumpled bed that Betty had deserted at dawn and snatched up the letter, reading it with a deep frown on his young face.

Old dears! it read,

 I shall simply pass out if I stay in this poisonous dump any longer, so Dudley Weston and I have decided to tie up. You needn't feel bad, because we were going to do it anyway as soon as commencement was over, and this will help out a little in one way, for nobody will expect Dad to give me a wedding if I just go off. We're thinking of making it companionate, so if things don't go right we can just quit anytime. That ought to make Mums feel better about it, but I'm sure you'll like Dud all right when he's really in the family. I'm sorry about Christmas, but I'll have plenty of money of course when I'm married, and I'll send some real presents when I get somewhere. Till then these things can do. Bye-bye. Let you know later when we get our plans made. Have a good time.

Betty

Chris cast a pitying eye toward his mother and tried to speak, but his voice choked up! He cleared his throat and tried again.

"I say, Muth, that's a rotten deal! Betts oughtta be whaled when we get her home again. She's a little fool! That's what she is. What she sees in that Dud Weston! He's just a loudmouthed boor! She thinks she'll have plenty of money when she marries him! Why, that poor fish is always broke! His dad gives him a smaller allowance than we get, and he's always spent it two or three months ahead. He goes around borrowing off the fellas. He borrowed two bucks off me just last week. I'll bet a hat he borras the money to get married. That kid'll find out whatta bad egg he is soon enough if she ever marries him! But we won't let 'er. We'll get busy, Mums, and stop it! Don't you worry, Mums, she can't uv got far. How long d'ya 'spose she's been gone? He couldn't 'a come way up here after her. He doesn't know the way. She musta walked ta the village 'nless she got the milkman to take her. Wait! I'll phone up there and see."

"Wait! Chris!" said his mother, suddenly sitting up, wiping her eyes, "We mustn't tell people! Not yet—anyway! We don't want anyone to know what a wild thing Betty is trying to do. We'll have to look out for your sister's reputation, you know, dear."

"Don't you worry, Muth! I'll be discreet all right. We gotta find out something to start on. We gotta work fast, you know. I'll just ask the milkman if my sister caught him all right or did she havta walk all the way to the early morning train, see? That'll make him think we were in on it."

"He'll think it very strange that we let her go down the lane alone so early in the morning."

"Well, let him think! I'll tell him the kid woke up early and slipped off so as not to wake us up! See? I'll fix it up. Don't you worry. No, Muth!" as she started to go downstairs with him, hindrance in her very attitude. "You lemme handle this! Dad said I was to be the man of the house. Now, you jus' stay here, an'—an' well, you jus' stay here an' *rest*! Now I'll han'l this all right. We haven't any time to waste, you know."

Eleanor sank back on the pillow with a quivering sob.

"All right, Chris. But you be very careful what you say, and *hurry*! I'll stay here and pray!"

"Aw! Now, *Muth*! It isn't as bad as that! You don't havta *pray*! I'm handling this all right, an' we're gonta get *results* right off the bat! You just wait, and *rest*! Take a good *rest*! Then you'll be all ready to make it nice for Betts when she gets back. Or bawl her out!" he added under his breath.

Chris went downstairs in three leaps, and she could hear his voice in the library below talking in low, grown-up tones.

But Eleanor was praying even while she held her breath to listen. She might be able to tell from the sound of Chris's voice what replies he had received.

It was fully five minutes before Chris returned.

His face was grave and thoughtful, and there was not so much assurance in his voice as when he went downstairs.

Eleanor rose on one elbow and eyed him eagerly, a new

dependence in her voice:

"Did she go with him?" she asked in a sharp, frightened voice. Little Betty! Her little daughter, guarded all her life, at least supposedly so, out alone with a strange milkman at four o'clock in the morning!

"They don't know," said Chris evasively. "He ain't got back yet. He was going over across the mountain to buy a coupla cows he heard of, and he won't be back till night. Whaddaya say, Muth, I hire a car down ta the village an' chase after him? I cud catch him in no time with only that team he drives, and then like as not Betts hired him to take her someplace to meet Dud Weston, an' I'd catch her before she met him, see? And bring her back."

"No!" said Eleanor sharply. "You mustn't leave here. You know your father said you mustn't even go down to skate while he was gone. He wanted you here! I should die if I didn't have you here. This is terrible! And besides, Chris, that would be a wild goose chase. You don't even know that Betty is with him, and while you were gone something might turn up that would tell us where she really is."

"But I've got a hunch she's with the milkman. Right now. See? At least I think it's worth trying."

"Look here, Chris. That is not to be thought of. We can't waste time going off on a hunch. And if you are going to do crazy things like that I can't trust you to manage for me. You can probably telephone and get that milkman by this time at the place where he was going. His wife will know where to telephone. Besides, I don't believe Betty has driven across any mountains in that old milk sled. She may have gone down to the village, but Betty would have been too impatient to ride a longer distance that way. She turned up her nose yesterday at having to ride in a sleigh like that with only straw on the floor for a seat. The thing to do is to find out if she went on the train. We must telephone to the station."

"I've already done that," said Chris in a half-offended tone. "The only morning train was the one Dad went for. There isn't another till two o'clock. The station wasn't open till eight o'clock, so they don't know whether any girl took that early train or not. But anyway, if Betts was on that train Dad'll see her. Dad'll take care of her. We'll likely get a telegram from Dad pretty soon saying she's along with him and for us not to worry."

Eleanor caught at the idea eagerly, but she did not feel like relaxing their efforts.

"We could send a telegram to that train, Chris!" she said, brightening. "We could let your father know. He'll understand just what to do."

"Now, look here, Muth," exclaimed Chris, raising his voice, "you don't understand about things. You gotta let me han'l this. Dad's train musta got away off we don't know where, an' what's the use o' bothering Dad? He left me in charge an' I'm gonna handle this. If Dad knew Betts had gone off with that half-baked simp he'd go off his nut. You know how crazy he was with that trouble about me, and Betts means ten thousand times more to him than I ever did—"

"Chris!"

"Yep! She does! She's a girl! I don't mind. But she does. And he'd hafta give up that 'mportant business he was going to tend to and go traipsing off no one knows where. And you know he said he simply had ta be down home tonight! And what could he do anyway? I ask you. Could he do more'n we're doing? You don't seem to realize she started from here! She didn't start from down there! And he'd hafta come back here, and then where would his 'mportant business be, I ask you. And mebbe, if he knew what Dud had done, leastways what he was gonta do, he go an' *kill* Dud, or hit his dad or something awful! You know how Dad is about Betts! You know he'd be awful angry. No. Muth, the thing for us to do is get busy, and right now I'm gonta get a long distance in for Dud Weston. If he's home I'll talk to him kinda like I wanted him to do a favor for Betts or something like that, see? And then I'll find out where he's gonta be tonight, an' then I'll send the p'lice to arrest him, see? Or something, so if Betts has gone down to Briardale ta meet him we'll stand her up! See?"

"But Chris, you don't even know that Dudley is at home. If he's meeting Betty somewhere, or if he came up here after her—"

"I'll eat my hat if Dud Weston ever took this long trip after Betts. He'd make her come somewhere. He's the laziest cuss in Briardale. However, I'll find out. I gotta buddy at home that's a regular sleuth fer finding out things. I'll put him onta this job by phone—"

"But Chris, you mustn't let people in Briardale know about your sister. Why, it would be simply awful! We must stop it before they ever get married! We *must*! And then there will be nothing for them to gossip about. You mustn't tell any boy about your sister's private affairs!"

"There you are again, Muth. It's evident you don't trust me. *I* wouldn't tell anything about my sister! I'd just let that fella know I wanted ta get pointers on Dud Weston. Now, Muth, I gotta get that call in fer Dud. It's our best bet ta find out first whether he's at home 'r not. If he is, we got plenty o' time ta let Dad know before he gets there, and he can get Betts before she sees him. He can nail Dud before he goes to meet her. See?"

"Oh!" groaned Eleanor, sinking down on the edge of the bed again. "Oh, I'm afraid it will *kill* your father!"

"That's it, Muth, we gotta get this thing in hand before Dad has to know. And I gotta get busy. Muth, you sit down and write out what Betts had on so's I can give a description if I hafta have her paged ur anything at a station ur hotel."

"But how do I know what she had on?" groaned the mother.

"Look in her closet and see what she left behind!" said the practical boy. "Did she wear her new fur coat?"

Given something practical to do Eleanor went to work, taking out the things in Betty's closet, running up to the attic to see which suitcase she had taken, writing down a probable description.

Jane appeared at the head of the stairs, looking silently in on her mother as she wrote.

"Aren't we ever going to have lunch?" she asked. "I'm starved. What are you and Chris fighting about?"

"Oh, Jane!" said her mother, her eyes filling with tears again. "You don't know what a dreadful thing has happened, dear."

"Sure, I do!" said Jane. "I'm not dumb. Betts is a selfish thing, that's what she is. She doesn't care whether we any of us have any Christmas or any good times anymore or anything." Jane was winking back the tears, and her voice sounded suddenly like a sob at the end of her sentence.

Eleanor turned and caught Jane in her arms and realized suddenly that it had been a long time since she had held Jane so. Her little girl had somehow grown hard and unloving and had not wanted babying. But now suddenly Jane buried her face on her mother's shoulder and cried like any little, dear girl whose good times were spoiled and who wanted to be comforted.

"Darling," said Eleanor, "never mind Christmas. We'll make all that up afterward if we can only find Betty. My dear, your sister is in great danger!"

"Well, she put herself there, didn't she? If she hadn't a wanted to she wouldn't have, would she? I wouldn't fuss about her. Let her go. We can have a better time without her. She always wanted the best things anyway, and she's been cross as two sticks ever since she came. She hated this place, and she wasn't going to get over it. She told me. And she didn't like ta work. It wasn't fair, and then she always got the biggest pieces of pie—I'm glad she's gone." And Jane shook the long dark forehead curl out of her eyes and glared up fiercely through her tears.

"My dear, my dear! What a terrible state of things between two sisters. But you must not talk that way. Even if Betty has done wrong and been selfish, now she is in great danger. We must do all we can to find her, and there will never be any happiness in this house till she is found. We love all our children. Now, Jane, dear, stop crying and stop thinking hard thoughts against Betty, and try to help me. Think! Did you ever hear Betty say anything about where she would go if she went away? Did she ever say she wanted to go?"

"I'll say she did!" said the little girl. "She couldn't get done talking about it. She told me once she was going ta write ta Dudley Weston and get him to rescue her from this poisonous dump. That's just what she said. She said Dudley would lie down and let her walk over him if she asked him."

"Have you any idea how she was planning to go? Did she suggest any way when she talked with you?"

The little girl shook her head:

"No, but you might find something in her drawer, some letter, or in some of her pockets. She had a letter from Dudley one day. I saw his name signed. Just as I came into her room, I was looking over her shoulder, and I saw it. It said, "Yours ta get drunk. Dud" and I was going to read more only she turned around and saw me and was awfully angry at me and said she'd tell you and Daddy if I didn't keep out of her room. But she hid the letter in her pocket. Why 'n't ya look?"

Jane went over to the bureau and began to rummage.

"What's this?" she asked, taking up the package Betty had left with her name on it. She broke the string and opened the paper.

"Her coral beads!" she said. "Well, she never liked them herself; she needn't think she's done anything great! But they always looked better on me than they did on her. I think she's just too mean for anything, anyway, to spoil all our Christmas, and Daddy gone, too. It's desperate!" And Jane broke down and cried again.

Eleanor was looking through the things in the closet, and she stopped and gazed at her little girl in dismay. Such deep-rooted hardness between two sisters! How had it come about? So unloving, so selfish, both of them! Why hadn't she known how things were going? Why hadn't she seen it before and done something to bring about a sweeter life in the home? Oh, she had been wrong! It had been her own fault! This must be a punishment for her own neglect.

But she had thought she was doing everything for them! They were being educated in the best of schools, with the most expensive teachers, and that class at the women's club had said that children must not be fussed over and noticed in every little wrong thing they did.

Suddenly she came on a couple of letters in Betty's old sweater pocket and brought them out to the light. They were only from Betty's friend Gipsy, but they shed a good deal of light on Betty's associates and opened Eleanor's eyes to a number of things, more than any amount of club lectures could have done.

She was sitting in a daze of sorrow looking at them when Chris came back. Word had come back from the Weston home that Dudley was away at a weekend party down at the shore.

"So that's that!" said Chris, frowning thoughtfully. "Mebbe he's there, and mebbe he isn't. If I only knew where that house party was, whose house— Aw, this is the limit, living away off up here! If I knew who was giving it, might be Gwen or Fran or Gyp Magilkey. 'F I only knew, I might telephone there and ask to speak to Dud. Maybe that's where Betts was going to meet him."

"Oh!" said Eleanor, looking up from her daze of trouble. "Why, it must be Gwen's house party. This letter I found in Betty's pocket speaks of a house party at Gwen's and a dance at Shillingsworth's. Isn't that the dancing pavilion down at Lancet Beach?"

"It sure is," said Chris excitedly. "Let me see that letter!"

He glanced through Gipsy's effusive epistle, flung it back into his mother's lap with a contemptuous "Say, isn't that just like *a fool girl*," and went off downstairs again. Eleanor felt a thrill of hope. Perhaps, after all, Betty was only going down to that house party and didn't really mean to get married. Perhaps she only said that to throw them off the track and worry them so they wouldn't make a fuss about the party afterward.

But in half an hour Chris came back with a really anxious look on his face.

"I had Gwen on the line all righty," he said, slumping into a chair near his mother. "But she didn't know a thing about Dud; said he promised to be there last evening to help put up laurel, but he hadn't turned up and hadn't sent any word. I asked who else was there, letting on I was a friend of Dud's and might wantta speak to 'em. They named over all Betts' class, but they didn't say a word about Betts so they can't be expecting 'em back there. So that's that! I'm up a tree! Where's Jane?"

"I sent her out with the children. She's so forlorn I thought it would do her good to get a little air. Don't you think we ought to try finding out about your father's train? Couldn't we wire him now? He ought to be getting into the city in an hour or so, and I wouldn't know where to reach him after he gets off the train. The office will be closed, you know, and he didn't have time to tell me where he would be—"

"I been keepin' the wires hot," said Chris efficiently. "I got the list of towns that early train stops at, and I've phoned three or four, but none of 'em have seen a girl of Betty's description. I was thinking of trying Springfield next, only that's not far enough away. Dud would never have come way up there for Betts. He wouldn't have gas enough. He never has any gas left in his car. Always hasta borrow ta get anywhere. Bah! But I gotta wire in now for that conductor of the early train. He'll know if a girl got on that early and where she was going to."

"Why yes," said Eleanor. "Why didn't we think of that before? Of course he'd know."

Jane appeared in the doorway with the twins behind her.

"I went down to the log cabin," said Jane solemnly, "and asked 'em if they had heard a strange sound in the night like anyone going down the lane or anything, or maybe early this morning, but they said no, they didn't hear a thing, that it mighta been a rabbit I heard, and the sick man said it couldn'ta been anything 'cause he's most always awake nights, and he'd a heard it if it hadaben. But I found some tracks!"

"Tracks!" said Chris eagerly. "What kinda tracks?"

"Tracks in the snow, 'bout the size of Betty's galoshes, where she musta broken through the crust of the snow."

"Where?" Chris was out following her like a real detective.

The tracks left the beaten path and went in a detour across the fields, giving wide berth to the log cabin and ending abruptly in a stretch of crust that was thicker than the rest because it was in a sheltered nook where the sun could not reach it and was strong enough to bear the weight of a light person. Chris tested it and then walked all around it searching till he came to the tracks again, fifty feet ahead on the southern slope of the hill, and followed them down till they ended in the highway. But they unmistakably turned toward the village. That was plain. He felt sure they were Betty's.

Chris hurried back to the house to tell his mother, and just as he entered the door he heard the telephone ringing.

It was an answer to his telegram to the morning train conductor. Yes, a young girl of Betty's description had boarded the train at the village station that morning. She was all alone and had paid her way as far as Springfield.

"Well, we got something at last!" said Chris as he hung up the receiver. "Gee! I never thought she'd be so near as that. I wish I'd telephoned there first! Good night! She's had time to make a great getaway. What time is it, five o'clock? Well, I can find out where she bought a ticket to from there, anyway, or if she didn't buy one I'll have her paged! I can find out if she was alone when she bought her ticket, too. Well, we're getting on!"

Chapter 21

When Betty got out of her train at Springfield and disappeared into the station she found that it was half past ten o'clock. That was three-quarters of an hour later than the timetable had said it would be, and she sighed contentedly. Three-quarters of an hour less to wait for Dudley.

She looked around eagerly. Perhaps he was even here already. Unconsciously she straightened her hat and tried to blink the sleep out of her eyes, for she had just woke up from one of the soundest sleeps she ever had and might have been carried on beyond this station if it had not been for the kindness of the conductor who woke her and helped her out.

As Dudley did not seem to be anywhere in immediate view, Betty sought and found the ladies' waiting room and began to repair the damages of travel. Her small vanity case, which she had been carefully hoarding during the days at the farm, did heavy duty, for Betty felt that she was getting back into her own world again and must look her best. Perhaps she applied a trifle more lipstick and rouge than was usual for her, for now there was no disapproving parent's eye upon her, and she experienced a daring delight in making her lips and cheeks as vivid as she had always longed to have them. She knew that her special type needed just this touch—at least that was what Dudley Weston had told her—to make her look distinguished and interesting. She surveyed her finished result with real pleasure. She really had a wicked look as she turned from the smoky little mirror in the ladies' room and picked up her suitcase to go back into the main waiting room. She hoped Dudley would come soon. She was deadly hungry, but of course it wouldn't do to eat before he came, for he might come any minute now.

She selected a seat where she could see all doors of entrance and settled down to wait, with the clock in full view.

She had just thirty-seven cents left after paying her fare to Springfield, and after waiting an hour with no results she walked over to the newsstand and purchased a five-cent bar of chocolate and a five-cent package of peanut butter cracker sandwiches.

She ate them hurriedly, prepared to hide them at once should Dudley enter either of the doors, for she did not want him to see that she had been eating and not waiting for him. But when she finished eating she seemed hungrier than before. The minutes dragged themselves slowly by, and at last the great clock hands in the station pointed to twelve, and various whistles and bells in the town set up a screeching and clanging to call attention to the fact that it was high noon.

Betty's cheeks grew hot at the thought that in a few minutes she would be actually off on her wedding trip with Dud. As each moment passed by she found her heart beating more wildly.

A sudden rush of memory made her think of her mother and father, her brothers and sisters. Strange she felt this way. She had not expected any such softness as this. If Dud would only come! Well, she would have something on him now, if he was late. He was always saying girls were late!

But the next half hour slipped away, slow-throbbing minute by slow-throbbing minute, and no Dudley.

Betty began to grow angry. Dudley had no right to keep her waiting so long! When she had come as far as this and kept her agreement she had a right to expect him to be there! It wasn't gallant in a bridegroom to keep her waiting. He really ought to have been there before her. He should have been there at early dawn to make things right!

Still, of course he might have had an accident with his car, a flat tire or something. Betty was not given to fears. She did not begin to think of anything like a real accident until the clock hands pointed to a quarter past two. Then she got up with her suitcase in her hand and walked briskly to each of the doors and windows in turn and looked out. Finally she went out and walked around the outside of the station, scanning each car parked in the block, but there was nothing like Dudley's loud combination of colors in the whole collection. Then she went back nervously and took her seat again, fearful lest he might have come and gone away mad because she was not right there at his first glance as he entered the station.

Her eyes were beginning to burn with constantly watching the opening doors and scanning the windows of the station. Her cheeks felt as hot as their color, and her lips felt cracked and fairly bleeding from her long walk in the wind in the morning. She felt dizzy and sick, and her head ached with great throbs. Dudley was spoiling it all!

Her hunger had long ago turned to a gnawing faintness as the afternoon wore on, and she began to wonder what she should do if Dudley did not come before night. How long could she go without food? What a fool she had been not to bring more than just the two or three tiny sandwiches she had managed to slip in her suitcase the afternoon before. It would have been easy to bring along plenty without exciting suspicion in the least. Doughnuts and cookies and gingerbread. There was always plenty on hand. Jane delighted to try her hand at the new things she had been learning how to make. How good it would be to walk into the dining room now and sit down to a good meal! If only nobody knew that she had gone away!

A train came rushing up, and they called out its stops. It was the train that went back to the little village below the farm. If she had the money she could get on it and go back. It would serve Dudley Weston right, keeping her waiting so long! She would have been almost willing to do it now; she was so angry with Dudley for being late. Yet of course she couldn't because she had no money.

She walked restlessly to the door and watched the people get on. No one would know her, of course. She would not know any of the passengers, yet it was comforting somehow to feel that that train was going back to where she had come from, back where her mother was, and home, and Christmas.

A sudden compunction assailed her for having gone away before Christmas. Of course she might have waited.

Probably if she got on the train now and told the conductor she hadn't money enough to get home but would send it to him he would likely let her ride. She could give him her wristwatch as collateral. But she wouldn't do it, of course.

The train began to move, and she looked around again hastily to see if Dudley was coming. There was no Dudley, and she took a couple of steps toward the last car, which was moving past her more rapidly now. And then she saw that she couldn't get on it even if she wanted to; it was moving too rapidly. It had gone past her the full length of the car.

She turned with a long, drawn sigh, half wishing she had got on. The deadly thought assailed her that perhaps Dud would stand her up! Perhaps he would not come at all. Perhaps he had gone down to Gwen's house party! And she like a fool was sitting alone in a strange station, moneyless and hungry, and utterly out with her family, while he danced the giddy hours away with Gwen!

Furious, she walked crisply across the station and out the opposite door. If she had only done something to get some more money! If she could sell her watch now, for instance, and hire a taxi—no it was too far for a taxi—but she could telephone home at least. Perhaps, if she asked them, they would reverse the call and let her talk to her father! That would be the last resort! Poor Dad. He would be furious, of course, but the approaching evening and the hunger and the anger were making her almost willing to stand his fury, if only she might get back to her own bed, something good to eat, and peace and safety! Out on her own, with nothing to do but wait in a station for somebody who did not come! Running away wasn't all it had promised to be.

During the little moment in which she had entered the platform, and gone through to the opposite side of the station, the night seemed to have come down. It startled her to look out upon the square and see the lights springing up on all sides, see the streets dim away vaguely into twilight, and the sky dark, with little occasional flakes drifting slowly, lazily down.

Her mind went back to the drive they had had in the snow when they came up to the farm, and she shuddered at the thought that this might be another night like that, with Dudley and his crazy roadster wallowing through the drifts.

She scanned the sky anxiously and then stepped back quickly into the shadow as a car came swooping up toward the station, with the air of intending to drive right up on the platform and go inside the door.

The car stopped a few feet from where she was standing, and she heard a girl's voice laughing raucously:

"Well, so long, Buddy! Thanks for the buggy ride! I'll love you always for this day! You saved my life. I'll tell the world! If I'd had to come on the train I'd uv been bored to death. I only wisht you was going the rest of the way!"

"Same here, darling! But no chance! I gotta skirt inside here, sore's a boil by this time. You'n I lingered a little long over our dinner. I'm late by just five hours! Sorry, but it can't be helped. 'Nother time possibly. Ef you come down my way again call me up an' I'll show you a wild night! So long, Peachy. I won't forgetya!"

The young man turned and came face-to-face with Betty trembling with anger. Her little delicate face was white beneath its makeup, and the white light of an electric arc suddenly leaping up shone upon her.

"Hello, Betts!" said Dudley easily. "On time after all! I wasn't counting on that! First time in yer life! Well, couldn't be helped. Had two flat tires and a blowout! Got a leak in the radiator, and water in the carburetor, and came through three thunderstorms and a fog. Gosh, but it's a heck of a journey! Hadn't been you, Thorny, I'd uv turned back! Think you're worth it?"

Betty, furious with anger, tottering with fatigue and hunger, perceived that Dudley had been drinking. Not enough to be stupid or angry, only enough to be loudmouthed.

"For mercy's sake, Dud, hush!" she said as she saw some passing people turn to look at them. "Lock your car, and come, let's get some dinner. I'm starved! I'm just about to pass out! I've waited for you ever since noon!"

"Good night! Thorny, I've just finished a meal! Couldn't eat another bite 'f I was to be 'lectrocuted for it. You run along an' get a bite while I get gas. We gotta beat it! I promised Gwen we'd be down ta th' house party soon's we could make it. Run along. Make it snappy. We oughtta get outta here!"

Betty's heart sank, and her fury rose. She was so angry that she wanted to cry. She was so tired and hungry that she wanted to run home. Dudley had been eating a good dinner with that other awful girl! He had not cared that she was waiting, hungry, anxious! And now he wanted her to go and eat alone! When she had waited all day!

And he was not offering to pay for it either! And she had but twenty-seven cents!

Yet, with all her despair and poverty she would not tell Dudley that she did not have money! Some terrible sense of pride descended upon her. She would rather starve than ask Dudley for money. She would not put herself in his power to that extent. Something innate told her that as soon as she did she would cheapen herself to him. She had always held him in her power, had carried a high hand and ordered him around. To tell him now that she was penniless would be to change their relations, to put herself in his power. She was trying to think what to do, whether she could get enough to satisfy her hunger out of twenty-seven cents.

"Oh," she said coldly. "I see! You preferred to have dinner with that girl! Perhaps I had better go back to my home, and you can marry her!" And she turned as if to go away, carrying her little head haughtily, holding her suitcase with a firm grasp, though the hand that held it trembled with weariness.

"Heck! Thorny, you're the limit! Didn't I come all this way after ya? What more da ya want? There's plentya girls I cud get, you know darn well!"

He was talking very loud now, and people were turning again to look at them. Betty shrank into her shadow and protested.

"Hush, Dud. You're making yourself a spectacle," she said in a low tone. "See, those people are coming this way just to listen."

"What's the dif?" said Dudley, speaking still louder. "It's none of their darn business! You're jealous, that's what's the matter, jus' plain jealous! Jealous of that poor little kid that I picked up on a lonely road, walkin' to Springfield jus' 'cause she didn't have the money! If you're going to develop a complex like that I better beat it!"

Betty was about to tell him he had, with her heart full of fury and her lips shaking so that she could scarcely speak, when suddenly a voice arrested them both, startling into their controversy like a voice of authority.

"Paging Miss Betty Thornton!" it said in the tone of a monotonous giant doing his duty. "Miss Betty Thornton of Briardale, Pennsylvania, will please come to the telephone in the office!"

The door of the station had swung wide, and the great megaphone, which was located on the wall opposite, seemed to be directed definitely at them. They started toward one another in a common fear, and Betty found herself clinging to Dudley's hand and trembling like a leaf. It was as if she had been caught and shamed before the whole world.

And while they stood silent, listening, the monotonous voice went on again:

"Paging Miss Betty Thornton of Briardale, Pennsylvania. Please come to the telephone in the office."

Suddenly Dudley Weston came alive.

"Get in there, quick!" he said roughly and pushed her toward the car, fairly lifting her into the seat and slamming the door.

"They're after us, Thorny! We gotta beat it!" he breathed and flung himself around to his own seat, starting the car with a jerk and dashing out among the taxicabs with a vehemence that set up a commotion among drivers and traffic police.

Betty was trembling still. She looked back as someone swung wide the door of the station again, and the sonorous voice pursued them: "Paging Miss Betty Thornton of Briar—"

The car swung around a corner, and the voice was lost in the multitudinous noises of the city. Betty felt as if she were being snatched from a helping hand that had been reached out to save her. She knew in her heart that if that voice had come a few minutes sooner, if it had come while she was sitting alone and forlorn in the station, she would have answered it, gladly, and flown back to home and Mother; or if it had come even afterward when she saw Dudley with that unspeakable girl, she would have turned and fled to the call as to a city of refuge.

554

As they turned another corner, barely escaping a crash with a big car, and reeled into line among the traffic, Betty clutched wildly at her companion's arm and cried convulsively:

"Take me back, Dudley, take me back at once. I've got to answer that telephone call! I've got to, don't you see? Someone might be sick or dead!"

"Let 'em die, then!" said the boy roughly. "You left 'em, didn't ya? Well, then don't go whining back. I got ya, and you're mine now! Shut up and leggo my arm! How cun I drive with you pulling my arm like that? You little fool you. Your yella, that's what you are! I useta think you had nerve, but you haven't any more pep than a mouse. Get over there!" and he shoved her roughly to the other side of the seat.

Betty froze into dignity.

"Dudley Weston, don't you *dare* touch me again!" she cried furiously. "And you take me back at once! I've got to answer that call. Take me back, I say! Or I'll jump out right here in traffic, and then you'll be responsible!"

For answer Dudley replied:

"Help yourself! You're Thorny all right!" and stepped on the gas, making the pedestrians scuttle to left and right wildly to get out of his way, and a traffic whistle pursued them as they vanished into the distance.

Betty sat back in her seat furious and helpless, the cold air keeping her alive and driving back the deadly faintness that assaulted her now and again. She shut her lips tight and sat silent and angry, mile after mile, with Dudley driving hard and fast.

How he got through the thick of the city without being arrested was nothing short of a miracle. Betty kept hoping he would be arrested, and then she might escape.

She was not frightened, for she was used to Dudley's wild driving, she was merely hungry and tired and angry, furiously angry. This was no romantic marriage as she had fancied it, driving like mad away from all that had until then been comforting, driving into an unknown night with an ungallant knight who swore at her every time he escaped running down a trolley car or colliding with a truck; with an empty stomach and another girl, in the background who had dined with her beloved, a blowsy girl, too, with a loud voice and bad English, and a sneer on her unwholesome face. To think he would care to stop for that girl—eat dinner with her—when he was on the way to meet his bride! Well, she wasn't sentimental, but this was the limit!

Chapter 22

Farther and farther from the city they drove, out into the empty country, with snow on the ground and snow beginning to come down from the sky now in earnest, in lazy whirls and fantastic drifts that gave a sense of power, terrible power, power to come down in flocks and droves pretty soon if it chose.

They were out in the country now with no moon, no stars, black leaden sky overhead, and only the light of the snow to guide them. There were occasional woods, dark as velvet, and only the streak of their own lamps to break it, and in one of these Dudley suddenly brought the car to a dead stop, so suddenly that it almost threw her off the seat.

"Now," said the gallant young bridegroom, "if you wantta jump out here's a good place to try it. You get out and walk back, and I'll go on to Gwen's house party. I'm sick of a grouch! You've lost your nerve! Get out!"

For one angry instant Betty was on the point of obeying. She put out her hand to open the door and looked out to the blackness of the woods, with the one gash of white where the lamps shone ahead, and she thought of the lamps going on without her. Only the little red taillight at the back, winking, winking, in the distance and vanishing, and she shuddered. Her voice broke, and tears came into her throat and eyes, angry tears that those gallant young eyes tried to conquer, and failed.

"I'm hungry!" wailed Betty like a frightened little child. "I'm not grouchy. I'm just—just—tired and hungry! I haven't had any—any—l–l–lunch, nor d–d–dinner!" Her voice was coming through real sobs now. "And you—you—you—b–b–b–rought that g–g–gr–rlll!"

"Oh, gosh! Yes, I thought that was it! Jealous little cat you are! Anything I hate is a sniveling woman! Anything I hate is a jealous little cat! I never thought you were like that! I wouldn'ta come if I had! I'd a sight rather stayed at Gwen's, only I had given my word of honor—" he swaggered.

"I'm not jealous!" said Betty, suddenly straightening up and dashing the tears away from her face, her bold look coming back into her eyes. "You think I'd be jealous of a thing like that? Fat and dowdy! She hadn't a bit of style! She was common! Very common! How could I think of being jealous of a thing like that? Why, she had dirty fingernails and looked as though she'd never had a shampoo or her hair waved. Her hair hung round her face like a row of pins in a paper. No, I'm not jealous! I'm just *disappointed* in you, Dudley Weston."

"I'll say you are! I'll say you're a peach! I'll say you're a beaut! You're the bee's knees and then some. I drive thousands of miles after you just to rescue you from a cruel family, and give up all my fun, and my midyear exams, and all my chance of graduating and feeling I have an education, and what for? I ask you. Just to get my eyes scratched out by a jealous little cat!"

Betty withdrew into her corner and closed her lips in a hard little line. This was a new Dudley! How she hated him! Was this what she was marrying?

"Well, are you going to get out?" asked Dudley loftily, after a long minute's silence.

"No," said Betty composedly in her very best princess style, "not in a place like this, of course."

"All righty!" said Dudley, preparing to start the car. "Last chance now ur never!" And they shot out into the road again and dashed through the night, but neither spoke for a long time.

At last after what seemed to Betty like an eternity where she had been regretting everything she had ever done since she was born, Dudley stopped the car and handed her a flask.

"Here!" he said, though still gruffly. "Put yerself around some of this. It's a wow! I got it on the way up. It oughtta bring ya outta yer grouch ef anything will. If it don't I'm done!"

She perceived that Dudley was making a drunken attempt to make up with her, and she took the flask eagerly and tipped it up to her lips.

The flask had apparently been recently replenished for it was nearly filled, with some hot stinging liquor that was new to Betty and burned her throat as she swallowed it. Immediately a sense of comfort pervaded her, and the clamor in her stomach was warmed and soothed.

"Hot stuff!" said Dudley, leaning over and taking the flask as she handed it back, a little frightened at the new feeling of exhilaration that began to tingle all over her tired body. Dudley took great swallows of the liquor, and the smell of it filled the car with a strange, sickening odor.

Dudley took a long drink and then lurched over with his arm around Betty and kissed her. The smell of his breath was hot and heavy. Betty felt a dizzy disgust at his touch.

"Hurry up, Dud," she said, trying to get her old imperious tone back again. "Let's go! I want some dinner, and then I'll feel all right!" What was the use in quarreling with Dudley? It was too late. She must make the best of things and get her old control over him.

"Awwright ole girl! Jus' you shay!" said Dudley, starting the car again with one arm still around her, crushing her to him.

Dudley drove wildly as usual, and before long they came to a town and a gas station.

"Gotta get gas, ole girl!" he said affably. "Shay, you got any dough? I haven't got mush more'n 'nough to pay fer gas. That darned kid pinched it off me. She gave me a lotta sob stuff about her folks turning her out, an' her not having any place ta go, till I shelled out all I had."

"Dudley! Do you mean we haven't any money? Why, what are we going to do? Do you mean you gave that girl all the money you had when you were coming to marry me?"

She was both frightened and angry again, and her voice had a helpless note in it.

"Oh, tha's all right, kid," he said comfortingly. "Got 'nough to get gas, and I'll telephone to the ole man and get him to wire me some money awwright! Donchoo worry, kid!"

"But I'm hungry!" said Betty, beginning to cry now without realizing it.

"That's tough luck, kid, but it won't take so long now ta get ta N'York. Are you broke, too?"

"I've only got twenty-seven cents!" said Betty with a quiver.

"That's awwright!" soothed Dudley. "Getta good meal fer that!"

So while Dudley bought gas and a package of cigarettes Betty climbed out and spent twenty-five of her twenty-seven cents on a cup of bitter coffee, a box of stale crackers, and an overripe banana.

"Have a cigarette!" said Dudley graciously as she got back into the car.

Betty took it eagerly and tried to get the usual thrill out of smoking, but somehow everything seemed to have gone stale like the crackers. All she wanted in the world was to lie down and go to sleep.

They drove on through the night, passing villages and larger towns more often now and shooting through their quiet streets or noisy thoroughfares alike regardless of life or limb.

"Oh, Dud, I wish you wouldn't drive so fast through these towns! We might get pinched!" said Betty after a particularly narrow hairbreadth escape.

" 'Smatter of you, Thorny?" inquired the gallant youth. "Getting soft? Losing yer nerve? Thought you liked a kick. This is nothing. Only fifty-five. Let's make it sixty." He stepped on the gas, and the car lurched out around a curve and almost into a staid old Ford driven by an elderly man.

Betty caught her breath and looked back expecting to see the Ford on its side, but her escort gave her far too much to think about, and she had to turn back and forget the old man and the Ford.

"Goin' to take a shortcut," said Dudley, swerving into a rough asphalt road that looked as if it were utterly out of repair.

"Oh, I wouldn't, Dud, not tonight!" cried Betty. "What if you should get a flat tire! What if we should have a blowout! Let's take the regular road!"

"Oh, I know you wouldn't. You'd wantta be all night and all next day on the road. You're yella, that's what's the matter with you. A fella I met tol' me this was a good road. I'm tryin' it, see? Take another drink! Brace ya up. Look at me! I'm not afraid to take a chance. You gotta keep up your end ur we can't make a go of it. Why, Thorny, you useta be a tough little egg. Wha's eatin' ya?"

"I think we'd get there quicker if we kept to the good road," answered Betty sulkily. "You make me tired the way you act."

"Oh, I do, do I? I make you tired, do I? Well, just for that we're goin' this road, see? An' we'll take it at seventy-five if I like. Or ninety, maybe. Wantta see me take this road at ninety an hour?"

That was a night to be remembered.

The rough road proved to be anything but a shortcut. Mile

after mile they careened along, over breaks that seemed like ditches, through snow that had blown in the way and never been cleared. Traffic had gone around the drifts, but Dudley went straight through and nearly stalled his engine. Twice he had to get out and work at the machinery with cursing lips and uncertain fingers. Then Betty discovered that though the flask had been emptied much to her relief several miles back, Dudley had more of the strange tangy, sickly smelling liquor in the back of his car, and each time he got out he replenished the flask.

He offered it to her every time he drank, but she refused. She had heard about drugged liquor that made people very sick, killed them sometimes, and tonight she somehow felt a strange reluctance to take a chance.

"Where did you get it, Dud?" she asked after the fifth refusal and his accompanying jeer at her new principles. "It tastes funny. Maybe it's poisoned."

"Great cats!" said Dudley. "I musta made a mistake an' brought along yer grandmother! Letcha off at the next town an' ya can walk back. Didn't know ya'd gone on the water wagon."

"Oh, cut it out, Dud!" said Betty, trying to assume her old superiority. "You're not pleasant!"

"Pleasant! Pleasant! I like that! When I came all the way—"

And so it went on, hour after hour, as the night waned, and morning began to dawn. Betty thought it never would end.

"Where are we going, Dud?" she asked at last, wearily. "I'm just ready to pass out. Aren't we ever going to get there? This road is so bumpy my back aches."

"Get there! Get there!" repeated Dudley drunkenly. "All you care is get there! Whaddaya think of me? I drove all last night—"

Betty looked at him in the early dawn of the cold, cheerless morning. His face was flushed in blotches, his eyes were bloodshot, his collar awry, his hair disheveled, his lips swollen. He had a wild look about him. She wondered why she had ever called him good looking. She shuddered and drew herself away, a feeling of utter disgust coming over her. She used to think it was manly to get a little drunk. But Dudley was more than a little drunk. He was beside himself, and he was driving like a madman. He was talking like a madman, swearing at her in the intervals.

"Tied to a skirt! That's what it is to be tied to a skirt!" he said. "Get me away up here, outta my way! Make me shpend all my dough gettin' gas. Then make a fuss about a little bitta road. Awright! We'll try another road!"

Suddenly, without any warning, he deliberately turned the car to the left. The road sloped down abruptly to another highway several roads below the one they were on.

Dudley had been drinking at intervals all night, but the last drink had been deeper and longer than all the rest, inasmuch as he had recently refilled his flask from the mysterious supply in the back of his car, and now he seemed to be utterly beyond reason. Betty had never seen him like this. She had never seen anyone quite so drunk and wild and angry as Dudley was now. Probably it was a combination of exhaustion from long driving and overstimulation from the bad liquor. He seemed quite like an insane person.

Betty, forgetting all her pride in being hard boiled and daring anything, was frightened beyond anything she had ever felt before. She cried out and sprang forward at the same time, trying to lay hands on the wheel and turn the car back into the road before it should be too late, but Dudley was only infuriated by this. He turned like a wild beast and glared at her, striking her hands from the wheel with a paralyzing blow and then dealing a stinging slap across her mouth and another over her eyes, till she huddled speechless with fear in her corner of the car too frightened to think. The last vision her eyes had caught as they received the blinding blow was a rim of crimson disk like a great fire opal, coming up above the distant mountain.

Dudley had begun to brake and had caught the wheel once more, but the car was beyond his control. Betty in her blindness and horror and pain could feel it hurtling down the sudden grade, could realize what it meant, had time to wonder what the swift end would be, and then to suddenly feel the eye of God upon her—God, standing down there in the valley, watching them come, knowing what was happening to them, knowing she had brought this all on herself, and yet looking at her in that same yearning way, as if He would have saved her from it if she had but let Him! God! Why, *God* could save her even yet, couldn't He, if He was a God?

"Oh, God!" she cried. But the awful curses of Dudley as he tried to direct his car into the road drowned out her voice. Had He heard? Had God heard?

And then the car turned over and all was blotted out.

Chapter 23

Back in Vermont there was consternation when the word came that the young woman who had answered the description of Miss Thornton, and who had been seen by several employees of the railroad in the station during the day, was not to be found. She had been paged for half an hour and had not been found.

"I knew I ought to have telegraphed your father the first moment we found she was gone!" cried Eleanor with a gasp of fear. "He will never forgive me! Our little girl gone and I didn't let him know! And now it is getting dark, and where can she be?"

She dropped down on the hard old sofa in the library and buried her face in her hands.

"Oh, good night, Muth! We're doing the best we can! If Betts was really in Springfield she can't be so far away from here yet! Likely she's gone to a hotel. I'll phone all the hotels and find out! You know we can get a detective in Springfield and get right on the job, if you're willing!"

"No," said Eleanor, springing to her feet. "I must tell your father before we do another thing. He will likely be in the office by this time. If he caught that train this morning he would have gone right on through. Call up the office—"

"But it's Saturday. The office is closed."

"Somebody might be there. Try it. Your father would be there, I'm sure, if he has reached the city."

So Chris tried the office.

But only the janitor answered. Yes, the office was closed. No, there wasn't anybody there! No, Mr. Thornton hadn't been in that day. Mr. Thornton was out of town for an extended stay.

"I toldya, Muth," said Chris, turning to his mother triumphantly. "Now you lemme handle this—"

"No, Chris. You must get the telegraph office and send a telegram to the train. If your father had to stay over in New York—I've been thinking it over and I believe he said he might have to stop there to see a man—but if he did stay over he would have taken the four o'clock from the Pennsylvania station. That's the train he always takes when he goes to New York. You must send a telegram to him on that train. That will get to him before he reaches home, and he will have time to think up what to do."

"Great cats, Muth, what can we say in a telegram that won't publish the whole thing to the world? He won't understand without a whole letter. Now I ask you, what can he do away off there?"

"Your father always knows what to do," said Eleanor firmly. "This is no time to worry about the world, but anyway nobody on the train will know anything about us. Here's a telegram I've written out. Send it quick, and then get Mr. Chalmers's number and ask for him. I want to talk to him. We can confide in him. If he isn't home get some other member of the firm. I've *got* to have help at once!"

But Chester did not get Eleanor's telegram. He was not on the four o'clock train from New York. He was speeding across his home city in search of a man who was about to leave for a Christmas vacation and was a very important factor in the contract that was to be signed. He had no time to send telegrams, nor receive them, and when later he remembered to send a message it merely read: "Business well in hand. Probably shall reach farm Monday night. Will keep you informed." But the message gave no clue to his whereabouts at the time.

The messages to the members of the firm brought equally poor returns, for everyone seemed to be off somewhere on this last Saturday before Christmas, and the message Eleanor left at each point—"Please have Mr. Thornton call up his wife as soon as he comes in"—lay scattered about Briardale and the city like so many useless fragments. Chester took no time to go anywhere except where he was obliged to go, and the small amount of sleep he snatched was taken at a little inconspicuous hotel where he happened to be when he got done Saturday night, and where he had never stayed before.

So the night came down, the awful first night of Betty's absence, and still they had managed to get no clue.

Eleanor walked up and down her room, or stared out of the window at the slow-moving flakes that wavered past the window, and thought and shuddered and blamed herself. And then she walked again and thought of the child psychology class and the things the teacher had warned them against. What utter folly they all seemed now, and how well she had followed their lead! "Let a child express itself."

Well, Betty was expressing herself!

Not once had they told the eager mothers what to do if a child went wrong and brought lifelong sorrow upon herself and her family! They had said if a child used bad words, you must not notice it. It was a phase. It would pass. They had said if a child rebelled against you, you must turn his attention to something else, soothe and engage him elsewhere, lead him to view the question from a pleasanter standpoint. But not once had they said anything about teaching your children right and wrong, teaching them to obey, to respect law and order. No, they had rather decried that attitude. No parent had a right to put limits upon his children. Who was to say what was right or wrong? The child's own inner sense would ultimately determine those things and so allow the young nature to develop without being warped or hindered or misshapen or biased according to ancient inherited dogmas and superstitions. Oh, she knew the phrases by heart! But they had never told her what to do when a child had gone wrong.

Well, right or wrong, Betty was gone. Where? The mother shuddered and knelt by her bed with wordless prayers upon her lips.

In the early dawn of the Sabbath morning Betty came to her senses with a breath of cold air blowing in her face. Somewhere in the air there was the vanishing sound of a crash, and there seemed to be splinters of glass all about her, for when she put out her hand feebly, she touched something sharp and brittle that crushed under her fingers, and afterward there was blood on her hand and face.

There were two men standing over where she was huddled, and before long they loosened the thing that confined her and lifted her out into the cold morning, stinging sharply on her cheeks, snow falling in great splotches on her forehead and eyes.

There was a large car standing a few feet away, and they opened the door and put her on the backseat, tenderly, as though there was something sad and terrible about it. Then they went back and left her there alone. She watched them idly, apathetically, from the window of the car, licking the snow from her lips where it had fallen and wondering what it was all about. She could see the two men working, bending over in the snow, lifting something, pulling, lifting again, and then they came toward her bearing something between them. They stopped and shook their heads and looked toward her, and laid it down, gently, oh, very gently, almost reverently. She wondered!

Why, it looked like Dudley! Where—? How? Where was she?

The two men came and asked her if she could sit up. It had not occurred to her that she was lying down until then. She said yes, and her voice sounded weak and far away, with a tremble in it. She wondered what was the matter with her.

The men lifted her into the front seat and tucked a rough blanket around her. They went back and picked up the thing that looked like Dudley and brought him and laid him in the backseat of the car, being very careful about it. She caught a glimpse of his face. It was ghastly, and streaked with blood. One arm hung limply down, and his hand was bleeding, too. Was there a cut across his cheek? She might have turned to look again, but she felt so weak and tired, and somehow her soul was revolted with the sight of him. She tried to shake off the daze and think back. Where had they been? What had happened? How had they got here in the road? She looked over to the broken car, scattered on the roadside, its bright-painted body splintered like a child's toy, its fenders ripped off and bent out of shape. How long ago was it that she and Dudley had been careening down that hill?

She closed her eyes with a dizzy memory and swooned away.

A long time afterward, it seemed, she came to herself again, and they were driving along a smooth road. There was snow only at the sides of the road now. The roadway was clear, and there were many cars coming and going, and houses and other buildings along the way.

The two men were talking. One of them was driving the car and the other sat in the backseat with the thing that was Dudley, holding him. She was glad she could not see behind her. She did not have to look. It sent a great wave of sickness over her to think of it. She heard the men saying something about a hospital. The nearest hospital.

"It might be a question of minutes whether the lad lives or dies," one said. "He's pretty far gone!"

Something froze within her. Suddenly the whole ugly business flashed across her consciousness. She and Dudley had been running away to get married, and they had come to this! And perhaps Dudley would die! Then would she be a murderer? And have her picture in the paper! And a terrible trial! And all the family have to come and hear the whole thing told out! They would tell how she had dropped her suitcase out of the window and stolen out of the house before daylight. They would have great big headlines in the newspapers: HIGH SCHOOL SENIOR RUNS AWAY WITH YOUTH WHO DIES IN SMASHUP! Father and Mother would be dragged through all that!

She thought of herself as she had been the night of the last high school dance, dressed in her rose petal taffeta. Betty Thornton, the star pupil of the school, the acknowledged beauty, the belle of the school! Herself, Betty, come to this!

She began to watch the way with a wild fascination. Dare she jump out and run away? Oh, she must not go to a hospital and have them ask her questions. She must never, never be discovered! And yet! Could Betty Thornton run away? When she had let Dud get into this mess, she would have to stand by!

She must have swooned away again, for the next time she knew anything the car had stopped in the din of a city street. In the distance was the outline of tall buildings against the sky, and in the immediate foreground loomed a many-storied brick building, which she seemed to understand was the hospital.

Some men in white linen coats hurried out, and two others came with a stretcher. She heard one of the men in the car say: "I thought we'd never get to New York with 'em! This here lad is far gone!"

So they were in New York at last! This was the way they had arrived! They had meant to be married in New York, and now Dudley was dying, dead perhaps already! It was ghastly! It couldn't be real! It must be she was asleep, dreaming. Perhaps she was really back in her bed at the farm having the nightmare!

The men in the linen coats had opened the car door and stepped in. They were lifting out Dudley and laying him on the stretcher. She tried to keep her eyes shut, but something made her look, and as she looked Dudley moaned, moving his swollen, cut lips. There was more blood on his face. It was horrible!

She closed her eyes and dropped her head sideways on the back of the seat and listened as they carried the stretcher with its ghastly burden up the steps and into the great building.

A hand touched her forehead, and then another hand was laid firmly about her shoulders. She looked up and saw a white-robed nurse looking at her kindly.

She looked down startled and saw a stretcher waiting to take her into the hospital. There was a smear of blood on one edge. She started to her feet in fright.

"Oh, no! I can walk!" she said. "Let me go home!"

"Are you able to walk?" asked the nurse kindly and helped her out of the car.

Betty's feet felt strange and weak. Her knees trembled. She stood uncertainly. One of the helpers came forward and put his arm about her, and the nurse helped her on the other side; so she walked, tremblingly, up those awful steps and into that grim building where they had taken that huddled form that was Dudley. Would she have to look at him?

The nurse put her into a wheelchair and pushed her down a long hall to an elevator. They went up several flights and she was wheeled down another hall to a little white room where they made her lie down on a white iron bed.

"But I've got to go—" protested Betty as she sank back on the pillow.

"The doctor must examine you," said the nurse, unfastening her coat and taking her hat off.

An interval followed in which Betty drowsed and realized

nothing. Then a doctor and another nurse came in and gave her a thorough examination, looking for broken bones.

"Does that hurt?" they asked her.

Betty assured them that it did not, although she had not much of an idea what it all meant. She had a feeling that she must please them all so that they would go away and let her alone and she might steal away from them. It was terribly hot around her now, and she was one big ache from head to foot.

"Mainly shock," she heard the doctor say. "Keep her quiet. Give her some nourishment. I've left a prescription."

The doctor went out, and the nurse gave her something in a spoon.

"I must get up," said Betty, trying to lift her head from the pillow.

"You'll have to have something to eat," said the nurse crisply. "I'll bring it." Betty reflected that she was faint. Perhaps that was the reason her legs felt so weak, and her arms and hands when she lifted them. It would be better to wait for breakfast. It wouldn't take long, and she remembered that she had no money.

The nurse brought hot milk and fed it to her in a spoon. It tasted good. She wondered that she had always despised hot milk.

Memories were beginning to drift into her mind. The morning she started. The place she had left her galoshes under a seat in the station in Springfield. Would they be there when she got back?

In a minute now when the nurse went out she would put on her shoes and her coat and hat and slip out. Nobody would know. They would think she was a visitor. The nurse had put her coat and hat in that peculiar long wardrobe at the foot of the bed. It would be easy to get away. And she would go to Aunt Florence's. Aunt Florence would help her. She wouldn't have to tell everything. She could make up some kind of an excuse for being in New York alone. She would think about it later when she got a little rested.

She closed her eyes and took the last few spoonfuls.

"Now," said the nurse, setting the cup and spoon down on the little stand by the bed, "you haven't told me your name yet. We have to have your name and address to keep our records."

Betty kept her eyes closed and breathed steadily. She didn't want to answer that question. Perhaps the nurse would think she was asleep.

The nurse brought her pad and pencil, and said:

"Now, what did you say your name was?" But Betty did not hear her. She seemed to be lying in her bed upstairs at the farm, with her father downstairs praying, and God standing out there somewhere in the room watching her.

The nurse went out in the hall.

"She dropped off to sleep before I got her address," she said to the head nurse. "Now, what'll I do? The doctor told me to phone her folks."

The head nurse consulted the card the doctor had given her:

"Better let her sleep," she said. "What her folks don't know won't hurt them, and the doctor's got her marked up as just needing to rest before she goes home."

So Betty slept.

From time to time the nurses flitted in and out of the little room where she had been taken for examination. They took her temperature, and they gave her medicine, and even fed her a few mouthfuls of broth, and still Betty slept.

She slept all through the long Sabbath day, while her mother was agonizing at the farm unable to get in touch with her father, while Chris kept the wires hot telephoning and telegraphing in various directions, while the children sat around disconsolately trying to amuse themselves, and Jane stood at the window and watched and grew strangely silent and mature.

It was Monday morning, bright and shining when Betty awoke.

She found that she had been undressed and put to bed properly. She stirred and found that she was able to move. She got up and stood upon her feet. They were shaky, but they would hold her. She could walk as well as ever.

She was nearly dressed when the nurse came in with her tray.

"Well!" said the nurse. She was a new one that Betty had not seen before. "Good morning. You're up already! And ready for the day. I hear you're to be dismissed this morning if you haven't any temperature. The doctor comes in about ten o'clock, and he'll look you over, and then I guess they'll let you go if he doesn't find any complications. I guess you'll be glad."

Betty smiled shyly.

"You're fortunate!" said the nurse. "The young man that was brought in the same time as you hasn't got conscious yet."

A horror filled Betty.

She did not feel like eating the breakfast that was spread before her, hungry as she was. She tried to ask a question, but it stuck in her throat.

"Is he— Then he isn't— He's—a–live yet?" she asked with blanching face.

"Oh, yes, he's alive. But he's got a fractured leg and arm and a fractured skull. They don't know, but they may have to trephine. They've sent for his folks. They found his driver's license and got 'em on the phone. The doctor wouldn't let anyone wake you. He said you'd be all right after you woke up, but you needed an unbroken rest."

Betty tried to eat a little of the fluffy omelet, but another question was sticking in her throat. Ought she to go and see Dud? Would they let her? It wouldn't be quite upright not to even ask about him. He had been unspeakable. It made her shudder to think of that terrible ride. She felt as if she never wanted to see him again. But she didn't want to run away and leave him. If he was dying she couldn't run away. Even if they thought she was the cause of his death! Even if they had her arrested for murder, she had no right to run away. It was yellow to do it. Something fine in her nature would not let her go without making some effort to help. She would have to stick by.

"Would they—" she paused to gather words— "could I go in and see him?"

"Oh, yes, I guess you could," said the nurse. "I could ask the head nurse. It couldn't do him a mite of harm I shouldn't think. He isn't conscious. Of course his folks aren't here yet—"

But Betty had to get to the bottom of this. She must know just how far she ought to be expected to go.

"Would I be allowed to—to—help him—any?"

The nurse gave her a keen look.

"What relation are you to him?" she asked curiously. "You ain't his sister, are you? You don't happen to be married to him, do you? You look awful young for that."

"Oh, no!" said Betty quickly, her cheeks growing scarlet. "I'm just a—just a—just an acquaintance. We were out taking a—a—ride together!"

"Mercy goodness!" said the nurse, aghast. "An' you were out at that time in the morning!"

Betty's cheeks flamed hotter.

"Oh, no," she said quickly, "it was early evening when we started," and then she realized that she was only making things worse.

"Good night!" said the nurse. "Then you musta lain on the roadside pretty near all night before anyone found you."

Betty looked down at her tray and poured cream on the dish of oatmeal.

"It was—pretty awful—I guess—" she tried. "I don't really remember much about it after the car began to go down the hill."

"Well, don't talk about it," said the nurse. "You best forget it as soon as you can. You've got to live, and you can't keep yourself upset

575

remembering things like that. I guess you could go in and look at him, but they won't let you stay. He's too sick. They won't let even his mother stay in the room when she comes. She'll mebbe take a room near here, but they don't let folks stay in the room much when a patient is so bad."

Betty brightened.

"You don't think I—that is, perhaps it would be polite for me to stay around till he was better. It doesn't seem just right to go off and leave him alone."

"Oh, my land, child! He ain't alone. His folks phoned for him to have a special nurse, two if necessary, and they're coming on this morning, too. They'll be here by noon or a little after. And even if you wanted, there wouldn't be any place for you to stay except the little sun parlor down the hall, and that's always full with visitors. This room is engaged for today. A girl. Operation. Appendicitis! She'll be in about three o'clock. The hospital's awful full now. You'd a been put in the ward if you'd been a regular case, but they had two women dying there last night, and one was hollering to beat the band. The doctor thought it would be better for you to rest in here, being as this wasn't occupied till today."

Betty shivered and drew a deep breath of thanksgiving. She had never realized before what depths of horrors there were that one might escape. She took another bite of the oatmeal and cream.

"I ought to pay something for all you've done for me here," she said, thinking aloud. "But I haven't got my pocketbook with me. I guess it got lost in the snow."

Betty remembered the meager two cents left in her pocketbook and wondered if that had been a lie. "I'll have to send something back when I get home."

"Oh, that'll be all right, I'm sure," said the nurse, smiling. "But don't your folks know about your accident? Aren't they coming to see you?"

"Why—my family"—Betty hesitated—"my family are out of town," she finished glibly, "and it wasn't worthwhile to worry them, you know. I—am—going to my aunt's. She didn't know just what day I was coming, so of course she won't worry."

"Well, that's fortunate, now isn't it? I always feel so sorry for the folks that have to worry. What pretty hair you have. It's naturally curly, isn't it? I always say that people that have naturally curly hair have the advantage of everybody else. Now, if you've finished your breakfast, I'll see if they will let you look at your friend."

She went out with the tray, and Betty felt suddenly cold and frightened and very young. Oh, if she only didn't ever have to see Dudley Weston again looking that way! It was too horrible! Why did people have to die anyway? What an awful world it was!

The nurse came back with permission for Betty to go to Dudley's room, and in fear and trembling she followed the nurse.

"He won't know you, you know," the nurse whispered as she opened the door, and Betty took a deep breath and stepped within the threshold casting frightened eyes at the bed.

But there was nothing of Dudley Weston there on the bed to recognize save the tip of his chin with the cleft in it, the cleft that used to make him so good looking. His hair had been cut away, and his head and face were swathed in bandages. Some of them were soaked in blood. His hands were bound up in gauze also, and one arm was in splints. There was a weight hanging at the foot of the bed from under the sheets, which the nurse explained was put there to keep the broken bone in place and stretch it so that if he got well one leg would not be shorter than the other.

If he got well!

She shivered at the thought of Dudley, bound up that way, with all those terrible possibilities hovering over him. Dudley the lithe, the athletic, the best dancer and tennis player in high school. Dudley, who was planning to be a polo player! Dudley whose pride was his grace of movement, his incessant activity! What if he should never walk again! What if one leg should be shorter than the other, like the Boyd boy who had to walk with a crutch! She could not picture Dudley a cripple.

Dudley was turning his head monotonously from side to side and babbling strange sentences that were utterly unintelligible. He frightened her and made her feel as if she were back in the car going down that steep incline while he shouted awful curses at the brakes! She began to cry softly and hid her face in her handkerchief, her little, crumpled, dirty handkerchief that had done overduty for the last forty-eight hours.

The nurse put her arm about her and led her from the room.

"I wouldn't feel so bad," she said comfortingly. "He might get well after all. The doctor said he had a chance."

A chance! Only a chance!

"If I only hadn't gone with him!" Betty sobbed, unaware that she was revealing herself.

"Well, now I wouldn't blame myself," soothed the nurse. "You know we can't help these things. What was to happen has to happen, I always say, and no good comes of blaming anybody. Like as not some other girl woulda gone if you hadn't uv."

Betty thought of the loud, coarse, common creature at Springfield and admitted to herself that this was probably true. Dudley Weston would always find a girl, of some kind. Yet she felt herself judged guilty by some finer moral judgment.

"You'd better lie down awhile now," said the nurse. "I'll just spread up the bed, and you can take a nice nap. You need it after going in there. It's kind of a strain, and you're sort of shaken up. You'll have plenty of time for a good rest before the doctor makes his rounds, and like as not he'll dismiss you."

Betty submitted to having her shoes taken off and being put to rest under a blanket. But as soon as the nurse's footsteps had died away down the hall she slipped up again and put on her shoes and her hat and coat. She did not want to wait for that doctor and more questions. She wanted to get away without having her name taken. She was fairly in a panic about it. It seemed as if her full senses had just come back to her. Also, she wanted to get away from Dudley in the room down the hall, moaning and turning his head from side to side. If she could do nothing she must get away. She could telephone afterward and find out how he was, but she must go quickly. If his father and mother were coming they would look after him.

She stole to the door and listened. There seemed to be nobody in the immediate vicinity of her room just then. There were two nurses down at the end of the hall walking, but their backs were turned. There was only an old woman with a mop and pail just going into the room next to hers.

She glanced down the hall in the other direction. The stairs were only a few feet away, with the elevator next to them, and the incessant bell sounding mysteriously in the passage. It seemed a propitious time to make an escape.

With another quick look around she opened the door, crossed the hall like a wraith, and slid into the stairway.

The stairs were white marble, a few steps and then a turn to a landing, then a few more steps and another turn. She was out of sight from the floor above in a moment.

Her knees felt shaky yet, but her fear of being held up and made to tell her name and address gave her strength to go on, down and around, turn after turn, floor after floor. She had no idea she had been brought up so far in that wheelchair in the elevator.

But at last she came to a hall that had a great arched doorway to the street and a row of patients sitting in line waiting to see the doctors.

She gave them one quick wild glance and hurried past them out through the door, into the noise and bustle of the street. No one had seemed to notice her; no one had tried to detain her or seemed to realize that she was a patient escaping before she had been dismissed, but she felt as if an army with banners were pursuing her.

At the first corner she turned and walked rapidly, feeling a little easier. Then suddenly she stopped, realizing that she did not know the name of that hospital. She could not send them money for what they had done for her, and she could not find out how Dudley was unless she knew where he was.

It took courage, but she turned back and went almost to the door till she was able to read the name on the great brick building. Then she walked to the corner on either side and read the signs of the streets and memorized them. She started on again, not caring which way she went, only to get out of that region. She kept repeating the names of the streets and the name of the hospital like a charm, and feeling very noble and satisfied with herself that she had compelled herself to go back and read those names.

Chapter 24

But after she had walked a good many blocks she suddenly began to feel very tired, as if she must sit right down on a doorstep and rest. She must get to Aunt Florence's at once and try to think what to do next. If she only had some money she could telephone Aunt Florence to come after her, but two cents wouldn't buy anything. Not anything! But a newspaper. And what would she want of a newspaper?

Well! She might buy a newspaper and look at the want advertisements and get a job. If she didn't feel so shaky all over that might be quite a thrill, something with a kick in it to tell forever after. Something she could even tell to Dudley with pride!

But somehow when she came to think about any kind of a kick she felt no enthusiasm. Her pep was all gone. She didn't seem to want anything but a bed to lie down upon. Perhaps she ought to have stayed longer in the hospital. She could have closed her eyes and pretended to be asleep if they came around asking for her name again. But then if Mr. and Mrs. Weston came in the room to see her they would know her. She wouldn't have to speak, or even look at them. They would know her at once and would probably telegraph

Dad and Mother, and there would be a mess in no time. No, she must fight this thing out with dignity. Having swung off from home she could not go back crestfallen and become subject to her parents again. That would be too humiliating!

So she began to take account of numbers, and discovered that she was walking downtown instead of uptown where Aunt Florence lived. Fortunately she knew Aunt Florence's address, away up in the hundred and eighties, on Riverside Drive. And this was only in the forties! It was going to be a long walk! Oh, if she only had a few pennies that she might take the bus!

After walking what seemed like weeks to her weary soul, she began to feel uneasy. Things did not look natural, and when she tried to cut across to where it seemed to her the right street ought to be, there loomed the park, wide and white and interminable. At last in desperation she went to a policeman.

It was quite against her ideas of what was proper for a modern young girl to have to ask advice from a policeman, but she was desperate, and little chills were beginning to creep down her back and up her ankles, clad only in their thin silk stockings, with thin little shoes on her feet.

"Yer wy off, miss," said the policeman, red haired and blue eyed and brusque, eyeing her trim little figure in its fur coat and modish little hat. "Ya mustav come up the wrong side of the pahk! Plenty of um does. You jus' stan' heah till a bus comes along goin' that wy, and you git on an' it'll tak' ye within two blocks uv yer house."

"Thank you," said Bett,y looking dismayed and hesitating at the curb.

"Right here, miss. I'll put ya on the right bus. Ya can't miss it."

Betty turned her big beautiful eyes upon him and seemed ready to cry.

"But—I've spent all my money," she said childishly. "I'll have to walk. Couldn't you tell me which way to walk?"

He looked her over thoughtfully from the crown of her pretty hat, which was pretty in spite of being somewhat battered, to the tip of her little scuffed patent leather shoe. He cast his blue eyes at the lowering sky and flicked a lazy snowflake from his sleeve.

"It's a good two miles, miss," he said. "Hundred and Eighty-Third Street. You can't make it across the pahk 'fore the storm breaks. We're due for more snow this afternoon. I better lend it to ya. I got a goil myself, ya know. The bus oughtta be comin' any minute. Heah she comes now. I'll jus' speak a woid to the driveh. He'll put ya off at the right place."

The bus was bearing down upon her as he spoke, and before she had time to protest he had signaled it and pressed a quarter in her hand.

"Oh, thank you," said Betty, "but won't you give me your address so I can return it? I couldn't let you—"

"Just bring it next time ya come this wy," he smiled. "Ask ennybody fer Pat."

He smiled and winked, and Betty found herself seated in the coach, with the conductor ringing up her fare.

Oh, it was good to sit down and rest, to close her eyes and forget just for an instant what an awful situation she was in. What would Dad and Mother say if they knew? But it would be all right when she got to Aunt Florence's. Aunt Florence wouldn't ask too many questions. She was a good sport. She wore imported hats and frocks and wasn't as straitlaced as Mother. She was Mother's youngest brother's wife, and Mother didn't quite approve of her, but Betty admired her with her whole soul. Aunt Florence belonged to the smart set of New York and went to nightclubs and never had a dull day. Betty had longed to visit her, but Dad and Mother had always managed to have a good excuse for declining all the New York invitations she had received.

It came to her as she rode along, through the white streets blurred with the scurrying flakes coming down closer together now, that she must arrange some tale to tell Aunt Florence before she reached the house. Well, why couldn't she just say that she was bored to death up there at the farm and took a notion to run away and spend Christmas in New York? From what she knew of Aunt Florence she would laugh and pinch her cheek, and maybe tell her to run and telephone to the folks so they wouldn't be scared, and say she was going to keep her the rest of the winter!

What a great thing that would be! To stay with Aunt Florence all winter during the lively season in New York, and go to nightclubs and plays and parties with her! My! That would be worth even the accident. Why hadn't she thought of just running away to New York? She could have pulled that off without Dudley Weston's help, and then all this awful mess wouldn't have happened.

And if she stayed the rest of the winter in New York, why, then everything would be quite smoothed over by spring, and Daddy would likely be only too glad to have her come home and to go back to Briardale, too. If she made that a condition of returning. Daddy would get over his social purity complex and maybe learn a thing or two in the bargain!

Betty's spirits were quite revived by the time the conductor motioned to her that she had reached her corner.

She got out in the falling snow and even enjoyed the refreshing bite of the flakes on her cheeks as she walked the few steps to her aunt's number.

As she stood waiting for the door to be opened she looked around with growing elation. The tall buildings filled her with joy. Apartment houses loomed in the background, and mansions were all about her. She had heard that a famous movie actress, of New York and Hollywood, owned the house two doors from here. Which was it, she wondered, up or down?

Then the door was opened grudgingly by an elderly woman in working garb.

Betty lifted her voice eagerly:

"Is my aunt—I mean is Mrs. Cassatt in?"

"No, Mrs. Cassatt ain't in."

Betty's face fell.

"Oh, well, I'll just come in and wait for her, then. When will she be back?"

"Mrs. Cassatt has gone to Palm Beach," said the woman frigidly. "She won't be back till spring."

Betty exclaimed in dismay:

"Oh, what shall I do? I've come to make her a visit. I didn't know she was going away. She said I was to come anytime I liked."

"Did you send her word you was coming, miss?" asked the woman, cruelly calm, eyeing her battered hat and the torn place on her fur coat.

"Why, no," said Betty. "I came in a great hurry, and I was going to surprise her!"

"She's been gone two weeks," said the woman. "There ain't anybody here but the caretakers."

"Well, I don't know what I'm going to do," said Betty. "You see, I've spent all my money. I haven't enough to get back home, and besides I've lost my suitcase on the way. I wonder if you could lend me some money till tomorrow. I could return it right away, you know."

The woman's eyes narrowed.

"That's a common dodge for beggars," she said. "You can't pull one like that off on me!"

Betty's cheeks flamed, and her eyes flashed. "I'm not a beggar!" she said haughtily. "I'm Mrs. Cassatt's niece, Betty Thornton from Briardale, Pennsylvania, and we are spending the winter up in Vermont at my father's old home on the Thornton farm."

"I never heard of no such people," said the woman dryly, her eyes hard and amused.

585

"Well, at least you can let me come in and telephone to my father to wire me some money, can't you?"

"We've had our orders to admit no one, miss!" said the woman curtly.

"Well, what am I to do?" asked Betty with her princess air.

"It's none of my concern, miss."

Betty stood stormily trying to think what to do.

"At least you can go in and telephone for me, then, can't you? Just say that Betty is here without money and will they tell her what to do, or wire some money or something? I can sit on the front steps till they come for me if you won't let me in the house. The number is—"

But the woman interrupted:

"No, miss, I won't do no telephoning for ye. I got no time to fool with beggars of any kind, and as for that old gag, you can't fool me. You're just tryin' to get into this house, and you ain't going to do it. As for settin' on the steps, just try it and I'll hand you over to the p'lice quicker'n you can think. Now, you better be moving on or I'll call the dog out. He's a p'lice dog and he's fierce. He don't like strangers!"

Betty tried to maintain her dignity, though the tears were very near to falling.

"I shall take care that my aunt knows how I was treated at her house when I was in trouble," she said as she whirled about and walked unsteadily down the steps.

"Help yourself," called the woman disagreeably. "I'm doing my duty, and ef you was doin' yours you wouldn't be here."

And with that wholesome truth she slammed the door and locked it noisily.

Betty walked out into the fast-falling snow and stared up and down the street, wondering what she should do now. She looked across the drive at the torpid black river with its border of dirty drifts, and wished she dared fling herself over one of those cliffs and down into the icy depths below. What was life worth anyway?

But life still had a hold on Betty, much as she might toy with the idea of youthful suicide. And when a big bus lumbered down and paused at her very side, she remembered the change from her quarter still in her purse and climbed on board. At least she could not continue to stand on the sidewalk in the snow.

As she settled back in her seat she realized that her feet were wet and her throat was beginning to burn roughly. Now she was getting a cold, she supposed. She must get somewhere out of the cold. There were chills going down her back again, and her limbs ached like a toothache. Her head ached and her eyeballs burned, and her soul burned with humiliation. To think she had been called a beggar and openly suspected of being a thief! Betty Thornton! How mortified Daddy and Mother would be!

And now she must sell her watch. It was the only thing she had that was worth much, but where should she go to sell it?

Following an impulse, she got off the bus in the shopping district and went into one of the largest department stores.

In the jewelry department where she made her request they eyed her suspiciously again. Betty flamed gorgeously as she looked the two men clearly in the eye while they took her watch and examined it.

She needed no rouge to make her cheeks vivid. The snow and the excitement and embarrassment had painted them crimson.

"Whose watch is this? Where did you get it?" asked one of the men.

"It is a very valuable watch," added the other man.

Betty looked up and tried to smile engagingly but only succeeded in looking frightened.

"It is mine. My father gave it to me. You'll find my name, Elizabeth Thornton, on the back of it. I wouldn't want to sell it permanently, you know. I wouldn't part with it for anything, but I spent all my money, and I must get enough to get home. I just want to leave my watch as security, and I'll be glad to pay something extra for your trouble, you know."

The two men looked at one another meaningfully and handed back her watch.

"We don't purchase secondhand jewelry," said the first man.

"You'd have to go to a pawnshop for that," said the second.

"Oh," said Betty pitifully. "Where is one? Could you send me to a respectable one? I thought they were all quite common places."

The two men did not smile.

"There is one around the corner, two blocks over and then turn to your right a block," said one of the men after a due pause. "It doubtless is common. But it is a pawnshop."

They bowed and left her standing amid the gorgeous display of jewels and silver and platinum, her little watch in her hand.

Slowly Betty walked out of the store, the two men standing together at a distance and following her with hard, suspicious eyes, like the Pharisees in sacred paintings.

Her feet were wet and cold. It seemed as if the bones were breaking in places when she walked. Her back ached, and her head was whirling and dizzy. The oatmeal and the egg she had taken at the hospital were long ago forgotten. Her stomach was empty, and she felt faint, but she was not hungry. She felt her throat growing sore again as she went out into the wet snow. She heard people saying that it was going to be a white Christmas, and wasn't it nice to have the fresh snow for tomorrow.

Christmas! Tomorrow was Christmas! And she was wandering about New York alone!

Of course she could always go back to the hospital, if she could walk there, for now she had not the price of another bus ride left. Yes, she could go back and grovel before Mr. and Mrs. Weston and disgrace her family forever. She could go back, and perhaps they would be glad to have Dudley marry her. She had heard that they said they wanted Dudley to marry young. She shuddered. She did not want to marry Dudley. She never wanted to see him again. That ride had cured her. She would never, never willingly go near him again. There were unspeakable things he had said and done on that awful ride that were burned into her memory and would always be there. She felt she would never be really happy again in this world. Yes, she could go back to the hospital and borrow money from Mrs. Weston. But she would rather to go over to one of those looming cliffs across the river and fling herself in than do that!

Having uttered that fiercely in her heart she went out into the snowy avenue, garlanded with holly and mistletoe, bordered with hemlocks and spruce and pine, filled with happy people going home with last packages. Christmas cheer everywhere and only Betty Thornton left out!

She turned around the corner and sought that pawnshop.

And then they gave her only ten dollars for her watch, her precious platinum watch with the little diamonds set about it. Would she ever see it again? Betty Thornton pawning her watch, her last year's Christmas gift from her father, to get money to go home!

"And when he had spent all. And when he had spent all!" Where had she heard that phrase, and why did it keep ringing over and over in her head now?

It had grown very dark while she was in the pawnshop. The old man with a hooked nose and a scraggly beard had kept her waiting a long time before he told her what he would give her for the watch, and when she faltered and told him it was very valuable and ought to bring more than that he swept it aside and told her he had more watches now than he knew what to do with, and people never came back for the things they pawned anyway. So she told him hastily that she would accept it and that she meant to send for her watch the very next day after Christmas!

When she came out of the shop the lights bewildered her, and she took the wrong turn and wandered eight or nine blocks out of her way before she discovered it. Frightened, she turned back again. She began to remember how her mother was afraid to have her out alone at night in city streets, and a strange kind of fright took possession of her. Betty Thornton, the little hard-boiled high school sport, was frightened all alone by herself in New York! She tried to shame herself out of it, but the tremor remained until at last she straggled into the great station, too weary to hardly drag one foot after the other.

It was fortunate perhaps that she should have gone to the restaurant before finding out what a ticket to the village below the farm would cost. But she was ready to drop with faintness and felt that food was the first consideration.

And then she was too weary to eat what she had ordered. She could only eat a little of the soup. When she tried the chocolate ice cream and the coconut cake that she had ordered, she found them too sweet, and the cold sent shivers down her back again. Her feet felt wet and cold, and her throat was decidedly sore now. Sore she was from head to foot, with a blinding headache.

When she gave up trying to eat and went to buy a ticket she found to her horror that she had not money enough to take her home.

She spread her money out before the ticket agent. There was a long line of impatient travelers behind her waiting their turn.

"That's all I have left," she said. "How far will it take me?"

The man counted it with a practiced eye.

"Take you to Weldon," he said. "That's thirty miles this side Wentworth."

The woman behind Betty reached out a gloved hand with a twenty-dollar bill clutched in it and waved it impatiently at the man behind the window:

"I want to get that next train!" she said in a loud tone. "All right!" said Betty wearily, "I'll go to Weldon." She had to wait nearly an hour for the next train. When she finally crept into a stuffy seat in the second-class car and curled up with her head on the window seat, she was too tired to think at all. She just wanted to keep still and try to endure the terrible pain in her back and the terrible ache in her head and the great mountain of a lump in her throat when she swallowed.

Fitfully she slept, apathetically she endured the hard seat, and the twist that came in her neck and shoulder from lying down against the windowsill, the chill that came from the crack under the window.

As the night went on the car grew very cold. If it had not been for her fur coat she would have perished. She was too far down in the depths of weariness and despondency to question what she should do in the morning. She had not even inquired what hour her train reached Weldon. It is doubtful if she would have taken in the added catastrophe if she had known it was due there at four o'clock in the morning.

However, a kindly overheated bearing delayed the train an hour and a half, and it was not until half past five that a long-suffering conductor hunted her up and shook her gently, though gruffly, telling her it was time to get out.

She stood dazedly on the platform of the little closed station and watched her train amble away into the white darkness of the chill before the dawn. When its last red twinkle died into the darkness she turned around and looked about her.

Everything was still and dark. There seemed to be no one about anywhere. White arc lights blazed overhead with that appalling brilliance that lights can assume in a deserted station in a lonely spot at unearthly hours. Little white houses with green shuttered windows huddled along a straggling street. The snow had fallen anew here, too, for all the trees were outlined in white velvet and stood out against the dark like the nerves of a skeleton. There was almost an uncanny stillness over the white dark world. And not a soul in sight!

Betty tried the door of the station. It was locked. Dim lights were burning inside. Perhaps someone slept there. But though she pounded on the door till her knuckles ached it brought no response. The telegraph machine clicked away to itself: *"Cluck-cluck-cluck! Cluck!—Cluck!"* Like a deaf old man who was snoring and would not listen. A little mouse inside ran across the station floor, and its plush feet echoed like a clatter in the empty room. It was weird.

In despair she turned away and walked to the end of the platform.

There was an arc light here and a signpost. She came nearer and read it: WENTWORTH 41 MILES! A finger pointed out through the village on a road well rutted by vehicles.

Chapter 25

She looked back at the station looming in the dark, with no seats offering friendly help. Not even a packing box to sit on! What should she do? She couldn't stand here till daylight. One lonely place was no better than another. Why not start on? She would be warmer than standing here in the wind.

So with feet that were stiff and sore from her day's walking, with flimsy shoes that were scarcely more than half-dry, with silk stockings of gauzy film, she stepped out into the snow and started on her journey. Forty-one miles! And then three on top of that to the farm! Would she be able to make it? Oh, if she only had her galoshes that she left behind the wastepaper basket in the waiting room in Springfield, years and years and years ago!

The new-fallen snow was soft and feathery, and the track had not yet been beaten through it. As she put her foot down, it would sink in some places up to her ankles. Her shoe was low cut, and the snow rushed in beneath her instep and nestled about her foot with a chilling embrace that was sickening. She became more conscious of her sore throat and her aching head, and with a wild thought of plunging through and getting somewhere quickly she started to run.

But running in a rough road was a most uncertain matter, and more than once she lost her footing and fell. Once she pitched sideways into a drift and plunged her arms into the snowbank beyond their depth. It was not easy to rise again, and when she did she found there was snow inside her sleeves and up her arms.

The hour too was almost uncanny, gray dawn fighting with the rising day, the streets of the little town deserted as if the inhabitants were long dead. She rose and fled along once more, now gaining a footing on a sidewalk that offered firmer walking. Here she could stamp the snow out of her shoes and shake it out of her sleeves. She even stood on one foot at a time and took off her shoes and emptied them, brushing off the snow from her icy feet. That made her feel a little more comfortable. And so she hurried on.

But even the sidewalks came to an end very soon, as the houses grew fewer and farther apart. At last she came to the beginning of the open country again. The sidewalk ended abruptly, in a great drift of snow like a barrier that must be surmounted before she could get into the road again. She was in despair. How could she go on? Her feet were terribly cold, and if they got wet again they would surely freeze stiff.

She retraced her steps till she came to a house where the way had been cleared in front of a gate to the road and a stepping-stone bridged the curb. She stood poised an instant before stepping out again into that horrible cold mass and tried to think of something she might do to keep her feet from actually freezing. If she only hadn't been too proud to wear her galoshes!

She was wearing a scarf of soft silk, long and wide, and very gauzy in texture, painted over with flowers. It had been a gift on her last birthday, and in her extravagant love of show she had been wearing it to school the day she was taken away. She looked at it now, dubiously, her lovely scarf! But it must be sacrificed. She would freeze if she did not do something.

Ruthlessly she unwound it from her neck and tore it in two. Then sitting down on the horse block, with a furtive glance toward the still-sleeping frame house set back from the road, she took off her little shoes and carefully wound each foot with the scarf. It took several experiments before she was able to get her foot back into her shoe with the added folds of silk, but at last she stumbled up to her feet again and started on. For a little while she did feel more comfortable, although the lumpy folds of silk make it hard to walk. But her feet were getting so numb now that a little thing like that did not seem to matter so much.

She had gone what seemed to her about ten miles, stumbling and falling, slipping back each step sometimes, till it seemed she made little progress, when she came at length to another signpost. Eagerly she read the mileage: WENTWORTH 39 MILES. All this long, cold, terrible way, and she had gone only two miles! How could she ever get there? Her feet were absolutely numb now. They were so cold that stinging pains were going up her limbs. She had a feeling that before long her feet would be frozen solid like icicles, and perhaps snap off at some careless step, and leave her lying there in the road with no one to know.

All at once home and Mother and Father and her siblings loomed large and dear in her life. Suppose she should die there in that lonely road, and not be found for days, and word never even get to her family that she had died. Strangers would pick her up and take her to the morgue!

She shuddered and plunged forward again with a sickening feeling that she must, even though it was no use. Every step she got nearer to Wentworth meant that much more of a chance that they would at least know sometime that she had tried to come home.

A wind had risen, gradually, blowing the snow around and flinging it into her face sharply, stingingly. It bit into her like venomous insects and added one more source of discomfort.

She had reached the top of a hill where the fields on either side were windswept and barren and where the snow had drifted over the fence tops and obliterated the lines of them completely. It had even eddied across the road, obliterated the tracks of the last few weeks, and wiped out the way for some distance into a smooth blanket of deep white. She paused at the brow of the hill and looked across in new dismay to the vague lines of snowcapped fences in the distance and tried to determine just where the road might be.

She took a few steps forward and found that the drifts were not so deep, that she could plunge through provided she kept in the track of the road. But the least misstep brought her down in snow beyond her depth. Then she would look back and try to get her bearings again, but the downward trend of the road had carried her out of sight of the fences behind, and she had nothing to guide her except that vast expanse of whiteness ahead going down to the valley, with vague tracings like quilting in a patchwork of snowfields.

Nevertheless she tried bravely to stumble on, frightened and weary. It seemed as though her heart was a pump that would not work, and her breath hurt in her chest, and stung maddeningly in her nostrils, as she labored.

The snow was growing deeper now, and she realized that she must be off the road again, or else the drifts were deeper. How was she ever to go on? Her feet felt like leaden weights, and once or twice when she fell she stayed down in the snow for a moment to rest and get her breath again. The pain in her throat was like a knife cutting when she tried to swallow, and her head ached as if it were going to burst. The tears were rolling down her cheeks, blinding her at times, yet she was not conscious of crying. Once she put up her hand to see why her cheeks were so cold and found the tears frozen on her lashes and her face.

It was just then, bewildered and frightened, that a new

predicament arose. She had stepped into snow a little deeper than she had yet found, and her numb feet refused to lift themselves and go another step. It was as if they had suddenly been turned to stone, loaded with lead, and all the efforts of the brain and heart could not make them take another futile step in that deadly white way.

Crying out at last with a weak little bleat like a lost lamb, Betty leaned forward with her hands against the snow to make one last effort and plunged forward, her arms sinking in to the shoulders. Snow inside her sleeves, snow inside all her garments, snow against her bare flesh! Snow that felt warm like a blanket compared to the chill of her flesh! Good snow! Kind snow! She lay upon it like a tired child in the arms of a great mother.

She thought of the stories she had read of quicksand and people sinking to their death. But this was not quicksand. It was more like a mammoth feather bed in which she was sinking, sinking down, and would soon be out of sight. If she opened her eyes she could look across the snow and down to those interminable white fields stretching their vastness away to the rim of the world and no help anywhere. She had taken herself out of the realm of her family, the only ones in the wide world who really loved her! Betty! A lost lamb on the snowy mountain.

The gray morning came up, with a sullen sky, the morning that was to have been Christmas Day, and Betty Thornton lay out alone on a billow of snow, slowly freezing to death.

She had read that people freezing to death did not suffer pain. It was true, then. She was satisfied to lie here and rest. The things that hurt, her chilled feet, the aching in her back, and the pull on her tired limbs and heart, were gone. Even the sting of the cold in her nostrils was not so bad when she did not have to breathe much, and her throat did not hurt so much if she did not try to swallow. She would go to sleep a little while, and perhaps when she woke up the sun would shine and the snow would be melted at least enough to show her the way.

She closed her eyes with a little sob and let her body rest down in the feathery bed of snow, and suddenly she could hear the family singing the old song, down in the living room of the farmhouse. Chris's baritone and Daddy's tenor. Jane singing also and Mother carrying the soprano all alone, her voice sounding weak and trembling like a sob in the end of the words, and Betty not there to help! She tried to open her lips and sing. Perhaps they would hear her and come to help her out. But when the sound came out in a little cracked squeak her throat hurt her so terribly that she had to give it up. But what were those words they were singing, the words she had formed with her lips but could not utter?

> *"While I draw this fleeting breath,*
> *When my eyelids close in death,*
> *When I rise to worlds unknown,*
> *See Thee on Thy judgment throne."*

Then she was dying. This was almost her last breath! Her eyelids were closing in death, and she was going to an unknown world. There would be a judgment throne, and she would be tried for all the things she had done that were wrong and for all the things she ought to have done that were right. And God would be there!

Suddenly she knew that God was there now, out there in the white fields just beyond; that He had been out there all the time looking at her in His kind, sad way, watching how far she had gone away from home. She had tried to get away from Him but she had only got away from those she knew and loved, and God who frightened her had come along. She could not get away from God!

She could hear her father praying now with agonized tones, kneeling on the snow out there, with his head bowed and tears in his voice, or was it in the living room at the farm he was kneeling?

She was not sure. It was not at home in Briardale, she was sure of that, for he never prayed in Briardale except sometimes in church, a very formal polite prayer that had not seemed like prayer at all and had not bothered her in the least. But he was praying now, in tones that tore her young heart: "Oh God, find my little Betty! Save my little Betty!" She could hear it over and over again, with the tears in his voice, and her mother sobbing in between; Jane sobbing too, and Chris wiping his eyes—and even little Doris and John crying, kneeling there beside the old sofa and crying, or was it out in the snow? She could not tell. Strange that she could see them all so plainly, hear them, too, and she could not make herself known to them. But perhaps she was already dead. Her feet were dead, anyway. It was a long time since she had felt them at all. And there was something packed away inside her lungs that made it hard to breathe. It hurt like a knife now when she tried.

And God was out there yet. She had not opened her eyes but He was there! Yes, she must be dead already, and this was the judgment God had come for. So, there *was* a God after all! The teachers in high school had not known. Was Dudley dead, too? Did he know, too, that there was a God? Would they be judged together for what they had tried to do?

It was just then, perhaps, that Betty suddenly grew up and became a woman.

~~~

Chester had not received any of the frantic messages that were sent to him. He had not gone to the places where he might reasonably have thought to go. He had found one or two important matters that must be attended to at once, and he had used every minute of time and attended to them, with the one object in view, to get back to the farm Monday evening and spend Christmas Eve with his family. He had not even taken time to call on the phone, he was going back so soon. Instead he took the time to purchase gifts—not the gifts he had planned for them on that evening when he had first known of his new prosperity, but sensible things that could be used on the farm and make the winter in the cold and isolation a delight. He telephoned an order for skis, and snowshoes and a new kind of sled for sledding and some better skates and warm sweaters, and a lot of games that could be played indoors on stormy days. He bent his every energy to getting back, that this Christmas might yet be one of the happiest that they had ever spent together.

He reached the farm about nine o'clock Christmas Eve and burst through the door with a shout of welcome.

They all came rushing to meet him, Eleanor with tears upon her face, eager expectancy in her look.

"Oh, have you found her?" she cried as he stooped to kiss her. "Where is Betty? Didn't you bring her back with you? Oh, *couldn't* you bring her back? Was it too late?"

She looked with blank eyes past him to the closed door where no Betty stood as she had hoped.

"Bring her back?" said Chester. "Back from where? Has Betty gone down to the village alone at this time of night? Surely you didn't let her go alone!"

It was a long time before they could make him understand, and finally Chris had to break in:

"Now, Muth, dear," he said gently, "you just wait, and let me han'l this! I'll tell Dad. He left me in charge!"

And so they finally made the whole terrible story clear.

It appeared that they had done every one of the things that he suggested eagerly as the story was unfolded. Yes, they had telephoned this one and that; yes, they had wired to all the stations. Yes, they had—

He walked the floor in his first frantic realization of truth that Betty had been gone three days, and no word had come from her.

It was too late to hope to stop the folly of a marriage. Too late to do anything but try to find her and keep her from further folly if possible.

"It is all my fault!" he exclaimed as he wheeled at one end of the room and started pacing back again. "I have not been the right kind of a father! I have not watched my children! I am like Eli. My children have become vile, and I have not restrained them! It is my fault, and now my punishment has come!"

"Oh, but I am her mother!" broke out Eleanor, sobbing as if her heart would break. "I have not been the right kind of a mother—"

"Stop!" said Chester, pausing before her and laying his hand on her bowed head. "You have been a wonderful mother! You have not gone out into the world to know the world as I have. You did not know—"

"Oh, I knew," said Eleanor, "but I did not believe it was true. I didn't think such things could ever happen to us. I thought people were exaggerating! Oh, if I could *only* go back and have Betty in my arms again, a little baby, I would do so differently. Those people who are teaching child psychology don't know. They ought to be told that they are doing mothers harm—"

"They are blathering idiots!" said Chester viciously. "But that does not let us off. We were brought up in the fear of the Lord, you and I, and somehow we have failed to hand it on to our children. They have lost the sense of sin! They have lost the sense of right and wrong. I saw that the night I went out after Betty! I saw that when I found Jane dancing a vulgar dance in a drugstore for the edification of a lot of dirty-minded fellows. I saw it later when the letter came—"

He became aware of Chris's miserable eyes upon him and little Jane's dark head down upon the arm of the sofa as she huddled in its corner, her eyes smoldering with unhappiness.

"But we must not think of that now. We must do something!

You have been wonderful, Chris, I'm proud of you. But now I think that we cannot any longer keep this thing quiet. I will try to get in touch with Mansfield, our New York man who handles all the office detective work. Perhaps he can think of something else to do. Chris, you say you tried to get in touch with the Westons, how lately?"

"This afternoon," said Chris, comforted that his father was satisfied with his action. "They are gone to New York, but the servant didn't know the address."

"Well, I'll get Mansfield at once if I can. It's a bad night, Christmas Eve, to expect to get anybody, but we'll be able to find out something. Perhaps they'll broadcast it tonight, though I'm afraid it is too late to get in now."

"Oh, Chester!" wailed Eleanor. "Must we do that?"

"I'm afraid we must, dear, if we want results. But I'll see what Mansfield says—"

"But Chester, you must have some supper." Eleanor sprang up and went toward the kitchen.

"No, Eleanor. Not now. I couldn't eat!" said Chester. "Not now. You go to bed. You look completely exhausted. I'll come up and tell you what he says when I get him."

"But just a cup of coffee—"

"No, Eleanor. Not now. I couldn't swallow it. I'll get something when I want it."

Chester went into the library and shut the door. They heard the telephone ringing now and then; they heard Chester's low voice talking and then long silences. The household settled to sleep at last, feeling the burden of responsibility rolled from their shoulders to a certain extent, feeling greatly comforted to have the husband and father at home again and undertaking.

But Chester, in the room below as he waited for Mansfield, who was reported to be out of town for a few hours, was kneeling beside his mother's old rocking chair, praying. By his side on his father's desk the old Bible was spread open, for Chester had been reading the word of God concerning Eli, trying to find some hope for his own sin. And when he could not find it he bowed in deep anguish and prayed, "Oh, God, forgive me! Have mercy upon me, a sinful father, that I have not seen nor knew what was coming to my children, and have not restrained them. Oh, God, have compassion on my little Betty! Oh, God, *find* my little Betty! *Save* my little Betty!"

Chapter 26

Out across the miles of snowy fields the echo of that prayer hovered in the air as it went up to the throne of God, its wavelengths lingering about through the gray dawn, while the father knelt and poured out his heart in the same words again and again: "Save my little Betty! Oh God, *find* my little Betty!" From heaven's broadcasting station perhaps that prayer went back till Betty's heart tuned in and heard—Betty, lying in the cold white snow, listening to her father's prayer that had gone up to God and was sent back to her. Betty, finding God still following her, standing apart, across the snows of Christmas morning!

All had gone blank out there on the snow. Betty could no longer hear her father's voice in prayer. She felt alone, forsaken! But God was still there. She could not rise nor look, for her body seemed to have gone dead, but she knew He was there.

Suddenly a hand touched her on the shoulder. She was surprised. She opened her eyes and saw a face bending over her and two pleasant eyes looking into hers.

"Are you God?" she thought she heard her own voice ask, her little frozen voice.

"No," said a kindly voice, "but I'm God's child! What are you doing here, sister?"

"My feet are dead," she answered out of the case of fire and ice in which her body seemed to be fastened. "I think perhaps they are broken off."

He stooped and lifted her in strong arms, and she felt the sucking bed of snow release her from its deadly hold.

She was too tired to look up, except for a glance at the kindly face and the pleasant eyes upon her, eyes that looked as though the sunshine was in behind them somewhere.

There was an old Ford standing out there in the road about five yards from the place where she had fallen. She wondered how it had got there without her hearing it. He put her in the backseat, brushing the snow from her garments. He unwound the tattered silk about her ankles that had slipped down farther and farther until they were mere ribbons cluttering about her feet.

"You poor kid!" he said as he unfastened the little inadequate shoes. "You poor kid! Your feet must be frozen!"

"Oh, are they there yet?" said Betty, rousing from the stupor into which she had immediately sunk. "I thought they were broken off!"

He cast a furtive, anxious glance at her flushed face and caught the hoarse rasp of her voice as she coughed. He took off his big driving gloves and took her cold, cold feet in both of his warm hands and rubbed them.

"You poor kid!" he said gently.

She laughed hoarsely.

"I ran away to get married," she said, laughing again deliriously, "and I left my galoshes in the station!"

He gave her a quick keen glance.

"Where do you live? Who are you?" he asked in a quiet voice, not at all as if it mattered or were anything to make her excited.

"I'm Betty Thornton," she babbled. "I live in Briardale when

I'm home, but we're spending the winter at the old farm beyond Wentworth. I'd better get out and go on. I'm on my way home. It's getting late and my head is hot and my feet are cold, or else it's the other way around."

The young man looked at her anxiously as he took out a suitcase and began to search for things.

"How long have you been on your way?" he asked, pulling out a pair of long gray woolen golf stockings and drawing them over her feet.

"Since the stars came out," said Betty unintelligibly. "The car rolled down the hill and the glass broke, and there was one star God had in His hand! God was there!"

She looked at the young man anxiously as if she wanted to be assured that she was right.

"Yes, God is always there," affirmed the young man quietly. "Now, drink this coffee. It's still hot."

He unscrewed the top of a thermos bottle and poured out the last few swallows of coffee. He tipped the little metal cup to her lips and she tried to swallow, but the knife was there in her throat.

"There's ice in my throat," she explained, looking at him wildly. "I shall have to wait till it melts."

"Drink the rest of this. It will help to melt the ice!" he urged, and Betty swallowed again, obediently, and sank back on the folded coat he had laid under her head.

She did not open her eyes when he tucked a blanket about her. She felt herself sinking into a deep place now that was as hot as she had been cold a little while before. She was thinking that God's child had kind eyes. They were nice eyes. They comforted her. She liked to hear him say, "Poor kid!"

While Chester was still upon his knees crying to God, confessing his sin, and praying for mercy on his child, the shabby Ford turned into the lane and plowed its way up to the old farm.

Betty's mother was the first one at the door.

She had come downstairs to prepare breakfast, anxious for her man, tiptoeing about lest she wake him, not daring to open the library door lest she disturb him, yet anxious to know what he had done during the night.

The throb of the car roused the house. Chris was down almost at once, and Jane, calling from upstairs at the window:

"It's Betts, Muth! But that's not Dudley Weston with her! Who can it be?"

Eleanor did not hear Jane. She had flung wide the door and with her hand fluttering to her throat was standing wide eyed looking out, her intuition telling her that this was no ordinary news that was about to be revealed.

"While they are yet speaking, I will hear," was the promise that Chester Thornton had read as he knelt before the old Bible.

He was still praying, "God, find my little Betty!" when John flung the library door wide and called excitedly:

"Dad, come quick! Betty's come home, and she's awful sick!"

They carried Betty upstairs to her bed in the bright Christmas morning, for the clouds had cleared and the sun was sparkling over everything, but Betty did not recognize it. She tossed on the big, cool bed and thought it was a field of snow. She looked in her mother's face and did not know her. Two white-robed nurses took up their station around her bed before long, and two noted physicians from New York came in consultation with the little country doctor from Wentworth, and all that skill and science could do was being done for Betty Thornton.

Downstairs the Christmas tree, partly decked in its tin stars and paper frills, stood neglected and desolate. The children stole by it without looking. It seemed a desecration now to think about Christmas with Betty so sick.

The white-haired minister drove up every day in the old Ford to find out how the little patient was doing. Once or twice he came up into the room and knelt beside Betty's bed and prayed, while her mother wept outside the door, and her father stood beside her, his arm about her and a look of utter anguish on his face. The minister's son did not come in. He did not want to intrude, but he always asked anxiously, "How is she?" when his father came back to the car.

The Christmas season passed without a celebration. Anxiety held the household in its grip. Even John and Doris learned how to sigh, and one day Eleanor caught Jane at the window crying.

"Betty had no right!" she explained when her mother asked what was the matter. "She had no right to spoil Christmas for us all. She oughtta uv thought of other people a little!"

"Hush, darling," said her mother. "If Betty will only come back I think perhaps she'll understand that now—"

"Come back?" said Jane with a quick catch of alarm. "Won't she come back?"

"We hope so, darling, but the doctor isn't sure!"

"Well, why did she have to do something to upset everybody else? If she wanted to be silly she'd oughtta uv found some way that wouldn't hurt her family."

"When people do wrong, Janie dear, they never do it alone. They always bring consequences on other people. We're all bound up in the bundle of life together, and a man or woman or girl or boy can't sin in any way without hurting others."

The day came when Betty turned feverish eyes upon them all and demanded:

"Where is God's child? I want to see him."

And for hours she kept asking the same question.

They did not know what she meant, and they sent for the old minister, who knelt beside her bed and prayed.

She stared at him with eager eyes.

"You are nice," she said, looking at him intently, "but you are not the child of God. He warmed my feet and brought me to my father's house. I want to see him. I want to ask him a question."

"Ah," said the minister, smiling kindly, "I think it is my son David that you mean. He is a child of God. I will send for him!"

And that night David Dunham left his studies in a far city and journeyed up to Vermont in answer to his father's call, but he did not borrow his roommate's Ford this time. He caught the fast express, and was at home as soon as steam and rail could bring him.

"Well, sister," he said, sitting down beside the bed and taking her little hot hand in his, "I am the child of God you sent for. What can I do for you?"

She turned her restless eyes upon him, and her voice was full of pleading:

"Oh, won't you ask God not to judge me for letting Dudley take that drive?"

"And who is Dudley?" asked David Dunham kindly.

"Dudley is the boy I was going to run away with, and he wouldn't have got killed if I hadn't gone."

There was great distress in her voice. Chester and Eleanor looked at one another in dismay. This was the first they had heard of Dudley. Had Dudley been killed? What terrible experience had their beloved child been passing through without them? Or was this some wild raving of delirium?

The anxious young voice went on:

"Won't you tell God not to look at me? He keeps looking at me all the time. He thinks I'm unclean! He thinks I'm foul! My father said so. And He keeps looking at me all the time. Won't you tell Him to stop?"

David Dunham turned his clear eyes on the sick girl. He took hold of the little hot hand that Betty held out pleadingly, with his big cool grasp, and spoke quietly, commandingly, to her:

"Listen, sister! Didn't you know that Jesus Christ has opened a fountain for sin and for uncleanness? Long ago He shed His blood to make a fountain to wash away our sins. He wants to make you clean, sister, that's why He is looking at you."

"But I'm afraid of blood!" she cried, clinging to his hand. "There was blood on Dudley Weston's head and face. There was blood on the stretcher they carried him on—I couldn't wash in blood!"

"This is Christ's blood, sister. It is not human blood. Human blood could not wash us from sin, but Jesus' blood can wash us whiter than snow!"

"Oh, did you have to be washed, too? It that why you look so much like God?"

"I certainly did, sister. We all have to be washed."

"But won't it hurt?" Betty's eyes were full of fear.

"I'll say it won't!" said the young man with a light in his face. "You just ask Him, and it's done, just like that!"

"You ask Him, won't you? I'm afraid."

David Dunham knelt by the side of the bed, the little hot hand still in his, and began to pray:

"Oh, God, our Father, in the name of Jesus, who died to make us clean from sin, please wash this young woman, and make her free from sin forever. Put her behind the blood now, and make her Thy child! Wash her and make her whiter than snow, for Jesus' sake who loved her and died for her."

When the prayer was ended she looked in his face eagerly.

"Is that all? Is it done?" she asked.

"Yes, it is done. You can trust Him to take care of all the rest."

"Then I'm going to sleep," she said with a sigh. "I was afraid to go to sleep before."

Her hand still in his, she closed her eyes and lay quiet.

Suddenly the big troubled eyes opened again.

"I ought to go back and tell Dudley," she said anxiously. "Dud doesn't know, and he's a *mess*!"

"Dudley shall be told," promised Dunham quickly, and the white lids fluttered down, content.

For a long time David Dunham knelt beside the bed with Betty's hand lying lightly within his own, his head bowed, his eyes closed. And Betty fell into the first natural sleep she had had since he brought her home.

The doctor had waved them all away and told them that if she could sleep a few hours there was hope, so the house was still as still could be. When Dunham at last came downstairs, his face wearing the look of one who had just had audience with the King, Chester met him with extended hand.

"I can't thank you enough," he said, his voice unsteady with feeling. "You've saved our little girl's life the doctor tells me. I shall never forget it. You are a wonderful young man."

David returned the handshake warmly.

"Don't say that, Mr. Thornton," he answered. "Say we have a wonderful God! It was God who reached down and gave peace to your daughter."

"It was you who made her ready to receive it."

"No," said David, "it was the Holy Spirit. He only used me as a humble instrument. And now, Mr. Thornton, who is this Dudley? I promised I would see him."

Chester's face grew hard.

"He is a vile little beast who is trying to lead my daughter astray," answered Chester fiercely. "It is his fault that she is lying there. I would rather have nothing to do with him. He is not worth it. I hope that Betty may never see his face again!"

"I surmised as much from what she told me on the way home, although I do not think she knew what she was saying," said Dunham. "But still, I'd like to keep my promise. Could you give me his address? I shall not of course mention you in the matter. I would do it wholly on my own initiative."

"Thank you," said Chester. "That's good of you, of course. I would really prefer not to have our family drawn into the matter at all. I do not know yet just how far Betty has involved herself. Of course she was not able to give any connected account of herself. She has been in delirium ever since you brought her home."

"I surmised from phrases she kept repeating on the way home that there had been some sort of an accident, and that the young man was in a hospital, either dead or dying. She kept saying over and over the name of the hospital and the street it was on. I am sure it must be in New York."

"You don't say!" said Chester, startled. "That's awkward! I suppose somebody ought to find out. The Westons are neighbors of ours in Pennsylvania, but people whom we don't much care for. We have not had much to do with them. I wonder if they know where their son is. I don't want to be unchristian, of course, but really the boy has been unspeakable, and I would like to spare Betty any connection with the matter if I could. However, we must not be inhuman—"

"Suppose you let me inquire into things," offered Dunham. "I am a stranger and can find out how things are before you make any move."

"Thank you! I'd be grateful for that," said Chester, bowing gravely, trying to keep the anger out of his voice. "You can't understand, perhaps, how bitter I am toward the young man who led my daughter into a situation like this. Or, if she was partly to blame, as I am afraid she was, who allowed her to go through this awful experience, who has compromised her—"

"I can understand!" said David quickly. "I'd like to go out and thrash him this minute myself. But it seems as if perhaps God may have taken it out of our hands and is dealing with him Himself."

Chapter 27

David did not lose time in locating the hospital where Dudley Weston was. It had been easy, for Betty had babbled the name and the streets over and over on the way home as if it had been a lesson she was memorizing, and David had written them down lest it might be important later. He inquired about the young man and found that he had just passed through an operation on the skull that they hoped was going to be successful, that he was doing as well as could be expected considering the injuries he had sustained, and that his parents were with him. David asked how soon he might receive visitors and was told that it would be at least a week before anyone outside his family would be admitted.

"And now," said David as he turned away from the telephone to face Chester who had been sitting near, "I guess there isn't anything to do but pray about it for a while. I'll just ask guidance. And when he's able to see me I'll run down to New York and try to get a heart-to-heart talk with him. I shouldn't think there was any obligation upon you to do anything just now either, Mr. Thornton. Your daughter is too ill for you to have time or thought for anything else. The lad is evidently being cared for and in need of nothing that we can do at present. Besides, you're not supposed to know what has happened. I should think you might well afford to wait until your daughter is able to tell you more about the situation. I'll keep you informed of what I may discover. And the way will open up. It always does, when we put the problems in His hands."

"I'm afraid I've never got in the habit of that," said Chester humbly. "It's going to be hard to have any sympathy whatever with such a young viper as that boy is."

At the doctor's request David Dunham stayed at the farm until Betty had passed the crisis and was decidedly on the way to improvement. He said that he did not care to risk having David away if she should suddenly ask for him, that he had been more valuable than any medicine. So David stayed, although it meant hard work when he got back to make up for the lost time.

But Betty did not ask for him again. She did not even seem to remember anything about what had passed between them when she finally woke up one morning with a weak smile and looked intelligently into her mother's face. She was almost like a baby for a few days, only able to smile a little and lift her hand a few inches to sign what she wanted. She seemed too weak and tired for words, a frail, sweet shadow of the Betty that had been. She crept slowly, hesitantly back to life again. And after a few days, when it was a thoroughly established fact that she was going to get well, David Dunham went back to his studies.

On his way he stopped over in New York and sought out the hospital. Somehow he managed to meet with Dudley Weston. Under guidance of the Lord, with Spirit-given tact and preparation on his knees, the young man waited until a favorable opportunity presented itself, with the elder Westons both away for the afternoon. In fact, it developed that they were not especially devoted to wasting much time in whiling away the weary hours of their only son while he stayed in the hospital.

It was like David Dunham to hunt around until he found an old schoolmate who had gone into medicine and was serving an apprenticeship in the very hospital where Dudley had been taken. Having reestablished his old friendship with the young intern by a few minutes' talk, and well knowing that an intern has no time for company, he said he would just stroll through the halls and wait around till his friend had some time off and they could go out together for lunch. There was a lad up in the private ward to whom he was taking a message. No, he wasn't a personal friend, in fact wasn't known to the young man, but he had a reason for wanting to meet him. Was there any way he could be casually introduced? The name was Weston, Dudley Weston.

The doctor eyed him curiously.

"Sure," he said. "I'll take you up. But you won't like him. He's not your kind, Dave! He's the very devil!"

"So I have been told," said David calmly.

They went up to the fourth floor, and the doctor knocked at Dudley Weston's door and went in.

"Hello, Weston, how are you?" greeted the doctor with his best hospital manner. "I want to take your temperature, if you don't mind."

"Just had my temperature taken half an hour ago," growled Dudley Weston, turning a frowning face and glaring at the door.

"Well, this is special," said the doctor, reaching for his thermometer. "I want it for my report, see?"

David stood just outside the doorway, studying the lad.

Dudley Weston's handsome countenance was still adorned with strips of plaster, and a cigarette was sticking out of one corner of his sensuous lips. The recent suffering through which he had passed had not sweetened either his temper or his expression.

"What the devil do you want to annoy me for?" said Dudley. "I should say, it was your business to get your figures from the nurses and not bother me again. Well, stick her in and get it over with."

The doctor got out his thermometer, talking as cheerfully as if he had been received with the utmost courtesy.

"Having a tough time of it, aren't you, Weston? I brought a friend along with me, thought he might amuse you a few minutes till I get off duty. He's the best man on skis I know outside of the regular professionals."

The frown that had been gathering like a quick storm on the boy's face was held at bay.

"Skis?" he said with a quick ungracious look, which nevertheless gave permission to David to enter.

So David, with his ready smile and his quick charm got entrance to Dudley Weston's room, and for half an hour sat and talked.

They spoke of several men who were noted in the various sports, and David knew them all, some of them being personal friends of whom he related little amusing incidents. Suddenly he turned to the invalid and said:

"I wonder if you know my best friend, the Lord Jesus Christ?"

Dudley Weston only stared, and his face grew hard and cynical.

"What are you?" he asked insolently. "A sky pilot? No real man would swallow that bunk!"

"I'm sorry," David answered gravely. "It's evident you don't know Him or you wouldn't talk that way. But there was a time when I didn't know Him, either. I met Christ, and He forgave my sins and washed me in His blood, and taught me that the existence I had led before wasn't really living at all. And I've found He is so wonderful that I want everybody I meet to know Him."

Dudley regarded his visitor with a supercilious smile:

"I pass," he said flippantly. "He's not my type. I prefer to keep my sins. Better snap out of it. Life is too brisk to put on that sob stuff and talk tommyrot like that!"

David took out a card.

"Sorry," he said pleasantly. "I'd like you to know Him. If you ever feel differently let me know. Here's my address. I'll be glad to introduce you."

"Not here!" said Dudley with a shrug of his one good shoulder. "Not my speed! Have a drink, Dunham? I've got some of the real thing in that bureau drawer in a flask. Be glad to have you try a pull at it."

"Thanks, no," said David evenly, "I wouldn't get a bit of kick out of it. That's not my speed, you know."

There was a twinkle in his eyes, but his mouth looked strong and firmly set. Dudley eyed him for an instant, half-inclined to think he was being laughed at, but then a diversion occurred.

There came a knock at the door, bold and assured, and without waiting for invitation two girls entered, showily and scantily attired. They wore heavy makeup and carried an atmosphere of scent—one would hardly call it perfume—that was as loud as their voices.

"Hello, Dud!" they called as they entered. "Got company? I thought you said you were all by yourself."

"So I was, Peachy. This is a new importation. Shows what I've come to. Make you acquainted with the parson. He's been trying to save my soul, but somehow it didn't take. Dunham, meet Peachy and Pearl. Now here's two girls that are just my speed. Sit down and have a little chat with us. Perhaps you'll get a kick out of it. Peach, get the flask, you know where it is, and let's have a regular time. Sit down, Parson! Get acquainted with the ladies!"

"Thank you," said David gravely, looking them over without a flicker. "But I'm afraid they wouldn't care for my line. I'll be going now, but remember, my offer holds good to the end."

He was gone; the three sending peals of laughter after him were not quite certain whether he had been kidding them or not. Had there or had there not been a twinkle in his eye as he said it?

"Whaddee mean, his line, Dud?" asked Peachy. "Whaddaya let him go for? He's a good looker if he is a parson."

⁓

"Well," said David to himself as he walked down the street and drew a long breath. "That's done—or—is it? The incident is closed, my promise is fulfilled, and if I'd done it on my own initiative I'd think I'd made a mighty bungle of it, but I've that promise, 'Ye have not chosen me, but I have chosen you.' I'll just roll the burden of it on Him now. Perhaps in eternity I'll know. But anyway, I had to go."

A little later he added to himself, "The young woman was right. He certainly is a mess! Poor girl! How did she come to get mixed up with him?"

Chapter 28

*B*etty crept slowly back to life, but there was something childlike and dependent, something sweet and new and yielding about her that the old Betty had not known. Eleanor felt as if she had her baby back again. Betty smiled when anything was done for her and showed almost none of the old impatience and irritation if she had to wait for something. And yet overall she seemed reserved and more mature, as if life had hit her hard and taught her something.

She talked very little and said nothing at all about her recent experience. They did not even know if she remembered it, or if it might not have been mercifully blotted out of her mind.

They rejoiced with trembling, however, and thanked God for her present gentleness. They were constantly fearful of possibilities in the future when Betty would be very well again. When Dudley Weston should be well, perhaps, too. What would be the next move? There would have to come a day in the near future, of course, when Betty must be questioned about her escapade. That is, provided she did not volunteer information. God grant there might not have to be any more terrible revelations!

So Betty came back from death's door, and the day arrived at last when she was to be brought downstairs for the first time.

It had been Eleanor's plan for her not to get up until after the midday meal, but Betty suddenly roused to interest and begged to be taken downstairs in the morning. This was rather a complication because the old minister, Dr. Dunham, was coming for the first lesson with the children. Eleanor had arranged to have them use the living room for a schoolroom, and the couch that Betty was to lie on was in that room.

"I'm afraid it will tire you, dear, the whole morning long and you having to listen."

"No, it will not tire me, Mums," said Betty, with more vigor than she had shown since she went away.

"If I get tired I'll just shut my eyes and pretend I'm not there. I'm tired of being away off here. It's time I got well!"

So they yielded to her urgency, and Chester carried her downstairs and settled her on the couch by the fireplace, somewhat apart from the little circle around the big table. There was a blackboard at the other end of the room, and on the table was a pile of beautiful new Bibles in soft leather bindings.

Dr. Dunham was already in the room and greeted Betty pleasantly but did not act as if she were a member of the class, and the room settled down to business.

"Now," said the minister when Eleanor had tiptoed out of the room and Chester had retired into the library. "Friends, we're going to try out a new kind of school, you and I. We're going to study history, literature, biography, biology, geology, chronology, astronomy, theology, geography, philosophy, and a lot of other -ologies, with maybe a touch of mathematics here and there, but we're going to study it all out of one Book.

"We may bring in other books occasionally as sidelights, but the whole study is to center around one Book. And if there is any difference of opinion between other books and other people and *our* Book, *it* is to be the criterion, because its Author is the only writer in the universe who can possibly know the *truth* about any of the subjects named! The reason that He is so well informed is that He is the originator of them all, and His name is God!

"I hope that as we go on with our study you will find that none of the subjects I have mentioned are really separate subjects but are merely classifications of one great theme, which together explain life.

"Now if you can bring to this study a belief in the Book that we are to take up, you will be able to enter deeper into the things of which it tells. But if not, you will only see the things that are on the surface. I do not mean an intellectual belief that comes from being convinced that the Book is logically true; I mean a *will* to accept every statement the Book gives. If you can do that you will have a key that will unlock a great many secret and beautiful treasures of knowing and wisdom that have been placed there for only those who believe. And if you can do that honestly, I can promise you that the proof of its truth will later be shown to you.

"I cannot do this for you. You will have to do it for yourselves. But you will be well repaid if you exercise this act of the will and come to your study believing the Book comes from God, and giving it opportunity to prove itself true. But even if you are unwilling to do this, the Book can show you many wonderful treasures and delights if you will give yourselves to a study of it. It is up to you, my friends, how much you get out of what we are about to do."

Betty was listening with closed eyes. No one was noticing her, but she did not miss a word.

At this stage Jane raised her hand.

"How can we believe that, when *anybody* might have written it?" she asked pertly.

The minister smiled.

"You think anybody might have written it?" he asked pleasantly.

"Try it and see. A great many have tried to write something like it and failed. But yes, Jane, you can believe it in spite of any doubts you may have, if you *will* to do so. People easily believe much more foolish things than that. You can say, 'I'm going to take this Book with a mind open to receive every word it says as absolute fact, and let it prove itself to my reasoning powers as I study, and begin to understand.' You have no right to doubt a book until you know what it says. The Bible is able to prove its truth to you if you will give it a chance to reveal itself to your spirit. You can't just understand the Bible with your mind alone, your spirit must enter into it, because it is written for your spirit to understand. If you were to try to get at the Bible through your body alone, if you were to take it and eat it and try to get it into your system in that way, you would not get anywhere with it. And why do you expect to understand it merely through your mind alone?"

Jane giggled.

"And now," said Dr. Dunham, "I am going to tell you a little story I once heard a great teacher tell that will illustrate one way we know the Bible is true. We will suppose a man in England makes his will. He leaves his property in trust for a good many years until it shall accumulate interest enough to amount to a certain very large sum. At that time it is to be divided between all his descendants who are then living. A copy of this will is filed with the English government at the time of the man's death, perhaps in some courthouse or government building in England. After a few years have passed, one of this man's sons decides to move to Spain. He desires to give his children the benefit of his father's will, so he gets a copy of it and takes it with him to Spain. There it is translated into Spanish and put on file, perhaps with the Spanish government. Another son moves to Germany, and he gets a copy of the will in German. Later another goes to Italy and the will is translated into Italian. Another to India, and perhaps another somewhere else. Each takes a copy of the will in the language of the country to which he is going, filing it for use of their descendants. Then one day a great fire destroys the building in which the original will is filed. The will is burned. At last the day comes when the property has reached the sum named in the will and the heirs make application to have it divided. But the original will is gone, and what can they do? They get together the wills that have been translated into the different languages and compare them. In this way they get an accurate copy of the original will, and by it the court divides the property. Now just such a thing happened with the Bible. We have not the original manuscripts on which the men wrote who were taught by God what to write. But as the years went by those original manuscripts were copied and recopied into many languages and scattered over the whole earth; scholars who have devoted their lives to the study have gathered these different copies and compared them. They find that they all agree! Here is a book"—he held up a little brown volume—"that tells about this investigation. It is written by one of the greatest scholars in the world, who has devoted forty-five years to looking into this matter. You will be interested to study this sometime. It was written to show that from the standpoint of a scholar we may know that we have the original word of God as it was given to holy men of old, moved by the Holy Spirit. That is what we call 'inspiration.' We shall talk of that later.

"Now, will you open your Bibles to the first chapter and the first verse of the first book, called Genesis, and we will have our first geography lesson."

There was a little rustle of excitement as the new Bibles were opened.

"Christopher, will you read the first verse?"

Chris read, almost embarrassedly:

"In the beginning God created the heaven and the earth."

The old minister interrupted him:

623

"You will remember we are going to take up our study of this Book with the idea of accepting all its statements and giving it a chance to prove them true. We must therefore if we are to get anywhere accept this as a fact."

Jane began to be restless. Her lip curled a trifle.

"What is it, Jane?" questioned the keen-eyed minister.

"Our teacher at school says that isn't so!" said Jane importantly. "She says God didn't make the earth or anything. She says it just developed out of matter and that there isn't any God, only just a force that makes things grow. She says that nobody believes that anymore, only ignorant people."

"Shut up, Jane, that's not polite!" admonished Chris in the tone of a mentor.

"Let her speak," said the teacher. "We want to understand all these things and get them cleared away out of our minds. Now, Jane, your teacher is wrong! There are a *great many* famous scholars who believe in God and His Book with all their hearts. One of them is coming to visit me this winter. He is the author of this brown book I showed you. Perhaps I can introduce him to you. He is considered by everybody to be the greatest living authority on ancient languages. He has spent many years in trying to find out these things, and he probably knows more than your teacher in school ever heard of. He has personally read all the ancient manuscripts and has given his whole life to this study. He knows forty-eight ancient languages, and in over twenty he can talk and write as well as read. He has written two remarkable books about the Bible showing that it is true, which someday I hope you'll read. And after you have read them you may like to send copies of them to your teacher to read.

"But now suppose we get back to our study of the statement that God made the heavens and the earth out of nothing, for that is what the word *create* in the Hebrew means, 'to make out of nothing.'"

The children looked incredulous but waited.

"Now, we do not know how many ages ago that was," went on the wise, pleasant voice, "but it was thousands, perhaps millions of years—"

"Why," broke in Betty, before she realized she was speaking, "why, I thought all people who believed in the Bible thought the earth was made only about five or six thousand years ago, and that it was all made in six days. And that *couldn't possibly* be, you know, for there are all those fossils and buried things that took simply ages to get that way."

The minister smiled leniently:

"There is room for all that, Betty, between the first and second verses of Genesis. We have been talking about what is sometimes called the pre-Adamite creation. Jane, will you read the second verse?"

Jane read:

"And the earth was without form, and void; and darkness was upon the face of the deep. And the Spirit of God moved upon the face of the waters."

"Now," said the minister, "in the Hebrew, which is the language in which this Old Testament was originally written, that word that has been translated 'was' means 'became.' It doesn't mean that it *was* so in the first place but that it *became* so after it was created on account of some great disaster or cataclysm resulting from God's wrath. There are some words that translated into other languages lose much of their strength, and this is one. The verse should read 'And the earth *became* without form.' There are passages in Isaiah and Jeremiah that have reference to this very thing having happened to 'the world that then was' as it is called. Jane, I've given you the Isaiah reference to read, and Christopher may take the one in Jeremiah. I'll give Doris and John each something to look up also. It is very interesting to study about the destruction of this first creation because of sin and how God had to make the world over again. Now, Jane will you read?"

The morning flew away before any of them realized it, and Betty did not want to go back to bed again when the class was over. She even sent Jane downstairs that afternoon for one of the new Bibles and got her to make a copy of all the references that she might look them up again.

"It's going to be kind of fun, I believe," vouchsafed Jane when she brought the Bible.

"I never heard anything like it," said Betty. "I don't believe they know these things in school. I wonder if he knows what he's talking about."

"Well, he sure had a good line and is interesting," said Chris, who was standing in the doorway. "But maybe it's all just baloney!"

That was the beginning of a new order of things.

The children took hold of their studies with avidity, and worked and played happily. They seemed to forget the life from which they had been so summarily withdrawn.

Betty grew stronger every day now and came regularly to the classes. Her father had been fearful that she would rebel against studying with the minister, but she went into the work without any question.

Chester and Eleanor looked on with delight. What a miracle had been wrought! Even Doris and John were eager and interested and went about memorizing Bible verses and vying with one another as to who could learn the day's portion first. All of them seemed simply fascinated by the new study. Even Chester and Eleanor began to drop into the classes.

"I had no idea what the Bible was like," said Chester humbly one day. "I have brought my children up in ignorance. They are simply little heathen. I am not much better! And I thought I knew the Bible well!"

"Well," Chester heard Chris say to Betty one day, "I don't know whether the old man has got it right or not, but it's darned interesting anyway. That about the pyramid being all told about in the Bible was great! Gee, I'd like to go over to Egypt and see that thing and crawl all through those passages. He says he's got a model of it; he's going to bring it over and show us."

The clear, cold weather had settled down upon them now, and the children spent many happy hours upon the ice or sledding down the old hill—coming in with faces glowing, healthy appetites, and minds alert for study. Even Betty took her part now again in the sports and seemed to be getting fully back to normal once more. Eleanor and Chester watched her with growing delight and began to hope her fearful experience was not to be so disastrous after all. Yet nothing had been said between them about her running away. Chester and Eleanor were both afraid to disturb the happy calm that seemed to have settled down upon the old farm and decided to let well enough alone and just ignore the circumstance for the present. Betty was noticeably maturing day by day.

One day Mrs. Dunham fell ill, however, and the lessons had to be interrupted. She was so ill that after a few days they sent for her son, and David came swiftly in answer to their call.

When she grew better Dr. Dunham came down with a heavy cold brought on by weariness and loss of sleep during his wife's illness, and David lingered on a few days longer.

It was at his father's request that he came up to the farm to conduct the classes for a time or two.

"Davy has one or two new discoveries in archaeology I want the children to hear about," explained the old minister when Chester came up one morning to see how he was getting on. "I want David to tell them, too, about the prophecies and the way they are being fulfilled over there in Europe today by the lining up of the nations; that shows the Coming of the Lord cannot be far away. He has a new book on the chronology of the Bible that I want him to show them. It makes things very clear. It's a kind of key to some of the sealed passages in Daniel. We must have it for reference. You know the Bible says that in the time of the end they shall be unsealed, and the wise shall understand these things, but none of the wicked shall understand."

"I never noticed that passage before," said Chester humbly. "I'm learning a lot this winter, including what a miserable father I have been."

"But Thornton, it's wonderful how your children are taking hold of this study," went on the minister. "It's given me an idea. I wish I was young and had money. I'd start such a school with the Bible as the basis of all studies. I understand there are several now, here and there, with much the same idea behind them."

"Well, why not come down to Briardale and start it there," said Chester. "I would dare to take my kiddies back home if I had such a school to send them to. We could have a winter school in Briardale and a summer one up at the farm. I believe I could get some other men to join with me and finance the thing, if only I could show them the result of it on my children. What do you say? Will you do it?"

"But there's my church," smiled the minister.

"Let some young man just starting take the church for the winter months," said Chester, "and you and David come and help me start a school in Briardale. You need to get busy out in the world. This is no time to hide away a wise man of God in the wilderness like this. Look at my children! Think what was happening to them! And there are millions of others in their condition."

"Not every father is awake to the condition of things," said Dunham.

"Well, I'll admit God sent me an eye opener," said Chester, "but there must be a few others who are worried about the state of things. I'll see what I can stir up."

David came up to the farm for a few days and began to teach more wonders to the eager students. He was "David" to them all now.

He took them out and taught them to use their skis, and they were wild with delight. They skated and sledded and had wonderful times together after the lessons were over, and then they came in and helped Eleanor cook and wash dishes.

One day Jane expressed their feeling:

"I'll say I'm glad Daddy kidnapped us all and brought us up here, aren't you, Betts?"

And Betty with a smiling face admitted she was.

Betty had received David shyly, almost silently at first, but after they had played together out-of-doors for a few days she began to talk with him a little more naturally. He wondered if she remembered any of the things she had said to him in her delirium. But one day when they had been sledding together and he was helping her up the hill again, she suddenly turned to him and said:

"Did you mean all those things you told me while I was sick, or did you just tell me that to quiet me?"

"I certainly meant every word," he said with a glad ring to his voice. "I have been wondering if you remembered."

"Oh, I couldn't forget that!" said Betty earnestly. "It had been so awful having God looking at me all the time. I could see just what He thought of me. But isn't He going to bring it all up sometime and judge me for it?"

"No. He says in His word that He'll forgive your transgressions and remember them no more."

"But it will always be there," said Betty sadly. "There'll always be those things that I have done! I'll always be unclean!"

"What God has washed cannot be unclean. 'As far as the east is from the west, so far hath he removed our transgressions from us,'" quoted David.

She was silent for a long time, and then she said timidly, as though she were not sure she ought to say it:

"But *you* will always think of me that way—as—unclean!"

"I will always think of you as one who is saved!" he said reverently, and his voice had a glad ring in it.

"Oh, will you!" she exclaimed with a light coming into her eyes. "I'm so glad! But oh! I wish I'd never known Dudley Weston!" She pressed her fingers over her eyes and gave a little shiver of horror at the remembrance.

When David Dunham went back to his work, he wrote to Betty every few days, and life began to take on a new look. She was no longer the haughty princess in exile. She walked the earth as if it were paved with flowers, and all day long she was singing.

Plans for the new Bible school went forward rapidly. Chester took a trip home and found three or four more men whose children were disappointing them. They were dubious, it is true, as to whether anything about the Bible could ever touch their young outlaws, but they were willing to be convinced, and Chester brought three of them up to the farm when he came back, along with Hannah who said she was homesick for her family. When the three fathers had listened in on the Bible studies for several hours they marveled and went away thoughtfully to tell others. And so the scheme for a Bible school grew.

The spring came on, and the snow melted at last. Arbutus and mountain laurel appeared, and the earth took on a loveliness that even surpassed the grandeur of the winter whiteness.

Chester went back home for part of each week now as the business claimed more of his time. But the family had elected to stay at the farm till summer was over. So the Bible lessons went steadily on. As the Book opened its treasures to them, the children changed and grew thoughtful and lovely of attitude. Eleanor was expressing this to their minister one day, and he smiled and said:

"The Lord has promised that His Word shall not return unto Him void but shall accomplish that for which He sent it. Your children are growing wise in the deepest lore of the ages. I think they are going to be among the wise, Mrs. Thornton."

As the summer drew to a close the plans for the new school began to mature. Money had been forthcoming. A building had been secured. The Dunhams promised to undertake the school and had found several other fine, wise spirits for teachers. Word had gone forth that the school would be open for students in the fall.

The exile was over.

The Thorntons were going back to Briardale again, but they were all reluctant to leave the farm and talked eagerly of their return next summer.

David had come up to help his father pack and spent much time at the farm. He and Betty were standing one day on the brow of a hill. The frost had already begun to fling scarlet banners of loveliness over the world in preparation for another winter. Betty's face was tender as she looked across the misty purple of the mountains.

"It's going to be strange going back," she mused. "I almost dread it. There won't be any of my old friends who will be in sympathy with me. I shall be practically alone. There are some I wish I never need see again. I'm glad the Westons have moved to New York. But Gyp and Fran will not understand. I used to be proud of being hard boiled, and they will think I am crazy. I shall be separated from everybody."

"That's the history of every child of God," said David quickly. "'Come out from among them, and be ye separate.' The church is a body of called-out ones. He has called us to be a royal generation, kings and priests unto Him. Isn't that good enough, Betty?" He looked at her earnestly, reaching out and gathering her hand into his. "You are very precious to me, Betty. I have loved you ever since I found you like a little lost lamb in the snow. Do you think you could ever love me? Do you think after the school is on its feet and things straighten out that you and I could go together through life? Could you love me, Betty?"

Betty lifted wondering, startled eyes that filled with humble tears.

"Oh, David," she said sadly, "I love you. Yes I love you. I didn't know there was anything like love before. I thought it was all bunk. But David, I'm not good enough for you. I'm"—she caught her breath in a sob and laid her face against his shoulder—"I'm *unclean*!"

"Whom Jesus Christ had cleansed is not unclean, Betty darling! 'The king's daughter is all glorious within.'" And he laid his lips reverently upon hers and drew her close to his heart.

The next day the Thorntons went back to their home to begin a new life. As they drove up to the house they saw a beautiful blue Mermaid Eight parked at the door.

"That," said Chester to Betty, "is by way of a birthday present. I saw how things were going, and I thought I'd like to get it in before it had to be a wedding gift."

A NEW NAME

Chapter 1

1920s,
Eastern United States

Murray Van Rensselaer had been waiting for an hour and a quarter in the reception room of the Blakeley Hospital.

He was not good at waiting. Things usually came at his call, or sometimes even anticipated his desires. It was incredible that he should suddenly find himself in such a maddening set of circumstances!

He still wore the great fur-lined overcoat in which he had arrived after the accident, but he seemed to be unaware of it as he paced excitedly up and down the stark leather-upholstered room.

Across the marble corridor he could just see the tip of white, starched linen that was the cap of the uniformed person with

bifocals who sat at the rolltop desk and presided over this fiendish place.

Three times he had pranced pompously across the tessellated
floor and demanded to know what had become of the patient
he had brought in. She had only looked him over coldly, impersonally, and reiterated that word would be sent to him as soon
as the examination was completed. Even his name, which he had
condescendingly mentioned, had failed to make the slightest
impression upon her. She had merely filed his immaculate calling
card and ordered him back to the reception room.

The tall clock in the corner, the only live thing in the room,
seemed to tick in eons, not seconds. He regarded it belligerently.
Why should a clock seem to have eyes that searched to your soul?
What was a clock doing there anyway, in a place where they
regarded not time, and were absorbed in their own terrible affairs?
The clock seemed to be the only connecting link with the outside world.

He strode nearer and read the silver plate of the donor,
inscribed in memory of "Elizabeth," and turned sharply back to
the door again with a haunting vision of the white-faced girl he
had brought in awhile before. Bessie! Little Bessie Chapparelle!
She was "Elizabeth" too.

What a cute kid she had been when he first knew her! Strange
that on this day of all days he should have come upon her
standing at that corner after all these years, suddenly grown up
and stunningly beautiful!

And now she lay crumpled, somewhere up in those distant marble halls!

He shuddered in his heavy coat and mopped the cold perspiration from his brows. If anything should happen to Bessie! And his fault! Everybody would of course say it was his fault! He knew he was a reckless driver. He knew he took chances, but he had always gotten by before! If she hadn't been so darned pretty, so surprisingly sweet and unusual, and like the child she used to be—and that truck coming around the corner at thirty-five miles an hour!

The air was full of antiseptics. It seemed to him that he had been breathing it in until his head was swimming, that cold, pungent, penetrating smell that dwelt within those white marble walls like a living spirit of the dead!

Gosh! What a place! Why did he stay? He could go home and telephone later. Nobody was compelling him to stay. Bessie was a poor girl with nobody to take her side. Nobody but her mother!

He halted in his excited walk. *Her mother!* If anything happened to Bessie, somebody would have to tell her mother!

A door opened far away in the upper marble regions, and the echo of a delirious cry shivered down through the corridors. Rubber wheels somewhere rolled a heavy object down a space and out of hearing; voices rose in a subdued murmur as if they passed a certain point and drifted away from the main speech, drifted down the stairs, vague, detached words. Then all was still again.

Something dragged at his heart. He had thought they were

coming, and now suddenly he was afraid to have them come. What a relief! Just a little longer respite till he could get ahold of himself. He wasn't at all fit, or things wouldn't get ahold of him this way. He had been going pretty hard since he left college. Too many highballs! Too late at night!—Too many cigarettes! The old man was right! If he hadn't been so infernally offensive in the way he put it! But one couldn't of course go that pace forever and not feel it.

What was it he had been thinking about when those voices passed that point above the stairs? Oh! Yes! Her mother! Someone would have to tell her mother! She was a woman with a kind twinkle in her eyes. One would find it terrible to quench that twinkle in her eyes! He remembered how she had bandaged his cut finger one day and given him a cookie. Those were happy days!—Ah! *There!* There was that sound of an opening door again!—Voices!—Footsteps! Listen! They were coming! Yes—they were coming! Rubber heels on marble treads! And now he was in a frenzy of fear.

Bessie, little blue-eyed Bessie with the gold hair all about her white face!—

The steps came on down the hall, and he held his breath in the shelter of a heavy tan-colored velvet curtain. He must get himself in hand before he faced anyone. If he only hadn't left his flask in the car! Oh, but of course! The car was wrecked! What was he thinking about? But there would be other flasks! If only he could get out of this!

The nurse came on down the hall. He could see her reflection in the plate glass of the front door that was within his vision as he stood with his back toward the desk. She was going straight to the desk with a message!

The front doorknob rattled.

He glared impatiently at the blurred interruption to his vision of the nurse. A sallow man with a bandaged head was fumbling with the doorknob, and the white uniform of the nurse was no longer plain. He held his breath and listened:

"Well, is there any change?" asked the voice behind the rolltop desk, impassively.

"Yes, she's dead!" answered the nurse.

"Well, you'd better go down to that man in the reception room. He's been pestering the life out of me. He thinks he's the only one—

"I can't!" said the nurse sharply. "I've got to call up the police station first. The doctor said—" She lowered her voice inaudibly. The man with the bandaged head had managed the doorknob at last.

The door swung wide, noiselessly, on its well-oiled hinges, letting in the bandaged man; and as he limped heavily in, a shadow slipped from the folds of the heavy curtain and passed behind him into the night.

Chapter 2

In the big white marble house on the avenue that Murray Van Rensselaer called home, the servants were lighting costly lamps and drawing silken shades. A little Pekingese pet came tiptoeing out with one man to see what was the matter with the light over the front entrance, stood for a brief second glancing up and down haughtily, barked sharply at a passerby, and retreated plumily into the dark of the entrance hall with an air of ownership, clicking off to find his mistress. Sweet perfumes drifted out from shadowy rooms where masses of hothouse flowers glowed in costly jardinières, and a wood fire flickered softly over deep-toned rugs and fine old polished woods, reflected from illuminated covers of many rare books behind leaded panes of glass. It flickered and lighted the dreary face of the haughty master of the house as he sat in a deep chair and watched the flames, and seemed to be watching the burning out of his own life in bitter disappointment.

The great dining room glittered with crystal and silver, and abounded in exquisite table linen, hand-wrought, beautiful and fine as a spider's web or a tracery of frost. The table was set for a large dinner, and a profusion of roses graced its center.

Ancestral portraits looked down from the walls.

At one end of the room, in a screened balcony behind great fronds of mammoth ferns, musicians were preparing to play, arranging music, speaking in low tones.

The footsteps of the servants were inaudible as they came and went over the deep pile of ancient rugs.

A deep-throated chime from a tall old clock in the hall called out the hour, and a bell somewhere in the distance rang sharply, imperatively.

A maid came noiselessly down the stairs and paused beside the library door, tapping gently.

"Mr. Van Rensselaer, Mrs. Van Rensselaer would like to see you at once if you're not busy."

The wistful look in the master's eyes changed at the summons into his habitual belligerence, and he rose with a sigh of impatience. He mounted the stairs like one going to a familiar stake.

Mrs. Van Rensselaer sat at her dressing table fresh from the hands of her maid, a perfectly groomed woman in the prime of her life. Not a wrinkle marred the loveliness of her complexion, not a line of tenderness, or suffering, or self-abnegation gave character to her exquisite features. She had been considered the most beautiful woman of the day when Charles Van Rensselaer married her, and she still retained her beauty. No one, not even her bitterest enemy, could say that she had aged or faded. Her face and her figure were her first concern. She never let anything come between her and her ambition to remain young and lovely.

If her meaningless beauty had long since palled upon the man who had worked hard in his younger days to win her hand, he nevertheless yielded her the pomp which she demanded; and if there was sometimes a note of mock ceremony in his voice, it was well guarded.

He stood in the violet shadow of her silken-shrouded lamp and watched her with a bitter sadness in his eyes. It was a moment when they might have met on common ground and drawn nearer to one another if she had but sensed it. But she was busy trying the effect of different earrings against her pearly tinted neck. Should it be the new rock crystals or the jade, or should she wear the Van Rensselaer emeralds after all?

She turned at last, as if just aware that he had come in, and spoke in an annoyed tone: "Charles, you really will have to speak to Murray again."

She turned to get the effect of the jewel and tilted her chin haughtily.

"He is simply *unspeakable!*"

She held up her hand mirror and turned her head the other way to get a look at the other ear.

Her husband drew a deep, fortifying breath, wet his lips nervously with the tip of his tongue the way a dog does when he is expecting a whipping, and braced himself for action.

"What's Murray been doing now?" he asked crisply, belligerently. There was fight in his eye and a set to his jaw, although the lean cheekbones just below the eyes seemed to wince as at a blow.

"Why, he's making himself conspicuous again with that lowdown De Flora woman. Marian Stewart has been telling me that he took her to the Assembly last night and danced every dance with her. And it's got to stop! I'm not going to have our name dragged in the dust by my own son."

"But I don't understand," said her husband dryly. "You didn't object when he did the same thing with the Countess Lenowski, and she was twice divorced. I spoke of it then, for it seemed to me morals were more in your line than mine, but you thought it was all right. I'm sure I don't see what you can expect of him now when you sanctioned that two years ago."

"Now, Charles! Don't be tiresome! The Countess Lenowski was a very different person. Rich as Croesus, and titled, and beautiful and young. You can't blame the poor child for being divorced from men who were seeking her merely for her money!"

"The Countess Lenowski is neither so young nor so innocent as she would have everybody believe, and I told you at the time that her beauty wasn't even skin deep. I don't get your fine distinctions. What's the matter with this De Flora woman? Isn't she rich? Doesn't your son think she's beautiful? And she's young enough. They say she's never been married at all, let alone divorced. I made a point to look into that."

"Now, Charles, you're being difficult! That's all there is to it. You're just trying to be difficult! And there's no use talking to you when you get difficult. You know as well as I do what that De Flora woman is. Some little insignificant movie actress, not even a star! With all Murray's money and family, of course, every little upstart is simply flinging herself at him, and you must speak to him! You really must. Let him know his allowance will stop and he can't have any more cars unless he behaves himself!"

"And why must I be the one to speak? I left all questions of social and moral obligations to you when he was young. I am sure it is late in the day for me to meddle now."

"Now, Charles, you are being difficult again. You are quibbling. I called you up to let you know that Murray needs advice, and you're to give it! That's all! It's time you were dressing. We have a dinner, you remember. The Arlingtons and the Schuylers. Do be ready. It's so tiresome to have to wait for you."

Thus dismissed, the head of the house looked at his wife's slim young back and well-cut coiffure with an expression of mingled scorn and despair, which she might have seen in her mirror if she had not been too much absorbed with her own image, but it is doubtful she would have understood if she had seen it. It was because he had long ago recognized her obtuseness in these fine points that Charles Van Rensselaer had been able to maintain his habitual air of studied mock politeness. Her name was Violet, and she knew she could count always on courtesy from him, no matter how his eyes mocked. With that she was content.

He watched her a full minute, noting the grace of movement as she turned her head from side to side perfecting the details of her contour, marked the luster of her amber hair, the sweep of lovely white shoulder against the low severe line of her dinner gown, looked almost wistfully, like a child, for something more, something tender, something gentler than her last words, less cold and formal; yet he knew he would not get it. He had always been watching for something more from her than he knew he could ever get; something more than he knew she possessed. Just because she was outwardly lovely, it seemed as if there must be something beautiful hidden within her somewhere that some miracle would sometime bring forth. The love of his early youth believed that, would always cling to it, thinking that sometime it would be revealed—yet knowing it was an impossibility for which he hoped.

With a sigh almost inaudible he turned and went down the heavily carpeted hall, followed by the trail of her impatient cold words: "Oh, are you there yet? Why won't you hurry? I know you'll be late!"

He shut the great mahogany door behind him with a dull thud. He would have liked to have slammed it, but the doors in that house could not slam. They were too heavy and too well hung on their oiled hinges. It shut him in like a vault to a costly room where everything had been done for his comfort, yet comfort was not. He did not hasten even yet. He went and stood at the window looking out, looking down to the area below, to the paved alleyway that ran between the blocks and gave access to the back door and the garage. A row of brick houses on the side street ended at that alleyway, and a light twinkled in a kitchen window where a woman's figure moved to and fro between a table and the stove—a pleasant, cheery scene reminding one of homecoming and sweet domesticity, a thing he had always yearned for yet never found since he was a little child in his father's home at the farm, with a gentle mother living and a house full of boisterous, loving brothers and sisters. He watched the woman wistfully. What if Violet had been a woman like that, who would set the table for supper and go about the stove preparing little dishes? He laughed aloud bitterly at the thought. Violet in her slim dinner gown, her dangling earrings, and her french bob, risking her lily-and-rose complexion over a fire!

He turned sharply back to his room, snapped on the electric light, and went and stood before the two great silver frames that adorned his dressing table. One held the picture of the lovely delicate woman, almost a girl in appearance, smart, artistic, perfect as the world counts perfection. It was a part of her pride that placed her picture in his room for others to see his devotion, and had it changed each time a new picture that pleased her was taken. His pleasure in her picture had long ago vanished, but he studied her face now with that yearning look in his own, as if again he searched for the thing that was not there, as if his eyes would force from the photograph a quality that the soul must be hiding.

Then with a long sigh he turned to the other frame—the young, careless, handsome face of his son, Murray Montgomery

Van Rensselaer. That honored name! How proud he had been when they gave it to his child! What dreams he had had that his son would add still more honor to that name!

He studied the handsome face intently, searching there for the thing he could not find in the mother's face. How alike they were, those two, who belonged to him, yet were to him almost as strangers—one might almost say as enemies sometimes, when they combined to break his will or his request.

Yet of the two the boy was nearest to him. There had been times when Murray was very young that they had grown almost close—fishing excursions, and a hike or two, a camping trip—rare times, broken up always by Violet, who demanded their attention and resented rough things for her son.

The boy's face was too slender, too girlish, almost effeminate, yet behind it there was a daredevil in his eyes that suggested something more rugged, more manly, perhaps, when he would settle down. The father kept wishing, hoping, that the thing he had not found to satisfy his longing in his wife would someday develop in his son, and then they might be all in all to one another.

With another deep sigh he turned away and began mechanically to dress for the evening, his mind not on what he was doing. But then why should it be when everything was laid out for him? It required no thought. He was thinking about Murray. How they had spoiled him between them! Violet indulging him and repressing all his natural bent toward simple, natural things, molding him into a young fop, insisting on alternately coddling and scolding him, never loving to him even in her indulgence, always cold and unsympathetic toward all that did not go the way she chose.

For himself, he had been so bitterly disappointed in the lad that the years had brought about an attitude of habitual disapproval, as high and as wide and as separating as any stone wall that was ever built. Yet the father's heart ached for his son, and the years were growing bleak with his denial. Why did the boy choose only folly? Scrapes in school and worse in college. Clubs and sports and drinking affairs. Speeding and women and idleness! What a life! What would the grandsire who had founded the ancient and honorable house and had given them the honored name think of such an heir? Yet what could one expect with a mother such as he had given his son?

He gave a last comprehensive survey of his well-groomed self and turned out the light. With deliberate intent he walked across to the window again and looked out to that bright little kitchen window across the alley.

Darkness had dropped down upon the city since he had lighted his room, evening complete, and the little bright window with its aproned figure moving steadily back and forth with brisk step between stove and table stood out clearly in the crisp night. He could see the knife in her hand as she stirred something in a pan on the stove. He could see the foaming pitcher of milk she put in the center of the white-draped table. He could see a griddle over the flame, with blue smoke rising from it. Pancakes. They were going to have pancakes for supper! His mother used to have pancakes for supper when he was a little lad out at the old farm, pancakes with maple syrup! How he wished he could go over there to the little two-story redbrick house and sit down at that white table and eat some. There would be syrup like amber perhaps in a glass pitcher, and how good they would taste! What would they say if he were to go over and ask if he might eat supper with them? What would Violet say if he should go? Leave her abominable, interminable dinner party and go over to that quiet kitchen to eat pancakes! Violet would think he was crazy—would perhaps take steps to put him in the insane asylum, would at least consult a physician. What a fraud life was! A man was never his own master in this world!

A servant tapped at the door.

"Mrs. Van Rensselaer says will you please come down at once. The guests have arrived."

There was a smack of insolence in the maid's voice. She knew who was mistress in that house.

As he turned away from the simple vision, a figure stole down the alley, furtively looking this way and that, and slipped like a shadow close to the bright kitchen window, peering in, a white anxious face, with a cap drawn low over the eyes, and a reckless set to the expensive coat worn desperately hunched above crouching shoulders.

If Charles Van Rensselaer had lingered just a second longer at the window, he might have seen that creeping figure, might have—!

But he turned sharply at the servant's call and went down to play the polished host, to entertain his unwelcome guests with witty sarcasm and sharp repartee, to give the lie to his heart sorrow, and one more proof to the world that he belonged to a great and old family and bore a name that meant riches and fame and honor wherever he went.

Chapter 3

When Murray Van Rensselaer slid out from the hospital door into the night, he had no fixed idea of where he was going or what he was going to do. His main thought was to get away.

It had been years since he had had to walk anywhere, much less run. There had always been the car. But the car was in pieces, and he dared not take a taxi. His feet, so long unused for real work, were nimble enough in dancing and in all sorts of sports, but now when necessity was upon him, somehow they seemed to fail him. They lagged when he would hasten forward. It seemed to him he crawled.

The blocks ahead of him looked miles away. When he came to another corner and rounded it into the next street he felt a great achievement, yet shrank from the new street, lest he meet some acquaintance. It was impressed on him with letters of fire, written with a pen of iron in his soul that he was a murderer, and he must escape from justice. Therefore his unwilling feet were carrying him through the night to a place he knew not, to a place he would not. It came to him suddenly that he despised himself for fleeing this way, but that he knew his own soul, and that it was not in him to stand and face a murder trial. He could not bear the scorn in his beautiful mother's face, the bitterness in his father's eyes. He shrank from the jeers or pity of his companions, from the gentle, sad eyes of Bessie's mother, from the memory of Bessie's white face. He could not face a court and a jury, nor fight to save his life. He could not bear the horror of the punishment that would be measured out to him. Even though money might make the penalty light, never again could he face the world and be proud of his old family name and carry out life with others with a high hand because he was Murray Van Rensselaer; because he had a right to be deferred to, and to rule others, because he had been born into a good and honorable and revered family. He had severed connection with that family! He had smirched the name he bore! He had ruined himself for life! He was a murderer!

These thoughts pursued him through the night as he hurried onward, not knowing where he went.

Cars shot by him in the street. Twice he ducked away because a familiar face looked out at him from some passing vehicle. Like a dart the thought went through him that he could go their way no longer, be in their world no more. He must always shy away from the face of man. He would never be free again! He had lost everything! The brand of Cain was upon him! Who was Cain?

Where had he heard that phrase, "the brand of Cain"?

And then he came within the shadow of his own home.

He had been busy with his terrible thoughts. He had not been thinking where he was going, not realizing where his frantic feet were carrying him. Now as he turned the corner sharply, almost knocking over another pedestrian in his flight, he saw the great marble structure ahead of him; its shaded lights, its dim familiar beauty, its aloofness, its pride, impressed him for the first time. What had he done? Brought down the pride of this great house! Blighted his own life! He did not want to come here! He must not come here! The marble of the walls was as unfriendly and aloof as the marble halls from which he had fled. The cold clarity of the ether still clung to his garments like the aroma of the grave. Why had his feet carried him here, where there was no hiding for him, no city of refuge in that costly marble edifice? His father and his mother were bitter against him anyway for past offenses. Little follies they seemed to him now beside the thing that he had so unwittingly done. Had some devil led him here to show him first what he had lost before it flung him far away from all he had held dear in life?

Yet he could not turn another way. It seemed he must go on. And now as he passed the house, across the way a shining car drew up, and people in evening coats got out and went in, and he remembered. There was to have been a dinner—his mother had begged him to come—Gwendolen Arlington—she was the girl in coral with the silver shoes—a pretty girl—how she would shrink from him now! She must not see him—! He shied around the corner as if some evil power propelled him in a vain attempt to get away into some dark cranny of the earth—Gwendolen—she would be sitting at his mother's table, in his place perhaps, and his chair vacant beside her—oh no, his mother would supply someone else, and he perhaps—where would he be? While the news boys on the street cried out his name in shame—and his mother smiled her painted smile, and his father said the glittering sarcasms he was famous for, and he—was out in the cold and dark—*forever*!

Not that he had ever cared particularly for home, until now, when it was taken from him! There had always been a hunger in his heart for something different. But now that he was suddenly alienated from all he knew, it became strangely precious.

Ah! Now he knew where the devil was carrying him. The old alley! Bessie's house! He knew deep in his heart he could not have gotten away without coming here. He would have to see it all to carry it with him forever, and always be seeing what he had destroyed. Yes, there was the kitchen window, the shutters open. Mrs. Chapparelle never closed those shutters while Bessie was out. It was a sort of signal that all was well in the house, and every child safely in when those shutters were closed. He could remember as a little boy when he watched from his fourth-story back nursery window, always with a feeling of disappointment when those shutters that shut out the cheeriness of the Chapparelle home were closed for the night.

Yes, and there was the flat stone where he and Bessie used to play jacks under the gutter pipe, just as of old. He hadn't been out in the alley since he came back from college, and that was before he went to Europe. It must be six or seven years now! How had he let these dear friends get away from him this way? His mother of course had managed at first. She never liked him to go to the side street for company—but later, he had chosen his own companions, and he might have gone back. Why hadn't he?

Somehow, as he made his stealthy way down the paved walled alley, thoughts came flocking, and questions demanded an answer as if they had a personality, and he was led where he would not.

Surely he did not want to come here now of all times. Come and see this home from which he had taken the sunshine, the home that he had wrecked and brought to sorrow! Yet he must.

Like a thief he stole close and laid his white face against the window pane, his eyes straining to see every detail, as if precious things had been lost from his sight and must be caught at, and all fragments possible rescued, as if he would in this swift vision make amends for all his years of neglect.

Yes, there she was, going about getting supper just as he remembered, stirring at a great bowl of batter. There would be pancakes. He could smell the appetizing crispness of the one she was baking to test, to see if the batter was just right. How he and Bessie used to hover and beg for these test cakes, and roll them around a bit of butter and eat them from their hands, delicious bits of brown hot crispness, like no other food he had ever tasted since. Buckwheats. That was the name they called them. They never had buckwheats at his home. Sometimes he had tried to get them at restaurants and hotels, but they brought him sections of pasty hot blankets instead that had no more resemblance to the real things than a paper rose to a real one. Yes, there was the pitcher of milk, foaming and rich, the glass syrup jug with the little silver squirrel on the lid to hold it up—how familiar and homely and dear it all was! And Bessie—Bessie—lying still and white in the hospital, and the police hunting the city over for her murderer!

Somebody must tell her mother!

He looked at the mother's face, a little thinner, a trifle grayer than when he knew her so well and she had tied up his cut finger. The crinkles in her hair where it waved over her small fine ears were sprinkled with many silver threads. He remembered thinking she had prettier ears than his mother, and wondering about it because he knew that his mother was considered very beautiful. She wore an apron with a bib. The kitten used to run after her and play with the apron strings sometimes, and pull them till they were untied and hung behind. There was an old cat curled sedately on a chair by the sink. Could that be the same kitten? How long did cats live? Life! Death! Bessie was dead, and there was her mother going about making hotcakes for supper, expecting Bessie to come in pretty soon and sit at that white table and eat them! But Bessie would never come in and eat at that table again. Bessie was dead, and he had killed her! He, her murderer, was daring to stand there and look in at that little piece of heaven on earth that he had ruined.

He groaned aloud and rested his forehead on the windowsill.

"Oh God! I never meant to do it!" The words were forced from his lips, perhaps the first prayer those lips had ever made. He did not know it was a prayer.

The cat stirred and pricked up its ears, opening its eyes toward the window, and Mrs. Chapparelle paused and glanced that way, but the white face visible but a moment before was resting on the windowsill out of sight.

The busy hum of the city murmured on outside the alley where he stood, but he heeded it not. He stood overwhelmed with a sense of shame. It was something he had never experienced before. Always anything he had done before, any scrape he found himself in, it had been sufficient to him to fall back on his family. The old, honored name that he bore had seen him through every difficulty so far, and might even this time if it were exerted to its utmost. Had Bessie been a stranger, it would probably have been his refuge still. But Bessie was not a stranger, and there was grace enough in his heart to know that never to his own self could he excuse, or pass over, what he had done to her and to her kind, sweet mother, who had so often mothered him in the years that were past.

A little tinkling bell broke the spell that was upon him—the old-fashioned doorbell in the Chapparelle kitchen just above the door that led to the front of the house. He started and lifted his head. He could see the vibration of the old bell on its rusty spring just as he had watched it in wonder the first time he had seen it as a child. Mrs. Chapparelle was hastening with her quick step to open the door. He caught the flutter of her apron as she passed into the hall. And what would she meet at the door? Were they bringing Bessie's body home, so soon—! Or was it merely someone sent to break the news? Oh, he ought to have prepared her for it. He ought to be in there now lying at her feet and begging her forgiveness, helping her to bear the awful sorrow that he had brought upon her. She had been kind to him, and he ought to be brave enough to face things and do anything there was to do— but instead he was flying down the alley on feet that trembled so much they could scarcely bear his weight, feet that were leaden and would not respond to the desperate need that was upon him, feet that seemed to clatter on the smooth cement as if they were made of steel. Someone would hear him. They would be after him. No one else would dash that way from a house of sorrow save a murderer! Coward! He was a *coward*! A sneak and a coward!

And he loved Bessie! Yes, he knew now that was why he was so glad when he saw her standing on the corner after all those years—glad she finally yielded to his request and rode with him, because she had suddenly seemed to him the desire of his heart, the conclusion of all the scattered loves and longings of his young life. How pretty she had been! And now she was dead!

His heart cried out to be with her, to cry into her little dead ear that he was sorry, to make her know before she was utterly gone, before her visible form was gone out of this earth, how he wished he was back in the childhood days with her to play with always. He drew a breath like a sob as he hurried along, and a passerby turned and looked after him. With a kind of sixth sense he understood that he had laid himself open to suspicion, and cut sharply down another turn into a labyrinth of streets, making hairbreadth escapes, dashing between taxis, scuttling down dark alleys, and across vacant lots, once diving through a garage in mad haste with the hope of finding a car he could hire, and then afraid to ask anyone about it. And all the time something in his soul was lashing him with scorn. Coward! Coward! it called him. Bearing a lofty name, wearing the insignia of wealth and culture, yet too low to go back and face his mistakes and follies, too low to face the woman he had robbed of her child and tell her how troubled his own heart was and confess his sin.

Murray Van Rensselaer had been used to boasting that he was not afraid of anything. But he was afraid now! He was fleeing from the retribution that he was sure was close upon his footsteps. Something in his heart wanted to go back and do the manly thing but could not! His very feet were afraid and would not obey. He had no power in him to do anything but flee!

Chapter 4

Sometime in the night he found himself walking along a country road. How he got there or what hour it was he did not know. He was wearier than he had ever been in his life before. The expensive shoes he was wearing were not built for the kind of jaunt he had been taking. He had been dressed for an afternoon of frivolity when he started out from home. There had been the possibility of stopping almost anywhere before dinnertime, and he had not intended a hike when he dressed. His shoes pierced him with stabs of pain every step he took. They were soaked with water from a stream he had forded somewhere. It was very hazy in his mind whether the stream had been in the gutter of the city where the outflow from a fire engine had been flooding down the street or whether he had sometime crossed a brook since he left the outskirts of town. Either of these things seemed possible. The part of him that did the thinking seemed to have been asleep and was just coming awake painfully.

He was wet to the skin with perspiration and was exhausted in every nerve and sinew. He wanted nothing in life so much as a hot shower and a bed for twenty-four hours. He was hungry and thirsty. Oh! *Thirsty!* He would give his life for a drink! Yet he dared not try to find one. And now he knew it had been a brook he had waded, for he remembered stooping down and lapping water from his hand. But it had not satisfied. He wanted something stronger. His nerves under the terrible strain of the last few hours were crying out for stimulant. He had not even a cigarette left—and he dared not go near enough to human habitation to purchase any. Oh yes, he had money, a whole roll of it. He felt in his pocket to make sure. He had taken it out of his bank that morning, cashed the whole of his allowance check, to pay several bills that had been hounding him, things he did not want Dad to know about. Of course there were those things he had bought for Bessie and had sent to her. He was glad he had done that much for her before he killed her. Yet what good would it ever do her now? She was dead. And her mother would never know where they came from. Indeed Bessie would not know either. He had told her they were for a friend and he wanted her help in selecting them. Perhaps Bessie would not have liked his gift after all. He had not thought of that before. Girls of her class—but she was not any class—no type that he knew—just one of her kind, so how could he judge? But somehow it dawned upon him that Bessie would not have taken expensive gifts even from him, an old friend. That entered his consciousness with a dull thud of disappointment. But then, Bessie would never know now that he had sent them. Or did they know after death? Was there a hereafter? He knew Mrs. Chapparelle believed in one. She used to talk about heaven as if it were another room, a best room, where she would one day go and dress up all the time in white. At least that was what his childish imagination had gleaned from the stories she used to read to him and Bessie. But then, if Bessie knew about the gifts, she would also know his heart—Wait! Would he want her to know his heart—all his life?

He groaned aloud and then held his breath lest the night had heard him. Oh, he was crazy! He must find a spot to lie down, or else he might as well go and give himself up to justice. He was not fit to protect himself. He was foolish with sleep.

He crept into a wood at last, on a hillside above the road, and threw himself down exhausted among some bushes quite hidden from the road in the darkness.

He was not conscious of anything as he drifted away into exhausted sleep. It was as if he with all his overwhelming burden of disgrace and horror and fear was being dragged down through the ooze of the earth out of sight forever, being obliterated, and glad that it was so.

He woke in the late morning with a sense of bewilderment and sickness upon him. The light was shining broad across his face and seemed focused upon his heavy, smarting eyes. He lay for an instant trying to think what it was all about, chilled to the bone and sore in every fiber. A ringing sound was in his ears, and when he tried to rise, the earth swam about him. His whole pampered being was crying out for food. Never in his life before had he missed a meal and gone so far and felt so much. What was it all about?

And then his memory reminded him sharply of the facts. He was a murderer, an outcast from his father's house upon the face of the earth, and it was necessary that he should go without food and go far, but where, and to what end? There would be no place that he could go but that he would have to move farther. Why not end it all here and be done with it? Perhaps that would be a good way to make amends to Bessie. He had killed her; he would kill himself, and if there was a place hereafter he would find her and tell her it was the only decent thing he could do, having sent her, to come himself and see that she was cared for. Yet when he toyed with the thought somewhat sentimentally in his misery, he knew he had not the courage to do it even for gallantry. And it seemed a useless kind of thing to do. Nothing was of any use anyway! Why had he ever gotten into such a mess? Only yesterday morning at this time he was starting off for the country club and an afternoon's golf. He took out his watch and looked at it. It had stopped! The hands were pointing to ten minutes after one. Probably he had forgotten to wind it. It must be later than that.

A sudden roar came down the road below him, growing in volume as it approached. He struggled to a sitting posture and looked out from his hiding place. It was a truck going down the road, and behind it came two other cars at a little distance apart. One carried a man in uniform. He could see the glitter of brass buttons and a touch of brightness on his cap. He drew back suddenly and crouched, his fear upon him once more. Perhaps that was an officer out to hunt for him. If it was late in the day, by this time the newspapers had gotten word of it! He could see the headlines: SON OF CHARLES VAN RENSSELAER A MURDERER! DRIVES GIRL TO HER DEATH. TAKES BODY TO HOSPITAL AND ESCAPES.

He shuddered, and a ghastly pallor settled upon him. Incredible that such a fate could have overtaken him in a few short hours, and he should have been reduced to hiding in the bushes for safety! He must get out of here, and at once! Now while there were no more cars in sight. The road appeared to be comparatively free from travelers. Perhaps he could keep under cover and get to some small town where he might venture to purchase some food. He certainly could not keep on walking without eating. He struggled to his feet in a panic and found every joint and muscle stiff and sore and his feet stinging with pain as soon as he stood upon them. He glanced down and saw that his handsome overcoat was torn in a jagged line from shoulder to hem, and a bit of fur was sticking out through the opening. That must have been done when he climbed that barbed-wire fence in the dark!

He passed his hand over his usually clean-shaven face and found it rough and bristly. He tried to smooth his hair and pull his hat down over his eyes, but even this movement was an effort.

How was he to go on? Yet he must. He was haunted by a prison cell and the electric chair, preceded by a long, drawn-out trial, in which his entire life would be spread to public gaze. His beautiful mother and haughty, sarcastic father would be dragged in the dust with their proud name and fame, and Mother Chapparelle in her black garments would sit and watch him with sad, forgiving eyes. Strange that he knew even now in his shame that her eyes would be forgiving through their sorrow.

Yet paramount to all this was the piercing, insistent fact that he was hungry. He had never quite known hunger before. He felt in his pockets in vain hope of finding a stray cigarette, but only old letters and programs, souvenirs of his carefree life, came to his hand. Then it came to him that he must destroy these, here where he was in shelter and the ground was wet. He could make a hasty fire and destroy everything that would identify him if he should be caught.

He felt for his little gold matchbox and, stooping painfully, lighted a small pile of letters and papers and bits of trinkets. He burned his tie and a couple of handkerchiefs with his initials. There were his watch and cufflinks, and the gold cigarette case, all bearing initials. He could throw those in the bushes if there was danger. Perhaps he had better get rid of them at once, however, while there was a chance. What if he should bury them? He looked about for something with which to dig. Digging had never been a pastime with him. He awkwardly turned up a few chunks of mud with his hands then took out his knife, a gold one attached to his watch chain, and burrowed a little farther, not getting much below the surface. He put the trinkets into his glove and laid them into the earth with a strange feeling that he was attending the burial of something precious. Then after he had walked a few steps he deliberately returned and unearthed the things, restoring them to his pocket. He had had a sudden realization that he was parting with what he might need badly. There was not enough money in his pocket to carry him far, nor keep him long, and these trinkets would help out. They were no more an identification than all the rest of him. Why throw them away? He looked regretfully at the ashes of his two fine handkerchiefs, the last he would ever have with that initial. And he would need them. He turned and looked back over the road he had traveled in the night and seemed to see all the things he was leaving, his home, his friends, his club, his comfortable living! What a fool he had been. If he had not angered his father and annoyed his mother, and "got in bad" with all his relations everywhere, they would have stood by him now and helped him out of this scrape somehow, just as they had always done before.

Then in the middle of the distance where the panorama of his life had been passing, there arose a face, smiling and sweet, with a rose flush on the cheeks, a light in the eyes, sunshine in the hair, and he remembered! As he looked the face grew white, and the lids fell over the blue eyes, and she was gone!

Sick with the memory, he turned and fled; on feet that were sore, with limbs that were aching, with eyes that were blinded with unaccustomed tears, he stumbled on across rough fields, through woods and meadows and more woods, always woods when he could strike them.

And coming out toward evening with a gnawing faintness at the pit of his stomach, where he could see across a valley, he noted a little trolley car like a toy in the distance sliding along the road, and a small village of neat little houses about a mile away. Eagerly he watched the car as it slid on across the land, almost as small as a fly it seemed, and soon it was a mere speck on the way to the village. Where there was one trolley there were more. Could he dare try for the next one and go to that village for something to eat? He could not go on much longer without food. Or else he would fall by the wayside, and the publicity which his mother so hated—that kind of publicity which was not pretty—would be sure to find him out. He must not drag down his mother's and his father's name. He must hold out to save them so much at least.

His mind had grown clearer through the day, as he had tramped painfully hour after hour and thought it out. He knew that the only thing to do was to get far away, to someplace where law could not find him out and fetch him back for punishment. To do that successfully he must disguise himself somehow. He must get rid of his clothes little by little and get other clothes. He must grow a beard and change his haircut and act a part. He had been good at acting a part for fun in the old days. He was always in demand for theatricals. Could he do it now when Fear was his master?

He stumbled across the meadows one by one, painfully over

the fences, and at last stood in the ditch by the side of the shining rails with the long, low sunset rays gilding them into bright gold. He waited with trembling knees and watched eagerly for the coming of the car, and when at last a faint hum and a distant whistle announced that it was not far off, he began to fairly shake in his anxiety. Would there be many people on board? Would he dare take the risk? Still, he must take it sometime, for he could not hold out much longer.

There were only three women on board, and they did not notice the haggard young fellow who stumbled into the backseat and pulled his hat down over his eyes. They were talking in clear intimate voices that carried a sense of their feeling at home in the car. They told about Mary's engagement, and how her future mother-in-law was giving a dinner for her, and how proud John was of her and was getting her a little Ford coupe to run around in. They talked of the weather and little pleasant everyday things that belonged to a world in which the man in the backseat had no part of. They whispered in lower tones of how it was rumored that Bob Sleighton was making money in bootlegging, and he got a glimpse for the first time in his life of how the quiet, respectable, nondrinking world think of people who break the law in that way. And then they told in detail how they scalloped oysters and made angel cake, and just the degree of brownness that a chicken should be when it was roasted right, until Murray Van Rensselaer, sitting so hungry in his backseat, could fairly smell them all as they came out of the oven, and felt as if he must cry like a child.

Chapter 5

It was dusk when he slid stealthily out of the car, having waited with his head turned toward the darkening window till each of the three women had gotten off at her particular corner. He had spotted a bakery window, and there he made his way, ordering everything they had on their meager menu. But then when he had gotten it, he could only eat a few bites, for somehow Bessie's white face as he carried her into the hospital kept coming between him and the food and sickened him. Somehow he could not get interested in eating any more, and he paid his bill and left a tip that the girl behind the counter did not in the least understand. She ran out to find him and give it back, but he had gone into a little haberdashery shop, and so she missed him.

He bought a cheap cap of plain tweed and a black necktie. Somehow it did not seem decent going around without any necktie. He walked three blocks and threw his old hat far into a vacant lot, then boarded the next trolley, and so went on, where he did not know. He had not known the name of the little town where he had eaten. He began to wonder where he was. He seemed a long way from home, but when a few minutes later the motor-man called a name, he recognized a town only about thirty miles from his home city. Was it possible he had walked all that time and only gotten thirty miles away? He must have been going in a circle! And the newspapers would have full descriptions of him by this time posted everywhere! He was not safe anywhere! What should he do? Where go? Why go anywhere?

He lifted his eyes in despair to the advertisements overhead, for it seemed to him that every man in the car was looking at him suspiciously. He tried to appear unconcerned. He felt his chin to see if his beard had grown any, but his face was unsuitably smooth. He tried to make himself read the advertisements, Chiclets and chewing gum, and baked beans. Toothpaste, and wallpaper, and cigarettes.

Then suddenly his attention was riveted on the sign just across from where he sat. The letters stood out so clearly in red and black on the white background as if they were fairly beckoning to get his attention, as if somebody had just written them to attract his eye; as if it were a burning message for his need: YE MUST BE BORN AGAIN!

A strange thing to be in a trolley car. He never stopped to wonder how it came there, or what it meant to the general public. He took it just for himself. It suggested a solution to his problem.

He must be born again. Sure! That was it, exactly what he needed! He could not live in the circle where he had been first born. He had ostracized himself. He had been disloyal to the code and cast a slur on the honorable name with which he had been born, and it was no more use for him to try to live as Murray Van Rensselaer any longer. He would just have to be born all over again into someone else. Born again! How did one do it? Well, he would have to be somebody else, make himself over, get new clothes first, of course, so he would look like a new man, and the clothes that he could find for what money he had would largely determine the kind of man he was to be made into. This cap was the start. It was a plain, cheap working man's cap. It was not the kind of cap that played much golf or polo, or was entitled to enter the best clubs, or drove an expensive car. It was a working man's cap, and a working man he must evidently be in the new life. It was a part of being born that you didn't choose where you should see the light of day, or who should be your parents. A strange pang shot through him at the thought of the parents whom he might not call his own anymore. The name he had borne he would no longer dare to mention. It was the name of a murderer now. He had dishonored it. He would have to have a new name before it would be safe for him to go among men.

A policeman boarded the car in a few minutes and eyed him sharply as he passed to the other end of the car. Murray found his whole body in a tremble. He slid to the back platform and dropped off the next time the car slowed down, and walked a painful distance till a kindly voice from a dilapidated old Ford offered him a ride. Because he felt ready to drop and saw no shelter nearby where he might sleep awhile, he accepted. It was too dark for the man to see his face clearly anyway. He seemed to be an old man and not particularly canny. A worldly wise man would scarcely have asked a stranger to ride at that time of night. So Murray climbed in beside him and sank into the seat, too weary almost to sigh.

But the old farmer was of a social nature and began to quiz him. How did he come to be walking? Was he going far? The young man easily settled that.

"Car broke down!" That was true enough. His car would never run again.

But the old man wanted to know where.

Not being acquainted with the roads around there, Murray could not lie intelligently, and he answered vaguely that he had been taking a cross-cut through a terrible road that did not seem to be much traveled.

"'Bout a mile back?" asked the stranger.

"About."

"Hmm! Copple's Lane, I reckon. In bad shape. Well, say, we might go back and hitch her on and tow her in. I ain't in any special hurry." And the man began to apply the thought to his brakes for a turn around.

The young man roused in alarm.

"Oh, no," he said energetically. "I've got an appointment. I'll have to hurry on. How far is it to a trolley or train? I'll be glad if you'll let me out at your home and direct me to the nearest trolley to the city. I'll send my man back for the car. It'll be all right," he added, reverting in his anxiety to the vernacular of his former life.

His worldly tone made its immediate impression. The stranger looked him over with increasing respect. This was a person from another world. He talked of his man as of a slave. The fur collar on the fine overcoat came under inspection. He didn't often have fur-lined passengers in his tin Lizzie.

"That's a fine warm coat you've got on," he admired frankly. "Guess you paid a pretty penny for that?"

The young man became instantly alarmed. Now, when this man got home and read his evening paper with a description of that very overcoat, he would go to his telephone and call up the police station. He must get rid of that coat at all costs. If the man had it in his possession perhaps he would not be so ready to make known the location of the owner.

"Don't remember what I paid," he answered nonchalantly. "But it doesn't matter. I have to get a new one. This one got all cut up in the wreck," and he brought to view the long rip where the coat had caught on some barbed wire when he tried to climb a fence.

The stranger looked at the jagged tear sharply.

"My wife could mend that," he said speculatively. "Ef you wantta stop at the house and leave it, she'll darn it up so you won't scarcely know it's been tore. Then when you get your car fixed up, you can come along back and get your coat. I'll loan you mine while you're gone. That's a mighty fine coat. I'd like to own one like it myself. Sorry you can't remember the price. Now I paid twenty-seven fifty at a bargain sale fer this here one, and it's a real good piece of cloth."

Young Van Rensselaer stared in the dark. He did not know there were coats for twenty-seven fifty.

"Nice coat," he said nonchalantly. "How'd you like to exchange? I'm going away tonight on a little trip, and I'm afraid I couldn't take the time to come back, and I wouldn't have time to wait to have it mended. I do hate to go with a torn coat, too."

"H'm!" said the man with a catch in his breath as if he could not believe his ears, but he did not mean to let anybody know it. "But that wouldn't be altogether fair. Your coat is lined with fur. It must have cost 'most fifty dollars."

"Oh, well, I've had it some time, you know, and your coat is new; that squares it all up. I'm satisfied if you are."

"It's a bargain!" said the man, stopping his car with alacrity, beginning to unbutton his overcoat. A bargain like that had better be taken up before the young gentleman retracted his offer.

Murray Van Rensselaer divested himself of his expensive coat and crawled into the harsh gray coat of the stranger, and said to himself eagerly, "Now I'm becoming a new man," but he shivered as the car shot forward and the chill air struck through him. Fur lining did make a difference. It never occurred to him before that there were men who could not have fur coats when they needed them for comfort. And now he was one of those men! How astonishing!

The new owner of the fur coat decided that it would be wise not to take the strange young man to his house. He would drop him at the first garage, which was a mile and a half nearer than his home. Then if he thought better of his exchange, he could not possibly hunt him up and demand his coat back again. So the young man was let out in the night before a little garage on the outskirts of town, and the Ford disappeared into the darkness, its taillight winking cunningly and whisking out of sight at the first corner. No chance for that fur coat to ever meet up with its former owner again. And Murray Van Rensselaer stood shivering in the road, waiting till his companion was out of sight that he, too, might vanish in another direction. He had no use for a garage, and he groaned in his spirit over the thought of walking farther with those infernally tight shoes. He almost had a wild notion of taking them off and going barefoot for a while.

Then suddenly a brilliant headlight mounted the hill at the top of the road, and a motorcycle roared into view, heading straight toward him. He could see the brass buttons on the man's uniform, and he dodged blindly out of the path of the light and ducked behind the garage in frantic haste, forgetful of his aching feet, and made great strides through the stubble of an old cornfield that seemed acres across, his heart beating wildly at the thought that perhaps the man with his overcoat had already stopped somewhere to telephone information about him. He was enveloped in panic once more and stumbled and fell and rose again regardless of the bruises and scratches, as if he were struggling for the victory in a football game. Only in this game his life was the stake.

A phrase that he had heard somewhere in his past came to his mind and haunted him. Like a chant it beat a rhythm in his brain as he dragged his weary body over miles of darkness.

"The mark of Cain!" it said. Over and over again: "The mark of Cain!"

Chapter 6

Grevet's was a fine old marble mansion just off the avenue with its name in gold script and heavy silken draperies at the plate-glass windows. It had the air of having caught and imprisoned the atmosphere of the old aristocracy that used to inhabit that section of the city. The quiet distinction of the house seemed to give added dignity to the fine old street, where memories of other days still lingered to remind old residents of a time when only the four hundred trod the sacred precincts of those noble mansions.

Inside the wrought-iron grill-work of its outer entrance, the quiet distinction became more intense. No footstep sounded from the deep pile of imported carpets that covered the floors. Gray floors, lofty walls done in pearl and gray and cream. Upholstery of velvet toning with the walls and floor. And light—wonderful perfect light—softly diffused from the walls themselves, seemingly, making it clear as the morning, yet soft with the radiance of moonlight. A pot of daffodils in one window, just where the silken curtain was slightly drawn to the street. A crystal bowl of parma violets on a tiny table of teakwood. An exquisite cushion of needlepoint blindingly intricate in its delicate design and minute stitches. One rare painting of an old Greek temple against a southern sky and sea. That was Grevet's.

And when you entered there was no one present at first. It was very still, like entering some secret hall of silence. You almost felt like an intruder unless you were of the favored ones who came often to have their wants supplied.

A period of overwhelming waiting, of hesitation lest you might have made a mistake after all, and then Madame, in a costume of stunning simplicity, would glance out from some inner sanctum, murmur a command, and out would come a slim attendant in black satin frock and hair, cut seemingly off the same piece of cloth, and demand your need, and later would come forth the mannequins and models wearing creations of distinction that would put the lily's garb to shame.

It was in the mysterious sidelines somewhere, from which they issued forth unexpectedly upon the purchaser of garments, that a group of these attendants stood conversing, just behind Madame's inner sanctum, in low tones because Madame might return at any moment, and Madame did not permit comments on the customers.

"She was a beautiful girl," said one whose high color under tired eyes, and boyish haircut on a mature head, were somehow oddly at variance. "She was *different!*"

"Yes, different!" spoke another crisply with an accent. "Quite different, and attractive, yes. But she had no style. She wore her hair like one who didn't care for style. Pretty, yes, but not at all the thing. *Quite out.* She didn't seem to belong to him at all. She was not like any of the girls he has brought here before."

"And yet she had distinction."

"Yes," hesitating, "distinction of a kind. But more the distinction of another universe."

"Oh, come down to earth, Miss Lancey," cried a round little model with face a shade too plump. "You're always up in the clouds. She had no style, and you know it. That coat she wore was one of those nineteen-ninety-eight coats in Simon's window. I see them every night when I go home. I knew it by those tricky little pockets. Quite cute they are, with good lines, but cheap and common, of course. She was nothing but a poor girl. Why try to make out she was something else? She has a good figure, of course, and pretty features, if one likes that angelic type, but no style in the world."

"She was stunning in the black velvet," broke in the first speaker stubbornly. "I can't help it—I think she had style. There was something—well, kind of gracious about her, as if she were a lady in disguise."

"Oh, Florence, you're so hopelessly romantic! That's way behind the times. You don't find Cinderellas nowadays. Things are more practical. If a lady *has* a disguise, she takes it off. That's more up to date."

"Well, you know yourself she was different. You can't say she wasn't perfectly at home with those clothes. She wore them like a princess."

"She had a beautiful form," put in an older salesperson. "That's a whole lot."

"It takes something more than form," said the girl persistently. "You know that Charlotte Bakerman had a form. They said she was perfect in every measurement, but she walked like a cow, and she carried herself like a gorilla in a tree when she sat down."

"Oh, this girl was graceful, if that's what you mean," conceded the fat one ungraciously.

"It wasn't just grace, either," persisted the champion of the unknown customer. "She didn't seem to be conscious she had on anything unusual at all. She walked the same way when she came in. She walked the same way when she went out in her nineteen ninety-eight. She sort of glorified it. And when she had on the Lanvin green ensemble, it was just as if she had always worn such things. It sort of seemed to belong to her, as if she was born with it, like a bird's feathers."

"I know what you mean," said the woman with tired eyes and artificial blush. "She wasn't thinking about her clothes. They weren't important to her. She would only care if they were suitable. And she would know at a glance without discussing it whether they were suitable. You saw how she looked at that flashy little sports frock, the one with the three shades of red stripes and a low red leather belt. She just turned away and said in a low tone: 'Oh, not that one, Murray!' as if it hurt her."

"Did she call him Murray?" asked the fat one greedily.

"Yes. They seemed to know each other real well. She was almost as if she might have been a sister, only we know he hasn't got any sisters. She might have been a country cousin."

"Perhaps he's going to marry her!" suggested the fat one.

"Nonsense!" said the first girl sharply. "She's not his kind. Imagine the magnificent Mrs. Van Rensselaer mothering anything that wore a nineteen-ninety-eight coat from Simon's! Can you? Besides, they say he's going to marry the Countess Lenowski when she gets her second divorce."

"I don't think *that* girl would marry a man like Murray Van Rensselaer," spoke the thoughtful one. "She has too much character. She had a remarkable face."

"Oh, you can't tell by a face," shrugged a slim one with sinuous body and a sharp black lock of hair pasted out on her cheek. "She can't be much, or she wouldn't let him buy her clothes."

"She didn't!" said the first speaker sharply. "I heard her say, 'I wouldn't think she would like that, Murray. It's too noticeable. I'm sure a nice girl wouldn't like that as well as the blue chiffon.'"

"Hmm!" said the slim one. "Looks as if she must be a relative or something. Did anybody get her name?"

"The address on the box was Elizabeth Chapparelle," contributed a pale little errand girl who had stood by listening.

"Elizabeth!" said the thoughtful one. "She looked like an Elizabeth."

"But if they weren't for her, that wouldn't have been her name," persisted the fat one.

"I thought I heard him call her Bessie once," said the little errand girl.

"Then he was buying for one of his old girls who is going to be married," suggested the slim one contemptuously. "Probably this girl is a friend of them both."

"Hush! Madame is coming! Which one did he take? The Lanvin green?"

"Both. He told Madame to send them both! Yes, Madame, I'm coming!"

A boy in a mulberry uniform with silver buttons entered.

"Say, Lena, take that to Madame, and tell her there's a mistake. The folks say they don't know anything about it."

Lena, the pale little errand girl, took the heavy box and walked slowly off to find Madame, studying the address on the box as she went.

"Why!" She paused by the thoughtful-eyed woman. "It's her. It's that girl!" Madame appeared suddenly with a frown.

"What's this, Lena? How many times have I told you not to stop to talk? Where are you carrying that box?"

"Thomas says there's a mistake in the address. The folks don't know anything about it."

"Where is Thomas? Send him to me. Here, Thomas. What's the matter? Couldn't you find the house? The address is perfectly plain."

"Sure, I found the house, Madame, but they wouldn't take it in. They said they didn't know anything about it. It wasn't theirs."

"Did they say Miss Chapparelle didn't live there? Who came to the door?"

"An old woman with white hair. Yes, she said Miss Chapparelle lived there. She said she was her daughter, but that package didn't belong to her. She said she never bought anything at this place."

"Well, you can take it right back," said Madame sharply. "Tell the woman the young lady knows all about it. Tell her it will explain itself when the young lady opens it. There's a card inside. And Thomas," she added, hurrying after him as he slid away to the door and speaking in a lower voice, "Thomas, you leave it there no matter what she says. It's all paid for, and I'm not going to be bothered this way. You're to leave it no matter what she says, you understand?"

"Sure, Madame, I understand. I'll leave it."

The neat little delivery car, with its one word, GREVET'S, in silver script on a mulberry background, slid away on its well-oiled wheels, and the service persons in their black satin straight frocks turned their black satin bobbed heads and looked meaningfully at one another with glances that said eagerly: "I told you so. That girl was different!" and Madame looked thoughtfully out of her side window into the blank brick wall of the next building and wondered how this was going to turn out. She did not want to have those expensive outfits returned, and she could not afford to anger young Van Rensselaer; he was too good a customer. He had expected her to carry out his instructions. It might be that she would have to go herself to explain the matter. Anyone could see that girl was too unsophisticated to understand. Her mother would probably be worse. She would have notions. Madame had had a mother once herself, so long ago she had forgotten many of her precepts, but she could understand. Madame was clever. This was going to be a case requiring clever action. But Madame was counting much upon Thomas. Thomas, too, could be clever on occasion. That was why he wore the silver buttons on the mulberry uniform and earned a good salary. Thomas knew that his silver buttons depended on his getting things across when Madame spoke to him as she had just done, and Madame believed Thomas would get this across.

In the early dusk of the evening when it came closing time at Grevet's, the service women in chic wraps and small cloche hats flocked stylishly out into the city and made their various ways home. The thoughtful one and the outspoken one wound their way together out toward the avenue and up toward obscure streets tucked in between finer ones, walking to save carfare; for even those who worked at Grevet's, there were circumstances in which it was wise in good weather to save carfare.

Their way led past the houses of wealth, a trifle longer perhaps, but pleasanter, with a touch of something in the air which their narrow lives had missed but which they liked to be near and enjoy if only in the passing. Their days at Grevet's had fostered this love of the beautiful and real, perhaps, that made a glimpse into the windows of the great a pleasant thing: the drifting of a rare lace curtain, the sight of masses of flowers within, the glow of a handsome lamp, and the mellow shadows of a costly room, the sound of fine machinery as the limousines passed almost noiselessly, the quiet perfect service of the butler at the door, the well-groomed women who got out of the cars and went in, delicately shod, to eat dinners that others had prepared, with no thought or worry about expense. These were more congenial surroundings to walk amid, even if it took one a block or two farther out of the way, than a crowded street full of common rushing people, jostling and worried like themselves, and the air full of the sordid things of life.

They were talking about the events of the day, as people will, the happenings of their little world, the only points of contact they had in common out of their separate lives.

"How much have you sold today, Mrs. Hanley?" questioned the girl eagerly. "I had the biggest sale this month yet."

The sad-eyed one smiled pleasantly.

"Oh, I had a pretty good day, Florence. This is always a good time of year, you know."

"Yes, I know. Everybody getting new things." She sighed with a fierce longing that she, too, might have plenty of money to get new things. A sigh like that was easily translatable by her companion. But for some reason Mrs. Hanley shrank tonight from the usual wail that the girl would soon bring up about the unfairness of the division of wealth in the world, perhaps because she, too, was wondering how to make both ends meet and get the new things that were necessary. She roused herself to change the subject. They were passing the Van Rensselaer mansion now, well known to both of them. She snatched at the first subject that presented itself.

"Why do you suppose Madame is so anxious to please that young man when everybody says he doesn't pay his bills?"

"Oh," said Florence almost bitterly, "she knows his dad'll pay 'em. It's everything to have a name like that. He could get away with almost anything if he just told people who he was."

"I suppose so," said Mrs. Hanley almost sadly. "But I hope that girl doesn't keep those clothes. She's too fine for such as he is."

"Yes, isn't she?" said Florence eagerly. "I suppose most folks would think we were crazy talking like that. He's considered a great catch. But somehow I couldn't see a girl like that getting soiled with being tied up to a man that's got talked about as much as he has. She's different. There aren't many like that living. That is the way she looks to me. Why, she's like some angel just walking the earth because she has to; at least that's the impression her face gave to me. Just as if she didn't mind things us other folks think so much about; she had higher, wonderful things to think about. I don't often see anyone that stirs me up this way and makes me think about my mother. I guess I ain't much myself, never expected to be, but when you see someone that is, you can't help but think!"

After that incoherent sentence, Florence, with a cheerful good night, turned off at her corner, and Mrs. Hanley went home to a little pent-up room high up in a fourth-rate boardinghouse, to wash off her makeup and prepare a tiny supper on a small gas stove, and be a mother for a few brief hours to her little crippled son, who lay on a tiny couch by the one window all day long and waited for her to come.

Chapter 7

More than four hundred miles away, a freight train bumped and jerked itself into the town of Marlborough and lumberingly came to a halt. With its final lurch of stopping, a hasty figure rolled from under one of the empty cars and hurried stiffly away into the shadows as if pursued by a fear that the train upon which he had been riding without a right might come after him and compel him to ride farther.

The train was over an hour late. It was due at five. It had been held up by a wreck ahead.

It was the first time that Murray Van Rensselaer had ever taken a journey under a freight car, and he felt sure it would be the last. Even though he might be hard pressed, he would never resort to that mode of travel again. That the breath of life was still in him was a miracle, and he crawled into the shadow of a hedge to take his bearings.

There were others who had stolen rides in that manner, for thousands of miles, and seemed to live through it. He had read about it in his childhood and always wanted to try it, and when the opportunity presented itself just in the time of his greatest need, with a cordon of policemen in the next block and his last dollar from the ample roll he started with spent, he had lost no time in availing himself of it. But he felt sure now that if he had been obliged to stay under that fearful rumbling car and bump over that uneven roadbed for another ten minutes, he would have died of horror, or else rolled off beneath those grinding, crunching wheels. His head was aching, as if those wheels were going around inside his brain. His back ached with an ache unspeakable, and his cramped legs ached as if they were being torn from his aching body. He had never known before how many places there were in a human body to ache.

He had eaten no breakfast nor dinner. There was no buffet in the private berth he had chosen, and he had no money in his pocket to purchase with if there had been. It was his first realization of what money meant, of what it was to be utterly without it. For the moment, the fear that was driving him in his flight was obliterated by the simple pangs of hunger and weariness. He had started for the far West, where he hoped to strike some remote cattle ranch where men herded whose pasts were shady, and where no questions were asked. He felt that his experience in polo would stand him in good stead among horses, and there he could live and be a new man. He had been planning all the way, taking his furtive path across the country, half on foot and half by suburban trolleys, until his money gave out and he was forced to try the present mode of transportation. He had entertained great hopes of a speedy arrival among other criminals, where he would be safe, when he crawled under that dirty freight car and settled himself for his journey. But now, with his head whirling and that desperate faintness at the pit of his stomach, he loathed the thought of going farther. If there had been a police station close at hand, he would have walked in gratefully and handed himself over to justice. This business of fleeing from justice was no good, no good in the world.

He stood in the shelter of a great privet hedge that towered darkly above him, and shivered in the raw November air, until the train had jolted itself back and forth several times and finally grumbled on its clattery way again. He had a strange fancy that the train was human and had discovered his absence, was trying to find him perhaps, and might still compel him to go on. He almost held his breath as car after car passed his hiding place. Each jolt and rumble of the train sent shivers down his spine and a wave of sickness over him, almost as if he had been back underneath that dreadful car above those grinding wheels. It was with relief unspeakable that he watched the ruby gleam of the taillight disappear at last down the track around a curve. He drew a long breath and tried to steady himself.

Down the road, across the tracks, some men were coming. He drew within his shelter until they were passed and then slid round the corner into a street that apparently led up over the brow of a hill.

He had no aim, and he wondered why he went anywhere. There was nowhere to go. No object in going. No money to buy bed or bread with, nothing on him worth pawning. He had long ago pawned the little trinkets left in his pockets when he started. Eventually this going must cease. One had to eat to live. One couldn't walk forever on sore feet and next to no shoes. Flesh and bones would not keep going indefinitely at command of the brain. Why should the brain bother them longer? Why not go up there on the hill somewhere and crawl out of sight and sleep? That would be an easy way to die, die while one slept. He must sleep. He was overpowered with it like a drug. If he only had a cigarette, it would hearten him up. It was three days since he had smoked— he who used to be always smoking, who smoked more cigarettes than any other fellow in his set. It was deadly doing without! And to think that the son of his father was reduced to this! Why, even the servants at home had plenty to eat and drink and *smoke*!

He plodded on up the street, not knowing where he was going, nor caring, scarcely knew that he was going. Just going because he had to. Some power beyond himself seemed to be driving him.

Suddenly a bright light shone out across the walk from a big stone building set back from the street. It was a church, he saw as he drew nearer, yet it had a curious attachment of other buildings huddled around it, a part of the church, yet not so churchly. He wondered vaguely if it might not be a parochial school of some sort.

There were lights in low windows near the ground and tall shrubs making shelter about, and from the open doorway there issued a most delectable odor, the smell of roasting meat.

Straight to the brightness and appetizing odor his lagging feet led him without his own conscious volition. It was something that he had to do, to go to that smell and that comfort, even though it led him into terrible danger. A moment more and he stood within the shelter of a great syringa bush looking down into the open window of a long, lit basement room, steadying himself with his trembling hand against the rough stone wall of the building, and just below his eager hand was a table with plates and plates full of the most delectable-looking rolls and rows of wonderful chocolate cakes and gleaming frosted nut cake.

He could hear voices in the distance, but no one was in sight, and he reached down suddenly and swiftly and with both hands gathered two little round white frosted cakes and a great big buttered roll and, sliding behind the syringa bush, began to eat them voraciously, snatching a bit from one hand and then the other.

He had never stolen anything before, and he was not conscious of stealing now. He ate because he was famished and must eat to live.

Down in the basement a church supper was in preparation.

Great roasts were in the parish oven; potatoes were boiling for the masher. The water was on for lima beans, and a table stood filled with rows of salad plates, on which one of the church mothers was carefully placing crisp lettuce and red-ripe tomatoes stuffed with celery and bits of nuts. Another church mother was ladling out mayonnaise from a great yellow bowl in which she had just made it. A kettle of delicious soup was keeping hot over the stove.

They never did things by halves in the Marlborough Presbyterian Church, and this was a very special occasion. It was the annual dinner of the Christian Endeavor Society, and they had always made a great deal of it. In addition to this, a new man was coming to town, a young man, well heralded, notable among young church workers in the city where he had spent his life, already known for his activity in Christian Endeavor work and all forms of social and uplift labor. They felt honored that he was coming to their midst. As a teller in the bank, he would have a good financial and social standing as well, and moreover his name was well remembered, as his father and mother used to live in Marlborough years before. There had been a letter commendatory and introductory from the city pastor to Rev. Dr. Harrison, the pastor of the Marlborough church, and the annual church affair had been postponed a week that it might be had on the night of his arrival, that he might be the guest of honor and be welcomed into their midst properly. Not a few of the girls in the Christian Endeavor had new dresses for the occasion, and the contributions for the dinner had been many and unusually generous. It seemed that all the girls were willing to make cakes galore, and each vied with the other to have the best confection of the culinary art that could be produced. Some of the mothers had offered their best linen and silver to make the tables gorgeous, and there had been much preparation for the program, music, speeches, and even a dramatic monologue. The vice president, who was poetically inclined, had written a poem that was intended as a sort of address of welcome to the stranger, and an introduction to their members, and many a clever hit and pun upon names embellished its verses. No one who had come to town in years had had the welcome that was being prepared for Allan Murray, the new teller in the Marlborough National Bank, and State Secretary of the Christian Endeavor Society in his home state.

The big basement dining room of the church was all in array with tables set in a hollow square. Two girls were putting on the finishing touches.

"Anita, oh, Anita! Has Hester May's sponge cake come yet?" called the taller of the two, a girl rather apt to wear many beads.

"Yes, it's here, Jane, real gummy chocolate frosting on top. Mmmm! Mmmm! I could hardly keep from cutting it. It looks luscious. Is your mother going to get here in time to make the coffee?"

"Oh yes, she'll be here in half an hour. You ought to put an apron on, Anita. You'll get something on that lovely blue crêpe dress. My, but you look scrumptious with that great white collar over the blue. Did you make that collar yourself? It's wonderful! Say, how did you embroider that? Right through the lace border and all? Oh, I see! My, I wish I was clever like you, Anita!"

"Oh, cut it, Jane! We haven't time for flattery! I've got to finish setting this table. Are the forks over there? Where's Joseph? Go ask him if we haven't any more forks. He washed them after the Ladies' Aid luncheon. Perhaps he put them away."

"They're in the lower drawer. I saw them when I got out the napkins to fold. Here they are. Wouldn't it be dreadful if the guest of honor didn't get here after all, when everything is coming out so fine? Did you know Mrs. Price was sending roses out of her conservatory? A great armful. I brought down mother's cut-glass bowl to put them in, and we'll put them at the speaker's table, right in front of Mr. Harrison and the guest. Oh dear, I hope he gets here all right!"

"Why, why shouldn't he, Jane? What an idea! Didn't he write and say he expected to arrive this afternoon? Mrs. Summers said she had his room all ready, and his trunk came last night, so of course he'll be here."

"But there's been an awful wreck on the road. Didn't you hear about it, Anita? Yes, it's terrible, they say. Doctor Jarvis telephoned he couldn't come to lunch. He went on a special relief train. It's somewhere down around Smith's Crossing. The rails spread, or something, and the express telescoped the way train, or else it was the other way round, and a lot of people got hurt, and some killed, or at least there was a rumor they did."

"Mercy!" said Anita, stopping in her work. "Why, that's awful! Allan Murray might have been on the train, you know."

"No, I guess not," said Jane. "He telegraphed last night he was arriving here late in the afternoon. That would mean he would take the train at Alton at noon. This wreck was the morning train. But then, he might have been delayed by it. You know it takes a long time to clear the tracks. Oh well, he's likely at Mrs. Summers' now unpacking, or we would have heard. We ought to stop talking and get to work. The celery has to be put in the glasses and the nuts in the dishes. One of those nut dishes is broken, too. Isn't there another dish up on that high shelf that will do?"

"I brought over some silver nut dishes. They will do for the middle table. Did they say any Marlborough people were on that train?"

"Yes, Dick Foster and some college friend coming home for the weekend, but they phoned they were all right. They were in the last car and only a little shaken up. Mr. Foster took the car and ran down to Smith's Crossing after them. Then there was that lame shoemaker from under the drugstore, that little shop, you know, and Mrs. Bly, the seamstress. Nobody knows anything about them. At least I didn't hear."

"Oh, Mrs. Bly," said Anita sympathetically. "I hope no harm came to her, poor thing. She's sewed for us ever since I was a child. Say, Jane, does your brother know this Mr. Murray? He went to the same college, didn't he?"

"Yes, but it was after Allan Murray left. He saw him once though. He was just adored in college. He was a great athlete, though very slender and wiry, Bob says, and he was awfully clever. Made Phi Beta Kappa and all that, and was president of the

YMCA, and head of the student gov, and stunningly handsome. Bob didn't say that though. It was Marietta's cousin said that. Her brother was in Allan Murray's class and brought him home once, and she thought him just a perfect Greek god, to hear her talk, but when I asked Bob about it, he said, oh yes, he was a looker he guessed. He never took particular notice. And I simply couldn't get a description, though I tried hard enough. He couldn't even remember the color of his eyes, said they were just eyes, and what difference did it make. But Marietta said he was dark and had very large dark eyes, slender—no, *lean*, that was the world she used— and awfully tanned and fit. She said he had a smile, too, that you never could forget, and fine white teeth, and was careful about his appearance, but not much of a dresser. She said he had worked his way through college. His father had lost money, and he was going in for thrift and didn't give much time to social things but was awfully good company."

"Hmm! That's just about what the minister said when he told us he wanted us to make him feel at home. I don't really approve of it myself, this taking a stranger and carrying him around on a little throne before you've tried him out, but when Mr. Harrison asked us to arrange this Christian Endeavor banquet on the night of his arrival to give him a kind of welcome to our town, why of course it had to be done. And of course Mr. Harrison knows what he's talking about, or he wouldn't suggest it. But it makes it just a little embarrassing for us girls to seem to be so very eager to welcome another young man into our midst that we fall all over ourselves to let him know it right off the first night."

"Now, Anita! You're always so fussy and prudish! As if he would think anything about it at all. Besides, his having been an active Christian Endeavorer in his home church and his father having been a member of our church years ago when he was a boy makes it kind of different—don't you think?"

"Oh, I suppose so," said Anita thoughtfully. "Only I do hope he won't be stuck on himself. The young men are all so sure of their welcome anyhow these days, it doesn't seem as if it was hardly necessary. And it's enough to turn a young man's head anyway to have the whole town bowing down to him this way. Teller in the town bank, taken in to board at one of the best houses in town just because Mrs. Summers knew his mother when she was a girl, and given a church supper on the night of his arrival. I'm sure I hope he will be worth it all, and that we won't spoil him right at the start."

"Oh, Anita! You're so funny! What do you care if he is spoiled, anyway, if we have a good time out of it? I'm sure I don't. And it'll be nice to have another fellow around; so many of our boys have gone off to college or to work in the city. And those that are left don't care a cent for the church affairs. I have to fairly hire Bob and Ben to come to anything we have here, and this Murray man, they say, is crazy about church work. If it proves true, I think the society will grow by leaps and bounds."

"Well, what kind of a growth is that? Just following after a new man! That's not healthy growth. When he goes, they'll go with him if that's what they come for. Who is that outside? Perhaps it's the man with the ice cream. It ought to be here by this time. Go out and look. It may be some of those tormenting boys that live across the street. And the cakes and rolls are all under that window. I declare, I should think church members would teach their children better than to *steal*! Go quick, Jane. I don't want to leave this butter now till I get it all cut in squares. But for pity's sake, forget that new man, or you'll be bowing down to him just like everybody else!"

"Oh, Anita! You're perfectly hopeless," giggled Jane as she fled up the basement stairs to the outside door to reconnoiter.

A moment more and Anita heard her friend's voice ring out clearly in an eagerly hospitable voice among the syringa bushes outside the chapel window:

"Isn't this Mr. Murray? Mr. Allan Murray? Won't you come right in? We're all expecting you."

Anita, cutting butter into squares in the pantry window in the basement, turned away with a curl of her pretty lip and slammed down the window. If Jane wanted to make a fool of herself with this stranger, she, Anita, was not going to be a party to it. And she carried the cakes to be cut to the far table in the kitchen quite away from the dining room and went to work with set lips and a haughty chin. The new man should not think *she* was after him, anyway.

Chapter 8

Outside the church Murray Van Rensselaer, somewhat fortified within by the stolen bun and the two frosted cakes, whose crumbs were yet upon his lips, started in astonishment.

Of the unexpectedly warm greeting he caught only one word, "Murray," his own name, and as he took it in, thinking at first that he had been recognized, it came to him what it would mean. The whole careful fabric of his intricate escape was undone. Unless he disappeared at once into the darkness, he would be brought speedily out into the light and have to explain. Some dratted girl he had probably met at a dance somewhere and didn't remember. But everybody knew him. That was the trouble with belonging to a family like his and being prominent in society and clubs and sports. His picture had been in the paper a thousand times—when he took the blue ribbon at the horse show, when he played golf with a visiting prince at Palm Beach, on his favorite pony playing polo, smashing the ball across the net to a world champion tennis player; the notable times were too numerous to mention. She didn't know. She hadn't seen the city papers yet or hadn't noticed. Probably didn't think it was the same name. It wouldn't take long for the news to travel, even four hundred miles. That was nothing. He must get out of here!

He made a wild dash in the other direction but came sharply in contact with a stiff branch of syringa, which jabbed him in the eye smartly, and for an instant the pain was so great that he could do nothing but stand still.

The girl in the doorway was tall and slim, and she stood where the light from the chapel shone full behind her and silhouetted a very pleasant outline. Also she knew that the light caught and scintillated from her crystal necklace, which hung to her very long indefinable waist, and that she presented thus a trim appearance. But she might as well have been short and fat for all he saw of her as he stood and held his eye and groped about with his other hand on what seemed an interminable stone wall behind him. Was there no way to get out of this?

Jane was not a girl to give up the vantage she had gained of being the first to welcome this new hero to town. He had backed off into the shrubbery, shy perhaps, and had not answered, but she was reasonably sure of her man. Of course it must be he. He was likely reconnoitering to be sure he was in the right place, and it wouldn't do to let him slip away. He might be one of those who were shy of an open welcome and needed to be caught or he would escape. So Jane proceeded to catch him.

With nimble feet she descended the three stone steps and was upon him before he knew it, with a slim white hand outheld.

"Your name is Murray, isn't it? I was sure it must be"—as he did not dissent. "Mine is Jane Freeman, and we're awfully glad you've come to town. We're expecting you to supper, you know, and you might as well come right in. Everybody else will be here pretty soon, and we'll just have that much more time to get acquainted. Won't the girls be humming though when they find out I met you first! But I had a sort of right, because my mother and your mother were schoolmates together, you know! Were you trying to find the right door? It is confusing here. Doctor Harrison's study is that door, and that one goes into the choir room, and this enters the kitchen and dining rooms. We go over to this other door and enter through the chapel. Everyone gets lost here at first."

"Yes, I guess I did lose my way," murmured Murray Van Rensselaer, feeling it imperative to say something, under the circumstances, and casting furtive glances behind him to see how he could get away.

"Come right around this way," went on Jane volubly. "Here's the path. Have you been over to Mrs. Summers' yet? Isn't she coming over? I thought she would have shown you the way."

"No, I haven't been to Mrs. Summers' yet," he said, catching eagerly at the idea. "But I really can't go in this way. I've—you see, there was a wreck on the road—"

"Oh, were you *really* in the wreck after all? How wonderful!

And you got through? How ever did you do it? Why, the relief train hasn't come back yet—at least it hadn't when I came over."

"Oh, I walked part of the way and got on the freight—"

"Oh really! How thrilling! Then you can tell us all about the wreck. We haven't heard much. Come right in and meet Anita. I want you to tell her about the wreck." But the young man halted firmly on the walk.

"Indeed," said he decidedly, "it's quite impossible. I'm a wreck myself. I've got to dress before I could possibly meet anybody, except in the dark, and I think you'll have to excuse me tonight. My trunk hasn't come yet, you know, and I'm really not fit to be seen. You don't know what a wreck is, I guess."

"Oh, were you really in it like that!" exclaimed Jane adoringly. "How wonderful that you escaped! But you're mistaken about your trunk. It came yesterday. Mrs. Summers told me this morning it had arrived, and it's over in your room. If you really must dress first, I'll show you the way to Mrs. Summers', but it wouldn't be necessary, you know. You would be all the more a hero. You could come right in the church dressing room and wash and comb your hair. It would be terribly interesting and dramatic for you to appear just as you came from the wreck, you know."

"Thank you," said the young man dryly. "Much too interesting for me. I'll just get over to my trunk, if you don't mind," he suggested soothingly. "Which way is the house? I won't have any trouble finding it. It's not far away, you say?"

"Oh no, it's right here," she said excitedly with a vague wave of her hand. "Come right across the lawn. It's shorter. I don't mind running over in the least. In fact, I've got to go and see if I can't borrow another vase for some roses that just arrived. You must be very tired after such an exciting afternoon. Was it very terrible at first? The shock, I mean?"

"Oh! Terrible? Yes, the wreck. Why, rather unpleasant at first, you know. The confusion and—and—"

"I suppose the women all screamed. They usually do when they are frightened. I never can see why. Now, I never scream. When I'm frightened I'm just as cool. My father says he can always trust me in a crisis because I keep still and do something. You look as if you were that way, too. But then men are, of course."

She was steering him swiftly toward a neat Queen Anne house of somewhat ancient date, perhaps, but very pretty and attractive, in spite of the fact that the maples with which it was surrounded were bare of leaves. There were little ruffled curtains at the window, and plants, and old-fashioned lamps with bright shades, and a gray-haired woman moving about in a bay window watering a fern. It was a picture of a sweet, quiet home, and something of its peace stole out into the November night with its soft lights like a welcome. Murray looked with hungry eyes. There would be beds in that house, and warmth, and a table with good things to eat. The bite he had stolen had only whetted his appetite. How good if he had a right to enter this home as the boy who was expected would do soon, welcomed, a festive supper prepared, perhaps a place where he might earn enough to live, and friends to make life worth the living. It was the first time in his life he had ever felt an urge to work. His father's business had seemed a bore to him. He had pitied him now and then when he happened to think of it at all, that he was old and had to go downtown every day to "work"—not that he had to. Murray knew his father could retire a good many times over and not feel it. But he had pitied him that he was old and therefore had nothing to interest him in life but dull business. Now business suddenly seemed a haven to be desired.

But all this was merely an undercurrent of thought while he was really casting about in his mind how he might rid himself of his pest of a girl, and was furtively observing the street and the lay of the bushes that he might suddenly dodge away and leave her in the darkness. He hesitated to do it lest she might even pursue him, and he felt that in case of fleeing his strength would probably leave him altogether, and he would drop beside some dreary bush and be overtaken.

He could not quite understand his attitude toward this girl. He had been somewhat of a lady-killer, and no girl had held terrors for him in the old life. He knew they always fell for him, and he could go any way he liked and they would follow. Now here was a girl, just a common little country girl, filling him with terror. She seemed to possess almost supernatural power over him, as if she had eyes that could see through to his soul and would expose him to the scorn of the world if he for one moment angered her and let her get a chance to look into his poor shaken mind. *Murray*

Van Rensselaer! Why, Murray, what's the matter with you? he said to himself. And then, *But I'm not Murray Van Rensselaer anymore. I'm a murderer fleeing from justice! I must get away!*

Then right before him, what he thought was a long french window turned into a glass door and opened in front of his unwilling feet, and there stood in the broad burst of light the woman with the gray hair whom he had seen through the window going about the room.

She stood there with a questioning look upon her face, and she had kind eyes—eyes like Mrs. Chapparelle's—*mother* eyes. They looked into the darkness of the yard as if they were waiting for him, searching, expecting him, and he found his feet would go no further. They would not take the dash into the darkness of the shrubbery that his situation required. They just stopped and waited. It had been growing in his consciousness for some time that this thing would happen pretty soon, that he would stop and get caught, and he wondered almost apathetically what he would do then. Just wait, and let them do with him what they pleased?

But Jane's voice rang out triumphantly: "He's come, Mrs. Summers. He didn't get hurt after all. He came through all right. Isn't that great? But he's all messed up, and he wants to clean up. I told him I was sure his trunk had come. It has, hasn't it?"

"Oh, is that you, Jane? Yes, his trunk has come," said the lady with a smile. Then she turned toward the shivering youth and put out both hands eagerly, taking his cold ones in hers that felt to him like warm little veined rose leaves. She drew him without his own volition across the brick terrace into the light.

"So this is Allan Murray!" she said, and her voice was like a mother's caress. "My dear boy! I'm so glad to have you with me! You don't know how precious your dear mother was to me! And I shall be so glad if you will let me take her place while you are here, as much as anyone could take the place of a woman like your mother!"

Now was the time for him to bolt, of course, if he was ever going to get away, just jerk his hands from her frail touch and bolt! But his feet didn't seem to understand. They just stood! And his eyes lingered hungrily on her loving ones. He longed, oh, how he wished that this woman really was a friend of his mother—that he had had a mother who could have been a friend of a woman like this one, that he might now be befriended by her. And his hands warmed to the soft vital touch of those little frail rose-leaf hands. They seemed to be warming his very soul, clear to the frightened center where he knew he was a murderer and an outlaw. But he hadn't vitality enough left to vanish. He would have been glad if some magic could have made him invisible, or if he could have suddenly died. But nothing like that happened to men who were in trouble.

Then, his hands and his feet having failed him in this predicament, he tried his lips, and to his surprise words came, fluently from long habit, with quite a nice sound to his voice, modest and grateful and polite and apologetic.

"So kind of you!" he murmured safely, the old vernacular

returning from habit to his lips. "But I'm not fit to be touched. It's been awful, you know—smoke and soot and cinders and broken things. I'm torn and dirty—I'm not fit to be seen!"

"Why, of course!" said the dear lady with understanding. "You don't want me to look you over and see how much you resemble your mother till you've had a bath and a shave. I know. I've had a boy of my own, you know. He died in the war"—with the breath of a sigh—"but come right up to your room. Everything is all ready, and there's plenty of hot water. The bathroom is right next to your room, and your room is at the top of the stairs on the right. There are towels and soap and everything you need. If I'd only had your trunk key, I would have presumed to take out your clothes and hang them in the closet for you. It would have been such a pleasure to get ready for a boy again. And it would have taken out the wrinkles. But I've my electric iron all ready, and I can press anything that needs it while you are taking your bath. Suppose I go up with you and you unlock the trunk and hand me out your suit, and I'll just give it a mite of a pressing while you're in the bathroom. It won't take a minute, and I'd love to."

She led him as she spoke to the foot of the stairs, where a soft light above invited to the quiet restfulness of upstairs, and a gleam of a white bathroom lured unspeakably his tired body. But his brain was functioning again. He saw a way of escape from this delightful but fearful situation.

"That's the trouble," he said. "I have lost my keys! They were in my bag, and the bag rolled down the embankment into the burning cars."

"Oh!"

"Ah!" from the two women as he hurried on.

"I am sorry to disappoint you, but I guess I'll have to forgo the supper. It will take too long to get that trunk open and get ready. You two just better go over to the church, and I'll stick around here and get shaped up for tomorrow. You know I've been through a pretty rough time and—"

"I know you have," broke in the gentle voice firmly, "but I'm afraid you'll really have to go to that supper. It's all been prepared as a welcome for you on account of your father and mother, you know, and it's pretty much for a church and a town to remember and love people like that through thirty years of absence. Besides, Mr. Harper, the president of the bank, will be there, and I don't suppose it would be a very good thing for your future as the new teller if you were to stay away. You see, really, they are honoring you and will be terribly disappointed—"

Murray Van Rensselaer began to feel as if he really were the person who was being waited for over at that church supper, and his natural savoir-faire came to his assistance.

"Oh, in that case of course," he said gallantly, "it wouldn't do to disappoint them, but how can I possibly manage it? You don't happen to have a suit of your son's that you'd be willing to loan me?"

He said it with just the right shade of depreciation and humility. It was a great favor, of course, to ask for the suit of her dead son. But she flashed a pleasant, tender look at him.

"No, dear, I haven't. I gave them all away where they would be useful. But I am sure we can get that trunk of yours open."

"Couldn't we pick the lock?" said Jane, wishing she still wore hair pins. It would be so romantic to lend the hair pin that opened the new hero's trunk.

But Mrs. Summers opened a little cabinet by the foot of the stairs and took out a hammer and screwdriver.

"I think we'll manage with these," she said pleasantly. "Jane, if you'll just take those two vases and that maple cake and run over to the church and tell them we'll be a few minutes late, but we're coming, then I needn't stop to go over just yet. Now, Allan Murray, come on!" she said, and started up the stairs.

Murray Van Rensselaer hesitated and looked toward the door, but the reluctant Jane, with arms full of cake and vases, was still filling it, eyeing him blissfully, and there was no escape that way. Perhaps if he once got in the room above with the door locked, he could climb from the window and get away in the dark. So he dragged himself up the stairs after his hospitable hostess and was ushered into a bedroom, the like of which for sweetness and restfulness had never met his eye before.

There were thin white smooth curtains at three low windows, a white bed with plump pillows that looked the best thing in the world for his weary body, a little stand beside it with a shaded lamp, and a Bible. Odd! A Bible! Across the room was a fireplace under a white mantel, and drawn up beside it under a tall shaded lamp was a big luxurious chair with a bookcase full of books beside it.

710

Then he turned to the inner side of the room, and there a bureau with a great mirror suddenly flung his own image back to him and startled him.

The last time he had seen himself in a mirror was at his tailor's trying on a new suit that had just been finished for his order. He could see the trim lines of his figure now, the sharp creases of well-pressed garments, the smart cut, the fine texture of the material, his own well-groomed appearance, his handsome careless face, shaven and sure of himself and his world, the grace of his every movement. He had not known he was particularly vain of himself, but now as he gazed on this forlorn, unshaven object, with bloodshot eyes, with coarse, ill-cut garments, and a shapeless cap crushed in his dirty, trembling hand, he was suddenly filled with a great shame.

Mrs. Summers was down on her knees beside a neat trunk, making strong, efficient strokes with a hammer on the lock.

I don't belong here! The words were as audible to his ears as if he had spoken them aloud, and he turned with a swift motion to glide out the door and away, but too late. The lock of the trunk had given way with a rasping sound, and Mrs. Summers rose with a little smile of triumph on her lips and looked toward him. He could not flee with those kind mother eyes upon him.

"Now, if you'll help me pull it out from the wall, we can open it," she said pleasantly, and there was nothing for him to do but acquiesce, although he really was very little help with that trunk, for his arms were weak, and when he stooped, a great dizziness came over him, so that he almost thought he was going to fall.

Mrs. Summers swung the top of the trunk open deftly.

"We can have Mr. Klingen, the locksmith, up in the morning to fix that lock before we put the trunk away in the attic for the winter," she said, smiling. "Now, which is the suit you want to wear tonight? This blue one right on top? We've got to hurry a little because it's getting late. And I'll tell you a secret. I've got three big pans of scalloped oysters downstairs piping hot and just ready to be eaten, and I want you to help me carry them over to the church. They're a surprise. They don't know they're going to have scalloped oysters. They think they're only having roast lamb and mashed potatoes, but I just thought I'd have a little celebration on myself, so I made these without telling. Do you like scalloped oysters?"

"Do I like scalloped oysters?" beamed Murray, forgetting his role of outlaw and realizing his empty stomach. "Lead me to 'em."

His hostess smiled appreciatively.

"All right, you hurry then, and I'll have your clothes up in a jiffy! Here's the bathroom, and this is the hot water." She turned the faucet on swiftly. "And this knob controls the shower. Bob always liked a shower. Do you?"

"I certainly do!" said Murray fervently.

"Well, now, hurry up! I'll have your suit up in no time. Let's run a race!"

She ran smiling down the stairs as if she were an old comrade, and he stood still in the cozy little bathroom with the steam of the nice, hot water rising in the white tub, and what seemed like a perfect army of clean, luxurious towels with big embroidered S's on them, and Turkish washrags with blue crocheted edges, and cakes of sweet-smelling soap all calling him to the bath that his aching body so much desired, and yet now was the time when he ought to be going! He *must* be going!

He glanced back from the door and down the stairs. He could just see an ironing board beyond the dining room door, right in the doorway, and the blue suit lying across it, the trousers folded in a most acceptable manner, and there was her step. She was standing right in the doorway with the iron in her hand and facing toward the stairs! He could not get away without passing her, at least not by going down the stairs. And, well—why not take a bath? He certainly needed it. There would be a way to get away later. And oh, scalloped oysters, and those good things he had seen through the windows! But of course he couldn't go to that supper! Still, there was the bath all ready, and no telling when he would ever get a chance again.

So he locked the door and began swiftly to take off the alien garments that in the three weeks of his wanderings he had managed to acquire. At least, here was a bath, and why not take the goods the gods provided?

Chapter 9

Murray Van Rensselaer was roused from the relaxation which the luxury of soap and water had brought to him by the sound of Mrs. Summers' voice and a tap at the bathroom door.

"Your suit is ready on the bed, and I took the liberty of laying out some underclothes and things that I found in the trunk. Will it take you long to dress? I don't want my oysters to get tough."

"I'll be with you in no time now," he called lightly as he scrubbed away feebly with one of the big Turkish towels. He was beginning to realize all he was in for. Where would he get shaving things? He was not used to shaving himself often, either. He had depended on his man so long. But perhaps that trunk would have some things in it. Darn it all! Suppose that suit didn't fit after she had taken so much trouble pressing it. He would simply have to make a dive out of the window if it didn't. Or wait. He could say they had sent the wrong trunk! Only how would she account for the fact that he hadn't noticed it when she took out the suit? Well, he needn't cross the bridge till he came to it.

He gathered up his coarse garments, enveloped himself in a towel, and with a hasty survey of the hall, made a dive into "his room," feeling as if he had already weathered several storms.

There on the bed lay garments, and fearfully he put forth his hand and examined them. They were pleasant garments, smooth and fine, not perhaps so fine as the heir of the house of Van Rensselaer had been used to wearing, and still, good enough to feel luxurious after the ones he had picked up by the way on his journeys and used as a disguise. He climbed tentatively into them and found that they fit very well—a little loose on his lean body, grown leaner now with enforced privation, but still a very respectable fit.

Everything was there, even to necktie and collar, even to buttons put onto the shirt. What a mother that woman was! Fancy his mother doing a thing like that, putting buttons on a shirt! And hunting out all those garments just as if she had been a man! Well, this woman was great! He had a passing regret that he could not remain and enjoy her longer, but at least he was thankful for this brief touch with a life like that. Well, he would remember it, and sometime, when—no! There would never be any time when he could, of course. He was a murderer and an outlaw. But if there had been, she would have been a sweet memory to put by to think of, a kind of ideal in a world that knew no ideals. There had been fellows in college, a few that looked as if they had homes and mothers like this. He hadn't realized then what made them different, but this must have been it. They had homes and mothers. He began to envy the chap whose name was Allan Murray. What a winter he would have in this room, sitting by that fire reading those books. He had never been much of a reader himself, but now as he slid his feet into the shoes that were a whole size too large for him and glanced up at the comfortable chair and the light and the gleaming blue and red and gold of the backs of those books, he thought it might be a pleasant occupation. In fact, almost anything that kept one at home and gave one rest and peace seemed heaven to him now. The bath had refreshed him and given him a brief spurt of strength, and now that he was again attired in clean garments, and looked fairly like a respectable young man once more, his courage rose. He had managed the old-fashioned razor very well indeed for one as unskilled in caring for himself as he was, and his clean-shaven face looked back at him now from the big old mahogany-framed mirror with a fairly steady glance. He wasn't so bad-looking after all. There were heavy shadows under his eyes, and he looked thin and tired, and there was an almost irritating resemblance to his mother in his face that he had never noticed before, but still, nobody would ever look upon him just casually and take him for a murderer. And here, for the time being, he was protected by another man's identity and name. If that chap Allan Murray only didn't turn up in the midst of proceedings, why, perhaps he could even venture to get a little dinner, if things didn't get too thick. Of course he could always bolt if there were any signs of the other fellow coming to life. It was to be hoped that he at least had sustained a sprained ankle in the wreck that would keep him till morning, or till a late train that night. He hated the idea of having to go off with the other fellow's clothes. They might be some he was fond of, and maybe he couldn't afford to buy many. But he had a good job ahead of him, and he'd probably pull through—teller of a bank! That must bring a fairly large salary. And anyhow, if a fellow was a murderer, why not be a thief also? One was an outlaw anyway. Might as well be hung for a sheep as a lamb. Besides, would that other fellow stop at a suit of clothes if his life was at stake? And the reputation of his fine old family? I ask you.

His meditations were broken by a pleasant voice chanting: "Are you ready, Allan Murray? My oysters will be tough if they have to wait another minute!" and there was that something in her voice that made him respond cheerily much in the same spirit:

"Yes, I'm coming, Mrs. Summers. Be with you immediately." And that was the first that his real inner consciousness knew or had admitted that he really meant to dare to go to that supper.

He snatched a nice white hairbrush and brushed his hair vigorously, parting it in a way he had never done before, and bungled a knot in the blue tie she had laid out; then, grasping a gray felt hat that seemed to wink at him from the tray of the trunk, he hurried downstairs, as pleasant-appearing a young man as ever one would need to see. He caught a glimpse of himself in a long old mirror between two windows in the living room as he came downstairs, and he said to himself: *Why, I don't look in the least like myself. I look a new man. Nobody would ever dream that I'm a murderer!*

He carried two pans of scalloped oysters across the lawn to the church, while Mrs. Summers walked beside him and carried the third and guided him to the church kitchen door. Now, here would be a good chance to escape when she went inside the kitchen, only he would simply have to take one of those pans of oysters with him, for they were making him giddy now with their delicious odor. He wished he had remembered to bring his old overcoat with him, for it was cold out here in the chill November air.

But Mrs. Summers gave him no chance to escape. She swung the door open and ushered him inside, where he was surrounded by a bevy of young people, who fairly took him into their arms with welcome and almost carried him on their shoulders into a great banquet hall, where tables were set with flowers and overflowing plates of good things, and the odors of wonderful food were more than a starving man could resist. He let them shut the door and draw him inside. Only when he lifted his eyes and met the eyes of one girl in blue whom they introduced as Anita, and who looked at him as if she knew he was a sham, and despised him, did he come to himself and wish he could run away.

But Anita dealt her glancing blows and passed indifferently, and he was hurried eagerly into the banquet room and placed in the seat of honor beside the minister, who had also just arrived.

There was a great excitement, for someone had just come in

with grave face and open evening paper, stating that the name of Allan Murray was among those who were seriously injured in the wreck.

Murray couldn't help feeling a twinge of relief and security as he heard that. At least he could eat his dinner in peace, without any more likelihood than there had been for the last three weeks that he would be apprehended and lodged in jail before the meal was over.

But his relief was but short-lived, for another difficulty approached. The minister leaned over, smiling, and said in a low tone: "Murray, they're going to call on you to ask a blessing."

Murray's heart stood still, and he felt a trembling sensation creeping over him, as if the enemy after a brief respite had him in sight again. Whatever a blessing was, he didn't know. If the man had asked him to "say grace," he might have understood. But a "blessing"! Well, whatever it was, he had best keep out of it, so, gripping his self-control together again, he endeavored to look as if nothing extraordinary had been asked of him and leaned engagingly toward the minister.

"Doctor, I hope you'll excuse me from doing anything tonight. I'm simply all in. That wreck—!"

"Oh, certainly," the minister hastened to assure him. "I shouldn't have asked, and of course everybody will understand. But you are so well known as an active Christian worker, you know, that it was only natural to feel it appropriate. Still, of course I understand. I'll just tell the young president of this affair how it is, and she'll excuse you. I guess you must have a good appetite by this time if you've just arrived from the wreck?" he finished kindly.

"I'll say!" said Murray, glad that there was one question he could answer truthfully.

Then, suddenly, a silence spread over the entire chattering company, and Murray looked up to see the girl in blue, the one who had looked through him with scorn, whom they called Anita, standing at the middle table on the opposite side of the room, about to speak.

"Mr. Harrison, will you ask God's blessing?"

Her voice rang clear, and her eyes seemed to sweep the speaker's table where he sat and touch him with a slight look of disapproval. Somehow he felt that that girl was suspecting him. It was almost like having a police officer standing over there looking at him. It gave him a feeling that if he should dare get up and try to slide away unnoticed, she would immediately call the whole company to order and have him arrested.

These things had for the moment engrossed his mind so that he had not taken in what the girl had been saying. But all at once he noticed that everybody in the room but himself was sitting with bent head in an attitude of prayer. At least, everybody except one girl. It was perhaps the ardent furtive glance of Jane's eyes raised from a bent head to watch him that finally called him to himself and made him involuntarily close his eyes and bend his head. He felt as if he had been caught thinking by Jane, and that there was no knowing but she would interpret his thoughts. She seemed so almost uncanny in her ability to creep into intimacy without encouragement.

But once his eyes closed, the words of Anita came back to him like an echo, especially that word "blessing." It was the same unusual word the minister had used, and he had used it in much the same phrase, "Ask a blessing." So this was what they meant—make a prayer! Gosh! Was that what they had wanted him to do? What he was supposed to be able to do? He had indeed assumed a difficult character, and one he would never have voluntarily chosen. What should he do about it? Would it happen again? And could he invent another excuse, or would that lay him open too much to suspicion? What did they say when they made a prayer over a table like that? Could he fake a prayer? He had tried faking almost everything. He was known at home as a great mimic. But to mimic something about which he knew nothing would be a more difficult task than any he had ever undertaken before. He set his mind to listen to the words that were being spoken.

The first thing he noticed about this "blessing" business was that the minister was talking in a conversational tone of voice, as if addressing some other mortal, though with a deferential tone as to One in authority, yet on a familiar, friendly basis. The tone was so intimate, so assured, as if addressed to One the speaker knew would delight to honor his request, that Murray actually opened the fringes of one eye a trifle to make sure the man by his side was not addressing a visible presence.

There was something beautiful and strong and tender about

the face of the minister with his eyes closed, standing there in the hush of the candlelit tables, the tips of his long, strong fingers touching the tablecloth, the candlelight flickering on his rugged face, peace upon his brow, that impressed Murray tremendously in the brief glance he dared take. And the words from those firm lips were no less awe-inspiring. A thrill of something he had never quite experienced before ran down his spine, a thrill not altogether unpleasant.

Those words! They sank into his soul like an altogether new lesson that was being learned. Could he ever repeat it and dare to try to get away with a prayer like that?

"We thank Thee for the new friend that has come among us to live, who is not a stranger, because he is the son of those whom we have long loved and known. We thank Thee for the beautiful lives of his honored father and mother, who at one time walked among us, and the fragrance of whose living still lingers in the memory of some of us who loved them. We thank Thee also that he is not only born of the flesh into the kingdom, but that he has been born again, of the Spirit, and therefore is our brother in Christ Jesus—"

There was more to that "blessing," although the stranger guest did not hear it. He felt somehow strangely ashamed as these statements of thanksgiving fell from the pastor's lips, as though he were being held to honor before One who knew better, who was looking him through and through with eyes that could not be deceived. So now there were two in that room whose eyes were hostile, who knew that he was false, that he did not belong there, the girl they called Anita and the Invisible One whose blessing was being invoked. And while he felt a reasonable assurance that he could escape and flee from the presence of that scornful girl, he knew in his heart that he could never get away from the other, who was the One they called God. God had never been anything in his life but a name to trifle with. Never once before had he felt any personality or reality to that name God. It filled him with amazement that was appalling in its strangeness. He felt that life until then had not prepared him for anything like a fact of this sort. Of course he knew there were discussions of this sort, but they had never come near enough to him for him even to have recognized an opinion about them before. Why they did now he did not understand. But he felt suddenly that he must get out of that room; even if he starved to death or was shot on the way, he must get away from there.

He opened his eyes cautiously, glanced about furtively for the nearest unguarded exit, and saw the eyes of Jane watching him greedily. She even met his glance with a feather of a smile flitting across her mobile young lips, a nice enough comradely smile, if he only had been in the mood to notice, and if she hadn't been so persistent and forward, but it annoyed him. He closed his eyes quickly as if they had not been opened, and when he tried to glance about again, he looked the other direction, where he thought he remembered seeing a door into a passageway.

But a dash of blue blocked the passageway. Somehow Anita, in the blue gown, had gotten there from her position at the other end of the room. She was standing, leaning against the door frame almost as if she were tired. Her shapely little head rested against the wall, and her eyes were closed. There was almost a weary look in the droop of her lips and the way she held the silver tray down by her side. Somehow she seemed different now when she was not looking at him. There was something attractive about her, a sweet, good look that made him think of something pleasant. What was it? Oh! *Bessie!*

Like a sharp knife the thought went through his heart. Yes, Bessie had a good, sweet look like this girl, and Bessie would have had eyes of scorn for anyone who was not true to the core. Up in heaven somewhere, if there was such a place as heaven—and now that he was sure he had lost it, he began to believe that there was—Bessie was looking down on him with scorn. A murderer, he was, and a coward! Here he was, sitting at a meal that was not his, wearing a suit and a name that were not his, hearing God's blessing invoked upon him and his, and too much of a coward to confess it and take his medicine. Obviously he could not steal out now with that blue dress blocking the way. He must stay here and face worse perhaps than if he had never run away. What had he let himself in for in assuming even for a brief hour another man's name and position in life? It was clear that this Allan Murray, whom he was supposed to be, was a religious man, had come from religious parents; so much of his newfound character he had learned from the minister's prayer. Now how was he to carry out a character like that and play the part? He with the burden of a murderer's conscience upon him!

The "blessing" was over, to his infinite relief, and a bevy of girls in white aprons, with fluttering ribbon badges and pretty trays, were set immediately astir. The minister turned to him with a question about the wreck, and he recalled vaguely that there had also been a word of thanksgiving in that prayer about the great escape he was supposed to have made. He grasped at the idea eagerly and tried to steer the conversation away from himself and into general lines of railroad accidents, switching almost immediately and unconsciously to the relative subject of automobile accidents, and then stopping short in the middle of a sentence, dumb, with the thought that he had killed Bessie in an automobile accident, and here he was talking about it—telling with vivid words how a man would drive and take risks and get used to it. Where was it he had heard that a guilty man could not help talking about his guilt and letting slip out to a trained detective the truth about himself?

His face grew white and strained, and the minister eyed him kindly.

"You're just about all in, aren't you?" he said sympathetically. "I know just how it is. One can't go through scenes like that without suffering, even though one escapes unscathed himself. I was on a train not long ago that struck a man and killed him. It was days before I could get rested. There is something terrible about the nerve strain of seeing others suffer."

And Murray thankfully assented and enjoyed a moment's quiet while he took a mouthful of the delicious fruit that stood in a long-stemmed glass on his plate.

But the minister's next sentence appalled him:

"Well, we won't expect a speech from you tonight, though I'll confess we had been hoping in that direction. You see, your fame has spread before you, and everybody is anxious to hear you. But I'll just introduce you to them sometime before the end of the program, and you can merely get up and let them see you officially. I know Mr. Harper will be expecting something of that sort, and I suppose you'll want to please him. You see, he makes a great deal of having found a Christian young man for a teller in his bank."

The minister looked at him kindly, evidently expecting a reply, and Murray managed to murmur, "I see," behind his napkin, but he felt that he would rather be hung at sunrise than attempt to make a speech under these circumstances. So that was his new character, was it? A Christian young man! A young Christian banker! How did young Christian bankers act? He was glad for the tip that showed him what was expected of him, but how in thunder was he to get away with this situation? A speech was an easy enough matter in his own set. It had never bothered him at all. In fact, he was much sought after for that sort of thing. Repartee and jest had been his strong points. He had stories bubbling full of snappy humor on his tongue's tip. But when he came to review them in his panic-stricken mind, he was appalled to discover that not one was suitable for a church supper on the lips of a young Christian banker! Oh gosh! If he only had a drink! Or a cigarette! Didn't any of these folks smoke? Weren't they going to pass the cigarettes pretty soon?

Chapter 10

Sometime about half past ten that supper was over. It seemed more like a week to the weary wanderer, though they professed to by hurrying through their program because he must be tired.

He really had had a very good time, in spite of the strangeness of the situation and his anxiety lest his double might appear on the scene at any moment to undo him. He had tried to think what he would say or do in case that should happen, but he could only plan to bolt through the nearest entrance, regardless of any parishioner who might be carrying potato salad or ice cream, and take advantage of the natural confusion that would arise in the event of the return of another hero.

Having settled that matter satisfactorily, his easy, fun-loving nature actually arose to a moderate degree of enjoyment of the occasion. He had always taken a chance, a big chance, and in this kindly, admiring atmosphere, his terror, which had driven him from one point to another during the last few weeks, had somewhat subsided. It was more than halfway likely that the man he was supposed to be was either hurt seriously or dead, seeing that they had had no direct word from him, and it was hardly probable he would appear at the supper at this late hour, even if he did get a later train to Marlborough. So, gradually, the tense muscles of his face relaxed, the alert look in his eyes changed to a normal twinkle, for he was a personable young man when he was in his own sphere, and his tongue loosened. As his inner man began to be satisfied with the excellent food, and he drank deeply of the black coffee with which they plied him, he found a feeble pleasure in his native wit. His conversation was not exactly what might have been termed "religious," but he managed to keep out of it many allusions that would not have fitted the gathering. He was by no means stupid, and some inner sense must have guided him, for he certainly was among a class of people to whom his previous experience gave him no clue. They were just as eager and just as vivacious over the life they were living and the work they were doing as ever the people with whom he was likely to associate were over their play. In fact, they seemed somehow to be happier, more satisfied, and he marveled as he grew more at his ease among them. He felt as if he had suddenly dropped out of his own universe and into a different world, run on entirely different principles. For instance, they talked intermittently, and with deep concern, about a man whom they called John, who was suffering with rheumatic fever. It appeared that they went every day to see him, that he was of great importance to their whole group; some of them spoke of having spent the night with him and of feeling intensely his suffering, as if it were their own, and of collecting a fund to surprise him with on his birthday. They spoke of him with honor and respect, as if he were one with many talents whom they deeply loved. They even spoke of his smile when they came into his sick room and of the hothouse roses that someone had sent him, how he enjoyed them. And then quite casually it came out that the man was an Italian day laborer, a member of a mission Sunday school which this church was supporting! Incredible story! Quite irrational people! Love a day laborer! A foreigner! Why, they had spoken of him as if he were one of their friends!

He looked into their faces and saw something beautiful; perhaps he would have named it "love" if he had known more about that virtue, or maybe he might have called it "spiritual" if he had been brought up to know anything but the material in life. As it was, he named it "strange" and let it go at that. But he liked it. They fascinated him. A wild fancy passed through his mind that if he ever had to be tried for murder, he would like it to be here, among a people who thought and talked as these people did. They thought him like themselves, and he was not. He did not even know what they meant by some of the things they said.

Between such weird thought as this, he certainly enjoyed his dinner, wineless and smokeless even though it was. There was a taste about everything that reminded him of the days when he used to go up to Maine as a little boy and spend the summers with his father's maiden sister, Aunt Rebecca, long since dead. Things had tasted that way there, wonderful, delectable, as if you wanted to eat on forever, as if they were all real and made with love. Odd how that word *love* kept coming to him. Ah! Yes, and there was Mrs. Chapparelle. She used to cook that way, too. It must be when people cooked with their own hands instead of hiring it out that it tasted that way. Mrs. Chapparelle and the pancakes, and the strawberry shortcake with cream, made of light puffy biscuit with luscious berries between and lots of sugar. Mrs. Chapparelle! Her face had begun to fade from his haunted brain since the night he had looked into her kitchen window and had seen her go briskly to the door in answer to the ring. What had she met when she opened that door? A white-robed nurse, and behind her men bearing a corpse? Or had they had the grace to send someone to break the news first?

The thought struck him suddenly from out of the cheerfulness of the evening, and he lifted a blanched face to Anita as she put before him his second helping of ice cream and another cup of coffee.

And he was a murderer! He had killed poor Bessie Chapparelle, a girl a good deal like this Anita girl, clean and fine, with high ideals. What would these people, these kind, good people, think of him if they knew? What would they do? Would they put handcuffs on him and send for the police? Or would they sit down and try to help him out of his trouble? He half wished that he dared put himself upon their mercy. That minister now. He looked like a real father! But of course he would have to uphold the law. And of course there wasn't anything to do but hang him when he had killed a girl like Bessie! Not that he cared about the hanging. His life was done. But for the sake of his mother, who had never taken much time out of her social duties to notice him, and the father who paid his bills and bailed him out, he was running away, he told himself, so that they would not have to suffer. Just how that was saving them from suffering he didn't quite ever try to explain to himself. He was running away so there would not be any trial to drag his father and mother through. That was it.

He ate his ice cream slowly, trying to get ahold of himself once more, and across the room Anita and Jane happened to be standing together for an instant in a doorway.

"Isn't he stunningly handsome, Anita? Aren't you just crazy about him?" whispered Jane effusively.

"He's good-looking enough," admitted Anita, "but I'm afraid he knows it too well."

"Well, how could he help it, looking like that?" responded the ardent Jane, and she flitted away to take him another plate of cake.

But the crowning act of his popularity came when Mr. Harper, president of the bank, senior elder in the church, and honored citizen, came around to speak with the young man and welcome him to the town. He had been detained and came in late, being rushed to his belated supper by the good women of the committee. He had only now found opportunity to find the new teller and speak to him.

Murray rose with a charming air of deference and respect and stood before the elder man with all the ease that his social breeding had given him. He listened with flattering attention while the bank president told him how glad he was to have a Christian young man in his employ, and how he hoped they would grow to be more than employer and employed.

Murray had dreaded this encounter if it should prove necessary, as he feared the president would have met his young teller before this occasion and would discover that he was not the right man. But Elliot Harper stood smiling and pleased, looking the young man over with apparently entire confidence, and Murray perceived that so far he was not discovered.

It was easy enough to assent and be deferential. The trouble would come when they began to ask him questions. He had settled it in his mind quite early in the evening that his strong point was to be as impersonal as possible, not to make any statements whatsoever about himself that could possibly not be in harmony with the character of the man he represented, as he thought they knew him, and to make a point of listening to others so well that they should think he had been talking. That was a little trick he learned long ago in college when he wanted to get on the right side of a professor. It came back quite naturally to him now.

So he stood with his handsome head slightly bowed in deference and his eyes fixed in eager attention, and the entire assembly fastened their eyes upon him and admired.

That might possibly be called the real moment when the town, at least those representatives of the town that were present, might be said to have opened their arms and taken him into their number. How he would meet Mr. Harper was the supreme test. With one accord they believed in Mr. Harper. He stood to them for integrity and success. They adored Mr. Harrison, their minister, and confided to him all their troubles; they had firm belief in his creed and his undoubted faith and spirituality; they knew him as a man of God and respected his wonderful mind and his consistent living. But they tremendously admired the keen mind, clear business ability, coupled with the staunch integrity, of their wealthy bank president, Elliot Harper. Therefore they awaited his leading before they entirely surrendered to the new young man who had come to live in their midst.

Murray Van Rensselaer felt it in the atmosphere as he sat down. He had not lived in an air of admiration all his life for nothing. This was his native breath, and it soothed his racked nerves and gave him that quiet satisfaction with himself that he had been accustomed to feeling ever since he was old enough to know that his father was Charles Van Rensselaer, the successful financier and heir of an ancient family.

He had stood the test, and the time was up. Now, anytime, in a moment or two, he could get away, melt into the darkness, and forget Marlborough. They would wonder and be indignant for a day or a week, but they would never find him nor know who he was. He would simply be gone. And then very likely in a day or two the other man whom he had been representing for the evening would either turn up or have a funeral or something, and they would discover his fraud. But there would in all probability be an interval in which he could get safely away and be no more. He had gained a dinner and a pleasant evening, a little respite in the nightmare that had pursued him since the accident, and he had a kindly feeling toward these people. They had been nice to him. They had showed him a genuineness that he could not help but admire. He liked every one of them, even the offish Anita, who had a delicate profile like Bessie's, and the ridiculous Jane, who could not take her eyes from him. Now that he was an outcast, he must treasure even such friendliness, for there would be little of that sort of thing left for him in the world going forward. He could not hope to hoodwink people this way the rest of his life.

He felt a sudden pang at the thought of throwing this all away. It had been wonderfully pleasant, so different from anything he had ever experienced among his own crowd—an atmosphere of loving kindness like what he used to find at the Chapparelles', which made the thought of stolen evenings spent in the company of Bessie seem wonderfully fresh and sweet and free from taint of any selfishness or sordidness. How different, for instance, these girls were from the girls at home. Even that Jane had an innocence about her that was refreshing. How he would enjoy lingering to play with these new people who treated him so charmingly, just as he had lingered sometimes in new summer resorts for a little while to study new types of girls and frolic awhile. It would be pleasant, *how* pleasant, to eat three good meals a day and have people speak kind words and try to forget that he was a murderer and an outlaw. If he were in a foreign land now, he might even dare it. But four hundred miles was a short distance where newspapers and telegraph and radio put everything within the same room, so to speak. No, he must get out, and get out quickly. There would likely be a late train, and perhaps his other self would arrive on it. If possible he would have to get away without going back to Mrs. Summers', but at least if he went back he must not linger there. He could make some excuse, run out for medicine to the drugstore, perhaps, or if worse came to worst, pretend to go up to bed and then steal away after she was asleep. There would be a way!

His resilient nature allowed him to feel wonderfully cheerful as he arose from the table at last and prepared to make his adieus.

But it was not easy, after all, to get away. Mrs. Summers came to him and asked him if he would mind carrying a basket home for her—she wouldn't be a minute—and then pressed him into service to gather up silver candlesticks and a few rare china dishes.

"You see, they're borrowed," she explained, "and I don't like to risk leaving them here lest someone will be careless with them in the morning before I could get over, or mix them up and take them to the wrong person. I wouldn't like them to get broken or lost under my care."

They walked together across the lawn under a belated moon that had struggled through the clouds and was casting silver slants over the jeweled brown of the withered grass.

"It's been so lovely having you here," said Mrs. Summers gently, "almost like having my boy back again. I kept looking at you and thinking, 'He's my boy. He's coming home every night, and I can take care of him just as I did with my own.'"

Murray's heart gave a strange lurch. Nobody had ever spoken to him like that. Love, except in a tawdry form, had never come his way, unless his father's gruffness and continual fault-finding might be called love. It certainly had been well disguised so that he had never thought of it in that light. It had rather seemed to him, when he thought about it at all, that he stood to his father more in the light of an obligation than anything else. His mother's love had been too self-centered and too irritable to interest him. There had been teachers occasionally who had been fond of him, but their interest had passed when he used them to slide out of schoolwork. There had been a nurse in his babyhood that he barely remembered, who used to comfort him when he was hurt or sleepy, and sometimes when he was sick cuddle him in her arms as if she cared for him, but that was so very far away. He had sometimes watched the look between Bessie Chapparelle and her mother when he would be there playing games in the evenings with Bessie, a look that had made him think of the word *love*, but that also was far away and very painful now to think about. Strange how one's thoughts will snatch a bit from every part of one's life and blend them together in an idea that takes but an instant to grasp, just as a painter will take a snatch of this and a dab of that color and blend them all into a tint, with no hint of the pink or the blue, or the black, or the yellow, or the white, that may have gone to form it, making just a plain gray cloud. Murray was doing more thinking these last few days than he had ever done in the whole of his life before. Life, as it were, was painting pictures on his mind; wonderful living truths that he had never seen before were flashing on the canvas of his brain, made up of the facts of his past life which at the time had passed over him unnoticed. He had gone from his cradle like one sliding downhill and taking no note of the landscape. But he found now that he had suddenly reached the bottom of the hill and had to climb up (if indeed he might ever attain to any heights again), that he knew every turn of the way he had come and wondered how he could have been oblivious before. It occurred to him that his experience might be called "growing up." Trouble had come, and he had grown up. Life had turned back on him and slapped him in the face, and he began to see things in life, now that he had lost them, that he had not even recognized before.

As he slipped his arm through the big basket and stood waiting for Mrs. Summers to decide whose cake pan the big square aluminum one was, he looked wistfully about him on the disarray of tables, kind of hungering in his heart to come here again and feast and bask in the cheery comforting atmosphere. Good and sweet and wholesome it all was, a sort of haven for his weary soul that was condemned to plod on throughout his days without a place for his foot to remain, forevermore. He had a strange, tired feeling in his throat as if he would like to cry, like a child who has come to the end of the good time, and whose bubbles are broken and vanished. There would be no more bubbles for him anymore. The bowl of soapsuds was broken.

And so as they walked toward the little cottage with its gleaming light awaiting them from the dining room window, he felt strangely sad and lonely, and he wished with all his heart that he might walk in and be this woman's boy. If only he could be born again into her home and claim her as his mother and take the place as her son and be a new man, with all his past forgotten! He thought—poor soul, he had not yet learned the subtlety of sin and the frailty of human nature—he thought if he could be in this environment, with such people about him, such a home to come to, and such a mother to love him, he could learn to fit it. If it hadn't been for the possibility of the other man coming, he would have dared to try it and keep up his masquerade.

Chapter 11

He helped her unpack the basket and put her things away, and he gave a wistful look about the pretty, cozy room. He had never supposed there were homes like this anywhere. There was nothing formal about the place, and yet there were bits of fine old furniture, pictures, and bric-a-brac that spoke of travel and taste. It just seemed a place where one would like to linger and where *home* had been impressed upon everything around like a lovely monogram worked into the very fabric of it.

"Now," said Mrs. Summers as she whirled about from the cake box, where she had been bestowing a dozen lovely frosted sponge cakes that had been left over and she had brought home, "you must get to bed! I know you are all worn out, and you've got to be on hand early tomorrow morning. What time did Mr. Harper say he wanted you at the bank? Was it nine o'clock? I thought so. So I won't keep you up but a minute more. I thought it would be nice if we just had a bit of a prayer together the first night, and a verse. I always like a verse for a pillow to sleep on, don't you? Even if it is late. Will you read, or shall I?" and she held out a little limp-covered book that looked, like everything else in the house, as if it had been used lovingly and often.

"Oh, *you*!" gasped Murray embarrassedly, looking at the book as if it had been a toad suddenly lifting its head in the way, and wondering what strange new ceremony now was being thrust at him. There seemed no end to the strange things they did in this pleasant, unusual place. Take that thing they called "blessing" and was a prayer! It was like that book his nurse used to read him in his childhood, called *Alice in Wonderland*. You never knew what you would be called upon to do next before you could eat or sleep. Did they do these things all the time, every day, or just once in a while, when they were initiating some new member? It must be a great deal of trouble to them to keep it up every day, and must take up a good deal of time.

"Very well," said Mrs. Summers. "You sit in that big chair, and I'll just read a little bit where I left off last night."

They did it every night, then! Like massaging one's face and putting on night garments, as his mother always did, lovely gauzy things with floating scarfs like wings. This must be a sort of massaging for the soul.

He settled down in the comfortable chair and watched the white fingers of the lady flutter open the leaves of the book, familiarly and lovingly.

He liked the shape of her lips as she spoke, the sound of her voice. There was fascination in watching her, so sweet and strong and pleasant.

"There was a man of the Pharisees, named Nicodemus, a ruler of the Jews: The same came to Jesus by night, and said unto him, Rabbi, we know that thou art a teacher come from God: for no man can do these miracles that thou doest, except God be with him."

Murray heard the words, but they meant nothing to him. He was not listening. He was thinking what it would have been like if he had been born into this home. Then suddenly into his thoughts came those words, so startling. Where had he heard them before? "Jesus answered and said unto him, Verily, verily, I say unto thee, Except a man be born again, he cannot see the kingdom of God."

Why! How very strange! Those were the words he had seen in the streetcar. Almost the identical words, "Ye must be born again!" He would never forget them, because that had seemed the only way out of his difficulty. And now she was reading again, this time identical: "Marvel not that I said unto thee, Ye must be born again."

Why! It was like someone answering his thoughts. What did it all mean? He listened and tried to get the sense. It appeared to be an argument between one named Nicodemus and one Jesus. There was talk of wind blowing and water and a Spirit. It was all Greek to him. A serpent lifted in the wilderness, of believing and perishing, and eternal life. He almost shuddered at that. Eternal life! Who would want to live forever when he was a murderer and an outcast? "For God sent not his Son into the world to *condemn* the world," went on the steady voice, "but that the world through him might be *saved*."

Astonishing words! They got him! Condemnation was what he was under. Saved! He almost groaned. Oh, if there were but a way for him to be saved from this that had come upon him!

"He that believeth on him is not condemned."

Strange words again, and of course it all meant nothing—nothing that could apply to his case. Depression came upon his soul again. The condemnation of the law overshadowed him. He looked restlessly toward the door. Oh, if he could get away now and go—go swiftly before condemnation overtook him and got him in its iron grip forever!

The little book was closed, and the astonishing little lady suddenly rose from her chair and knelt down beside it. He was embarrassed beyond measure. He wanted to do the proper thing and excite no suspicions, but how was one to know what to do in a situation like this? Kneeling down in a parlor beside a Morris chair! How could anyone possibly know that that was the thing expected? Or was it expected?

Then he began slowly, noiselessly, to move his weary, stiffened muscles, endeavoring to transfer his body into a kneeling posture without the slightest sound, the least possible hint that he had not of course been kneeling from the start.

Strange happening for this onetime social star to be kneeling now in this humble cottage, hearing himself (or what was supposed to be himself) prayed for earnestly, tenderly, with loving chains of prayer "binding his soul about the feet of God." He grew red and embarrassed. He felt tears stinging his eyes. How was it that a possibility of anything like this being done anywhere in the universe for him never entered his mind before? It was indeed as if he was born into a new universe, and yet he still had the consciousness of his old self, his old guilt, upon him. It was intolerable. He never had felt so mean in his life as while he knelt there, hearing himself brought to the presence of God and knowing that he had cheated this wonderful woman who was praying for him, and that he was soon going to steal from her house in the night and never be seen by her anymore. What would she think? And how would she meet her God the next time she prayed? Would she curse him, perhaps, and would worse punishment come upon him than had come already? And how would a God feel about it? He had never been much concerned about God, whether He was or was not, but now he suddenly knew as this woman talked with Him with that assurance, that face-to-face acquaintance, that intimacy of voice, that there *was* a God. Whatever anybody might say, he knew now that there *was*! It was as if he had seen Him, he had felt Him, anyway, in a strange convincing power like the look from a great man's eyes, whom one had never met before, nor heard much of, yet recognizes at the first glimpse as being mighty! Well! There was a Power he hadn't counted on! The Power of God! He knew the details of the power of the law. But what if he also was in danger from the Power of God? What if this deception, just for the sake of a bath and a supper, should anger God and turn the vengeance of heaven and hell upon his soul? He vaguely knew that there were yet unfathomable depths of misery that he had not even tapped the surface of, and his burden seemed greater than he could bear. If he only might become someone else, be born again, as the book had said, so that no one would ever recognize him, not even God! But would that be possible? Could one be born at all without God about?

Floundering amid these perplexities, he suddenly became aware that the lady had risen, and, red with embarrassment, aware of tears upon his face which he could not somehow wipe away quickly enough, he struggled to his own feet.

She was not looking at him. She had moved across the room to a pitcher of ice water she had prepared before she began to read, and now she poured a glass and handed it to him. He was struck with the look of peace upon her lips. It seemed a look that no one he had ever known before had worn. Wait, yes, Mrs. Chapparelle sometimes had looked that way, even when they had very little for supper. Once he had stayed with them when there were only potatoes and corn bread. No butter, only salt for the potatoes, and a little milk, two glasses, one for him and one for Bessie. She must have gone without herself, and yet she had that look of peace upon her lips! Had even smiled! What was it? Talking with God that made it?

He got himself up the little white staircase with the mahogany-painted rail and the softly carpeted treads of gray carpet, and locked himself inside his room. He knew he had said good night and agreed upon something about when he would come to breakfast in the morning. As he did not intend to be present at breakfast the next morning, he had paid little heed to what she had said. His soul was in turmoil, and he was weary to the bone. He dropped into the big chair and gazed sadly about him on the pretty room.

He had it in mind to make a little stir of preparation for bed and then wait quietly until the house was still and he could steal down the stairs or out the window, whichever seemed the easiest way, and be seen no more. But he felt a heaviness upon him that was overpowering. He looked at the white bed with the plump pillows and the smooth sheets that had been turned back for his use. His eyes dwelt upon the softness of blankets and the immaculate cleanness of everything, and he longed with inexpressible longing to get into it and go to sleep, but he knew he must not yield. He knew that it would not be safe for him to linger till the morning. The news of him would have spread even by this time, and someone somewhere would say that he knew that the man he was supposed to be was dead or hurt, or else was coming in the morning. No, he must get up and get into his coarse clothes at once and be ready to depart. It would not do to be quiet now and noisy later. She would think it strange of him to be long in getting to bed. He must hurry! He took off the shoes that were a bit too large for him and crinkled his tired toes luxuriously. He took off the suit that was not his and folded it for the trunk tray. He took off the collar and necktie and put them back in the trunk. Then he looked at the pile of soiled underwear that he had brought back from the bathroom after his bath, and his soul rebelled. If the fellow he was supposed to be ever came back from the wreck and got his good job and his good home, he might thank his lucky stars and not bother if he was minus a pair of undergarments. He couldn't go in those soiled, tattered things any longer. And besides, if he was a murderer, why not be a thief, too, to that extent, anyway? He was sure if he was in the other fellow's place he wouldn't begrudge a poor lost soul a few of his clothes.

So he gathered the soiled clothes into a bundle, laid them on the coals that were still red in his fireplace, and watched them blaze up into flames with weary satisfaction. Then he turned out the light and tiptoed over to the window. He raised the shade and looked out to reconnoiter.

The window overlooked the street, and there was a great arc light hung in the trees, so that it shone full upon his windows. Moreover, there were people passing, and cars flying by, not a few. Marlborough had by no means gone to bed, even though the Presbyterian church social was over and the last member of the committee gone to her home. It was no use to try to escape yet. He must wait till after midnight.

So he tiptoed back, intending to turn on the light and begin to get together the rest of his things. But the flickering firelight from a charred stick that had broken in two and fallen apart to blaze up again feebly fell invitingly over the white bed and played with the shadows over the pillow. An inexpressible longing came over him to just see how it felt to lie down in that soft clean whiteness and rest for five minutes. He would not stay for more than five minutes or he might fall asleep, and that would be disastrous, but he must rest a moment or two while he was waiting, or he would not be able to travel—he was so tired. He would open the window so that when he was ready to go, he would not be making a noise again, and then he would rest.

So, just as he was, he lay cautiously down and drew the soft blankets around him, with the fragrant sheet against his face, and closed his weary eyes.

The night wind stole softly in and breathed restfully upon him, filling his lungs with clean, pure air and fanning his hot forehead, and the little charred stick collapsed with a soft shudder and went out, leaving the room in darkness, and Murray Van Rensselaer slept.

Chapter 12

When he awoke eons might have passed. He didn't know where he was, and a broad band of sun was streaming across his bed. The wind was blowing the muslin curtain out like a streamer across the room, and Mrs. Summers was tapping at the door with crisp, decided knocks, and calling to him: "Mr. Murray! Mr. Murray! I'm sorry to have to disturb you, but it's getting very late. You ought to be eating your breakfast this minute. You don't want to be late the first morning, you know!"

He opened blinded eyes and tried to locate himself. Who in thunder was Mr. Murray, and why didn't he want to be late the first morning? Was that his man calling him? No, it was a woman's voice. He blinked toward the window and saw the outlines of a church against the brightness of the sunny sky and saw people going down a strange street. He turned his head on his pillow and closed his eyes. What the dickens did it matter, anyhow? He was tired and was going to sleep this heaviness off. He must have been out late the night before. Hitting the pace pretty hard again! Must be at some club, or one of the fellows took him home. What was the little old idea, anyhow, trying to wake him up? Couldn't they let a fellow sleep till he was ready to wake up?

But the knocking continued, and he was about to tell the person at the door what he thought of him in most forcible language, when he opened his eyes again with his face the other way and saw the old rough coat he had been wearing for the past three weeks lying across the nice comfortable chair by the side of the fireplace awaiting him. Then it all came back to him like a slap in the face.

He sprang to a sitting posture and gazed hurriedly about him, a growing alarm in his eyes.

"Mr. Murray! Mr. Murray! Are you awake? Breakfast is ready. It's very late!" reiterated the pleasant but firm voice. "I'm afraid Mr. Harper will think—are you almost ready?"

"Oh—I—why, yes, Mrs. Summers," he answered then, half abashed, with a growing comprehension in his tone. "Why, yes," crisply, "I'll be with you in just a moment. I'm nearly dressed. I must have overslept."

Mrs. Summers, relieved, retired from the door, and Murray slid cautiously from the bed and grasped what garments came to hand, which proved to be the suit he had worn the night before. He couldn't go down in those old rags in broad daylight, of course. He had to make a getaway the best way possible, now that he had messed all his plans by falling asleep. Poor old guy, he would miss a suit also, but what's a suit of clothes in an emergency!

Murray dressed at lightning speed, giving little time to the brushing of hair or arrangement of tie, and was soon hurrying downstairs.

She had his coffee all poured, and there was oatmeal with cream and granulated sugar. There was half a grapefruit, too, all cut and ready for eating, and he was hungry as a bear. Yet in spite of all her talk about hurrying, she stopped to say that prayer before eating. Odd. It seemed to be a matter of course, like breathing—a habit that one couldn't stop. He almost bungled things by beginning a bite of his fruit in the middle of it. But she didn't seem to notice. She was bringing hot buttered toast and scrambled eggs and wonderful-looking fried potatoes. He could have hugged her, they all looked so good, and he had been hungry, hungry, hungry so many days before that!

Then right into the middle of that wonderful breakfast there came a sharp ring at the door. He became conscious that he had heard a high-power car drive by and stop, and panic seized him. He was caught at last, caught in his own trap, baited by sleep. What a fool he had been! He set down his cup of coffee and sprang to his feet, looking wildly about him.

"I must go!" he murmured vaguely, feeling he must say something to his hostess.

But she was already on her feet, going swiftly to the door.

"Get your coat and hat," she said in a low tone as she went.

"Too bad, right in the middle of your breakfast. But he won't want to wait—"

He dashed toward the stairs, thinking to make his escape out of a window from above somewhere while the officers entered below, but almost ran into the arms of Mr. Elliot Harper, smiling and affable, with extended hand.

"Sorry to have to hurry you the first day," he said pleasantly, "but I didn't think to mention it last night. There's a conference this morning, and I thought I'd like to have you attend. I drove around in the car to pick you up. Don't let me take you away till you've finished breakfast, however—!"

"Oh, I've finished," said the young man, uneasily glancing up the stairs and wondering if his best chance lay up there or through the kitchen door. He seemed to be always just about to make a dash and escape. It was amusing when one stopped to think of it, how he got more and more tangled in a web. Hang it all! If he only hadn't fallen asleep last night! If he only could think of a reasonable excuse to get away! It wouldn't do to just bolt with this keen-eyed businessman watching him. He was the kind to set the machinery of the law moving swiftly. He must use guile.

"I meant to go back and polish my shoes," he said deprecatingly. "If you can wait just a moment—"

"Oh, let that go till we get to the bank!" said the president genially. "There's a boy down there just dotes on polishing shoes. Save your strength, and let him do it. This your hat? I'm sorry to hurry you, but I promised to see a man before the conference, and the time's getting short. If you can just as well come now, I'll take it as a favor. . . ."

He went. How could he do otherwise with Mrs. Summers smilingly blocking the way of escape upstairs, and the determined bank president urging him toward the door? He would just ride down to the bank. There could be no danger in that, and then while Harper was seeing his man he would melt away quietly into the landscape and be seen no more.

He climbed into the luxurious car with a sense of pleasure as of coming to his own surroundings once more and rode down the pretty village street, his companion meanwhile drawing his attention to the buildings they were passing.

"This is the minister's house. You'll like Mr. Harrison, I'm sure. He's a marvelous, humble, great man. If it weren't for his humility, he'd be nabbed up by some of the great city churches. Here the senior elder lives. He has two daughters you'll meet. Nice girls. One's engaged to my nephew. The big stone house on your right belongs to Earl Atherton, one of our directors. Made his money in oil. Keen man. Next is the Stapletons'. Have a son in Harvard. You must have heard of him in athletics, Norton Stapleton. Fine lad! Good sense of balance. Comes home every year still unspoiled. Says he's coming back to go in business with his dad. Not many like him. Over there's the Farrington-Smiths'. You won't care for them. The girls all smoke cigarettes and drink, and the boys are a speedy lot. The town as a whole disapproves of them. They moved here from the city, but I hear they don't care for it, call it dull.

They'll probably invite you. They are trying hard to get in with our best people, and the girls are really quite attractive in a dashing, bold sort of way, but you won't want to accept. Thought it was just as well to let you know how the land lies. There! That's the bank in the distance, that gray-stone front. We've made it on time after all. Now we'll go right in, and I'll introduce you to the vice president. He'll take you to our conference room. Mr. Van Lennup, I wrote you about him, you know. He's immensely pleased at your coming. He was another one who knew your father, you know. This way. Walk right in this side door!"

There was no escape, though he glanced furtively either way. The street was full of passersby, and the sunlight was broad and clear. A man suddenly dashing away from his companions would excite much attention in the quiet town. He could not hope to make any possible getaway that way. He must bide his time and watch for a side door, a byway somewhere.

They led him across a marble floor down aisles of mahogany partitions, through silently swinging doors to an office beyond, where he was introduced to the vice president. They went down a marble hall to an elevator and shot up several stories to a dim and silent room with thick velvet underfoot and a polished table of noble proportions set about with lordly chairs. He perceived that he was in the inner sanctum of the directors of the bank, and when the heavy door swung back with something like a soft sigh, he felt as if prison walls had closed behind him.

A young man who had been writing at the table rose, went to

the wide plate-glass window, and drew up the shade a little higher. Murray perceived that the window overlooked the street and was too many stories above it to allow climbing out and escaping that way. He was evidently in for a directors' conference unless there might be a chance when the others were all coming in for him to slip out as they entered and make his way by the stairs to the regions below. Strange, he hadn't expected this town was large enough to boast of high office buildings for its banks. But then, he had seen it only in the dark. It must be larger than he had supposed.

Then the vice president shoved forward a chair for him to be seated and paralyzed him by remarking: "They tell me you were in college with Emory Hale, and that you two went to France together. That'll be pleasant for both of you, won't it? Emory has, I think, decided to remain in Marlborough all winter. He is doing some intensive study along scientific lines, you know, and thinks Marlborough's quiet will be a favorable atmosphere for his work. He's going to write a book, you know. Great head he has. By the way, you knew his father was one of our directors? He'll be here this morning. I met him as I came down. He says Emory wrote home that it had a great deal to do with his decision for the winter, your being here!"

Murray's brow grew moist with a cold perspiration, and he sidled over to the window as his companion turned to greet a newcomer. Perhaps, after all, the window was his best chance. Perhaps it was the best thing to risk it. They couldn't arrest a dead man, could they, even if they did recognize him? But yet, if he should break both legs, say, and have to lie in the hospital and have officers visiting him. . . Hang it all! However did he get into a scrape like this? All for a row of buns and cakes! And a foolish girl who thought she recognized him! If he ever got out of this, he would run so far and so fast that nobody would ever catch up with him again. He would change clothes with the first beggar whom he met and chop wood for a living. He would do something so that he would never again run the risk of being recognized and hauled back to his home for disgrace.

And then the door opened, and half a dozen clean-shaven, successful-looking men entered, followed almost immediately by several more, and the conference convened.

He was given a chair at the far side of the table away from both window and door, and surrounded by strong, able-bodied men, who acknowledged the introductions to him with pleasant courtesy and the right hand of welcome. Before he knew it, he found himself glowing with the warmth of their friendliness and his heart aching almost to bursting that he could not stay and take refuge behind all this genial welcome. If only he were sure that that bird Allan Murray was dead, really dead, so he could never come to life and turn up inconveniently any old time, he believed he would chance it. He would take his name and his place and make a new spot for himself in the world and try to make something of himself worthwhile. A tingle of ambition burned in his veins. It intrigued him to watch all these businessmen who seemed so keen about their part in the work of the world. He had never touched the world of business much. He had not supposed it would interest him. He found himself wondering what his superior, sarcastic father would think of him if he should succeed in business someday and, having made a fortune, should return home and let him know what he had done. And then it came to him that even if he did make a new name and fortune, he would never dare return. He would only bring shame and disgrace upon his father and mother, because he was a murderer, and even if they tried to protect him, they would have to do it by hustling him off out of the world again where he would be safe.

A wave of shame brought the color into his pale face, and he looked quickly around the group of earnest men to see if any of them had noticed him, but they were intent upon some knotty discussion that seemed to have to be decided at once before they could proceed with the day's program, and he retired into his own thoughts once more and tried to plan an escape to be put into effect as soon as he should be freed from the zealous watchfulness of these men who thought he was their new teller. There was that Emory Hale, too, they had talked about, who was supposed to have been with him in France. He must get away before he turned up.

Two hours later he thought his moment had come.

They had all just come down in the elevator, and he was about to be shown to the location of his new duties. He came out of the elevator last and noticed an open door at the end of the hall only a few feet away and an alcove with a chair obviously for the comfort of the elevator boy during slow times. Deftly he swung himself back into this alcove till the other men had passed and the boy had clashed the steel door of the elevator shut and whirled away into the upper regions for another load. For a brief instant the coast was clear, and he glided to the doorway and was about to pass out into the sunshine, regardless of the fact that he was hatless. A second more and he could have drawn a full breath of relief, dashed around the corner, and sped up till he was somewhere out of town in the wide-open country.

But in that instant's passing he came face-to-face with Jane, smartly coated and hatted in green, with brown fur around her neck, the color of her eyes and hair, and unmistakable joy in her eyes.

"Why, Allan Murray!" she cried. "Good morning! Where are you going without your hat? You look as if you were running away from school."

He came to himself with a click in his heart that reminded him of prison bars and bolts, and turned to greet her.

Somehow he summoned a smile to his ashy lips.

"Not at all," he answered cheerfully, glancing behind him at the still-empty hallway. "I was—ah—just looking for the postman." A door opened somewhere up the hall, and footsteps came out briskly.

"Excuse me," he said to the lingering girl, "I must go back. We're very busy this morning. I can't stop!"

He turned and dashed back again, coming suddenly face-to-face with Elliot Harper, who surveyed him in mild surprise.

"Oh, is that you, Murray? I was just going back for you! I must have missed you somehow."

"Yes," said nimble Murray, "I just stepped to the door to get my bearings! I always like to know how the land lies, that is, the building I'm in, you know."

"Well, we'll go right in now. McCutcheon is ready to show you your duties. We go through this side door."

Murray followed him because there was nothing else he dared do, and the steel gateway swung to with a click behind him as he entered the inner precincts of the bank itself. And once more he heard dimly the echo of bolts and bars and approaching prison walls about him. He walked to the little grated window that was to be his, so cell-like with its heavy grill, and saw an open drawer with piles of clean money lying ready for his unskilled hand. He felt almost frightened as he stood and listened, but he kept his calm exterior. It was part of his noble heritage that he could be calm under trying circumstances. He was even jaunty with a feeble joke upon his mobile lips and a pleasant grin toward the man who was endeavoring to teach him what he had to do. The trouble was the man seemed to take it for granted that he already knew a great deal about the matter, and he had to assent and act as if he did. Here he was, a new man, new name, new station, new portion in life. Yet the odds were so against him, the chances so great that he would soon be caught and put under lock and key for an impostor, that he would have given anything just then even to be back riding under the freight train and dodging policemen at every turn of his way.

Chapter 13

The day that Bessie Chapparelle had met her old playmate, Murray Van Rensselaer, for the first time in seven years had been her birthday. She was twenty-one years old and feeling very staid indeed. It is odd how very old twenty-one can make itself seem when one reaches that milestone in the walk of life. A girl never feels half so grown-up at twenty-five as when she reaches twenty-one. And Bessie was counting back over the years in the way a girl will, thinking of the bright and sad epochs, and looking ahead eagerly to what she still hoped to attain. She was wondering how long it would be before she could give her beloved mother some of the luxuries she longed for her to have, and as she stood on the street corner waiting for a trolley, she watched the shining wheels of a new car come flashing down the street and wished she were well enough off to begin to buy a car. Just a little Ford roadster, of course, or maybe a coupe. A second hand one, too, but there were plenty of nice, cheap, second hand ones. It would be so nice to take Mother for a ride in the park in the evenings when she got home from her work. They could prepare a lunch and eat it on the way in the long summer twilights. What wonderful times they could have together! Mother needed to get out more. She was just stuck in the house sewing, sewing, sewing all the time. Pretty soon she would be able to earn enough so that Mother would not have to sew so much, perhaps not at all. Mother was getting to the age when she ought to rest more and have leisure for reading. The housework was really all she ought to be doing. If only she could get a raise within a year and manage to buy some kind of a car so they could take rides!

Bessie Chapparelle had been tremendously busy during those seven years since she and Murray Van Rensselaer used to play games together in the evenings and listen to the books her mother read aloud to them when they grew tired of chess and cards and crokinole. Murray had gone off to prep school, and Bessie had studied hard in high school. She had not even seen him at vacations. He had been away at a camp somewhere in the West or visiting with some schoolmate. He had remembered her graduation day, for they had talked about it before he left, and he had sent back a great sheaf of roses, which were brought up to her on the platform after she read her essay. Everybody wondered and exclaimed over the beauty and quantity of those roses, sent across the continent with a characteristic greeting tied on the card: *Hello, Pal, I knew you'd win out! Murray.*

The roses had brought other roses to her cheeks and a starry look to her eyes as she came forward with wonder in her face and received the two tributes of flowers, one of tiny sweetheart rosebuds and forget-me-nots, small and exquisite, and this other great armful of seashell-pink roses with hearts of gold. She was almost smothered behind their lavish glory, and her little white dress, simple and lovely, made by her mother, looked like a princess's robe as she stood with simple grace and bowed with a gravely pleased smile toward the audience. She took the roses over her arm and looked out from above them, a fitting setting for her happy face, but the little nosegay of sweethearts and forget-me-nots she held close to her lips with a motion of caressing, for she knew they came from her mother. They were like the flowers her mother had received from her father long ago when he was courting her, and they meant much to the girl, who had listened, fascinated by the tales of her mother's girlhood, and treasured every story and incident as if it had been a part of her very own life story. Oh, she knew who sent the forget-me-nots and sweetheart rosebuds! No one but her dear, toiling mother could have done that, and it filled her heart with tender joy to get them, for she knew they meant much sacrifice, and many hours' overwork, far into the night, perhaps, to earn the money for those costly little blossoms. She knew how much they cost, too, for she had often wanted to buy some for her mother and had not dared. But she did not know nor guess who had sent the larger mass of roses, not till she got by herself in the dressing room for a second and read the brief inscription on the card and Murray's name. Then something glowed in her face that had not been there before, a dreamy, lovely wonder, the foreshadowing of something she could not name and did not understand—a great gladness that Murray, her playmate, had not forgotten her after all this time, a revelling in the lavishness of his gift, and the wonder of the rare flowers, which she knew were more costly than anything else she had ever had in her life before. Not that she measured gifts by costliness or prized them more for that, but her life had been full of anxious planning to make a penny go as far as possible for the dear mother who toiled so hard to give her an education and all that she needed, and money to her meant toil and self-sacrifice and love. She would not have been a girl if it had not given her a thrill to know that her flowers were more wonderful than any flowers that had been sent up to that platform that day. Not that she was proud or jealous, but it was so nice to have them all see that somebody cared.

It was only a moment she had for such reflection, and then the girls came trooping in, and she had barely time to hide the little white card in the folds of her dress before they all demanded to know who sent them. They had not expected her to have such flowers. They were almost jealous of her. She was a brilliant scholar—was not that enough?

She had been popular enough, though too busy to form the friendships that make for many flowers at such a time. They had conceded her right to the place of honor because of her scholarship, but they felt it their right to shine before the public in other ways.

But Bessie was radiantly happy and gave them each a rose, such wonderful roses! They all openly declared there had never been such roses at a high school commencement before in all their knowledge. And she went her way without ever having told them the name of the sender, just vaguely saying, "Oh, from a friend away out West!" and they looked at one another wonderingly as she passed out of the dressing room and into the cool dusk of the night, where her mother waited in the shadow of the hedge for her. Then she had friends out West! Strange she never mentioned anyone before! Yet when they stopped to think, they realized Bessie never talked about herself. She was always quietly interested in the others, when she was not too busy studying to give attention to their chatter. And perhaps they had not given her much opportunity to talk, either. They never realized it before.

Then she passed from their knowledge, except for an occasional greeting on the street. They were fluttering off to the seashore and the mountains, and later on to college. But Bessie went to work.

Her first job was as a substitute in an office where a valued secretary had to be away for several months with an invalid mother.

She did not know shorthand and had only as much skill on the typewriter as one can acquire in high school, and with no machine of one's own, but she worked so diligently at night school and applied herself so carefully to the typewriter in the office that long before the absent secretary returned, she had become a valued asset to that office.

As fast as a helper in an office can climb, she had climbed, working evenings on a business course, and getting in a little culture also along the way. But she had not had time nor money for parties and the good times other young people had. One cannot study hard in the evening and take courses at a night school, then get up early and work conscientiously all day, and yet go out to dances and theaters.

Moreover, her life interest was not in such things. She had been brought up in an old-fashioned way, in the way that is condescendingly referred to as "Victorian." She still believed in the Bible and honored her mother. She still believed in keeping the laws of the land and the law of purity and self-respect. She had not bobbed her hair nor put makeup on her face, nor gone to any extreme in dress.

And yet when Murray Van Rensselaer saw her standing on that corner that morning of her twenty-first birthday, waiting for her trolley, she was sufficiently attractive to make him look twice and slow down his speed, even before he recognized her for the playmate of his childhood's days.

There had been no more roses, no letters even passing between them, and Bessie had come to look back upon her memory of him as a thing of the past, over forever. She still kept the crumpled rose leaves folded away in tissue paper in her handkerchief box and smiled at them now and then as she took her best handkerchiefs out for some formal occasion, drawing a breath of their old fragrance, like dried spices, whose strength was so nearly gone that it was scarcely recognizable. Just sweet and old and dear, like all the pleasant things of her little girlhood. Life had been too real and serious for her to regret the absence of her former friend or even to feel hurt at his forgetfulness. He had passed into college life and travels abroad. Now and then his name was in the paper in connection with college sports, and later as a guest of some young prince or lord abroad. She and her mother read these articles with interest and a pleasant smile, but there was no bitterness nor jealousy in their thought of the boy who used to find a refuge in their kitchen on many a stormy evening when his family had left him alone with servants, and he had stolen away for a little real pleasure in their cozy home. It was what was to have been expected when he grew up. Was he not Murray Van Rensselaer? He would have no time now, of course, for cozy pancake suppers and simple stories read aloud. His world expected other things of him. He was theirs no longer. But they had loved the little boy who had loved them, and for his sake they were interested in the young man he had become, and now and then talked of him as they turned out their own lights and looked across the intervening alley to the blazing lights in the big house where his mother entertained the great ones of the city.

His coming back to his own city had been heralded in the papers, of course, and often his name was mentioned in the society columns, yet never had it happened that they had met until this morning. And Bessie was heart-whole and happy, not expecting young millionaire princes to drop down on her doorstep and continue a friendship begun in lonely babyhood. She was much too sane and sensible a girl to expect or even wish for such a thing. Her mind now was set upon success in her business world and her ambition to put her mother into more comfortable circumstances.

She met him with a smile of real pleasure, because he had cared to stop and recognize her for old times' sake, yet there was just the least tinge of reserve about her that set a wall between them from the start. He had recognized her with a blaze of unmistakable joy and surprise on his face and brought his car to such an abrupt stop that a taxi behind him very nearly ran up on the top of his car and climbed over him, its driver reproaching him loudly in no uncertain terms. But Murray had sprung from his car and taken her by the hand, his eyes devouring her lovely face, taking in every detail of her expression. Clear, unspoiled eyes, with the old glad light in them; fresh, healthy skin, like velvet, flushed softly at the unexpected meeting; lips that were red enough without the help of lipstick; and hair coiled low and arranged modishly, yet without the mannish ugliness put on by so many girls of the day; trim lines of a plain tailored suit; unconscious grace, truth, and goodness in her looks. To look at her was like going into the glory of a summer day after the garishness of a night in a cabaret.

He would have stood a long time holding her hand and finding out all that had been happening to her during the interval while they had been separated, but the traffic officer appeared on the scene and demanded that he move his car at once. He was not allowed to park in that particular spot where he had chosen to stop and spring to the pavement.

"Where are you going? Can't I take you there?" he pleaded, with one foot on the running board and his eyes still upon her face.

She tried to say she would wait for the trolley—it was not far away now—but he waved her excuses aside, said he had nothing in the world to do that morning, and before she realized it she was seated in the beautiful car whose approach she had watched so short a time before. As she sank down upon the cushions, she thought how wonderful it would be if sometime she could buy a car like this. Not with such a wonderful finish, perhaps, but just as good springs and just as fine machinery. How her mother would enjoy it!

The car moved swiftly out of the traffic into a side street, where they had comparatively a free course, and then the young man had turned to look at her again with that deep approval that had marked his first recognition.

"Where did you say you wanted to go?" he asked, watching the play of expression on her face and wondering about it. She did not seem like the girls he knew. She was so utterly like herself as he used to know her when they were children, that it seemed impossible.

"You don't have to get somewhere immediately, do you?" he asked eagerly. "Couldn't we have a little spin first?"

She hesitated, her better judgment warning her against it. Already she was reproaching herself for having gotten into the car. She knew her mother would have felt it was not wise. They were not of the same walk of life. It would be better to let him go his way. Yet he had been so insistent, and the traffic officer so urgent to clear the way. There seemed nothing else to do.

"Why, I was going to the library for a book I need this evening in my study," she said pleasantly. "My employer is out of town and gave me a vacation. I'm making use of it doing some little things I never have time for."

"I see," said Murray with his pleasant, easy smile that took everything for granted. "Then I'm sure I'm one of the things you haven't taken time for in a good many years. You'll just give a little of your time, won't you? Suppose we go toward the park, where we'll have more room."

While she hesitated, he shot his car up a cross street and was soon whirling on the boulevard toward the entrance of the park, enjoying the light in her eyes as the car rolled smoothly over the asphalt. It was so apparent that she loved the ride! She looked as she used to look when he brought her over the canary in the gold cage that he had bought with some of his spending money one Christmas. He began to wonder why he had let this delightful friend of his drop out of his acquaintance. Why, come to think of it, he had not seen her since the night his mother made him so mad telling him he was disgracing the family by running to play with little "alley" girls, that he was too big to play with low-born people anymore. He remembered how he tried to explain that Bessie did not live in the alley, as his mother's maid had informed her, but just *across* the alley, and how he tried to force her to go to the window and look out across the back area, where she could see quite plainly the neat two-story brick house, with the white sheer curtains at the windows, and a geranium between the curtains. It had all looked so pleasant to him he felt sure his mother would understand for once if she would only look. He could not bear that she should think such thoughts about these cozy friends of his who had given so many happy hours to him that his mother would have left desolate. But she shook him off angrily and sent him from the room.

That had been the last time he had seen Bessie. They told him the next day that he was to go to a summer camp, and from there he was sent to boarding school in the far West. It had all been very exciting at first, and he had never connected his mother's talk with his sudden migration. Perhaps the thought only vaguely presented itself in his mind now as a link in the chain of his life. He was not inclined to analyzing things, just drifting with the tide and getting as much fun out of it all as possible. But now, with Bessie before him, he wondered why it was that he had allowed seven whole years to drift by apart from her. Here she had been ripening into this perfect peach of a girl, and he might have been enjoying her company all this time. Instead he had solaced his idle hours with anyone who happened to drift his way. Bah! What a group they had been, some of them! Something in him knew that this girl was never like those. Something she had had as a little girl that he admired and enjoyed had stayed with her yet. He was not like that. He was sure he was not. He was quite certain he had been rather a fine chap in those early days before the evil of life had been revealed to him. A faint little wish that he might have stayed as he was then faltered through his carefree mind, only he flippantly felt that of course that would have been impossible.

Bessie was enjoying her ride. She exclaimed over the beauty of the foliage, where some of the autumn's tints were still left clinging to the branches. She drank in the beauty of cloud and distant river, and her cheeks took on that delicate flush of delight that he had noticed in her long ago. He marveled that a human cheek could vary in its coloring so exquisitely. He had unconsciously come to feel that such alive-looking flesh could only be on the face of a child. Every woman he knew wore her expressions like a mask that never varied, no matter what emotion might cross her countenance. The mask was always there, smooth and creamy and delicate and unmoved. He had come to feel it was a state that came with maturity. But this girl's face was like a rose whose color came and went in delicate shadings and seemed to be a part of the vivid expression as she talked, as the petals of a rose showed deeper coloring at their base when the wind played with them and threw the lights and shadows in different curves and tintings.

Murray as a rule did little thinking, and he would have been surprised and thought it clever if someone had put this idea into words for him. But the impression was there in his mind as they talked. And then he fell to wondering how she would look in beautiful garments, rich silks and velvets and furs. She was simply and suitably dressed, and might be said to adorn her garments, but she would be superb in cloth of silver and jewels. How he would enjoy putting her in her right setting! Here was a girl who would adorn any garment, and whose face and figure warranted the very greatest designers in fashion's world.

An idea came to Murray.

They often came that way by impulse, and sometimes they had their origin in the very best impulses. He leaned toward her with a quick, confidential air. They were on their way back now, for the girl had suggested that she had taken enough of his time.

"I wonder if you won't do something for me?" he said in his boyish, pleasant tone that reminded her of other days together.

"Why, surely, if I can," she complied pleasantly.

"You certainly can," he answered cheerfully. "No one could do it better. I want you to come with me to a shop I know and help me to select something for a gift for a friend of mine. You are her figure to an inch, and you have her coloring, too. I want to see how it will look on you before I buy it."

There was perhaps just the least shade of reserve in her voice as she graciously assented. Naturally she could not help wondering who the gift was for. Not his mother, or he would have said so. He had no sister, she knew. A cousin, perhaps? No, he would have called her cousin. Well, it was of no consequence, of course. It gave her just the least little bit of an embarrassed feeling. How could she select something for one in his station of life? But she could at least tell what she thought was pretty. It was on the whole quite exciting, come to think of it, to help in the selection of something where money did not have to be considered—just for once to let her taste rule. It would be wonderful!

Then they turned from the avenue onto the quieter street and drew up suddenly before Grevet's. She drew her breath with pleasure. Ah! Grevet's! She had often wondered what a shop like this was like inside, and now she was to know! It was like playing a game, to have a legitimate reason for inspecting some of the costly wares that were here exclusively displayed. She stepped from the car with quiet composure, however, and no one would have dreamed that this was her first entrance into these distinguished precincts.

Chapter 14

In a little cottage on the outskirts of a straggling town about half a mile from the scene of the railroad wreck, a sick man lay tossing on a hard little bed in a small room that could not easily be spared from the needs of a large family. A white-capped nurse, brought in by the railroad, stooped over him to straighten the coarse sheet and quilt spread over him, and tried to quiet his restless murmurings.

"Teller!" he murmured deliriously. "Teller!"

"Tell who?" asked the cool, clear voice of the nurse.

"M'ry!" he mumbled thickly. "Teller!"

"You want me to tell Mary?" asked the nurse crisply.

The heavy eyes of the man on the bed opened uncomprehendingly and tried to focus on her face.

"Yeh! Teller! M'ry. Bank!"

"Mary Banks?" asked the nurse capably. "You want me to send word to Mary Banks?"

The patient breathed what seemed like assent.

"Where?" asked the nurse clearly, taking up the pencil that lay by her report and writing in clear little script, "Miss Mary Banks."

"Bank!" said the patient drowsily. "Bank! Teller!"

"Yes, I will tell her," responded the nurse. "Where—does—she—live?" enunciating slowly and distinctly.

The man's head paused in its restless turning, and the eyes tried to focus on her face again, as if he were called back by her words from some far wandering.

"Marlborough!" He spoke the word clearly and drowsed off again as if he were relieved.

That night by the light of a sickly gas lamp whose forked flame she had shaded with a newspaper from the patient's eyes, she wrote a note to Mary Banks in Marlborough, telling her that a young man with curly red hair and a tweed suit was calling for her and asking that she be told that he had been injured in a wreck. She stated that the patient's condition was serious and that if he had any friends, they had better come at once. It was impossible to find any clue to his name, as he wore no coat when he was picked up, having evidently pulled it off to assist others worse injured than himself and having fainted before he got back to it. The pockets of his trousers had nothing in them but a little money, a railroad ticket, a knife, a few keys, and a watch marked with the initials A.M.

The letter was given to the doctor to mail the next morning when he came on his rounds, and in due time it reached the

Marlborough post office. After reposing some days in the general delivery box, it was finally put up in a glass frame in the outer post office among uncalled-for letters. But the patient lay in a deep deathlike stupor, and knew nothing of all this. After his efforts to speak that one word, Marlborough, he had seemed satisfied, and the doctor and nurse tried in vain to rouse him again to consciousness of the world about him. It was thought that he had been injured around his head and that an operation might be necessary, but the doctor hesitated to take that step without first consulting with some of the sick man's friends or relatives. The doctor even went so far as to write a note to a fellow physician in the town of Marlborough, asking him to look up this "Mary Banks" and endeavor to get a line on the man and his friends, if possible.

But no Mary Banks could be found in all the town of Marlborough. Strange as it may seem, however, a young woman of romantic tendencies, by the name of Banks, who admitted that her middle name was Marie—Rose Marie Banks—was at last discovered, and induced to take the journey of some thirty miles to the bedside of the unconscious man, that she might identify him. It was a handsome young doctor who entreated her, anxiously, to please a former head and great colleague in the profession. He had just bought a new shiny blue car, and the day was fine. Rose Marie consented to go "just for the ride" and alighted happily before the cottage, stood an awed moment beside the sickbed, and gazed half frightened on the solemnity of the living death before her. Then she shrank back with a "No, I ain't never seen him before," and hurried out to the waiting car, glad to be back in the sunshine of life once more. The sick man lay burning with fever and moaning incoherent words to the distracted nurse, who had done her best, and the days went on and on monotonously.

Chapter 15

*I*t was strange how many circumstances could combine to hedge in Murray Van Rensselaer's pathway so that there was no way of escape.

They led him into the mahogany-lined cage with its bronze bars at the little window and inducted him into the mysteries of the duty of a bank teller, and he was fascinated. It was like a new game. He always was dead to the world for a time when he met with a new form of amusement. They never could get him to pay attention to anything else until he had followed out its intricacies and become master of its technique. And this playing with crisp new bills of fascinating denominations and coins in a tray of little compartments was the best he had ever tried. Poker chips and mah-jongg tiles weren't nearly as interesting. These were real. They suddenly seemed the implements with which the world's big battles were fought. He had a vague perception of why his father stayed in the game of business when he had enough money to buy himself out many times. It was for the fascination of it.

Also, as he cashed checks and counted money, he had a realization that he was doing something for the first time in his life that was really worthwhile to the world. Just why it was valuable to the world for him to stand there and hand out money in return for checks he did not figure out. He only knew he liked it immensely. He felt as if he were doing these people a personal favor to give them money when they asked for it. He was so smiling and affable, and took so much trouble to give the fussy old lady exactly the right number of five- and ten-cent pieces that she asked for in change, and was so pleasant to the children who came with their Christmas savings accounts and had to have different things explained to them, that the other officials, watching him furtively as they went about their own business, raised approving eyebrows at one another. They nodded as they passed with a tilt of the head toward the new member of their corps, as much as to say: "He'll do all right; he's going to be a success."

It is true he often did not know how to explain the things they asked of him and had to make them up or manage to get out of answering entirely. He asked very few questions, however, of his fellow workers, for he did not wish them to suspect he did not know it all. Only now and then he would say: "Oh, I say, Warren," to the man who had been assigned to coach him, "just what is your custom here about this?" making it quite plain that where he came from they had a method of their own, and he did not wish to vary from the usual habit here.

It was remarkable how often he could skate like that on thin ice and not fall through. Of course his college practice had made his mind nimble in subterfuges, but on the other hand, the situation was quite different from any he had ever met with before. He found it the more interesting because of these various hazards, and he came to feel a new elation over each person whom he succeeded in serving satisfactorily without help. It was quite a miracle that he made no more mistakes than he did.

The morning passed swiftly, and when he was told that it was the noon hour, he came to himself with a sudden realization that now was his chance to escape. He had almost forgotten that he had wanted to escape—*needed* to. He was enjoying himself hugely and liked the idea of going on and becoming a banker. He saw himself winning out and becoming a champion in the game of banking—just as he had won out and become a champion in tennis and golf and polo.

But with the relief from his little cage window and the piles of fascinating coins came the remembrance of his terrible situation, came as if it were new all over again, and settled down upon his soul in crushing contrast to the happiness of the morning. Why, men had liked him, been pleased with what he did, showed him that he was going to be a success. The long lines of men and women, even boys and girls, outside his window, looking at him as if he were someone who held their fate in his hand, had eyed him with pleasant cordiality. Everywhere men had acknowledged his smile, as if it were worth something to know him. He had been used to all that, of course, at home, only there had been a new tang to this friendliness—a kind of respect that had never been granted to him before. Was it because he was doing real work? Or was it partly because of what they thought he was—that religious business that almost everyone managed to get in a hint about? He did not quite understand it, but it somehow gave him a new angle on life, a new respect for righteousness and right living. How odd that he had never thought before that there were compensations in being what men called "good."

But to have experienced this new deference and then to be let down to reality again was a tremendous blow. Of course he had known it was not his; he was only sort of playing at being a man and a bank employee, but it had been great! And now he had to go out and sneak away like a thief and disappear! He looked down at the piles of money he was leaving with a wistful regret. Suppose he was a thief! Suppose he should sweep all that with one good motion into his pocket and disappear. He could do it. It would be a good game, interesting to see if he could get away with it, but how loathsome to think about afterward! He almost shivered at the thought of himself doing a thing like that. That money had come to have a sort of personality and value of its own apart from what it might be worth to him personally. He had never looked at money before in any but the light of his own needs. There had always been plenty of it so far as he was concerned, and he had always seemed to feel he had a right to as much as he pleased. But now he suddenly saw that money was a necessity to the daily life of the community. He had seen it pay a gas bill and a telephone bill today, and he had seen small checks brought forth from worn wallets in trembling hands, and the cash carried away with a look that showed it was to be used for stern necessity. One could tell by the shabbiness of some of the owners that with them a little money had to go a long way.

Now all this swept through his mind in a kind of hurried surge as he turned to follow the man Warren out to lunch. He knew none of the words to express these thoughts to himself, but the thoughts themselves left their impression on his soul as they surged through him.

And now, the murderer, who had played at being a bank teller for a brief time, must go out supposedly to lunch, must shake this man Warren somehow and get away, never to return, and he did not want to go. He did not want to go back to being a runaway murderer. He felt like a small boy who wanted somebody to show him the way home and comfort him. He decided the quickest way to shake Warren was to say that he must run back to Mrs. Summers' for lunch, as she would be expecting him, and he needed to get something he had left in his other coat, some papers he must show to Mr. Harper at once.

But he found no opportunity for such stratagem. The man Warren was in complete command of the situation. He was sent by Mr. Harper to bring Murray to the top floor, where lunch was to be served to the directors today, and where the president was awaiting him and wanted him to sit beside him. They were joined almost at once by one or two others who had been more or less in his vicinity all the morning, so there was no chance whatever of escape unless he wished to try the astonishing method of making a dash. This matter of making a bold dash had become almost an obsession in his mind. He saw it was a thing that was impossible. They would think he was crazy. They would immediately cry out. He would be caught at once and have to explain. It might work in the darkness, perhaps, but not in broad daylight in a bank. So he followed meekly and was shot up in the elevator to the top floor and given a fine lunch and more of the pleasant deference that had soothed his overwrought nerves all the morning, until he was even able to rally and make several bright sallies in response to the conversation of the men about him. He could see again that they liked him and were pleased with his ready speech.

Back to the window again and the pleasant game that was so fascinating. There was only one unpleasant occurrence, just before closing time, when the girl Anita came in to make a deposit and looked at him with her clear eyes. A distant, formal recognition she gave him, but no more, and again he felt her likeness to Bessie, poor Bessie Chapparelle, with her white face against his shoulder as he carried her into the hospital.

It swept over him with a sickening thud: Bessie was dead. Why hadn't he gone back to Bessie Chapparelle long ago? This girl Anita had that same sweet reserve about her that Bessie had put between himself and her while they were driving. He had wanted to break down that reserve, but he liked her for it. He could see that Anita would be a good girl to know. She would be somewhat like Bessie, perhaps. But because of Bessie he shrank from even looking at her. And somehow that odd fancy that she could look through him, that she might even read that he had killed a girl, took more and more possession of his mind. He must get away from this town!

But Mr. Harper came to him just at closing time, and said he wanted to take him home to dinner that night, that there were one or two matters he wanted to talk over with him, and besides his wife and daughters were most anxious to meet him. They would leave the bank around five o'clock. His duties would be about over for the day then, and they would take a little drive around the town and vicinity of Marlborough, if that was agreeable to the young man. Then they would drive to the Harper home and dine and spend the evening.

There was nothing to do but assent, of course, but his mind was so troubled trying to think how to get away that he scarcely paid heed to the routine of his work, which they were trying to teach him, and once or twice made bad calculations which he knew must have made them wonder that he did not know better. He saw they were being very nice to him, but he fancied a look of surprise passed over their faces that he had not understood more quickly.

The day's agenda was carried out without a break. He actually went through that entire day, ride and dinner and evening and all, and was returned to Mrs. Summers' house late that night and ushered to the very door, which she herself opened for him, so that there was no instant in which he could have gotten away unnoticed.

As he stood by the bedroom window in the soft light of the little bed lamp and looked out into the pleasant street once more, as he had done twenty-four long hours before, he was amazed at the supervision that had followed him from early morning to late at night. It seemed almost uncanny. He was beginning to wonder if perhaps there was some secret reason for it, that he should be caught in this maze of deceit, and then to add this also to his already-heavy offense. Could it be possible that a kind Providence, or some other great unseen Power, if there was such a thing in the universe, had provided this way of escape from his terrible situation and prepared a new place and a new name for his wayward self to begin again?

He looked around the pleasant, friendly little room that seemed already to have somehow become his, to the deep easy chair with the soft light falling on a magazine laid close at hand, to the comfortable white bed, with its sheets turned down again, ready for his entrance, and suddenly his heart failed him. How could he go out into the world again and hide away from men when here was this home and this place in the world awaiting him? He would never find another place where everything would be so easy to fit into. He might stay at least until something was heard of the other fellow. He would take pains to inquire about that wreck. He would profess to be anxious about some of his fellow passengers, and they would talk, and he would find out a lot of things—where the other fellow really lived—and perhaps there would be a way of tracing him. If he had really died, the way would be clear for him. The man seemed to have come from a distance, from the way they spoke of his trains, and his trunk coming on ahead. It was likely there would be a good chance of his never being found out. Why not take the chance?

Now, Murray Van Rensselaer had been taking chances all his life. He loved chances. He was a born gambler in life, and if it had not been for the white face of Bessie Chapparelle that haunted him everywhere he turned and suddenly appeared to him out of the most unexpected thoughts and occurrences, he would have just delighted in entering into this situation and seeing if he could get away with it. The little white haunting face spoiled everything for him everywhere. There had never been anything in his life before that really took the fun and the excitement out of living.

There was one other occurrence of the day that set its searing touch upon his troubled mind, and that was when he had been returning from lunch. He had lifted his eyes to the wall beyond the table where patrons were standing writing checks and had seen a large sign hanging on that wall beyond the table in full sight of all who entered the bank, bearing the picture of a young man, and underneath the picture the words, in large letters, $5,000 REWARD—

He read no more. To his distorted vision the picture seemed to be one of himself. Yet he was not near enough to see it, and he dared not go nearer. It had been like a nemesis staring him in the face all the afternoon as he worked away at the game of money, every time he looked up, and tried not to see the sign upon the wall with the face and the words upon it, yet always saw them.

He thought of the sign now as he stood by the window and looked out, thinking how he could get across that tin roof silently, and down to the ground by way of the rose trellis.

Then the thought presented itself that perhaps, after all, he was safer there, in the bank, even if it proved to be his own picture staring across at him, than he would be out in the world trying to run away from people who were hunting for him and wanting to get that reward. No one would think of looking for that face behind the teller's window. He was bearing an honored name, and behind that name he was safe. He must stay. That is, unless the other man turned up, and then—? Well, then it would be time enough to decide what to do. At least his situation could be no worse than it was now. He would go to bed and to sleep like other people, and tomorrow he would get up and go to the bank and play that enticing game of money again and see if he could get away with it all. At least it would keep his mind occupied, so that he would not always have to see Bessie Chapparelle lying huddled beneath that overturned car.

He turned from the window and looked toward the tempting bed again. He was not used to resisting temptations. It had been his habit always to do exactly as he pleased, no matter what the consequences. Let the consequences take care of themselves when they had arrived. Ten to one they would never arrive. It had been his experience that if you kept enough things going, there was no room for consequences. Habit is a tremendous power. Even in the face of a possible arrest for murder, it swayed him now. And he was tired—deadly tired. The excitement of the day, added to the excitement of the days that had gone before, had exhausted him. Add to that the fact that he had been without stimulants of any kind, unless you could call coffee a stimulant. It was a strange thing, all these people who did not drink and did not approve of smoking. How did they get that way?

He had thought that as soon as he got out in the world again somehow he would manage to get a pack of cigarettes. But at the breakfast table Mrs. Summers had told him how the one thing that had held her back at first from being ready to take him in was that she hated smoking in her house, but when Mr. Harper had boasted that he was a young man who never smoked, that decided her.

"And he was so pleased about it," she added. "You know, though he smokes himself, he said it was a sign of great strength of character in you that you had gone all through the war even without smoking, and you were said not to be a sissy, either."

He had paid little heed to her words while he was eating breakfast, because his mind was engrossed with how he could get away, but down at the bank Mr. Harper, at noon, lighting his cigar, looked at him apologetically and said: "I know you don't smoke, Murray, but I hope you'll pardon us older fellows who began too young in life to cut it out now. I admire your strength tremendously."

He had opened his mouth to disclaim any such strength, to say that they had been misinformed, for his whole system was crying out for the comfort of a smoke, but a distraction suddenly occurred, and caution held him back from contradicting it later. Besides, the entire company seemed to have heard it about him that he did not smoke, and he dared not attempt to invent a story that would show they were mistaken. If he was supposed to be that kind of young man, better let it stand. He could all the more easily slip away unobserved without their immediate alarm.

So now in the quiet of his own room, he longed fiercely for a smoke. But he had not a cent in his pocket. There had not been a chance for an instant all day when he could have purchased cigarettes unobserved, and if he had them in his hand he would not dare to smoke there in Mrs. Summers' house. She hated it. She would smell it. She would think him a hypocrite. Somehow he did not want Mrs. Summers to think ill of him. Of course he was a hypocrite, but somehow he didn't want her to know it. She had been kind to him, and he liked her. She was what seemed to him like a real mother, and he reverenced her. If he stayed and enjoyed her home and the position which he was supposed to fill, he would also have to live up to the character he was supposed to be, and that would include not smoking, even when he got a chance and the money to purchase the smokes. Could he stand it? Was it worth the trouble?

And yet when he came to think about it, was not that perhaps the very best disguise he could have, not to smoke? He had been an inveterate smoker. Everybody who knew him knew that. If he was made over into a new man, the old man in him unrecognizable, he must seek to obliterate all signs of the old man. Well, could he do it?

He had settled down into the big chair to think, to decide what to do, and suddenly a great drowsiness overtook him. With a quick impulse of old habit he got up and began to undress without more protest. He would have another good night's rest before he did anything about it anyway. He could not run far with sleep like this in possession of his faculties. And in three minutes he snapped out the light and was in bed. At least he was probably safe till morning. The man Murray could not very well turn up at that time of night.

Chapter 16

Murray wondered again the next morning when Warren stepped in with a note from Mr. Harper while he was eating his breakfast, and insisted on waiting and walking down to the bank with him. It did seem uncanny. Were all these people in collusion somehow to prevent his being left alone an instant?

It would have been a startling thought to him had someone suggested that each one was working out the divine will for his good, and that though he might flee to the uttermost part of the earth, even there an all-seeing care would be about him, reaching to draw him to a God he had never known.

Murray liked Warren. He seemed quite companionable. He wondered if he played golf or had a car. But it annoyed him to be under such continual supervision. Although he had about decided to remain in Marlborough for the present, at least until he got his first week's pay, if that were possible, still he did not like the feeling that he was being forced to do this. He cast about in his mind for an excuse that would leave him free, but Warren was so altogether genial that there seemed nothing else to do but make the best of it. Surely they would not have lunch parties on the roof of the bank building every day of the week. There would certainly come a letup sometime.

So they walked downtown together, and Murray discovered that Warren was married and lived in a little cottage two blocks above Mrs. Summers. Warren said they wanted him to come to dinner some night just as soon as Elizabeth got back. Elizabeth was away in Vermont, visiting her mother.

Elizabeth! Would he never get away from thoughts of Bessie Chapparelle?

Warren confided in Murray that he was saving for a car, just a little coupe—he couldn't afford anything else yet—but it would be nice for Elizabeth to take the baby out in. There was a nice, eager, domestic air about him that was different from anything Murray had experienced among his young men friends, even the married ones. He did not remember that any of them had babies, or if they had they did not speak about them. They were tucked away somewhere with their nurses out of sight till they should be old enough to burst upon the world full-fledged in athletics or society. There was something pleasant about the thought of a girl taking her baby out for a ride in a little coupe, even if it was a cheap one. And a cottage! He had never been to dinner at a cottage. It occurred to him that Bessie would have been the kind of mother who would have taken her baby out for a ride. Bessie! Oh Bessie! Why had he not thought of Bessie before and kept in touch with her? But when he did find her, he had killed her! He had thought this terrible depression at remembrance of her would pass away in a few days, but it did not. It only grew worse! Someday it might drive him mad! This was no way to begin a day!

But he entered the bank committed to take a hike with Warren that afternoon after closing time, and Warren was to come home to dinner that night with him. Mrs. Summers had asked him at the breakfast table. So the pleasant ties that were binding him to Marlborough multiplied and weakened his purpose of leaving, and from day to day he held on, each day thinking to go the next. If he had had money, even a little, or any sense of where he might go, it would have been different, perhaps, for ever over him hung the fear of the return of the real Murray, though each day, no, each hour that passed in security weakened his realization of it and at times almost obliterated the thought of it as a possibility.

Then there began to happen the strangest things that he had to do, things utterly alien to all of his former life.

There was the first Sunday. It came like a shock to him.

Saturday afternoon he and Warren took a hike, and on the way back he asked when Murray would like to go again.

"Why not tomorrow?" answered Murray, remembering that there would be no bank open on Sunday.

"Why, that's Sunday, old man," said Warren, laughing.

There was such a look of amusement on Warren's face that

it warned Murray. Sunday! What the dickens difference did that make, he wondered. But he caught himself quickly. It must make some difference or Warren would not look like that, so he responded with a laugh.

"Oh, that's so. Got my dates mixed, didn't I? Well, let's see. What do we do in Marlborough? How is the day laid out on Sunday? Much doing?"

"Well, not much time for idling, of course. We have our Ushers' Association meeting in the morning before church. They'll be sure to elect you to that. They were speaking about it."

"Ushers' Association?" said Murray, puzzled.

"Yes, I s'pose you belonged at home. In fact, they said you did. Well, we meet at quarter to ten. Then the regular morning service is quarter to eleven, and Sunday school is in the afternoon. Have they asked you to take a class yet? Well, they will. Then the Christian Endeavor meets at seven. They're planning to make you president at the next election. Perhaps I oughtn't to tell you that, but it's a foregone conclusion, of course. And the evening service is eight o'clock. Of course, it's short and snappy and gets out by nine fifteen, but it's a full day. Not much time left for your family if you go to everything."

"No, I suppose not," murmured Murray, trying to keep the amazement out of his voice. It was his policy to agree with everybody, as far as possible, until he had further insight, but was it possible that grown men and women went to Sunday school? Some nurse of his childhood had taken him for a few months once when he was quite young, but he had always supposed it was a matter merely for children. Yet Warren spoke as if he went to Sunday school. What was he letting himself in for if he stayed in this strange place? Could he possibly go through with it? And what were these "services" that he spoke of? Just *church*? Well, he could get out of that probably. Say he had a headache.

But when Sunday morning came and he sat down at the little round breakfast table opposite Mrs. Summers and ate the delicate omelet, fresh brown bread, sweet baked apples with cream, and drank the amber coffee that composed the Sunday breakfast and heard her talk, it was not so easy to get out of it.

"There's an article in this week's *Presbyterian* I'd like you to read. It speaks of that very subject we were talking about last night. You'll have plenty of time to read it before we go to church. I left it over on the Morris chair for you," she said. It was very plain she was counting on his going to church. Indeed, he had been made to understand everywhere all the week from many different people that church was where he was expected to be whenever there was service there, and he sighed and wondered how long he would be able to keep up this religious bluff. If he only had thought to profess to be going to spend the weekend with some old friend a few miles away, it would have given him freedom for a few hours, at least, and a start of almost two days on his pursuers, in case he decided not to return.

But then there was the old question again: Where could he go, how would he get another name, and why try to find a better place of hiding when this one seemed fairly crying out for him? Then, too, where would justice be less likely to search for him than in a church?

So he settled into the Morris chair with a sigh and took up the paper to read an article, the like of which he had never read nor heard before, and the meaning of which touched him no more than if it were written in a foreign tongue.

The article was about church unity. He gathered there was a discussion of some sort around, some theological crisis imminent. The article was couched in terms he had never even heard before, so far as he remembered—the Atonement, Calvary, the Authenticity of the Scriptures, the Virgin Birth, the New Birth, the Miracles. What was it all about, anyway? There seemed no sense to it. He read it over again, trying to get a few phrases in case someone began to talk in this strange jargon, and he was evidently expected to be a connoisseur in such things. He must master enough to put him beyond suspicion.

Take, for instance, that phrase "the new birth"; how strangely like the sentence he had seen in the trolley car, "Ye must be born again!" It had come from the Bible. He had discovered that the first night he spent in this house. There must be some slogan like that in all this discussion. He was rather interested to know what it all meant. It fitted so precisely in with his own needs. He was trying so hard to be born again, and he felt so uncertain whether he was going to succeed or not. Perhaps if he read this paper he would discover something more about it. At any rate it would make the good lady with whom he lived feel that he was interested in what she had been saying, and he had taken good care that she did the talking when she got on such topics, too. So he asked if he might take the paper up to his room for further perusal. Mrs. Summers said yes, of course, but it was time to start to church, and he must get his hat and come right down. And in spite of his desire to remain at home, he found himself yielding to her firm but pleasantly expressed wishes.

The sermon that morning was short and direct. The text was, "We must all appear before the judgment seat of Christ to give account of the deeds done in the body," and from the time those firm, mobile lips of the pastor began to repeat the words, and the clear, almost piercing eyes began to look straight down at him from the pulpit, Murray never took his eyes from the preacher's face.

It was, perhaps, the first real sermon he had ever listened to in his life. Oh, he had been to church now and then through the years, of course—mostly to weddings, now and then to a funeral, occasionally a vesper service where something unusual was going on and his mother wished him to escort her, once or twice to a baccalaureate sermon. That was all. Never to hear a direct appeal of the gospel. It was all new to him.

The minister was an unusual man. He knew scripture by heart, chapter after chapter. When he read the lesson he scarcely looked at the page, but repeated the words as if it were something he had seen happen, or had heard spoken, and about which he was merely telling in clear, convincing tones. His sermon was rich in quotations. The quotations clinched every statement that he made. Murray heard for the first time about the great white throne and the books to be opened, and the *other* book that was to be opened, where inside were written names, the Lamb's Book of Life. And whoever's name was not found written there was to go away into everlasting punishment.

Everlasting punishment! That was what he was under now. Life as himself, the Murray Van Rensselaer that he had started out to be, was done with so far as this life was concerned. His punishment could only end with death, and now this that the preacher was saying made it pretty sure that it would not end even then. He had somehow felt all along ever since the accident that if he could only die, all this trouble would be over, and he would have a square deal, as he called it, again, but it seemed not. It seemed things of this life were carried over into the next. If what this preacher said was true, all this about the books and the dead, small and great, being judged out of what was written against them, why, then there was no chance for him. The preacher further stated that those whose names were written in that other book, who were not to be punished, were the "born again ones." That was what that "born again" meant that he had been hearing about so much. Or what was it, after all? Nobody had said. The "born again ones." He had been trying to be born again and had taken a new name, but what were the chances that Allan Murray any more than Murray Van Rensselaer would be a born again one? Well, pretty good, if all they said about him were true, only if he was dead he would be over there himself and would preempt his own name, and besides, Murray had a sudden realization that there would be no chance of deception over there in the other world.

The preacher's words were very clear, very simple, very convincing. The words he repeated from the Bible were still more awe-inspiring. Murray walked silently back to the house beside Mrs. Summers with a deep depression upon him. He felt that he had taken out from that church the heavy burden of an unforgiven sin—that there was no place of repentance, though he might carefully seek it with tears, and that he must bear the consequences of his sin through all eternity.

He could not understand his feeling. It was not at all like himself, and he could not shake it off. He sat in his room for a few minutes looking into the red glow of the coals on his hearth and thinking about it, while Mrs. Summers put the dinner on the table. It somehow did not seem fair. When you came to consider it, he had not meant to be a murderer. There was not anyone he would have protected sooner than Bessie. He was just having a good time. It was not quite fair for him to bear unforgivable punishment the rest of his life for a thing he had not meant to do. Of course the law of the land was that way. It had to be to protect everybody. But the law had no right to you after you were dead. You had satisfied it. But if, after having escaped punishment in this life, he had yet to meet the judgment seat of an angry God, what hope had he?

He dwelt for a moment upon those whose names were written

in the other book, the "born again" ones. Mrs. Summers was likely one of those, if there was any such thing. Yes, and Mrs. Chapparelle. She read the Bible and believed it. He remembered the stories she read them Sunday afternoons. And was Bessie? Yes, she must have been. It must have been that which gave her that look of set-apartness, that sort of peace in her eyes—well, these were odd things he was thinking about. Strange they never came his way before. He had never really taken it in before what it would be to die—to be done with this earth forever! Bessie was gone! And he would be judged for it! Even if he escaped a court of justice, he would be judged. What was the use? Why not go home and take his chances? But no, that would drag his mother and father through all that muck. . . . Bah! He would stay where he was—awhile.

The little tinkling bell broke in upon his thoughts, and he found he was tremendously hungry, in spite of his serious thoughts. Fried chicken and mashed potatoes, and gravy over delicately browned slices of toast! A quivering mold of currant jelly! Little white onions in a cream dressing, a custard pie for desert. It all had a wonderful taste that seemed better than anything he knew, and he really enjoyed sitting there with her eating it. It seemed so cozy and pleasant. Even the blessing at the beginning was rather a pleasant novelty. She had asked him again to take the head of the table and ask the blessing, but he had looked at her with a most engaging smile and said, "Oh, you say it, won't you? I like to hear you." And she had smiled and complied, so now he was not anymore worried about that. If ever he were asked, he had learned what words were used. He could get away with it, though somehow he did not like to be faking a thing like that. It was strange, but he did not. He had never felt so before about anything. He wondered why.

He helped Mrs. Summers carry the dishes out to the kitchen, and while he was doing it the doorbell rang, and Jane presented herself. She announced that she had come as a representative of her class to ask Mr. Murray to be their teacher. She flattered him with her beseeching eyes while she pleaded with him not to say no.

"Class? What class?" he asked blankly, wondering what dog-gone thing he was going to run into now.

"Why, our Sunday school class. There are twelve of us girls. You know our teacher was Miss Phelps, and she's gone away for the winter to California. Perhaps she won't ever come back. Her sister lives out there. She resigned the class before she went away, and we haven't elected anyone else to fill her place. We were sort of waiting to see if you wouldn't take it. I hope nobody else has gotten ahead of us. I tried to see you this morning, but there were so many people speaking to you. Now, you *will* be our teacher, *won't* you?"

Chapter 17

Murray was appalled! He was aghast! He simply could not take this extraordinary request seriously. It seemed as if he must somehow get back to his former companions and tell them the joke. They wanted him to teach a Sunday school class of young ladies! Was ever anything more terribly ludicrous in all the world?

But he managed to keep a perfectly courteous face while he let her talk on for a minute or two, and while he summoned his senses and tried to figure out a line of safe reply that would not be inconsistent with his supposed character, the doorbell rang again. Ah! Now! Perhaps here was deliverance!

The caller proved to be the Sunday school superintendent, Mr. Marlowe.

"Mr. Murray, I hope I'm not too late," he began, after the introductions. "I've been away in New York all the week. I just got back late last night, and I missed you this morning at the service.

Mr. Harrison had some things to talk over, and when I looked around, you were gone. I've come over to see if you won't take a class of boys in our Sunday school. I've sort of been saving them for you. They're bright little chaps about ten years old and up to no good, of course, but they need a young man of your caliber, and I've just eased them along with some of the elders for a few Sundays until you would arrive. I do hope you'll be interested in them. They are one of the most promising classes in the school, and just at an age when they need the touch of a young man."

"Now, Mr. Marlow," pouted Jane, as soon as she could break into the conversation, "Mr. Murray is going to take *our* class, *aren't* you, Mr. Murray? I came over *first*, Mr. Marlowe. We've had it in mind ever since we heard Mr. Murray was coming, and the girls are *just crazy* to have him. . . ."

The superintendent turned a keen, scrutinizing glance on Murray.

"Well, that's up to you, Mr. Murray, of course. Which do you prefer to teach? The young ladies or the kids? Of course I've no wish to bias you if the girls have gotten their request in before me, but I certainly shall be disappointed. It isn't everybody who can teach these boys."

Murray was going to say eagerly that he had never taught young ladies in his life, nor anybody else, till it suddenly occurred to him that he did not know what reports of his exploits in Sunday school teaching had reached Marlborough. He must proceed carefully. He caught his sentence between his teeth and whirled it around.

"With all due apology to the young ladies," he said gracefully, turning a look on Jane that almost made her forgive him for what he was saying, "I think I'd fit better with the kids, if I'm to teach at all. You see—I'm"—he floundered for an explanation—"I'm just crazy about kids, you know!"

"Oh, Mr. Murray!" pouted Jane stormily.

The superintendent brightened.

"Well, I certainly am thankful," he said. "I didn't know what to do with those little devils! They spoiled the whole service last Sunday. They had little tin pickles from some canning factory, and they sent them whizzing all over the room. One hit an old lady's eye and made no end of trouble. I'll be grateful forever if you can see your way clear to taking them right on this afternoon."

"Oh!" gasped Murray. "Really, I—you know—I—"

"Yes, I know what you're going to say. You haven't had any chance this week to study the lesson. They all say that the first time, but it doesn't matter in the least. You can tell them a story, can't you? You can at least keep them from raising a mob or stealing the minister's hat. I'm about at the end of my rope, so far as they are concerned. Perhaps I'm not giving them a very high recommendation, but I heard of you before you came, that you were eager for a hard job, so here it is! Will you come over and get acquainted with them? Let the lesson take care of itself. Anyhow, they will teach it to you, if you ask questions. They are bright little chaps, if they are bad, and they've been well taught."

It was a strange thing, perhaps the strangest of all the strange things that had yet happened to Murray Van Rensselaer, that fifteen minutes later he found himself sitting in front of a class of well-dressed, squirming, whispering lads who eyed him with a challenge and were prepared to "beat him to it," as they phrased it.

What he was going to say to them, how he was going to hold them through the half hour for which he was responsible for their actions, he did not know, but he certainly was not going to let seven kids beat him, and besides, had he not a reputation connected with his new name which he must keep up? He wasn't going to be under suspicion because he could not bluff a good Sunday school teacher's line. That suggestion about letting the boys do the teaching had been a good thing. He would try that out.

During an interval when a hymn was announced, he overheard two of the boys talking about the football scores in the last night's papers, and as soon as the superintendent announced that the classes would turn to the lesson, he collected the attention of his young hopefuls with one amazing offhand question.

"You fellas ever see a big Army and Navy game?"

This, perhaps, was not the most approved method for opening a lesson in Acts, but it got them. The seven young imps altogether dropped the various schemes of torment which they had planned for this first Sunday with their new teacher and leaned forward eagerly.

"Naw! D'jou?"

A moment later and Murray was launched on a vivid and exciting description of the last Army and Navy football game he had seen, and for twenty brisk minutes he had the undivided attention of the most "difficult" class in the Sunday school.

"He'll do," whispered Marlowe to the minister as they stood together on the platform looking toward Murray, with his head and shoulders down and the knot of seven heads gathered around him. "We picked the right man all right. He's got 'em from the word *go.*"

The minister nodded with shining eyes.

"It looks that way. It certainly does," he beamed, and the two good men turned to other problems, fully satisfied that the seven worst little devils were well started on the way to heaven, led by this wonderful young Christian, who had not yet stopped at anything he had been asked to do. They began to plan how much more they could get him to do in places where they desperately needed help.

The superintendent's warning bell rang before Murray suddenly came out of that football game and realized that something had been said about a "lesson"—that, in fact, the lesson was supposed to have been the principal thing for which they were here as teacher and pupils. It would not do to ignore that utterly. Some of these young scamps would be sure to go home and tell, and his good name, of which he was beginning to be a little proud, would be damaged if he made no attempt at all to teach something sort of ethical. That was his idea of Sunday school teaching. "Boys, you must grow up to be good citizens," or something of that sort. He supposed there was some kind of a code, or formula, for the thing, and he recalled that he was to ask the boys to tell him, so he straightened back and began: "But we must get at our lesson, kids; the time is almost up."

"Aw shucks!" spoke up the boldest child impudently. "We don't want 'ny lesson. We want you to tell us more about that game."

"I've talked enough; now it's your turn. What's your lesson about? Who can tell me? I'm a stranger here, you know."

"'Bout Paul," said another boy, whom they called "Skid" Jenkins.

"No, 'twas Saul," said "Gid" Porter.

"It was Saul first," explained Jimmy Brower. "He got diffrunt after a while. Then he got a new name."

"I see," said Murray, fencing for time. What a strange lesson. Who was this Paul, he wondered. Not Paul Revere, of riding fame? He searched his scant knowledge of history in vain. Of Bible lore he knew not the slightest shred.

"Well, he was Paul the longest, anyhow," insisted Skid. "Everybody calls him Paul. You don't never hear him called Saul."

"Tell me more about him," said Murray. "What did he do?"

"Why, he was *fierce!*" said Jimmy earnestly. "He *killed* folks!"

The teacher sat up sharply and drew a deep breath. *He* had killed some one.

"Yes," said Skid, "he went right into their houses and took 'em to the magistrates and had 'em whipped and sent to prison, and burned their houses and took their kids'n everything, an' he was the one that held the men's sweaters when they was stoning Stephen, ya know. Gee, I'd like to a been living then! It musta been great! When they didn't like what anybody said, they just stoned 'em dead! We had Stephen last Sunday. And Saul—I mean Paul—but he was Saul then when he held the clothes—he was to blame, ya know. He coulda stopped 'em stoning Stephen ef he'd wanted. He was some kinda officer, ya know. But he didn't, 'cause he didn't wantta. Ya know he thought he's doin' right? That'uz before he was born again." He looked at his new teacher for approval and found a flattering attention. Murray's face was white, and beads of perspiration were standing on his brow, but he summoned a wan smile of approbation and murmured faintly: "Yes? How was that?"

Jerry Pettingill raised a smudgy hand.

"Lemme tell. He's talked long enough. It's my turn."

Murray turned his eyes nervously to this new boy, and he continued with the tale.

"He was on his way t'rest a lotta folks, an' the lightnin' struck him blind, an' the soldiers he had with him didn't see no one, just heard a voice, an' they didn't know whatta think, an' Saul—no, Paul—"

"He *wasn't* Paul yet—"

"Well, he was right away then, 'cause when he heard God he got borned again."

"What is 'born again'?" came from the lips of the unwilling teacher, almost without his own consent. He had no idea that these children could explain, and yet he somehow had to ask that question. He wanted to see what they would say.

"It's givin' yerself up to God!" said Skid cheerfully.

"It's quit doin' whatcher doin' an' doin' the other thing. Sayin' yer sorry an' all that. Only Saul, he said he didn't know. He thought he was doin' good," said another boy.

"Ya can't born yerself," broke in young Gideon. "The teacher said so last Sunday. He said God had to do it. God borned Saul all over and made him a new heart inside him when he said he wouldn't do them things anymore."

"Aw, well, what's that? I didn't say ya could, did I?" broke in Skid. "Saul, he was blind when he got up, an' he had to go on crutches to the city—"

"Aw, git out! Whatcher givin' us? They don't havta go on crutches when they're blind, and God sent a man to pray about him, and then he said, 'Brother Saul, receive thy sight,' an' after that he wasn't blind anymore, an' he was born again. He was a new man then, ya know, an' he didn't kill folks anymore, an' he went and got to be a preacher."

The superintendent's bell brought the narrative to a sharp close, and the new teacher sat back white and exhausted, the strength gone out of him. Even the kids were talking about killing people. What a lesson! How did the little devils learn all about it, anyway? Why had he ever stayed in this awful place? Why had he ever taken this terrible class?

"Well, you certainly are a winner, Murray," said the superintendent, slapping him admiringly on the shoulder. "You had 'em from the word *go*! I never saw the like of you!"

Murray turned a tired face toward Marlowe.

"You didn't need a teacher for this class, man! They can teach circles around any man you'd put on the job. I never saw the like! What you'd better do is give each one of those little devils a class to teach. Then you could all quit. I didn't teach that class; they taught it themselves."

The superintendent grinned at the minister, who was standing just behind Murray, and the minister grinned back knowingly.

"We're glad this young man has come to live among us," he said with a loving hand on Murray's shoulder, and somehow Murray felt suddenly like laying his head down on the minister's shoulder and crying. When he finally got away from them all, he went to his room and buried his face in the pillow and slept. He felt all worn out. He had never taken a nap in the daytime before in his life, but he certainly slept that afternoon.

It was quite dark when he woke up and heard Mrs. Summers calling him to come down to supper.

She had a little tea table drawn up in front of the fire in the living room, with a big easy chair for him and the Morris chair for herself. There were cups of hot bouillon with little squares of toast to eat with it and sandwiches with thin slivers of chicken on a crisp bit of lettuce. There were more sandwiches with nuts and raisins and cream cheese between, and cups of delicious cocoa, and there were little round white frosted cakes to finish off with. Murray thought it was the nicest meal he ever tasted, eaten that way before the fire, with the flickering firelight playing over Mrs. Summers' pretty white hair and the soft light from the deep shaded lamp over the little white-draped table. Cozy and homey. He found himself longing for something like this to have been in his past.

Mrs. Summers talked about the Sunday school lesson, discussed two or three questions that had been brought up in her class of young men concerning Paul's conversion, and Murray was surprised to find that he actually could make intelligent replies on the subject.

But then it all had to be broken up by the entrance of someone coming for him to go to Christian Endeavor. This time it was a stranger, the vice president of the Christian Endeavor, come to ask him to talk a few minutes. He really must do something about this. He was getting in too deep, going beyond his depth. It might be all well enough to pretend to teach a class of kids something he knew nothing about, but make an address in a religious meeting he could not—at least not yet. He had to draw the line somewhere.

So he summoned all his graces and made a most eloquent excuse. He had not been very well lately, had been overworking before he came here, and his physician had warned him he must go a little slower. Added to that had been the nervous strain of the wreck. If they would kindly excuse him from doing any public speaking for a month or so, at least until he had had a chance to pick up a little and get himself in hand. He felt that it was owed to the bank that he put his whole strength there for the present, till he was in the running and felt acquainted with his work, and so on and so on.

The young vice president smiled and regretted this was so, but said of course he understood. They would not bother him until he was ready, though everybody was crazy to hear him—they had heard so much about him. Didn't he even want to lead a prayer meeting? Well, of course. Yes, it was fair to the bank that he give all his strength there at present. Well, he would come over to the meeting anyway, wouldn't he?

And with a wistful glance at the easy chair and the firelight on Mrs. Summers' hair, he allowed himself to be dragged away with the understanding that he would meet his landlady in her pew for the evening church service. Gosh! Four church services, with a prospect of five for the next Sunday if they carried out their suggestion about the Ushers' Association! Could you beat it? He would have to bolt before next Sunday! He must manage it after he got his week's salary next Saturday. That would give him a little more money to start with. He would work his plans with that end in view. It certainly was too bad to leave when his disguise seemed to be working so perfectly, and seemed likely to be permanent, but he could not keep on this way. It might have been all right if he had anything to go on, but one could not jump into new surroundings like this and take on the knowledge that belonged to them. That was out of the question. It was all bosh about being born again. You could not do it. Maybe if you worked at it for years and studied hard you could. But it seemed like a hopeless undertaking.

That evening the sermon was on the Atonement. He recognized the word and sat up eagerly to discover what it meant.

That was a sermon of no uncertain sound. It pointed the way of salvation clearly and plainly, with many more quotations from scripture, so that the wayfaring man, though a fool, need not err in that, and Murray Van Rensselaer was both of those. He learned the meaning of the word *Calvary*, too, and heard the story of the cross for the first time clearly told. Before that it had been more or less a vague fairy tale to him. Of course one could not live in the world of civilization without having heard about Christ and the cross, but it had meant nothing to him. He was as much of a heathen as anyone could be and live in the United States of America.

He heard how all men were sinners. That was made most plain in terms that reminded him of the morning sermon about the judgment. He did not dispute that fact in his mind. He knew that he was a sinner. Since he had run away from the hospital, his sin had loomed large, but he named it by the name of murder and counted it done against a human law. Now he began to see that there was sin behind that. There were worse things in his life than even killing Bessie had been, if one was to believe all that the preacher said. It was an unpleasant sensation, this listening to these keen, convincing sentences, and trying them by his own experiences and finding they were true. He heard for the first time of the love of God in sending a Savior to the world. This thought was pressed home till He became a personal Savior, just for himself, as if he had been the only one who needed Him, or the only one who would have accepted Him. The minister told a story of two sisters, one of whom was stung by a bee, and the other fled away, crying, "Oh, I'm afraid it will sting me, too!" but the first sister called, "You needn't be afraid, Mary; it has left its sting in my cheek! It can't sting you anymore!" And Murray Van Rensselaer learned that his sin had left its sting in Jesus Christ and could hurt him no more. Strange thing! The sin from whose consequences he was fleeing away had left its sting in the body of the Lord Christ when He was nailed to the cross hundreds of years ago, and could harm him no more! Could not have the power to shut him out from eternal life, as it was now shutting him out from earthly life and all that he loved. Strange! Could this thing be true? There was one condition, however. One had to *believe*! How could one believe a thing like that? It was too good to be true. Besides, if it were true, why had no one ever told it to him before?

Murray went home in a dazed state of mind, home to the deep chair by the firelight, to Mrs. Summers' gentle benediction of a prayer before he went up to his room. And then he lay down in his bed to toss and think, and half decided to get up and creep away in the night from this place where such strange things were told and such peculiar living expected of one. What would they ask of him next?

Chapter 18

The next thing they asked him to do was to let them elect him state president of the Christian Endeavor Society.

It meant nothing whatever to him when they told him, because he did not know what Christian Endeavor even stood for at that time, but he smiled and turned it down flat with the excuse that he could not give any more time to outside things. He owed his whole energy to the bank. Mr. Harper would not like it if he accepted other duties here and there.

Then it developed that Mr. Harper *would* like it very much. It was just what Mr. Harper wanted of his bank teller, to be prominent in social and religious matters. A committee had waited upon Mr. Harper, and he came himself to plead with the young man, stressing that he would like him to accept as a personal favor to himself. He felt it would give their bank a good standing to have their employees identified with such organizations.

The young committee pleaded eagerly and promised to do all the work for him. They would prepare all the programs and suggest competent helpers on each committee who understood their work thoroughly. There really would be little left for him to do but preside at the state conventions and attend a county convention now and then. Wouldn't he stretch a point and take the office? They needed him terribly just now, having lost a wonderful president through serious illness.

It sounded easy. He did not imagine it meant much but calling a meeting to order now and then, and as there was a vice president, he could always get out of it on the score of pressing business when he did not want to go. So Murray "stretched a point" and said yes. He was beginning to enjoy the prestige given by these various activities which they had pressed upon him. He had almost forgotten that he was an outlaw. For the time being he seemed to himself to have become Allan Murray. He was quite pleased with himself that he was fitting down into the groove so well. Even the religious part was not so irksome as he had felt at first. He might in time come to enjoy it a little. He had not slipped away that next Saturday night. He had lived very tolerably through three more Sundays. He was even becoming somewhat fond of those seven little devils in his Sunday school class. His popularity as a Sunday school teacher was evidenced by the fact that seven other little devils, seven times worse than the first seven, had joined themselves to the knot that closed around him for a brief half hour every Sunday afternoon. There was even talk of giving him a room by himself next to the Primary room.

Fearing that he never would be able to teach a lesson, he had conceived the idea of offering a prize of a story to the class after they had told him the lesson for the day. This relieved him of any responsibility in the matter of the teaching, and kept excellent order in the class. All he had to do was to have a hairbreadth experience ready to relate during the last ten minutes of the session.

But Mrs. Summers, wise in her day and generation, perhaps wiser than Murray ever suspected, brought to bear her gentle heaven-guided influence upon the young teacher. If she suspected his need, she never told anybody but her heavenly Father, but she quietly hunted out little bits here and there about the lesson—illustrations, an unusual page from the *Sunday School Times*, a magazine article with a tale that covered a point in the lesson, now and then an open Bible dictionary with a marked paragraph—and laid them on his reading table under the lighted lamp.

"I found such a wonderful story today when I was studying for my Sunday school class," she would say while she passed him the puffy little biscuits and honey at the supper table. "I thought you might like to use it for your boys. I took the liberty of laying it up on your table, with the verses marked in the Bible where it fits. You have so little time; it is only right the rest of us should help you in the wonderful work you are doing in that Sunday school class."

He thanked her, and then because he did not like to seem ungrateful, and he was afraid he might be asked what he thought of it, he read what she had left there and was surprised to find himself getting interested. Strange how a dull thing grew fascinating if you just once gave your mind to it. He wondered if that were true of all dull things. He actually grew interested in getting ready for his Sunday school class. There were times when he even preferred it to going out socially, although that was where he naturally shone, it being more his native element.

Yet he often felt a constraint when he went out to dinner or to a social gathering. There were very few invitations to the kind of thing to which he had been accustomed. The whole community seemed to be pretty well affected by the sentiments of that Presbyterian church. They did not seem to know how to play cards, not the ones who were active, and they did not seem to think of dancing when they got together. Not that he missed those things. He was rather more interested in the novelty of their talk and their games, and their music, which was some of it really good. It appeared that the girl Anita was quite a fine musician. She had been away for a number of years studying. Yet he was always a little bit afraid of Anita. Was it because she reminded him of Bessie, or because she seemed to not quite trust him? He could not tell. When he was in the same company with her, he found himself always trying to put his best foot forward. It annoyed him. She seemed to be always looking through him and saying: "You are not what you are trying to seem at all. You are an impostor! You have stolen a dead man's name and character, and you killed a girl once! Someday you will kill the good man's good name, too, and everybody will find out that you are a murderer!" When these thoughts came through his mind, he would turn away from her clear eyes, and a sharp thought of Bessie like an intense pain would go through his soul. At such times he was ready to give it all up and run away. Yet he stayed on.

He was flooded with invitations to dinners and teas and evening gatherings, little musicals and concerts, and always at these gatherings there was the tang of excitement lest he should be found out. He was growing more and more skillful in evading direct questions and bantering gaiety intended to draw him out. He came to be known as a young man of great reserve. He never talked about himself. They began to notice that. All they knew about him they had heard from others before he came. They liked him all the better for this, and perhaps the mystery that this method gradually put about him made him even more fascinating to the girls. All except Anita.

Anita kept her own counsel. She was polite and pleasant, consulting with him when it was necessary, that is, when she could not get someone else to do it for her, but never taking him into the gracious circle of her close acquaintances. Jane often asked her why she had to be so stiff. Jane was more effusive than ever about the young hero of the town. But Anita closed her lips and went about her business, as charming as ever and just as distant. It intrigued Murray. He never had had a girl act like that to him. If it had not been for the fact that she reminded him unpleasantly of Bessie and made him uncomfortable every time he came in her vicinity, he would have set to work in earnest to do something about it, but he really was very busy and almost happy at the bank and was quite content to let her go her way. His work at the bank was growing more and more fascinating to him. He was like a child who is permitted to work over machinery and feel that he is doing real work with it. He fairly beamed when his accounts came out just right, and he loved being a wheel that worked the machinery of this big clean bank. While he was there he forgot all that was past in his life, forgot that any minute a stranger might walk in and announce himself as the real Allan Murray, and he would have to flee. In the sweet wholesomeness of the monotony of work, it seemed impossible that such things as courts of justice could reach a long arm after him and place him in jail and try him for his life.

He liked most of the men with whom he was associated; also he liked Mrs. Summers. The little talks they had at night before he went up to his room gave him something like comfort. It was a new thing, and he enjoyed it. He even let her talk about religious questions and sometimes asked her a shy question now and then, though most of all he was afraid to venture questions lest he reveal his utter ignorance and lay himself open to suspicion. More and more as the days went by he began to cling to the new life he was carving out for himself and to dread to lose it. The respect of men, which he had never cared about in his other days, was sweet to him now. To have lost his first inheritance gave him a great regard for the one into which he had dropped unawares. It was not his, but he had none now, and he must not let them take this one away from him. He flattered himself now and then that he had been born again, as the sign in that trolley car had advised. He was like a little child learning a new world, but he was learning it, and he liked it.

Into the midst of this growing happiness and assurance entered the State Christian Endeavor Convention.

It was to be held in a nearby city. He had not understood that he would have to go away to a strange place when he took the office, but it was too late to refuse now. He must risk it. Still, it worried him some. Here in Marlborough he was known, now, and would not easily be taken for someone else. Practically everybody in town knew him or knew who he was. He would not likely be mistaken or arrested for anyone else, even if his picture were put up in the bank right opposite his own window. He had by this time ventured to look the picture of the advertised man on the wall fully in the face and discovered it did not look in the least like himself, so he had grown more relaxed about such things. If all this time had passed and nothing had come out about him, surely his father had found a way to hush things up. Poor Dad! He wished he dared send him word that he was all right and on the way to being a man. But he must not. It might only precipitate a catastrophe. He was dead and had been born again. He must be dead to all his old life if he hoped to escape its punishment.

He journeyed to the convention in company with a large party from the Marlborough churches, who hovered around him and made him feel almost like a peacock with all their adulation. They pinned badges on him, chattered to him about their committee work, asked his advice about things he had never heard of before, and it amused him wonderfully to see what answers he could give them that would satisfy them, and at the same time would in no way give himself away.

But when they arrived at the strange city and went together to the convention hall, and Murray saw for the first time the great auditorium, with its bunting and streamers and banners and mottoes, his heart began to fail him. A kind of sick feeling came over him. It appalled him that he was to be made conspicuous in a great public assembly like this. He never imagined that it was to be a thing of this sort. He began to realize what a fool he had been to get into a fix like this—what an unutterable fool that he did not clear out entirely. He did not belong among people like this. He could never learn their ways, and inevitably sometime, probably soon, he would be found out. Every day, every hour he remained would only make the outcome more unspeakable. This business of being born again was an impossible proposition from the start. One could not work it. He ought to go. He would go at once! This was as good a time as any. Much better than in Marlborough, for no one around would recognize him, and he could get far away before his absence was discovered.

He cast a quick glance around him, and saw that his delegation were all being seated up near the front of the auditorium. With swift steps he marched down the aisle and out the door and came face-to-face with the man who was to lead the devotional meeting, to whom he had just been introduced.

"I was looking for you, Murray," he said. "You're wanted at once up on the platform. They want to consult you about the appointment of the committees before the meeting opens. Better hurry! It's time to begin."

Baffled again, Murray turned back up the aisle, resolving to find some excuse to slip out the side door, which he could see opening from the platform. There was to be a devotional meeting. He had heard talk about selecting hymns. He would slip out while they were singing. At any rate, there was no escape here just now, for the leader of the devotional meeting was just behind him.

So he went to the platform, bowed, smiled, and tried to conduct himself in an altogether happy and carefree manner, assenting to all the suggestions about committees, listening to reasons for certain appointments as if he knew all about it and was interested, with that flattering deference that was second nature to him. But his eyes kept turning constantly to the door at the left of the platform, and when they were finally through with him and motioned him to a seat in the center of the platform, he sank into the big chair of honor with relief. Now, at last, his release was at hand! When they arose to sing the first hymn, he would look up as if someone beckoned. No matter where that door led to, he would get out of sight somewhere and stay hidden until this infernal convention was over, and he could safely vanish into the world again.

Someone handed him a hymnbook open to the hymn. He

was not acquainted with any hymns, but it struck him as strange that this one should be about hiding. He accepted the book, as he did all things when he was conscious of his predicament, merely as a mask to keep him from suspicion, and he pretended to sing, although he had never heard the tune before.

"Oh, safe to the Rock that is higher than I,
My soul in its sorrow and anguish would fly;
So sinful, so weary, Thine, Thine would I be;
Thou blest 'Rock of Ages,' I'm hiding in Thee!"

Murray Van Rensselaer had never heard of the Rock of Ages except in connection with an insurance company. He did not understand even vaguely the reference, but as his lips formed the words which his eyes conveyed to his brain from the book, his heart seemed to grasp for them and be saying them in earnest. Hiding! Oh, if there were only some hiding for him! Sinful? Yes, he must be sinful! He had never thought he was very bad in the days that were past, but somehow since he had been in this region where everybody talked about Right and Wrong as if they were personified, and where all the standards of living were so different, it had begun to dawn upon him that if these standards were true, then he personally was a sinner. It was not just his having been responsible for Bessie's death. It was not even his running away when he found he had killed her. Nor yet was it his allowing these good people to think he was Allan Murray—a Christian with a long record of good deeds and right living behind him. It was something behind all that—something that had to do with the Power they called God and with that vague Person they called Jesus, who was God's Son. It was dawning upon him that he had something to do with God! He had never expected that he would ever have anything in the remotest way connected with God, and now suddenly it seemed as if God was there all the time, behind everything, and had not been pleased with his relation to life. It seemed that God had been there dealing with him even before he was born into the family of Van Rensselaer. Before being Van Rensselaer's child, he was God's child! His father had bitterly berated him for the way he had misused and been disloyal to the fine old name of Van Rensselaer; how would God speak to him sometime about the way he had treated Him?

"Hiding in Thee! Hiding in Thee!" sang the gathering throng earnestly and joyously, and he shuddered as his lips joined with theirs. Hiding in God! How could he hide in God? It would be like taking refuge in a court of justice and expecting them to protect him from his own sin!

He recalled the first lesson his Sunday school class had taught him about Saul who was Paul, when a light shined round about him and he met the Lord on the way to Damascus. He had heard more of him since, in sermons, and in the Bible readings, and in his talks with Mrs. Summers. One could not hear a story like that referred to again and again without getting the real meaning into his soul, but never before had it come home to him as a thing that really happened, and that might happen again, as it did while he sat there singing. It seemed to him that he was suddenly seeing the Lord—that for the first time he had been halted in his giddy life and made to see that he was fighting against the Lord God, that his whole life had been a rebellion against the Power that had created him, just as his whole former life at home had been a life apart from the parents who had given him life and supported him. It was not the decent thing at all. He had never thought of it so before. He would not have done it if he had ever thought of it that way. Of course his father had told him in a way—a bitter way, cursed at him, but given him the money to pay for his follies just the same. And he had not been honest with his father! He had not been honest with the law of the land either! He had broken it again and again, and counted it something to be proud of when he got away without having to pay a fine. All his life he had run away from fines and punishments. So far as law was concerned, he had been many times guilty. And then when one went further and thought about the laws of God, why, he did not even know what they were. He had never inquired before until a Sunday school session had forced the Ten Commandments to his attention. Of course he had always heard of the Ten Commandments, but they had seemed as archaic as the tomb of some Egyptian pharaoh. He had no notion whatever that anybody connected them with any duties of life today, until Mrs. Summers had discussed the subject briefly one night in that mild impersonal way of hers.

But now as he sat on that platform, singing those words about a hiding place for a soul that was sinful and weary, he knew that he ought to have known those commandments. He ought to have found out God's will for him. He knew that the right name for the state he was in was sin, and he felt an overwhelming burden from the knowledge. He was hearing God's voice speak to him, "It is hard for thee to kick against the pricks," and he did not understand it any better than Saul had done as he lay blinded on the way to Damascus.

The singing had ceased, and he realized that he had not yet slipped away. This was to be a devotional meeting. Perhaps during a prayer he might find a better opportunity.

Startling into his troubled thoughts came the words of the leader: "I am going to ask our new president, Mr. Allan Murray, to lead us in the opening prayer—"

Chapter 19

Never in his life had Murray Van Rensselaer been asked to make a speech or do a stunt that he had been known to refuse or be inadequate to the occasion. It had been his boast that a fellow could always say something if he would just have his wits about him, but the time had come when wits would not serve him. He was suddenly confronted with the Lord God and told to speak to Him before many witnesses! A great swelling horror arose around him like a cloud of enemies about to throttle him. His speech went from him, and his strength, also his self-confidence. A few weeks back he might have jumped to his feet and rattled off a pleasant little prayer, appropriate in its petitions, correct in its address and setting, and felt smart about having risen to the occasion. Not so now. He felt himself to be sitting confused and ashamed before the Lord, and he had nothing to say.

He was in dire straits. He realized fully that if he did not do what he was asked, his mask was off, and before all this assembled multitude he would be discovered and brought to shame. Yet he dared not say off a prayer that he did not mean. So much he had grown in the knowledge of the Holy One. He knew it would be blasphemy.

There was a dead silence in the room, a settling down of awe and waiting, half-bowed heads, trying to glimpse the new president before the prayer began, yet reverently waiting for him to address the great high throne of God for them.

A panic came upon him. He dared not sit still. Old habit of responding to any challenge, no matter how daring, goaded him; fear got him to his unwilling feet, and there he stood.

The silence grew. The heads were bent reverently now. Such a young man to be such a great leader, they thought. Such a deep spiritual look upon his face!

Murray stood there and faced God, his voice all gone!

Then the audience seemed to melt away behind a great misty cloud. A radiance was before his closed eyes, and his voice came back. Unwillingly it had to speak, to recognize the Presence in which he stood.

"Oh, God!—"

A wave of sympathy came up from the audience inaudibly, as incense from an altar. Murray felt the uplift of their spirits, as if they were far away, yet pressing him forward.

"You know I am not worthy to speak for this people—" He paused. His forehead was damp with the mighty physical effort of the words, as if they were drawn forth from his very soul.

"You know I am a sinful man—"

He felt as if he stood in the courtroom at last, confessing himself guilty before the world. Now his mother would know! Now his father would know! Now Bessie's mother and Mrs. Summers, and all of them would know, but he was glad! Already his soul felt lighter! The burden was going!

"You know I am not what they think!" he burst forth. "I am not able to preside at a meeting like this. Won't *You* take my place, oh God? Won't *You* lead these people, and won't *You* help me and tell me what to do? I am willing for You to do what You like with me. I'm *hiding* in You!"

He hesitated. Then he added what he had heard in prayers ever since he came to Marlborough, what Mrs. Summers always closed her evening petition with—"For Jesus Christ's sake. Amen."

Two ministers at the back of the church whispered to one another softly.

"A most remarkable prayer!" said one.

"Yes, and a most remarkable young man, they say!" said the other. "A wonder in this age that his head is not turned with all the praise he is receiving. How humble he is!"

Murray slumped into his seat with a sense of exhaustion upon him and dropped his head upon his shielding hand. The leader in a sweet tenor voice started softly the hymn:

"Have Thine own way, Lord, have Thine own way!
Thou are the potter, I am the clay;

Mold me and make me after Thy will,
While I am waiting, yielded and still."

The many voices took it up and it swept through the room like a prayer, softly, tenderly, the words clear and distinct. Murray had never heard anything like it before.

"Have Thine own way, Lord! Have Thine own way!
Search me and try me, Master, today!
Whiter than snow, Lord, wash me just now,
As in Thy presence humbly I bow."

Murray felt a great longing sweep over him to be washed whiter than snow. He had never heard talk like this, but it filled his need. He felt soiled inside. He did not understand it at all, but he seemed to have been wandering for a long time in filth, and now he realized that what he needed was cleansing. His own soul began to cry out with the spirit of the prayer song that was trembling about him from all these people, who seemed to know the words and by some miracle to all feel the same way that he did. Why! Were they all praying for him?

—"wounded and weary, help me I pray!
Power, all power, surely is Thine!
Touch me and heal me, Savior divine!"

They sang with such assurance, as if they knew He could and would do what they asked. Dared he ask, too? Were there conditions to such assurance? Would God take a man who had killed a girl and then gone on masquerading as a Christian just to save his skin?

"Have Thine own way, Lord! Have Thine own way!" went on the quiet prayer. Ah! That was the condition. Surrender! Well, he was ready. That was what that fellow Saul did, just said, "Lord, what wilt Thou have me to do?" He could ask that.

"Hold o'er my being absolute sway!" went on the song. Yes, he could echo that. He was ready for anything, if there was only a way out of this awful hole he was in. He was sick of himself and his own way. It had never been much but froth. He saw that now. Why had he not seen it before?

"Fill with Thy Spirit till all shall see
Christ only, always, living in me!"

What would that be like? Filled with Christ's Spirit! And men looking at him would see Christ, not Murray Van Rensselaer anymore. He understood. That was just what he had been trying to put across about Allan Murray, and he had almost done it. That was the reason why he had not been able to get away, because men looking at him had seen Allan Murray and taken him for what they expected Allan Murray to be! Ah! But this was to be Jesus Christ! Could he possibly get away with that? Only this was not to be a getaway. It was to be real. He was to surrender and let Jesus Christ live in him. Just cut out the things he wanted as if they were not, and let the Spirit of Christ do with him what He liked. Would that be unbearable? What was there he cared for anyway now? Why! He *wanted* to do this! He *wanted* to be made over! He *wanted* to die to the old life forever and be made new, and this seemed to be the only way to do it: *Could this be the new birth?*

There were other voices praying now, just short sentence prayers, tender and pleading, and all with an assurance as if the Lord to whom they prayed was quite near. They prayed for the young leader, that the Holy Spirit might be poured out upon him, and Murray sat with bowed head in great wonder and humility, and spoke within himself: "Oh God! Hear them! Hear them! *Let me be Your child, too!*" Surely, then, before the Throne, mention was made of Murray Van Rensselaer's name, and it was said of him, "For behold, he prayeth!"

Murray went through the rest of that convention in a daze of joy and wonder. He was not aware that he was doing an amazing thing, really an outrageous thing when one came to think of it. He had not the slightest perception of the gigantic fraud he was perpetrating upon an adoring public. He was absorbed in the thing that had come to pass within his own soul.

Every prayer that ascended to heaven, every song that was sung, every speech that was made, he drank in like the milk of a newborn babe. It all seemed to be happening for him. He was learning great things about this Savior that was his. He was finding out new facts about the indwelling of the Holy Spirit. For before he was like some of the early Christians, who said, "We have not so much as heard whether there be any Holy Ghost." He was but a babe in the truth.

For the rest he did as he was told. They asked him to preside at the meeting, and with gravity and humility he took his place, not realizing at all that it was presumption in him and that he was a false deceiver. His entire mind was engrossed with the wonder that had been wrought in himself. He went through the entire two days as one goes through a fire or an earthquake or any other sudden cataclysm which changes everything normal, and where one has to act for the moment. He had no consciousness for the time being of the past or its consequences, or that he was in the least responsible for them now. Deep in his mind he knew they were to be dealt with sometime, but he seemed to sense as the babe senses its mother's care that he now had a Savior to deal with those things for him. He was a new creature in Christ. Old things were passed away, and all things were become new!

They were wonderfully kind and helpful to him. They had all the matters of business carefully thought out and written up on little cards, with the hours neatly penned, and what he had to say about each item of business. They handed him a new card at the beginning of each session, and they thought him so modest that he kept in the background and did not try to shine when everybody was ready to bow down to him. He asked intelligent questions now and then about matters of business, and he carried them through without a hitch when it came to voting and appointing committees.

Somehow, too, he got through the introductions that were a part of his duty, though none of the speakers were at all known to him. They would say, "Now the next is Scarlett, from Green County. You know, the fellow that made his mark getting hold of the foreigners in his district and forming them into a society, and finally into the nucleus of a church. Great fellow, Scarlett! Give him the best send-off you can! He isn't very prepossessing in appearance, but he's a live wire!"

And Murray would get up and revamp these remarks into the finest kind of a "send-off," in his own peculiarly happy phrasing, and then sit down and wonder as some plain little man with clothes from a cheap department store and an unspeakable necktie would get up and tell in horrendous English of the souls that had been saved and the workers that had developed in his little corner of the vineyard. Murray found his eyes all dewy and his voice husky when the Scarlett man was done, and he turned for his next cue to his mentor.

"Whipple of China. Yes, *the* Whipple! Stuck by his mission when the mob was burning his school and came through. He's back, you know. Got it all built up again. Raised the money himself—but he'll tell about that, of course."

And Murray would get up and say: "It ill befits me to try to say anything in introducing Mr. Whipple, of China. You all know of his thrilling escape and of his wonderful success in rebuilding the work that the enemy had pulled down. I am sure you want to hear him tell his own story, and I will not take one moment of his precious time in anticipating it. Mr. Whipple."

Then he would sit down again to listen to a tale of God's care for His own, more thrilling than any that had ever come his way in story, drama, or life. And this was what men who knew the Lord had been doing with their lives! While he had been driveling his away in childish nonsense, they had been risking their lives for the sake of telling the story of salvation. Salvation! Oh, *salvation*! What a great word! He seemed never to have heard it before. What if someone had shouted that in his ear as he started away in the night from that hospital door? If it had been whispered behind him as he stood by Mrs. Chapparelle's kitchen window and watched her go away to answer the doorbell! If he could have heard it as he lay under the freight car and rode over the tortuous way! That there *was* salvation! Salvation for him! Why, he had not even realized then that he was a sinner. He had only thought of the consequences of his sin if he were found out. He had felt sorry for having hurt Bessie and her mother, of course, but he had no sense of personal sin. And now he had. Now he knew what the burden had been that weighed him down, growing gradually heavier and heavier through the weeks. And now it was gone! He wanted to run and shout that there was such a word as *salvation*, and that it was his! He did not quite know how he got it nor what it was, but he knew it was his, and that he had surrendered himself for life. He was not his own anymore. He belonged to Someone who would undertake for him. His old self was dead, and Christ had promised to see to all that. There would be things for him to do, of course, when this meeting was over. He did not know what they were, but he would be shown. He was like a person blinded now, groping, being led. It came to him that he was like Saul of Tarsus, waiting there in the street called Straight for someone to say, "Brother Saul, receive thy sight!" Strange what an impression that first Bible story of his life had made upon him! It probably would not have been remembered if he had not heard it in such a peculiar way, first taught by his wild little Sunday school class, and then read slowly, with original comments, by Mrs. Summers not many nights later at her evening worship. He realized that he had gotten a great deal of knowledge from Mrs. Summers. He put that away in his mind for future gratitude and absorbed himself in listening to the speakers, who one and all seemed to have the same power and impetus behind their lives, whether they were from China or Oklahoma or Sayres' Corners. Not all of them could speak good grammar. Not all of them knew how to turn a finished phrase, but all knew the Lord Jesus Christ and seemed glad about it. Strange there could have been so many people in the world who knew and loved these things and believed in a life that was invisible and eternal, and he had never come in contact with any of them before! He had known church people, not a few. His mother went to church sometimes, professed to be a member of one of the most fashionable congregations in his home city, but he felt positive his mother knew nothing of surrender to Christ. Why had no one ever told people in his home circle? His father! Did his father know?

It was undoubtedly Murray's absorption in the great new peace that had come to his soul through simple self-surrender that carried him through the services of those days without self-consciousness or fear. His quiet self-effacement made a deep impression on all. He did not seem to realize that he had evaded all attempts to bring him into the limelight. He had been so entirely taken up with his new thoughts that the old situation that had haunted him for weeks was gone for the time.

They came home on the midnight train, and it happened that the man from China was riding on that same train to the city farther on and sat with Murray.

Now Murray had never talked with a man face-to-face who had been through so many hairbreadth escapes as this man from China. Neither had he ever talked with a man or known a man who was so altogether devoted to his cause. So it came about that he sat an entranced listener again to the words of a disciple who had given his life to preaching the gospel in China.

"And how did you feel the night they surrounded the mission with the fire burning all about you, and creeping in the ceiling above?" asked Murray wonderingly. To think that a man had been through that and could sit calmly and talk about it.

"Oh, well, I had to work all the time, of course, stamping out the fire that fell all around, but I kept all the time thinking in the back of my mind that perhaps I'd see the Lord Jesus Himself pretty soon. That was a great thought. There was only one thing held me back. I didn't want to go till I had told a few more people about Him. I couldn't bear to go when there were so few of us telling the story, don't you see? Why, in China, do you know how many thousands of people there are to just one missionary? People I mean who have *never even heard* the name of *Jesus?*"

"No," said Murray, "but I'm beginning to get a sense of how many thousands there are in my own land who don't know Him, and haven't even got one missionary *to the whole bunch of them*! I'm wondering if you could even *get at* some of them to tell them, they're so full of their own matters. Take my own home city, now—"

Murray had forgotten that he was Allan Murray now of Marlborough. He was thinking of his home and father and mother, and the fashionable circle from which he had fled. There is no telling what he might have said had not someone plucked him by the sleeve and called: "Hey, Murray! This is our station! Aren't you going to get out? Not going on to China tonight, are you?" And they hustled him off into the night, with the stars looking down and a strange feeling that all the earth had been made over anew for him.

Murray undressed in a dream. He had not heard any of the nice things they had said about him as they walked down the silent street to Mrs. Summers' door. He had answered only in monosyllables. He had been thinking that when one got to know the news the next thing was to tell it, and how was that going to work out with the life he had left behind him and the mess that he was in? What was the thing for him to do next?

He did not see the pile of mail lying on his bureau. If he had he would probably have paid very little heed to it. He had gotten over the sudden shock that it gave him to see mail addressed to Allan Murray awaiting him. There had been letters several times, most of them circulars, one or two business letters. He had pried them open carefully to discover any possible clue to the situation and then sealed them and put them carefully away in the trunk. Opening the letters even of a dead man was not to his taste, but in this case it seemed almost necessary if he were to remain where he was.

However, the mail lay unnoticed till morning. He turned out the light and knelt awkwardly by his bed. It is a strange thing when a man kneels for the first time before his Maker. Murray dropped down and hid his face in the pillow, as if he were coming to a refuge, yet did not know what to say.

He knelt a moment quietly waiting, and then he said aloud in a low clear voice, as if there were someone else visible in the room:

"Lord, what do You want me to do now?"

In the morning he saw the letters. It was Sunday morning. He remembered that at once, for a bell was ringing off in the distance somewhere. And then his glance wandered to the little pile of letters lying on the bureau. They seemed to recall him to himself. He reached out and got them. Several circulars. There had been mail before from the same firms. Two letters bore the names of Christian Endeavor County Secretaries, and the last in the pile said, in a clear hand, written in the upper left-hand corner: "If not called for in five days, please return to Mr. Allan Murray."

Chapter 20

When Mrs. Chapparelle left her kitchen and the white face pressed against the windowpane and hurried to answer the wheezy old doorbell, her only thought was to hurry and get back to her hot griddle. She knew it was almost smoking hot now, and she wanted to try a little batter to see if there was just the right amount of baking soda in it before Bessie came.

She glanced at the clock as she passed through the door. It was late for Bessie already. What could have kept her? But then, she must have lingered longer at the library, for this was her vacation, and books were always such a temptation to her dear girl. How she wished she were able to buy more of them for her very own.

This would be Bessie, of course. She must have forgotten her key. Strange! Bessie never forgot things like that.

But it was not Bessie standing in the dusky street, with the big glaring arc light casting long shadows on the step. It was the same boy with the silver buttons and the mulberry uniform who had been there that afternoon with the two great big suit boxes, and insisted on leaving them there for a Miss Elizabeth Chapparelle. She had told him very decidedly that nothing of the sort belonged there, and that she could not inform him where they should go. She had even looked in the telephone book for another Chapparelle, but had not found any. Then she had told him that he had better go back to the shop and get further information. Now! Here was that boy again! What could be the meaning of it? She wished Bessie would come home while he was here and tell him herself that the packages were not hers. Bessie might know to whom they belonged.

But the boy was under orders this time.

"Lady, they're a present," he announced with a knowing wink. "I knowed I was right the first time. I've lived in this city since I was born, and I get around some every day. You can't kid me about an *ad*-dress! This here delivery belongs here, and don't belong nowheres else."

Mrs. Chapparelle was quite indignant.

"I'm sorry," she said firmly, "but I'm sure there's a mistake. There is no one who would send my daughter a gift from that shop. I cannot receive it. I cannot be responsible for goods kept here that do not belong to us. You must take it back and say the people would not receive it."

"Say, lady, would you want me to lose my job? You don't know Madame! She said I was to leave it, see? And when Madame says leave it, I leave it. You c'n fight it out yerself with Madame, but I ain't risking my job. You'll find the young lady will know all about it, and I'm leaving it. It's all paid for, lady, so don'tcha worry."

He dropped the package swiftly and returned to the street, where he lost no time at all in swinging himself into the mulberry car with the silver script lettering and glided away from the door, leaving the usually capable Mrs. Chapparelle standing annoyed and hesitating in the open door, a spatula in one hand and the two big boxes at her feet. What in the world could have happened to bring about this ridiculous situation? Now here were likely some very valuable garments that would most certainly have cost a great deal of money, landed at her feet for safekeeping. She disliked keeping them even until morning. Something might happen to them. The house might catch on fire and the clothes be destroyed, and she would be responsible. It would not matter so much if they had money to pay for such things, but they had not, and would be in real trouble if anything was damaged. It was likely the freak of the delivery boy, who did not want to bother to take the things back, and thought this an easy way out of it. She would not stand it. She would call up the shop at once and demand that they come for their property. It was not much after six. If she telephoned at once, she might catch them before closing.

She closed the door and, stooping, read the name and address on the boxes. Grevet's. She studied the telephone book and was soon talking with one of the employees in the office.

"No, ma'am. I don't know anything about it, ma'am. The shop

is closed. Madame is gone. You'll have to call again in the morning, ma'am. I'm only one of the service girls. I don't know anything about it."

She hung up and turned annoyed eyes toward the front door, wishing Bessie would come. How late it was! Why should Bessie be so late? It could not be possible that the child had been saving up money and had bought something for her to surprise her. She surely would not be so shortsighted. It would not be like Bessie. Bessie would know that she would not like it. And Bessie would never go and get anything for herself, either, at a shop like that. It would cost a fortune. As for it being a present, as the boy had said, that was all nonsense. Who would ever send Bessie a present from Grevet's? Nobody had any right to send Bessie presents. No, it was a mistake, of course. They would open it before long when Bessie came and find out if there was any clue to its owner. Just now she could smell the griddle burning, so she dropped the boxes on a chair in the front room and fled back to her kitchen.

The griddle was sending up blue smoke, and she quickly turned down the gas and mopped off the burning grease with an old dishcloth, promptly subduing her griddle back to its smooth, steady heat again. The batter hissed and sputtered and flowed out on the black griddle, shaping itself into a smooth round cake and puffing at once into lovely lightness, with even, little bubbles all over its gray-white surface. Her practiced eye watched it rise and knew that the cake was just right, just enough soda, just light enough, and just enough milk to give it a crisp brownness. She slid a deft spatula under its curling edges, flopped it over exactly in its own spot, its surface evenly browned. Then she turned her attention to the amber syrup bubbling slowly to just the right consistency of limpid clearness. She shoved the coffeepot to the back of the stove, lifted the cake to a hot plate on the top of the oven, tore a bit out of it and tasted it to make sure it was perfect, and then looked at the clock. Why, it was a quarter to eight! Was it possible? What had become of Bessie? How could she stay out so late? She knew her mother would worry! What should she do?

Often she had rehearsed in her mind through the years what she would do if anything happened ever that Bessie did not come home some evening. She would go about it in a most systematic way. She would phone the office to see if she was there. She would ask the janitor if he knew when she left the building, and who was she with? She would phone the other girls in the office. She had carefully gleaned their addresses one by one from her unsuspecting daughter to be prepared for such a time of trouble. Failing in getting any help from the girls or their employer, she would phone the nearest police station, and the big radio stations, and ask for help.

All this carefully planned program began to rush before her mind now as if a scroll with it written out had been unfolded. How many mothers have been through such a time of anxiety, and had a similar plan present itself, and say, "Here, now, is the time to use me," and yet the mother hesitates. So this mother waited and hesitated. Bessie was so careful and so sensible. Bessie had so much common sense. Terrible things did not happen in the world very often. There was some little simple explanation to this delay, and Bessie would surely walk in after five minutes more. Bessie would hate so to have her make a fuss, as if she could not take care of herself. Yet she might have telephoned if she had to stay.

So the mother reasoned and shoved back the griddle, turned the gas very low, heated the oven, and put away the rest of the meal to keep hot; finally abandoning clock, griddle, oven, and all, she went into the little dark front room to sit at the window, as mothers will, and look out and watch the passersby, waiting for the loved one.

The clock struck eight, and Bessie did not come. There lay those two strange boxes. They could have no connection, of course, with Bessie's being late, and yet they annoyed her. Bessie would be annoyed, too, when she came and found them. Perhaps she would not talk about them till her daughter had eaten her supper. Of course, she would soon come, and they would be eating pancakes and syrup, and she would take a deep breath again and know that all was well.

Was that the clock striking the half hour? Oh, what could have happened to Bessie? Never had she stayed away like this before without telephoning. Of course it was not late for a grown girl to be out in the bright city streets, but Bessie always let her know where she was. There had not been anything planned for this evening. She had been going to the library. Perhaps somehow she had gotten locked in the library through lingering too long. How could she find out? Would there be a night watchman who would go and search for her? What was the name of the library Bessie went to? She searched her brain for the right name as she strained her eyes to the street, which seemed full of strangers passing, but no sign of her girl. She went to the kitchen, warm and cozy and safe, with the batter waiting in a yellow bowl on the tiny old-fashioned marble-topped table beside the stove. The first buckwheats of the season, and Bessie loved them so! She looked in a panic at the clock, which was nearing a quarter to nine, and went hurriedly for the telephone book to look up a number. She really could not remain inactive any longer. She had set nine o'clock as her limit to wait, but she must be ready with numbers to call when the first stroke rang. Bessie would not let her go later than nine without phoning. There was a kind of pact between them that she would not get anxious nor do anything foolish till after nine.

She had written out the numbers of three libraries and the police station, and it was three minutes to nine when she heard the front door open. She was so frightened she was trembling, and for a moment her voice went down in her throat somehow, and she could not call. She would hear a voice. Was it Bessie?

"I'm quite all right now, thank you—" It sounded weak and tired. She got to her feet and stood as the kitchen door opened and Bessie walked in.

"I'm so sorry, Mother! You were frightened. But I couldn't help it. Have you had supper? I'm nearly famished. Couldn't we have supper first and let me tell you all about it afterward?"

Bessie sat down by the table and began to take off her hat. Her face looked white and tired, whiter than her mother had ever seen her look before, but she was smiling. Her mother rushed over and clasped her in her arms.

"My little girl!" she whispered softly with her face against her soft hair. "You're sure you're all right?"

"All right, Mother dearie, only so hungry—and a little tired," and she put her arm down on the white table and laid her head upon it. "Cakes! I'm so glad there are cakes! It didn't hurt them to wait, did it? I'm sorry I troubled you. I just know you have been all worried up."

Mrs. Chapparelle smiled and poured a foaming glass of milk.

"Drink some of this quick, dearie. It will hearten you up, and I've got the griddle keeping warm. It won't be a second now till I'll have a piping-hot cake for you."

Bessie drank the milk slowly, and the color began to creep into her cheeks faintly, but there was a sad, troubled look around her eyes. Her mother watched her furtively as she went briskly about getting the supper on the table. She knew something unusual had happened.

But she's here, dear Lord, safe and sound! she said in her heart thankfully as she felt the glad tears come into her eyes.

Mrs. Chapparelle did not ask questions. They talked, not much, about the little occurrences of the mother's day. Yes, the man came to take the ashes, and he only charged fifty cents. He was coming every week now, and they were to pay by the month.

And Mrs. Herron called up and wanted some more towels initialed for Lila's hope chest. She wanted the script letters, and they were worth more to embroider. The little girl next door had been taken to the hospital to have her tonsils taken out, and the milkman had left an extra pint of milk by mistake, so there was plenty to drink with the buckwheats. "And there! I meant to shut that window," the mother added as she hurried over to the corner of the kitchen. "Do you know I thought I saw a man's face looking in awhile ago, just before I began to get worried about you."

"Well, I've often told you, Mother, I think you should shut that blind before dark, especially when you're alone."

Bessie's color was better now. She was sitting up and eating cakes with relish. The droop was going out of her slender figure.

"Oh yes, and a very rude boy brought some packages here this afternoon which he insisted belonged to Miss Elizabeth Chapparelle. You didn't buy anything today, did you?"

"Not a thing, Mother dear. I didn't have but fifty cents in my purse when I started. You know it's almost payday," she rippled out with a voice like falling water, as if it were a joke between them.

"Well, I told him they weren't yours, of course, and I packed him off with his packages. But just when you ought to have been coming back, didn't he arrive again with his parcels and insist upon leaving them. He said he would lose his job if he took them back, that Madame told him not to bring them back, they were paid for, and they were a present. The lazy little scamp didn't want to go back tonight, I suppose, and he actually went away and left them with me right while I was telling him he shouldn't, just sailed away in his delivery car and left me standing with the things at my feet. I was all upset about it. They may be valuable things, and somebody fuming now about them. Maybe we ought to call up the Madame and find out where they really belong and telephone the owners so they can come and get them. Very likely somebody wanted them at once to wear tonight or pack up or something. I tried Grevet's, but they didn't answer. They said the shop was closed—"

"Grevet's!" Bessie lifted eyes wide with alarm, and her face grew white again. "You don't mean they came from Grevet's?"

"Why, yes," said her mother, puzzled. "You don't mean you know anything about them?"

"Where are they, Mother? I must see them first. If it's what I think it is, there's a mistake, and I ought to hunt up the right people at once—"

She rose from the chair and swayed slightly, catching at the table to steady herself.

"Bessie, *you are sick*!" cried her mother. "Something has happened. What is it? You must tell me at once, and you must lie right down."

She caught the girl in her arms and drew her toward an old-fashioned bench in the corner of the kitchen.

"What is it, Bessie? Tell me quick! What has happened? You can't hide it from me any longer!"

"Don't get worried, Mother," said Bessie, allowing her mother to draw her down on the bench. "It wasn't much. Just a little accident. I wasn't hurt, not much more than scared, I fancy. They took me to the hospital and looked me over thoroughly, and they insisted on keeping me there until a nurse could come home with me. That's why I was so late. You see—"

"But why didn't you telephone me?"

"Well, I started to, but the nurse wouldn't let me. She wanted to do it herself, and I was afraid she would frighten you, so I concluded it was better to wait a little and come myself."

"But what was the accident? You are hurt. I *know* you are *hurt*!"

"No, truly, Mother dear, I'm all right now, only a little shaken up. I was riding in an automobile with Murray Van Rensselaer, and a big truck came around a corner and ran into us and overturned us!"

The mother's cheeks were flushed and her eyes bright with anxiety.

"You were riding with *Murray Van Rensselaer*? But *where* is Murray *now*? Was he hurt, too? Did they take him to the hospital?"

"Why, no, I think not, that is—I don't know. The nurse thought he was all right. They said he was very impatient to know how I was, but when I came down they couldn't find him—"

"Oh!" said the mother indignantly. "He probably had some social engagement. One of his mother's dinners. I could see the cars arriving tonight, and the flowers, and things from the caterer's—!"

"Don't, Mother!" The girl sprang away from her. "Don't! He *may* have been hurt. He didn't seem like that kind of man. Perhaps he went away to a doctor himself."

"Well, I hope he did. For the sake of our old regard for him when he was a boy, I sincerely hope he had some good reason for deserting you after he had gotten you smashed up in an accident. How on earth did you come to be riding with him? I thought you would never condescend to do that after the way he has treated you all these years."

"Mother, I must see those packages, please! I'll tell you the whole story as soon as I've got that fixed up, but I must understand what has happened."

"You lie down, and I'll bring them," commanded her mother gently, and went away to get the boxes.

When she returned, Bessie stared at them gravely.

"I'll have to open them, I guess," she said at length. "There ought to be some card inside that will perhaps give the address."

"He said there was a card inside," said the mother as she began to untie the knots carefully.

They turned the soft wrappings of tissue back and discovered lovely gowns inside, sumptuous in their texture, exquisite in their simplicity.

"Oh, Bessie, if your father had lived, you could have had things like that!" wailed the mother's heart as she caught the first glimpse of shimmering silk and deep velvet.

"I'm just as happy without them, Mother," said Bessie serenely, slipping the card from the little white envelope.

There was nothing written on the card except his engraved

name. It told her nothing. She would have to search out Madame Grevet and find the true owner.

"I think she lives somewhere in the city. I'm almost sure someone pointed out her house to me one day. Let's have a look at the telephone book."

She was almost nervously anxious to get those gifts for Murray's dear friend out of the house. She did not want even to tell her story to her anxious mother until the matter was all set right.

But Madame Grevet was not to be found. She must have a private number. An appeal to the janitor of the shop brought no further help. He did not know her number, and anyway, if she had one she would be out. She was always out when she was at home, he said.

Bessie, exhausted, finally gave it up.

"We'll just have to let Murray know, Mother, and I hate that. Won't you call up?"

"No, I *will not!*" said Mrs. Chapparelle crisply. "Let them wait for their things till the shop comes after them again. It's not your fault that they insisted on bringing them here. We're not responsible. If Murray hadn't run away from you, I might feel differently, but as it is, I think it is not necessary for either you or me to run after them. People who have dresses like that can exist for another night without one more."

"But Mother, he was very anxious to have them delivered tonight. I heard him tell the saleswoman."

"That makes no difference, child; you are going to bed. I'll tie those boxes up and take good care of them, and tomorrow I'll telephone Grevet's to come for their property, but you are not to worry another minute about them. Now let me help you upstairs, and I'll give you an arnica rub, and you may tell me very briefly how you came to be riding in Murray Van Rensselaer's automobile. Then we're going to thank the heavenly Father and go to sleep. Now come, darling."

Chapter 21

But the morning brought no solution to the difficulty. Madame Grevet professed to be too busy to come to the telephone and sent a snippy service girl to negotiate.

Mrs. Chapparelle spoke to her gently, as a lady should, taking it as a matter of course that she would wish to set a mistake right. The girl was insolent, and when at last Mrs. Chapparelle's continued protest brought the Madame to the telephone, things were even worse. The Madame declared that it was not for her to meddle in all Mr. Van Rensselaer's many love affairs. The clothes were paid for and the money in the bank. Her responsibility was at an end. They would have to settle their lovers' quarrel themselves. No, she could not on any consideration take back the things. She did not do business in that way. If they wanted money, they must apply to Mr. Van Rensselaer himself for it, not to her. With which insult she hung up the receiver sharply.

Bessie, standing near the telephone, had heard it all. Her face was very white and haughty. Her eyes seemed darker, almost black, with a kind of blue fire in them. She began to dress at once, rapidly, in spite of her mother's protests.

"What are you going to do, Bessie—you mustn't get up! You are not fit to be out of bed."

"I must, Mother. Don't you see I must? I cannot have that woman thinking those things."

"But Bessie, you can't carry those boxes down there yourself. You oughtn't to go out today at all."

"I'll hire a taxi and take them down, Mother. Now, don't you worry about me. I'm quite all right. I only needed this to strengthen me. No, you don't need to go with me," she protested, as her mother began to unfasten her work dress and take down her Sunday crêpe de chine. "I think it is just as well that you shouldn't. I'm not going to make a scene. I'll be a lady, Mother dear. But that woman has got to understand that I am not that kind of a girl!"

Bessie finished dressing hastily and looked every inch a lady herself as she ran downstairs to call a taxi.

She obediently drank the glass of milk her mother handed her and let the driver carry out her boxes, departing in state, with a promise to return immediately.

She walked into Grevet's clad in righteous indignation, quietly, almost haughtily. She was not wearing the bargain coat this time. She had chosen to put on a little matching suit that her mother had made her from a beautiful piece of dark blue silk material, a touch of exquisite embroidery on the tunic where it showed in front, a touch of really fine fur on the collar. In lines and style it might have come from Grevet's itself, so unique and pleasing was the whole effect. The salespersons were puzzled and looked at her with new respect. Madame came forward smiling before she recognized her and halted half perplexed. The driver had set the boxes down inside the door and touched his cap with a smile for the tip she had given him. This girl had an air about her that somehow took the condescension from Madame's manner.

"There has been some mistake," Bessie said gravely. "I came here yesterday with Mr. Van Rensselaer to help him select a gift for a friend. The purchase has been sent to me instead of the lady for whom it was intended. I have brought it back. I am sorry I cannot give you the correct name and address, but Mr. Van Rensselaer did not happen to mention it. I have a kind of dim memory that he called her Gertrude, if that will help you any, but I am not quite sure. It didn't matter to me to remember, you know."

Bessie spoke with a grave air of finality.

Madame regarded the girl with a lenient, knowing smile.

"I think you will find the garments are yours, my dear. Mr. Van Rensselaer distinctly told me they were to be sent to you and wrote out your address himself while you were changing."

Bessie drew herself up with heightened color.

"Then he wrote it absent-mindedly," she said. "Mr. Van Rensselaer does not buy clothes for me. We are just acquaintances, old schoolmates. I haven't seen him in years till I met him on the street yesterday, and he asked me to stop a few minutes and help him select this gift for his friend. You will find he will be very much annoyed about this if he finds out you have sent it to me. I brought it right back so that you might call him up and ask him at once to give you the address again. I would not care to have him know it had been sent to my house."

The madame smiled again that aggravating smile.

"Mademoiselle had better call him up herself, and then she will discover that what I have told her is true."

"I do not wish to call him up," said Bessie haughtily, "and I decline to have anything further to do with the matter!" She turned toward the door.

Madame took one step toward her.

"One moment, mademoiselle! Does mademoiselle realize that if she leaves the goods here the gentleman will know nothing except that she has received them? The goods are paid for, and my responsibility is at an end."

"Your responsibility is not over until you have let him know that the purchase was not accepted at the address to which you sent it."

Bessie looked steadily at her adversary and spoke in a controlled voice. She was almost on the verge of tears, and she felt herself trembling from head to foot, but she managed to open the door and walk steadily out and down the street.

She felt degraded. To think that that woman had dared to place her on a footing with those women of another world than hers, who lived like parasites on what they could get out of their various lovers! It was maddening that she could not succeed in convincing the woman that she had made a mistake. The worst of it was, though, that she was almost convinced herself that it was not a mistake. Deep in her heart had crept a wild fear that it was true that Murray had sent those things as a gift to herself. That he had dared to insult her that way! To set her down as one of the cheap little butterflies with whom rumor said he played around continually. He had thought he could take her for a ride and toss her a costly gift and have her at his feet whenever he wanted her! He had not remembered the days of their childhood, when they played and read together and respected the fine things of life. He had professed to love her mother and to feel a warm comradely friendship for her, and here now he had shown that he did not even respect her. He thought because she lived in a small two-story house at the back of his father's grand mansion that he could treat her as he pleased!

Well, if he had dared to do this thing, of course it had been easy for him to run away from her in the hospital after he had been the cause of her getting all shaken up that way! Her heart felt like lead as she walked along slowly in the sunshine of the bright November morning. She realized that she had been struggling against all evidence to excuse Murray for not having brought her home, or come to tell her mother about the accident, or even calling up on the telephone this morning to find out if she was all right. She could not understand it. Murray! Her old friend, turned yellow like this! Disgusting! Terrible! Why believe in anybody anymore? But then she ought to have known better than to expect anything from a spoiled boy who had had no upbringing and too much money all his life. It was just what was to be expected every time with a mother like that beautiful doll-faced Mrs. Van Rensselaer. After all, she had known for years that Murray would never be anything to her, not even a friend. Why mourn this way, just because for a brief hour he had chosen to revive old acquaintance, amuse himself with his former playmate, and then vanish?

So reasoning, she went toward home, but her mind was by no means at rest. Another spirit kept continually whispering to her:

"But suppose that Murray was hurt himself! Suppose he is lying now in a hospital, unconscious perhaps, while you are enraged at him? This is not a Christian way to look at the matter. And besides, somehow you have got to let him know that you did not keep those dresses. If he really did try to present them to you, he has got to be made to understand that you are not that kind of girl."

When she reached home it was all to be argued over again with her mother, who was as disturbed as she about the matter. That anybody should dare to misunderstand her dear girl! That was more than the mother could bear. For Murray Van Rensselaer the boy she had always had a tender place in her heart, but for Murray Van Rensselaer the young man who had apparently forgotten his old friends for years, and now that he had chanced upon them again for an hour, had insulted them, she had little charity. It was the way of his world, of course, but she resented it. She did not covet his friendship for her girl, for well she knew how far apart they would have grown, and well she knew the follies and temptations of the life that he with his money and his fast friends had in all probability lived. No, if she had known of his proximity she would have hidden her girl, if it had been possible, rather than have had her come into contact with him again, rather than run the risk of Bessie's heart being touched by one who could never be anything more than an acquaintance to her.

But now that they had met, and he had tried to open the friendship once more by asking her to ride with him, the mother resented hotly both the way in which he had left her alone in the hospital and also the gift that he had presumed to send her. For that he had intended it for Bessie she was now well convinced. Did he think to bind her to him by costly gifts, yet toss her aside whenever the fancy took him? Did he consider her so low that he might pay off an obligation of courtesy by one of money? Having decided in her heart that he probably was worse than good for nothing, she proceeded to cast him out of her love, although she had really loved him when he was a little boy. He had seemed so lonesome, so interesting, so manly besides, and he had taken so kindly to her mothering. Well, that was past, and she must protect her precious girl at all costs. He was a child of luxury now. He was spoiled, and that was all there was to it. If he had been born to a different family, or his parents had lost their money and their prestige when he was small, there might have been some hope for him, but of course it was a foregone conclusion that he would be spoiled, and only of the world. What could one expect?

They argued ways and means for a long time, and finally Bessie sat down and wrote a frigid little note:

My dear Mr. Van Rensselaer:

I feel that you ought to know that the purchases you made at Grevet's yesterday were by some strange mistake sent to my address. The delivery man insisted upon leaving them here with my mother before I reached home, though she told him they were not ours. I took them back this morning, and the woman was very disagreeable about it and declared you had given no other address. I advised her to communicate with you at once. I hope your friend has suffered no inconvenience from the delay.

Sincerely,
Elizabeth Chapparelle

After the note was dispatched, Bessie felt better. Surely Murray could not misconstrue such a letter into an invitation to open the friendship again. If he tried that, she could easily show him that she wanted nothing from him. But she had done her duty toward the beautiful clothes, and now she could perhaps adjust her mind to think better of him. If possible, she wanted to think well of him because as an old friend he had figured largely in her childhood days, and she did not like to have anything haloed by her school days turn out to be common clay. He might go his way and forget her forever if he would only let her think well of him. She wanted to respect him with all her heart, but she did not see exactly how she was ever going to do it again. Supposing even that he had not meant to insult her with a costly gift without asking permission—and such a gift—a gift of clothing! There was still the fact that he had deserted her after getting her into an accident. She would not have supposed even a spoiled heartless flirt would do a thing like that to an old friend. Yet he seemed to have done it.

The hours went by, and she lay on the bench in the kitchen and pretended to read, but in reality she was listening for a ring at the door or the telephone. Yet none came. She stayed on the bench for two reasons. First, to satisfy her mother, who persisted in being anxious about her on account of the accident, and second, because she really felt quite weak and shaken up. Tomorrow her employer would be back in the office, and she must go to work again. The precious two days' vacation was going fast, and had all been spoiled. She felt almost bitter about it; there had been so much joy in its anticipation, but she did not want her mother to realize that. Mother was happy in just having her home with her.

So the letter was mailed, and Bessie waited, thinking surely when he got it he would call up or come around with a belated apology. She could not fully rest until she knew he understood that she was not the kind of girl to whom he could send such presents.

Days passed. A week. Two weeks. Three. Nothing was heard of Murray. Bessie and her mother began to wonder whether after all they ought not to have taken the boxes around to the Van Rensselaer house. Finally Bessie settled down to the belief that Murray was angry that she had not accepted his presents and had decided to drop her. Well, so she was content. She wanted no friendship with a man like that. She was glad if he felt that way. She was glad he knew he could not treat her the way he evidently treated other girls.

She settled back into the pleasant routine of her life, with the big ambition ahead to put her mother into more comfort, with opportunity for rest, and she succeeded pretty well in forgetting the one bright day with her old friend that had ended so disastrously. Only far back in her mind was a little crisp disappointment that her only old friend, whom she had so long idealized, had turned out to be such a hopeless failure, and sometimes in the dark at night when she was trying to go to sleep, her cheeks burned at the thought that she had accepted him so readily and jumped into his car at the first bidding. How she would like to go back to that bright twenty-first-birthday afternoon and haughtily decline that invitation to ride! Sometimes her pride fairly cried out for the chance.

Then one morning Mrs. Chapparelle, scanning the paper as was her habit for bits of news to give her child while she ate her breakfast before going to the office, came upon a little article tucked down in the society columns.

It is beginning to be an interesting question, "What has

become of Murray Van Rensselaer?" He isn't at his home, and he hasn't gone abroad, at least not according to any of the recent sailing lists of vessels. He is not registered at his club, and he has not been seen at any of the popular southern resorts. His family decline to talk. Polo season is coming on, and Murray Van Rensselaer has disappeared! Everybody is asking what are we going to do without Murray? Perhaps a certain lively countess could give information! Who knows?

Bessie looked up, startled, indignant.

"That's disgusting!" she said darkly. "No matter what he is, they haven't a right to meddle in people's private affairs that way and print it all out before the public!"

She did not eat any more breakfast. She began hurriedly to prepare for the office. Her mother watched her anxiously. Could it be possible that Bessie was still thinking about Murray? If so, she was glad she had stumbled on the article. She ought to understand fully just what he was. That detail about the countess, of course, might not be anything but a bit of venom from a jealous rival. But she was glad she had read it.

"Bessie," she began anxiously as the girl went to the hall closet for her overshoes, "are you sure you are dressed warmly enough for this stormy day?"

"Mother," said the girl crisply, "don't you think it would be a good thing if you began to call me Elizabeth now?"

There was a grown-up pucker on the white brow as if the child were feeling her years. The wise mother looked up quickly and smiled, sensing the feeling of annoyance that had come upon her since the reading of the article about her old friend. How her mother's heart understood and sympathized. Another mother might have felt hurt, but not this one, who had been a companion to her child all the way and understood every lifting of a lash, every glint in the deep blue of her eyes, every shade of expression on the dear face.

"Well, maybe," she agreed pleasantly. "I used to wonder whether we wouldn't be sorry we had nicknamed you. I don't know if I ever could get used to Elizabeth now. Bessie was a sweet little name when he called you that. It just fitted you!" There was wistfulness in her voice that reached through the clouds over her daughter's spirit.

"You dear little mother, you needn't ever try. So it is a sweet little name, and I don't ever want to change it. I wouldn't like you to say 'Elizabeth' anyway. It would sound as if you were scolding. Now, I'm not cross anymore. Good-bye, Mother dearie, and don't you even dare to *think* Elizabeth while I'm gone."

She kissed her mother tenderly and was gone, but all day the mother turned it over in her mind. Had it been wrong that she took that little lonely boy in years ago and let him be her daughter's playmate for a while? Was it going to blight her bright spirit after all this time? No. Surely it was only a bit of pride that was hurt, not her sweet, strong spirit!

But the girl thought about it all day long. Could not get

away from that bit of news in the society column. Was Murray really missing? What had become of him? Didn't they really know where he was? Could he be in a hospital unconscious somewhere? Oughtn't she perhaps to do something about it? What could she do? By night she had fully decided that she would do something.

Chapter 22

The first thing she did about it was to stop at a public telephone on her way home and call up her mother to tell her she might be delayed a few minutes with some extra work, and not to worry. Then with a heart that beat twice as quickly as it usually did, she turned the pages of the telephone book rapidly and found the Van Rensselaer number.

Ordinarily she would have consulted her mother before taking as decided a step as this, but something told her that her mother's sense of protection toward her would bias her judgment in this matter. She was a girl who prayed a great deal, and had great faith in prayer. She had been quietly praying all day long in her heart for guidance in this matter, and she believed she was doing the right thing. No need to trouble her mother with it yet. She would tell her before long, of course, but Mother might be alarmed and think she was more troubled than she really was, so she decided not to tell her yet. Besides, this was something that must be done at once if it really was necessary to do at all. She was going to find out.

The ring was answered promptly enough, evidently by a house servant.

No, Mr. Murray Van Rensselaer was not in. No, he was not *at home*. No, they could not tell her just when he would be at home, nor where she could reach him by phone.

There was a pause. She found her heart beating very wildly indeed. It seemed as though it would choke her. Then it was true! They really did not know where he was! But this was only a servant. Probably he would not know. She ought to get one of the family. After all, what had she to tell that would do them any good if they really were looking for him? Only that he had had an automobile accident and had disappeared from the hospital. Would that do them any good? Could they trace him from there if he had been injured?

The thought of Murray alone, delirious, perhaps, in a hospital, and his mother worrying, if such mothers ever worried, set her fluttering voice to going again.

"May I speak to Mrs. Van Rensselaer?"

"Mrs. Van Rensselaer will be dressing now," said the impersonal voice of the butler. "We don't disturb her when she's dressing unless it's for something very important."

"This is most important!" said Elizabeth firmly. She had started it; now she would see it through.

"Wait a minute. I'll put you on the other phone, and you can talk to the maid."

She heard a click, and a voice with a French accent answered her.

"Mrs. Van Rensselaer is having a shampoo and a wave now. Could you leave a message?"

"I'm afraid not," said Bessie desperately. "Do you think she could see me if I stopped by in about half an hour? Just for five minutes?"

"She might," said the maid. "You'd have to be very brief; she's giffing a dinner tonight. She'll not haf mooch time."

"I'll be brief," said the girl with relief in her voice.

"Who shall I say called?"

"Oh, Miss Chapparelle. But she won't know me."

❧

Bessie was waiting in a small reception room to the right of the front door when the maid came down and eyed her from head to foot appraisingly. She was sorry she had not waited to dress instead of coming straight up from the office.

"Mrs. Van Rensselaer says she don't know you. Who are you?"

Bessie's cheeks were burning. Now that she was here, she felt that she had intruded, and yet her conscience would not let her run away with her errand uncompleted. She stood her ground with her gravest little manner of self-respecting confidence.

"She would not know me." She smiled. "I'm only a neighbor who used to know Murray when we were children. I had something to tell her I felt she perhaps would be glad to know."

"Are you an agent? Because she won't see agents."

"Mercy, no!" said Bessie, smiling. "Tell her I won't keep her a moment. I would send a message if I could—but—I think I ought to speak with her."

The merciless eye of the maid gave her one more searching look and sped away up the stairs again. A slight movement in a great room like a library across the wide, beautiful hall drew the girl's attention, as if someone were over there listening. Perhaps it was Murray. Perhaps she was making a fool of herself. But it was too late now. She must see this thing through. It was always wrong to do a big thing like this on impulse. She ought to have talked it over with her mother first. But she had prayed! And it had seemed so right, so impossible not to do it. Well, the maid was coming back.

"Madame says she can't see you. She says she has no time to listen to complaints from the girls that hang on to her son. She says she remembers you now. You're the girl she sent him away from to boarding school to get rid of years ago!"

"That will do, Marie!" said the stern voice of the master of the house. "You may go back to Mrs. Van Rensselaer!"

The maid gave a frightened glance behind her and sped away up the stairs in a hurry. The occasions were seldom when the master interfered with his wife's servants, but when he did, he did it thoroughly. Marie had no wish to incur his disfavor. Who could know the master was in that room?

Mr. Van Rensselaer came out from the shadow of the dimly lit doorway and approached Bessie, eyeing her keenly.

"You had something to say about my son?" he asked in a courteous tone.

Bessie lifted eyes that were bright with unshed tears of wrath and mortification, but she answered firmly and with a tone of dignity: "Yes, Mr. Van Rensselaer. Will you tell me, is it true that your son is away and you do not know where he is?"

The father gave her a startled look.

"Why should you ask that?"

"Because I happened to read an article in the paper this morning that implied that. If it is not true, just tell me, and I will go about my own affairs. I did not *want* to come here. I thought I ought to."

"But if it were true, why should that interest you?"

"Because I was there at the time of the accident." She spoke in a low clear voice, very haughtily, her manner quite aloof. "I thought perhaps you might not know."

"Accident?" he said sharply. "Step into this room, please, won't you? We shall not be disturbed in here."

He drew a deep, luxurious chair for her before a softly flickering fire and turned on the electric light, looking keenly into her face.

"Now, will you first tell me who you are?"

Bessie was quite herself again. She was resolved to tell her story clearly in every detail as quickly as possible and then leave this dreadful house, forever, she hoped. How awful that she should be mixed up in a thing like this and be so misunderstood.

"I am Elizabeth Chapparelle, from the next street. Our house

873

is just behind yours. I used sometimes to play with Murray when we were little children. We were in the same classes in school for a while."

"I see," said the father, studying her speaking face. "Could that possibly be your kitchen window that I can see from the back of the house?"

"Probably." Bessie was in no mood to discuss the relative position of their houses. "I had not seen your son for several years, until the day of the accident."

The father started sharply now and came to attention.

"Will you tell it to me in detail just as it happened, please?" he asked. "Begin when you met him, and tell me everything."

Bessie noticed that he had not said whether he knew of the accident or not. He wanted to get every detail from her without letting her know anything. Well, that was all she wanted, too.

"I was standing on the corner of the avenue waiting for the trolley at two o'clock, three weeks ago today. I noticed a car coming down the avenue and was admiring it. I did not see who was driving it until Murray stopped the car and spoke to me. I had not seen him for years before then."

An alert movement of the father showed that he was giving all attention.

"The traffic was congested, and the policeman wanted him to move on, so he asked me to get in and let him take me to wherever I was going. There was no time to hesitate, so I got in, not intending to go but a block or two till I could be polite and make him let me out. The car seemed to go pretty fast—" She hesitated and looked troubled, as if she thought she were at fault for being in the car at all.

"It does," said Mr. Van Rensselaer dryly. "It has a habit of going fast."

Elizabeth lifted troubled eyes to find a shadow of a twinkle in the eyes that met hers. She hurried on:

"I told him I was going to the library, but he asked me to take a spin in the park, just a few minutes, to talk over old school days. He did not really wait for me to say whether I would. He just went—"

She was quite the most conscientious girl the father had met in thirty-five years. He wondered where she was brought up. He wondered if it could be genuine.

"Then when I said I must go back, he asked me if I would just stop at a shop and help him pick out a gift for a friend. Of course I consented. It was on our way from Grevet's to the library that the truck ran into us. We were overturned."

"Murray was *hurt*?" There was a sharp ring of pain in the father's tone, the first evidence of anxiety he had shown.

"I don't know," said Elizabeth. "I didn't think so at first, because they said he took me to the hospital. But after I read *that* in the paper, I thought if he had really disappeared perhaps he was hurt, and was somewhere in a hospital unconscious, and I ought to tell somebody. They say he brought me to the hospital in a taxi, so his car must have been wrecked."

The father's jaw hardened.

"What became of him after he brought you to the hospital? Were you hurt?"

"Not much, only shaken up, I guess, but I was some time coming to consciousness, and when they took me downstairs again they couldn't find him. They said he had been very anxious and impatient to know how I was, so I supposed perhaps he had an appointment and had to go. I went home. I thought probably he would call up to know how I was, but when he didn't, I decided he must have found out at the hospital that I was all right and hadn't thought anything more of it."

"H'm! That would have been a very gentlemanly thing to do, of course, get a girl smashed up and then go off without finding out whether she was dead or alive! I'm sure I hope that's not what my son did, but there's no telling!"

"Oh, we were not close at all, you know," explained the girl. "It was seven years since I had seen him. It was just the ordinary acquaintance of schoolmates."

"I can't see that that alters the discourtesy. But go on."

"Why, that's all," said the girl, suddenly feeling as if she had been very foolish indeed to come. "I—just thought—if you didn't know where he was—that perhaps I was the last one who had seen him, and you would want to make some inquiries if you knew there had been an accident. But of course it was foolish. You probably know all about him, and I beg you won't say anything to him about me. I'm sorry I have troubled you. I'm always doing something impulsive! I hope you will pardon my intrusion—" She turned quickly toward the door with an odd little look of sweet dignity. She felt she was almost on the verge of tears and must get away quickly, or she would break down right here before him.

"Wait a minute!" said the man sharply. "What did you say your name was?"

"Oh, please, it doesn't matter," she said with her hand on the doorknob.

"Excuse me, it does matter. I might want to ask some more questions. You've guessed right about Murray; I don't know where he is. I am taking it for granted that he will turn up all right, as he usually does, but at the same time there may be something in what you have suggested, and I'll look around and make sure. In the meantime, may I ask you to keep this just between ourselves?"

"Certainly," said the girl.

"And—I wouldn't try to see Mrs. Van Rensselaer again— she's—rather excitable—"

"I certainly shall not!" said Elizabeth, her cheeks growing very red at the remembrance of the insult.

"And I'm sorry that you had to endure such impudence from that cat of a maid. She's insufferable!"

"That doesn't—matter—" She turned toward the door again, wishing she were out on the sidewalk now in the cool air. Her heart was beating so fast again, and she was sure she was going to cry!

Perhaps the dewy look about her eyes gave warning of this, for the man suddenly changed his tone toward her:

"Look here, young lady, don't take this thing too seriously. You've done an awfully sporty thing, coming here to tell me this, after the way that young rascal of a son of mine treated you. There's just a chance that you may be right, and he is unconscious in a hospital somewhere. I shall leave no stone unturned, of course, to make sure. But in the meanwhile we'll keep this thing quiet. Now please give me your name. I'll keep it to myself, understand, and I won't let the kid know you've been here either, if you don't want me to. Chapparelle, you say, Elizabeth Chapparelle? Your father living? I used to know a man in business by that name, but that's a good many years ago. Fine chap he was, too."

"My father has been dead a good many years," said Elizabeth with a delicate withdrawal in her voice.

"You live on Maplewood Avenue? What number? You won't mind if I drop in perhaps, to ask you a few more questions, in case anything turns up?"

"Of course," said Elizabeth.

"By the way, what was the name of that hospital? And about what time did the accident occur? You understand, you know, that we're going to keep this out of the papers. And by the way, who else knows all this?"

"Nobody but my mother."

"Your mother?" There was speculation in the tone, a rising inflection.

"You needn't be afraid of my mother!" she said haughtily. "She was quite annoyed with me for having gotten into the car at all, and she is terrified at what might have happened."

"Too bad!" said the father with sudden sympathy. "I'm sorry you've had all this trouble. Wait! I'm going to ring for my car and send you around."

"Indeed, no!" said the girl firmly. "I should much prefer to walk. It's only a step anyway."

He opened the door for her himself and thanked her again most cordially, and she gave him a faint fleeting smile in acknowledgment.

He stood for a moment watching her walk away in the darkness. There was a sweet girl! Why couldn't Murray get her for a friend, instead of smashing her up! Just like Murray to lose his head over a countess and a dance-hall favorite and let a peach of a girl blossom at his feet and never notice her! Oh well, life was a disappointment anyway, whichever way you turned. Now here was Murray! What a bitter disappointment he was! Just when he might have been a comfort. Of course there was a slight possibility of his being injured somehow, but if he had been able to take a girl to the hospital, he couldn't have been very badly off. No, he was probably off with the fellows somewhere having a good time, or off with his countess or his latest fancy! What a son! But he must do his duty as a father anyway. So Murray's new car was wrecked! That was probably the reason Murray did not come home. He was waiting till his father's fury should blow over. Of course the car was covered by insurance, but what kind of a thing was that to do, wreck a new car all to bits the first week!

So he called up the Blakely Hospital first, and it being about the same hour as the accident, he got the same stiff-arched nurse with double lenses who had been on duty at the desk that day.

"Yes, sir, I was here when they came in. Yes, I remember him. Kind of a snob he was. Good-looking. They always are lookers when they're that way, but looks aren't everything. He thought he owned the earth. Said his name was Van something, as if that made any difference here! What's that? Yes, I guess it was Van Rensselaer. One of those millionaire families that think they come of a different race from the rest of us. Oh yes, I remember him. He pranced around here and got upset because we couldn't stop the whole hospital for his benefit. And then he got mad and left before his girl came down after all. Yes, she was a pretty little thing. No, I don't know what the doctor said about her. I guess she was pretty bad at first. They mighta thought she was going to die. I don't know. But they took her home, and I guess she's all right. No, I didn't see the young man go out. There was another patient come in to get a wound dressed, and about that time the nurse come down to report on the case, but she had to call the police station first about a drunk they had brought in, and when she went to say the girl was coming round all right, the young fella was gone."

The father thanked her and hung up. He sat thoughtfully for a few minutes in his big chair, trying to work it all out. Then he picked up the telephone again and went the rounds of the hospitals, but found no trace of any patient in any of them who fit the description of his son. After more thought he even called up the countess, and a few of the other various stars and favorites, without giving his name of course, but each of them professed not to have seen Murray. So that was that! Of course, if Murray was in hiding, he wouldn't have let anybody find him, and they would be in league with him. Well!

So he called up a very extra-secret detective, a private one, who frequented fashionable haunts, and was one of the crowd, knew everybody, and was known, but not in his secret capacity except to a few.

"That you, Eddie? Well, I want you to hunt up Murray. He's off somewhere. Just found out he had a wreck with his new car. Guess he's lying low till it blows over. We had a few words about some bills the other day, and he got upset. But something has come up I want him to sign. You just look around and get hold of him. Tell him I won't say anything about the car or the bills. Tell him I'm in need of him. Get me, Eddie? All right. Let me hear from you as early as convenient, even if it's in the night. The business is important and immediate. All right, Eddie. You understand."

He hung up with a tolerable feeling of ease. He had done his best, and Murray would likely turn up tonight or in the morning. Of course his mother would rave again if he didn't come to her bore of a dinner. But then, she always raved about something. It might as well be one thing as another.

He got up and went to the window, looking out into the dark street, and there came to him a vision of the girl as she had walked away, slim and proud. He knew what she was thinking. She was afraid that they thought her one of the girls who ran after Murray. But strange to say, he did not. If he had, he would not have taken the trouble to rebuke Marie when she uttered her impudent remark. Girls who ran after boys were fools. They deserved all they got. But this girl was different. One could see that at a glance; one could tell it by the first word from her gentle lips. She was the kind of a girl who grew up in the country and went to church on Sundays. She had eyes that saw birds and flowers in spring and loved them. He had known such a girl once when he was a boy in the country, and he had been the worst kind of a fool that he did not stay on the farm and marry her and have a big happy home full of loving kindness and children's voices, and a wide hearth with a big log fire and pancakes for supper. Buckwheat pancakes and maple syrup.

Deliberately he turned away from the window and walked upstairs to his own back room, where he switched off the light, drew up the shade, and looked out across the back alley to the bright little kitchen window with the table with the snowy cloth. There was a pie on the table tonight, and it looked like an apple pie, with the crust all dusted over with powdered sugar, the kind his mother used to make. There would be cottage cheese with the pie, perhaps. Oh! Someone had come to the window and was closing the blinds. It was the girl! She had taken her hat off and laid it on the corner of the table, and her bright hair gleamed in the light from the streetlamps as she bent her head to release the fastening of the blind. Then she straightened up, pulled the shutters closed with a slam, and shot the bolt across with a click. As if she knew she was shutting him out, and she wanted to do it!

Chapter 23

Before Murray could quite take in all that that letter might mean to him, Mrs. Summers knocked on his door.

"Mr. Murray, Doctor Harrison wants to speak with you on the phone. He tried to get you twice last night before you came in. I forgot to tell you about it—it was so late. Can you come right down? He seems to be in a good deal of a hurry."

"Sure! I'll be there in half a second!" said Murray, springing out of bed and drawing on some garments hastily.

He hurried down to the telephone.

The minister's voice came anxiously to him:

"Murray, is that you? Well, I've been trying to get you. You know your church letter came while you were away at the convention."

"Letter?" said Murray, quite innocently, and thought sharply of the letter upstairs. Things were closing in around him. The minister probably had one, too.

"Yes, your letter. It ought to have reached here sooner, but it seems to have been misdirected and gone around by the dead letter office. However, it got here in time for the season meeting, and I wanted to tell you that we accepted it, of course, and that we are counting you in with the others this morning. There'll be quite an accession. We would rather have had you present at the session meeting, of course, but it will be all right. There's really no need. Today is our communion service. You know that, of course. All you need to do is to come forward when your name is called. But I didn't want to take you unaware."

Accession! Come forward when your name is called! What the dickens was the man talking about? He could think of nothing but the astounding situation in which he had placed himself, and that letter upstairs. Then the minister hadn't gotten one yet. But he would soon. He must prevent anything more. At least he could confess before the whole thing was brought down around his ears.

"Yes," he was saying to Doctor Harrison, "yes. That'll be quite all right with me, Doctor," and he had not the slightest idea what it was all about. Some collection they were going to take up probably, that they wanted an unusual number of ushers. Well, it would not do any harm for him to do one more thing, but he simply must do something about this right off at once.

"Doctor Harrison!" he shouted, just as the hurried minister was about to hang up. "I want to have a little talk with you. When can I see you?"

"Yes?" said the minister anxiously. "Why, not before services, I'm afraid. Suppose we say after service, or perhaps after dinner would be better. We'll have more time then. Anytime after dinner before Sunday school. I'll be glad to see you. I have two or three schemes I want you to help me carry through."

He turned with a dazed look from the telephone and met Mrs. Summers' pleasant smile.

"Mr. Murray, I've put your breakfast on a tray, so you can eat while you finish dressing. There isn't much time, you know. Suppose you just carry it up with you and take a bite and a sip while you comb your hair."

He obediently took the tray to his room, but he did not eat anything. His mind was filled with confusion and wondering what he ought to do. One thing became plain to him as he glanced at his watch and saw that it was almost time for church to begin. He had just promised the minister he would officiate at some kind of an affair in the church, and he certainly must be there on time to find out what kind of an ordeal he was to be put through now. But this was the last one of those he would ever endure. Truth for him from now on. After he had talked with the minister and made a clean breast of things, he would clear out. Last week if he had been in these same circumstances, he would have cleared out without waiting for the talk with the minister, but today it was different. Something in him had changed, something that affected his whole life, and he could not somehow even think of running away. Some kind of confession and restitution must be made, so far as he was able, before he could be done with the past.

He was all in confusion as to what or how it must be done, but he knew that he must stay by the situation and clear it up. It was a part of the self-surrender of the day before.

He hurried through his shaving and dressing; as he tossed wildly among the collars and neckties that belonged to another man, in the trunk that was not his, he began to wonder about Allan Murray and what he was going to say to him. That he had also to account to him was another settled fact in his mind. The letter that lay facedown on his bed was like the presence of a stranger in the room, something that had to be faced. As a last act before he left the room, he swept his letters into the bureau drawer, took one swallow of coffee, and hurried down to where Mrs. Summers stood waiting for him at the front door.

"We're late!" he said anxiously, and there was a strained look around his eyes.

"The bell is still tolling," she replied. "We'll get there before the doxology. You look tired. Did you have a pleasant convention?"

"It was wonderful!" he said, and then realized that he was not thinking of the convention at all, but of his own experience. It gave him comfort that in the midst of the perplexities that seemed pressing him on every side, he could still thrill to the thought of that experience. It was not just imagination. It was real. It had stayed with him over night! It was his! Whatever came he would have this always, this sense of forgiveness and redemption from the blackness of darkness!

He escorted Mrs. Summers to her seat, as he had been doing ever since his arrival in Marlborough, and after he had settled himself, he realized that perhaps he ought to have inquired what was wanted of him and where he ought to be when needed. Then he remembered that the minister had said he need do nothing but come forward when his name was called, so he settled back once more and gave attention to the thought of that letter at home in his bureau drawer and what he ought to do about it. All through the opening hymn and prayer he was thinking and praying, *Lord, my Lord,* my new Lord, *show me what to do next!*

Through the anthem and the scripture reading and collection, he kept on with the same prayer. He roused to the consciousness that the collection was being taken without his aid, and without any apparent need of him, and decided that the minister had not had need of him after all. Or perhaps there was to be a circular or something passed around at the close. That was maybe what he had meant by "letter," probably a letter from the pastor to the people, a sort of circular.

Then all at once something took place quite out of the routine of service with which he had come to be familiar since he had been in Marlborough. A white-haired man named McCracken, whose name he had heard spoken with the title of "elder," though he had never understood what it meant, came forward and began to read names. He had been too much absorbed in his own thoughts to have heard what the minister said beforehand about it. But as the names were read he sat up and gave his attention. This likely was where he was supposed to come in. He noticed that the people got up and came forward as their names were called, and he wondered what they were supposed to be going to do. He would just watch the others. Perhaps they were to pass those "letters" around, whatever they were, and probably somebody would tell him which aisle they wanted him to take. He would just have to feel his way once more, as he had been doing all these weeks, and get away with the situation, but he resolved that not another day should pass before this sort of thing ended.

But as the names went on and the people responded, there began to be a strange assortment down there in front of the pulpit. There were young men and maidens, old men, and actually children. Some twenty-five or thirty quite young people came forward; one little boy only ten years old came down the aisle on crutches, with a smiling face and a light in his eyes. Murray wondered why they selected a lame boy to pass things, and such a little fellow! And if they were going to have children do it, why didn't they have them all children? It would be much more uniform. And there were some women, too. Odd! But they did a great many strange things in this church. Probably there would be some logical explanation of this also when he came to understand it.

"And from the First Presbyterian Church of Westervelt, Ohio, Mr. Allan Murray—"

Murray arose with a strange look around the church, a kind of sweeping glance, as if he were in search of somebody. Somehow it seemed to him that perhaps while he sat there the real Allan Murray had entered and might be coming down the aisle, but as his glance came back to the pulpit, Doctor Harrison nodded to his questioning look and seemed to beckon him, and he found himself walking down the aisle and standing with the rest. He did not know what he was about to do, but he had a strange serenity concerning it. He was not going of his own volition. It was as if he were being led. He thought of Saul with scales on his eyes, being led into the street called Straight by his soldiers and companions, and his spirit waited for what was about to happen to him.

The minister came to the front of the platform and looked down upon them with his pleasant smile. It came to Murray that he stood there to represent God. That was a strange feeling. He had never thought about a preacher in that way before. He had had very little ever to do with ministers. And then the minister spoke, in his strong, kind, grave voice:

"Friends, you are here to make a profession of your religious faith and enter into an everlasting covenant. We trust you have well considered what you are about to do, and so are prepared to give yourselves away, a living sacrifice, holy and acceptable to God through Jesus Christ."

Murray stared at the minister in wonder. How did the man know that that was what was in his heart? Was it in the hearts of these others? These men and women—and also these little children? He looked about upon them wonderingly. Had the same Spirit drawn them that had touched his heart? He felt a sudden burgeoning of interest in them, as if they were newfound brothers and sisters. What a strange thing! That little boy with the turned-up nose and freckles, the red hair that needed cutting, and the collar that was not exactly clean, was his brother. He had been born into a new family. He looked at the boy again and saw something in his face, a wistful, earnest look on the rough little, tough little countenance, and all at once he knew that humanity was the next greatest thing to God. Why had he not known that before? Why had he always thought the only thing worthwhile was having a good name and doing the latest thing that had been heard of? Oh, how he had wasted his time!

The minister's voice came into his thoughts just then again.

"Having examined and assented to our Articles of Faith, you will now profess them before these witnesses."

Murray had not examined any Articles of Faith, had not the least idea what they were. He listened intently.

"We believe in the Father, the Son, and the Holy Ghost, the true God.

"We believe that God has revealed the scriptures as our only infallible rule of faith and practice.

"We believe that all mankind are by nature lost sinners.

"We believe that Jesus, the Son, died to atone for sin.

"We believe that whosoever repents and believes in Jesus will be saved."

Ah! thought Murray. *That means me!*

"We believe that repentance and faith are the work of the Holy Ghost, showing themselves in forsaking sin and in loving God and man."

Oh! thought Murray. *That means me again. Was that who did it all for me? The Holy Ghost! And I have never known what that was before! There is a great deal I need to know!*

"We believe," went on the minister in clear tones, "that the Sabbath is to be kept holy.

"We believe that Baptism and the Lord's Supper are both duties and privileges."

At that moment Murray noticed for the first time that there was a table down before the pulpit, covered over with a fine white cloth of damask. The Lord's Supper! A solemn awe seemed to come over the room. It was something like the Holy Grail that he had had to write an essay on in school once.

"We believe," went on the minister again, "that there will be a resurrection and judgment, when the wicked shall go away into everlasting punishment, and the righteous into life eternal."

Ah! That Judgment Day! Did this change that had come to him mean a difference at the judgment? The born again ones were those whose names were written in that "other book," he remembered. Then he was one of those!

"These things you believe?" The minister seemed to be looking straight at him, and he found himself assenting. In his heart he knew that he accepted these things. They were new to him, but he meant to believe them. They were a part of the new world into which he had been born, and of course he believed them.

"You will now enter into covenant with God and this church."

Still the minister was looking at him. He thrilled with the thought of what had been said to him. Enter into a covenant with God!

"In the presence of God and this assembly, you solemnly embrace the Father, the Son, and the Holy Ghost as your God forever. You humbly and cheerfully consecrate your entire selves to His glory; to walk in all His commandments, assisted by His Spirit; to maintain private and family prayer; to keep holy the Sabbath; to honor your profession by a life of piety toward God and benevolence toward your fellow man—"

The solemn vows unfolded before his mind with a newness that was startling, and yet they all seemed natural to him, these vows that he was asked to take.

He saw the rest of the congregation rise, taking vows to watch over these who had just joined themselves to their number. He wondered how long things like this had been going on, and why he had been so ignorant of them. And then the words of the solemn charge struck deep into his soul:

"You have now entered into perpetual obligation." What tremendous words!

"These vows will abide upon you always. You must now be servants of God. From this day forward the world will take note of your life, to honor or dishonor Christ accordingly."

Murray caught his breath and looked around at the people

from a new point of view. Then he was responsible for what they thought of him! He was dishonoring Christ his Savior if he did not walk rightly! Why, it was just a new family whose honor he must regard. His father had berated him often for dishonoring the old name of Van Rensselaer, and bitterly now he knew how he had dishonored it. Strange he had not seen it before, nor cared, nor tried to do differently. He almost trembled at the thought that his life was nothing but dishonor from beginning to end.

The minister was giving the new members the right hand of fellowship, and as he moved from one to another, taking each one's hand in a quick warm clasp, he went repeating the Bible, giving each one a verse. Murray listened to them, recognizing them as words of scripture, because for the last few weeks he had heard Mrs. Summers read the Bible every evening. But now he was hearing them as if they were just new and handed down from the Lord that day, for the minister had a way of making a verse of scripture speak to the soul as he repeated it. And when he came to Murray, he grasped his hand and held it and looked straight into his eyes as he said:

"To him that overcometh will I give to eat of the hidden manna, and will give him a white stone, and in the stone a new name written, which no man knoweth saving he that receiveth it."

Murray stood as one transfixed while he heard these remarkable words. That they were sent direct from heaven for him he never could doubt. A new name! That was what he had been searching for. He had sinned and dishonored the old name with which he was born. There had been no hope for him. Then he had found a Savior, and he had been born again with a new name! It was all too wonderful to believe! He wanted to shout in his joy.

Every one of those new members had verses given them, as wonderful and perhaps fully as fitted to the needs of the special soul, but Murray heard none of them. He was exulting in his own. To him that overcometh! Ah! Could he overcome, now that he was born again?

Then began that wonderful benediction:

"Now unto Him who is able to keep you from falling—"

Ah! Then He was able. Then he might overcome!

"And to present you faultless—"

Faultless! What miracle was this? Every word was burned brightly into his soul. He didn't have to do anything at all. It was all to be done for him by One who was able!

"—before the presence of His glory with exceeding joy!"

Murray stood with bowed head and a great sense of thanksgiving. He did not notice the little stir around him at first as the new members went back to their seats. Someone found Murray a seat near to the front, and he sat down and looked around him as if his eyes had just been opened to the world. Then he saw that white-covered table again. Four of the elders were lifting off the cloth that covered it. He saw the shining silver of the communion service. Then the minister's voice again:

"The Lord Jesus, the same night in which He was betrayed, took bread; and when He had given thanks He brake it and said,

Take, eat, this is My body, broken for you; this do in remembrance of me. After the same manner also, He took the cup when He had supped, saying, This cup is the new testament in My blood; this do ye, as oft as ye drink it in remembrance of Me. For as often as ye eat this bread and drink this cup, ye do show the Lord's death till He come.

"But let a man examine himself, and so let him eat of that bread and drink of that cup. For he that eateth and drinketh unworthily, eateth and drinketh damnation to himself.

"If we confess our sins He is faithful and just to forgive us our sins, and to cleanse us from all unrighteousness. The blood of Jesus Christ, His Son, cleanseth us from all sin."

It was just at this point that Murray rose to his feet. It was as though the scales had fallen from his eyes, and he understood. He saw for the first time what he had been and what Christ was. And now he knew what it was he had to do. He had come to the Lord's table, and he was unworthy!

He took one step forward, and the minister looked up, astonished, yet feeling that there must be something important. He had great respect for this young man who had come to their midst so highly recommended.

The minister stepped to meet him and bent his tall head to listen.

"There is something I must say!" said Murray earnestly in a low tone. "Now!" he added insistently. The minister laid his hand upon the young man's shoulder and was about to suggest that he wait until the close of the service, but he saw something in Murray's face that made him desist. Perhaps the Spirit gave him a vision of this soul's need. He straightened up and said in his usual voice, quite clearly, so that everybody could hear: "Our brother has a word to tell us. We will hear it just now."

Murray turned and faced the people who had taken him in so openheartedly and let him know that they honored him. There, almost in the center of the church, facing him with admiring interest and not a little pride, sat Mr. Elliot Harper, his superior in the bank, with three or four lesser dignitaries connected with the bank not far behind him. There, a little to the right, was a group of young people who had the day before hung upon his every word and given him all the honor and respect that one human being can give to another. There, a few seats to the left, sat Mrs. Summers, with her kindly eyes upon him, thinking no doubt he was about to tell some touching incident of the convention, in which he had carried so great a part. And there, beside him, with confidence and interest in his eyes, waited the pastor, sure that they were to hear something that would lift their souls nearer to Christ. And he, what had he to tell? For one brief instant he wavered, and then the memory of those quoted words came back, "He that eateth and drinketh unworthily—" He must not begin the new life wrong, no, not if it shattered every beautiful thing that could ever come to him again. Not if it robbed him of friends and livelihood and freedom. No, this was the great moment of his life, the turning point.

But then came those other words, just heard: "If we confess—He is faithful to *forgive* our sins, and to *cleanse* us." Oh, to be cleansed!

So out of his heart he spoke!

Chapter 24

"I can't let this go on any longer!"

His voice was husky with a kind of anguish. The church grew very still. Everybody stopped thinking idle thoughts and gave attention.

"I'm not the man you think I am. My name is not Allan Murray. I don't know where he is nor what he is. I didn't mean to deceive you. I arrived here when you expected him, and you took it for granted I was he. I tried several times to get away quietly because I was ashamed, but you blocked my way by some new kindness, and because I was a wanderer from home and needed a home and a new name, I finally stayed. Then you made me president of that society, and I wasn't big enough! I knew I couldn't get away with that, and I meant to run away. But the Lord stopped me. He met me right there and showed me what a Savior He was. I guess I was like Saul. My Sunday school class taught me about him—"

Four boys in the back of the church who had been snickering softly over a picture they had drawn in the back of the hymnbook looked wonderingly at one another and got red in the face and watery round the eyes.

"So I gave myself up to the Lord, and He forgave my sin. Will you? I know it's a great deal to ask of you, but I had to ask it before I came down here when Doctor Harrison called my name because he told me to, but I believed all those things he asked us, and I meant it when I took that vow with all my heart." Then he turned to the minister: "I know I'm unworthy, but you said He would forgive if we confessed our sin, and I'm taking you at your word. I'm glad I came here this morning, and I'm glad I took those vows. They are going to be permanent for me. I'd like to have a part in this ceremony you're going to have here. I'd like to be counted in if you think it's all right, Doctor?" He looked at the minister again. "And then I'm going back to face some hard things at home, but I'd like to be counted in with you all this morning if I may. You said the Lord would give me a new name, one that belongs to me this time, and I want it. You took me in because you thought you knew my earthly father; will you forgive me because I want your heavenly Father to be my Father, too? I'm sorry I interrupted the service, but I couldn't go on without letting you know first."

He would have dropped into the front seat, but the minister's arm was around him, and the minister drew him close to his side and said with a joyous voice: "'There is therefore now no condemnation to them that are in Christ Jesus.' 'Beloved, now are we the sons of God, and it doth not yet appear what we shall be: but we know that, when He shall appear, we shall be like Him; for we shall see him as He is.' Let us pray."

And then with his arm still around Murray, standing together as they were, with Murray's head bowed reverently, and such a light of love in that pastor's face, Doctor Harrison prayed as he had never prayed before. Murray felt himself prayed for as Ananias must have prayed for Saul! Ah! if Murray's companions, back in his home city that day killing time in their various frivolities, could have looked into that church and seen their former companion, they would have stared in amazement and perhaps remained to ridicule. But in that audience there was not one who looked critically upon the young man. It was too much like a scene out of the New Testament. One could almost seem to see a flame of Pentecost coming down. Mrs. Summers sat wiping away the happy tears, for she had spent many hours in praying for the dear boy under her roof. There were others weeping and many who were led to look into their own hearts and lives through Murray's words, finding themselves unworthy also.

"And now," said the minister, "let all who will forgive our dear brother and take him into our full fellowship stand with me and join with us in singing 'Blest Be the Tie That Binds,' and then we will partake of the Lord's Supper together."

Such a volume of song went up from the hearts of those

Christian people as must have made the angels rejoice. Murray, looking up in wonder, could not see a single person sitting down. All were on their feet. He was overpowered with the wonder of it.

He knew he would never forget the beautiful communion service that followed. No other could ever be so beautiful. The choir sang softly and reverently bits of hymns that he had never heard before, but that they voiced so sweetly and distinctly that they sank into his soul to be a part of the picture of this day that was to stay with him to the day of his death.

They flocked around him when the service was over, some with tears in their eyes, and wrung his hand, and shyly said they were glad he knew the Lord. Even Elliot Harper, dazed and a bit mortified though he was, that something had been "put over on him" before the world, had the good grace or the Christianity to come over and shake his hand: "Well, sir, you gave us a surprise, but I admire your nerve and your frankness. You did the right thing. Come and talk it over tomorrow. You're a good business-man, whatever your name is, and I'm not sure but we can get together in spite of this."

Elliot Harper was a good man in many ways, but he couldn't help thinking that perhaps it would be a good thing for the bank to have it known that a young man in their employ had been so out-and-out honest as to make public confession at the communion table. That bank was a little idol that he had set up unawares.

But perhaps the greatest surprise of all that he had was to find the girl Anita standing quietly in the aisle up which he had to pass to Mrs. Summers, who was waiting for him.

She put out her hand and said frankly: "I'm glad you did that, and I want you to know I'm very glad you've found Christ."

He looked at her in surprise.

"You are?" he said, amazed. "I wouldn't suppose you'd care. I always felt you didn't trust me."

She gave a quick glance around to see if anyone was listening and then lifted clear eyes to his face.

"I went to school with Allan Murray's sister," she said. "He came down to commencement, and I saw him several times. He has curly red hair and brown eyes, and he is *taller* than you."

Murray gave her clear glance back again, and then his face broke into a radiant grin.

"You certainly had it on me," he said, his eyes twinkling. "I might have known I couldn't get away with a thing like that anywhere on the face of this little globe. But say, why didn't you give me away?"

Anita was nearer liking him then than she had ever been before. She looked at him with a warm, friendly smile.

"I had a notion it might be better to let the Lord work it out," she said.

"He has!" said Murray soberly. "I shall never cease to thank God for bringing me here."

"There's one thing more," said Anita gravely. "I wish you would tell me just how much Allan Murray had to do with this."

"Allan Murray! Why, not one thing, only that I have been

using his name and his things and his position."

"And you don't know where he is? You have no evidence that he was killed in that wreck?" There was an undertone of deep anxiety in her voice.

He gave her a quick, comprehending glance.

"I don't know a thing yet," he said gravely. "I've been wondering that myself every day I've been here, and wishing I knew, but I'm going to make it my next business to find out. Within the next twenty-four hours, if possible. I'll let you know the result if you would like me to."

"I wish you would," said Anita, her eyes cast down. "His sister was very dear to me. She died two years ago, and I've lost trace of him since. But I know there are none of his immediate family living." She was trying to excuse her deep interest, and Murray answered heartily: "I'll lose no time in letting you know when I find him," he promised. "I think he is alive. I have reason—but I can't tell you about that yet."

He noticed a look of relief in her face as he spoke, but several people who had been talking with the minister came down the aisle just then and separated them, and he went on to where Mrs. Summers waited for him.

Half shyly he looked up, suddenly remembering that he must not be too confident. He was no longer Allan Murray, the Christian, whose name brought only honor. Perhaps Mrs. Summers would not feel like taking him back to her house now.

"Are you going to forgive me, too"—he hesitated—"Mother?"

"My dear boy!" she said warmly, slipping her hand into his unobtrusively and squeezing his fingers gently with her warm rose-leaf grasp.

He had a choking sensation in his throat as if he were going to cry like a child. It was so good to be forgiven and loved. This was real mother-love!

"Did you suppose I was going to stop caring for you just because you had a new name? You are not Allan Murray, but you are my boy, and you always will be."

"That is great of you," he said huskily, because somehow his throat seemed choked with tears. "I appreciate that more than you can ever know! I'm not Allan Murray, but you may call me Murray. That's my own first name. That's how it all came about. That girl came out and called me Mr. Murray, and for the first instant I thought someone had recognized me!"

"How strange!" she said. "What a coincidence! The Lord must really have sent you here."

"Well, I rather think He did," said Murray. "I don't know anywhere else I've ever been where I could have gone and met *Him* and been taught about Him the way I have here. It's been a miracle—that's all there is to it."

They were walking across the path to her house now apart from all the other people. There were still groups of people here and there talking with one another about the wonderful service and the astounding revelation concerning the stranger in their midst. Jane had met Anita at the door of the church. There were traces of tears of excitement on her cheeks.

"Oh, don't you just *adore* him, Anita!" she greeted her friend. "Wasn't that simply *great* of him to be willing to come forward like that and tell the truth?"

"Don't be blasphemous, Jane," said Anita crisply. "He's not a god, or he wouldn't have gone around lying for weeks."

"Oh now, Anita! There you go! I think that's unchristian! I thought you stood up to say you were willing to forgive him."

"Forgiving's one thing, and worshipping's another, Jane. Don't be a fool! That's the one thing about you I can't abide, Jane. You will be so awfully silly! Why don't you say you're glad he found out what a sinner he was? Why don't you rejoice a little in the Lord, and worship *Him* for His saving power? We don't have miracles like that every day. It's really something worth talking about and worth giving God a little extra worship and adoration."

"Oh, mercy! Anita! You're always so long-faced! I think you talk a little too intimately about God—I really do! Of course *I* understand you, but some people mightn't think you were a Christian, you are so free talking about religion."

Anita's answer was a hearty, ringing laugh as she turned into her own gate.

"Oh, Jane, you're unspeakable! Well, good-bye! See you at Sunday school!" And Jane went on her gushing way, thinking how handsome the hero of the hour had been that morning, and losing the real significance of the occurrence entirely.

The minister had been detained with a messenger, who asked

him to come at once to the bedside of a dying woman, and Murray had slipped away without a word from him, but later he came back across the lawn to Mrs. Summers' cottage and took the young man by both hands.

"Dear brother," he said, "I want you to know how glad I am that you gave that confession and testimony this morning. Aside from your own part in it, and the joy you have set ringing in heaven over a sinner that repents, you did more in that brief confession to show my people what sin and true repentance means, and what the communion service stands for, than I could have done in a year of sermons. I've come over to congratulate you on your new birth, my boy, and to offer my services in any way I can be a help to you in the further reconstruction of your life, and the hard things you have to meet from your past."

There with the minister and Mrs. Summers, while the dinner waited in the oven, Murray told them his story. Briefly, with very few details of his home, beyond the fact of his name, and that he had been the means of killing a girl in an automobile accident and had run away from justice to protect the family name from being dragged through the criminal courts.

"But I'm going back at once," he said firmly. "It was all as plain as day to me while I sat in the service this morning. I asked God to show me what to do next, and that was what He seemed to tell me. I'm afraid I made a mess of your service, not understanding just what came next and where would be the proper time to interrupt you. But I just couldn't go on and take that communion with that on my soul!"

"You did right, brother. I'm glad you did just what you did," said Doctor Harrison sincerely.

"Well, I've got to make everything clean and clear, and then I don't care what comes to me. I'll have to suffer the penalty of the law, of course—that's right—but now I know I'm not going into it alone. I've got to go to the girl's mother and confess and ask her forgiveness, and then I'm going to give myself up. It's the only right thing, of course. I ought to have seen that before. But first I've got to hunt up that Allan Murray and make things right with him while I'm free. And that reminds me. Mrs. Summers, there's a letter upstairs among those you laid on my bureau that seems to be from him. I'll run up and get it."

He was gone up the stairs with a bound, and the minister sat and smiled at Mrs. Summers indulgently.

"Well, Mrs. Summers, he's a dear boy, isn't he? And our Lord is a wonderful God. He worketh mighty miracles and wonders. Now, I wonder what can have become of that man Murray! I feel responsible for him. I wrote his pastor that he was here, and he was all they had said he was and more. I wonder if we shall like the real man as much as his substitute."

"I wonder!" said Mrs. Summers sadly. She was looking ahead and knowing that this boy, too, she must give up.

Murray came down with the letter, and Mrs. Summers tore it open and read it aloud:

"My dear Mrs. Summers:

"You will have been wondering why I have not written
you before, but since the first word that my nurse says she sent
you I have been quite seriously ill. There was some kind of a
pressure on the brain, and they had to operate.

"But I am getting on finely now, and hope soon to be
up and around again. I am writing Mr. Harper tomorrow.
They won't let me write but one letter a day yet. Of course he
has probably had to fill my place with someone else, and if so,
there will likely be no further chance for me in Marlborough.
In which case I shall have to ask you to forward my trunk to
me, and to send me the bill for whatever I owe you. I hope
you have not had to lose rent on my room all this time, and
if you have I shall want to pay for whatever you have lost
through my illness.

"If, however, it should prove that there is still an opening
for me in Marlborough, the doctor says that I may promise
to come around the first of the year, if all goes well, and I
certainly shall be glad to get into a real home again, if such
be the Lord's will.

"I shall be glad to hear from you about the room and my
trunk, which I am not sure ever reached you. I am a little
puzzled that I have heard nothing from any of you, but I
suppose you have been busy, and perhaps there has been some
mistake about my address, and my mail has been forwarded
to you. If so, will you kindly send it to me, as there may be

something that needs immediate attention.

"I am taking it for granted that you know all the details of the wreck which changed all my plans, even better than I do, but thank God, I am told that I shall be as good as new again in a few weeks.

"Hoping to hear from you at your earliest convenience, and thanking you for any trouble you may have had with my belongings,

"Very sincerely,

"Allan Murray"

There was silence in the cheery little parlor as she finished reading the letter. Each one was thinking, perhaps the same thoughts. How very strange that this letter should have arrived just at this time!

"But it came several days ago," said Mrs. Summers, looking at the postmark. "I must have taken that up and put it on the bureau with the rest of the letters the morning you left for the convention. Strange I didn't notice his name!"

It was as if she had read their minds and was answering their thoughts.

"Hmm!" said the minister thoughtfully. "The Lord never makes a mistake in His dates. He meant this should all come about for His glory. Where was that written from, Mrs. Summers?"

"Why, it's Wood's Corners! That's not far away! To think he has been there so near, all this time!"

"How far is that?" asked Murray gravely.

"Between twenty and twenty-five miles," said the minister. "He will have thought it strange that none of his father's old friends came over to see him. Did you never get any word from him before, Mrs. Summers? He says his nurse wrote to you."

"Nothing at all," said Mrs. Summers thoughtfully.

"I must go at once!" said Murray, rising hastily. "You will excuse me, I know. There is no time to waste to make this thing right. Something might happen to stop me!"

"You must have your dinner first!" said Mrs. Summers, hurrying toward the kitchen. "Doctor Harrison, you had better stay here and eat dinner with us. Just telephone your wife that I've kept you."

But Murray was at the door already.

"Wait, young brother," said the minister, placing a detaining hand on his arm. "You've a duty here not yet finished, I take it. You've a Sunday school class to teach in a few minutes, and it is a very critical time for those boys. They will have heard of your confession this morning, and their hearts will be very impressionable."

"Doctor Harrison, I can't teach a Sunday school class. I never *did* teach! *They taught me!* You surely would not have me go before them again, now that they know what a fake I am! I have nothing to teach them!"

"You can teach them how to confess their sins, can't you? You can show them the way to Jesus, I'm sure, now that you have found it yourself? You have not finished your confession here until you have met your class and made it right with them, my boy. I'm counting on your testimony to bring those boys to the Lord Jesus."

Murray's face softened.

"Could I do that?" he asked thoughtfully, with a luminous look in his eyes. "Would you trust me to do that when I will in all probability be in jail next Sunday?"

"You could do that, my son, and I will trust you to do it. I want you to do it. It will make the jail bright around you to remember that you had this opportunity to testify before the opportunity passed by forever. You have made an impression on those boys, and you must make sure that it is not spoiled. Tell them the truth. Show them how Jesus forgives. Show them that it is better to confess soon than late."

So Murray taught his Sunday school class, taught it in such a way that every boy in the class felt before it was over that he had been personally brought before the judgment seat of God and tried. Taught it so well that several boys went home and took out personal and private sins that had been hidden deep in their hearts and renounced them in boyish prayers, in dark rooms at night, after the rest of the house was sleeping. Taught it so powerfully that the superintendent nodded toward the class and said in a low tone to the minister, "What are we going to do about that young man? Isn't there some way to keep him here? The real man can't possibly take his place now. Those boys will resent his presence, no matter how fine he is."

A moment later the minister stood behind that class for a

moment and noticed the sober, thoughtful faces of the boys. The usual restless merriment was not present. The boys had been in touch for a half hour with the vital things of the soul and had no time for trifling. He watched them a moment as the closing hymn was announced. Then he laid a hand on the shoulder of the teacher.

"Now, Murray," he said, using his first name familiarly with a fatherly accent, "I'm ready to take you over to Wood's Corners. We'll just slip out this door while they're singing. We'll have plenty of time to get back for the evening service. Mrs. Summers has prepared us a lunch we can eat on the way back, and so we needn't hurry."

Chapter 25

It was very still in the small gloomy room of the little country hospital where the sick man had been taken when it had been determined to operate on him. The woman down the hall who had been having hysterics every two or three days had been moved to the next floor, and her penetrating voice was not so constantly an annoyance. The baby across the hall was too desperately ill to cry, and the other patients had dropped off to sleep. The hall was almost as quiet as night.

The patient lay with his eyes closed and a discouraged droop to his nicely chiseled mouth. His red curls had been clipped close under the bandages, but one could see they were red. He had long, capable fingers, but they lay pallid and transparent on the cheap coverlet, as if they never would work again. His whole attitude revealed utter defeat and discouragement. As he lay there, still as death and almost as rigid, a tear stole slowly out from under the long, dark lashes. A weak, warm tear. He brushed it away impatiently with his long, thin hand and turned over with a quick-drawn sigh. Even the effort of turning over was a difficult and slow performance. He felt so unacquainted with the muscles of his heavy, inert body. He wondered if he ever again would walk around and do things like other people.

As if she had heard him far out in the hall, the nurse opened the door and came in. It annoyed him that he could not even sigh without being watched.

"Did you call, Mr. Murray?"

"No, Nurse."

"Did you want anything, Mr. Murray?"

"Yes, I want a great many things!" he snapped unexpectedly. "I want to get up and walk around and go to my work." He had almost said, "I want to go home," only he remembered in time that he had no home to go to. No one to care where he went.

"I want my mail!" he added suddenly. "I think it's time this monkey business stopped! I suppose the doctor has told you I mustn't have my mail yet. He's afraid there'll be something disturbing in it. But that isn't possible. I haven't any near relatives left. They're all dead. I suppose I've lost my job long ago, so it can't be anything disturbing about business, and I haven't any girl anywhere that cares a cent about me or I about her, so you see there's really no danger in letting me have it. In fact, I *will* have it! I wish you would go and get it right away. Tell the doctor I demand it. There would surely be something to interest me for a few minutes and make me forget this monotonous room and the squeak of your rubber heels on the hall floor!"

He had red hair, but he had not been savage like this before. He had just reached the limit of his nerves, and he was angry at that tear. It had probably left a wide track on his cheek, and that abominable nurse, who knew everything and thought of everything and presumed to manage him, would know he had been crying like a baby. Yes, she was looking hard at him now, as if she saw it. He felt it wet and cold on his cheek where he had not wiped it off thoroughly.

The nurse came a step nearer.

"I'm real sorry about your mail," she said sympathetically, "but your suspicions are all wrong. The doctor asked me this morning if I couldn't find out someone to write to about your mail. There truly hasn't been a bit of mail since you came here. And the head nurse wrote to that address you gave her, I'm sure, for I saw her addressing the letter. Isn't it likely they have made some mistake about the address? I wouldn't fret about it if I were you. You'll forget it all when you get well. Wouldn't you like me to read to you awhile? There's a real good story in the Sunday paper. I'll get it if you want me to."

"No thanks!" he said curtly. "I don't read stories in Sunday papers, and besides, you can't sugarcoat things with a story. And you're mistaken when you say I'll forget it. I'll never forget it, and I'll never get well, either! I can see that plain enough!"

With that he turned his face to the wall and shut his

nice brown eyes again.

The nurse waited a few minutes, fussing around the immaculate room, giving him his medicine, taking his temperature, and writing something on the chart. Then she went away again, and he sighed. All by himself he sighed! And sighed! He tried to pray, but it only turned out in a sigh. But perhaps it reached to heaven, for God heard the sighs and tears of his poor foolish children of Israel, and would He not hear a sigh today, even it if really ought to have been a prayer?

"I'm all alone!" he said, quite like a sobbing child. "I'm all alone! And *what's the use?*"

Then the nurse opened the door softly and looked in. It was growing dusky in the room, and the shadows were thick over where he lay. But there was something electric in the way she turned the knob, like well-suppressed excitement.

"There is someone to see you," she said, in what she meant to make quite a colorless voice. The doctor had said it would not do to excite the patient.

"Someone to see *me?*" glowered the man on the bed. "There *couldn't* be! There *isn't* anybody. Who *is* it?"

"One of them is a minister. He looks very nice."

"Oh!" groaned the patient disappointedly. "Is that all? Who told him to come?"

"Nobody," said the nurse cheerfully. "He's not from the village. They came in a car. There's a young man with him. You'd better let them come up. They look real jolly."

"Did they know my name?" He glared, opening his eyes at this.

"Oh yes, and they said there had been a letter from you or about you or something. They came from a place called Marlborough."

"Well, that's different!" said the patient with a jerk. "Can't you straighten this place up a bit? It looks like an awful hole. Is my face clean? It feels all prickly."

"I'll wash it," said the nurse brightly. She was quite gleeful over these interesting-looking visitors.

"You can show the minister up," said the patient. "I don't know the other one."

"But he's the one that asked after you. He seems real pleasant. He was quite anxious to see you. The minister called him Murray. Perhaps he's some relative."

"I haven't any!" growled the man, "but you can bring him, too, if he's so anxious to come."

He glared out from under his bandages at his visitors with anything but a welcoming smile. It was too late for smiling. They should have come weeks ago.

They stood beside his bed and introduced themselves, the nurse hovering nearby till she should be sure that all was well with her patient.

"My name is Harrison. I'm the preacher from Marlborough you wrote to several months ago. I've just found out today where you were, and I'm mighty sorry I couldn't have been around to help you sooner. I'll just let this young brother explain, and then we'll all talk about it some more."

The minister put a big, kind, brotherly hand on the weak white hand of Allan Murray and then dropped back to the other end of the little room and sat down on the stiff white chair. Murray stepped closer to the bed.

"And I'm a man that stole something from you, and I'm come to bring it back again, and to ask your forgiveness."

"Well, I'm sure I didn't know it, and you're welcome to it, whatever it was. It wouldn't have been much good to me, you see. Keep it if you like, and say no more about it." There was not much welcome nor forgiveness in his glance.

"But you see, I'm to blame for the whole thing," explained Murray gently, "and I want to tell you about it. Are you strong enough to listen today, or ought I to wait?"

"Go on!" growled the patient impatiently.

The nurse was still hovering, openmouthed. This was too unusual a morsel of news to miss. She could not tear herself away.

"You see, I was a renegade anyway—" began Murray.

"What did you steal?" the patient interrupted, raising his voice nervously.

"I stole your name, and I stole your job, and I've been living at your boarding place and using your things!"

"Well, you certainly did a smashing business! As I say, it didn't matter much to me, you see, if you could get away with it."

"But I didn't get away with it—that's it. I was held up."

"Who held you up?"

"God."

The patient eyed his visitor a moment, and a strange softened expression began to melt into his face.

"Sit down," he said. "Now, begin and tell."

"Well, you see, my name's Murray, too, my first name. Murray Van Rensselaer. Son of Charles Van Rensselaer. You've probably heard of him. Well, I broke a law, and then I didn't like the idea of facing the consequences, so I ran away. I don't know why I ran away. I hadn't been used to running away from things. I always faced them outright. But anyhow, that doesn't matter to you. I ran away, and after I got away I couldn't quite see coming back, *ever*. I had some money, and for a few days I kept out of sight and got as far as I could away from home. The day of your wreck I'd been traveling under a freight car because I hadn't any money, and we landed in Marlborough just at dark. Ever try traveling that way? Well, don't. It isn't what it's cracked up to be. When the train stopped at a crossing, I rolled off more dead than alive. I was all in. I hadn't had anything to eat all day, and I kept seeing cops everywhere I turned. So I hid till the train went on, and then I crawled off in the dark up a hill.

"By and by I spotted a light, and came to it through the dark, because I was so sick of going on I couldn't go a step further.

"There was an open window, and down just below me on a table in a basement I saw a row of cakes and bread. There didn't seem to be anybody around, so I put my hand in and took some and began to eat. I didn't call it stealing. I was starved."

The patient's eyes were watching Murray intently, and in the back of the room the minister was watching the patient.

"It turned out to be a church, and they were getting ready a big dinner to welcome *you*!"

A light shot into the eyes of the man on the pillow that seemed to suddenly illuminate his whole face. A surprised, glad light.

"A girl rushed out and called me Mr. Murray, and I tried to beat it, but it was all dark behind me, and my eyes were blinded looking at the lighted room, so I only got deeper in behind the bushes and ran against more church wall, and the girl followed me, laughing, and said she would show me the way, and that they were waiting for me. She said they had been so afraid I was caught in the wreck. She tried to pull me into the church, but I held back and said I was too dirty to go in, that my clothes were all torn and soiled. I said I had lost my baggage in the wreck. It seemed to be providential, that wreck, and I used it for all it was worth, for you see at first I thought I must have met that girl at a dance somewhere, and she recognized me and hadn't heard yet what trouble I was in. So I wanted to get away before she found out.

"But she said my trunk had come, and somebody named Summers was expecting me, and I could go right over to my room and get dressed, but I must hurry, because it was late. I tried to get directions, but she insisted on walking over there with me. I couldn't shake her. She seemed to think she had some special connection with me because her mother, she said, had known my mother.

"When we got to Mrs. Summers' house, she opened the door

herself and pulled me right in before I could slide away in the darkness. Of course I could have broken away, but that would have roused suspicion, and anything I *didn't* want was an outcry and the police on me; so I went in, and she took me up to the room she had gotten ready for you, and she actually smashed the lock on the trunk and went so far as pressing a pair of *your trousers* for me to put on, while I was taking a bath!"

By this time Allan Murray's eyes were dancing, and there was actually a little pucker of a smile in one corner of his mouth.

Murray hurried on with his story.

"There was no alternative but to get into some clothes and pretend to please the lady, for she was so insistent. You better believe I was glad of that hot bath, too, and I was still hungry as a bear. I hadn't eaten much for two days, and there didn't seem any way to get rid of her, so I helped her carry the scalloped oysters to the church, thinking I could slide out easily there. Boy! Those oysters had some delicious odor! I couldn't resist them. I almost took the pan and bolted before I got in, only there were too many people around watching."

The minister was smiling broadly now in the background, and Allan Murray was all attention. He had lost his sinister glare.

"Well, I got in there, and I couldn't get out. They introduced me right and left as Allan Murray, and I didn't dare deny it. I never realized before what a coward I was till I got into that fix, and then the doctor here asked me to 'ask a blessing,' and I didn't know what he meant. I never hailed with a gang like that before, and I hadn't been used to blessings."

The patient suddenly threw his head back and laughed.

"I found out I was a great Christian worker, and that I was the new teller in the Marlborough Bank, and that everybody was grateful that I hadn't been killed in the wreck," went on Murray with a flitting smile, "but I was mighty uncomfortable. There didn't come any good opportunity of getting out of there, however, and so I stuck it out, to my surprise, and got away with it! Even when Mr. Harper, the president of the bank, came to me and began to say how glad he was, I *got away with it*! Am I tiring you?"

"Go on!" shouted Allan Murray eagerly.

"Well, they herded me over to Mrs. Summers' again and sent me up to bed. There wasn't a second's chance to get away all that time without arousing the town, so I decided to wait till my hostess was asleep. But I made the mistake of lying down on the softest bed I ever touched, and boy! I was tired! And the next thing I knew they were calling me down to breakfast, and Mr. Harper was down there in his car waiting to take me to the bank.

"All day long they kept it up—for days. Never left me alone a second. I expected you to turn up every half hour, and I was worn to a thread with trying to keep up my part. At first I thought I'd stay till I got my first week's pay, but afterward I decided that as I had no name of my own I dared use, and as yours didn't seem to be needed by anyone, here was a perfectly good name and job, and I couldn't hide anywhere better than by taking another person's identity. So I settled down to be almost content in a condition like that! I was used to taking chances in anything that came along, and I suppose I just fell into it naturally.

"Then one day they did a dreadful thing. They made me president of the State Society, Christian Endeavor, you know. They say you know all about that."

Allan Murray's eyes lighted with keen appreciation of the situation in which his double was placed.

"I didn't know what it was like from a polo club, so when they made a great fuss about it, I said all right. But when I got to that state convention and saw what I was up against, I decided to beat it while they were singing the first hymn. And brother, I got the door in my sight, and my foot stretched out to take the first step toward it when God met me! Somehow He got it across to me that it was *He*, and I was a poor wretch of a sinner! And He wouldn't let me get out of that building! They were singing a hymn about hiding, and I was trying to hide, and right there, just as God stopped me, they asked me to make the opening prayer! Perhaps you wouldn't realize what that was like, being asked to pray before hundreds of people when you hadn't ever opened your mouth or your soul in prayer in your life! But I had to get up. And there I was facing God! I forgot all about the audience and just talked to God. I told Him what a wretch I was. I knew it then. I'd never known it before, but I knew it then. And when I sat down God talked with me! Sometimes it was in a prayer He spoke, sometimes in a Bible reading, or somebody's speech, but it came right home to me, and I found out I was a lost sinner, and only Jesus Christ

could save me. I'd seen something about being born again, before
I knew what it meant, and I'd wished I could begin life over with
a new name and all, but I didn't know how, see? But somehow I've
found out, and everything is different. I made a clean breast of
everything this morning in church, and then I found your letter to
Mrs. Summers. It got up in my room by mistake while I was away,
you see. So as soon as we could we came to hunt you up. Now, Mr.
Murray, can you see your way clear to forgive the rotten deal I gave
you? I've done my best to square things up, and if there's anything
else you'd like me to do, I'm ready. I belong to a new family now,
and I hope I'm going to honor it more than I did the first one. I've
heard ever since I've been in Marlborough what a great Christian
you are, and I'm going to try all my life to be like you, to make up
for the rotten way I masqueraded as you before I knew the Lord.
Can you forgive me?"

Allan Murray reached out a long, thin hand and grasped the
warm, firm one of Murray.

"I'll forgive you all right, brother, and from all I can see, you
put over a pretty good effort at being me. Now you better try
one better. Follow Christ, not me! I've found out the last few
weeks that I hadn't as much religion as I thought I had. When
everybody seemed to desert me and the good prospect I had was
lost, and I seemed to be lying on the very verge of the grave, I lost
hope and began to doubt the Lord. It was pretty tough lying here
not knowing what was going on anywhere and thinking nobody
cared. But I guess you've begun to make me see what it was all for.

It must have been a test, and I didn't stand it so very well either. I can see now. But if it's helped to bring a fellow like you to the light, it's worth all the suffering!"

Murray grasped both the other man's hands and held them.

"You're the right stuff, all right," he said. "Some fellows I know would have been too angry to speak to me for what I had done. But say, you're all wrong about nobody thinking about you. There's one. There's a girl. She wanted to know how you were. Her name is Anita. I don't know the rest of it. She went to school with your sister, and she was interested enough to ask me to find out about you and let her know. She'll be down to see you someday, or I'll miss my guess. And say, she's a good sport! She knew I wasn't you all the time. She remembered you had red hair. And she never told."

"She *is* a good sport," smiled the sick man. "You tell her I remember who she was. She played tennis with the champions and wouldn't take a handicap. And she gave up her place in a crowded hall once that a little lame girl might see! I wish she would come and see me. It would remind me of my little sister, Betty, who used to love her dearly."

"Yes," said the minister, rising and coming to the front, "Anita is a good sport. She's the best girl in the town of Marlborough. I could tell you a whole lot more things about her, but I haven't time now. I've got to get back to my evening service. The question is, how soon can we hope to be able to move you to Marlborough, where we can look after you personally? There's a whole church waiting to welcome you. I know, for look at the way they welcomed the man who came in your place! We love him, and we're going to love you just as much." He put his arm lovingly around Murray's shoulder.

"It looks to me as though I shall have a hard time keeping up with the pace you've set," said the sick man, trying to smile.

"No, you won't. Oh no! Don't you think it for a minute. You were born to it, but I've just been a great big bluff. Well, good-bye. You don't know how much easier you've made the rest for me, now that I know you don't hold this against me. I'll think of you in my room and teaching my class. I'm glad you're the kind of fellow you are. I shan't be jealous of you. I shall like to think about it."

"Nonsense! Man! Don't talk that way. You're coming to see me soon again, and we'll work things out together. I've a fancy you and I are going to be awfully good friends."

"I wish I could," said Murray wistfully, "but I've got an entirely different proposition to face. I'm going back home and give myself up for getting a young woman killed in an automobile accident, and I don't expect to see freedom again this side of heaven. But sometimes you think of me and work a little harder just for my sake, because I can't."

"Look here, brother," said Allan Murray, raising himself on one elbow and looking earnestly at Murray, "don't you talk like that! The Lord never saved you just to see you imprisoned for life. I'm going to get well in a few days now, and I'm going to spend time seeing you through. I'll begin right now by praying, and don't you give up!"

But Murray looked up with a bright smile.

"It's all right, you know, buddy. I belong to the Lord Christ now, and *what He wants is to go, from now on*, with me. I'm ready to face it all if that's what He wants for the honor of His name. That kind of living makes even dying worthwhile."

When they were gone and the nurse came in to turn on the lights and give him his medicine, Allan Murray was lying with wide-open eyes and an eager expression on his face.

"Nurse, how soon can I get up? I've a great deal to do, and it ought to be done soon."

The nurse looked up with a knowing smile.

"I don't know," she said brightly, "but I'll ask the doctor in the morning. I knew the best tonic in the world for you was to get in touch with the world again."

"It isn't the world," said Allan Murray contradictorily. "It's something better this time. *I'm needed.*"

Chapter 26

Murray Van Rensselaer had never held such sweet conversation with a man as he held with the minister on that ride home. Murray had never supposed there could be such a man as that minister, so strong and fearless, yet so tender and gentle, so wise and far-seeing, yet able to laugh and see a joke quicker than most: so wholly given up to the will of God. That was the secret of it all, really. He recognized that, untaught in holy things though he was.

And the minister on his part had conceived a great love for the young man who had come into their church under such peculiar circumstances. Somehow it seemed as though the Lord Himself had sent him and was caring for him in a special way. For it was no one's fault that Murray Van Rensselaer was taken into the church of God without the usual formalities and without knowledge of what he was doing. Not that there are not many thousands of young people swept into the church without any adequate idea of what they are doing, but they at least know enough to know that they are, as they call it, "joining the church." Murray did not know by that name that was what he himself was doing, but in heart he belonged to the Savior, body and soul. The work had been done in preparation wholly by the Holy Spirit Himself. Murray was in every sense begotten of the Spirit. Born anew.

As they rode along in the early dusk of the mid-winter afternoon, the minister marveled at this newborn Christian and the simple, childlike way in which he had grasped great truths and accepted them, which even scholars found difficult to believe. Taught of God, that was what he was. Not with the knowledge of men, but of the Spirit.

They rode into Marlborough five minutes before the evening service and stopped only long enough to pick up Mrs. Summers and move on to the church.

The news of Murray's confession had spread throughout the town that day, and the church was crowded. After the service the minister came down among the audience to speak to one and another, and happening to stand near Murray for a moment, he leaned over and whispered: "What a pity! See, Murray, all these people, and how you might influence them—*if you only hadn't to leave us!*"

"I know," said Murray, and his eyes drooped sadly; then, lifting his gaze anxiously, he said, "Do you suppose that heaven will have any way to make up for all the opportunities I've wasted here?"

Mrs. Summers and Murray sat by the fire a long time that night and talked after Mr. Harper had left.

Mr. Harper had come to say to Murray that he had entire confidence in him and felt that all would still be well in every way for his position in the bank, but he advised him to say no more about his past. One confession was enough. He needn't be telling it all the time. It would soon be forgotten, and everything would be as before.

Murray waited until he was all through, and then he looked him straight in the eye.

"That's all very kind of you, Mr. Harper. I know you're saying that for my sake. But I don't want it to be as it was before. It couldn't be. I've found out I was all wrong, and I'll have to be telling what God has done for me the rest of the time I have to live. As for the bank, I've *got* to leave you. You're very kind to ask me to stay after the way I've treated you and deceived you. I'm sorry to have to go away right off without waiting till you get a temporary person in my place, but you see it's just this way. I'm wanted by the state to answer a criminal charge, and there are some things that I must do to make right a cowardly thing I did, before I'm put where there is no chance for me to make anything right. Now that there are so many people who know who I am, there is no guarantee that I may not be arrested any minute, or else I would wait till you can fill my place. But I was with Allan

Murray this afternoon, and he thinks he will soon be able to come to you, if you still want him. He is a better man than I am. And everything will be all right for you when he comes."

But Mr. Harper was not to be appeased. He had taken a liking to this young man. He fit perfectly in with his schemes for the bank. The other might be all right, but he wanted this one. He was under no obligation to Allan Murray, since he did not come at the time arranged, and besides, there was room in the bank for another person if it came to that, of course. It was with great reluctance that he finally withdrew and left Mrs. Summers and Murray to have their last talk together.

It was then that Murray told her about Bessie and Mrs. Chapparelle. Told of his own home and his lonely childhood, though that was merely seen between the lines, not put into words. Told of the brightness of the little cozy home around the corner, and of the little girl who had been so sweet and cheerful a friend, then of the years between, and finally of his finding her that afternoon and taking her for a ride. He did not tell of their visit to Grevet's. He did not realize himself what part that incident had played in the tragedy of the fateful afternoon. But he told of his long wait in the hospital and finally of the approach of the nurse with the sad news, and his flight.

As he put it all into words, his own disloyalty and cowardice arose before him in their true light, and his shame and sorrow came upon him so powerfully that once he put his head down on the little tea table and groaned aloud. Then the little warm rose-leaf hand of the woman was laid upon his head tenderly, and he felt the comfort of her loving spirit.

They read together for the last time the precious fourteenth chapter of John, which has been the stay and comfort of so many saints in trouble throughout the ages, and then they knelt and prayed together. Mrs. Summers prayed for Murray, and finally Murray lifted a sorrowful voice and prayed, "Oh, God! Bless her—and help me!" Just a whisper of a prayer, but it must have reached the throne.

In the morning he drove away in the minister's car. The minister would only have it so.

"You are not safe in the train, son. They might get you arrested before your work is done."

The minister would have gone along, but Murray said no.

"I must face the music alone, you know. It was I who ran away from it, not you. And I'm not going to take you away from your busy days. But I'll send the car back safely, and I'll let you know how it turns out. I'll let you both know."

So he drove away.

Chapter 27

Mrs. Chapparelle was in the kitchen making pancakes again when Mr. Van Rensselaer came to the front door. She had to push the griddle back just as she had done once before, lest it burn.

The caller said he would like to see Miss Elizabeth, and she showed him into the pretty little living room, with its small upright piano and its few simple furnishings. He sat down and looked around him while he waited for the girl, for her mother said it was almost time for her to arrive home. Mrs. Chapparelle had gone back to her kitchen. She knew who the visitor was, although he had not given his name, and she had no desire to talk with him until Bessie came. She had little patience with Murray's parents. She thought they were to blame for what he was. Also she had not approved of Bessie's visit at the big house. She thought it had been unnecessary. Very likely that aristocrat had come to offer Bessie money or something, for her information, or else to bribe her not to say anything. She shoved the griddle back over the flame with a click and stirred her batter vigorously. The less she had to do with wealthy aristocrats the better!

Then the bell rang again, and she hurried to the door. Bessie must have forgotten her key.

Mr. Van Rensselaer had been looking over everything most carefully and approving of it all. There was taste in every article in the room. The one oriental rug before the couch was a fine old piece, and the couch itself was covered with pretty, comfortable-looking pillows. There was a tall reading lamp gracefully shaded over the chair where he sat, and there were books and magazines and a few fine photographs. It all had a homelike look, as if the room was used and loved.

A frown of annoyance gathered on his brow when the bell rang. He had hoped there would be no other visitor. Perhaps he could get the girl to take him out in the kitchen, where they could talk uninterrupted. He would like to see that kitchen. But then perhaps this was the girl herself.

Mrs. Chapparelle opened the door, and someone stepped in from the shadow of the front porch. She glanced at him, astonished.

"Why, *Murray*! Is it *you*?"

He looked so white and tired she felt sorry for him. But why should he come here after all these weeks? Had he then really been ill somewhere?

"Yes, Mrs. Chapparelle, it's Murray. But I'm afraid you don't want to see me."

"You look so white! Have you been ill?" she evaded.

"No, Mrs. Chapparelle, I've only been a fool and a coward and—a murderer—" he added bitterly.

"Murray!" She spoke in a startled voice.

"Yes, I know that's what you've been calling me, and coward, too, and I deserve it all and more. But thank God, He stopped me and brought me back. I'm going down now to give myself up and confess. But I had to stop here first to tell you and ask you to forgive me. I don't suppose you'll find it easy, and perhaps you won't give me that comfort. But I knew you were a Christian woman, and I thought perhaps— Well, anyway, I wanted you to know that God has forgiven my sins, and I belong to Him now. I thought that might make some difference to you. You were good to me when I was a kid—!"

At the first word from his son's voice, the father stiffened in his chair and grew alert, listening with all his senses strained. As the boy went on, an icy thrill went around his heart. What had Murray done now? A murderer? There had never been a murderer in the Van Rensselaer family to his knowledge. He tried to rise, but his muscles would not obey him. He found himself suddenly weak.

Murray's voice was going on haltingly. He seemed to be struggling with deep emotion.

"I thought I wanted you to know that I loved Bessie! I've always loved her, only she grew out of my life. Of course, I never was good enough for her, and she wouldn't probably have looked at me. I couldn't have hoped to marry her. She was a flower, a saint from heaven! But I loved her, and I shall always love her! If I were free—but there's no use talking of that. I don't want to be free! I want to pay all the penalty I can for what I did. But I do want you to know that I did not do it carelessly. I was not driving fast. My carelessness was in paying more heed to her than to what was going on around me. But I'm not excusing myself, only I didn't want you to think I was careless of her, or that I had been drinking!"

"Murray, what on earth do you mean, child!" broke in Mrs. Chapparelle. "Come into the kitchen, dear, and sit down, and let me give you a cup of tea! Why, your hands are like ice. Come with me!"

Mr. Van Rensselaer had got to his feet somehow and was standing in the doorway by this time, but neither of the two saw him. Mrs. Chapparelle had hold of Murray's hand and was drawing him toward the kitchen door. But just at that moment a key turned in the front door, and Bessie entered, all fresh and rosy from the sharp winter air.

Holding each other's hands, the mother and the young man turned with startled looks and faced her. None of them saw the shaken man standing in the doorway with a hand on a curtain on either side, looking at them all with growing comprehension and apprehension in his eyes.

The young man and the girl saw only each other.

"Bessie!" said Murray with a sudden light of wonder in his

eyes. "Bessie? You are not dead!" He dropped the mother's hands and stood an instant watching her to see if she were surely not an apparition.

"Murray!" There was great gladness in the girl's voice. A melting of the wall that had grown up through the years.

And then he had her in his arms. Her face was against his chest. His face was buried in her hair, her sweet bright hair. The others standing by did not exist for them.

The griddle in the kitchen had not been shoved far enough back. There was flame still under it. It sent up a strong odor of burning grease, and suddenly Mrs. Chapparelle, eyes blinded with wondering happy tears, hurried into the kitchen to see to it, mindful that she was not needed in the hall just then. She had forgotten entirely the visitor in the parlor, who was shamelessly happy at what he was witnessing.

He became aware that he ought not to stand there watching those two, at the same moment that Mrs. Chapparelle remembered his existence and hurried back to try to help out the situation. Murray and Bessie came to their senses about the same moment also, and there they all four stood and looked at one another, ashamed and confused, yet happy.

It took the man of the world to recover first.

"Well, my son," he said in a pleased voice, "you seem to have done something worthy of your family name at last!"

"Yes, Father, isn't it great? But everything's going to be different from now on. Oh boy! Mother Chapparelle! I just realized. I haven't got to give myself up after all, have I? I'm not a murderer! She's alive! And she loves me!"

They sobered down after a while, and Murray told them his story.

Mr. Van Rensselaer called up his house and said he was unavoidably detained and could not return until late that evening, and they all sat down in the little white kitchen and ate pancakes and talked. For hours it seemed they were eating and talking. Mrs. Chapparelle had to get more syrup and use the rest of the batter she had saved for the next meal and stir up more cakes. Mr. Van Rensselaer thought he had not been so happy since he was a little boy at home with his own mother.

The father did not talk much. He watched his boy. He listened to the wonderful story that fell from his lips, and in another language his sorrowful, hungry soul kept crying over and over to himself as the father of old, *"This my son was dead, and is alive again; he was lost, and is found!"* He began to rejoice that he would be able to kill the fatted calf for him. Nothing was too good for Murray now.

Then he turned his eyes to the lovely girl who sat with starry eyes and watched her lover who had come back through the years to fulfill the promise of the roses he had given her long ago. Come back a new Murray, with a new Name upon his lips, a Name that was above every name dear to her!

GRACE LIVINGSTON HILL (1865–1947) is known as the pioneer of Christian romance. Grace wrote more than one hundred faith-inspired books during her lifetime. When her first husband died, leaving her with two daughters to raise, writing became a way to make a living, but she always recognized storytelling as a way to share her faith in God. She has touched countless lives through the years and continues to touch lives today. Her books feature moving stories, delightful characters, and love in its purest form.

GRACE LIVINGSTON HILL (1865–1947), known as the queen of Christian romance, wrote more than one hundred and fifty faith-inspired books during her lifetime. When her first husband died, leaving her with two daughters to raise, writing became a way to make a living. But she always recognized storytelling as a way to share her faith in God. She has touched countless lives through the years and continues to touch lives today. Her books feature romance, action, delightful characters, and love in its purest form.

**Look for these other great
Grace Livingston Hill titles
from Barbour Publishing**